D1097701

Stevenson • Watters • Leyh • Allen • Nowak • Pietsch • Laiho

LUMBERJANES ™

TO THE MAX EDITION

VOLUME THREE

BOOM!
BOX ™

BOOM! BOX™

LUMBERJANES TO THE MAX EDITION Volume Three, June 2017. Published by BOOM! Box, a division of Boom Entertainment, Inc. Lumberjanes is ™ & © 2017 Shannon Watters, Grace Ellis, Noelle Stevenson & Brooke Allen. Originally published in single magazine form as LUMBERJANES No. 13, 18-24. ™ & © 2015, 2016 Shannon Watters, Grace Ellis, Noelle Stevenson & Brooke Allen. All rights reserved. BOOM! Box™ and the BOOM! Box logo are trademarks of Boom Entertainment, Inc., registered in various countries and categories. All characters, events, and institutions depicted herein are fictional. Any similarity between any of the names, characters, persons, events, and/or institutions in this publication to actual names, characters, and persons, whether living or dead, events, and/or institutions is unintended and purely coincidental. BOOM! Box does not read or accept unsolicited submissions of ideas, stories, or artwork.

BOOM! Studios, 5670 Wilshire Boulevard, Suite 450, Los Angeles, CA 90036-5679. Printed in China. First Printing.

ISBN: 978-1-68415-003-8, eISBN: 978-1-61398-674-5

THIS LUMBERJANES FIELD MANUAL BELONGS TO:

NAME:_____

TROOP:_____

DATE INVESTED:_____

FIELD MANUAL TABLE OF CONTENTS

LUMBERJANES
FIELD MANUAL

For the Advanced Program

Tenth Edition • April 1984

Prepared for the

**Miss Qiunzella Thiskwin
Penniquiqul Thistle Crumpet's**

CAMP FOR ~~GIRLS~~ HARDCORE LADY-TYPES

"Friendship to the Max!"

WITHDRAWN

A MESSAGE FROM THE LUMBERJANES HIGH COUNCIL

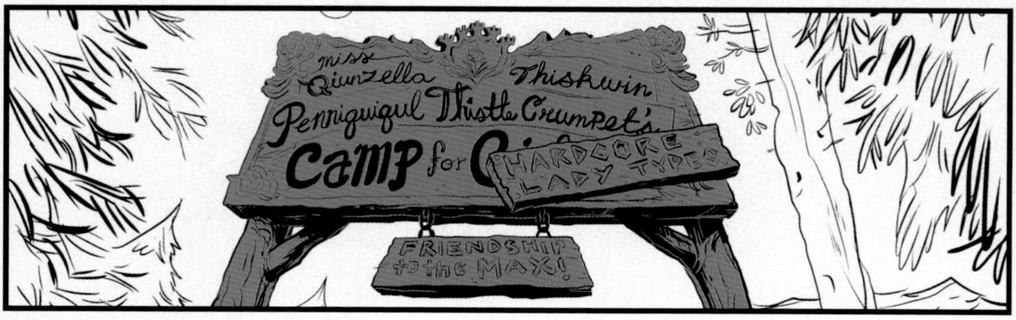
Miss Quinzella Thiskwin Penniquiqul Thistle Crumpet's
Camp for
HARDCORE LADY TYPES
FRIENDSHIP to the MAX!

Life is amazing. There are so many people and things around us that have the ability to experience life—to breath the air that we all share, to experience the emotions we enjoy from day-to-day, to forge connections that last.

Sometimes, it's hard to remember why we should wake up each day with a smile. One of the biggest lessons that we've learned over the years, and that we hope to pass on to our campers, is the joy of experiencing life. The joy of getting your hands dirty in a garden, of jumping in a lake, of overcoming a task after years of trying…those are the moments that make life amazing.

To all of our Lumberjanes: we hope that you will feel the same thrill of waking up in your bunk on the last day of camp, as you did on your first, and that even when you travel home again, with all of the lessons you learned and the memories of camp fresh in your mind, you will wake up in your own bed with a smile, too. Every day is as precious as you are, Lumberjane, and we hope that you cherish it as much as we cherish you.

There are many things to do at camp, and there are many things that we hope to teach you in your time here. Nothing at this camp will be more a gift than the friendships that you develop here. Keep your friends close. Learn to stretch out your arms and run past your comfort zone with someone by your side. Learn what it means to be by someone else's side, to support them in any adventure that life decides to throw at you in your time with us…And in your time outside camp.

No matter what might be thrown your way, or what kind of darkness could be lurking in the shadows, know that life is amazing. That for every hardship you come across, there will be endless amazing takeaways from each experience, which will only help you live your life to its fullest potential. We look forward to seeing what is to come in the next few months, and we hope that you do, too.

THE LUMBERJANES PLEDGE

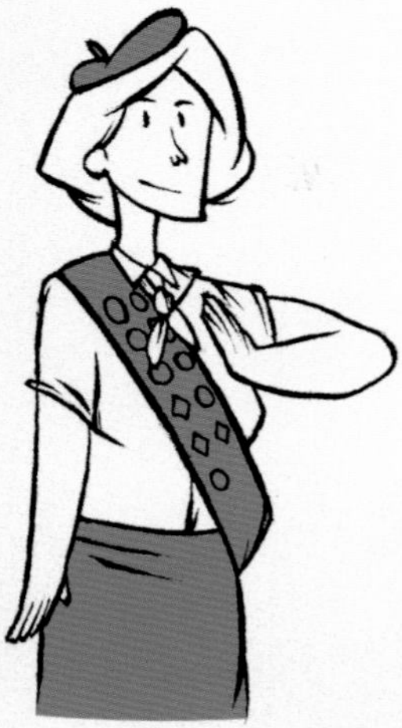

I solemnly swear to do my best
Every day, and in all that I do,
To be brave and strong,
To be truthful and compassionate,
To be interesting and interested,
To pay attention and question
The world around me,
To think of others first,
To always help and protect my friends,
[redacted]
And to make the world a better place
For Lumberjane scouts
And for everyone else.

THEN THERE'S A LINE ABOUT GOD, OR WHATEVER

LUMBERJANES ™
TO THE MAX EDITION

Created by **Shannon Watters, Grace Ellis, Noelle Stevenson & Brooke Allen**

Written by
Noelle Stevenson & Shannon Watters
(Chapter Seventeen)
Shannon Watters & Kat Leyh
(Chapters Eighteen through Twenty-Four)

Illustrated by
Brooke Allen
(Chapter Seventeen)
Carolyn Nowak
(Chapters Eighteen through Twenty)
Carey Pietsch
(Chapters Twenty-One through Twenty-Four)

Colors by
Maarta Laiho

Letters by
Aubrey Aiese

Design by
Kelsey Dieterich

"Band Camp"

Written by	Illustrated by	Letters by
Shannon Watters	**Ayme Sotuyo**	**Britt Wilson**

Character Designs by
Noelle Stevenson & Brooke Allen

Badge Designs by
Scott Newman & Kelsey Dieterich

Editors
Whitney Leopard & Dafna Pleban

Special thanks to **Kelsey Pate** *for giving the Lumberjanes their name.*

LUMBERJANES FIELD MANUAL

CHAPTER SEVENTEEN

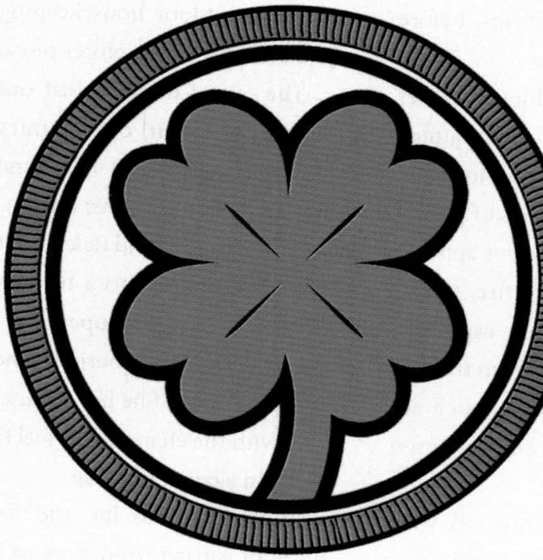

Lumberjanes "Out-of-Doors" Program Field

BEGINNER'S LUCK BADGE

"Everyone Starts Somewhere"

Every story has a beginning, and every race has a starting line. You don't finish things halfway through: you begin at the beginning and complete them start to finish. Nature is a great place to gain experience in the light of the sun, but a true Lumberjane knows the importance of learning things from square one. It is at Lumberjanes Camp that our Lumberjane Scouts will learn new skills and lessons. We don't expect every camper to come to us with knowledge already in their heads, and we find that one of the joys of camp is being able to pass on knowledge to your fellow campers.

The *Beginner's Luck* badge is for the Lumberjane who jumps feet-first into the unknown. The Lumberjane who is willing to learn as they go , who takes the experiences and lessons of others and applies them in their day-to-day life at camp. The *Beginner's Luck* badge can be earned by multiple methods: either by jumping into a course or curriculum without any prior knowledge, and using already acquired skills and gumption to come out with top marks, or through a series of tests that are set up by a scout's counselor. The latter is not only the most popular way to earn the badge, but is also often accepted as the most enjoyable method, since oftentimes the tests will involve working together with your cabin—with your friends.

The history of the *Beginner's Luck* badge goes back to the beginning of Lumberjane history. It is, in fact, one of the original badges from the founding of the camp, just with a better name. Back then, the *Beginner's Luck* badge was referred to as the *Guppy* badge, but after much deliberation, it was decided that while the scouts applying for the badge may in fact be the 'guppies' of their given activity, the skills needed to earn the badge were better described by *Beginner's Luck*. The biggest and most important lesson to keep in mind with this badge is that while everyone has to start at the beginning, and while you might be able to skip a step or two, you won't know which steps until you start.

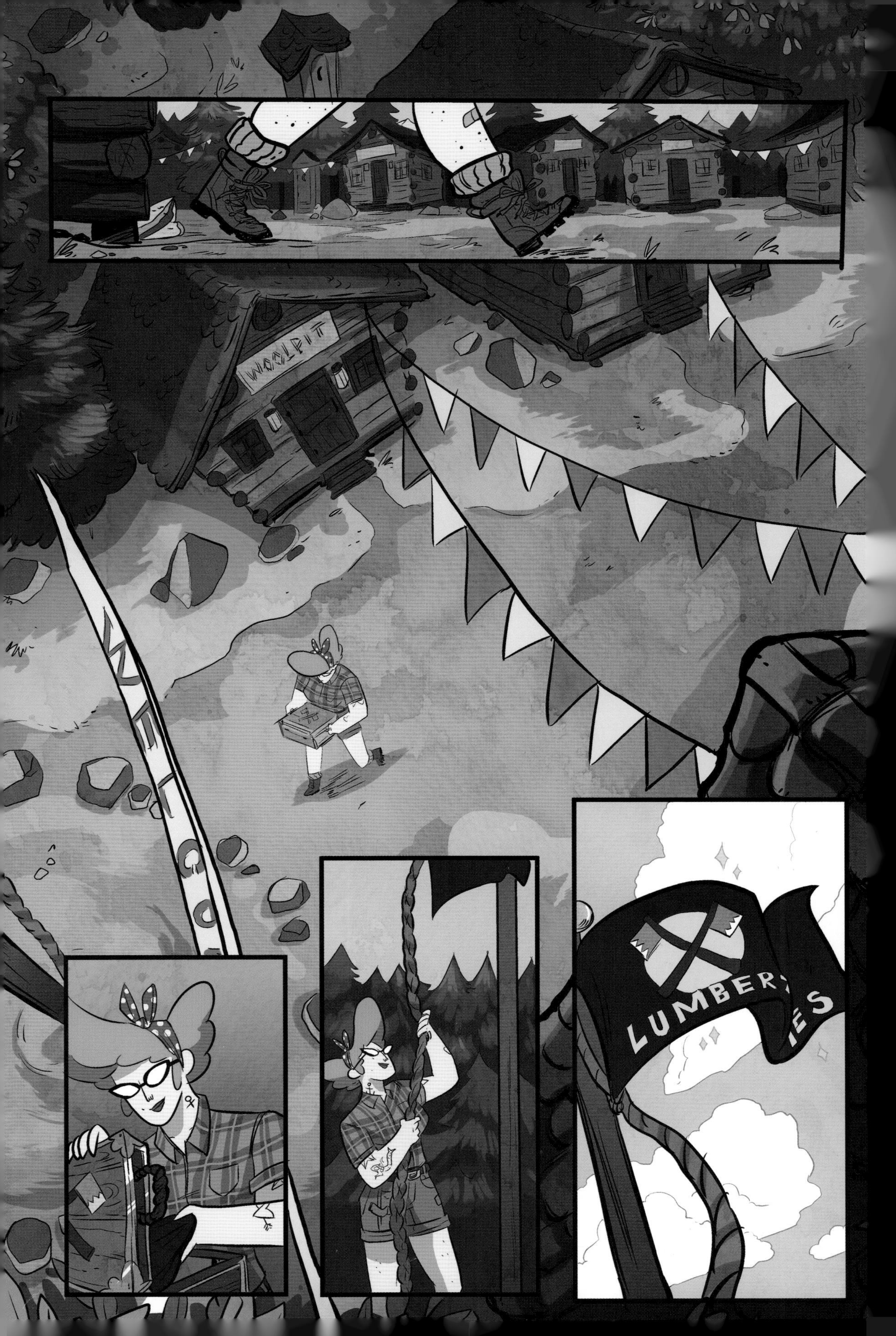
WOOLPIT
LUMBER
ES

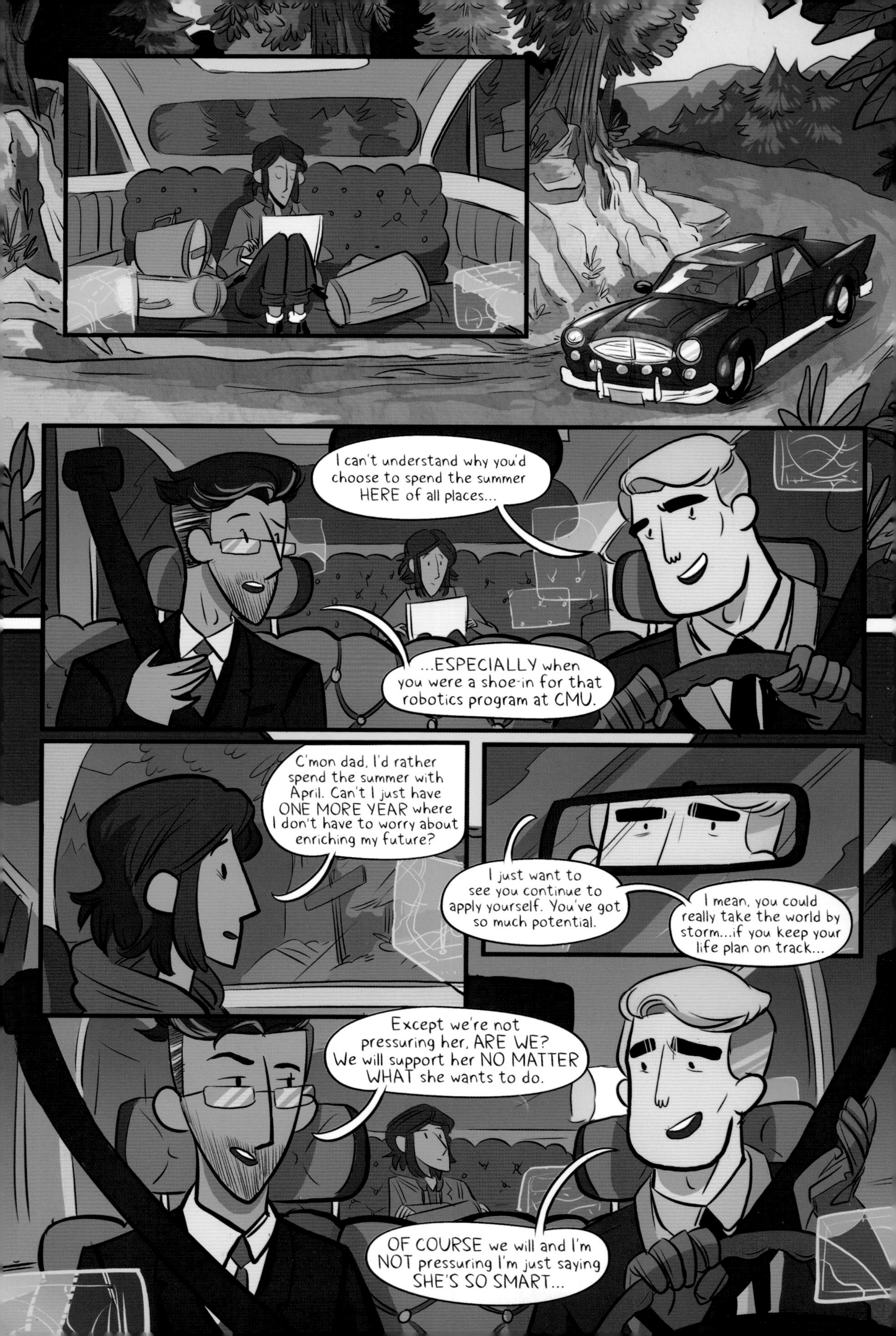
I can't understand why you'd choose to spend the summer HERE of all places...
...ESPECIALLY when you were a shoe-in for that robotics program at CMU.
C'mon dad, I'd rather spend the summer with April. Can't I just have ONE MORE YEAR where I don't have to worry about enriching my future?
I just want to see you continue to apply yourself. You've got so much potential.
I mean, you could really take the world by storm...if you keep your life plan on track...
Except we're not pressuring her, ARE WE? We will support her NO MATTER WHAT she wants to do.
OF COURSE we will and I'm NOT pressuring I'm just saying SHE'S SO SMART...

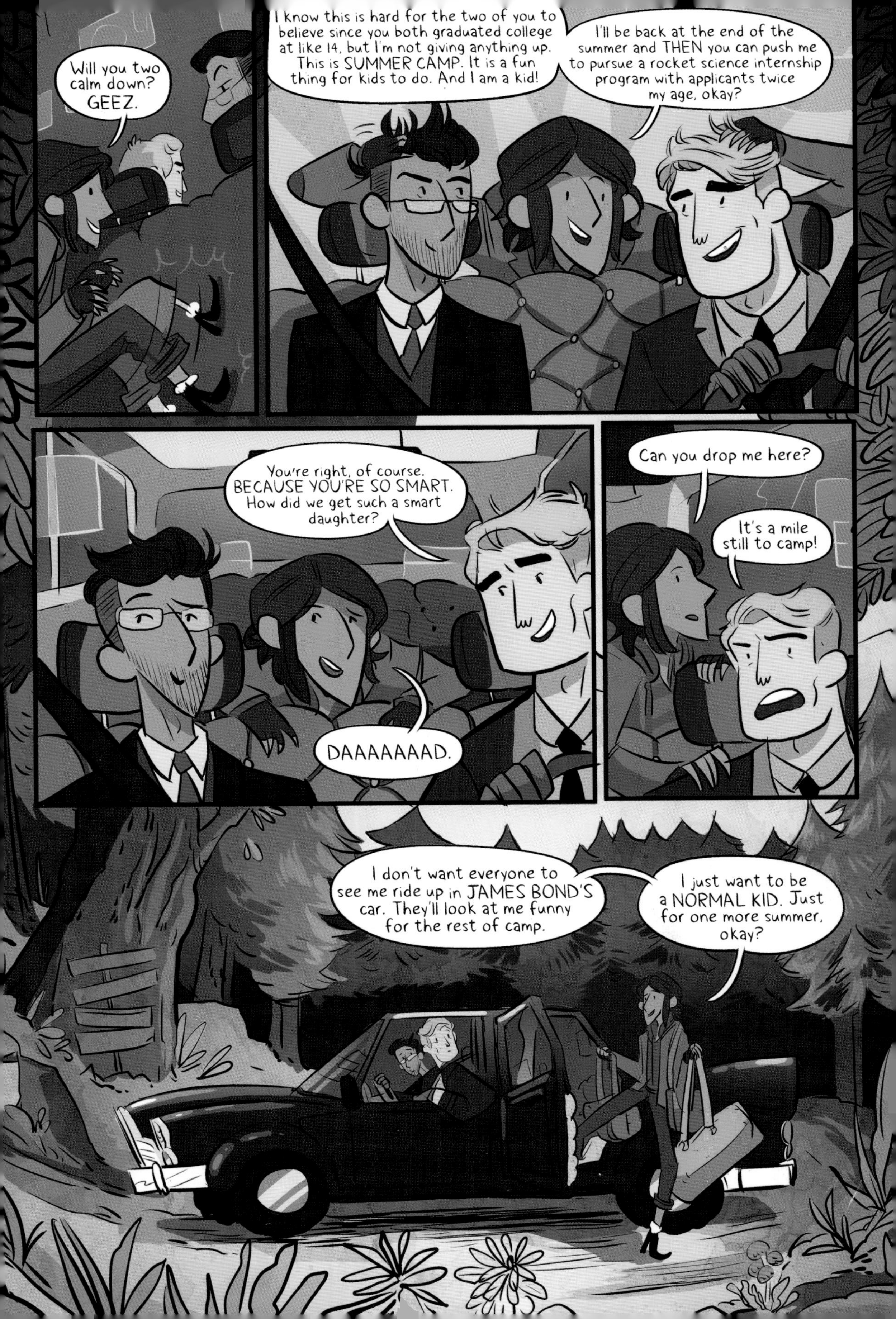

Will you two calm down? GEEZ.
I know this is hard for the two of you to believe since you both graduated college at like 14, but I'm not giving anything up. This is SUMMER CAMP. It is a fun thing for kids to do. And I am a kid!
I'll be back at the end of the summer and THEN you can push me to pursue a rocket science internship program with applicants twice my age, okay?
You're right, of course. BECAUSE YOU'RE SO SMART. How did we get such a smart daughter?
DAAAAAAAD.
Can you drop me here?
It's a mile still to camp!
I don't want everyone to see me ride up in JAMES BOND'S car. They'll look at me funny for the rest of camp.
I just want to be a NORMAL KID. Just for one more summer, okay?

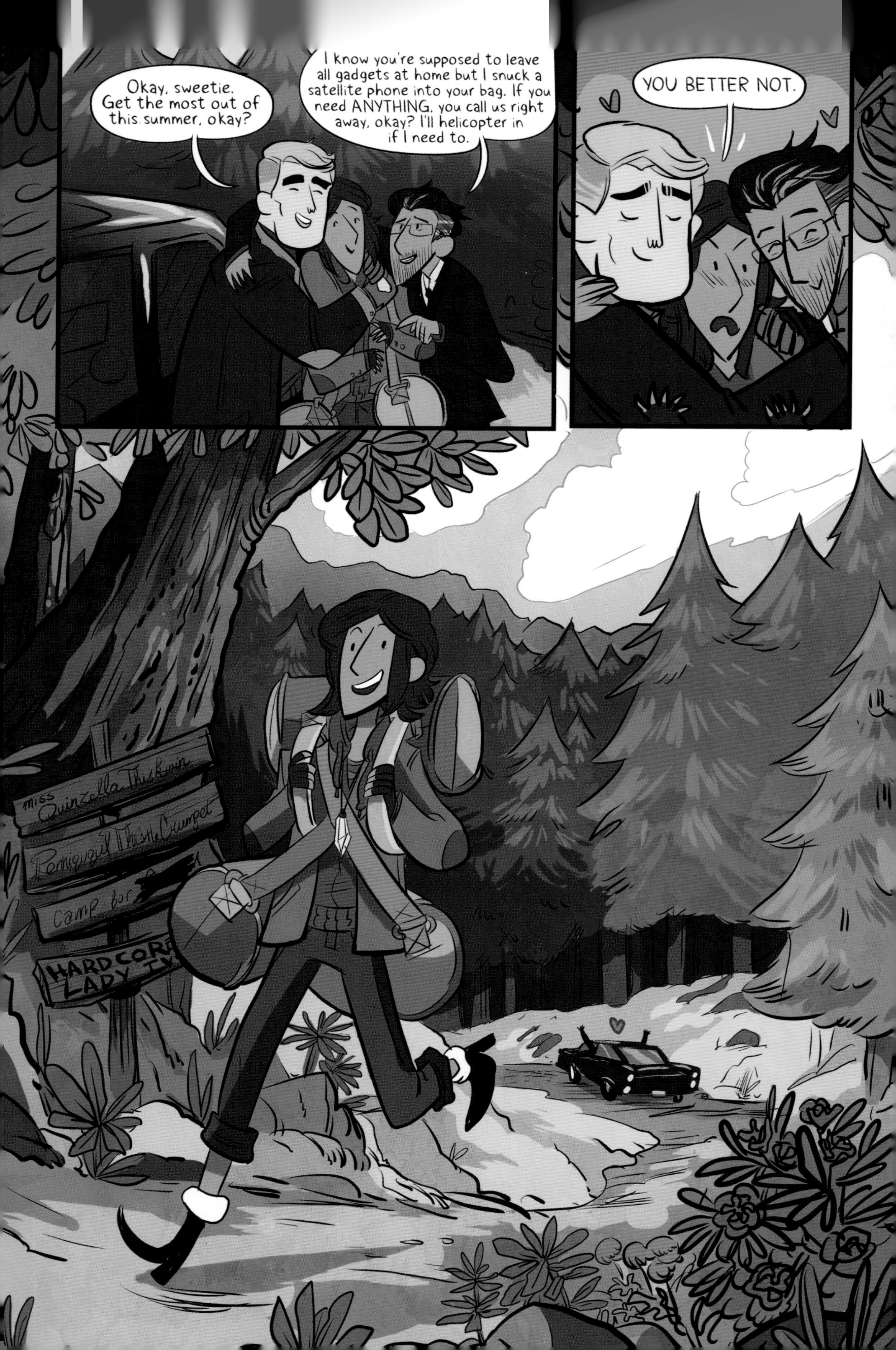
Okay, sweetie. Get the most out of this summer, okay?
I know you're supposed to leave all gadgets at home but I snuck a satellite phone into your bag. If you need ANYTHING, you call us right away, okay? I'll helicopter in if I need to.
YOU BETTER NOT.
Miss Quinzella Thiskwin
Penniquiqul Thistle Crumpet
Camp for
LADY

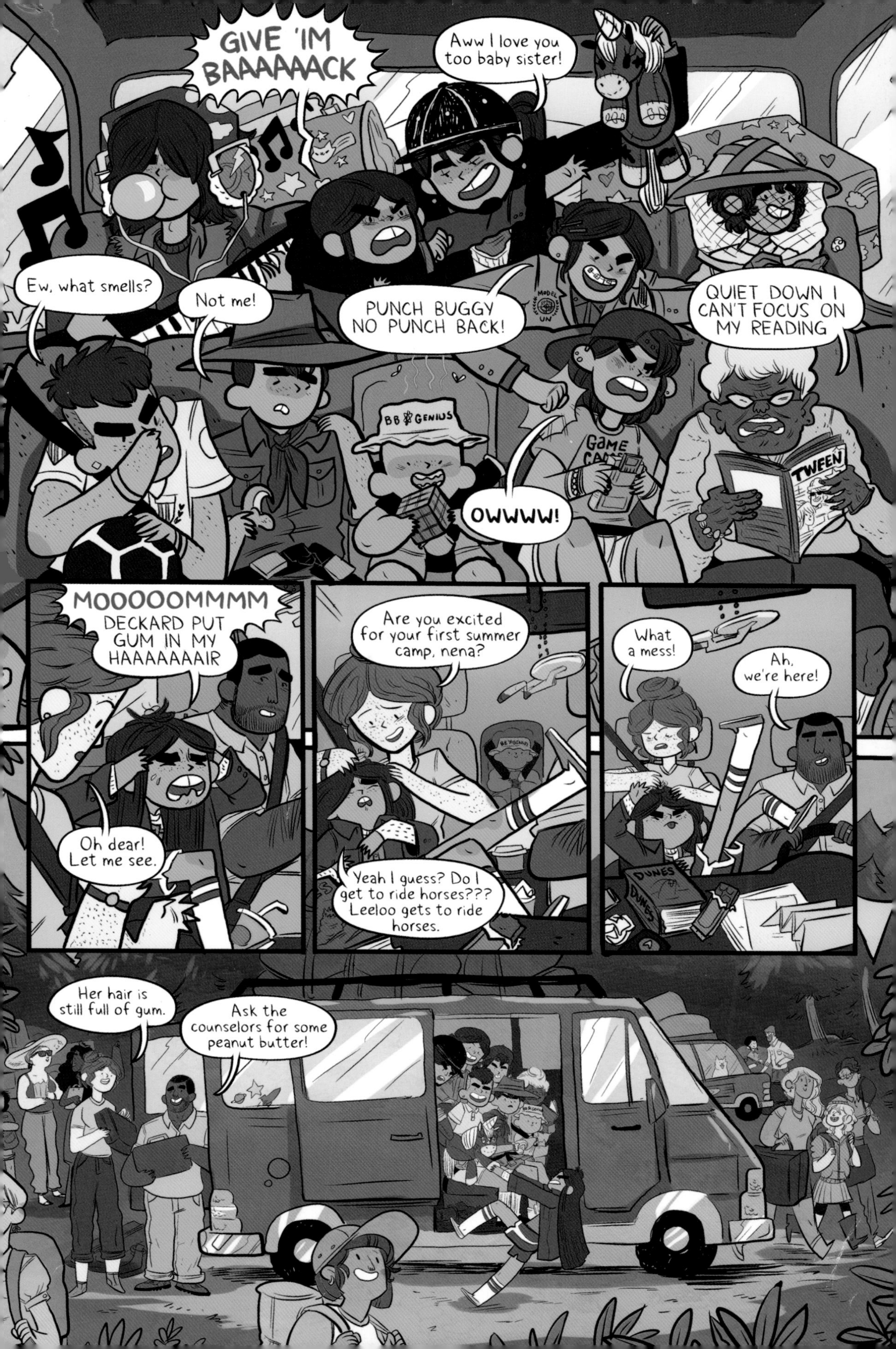
GIVE 'IM BAAAAAACK
Aww I love you too baby sister!
Ew, what smells?
Not me!
PUNCH BUGGY NO PUNCH BACK!
QUIET DOWN I CAN'T FOCUS ON MY READING
BB GENIUS
GAME
TWEEN
OWWWW!
MOOOOOMMMM DECKARD PUT GUM IN MY HAAAAAAAIR
Oh dear! Let me see.
Are you excited for your first summer camp, nena?
Yeah I guess? Do I get to ride horses??? Leeloo gets to ride horses.
What a mess!
Ah, we're here!
DUNES
Her hair is still full of gum.
Ask the counselors for some peanut butter!

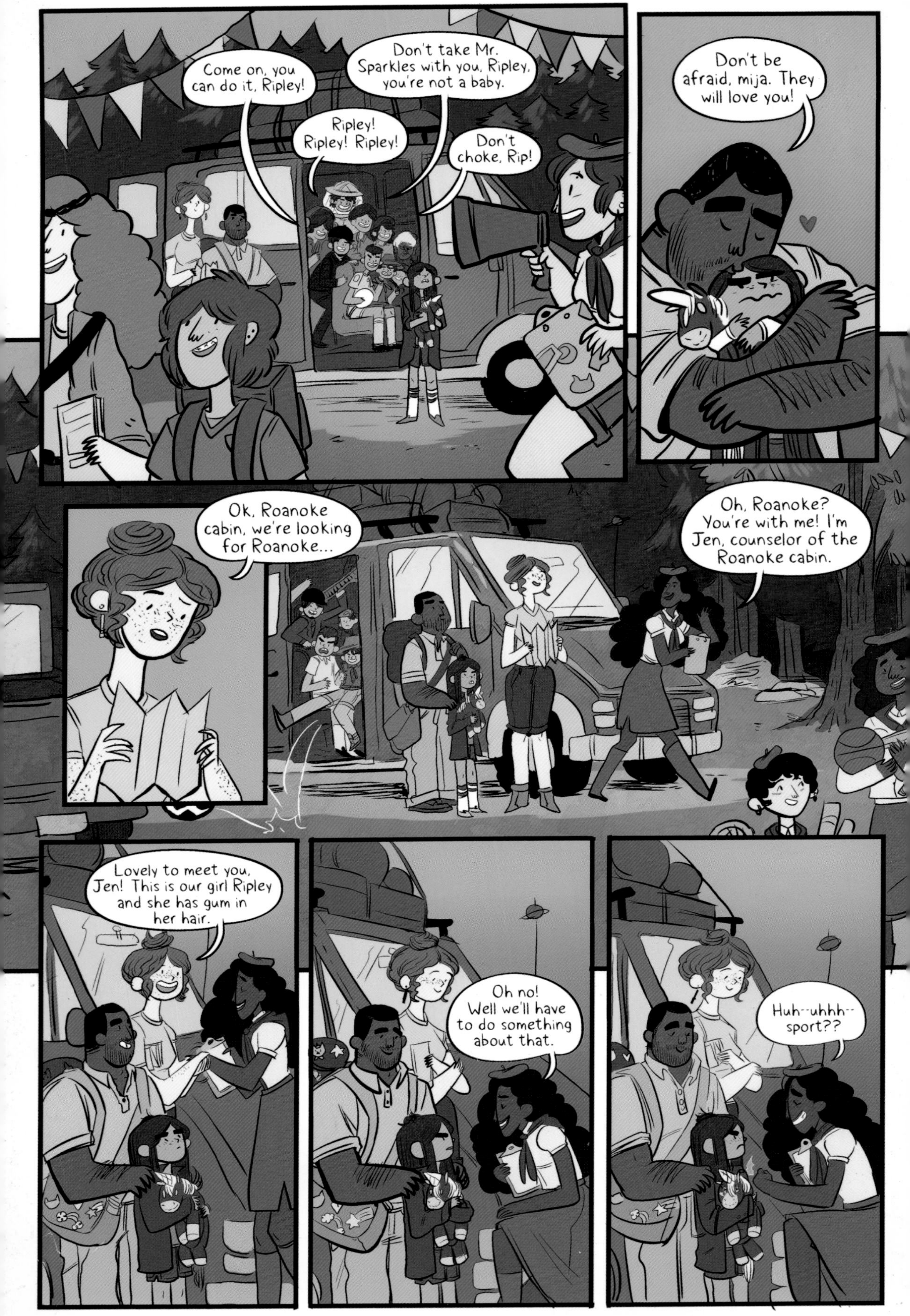
Come on, you can do it, Ripley!
Ripley! Ripley! Ripley!
Don't take Mr. Sparkles with you, Ripley, you're not a baby.
Don't choke, Rip!
Don't be afraid, mija. They will love you!
Ok, Roanoke cabin, we're looking for Roanoke...
Oh, Roanoke? You're with me! I'm Jen, counselor of the Roanoke cabin.
Lovely to meet you, Jen! This is our girl Ripley and she has gum in her hair.
Oh no! Well we'll have to do something about that.
Huh--uhhh-- sport??

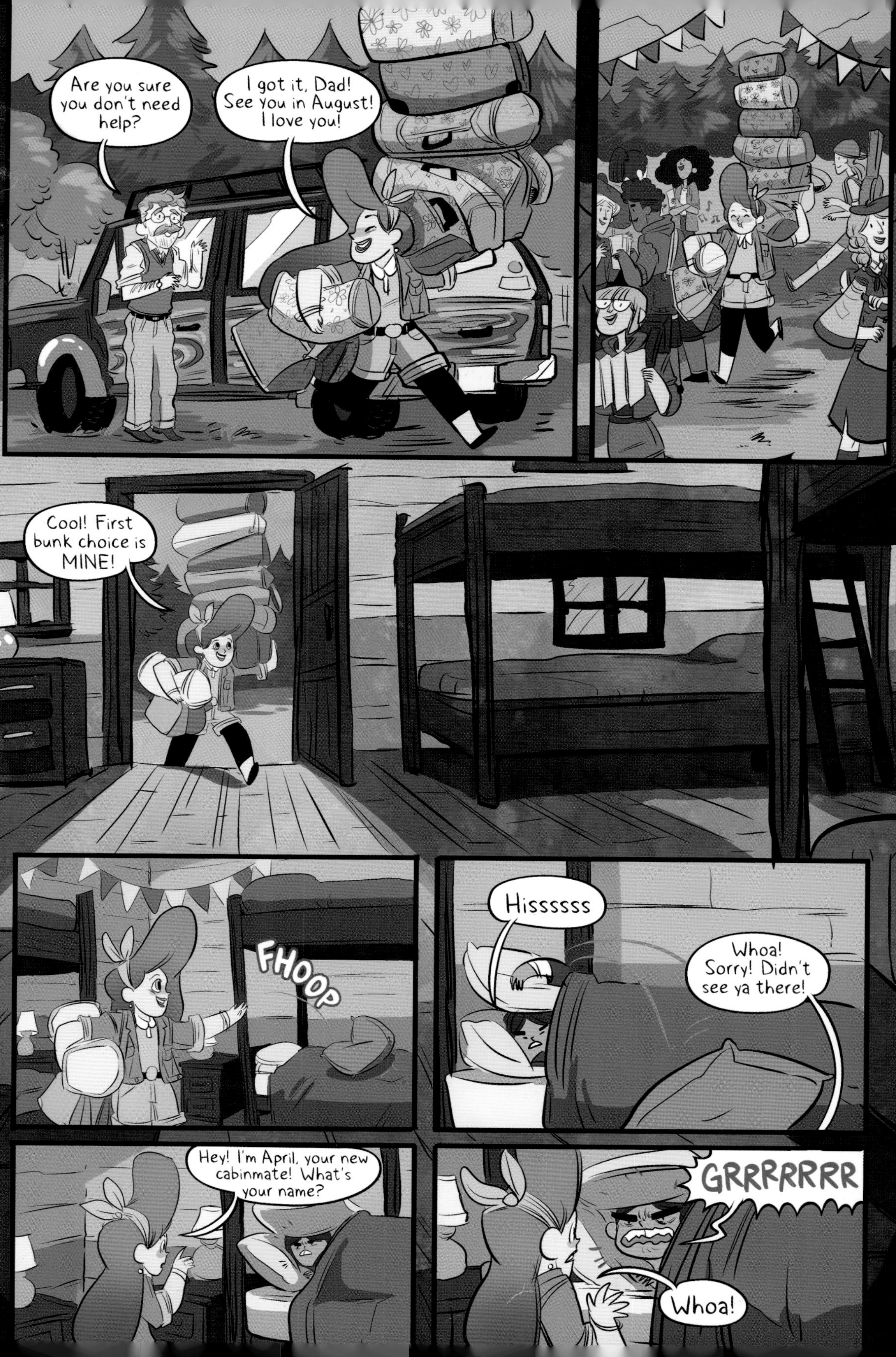
Are you sure you don't need help?
I got it, Dad! See you in August! I love you!
Cool! First bunk choice is MINE!
FHOOP
Hissssss
Whoa! Sorry! Didn't see ya there!
Hey! I'm April, your new cabinmate! What's your name?
GRRRRRRR
Whoa!

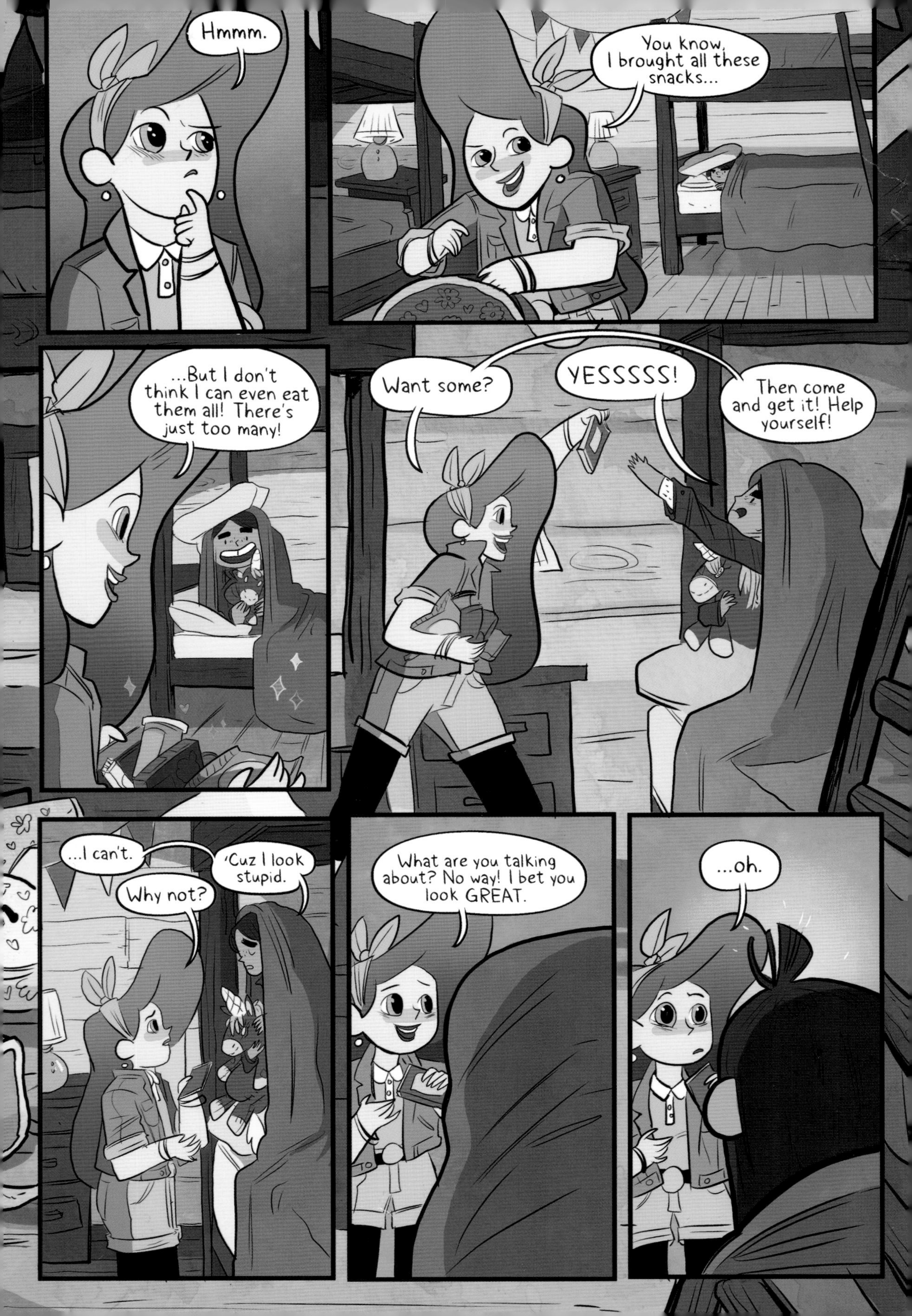
Hmmm.
You know, I brought all these snacks...
...But I don't think I can even eat them all! There's just too many!
Want some?
YESSSSS!
Then come and get it! Help yourself!
...I can't.
Why not?
'Cuz I look stupid.
What are you talking about? No way! I bet you look GREAT.
...oh.

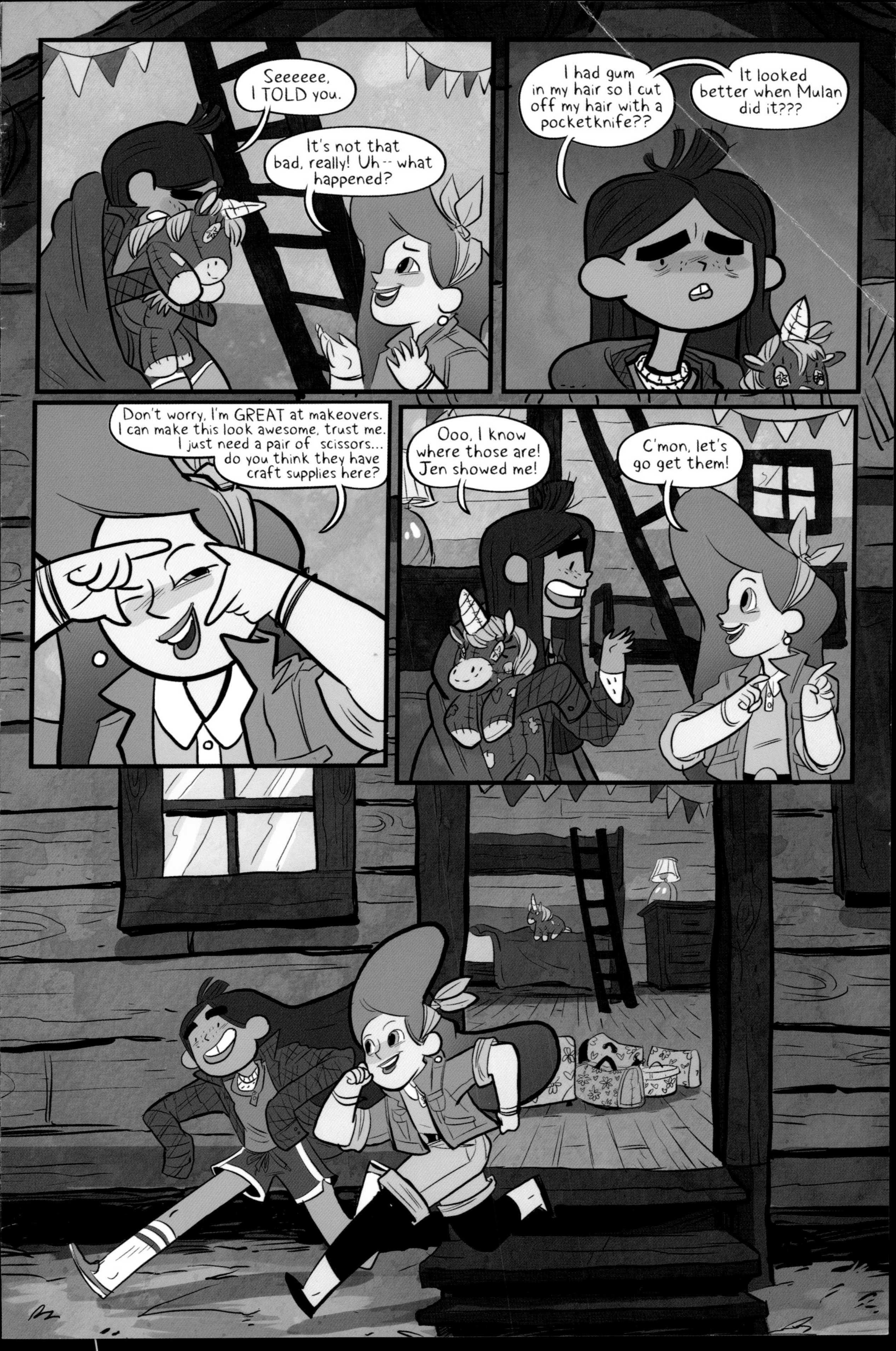

Seeeeee, I TOLD you.
It's not that bad, really! Uh -- what happened?
I had gum in my hair so I cut off my hair with a pocketknife??
It looked better when Mulan did it???
Don't worry, I'm GREAT at makeovers. I can make this look awesome, trust me. I just need a pair of scissors... do you think they have craft supplies here?
Ooo, I know where those are! Jen showed me!
C'mon, let's go get them!

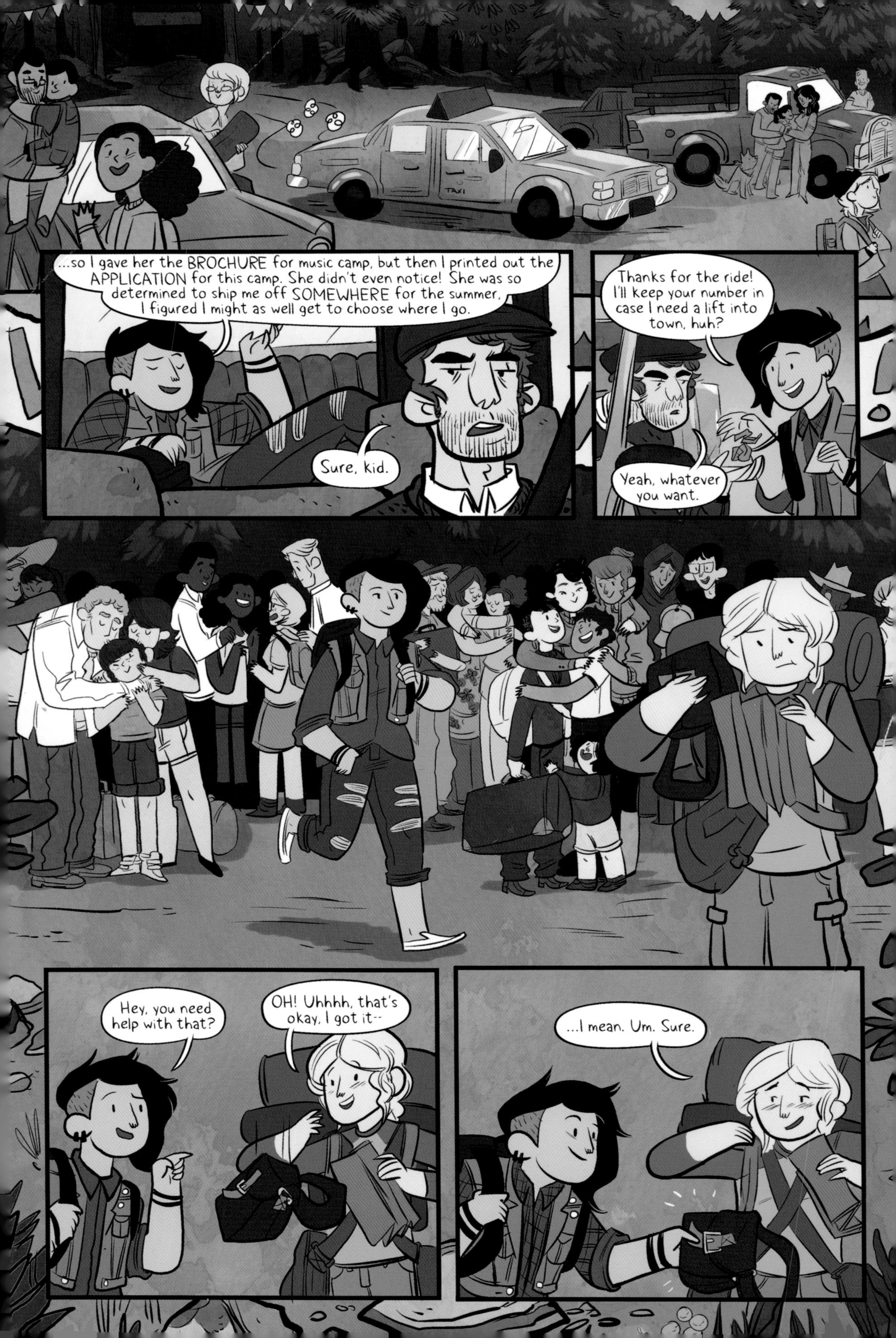
...so I gave her the BROCHURE for music camp, but then I printed out the APPLICATION for this camp. She didn't even notice! She was so determined to ship me off SOMEWHERE for the summer, I figured I might as well get to choose where I go.
Sure, kid.
Thanks for the ride! I'll keep your number in case I need a lift into town, huh?
Yeah, whatever you want.
Hey, you need help with that?
OH! Uhhhh, that's okay, I got it--
...I mean. Um. Sure.
TAXI

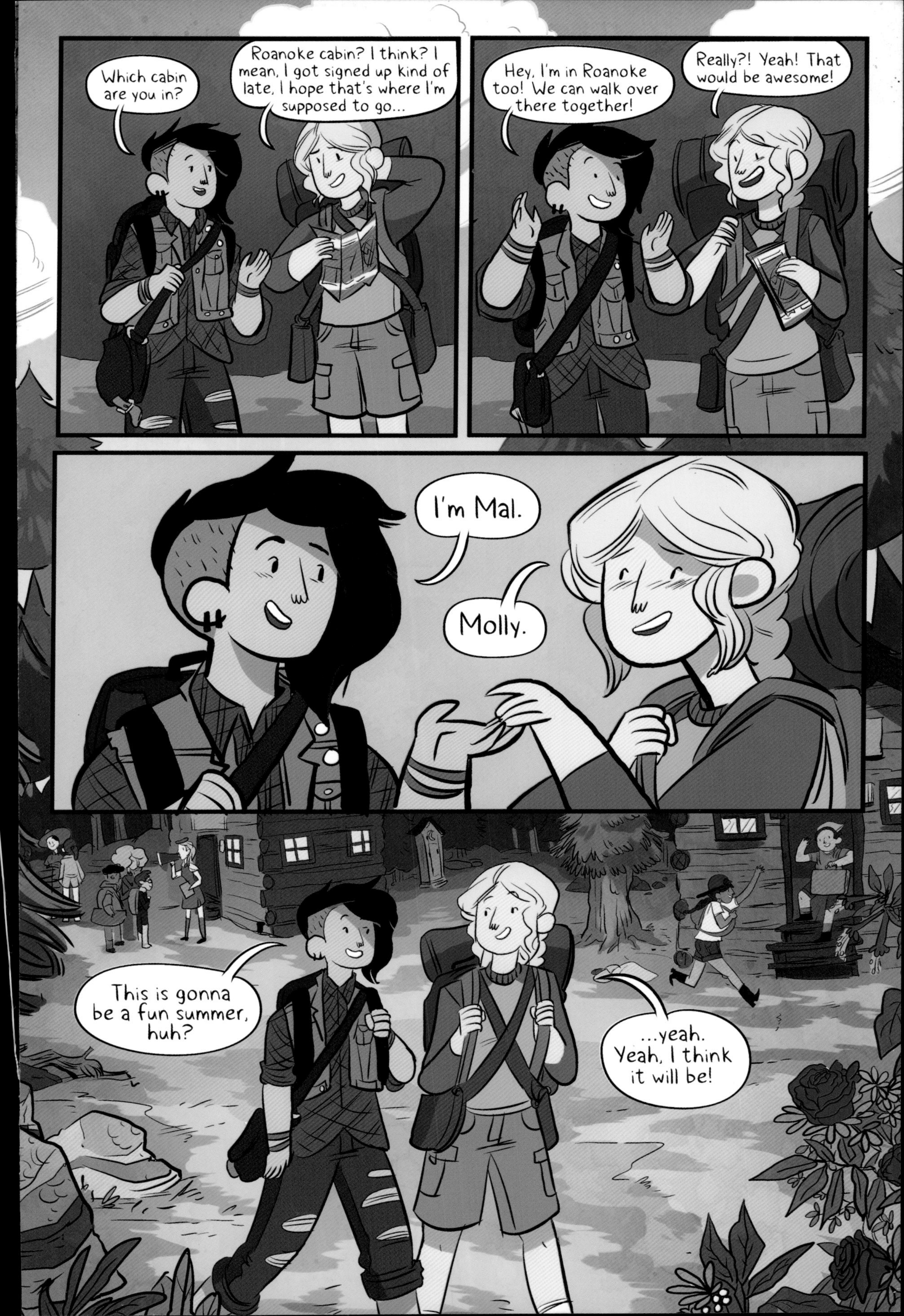
Which cabin are you in?
Roanoke cabin? I think? I mean, I got signed up kind of late, I hope that's where I'm supposed to go...
Hey, I'm in Roanoke too! We can walk over there together!
Really?! Yeah! That would be awesome!
I'm Mal.
Molly.
This is gonna be a fun summer, huh?
...yeah. Yeah, I think it will be!

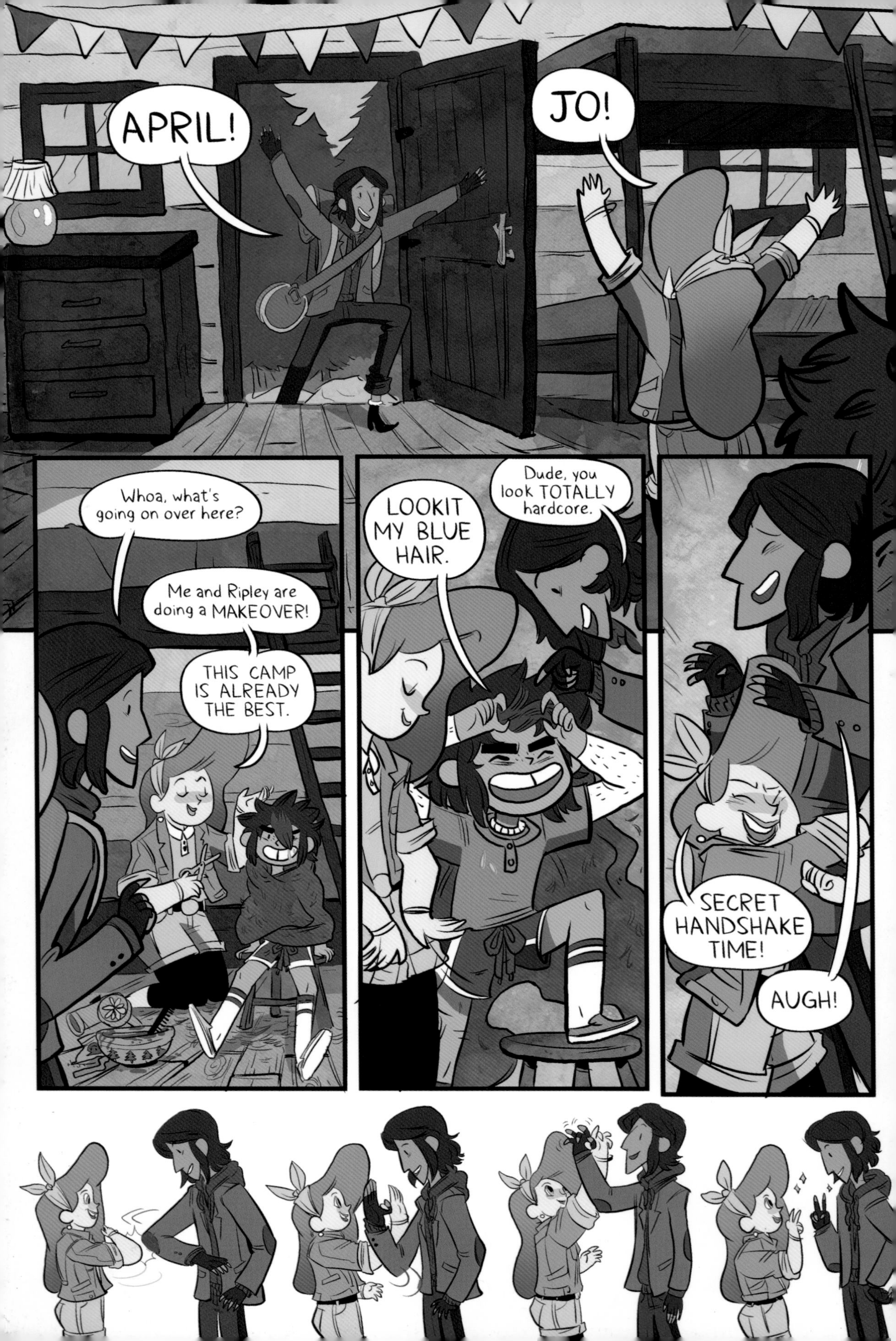
APRIL!
JO!
Whoa, what's going on over here?
Me and Ripley are doing a MAKEOVER!
THIS CAMP IS ALREADY THE BEST.
LOOKIT MY BLUE HAIR.
Dude, you look TOTALLY hardcore.
SECRET HANDSHAKE TIME!
AUGH!

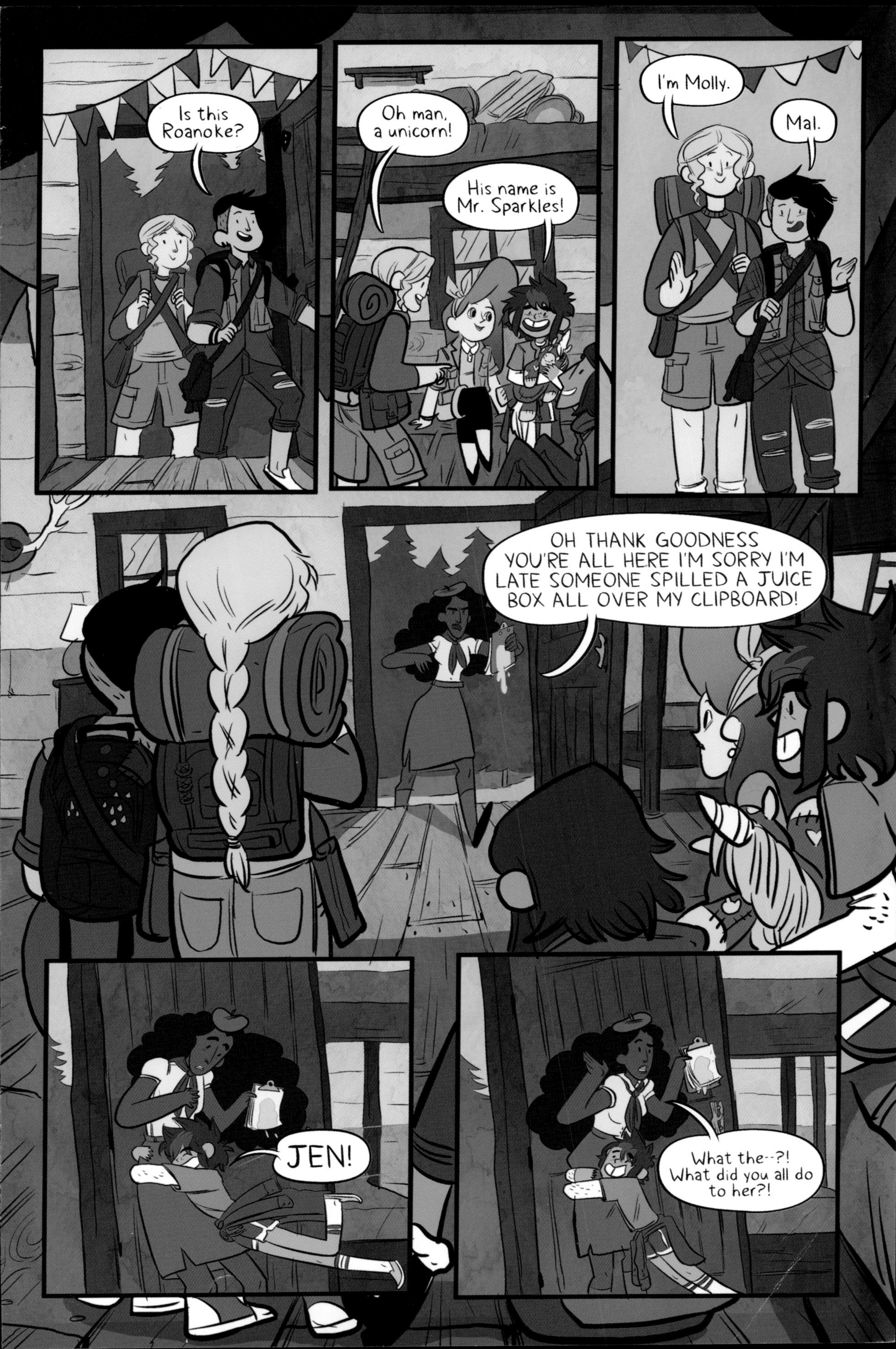
Is this Roanoke?
Oh man, a unicorn!
His name is Mr. Sparkles!
I'm Molly.
Mal.
OH THANK GOODNESS YOU'RE ALL HERE I'M SORRY I'M LATE SOMEONE SPILLED A JUICE BOX ALL OVER MY CLIPBOARD!
JEN!
What the--?! What did you all do to her?!

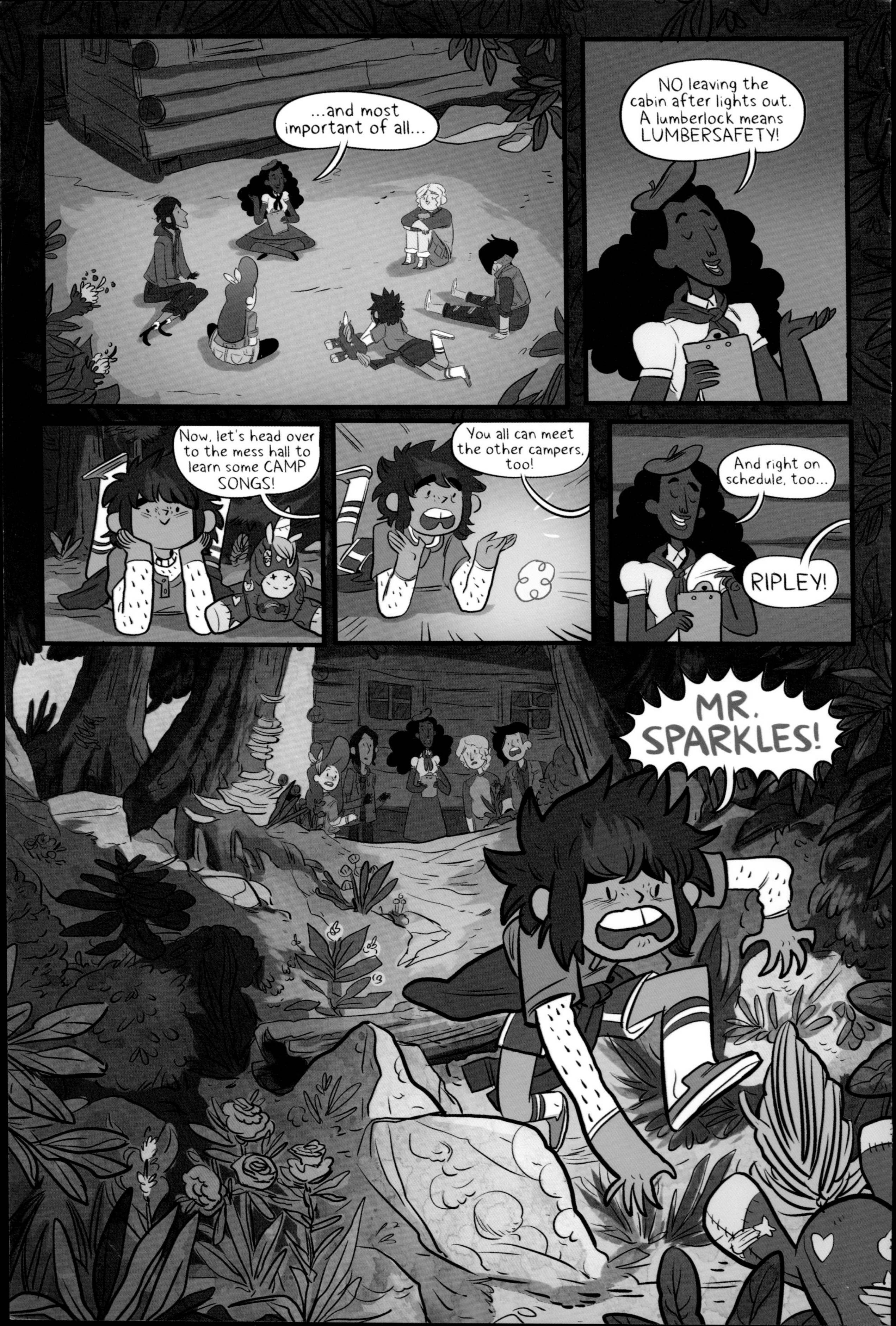
...and most important of all...
NO leaving the cabin after lights out. A lumberlock means LUMBERSAFETY!
Now, let's head over to the mess hall to learn some CAMP SONGS!
You all can meet the other campers, too!
And right on schedule, too...
RIPLEY!
MR. SPARKLES!

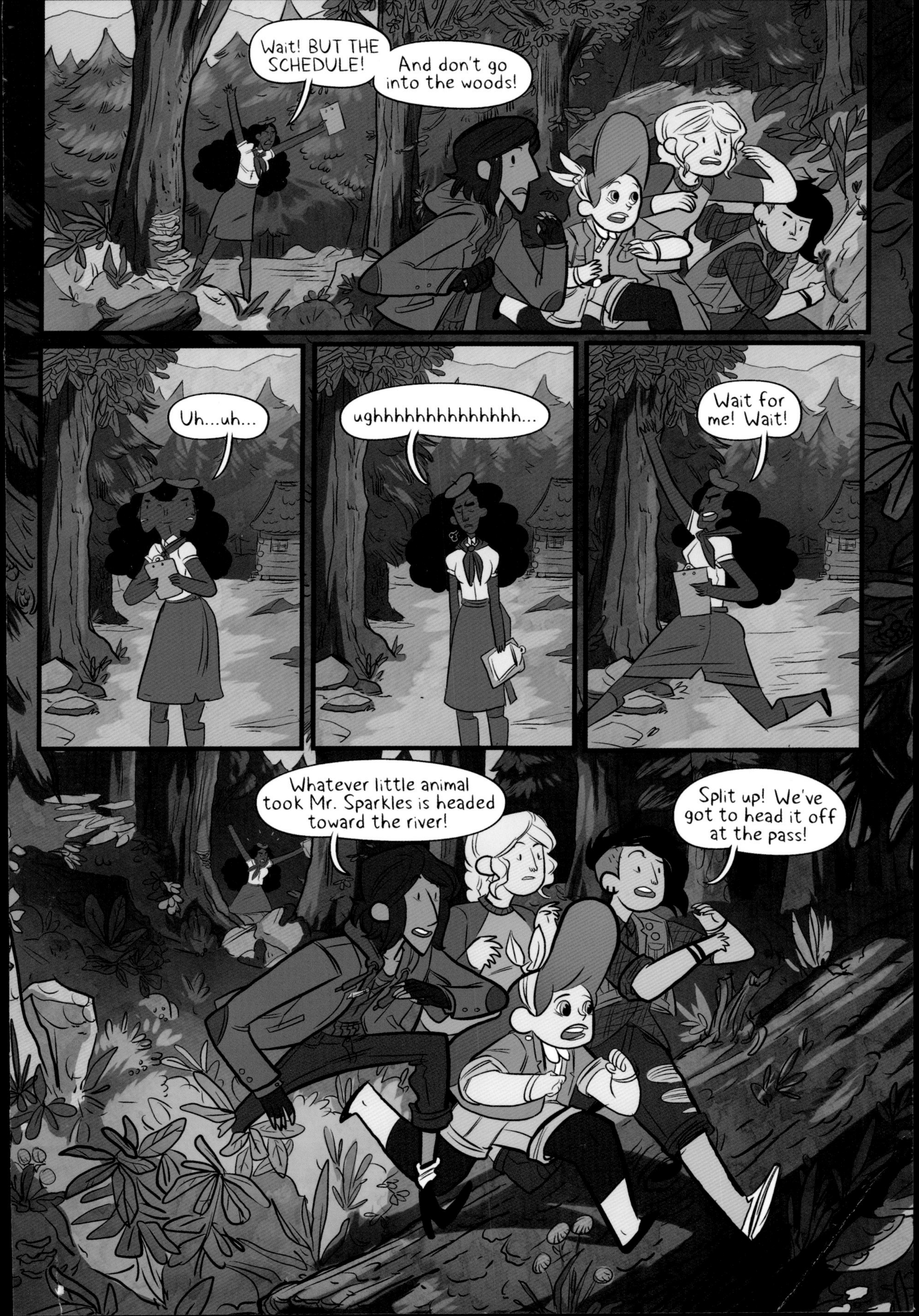
Wait! BUT THE SCHEDULE!
And don't go into the woods!
Uh...uh...
ughhhhhhhhhhhhhh...
Wait for me! Wait!
Whatever little animal took Mr. Sparkles is headed toward the river!
Split up! We've got to head it off at the pass!

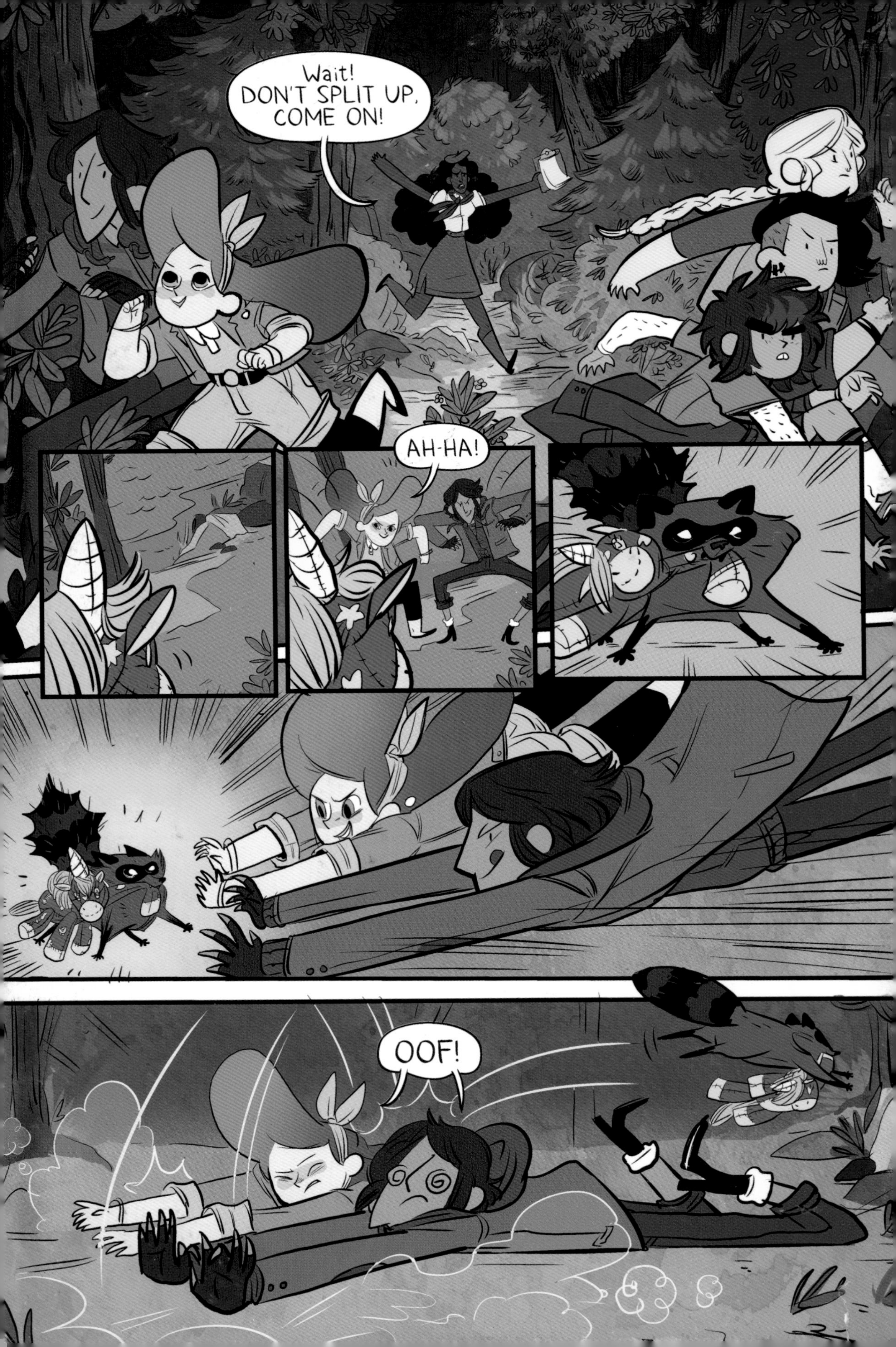
Wait!
DON'T SPLIT UP,
COME ON!
AH-HA!
OOF!

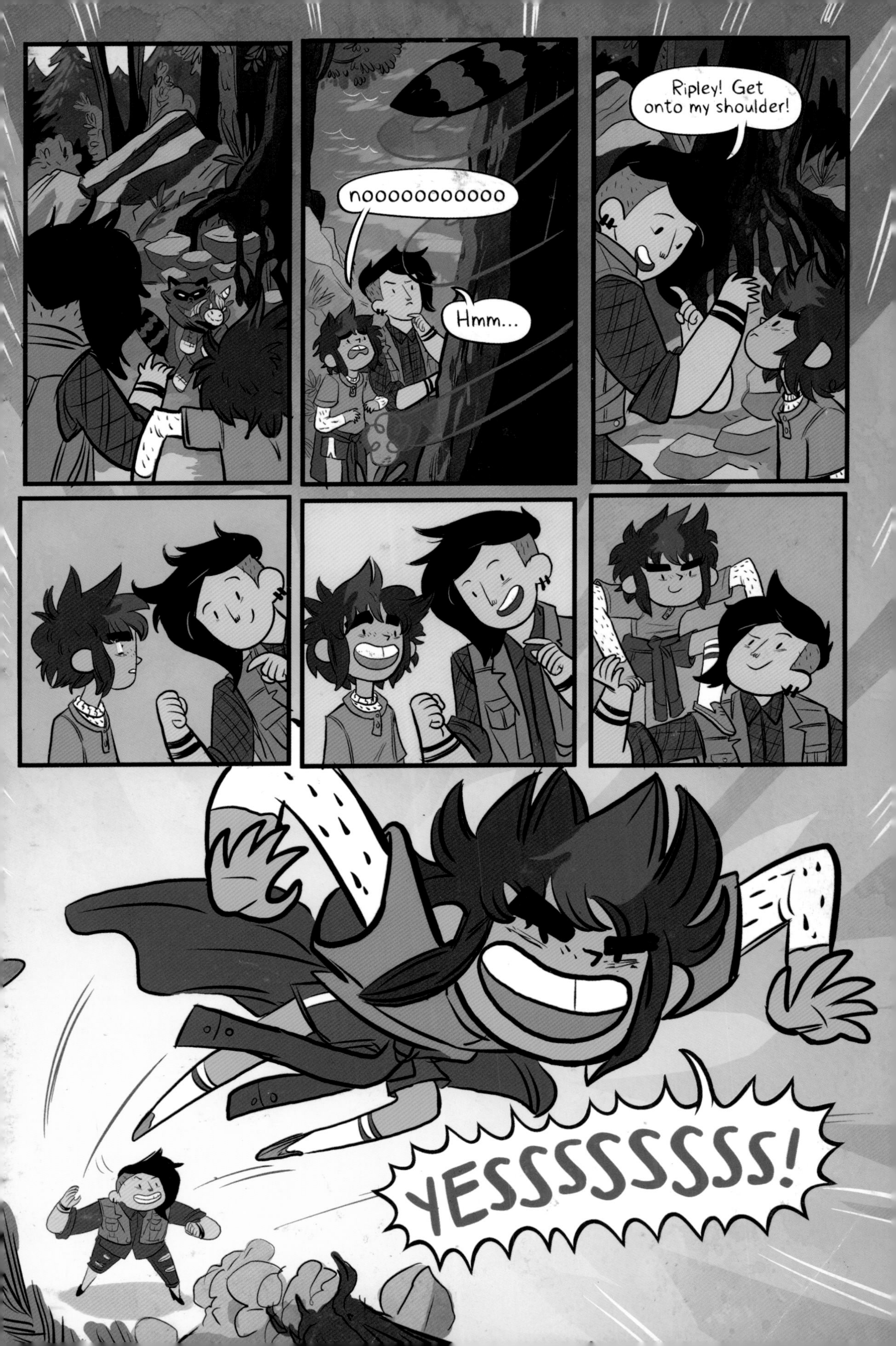
noooooooooooo
Hmm...
Ripley! Get onto my shoulder!
YESSSSSSSSS!

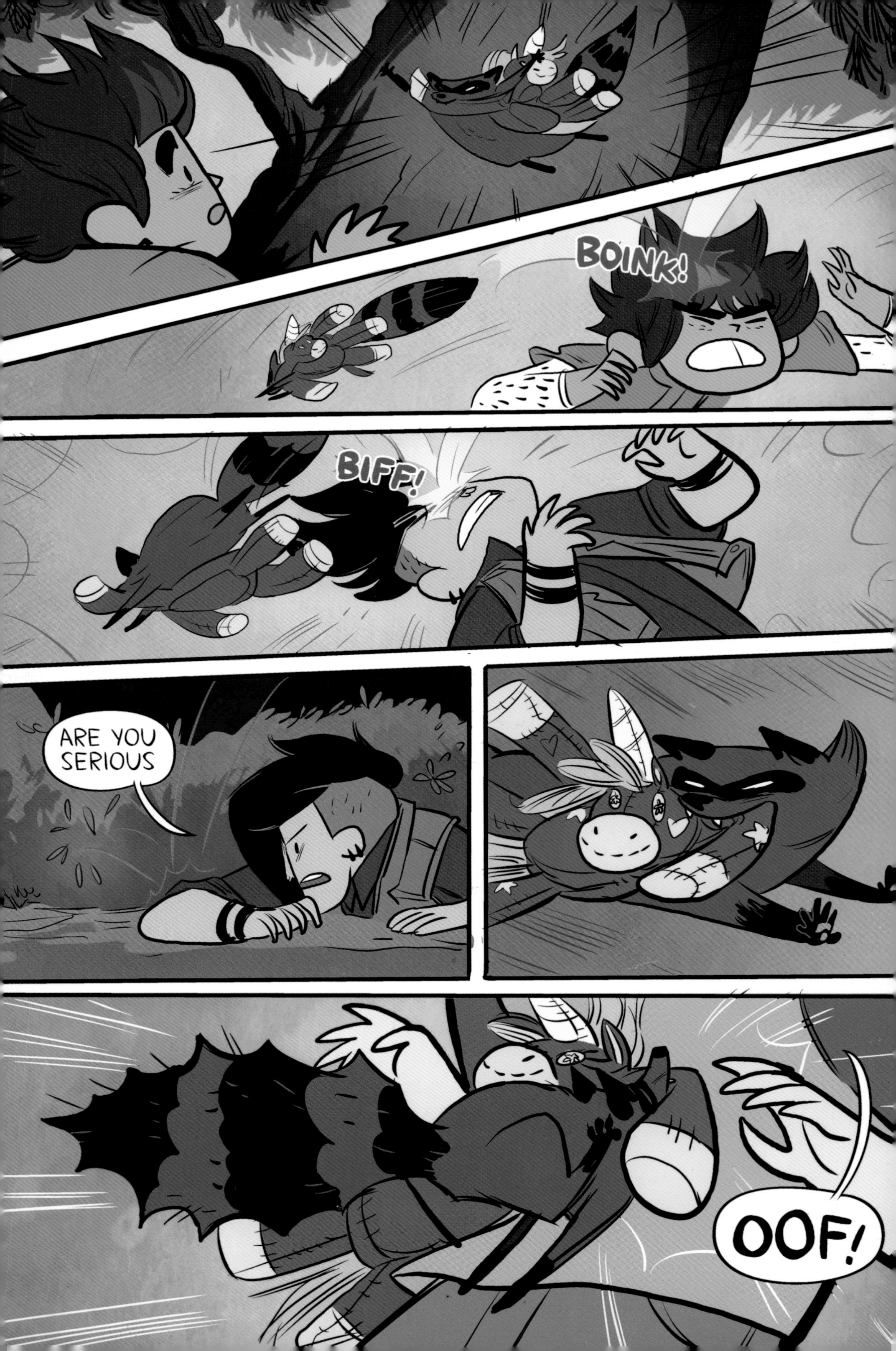
BOINK!
BIFF!
ARE YOU SERIOUS
OOF!

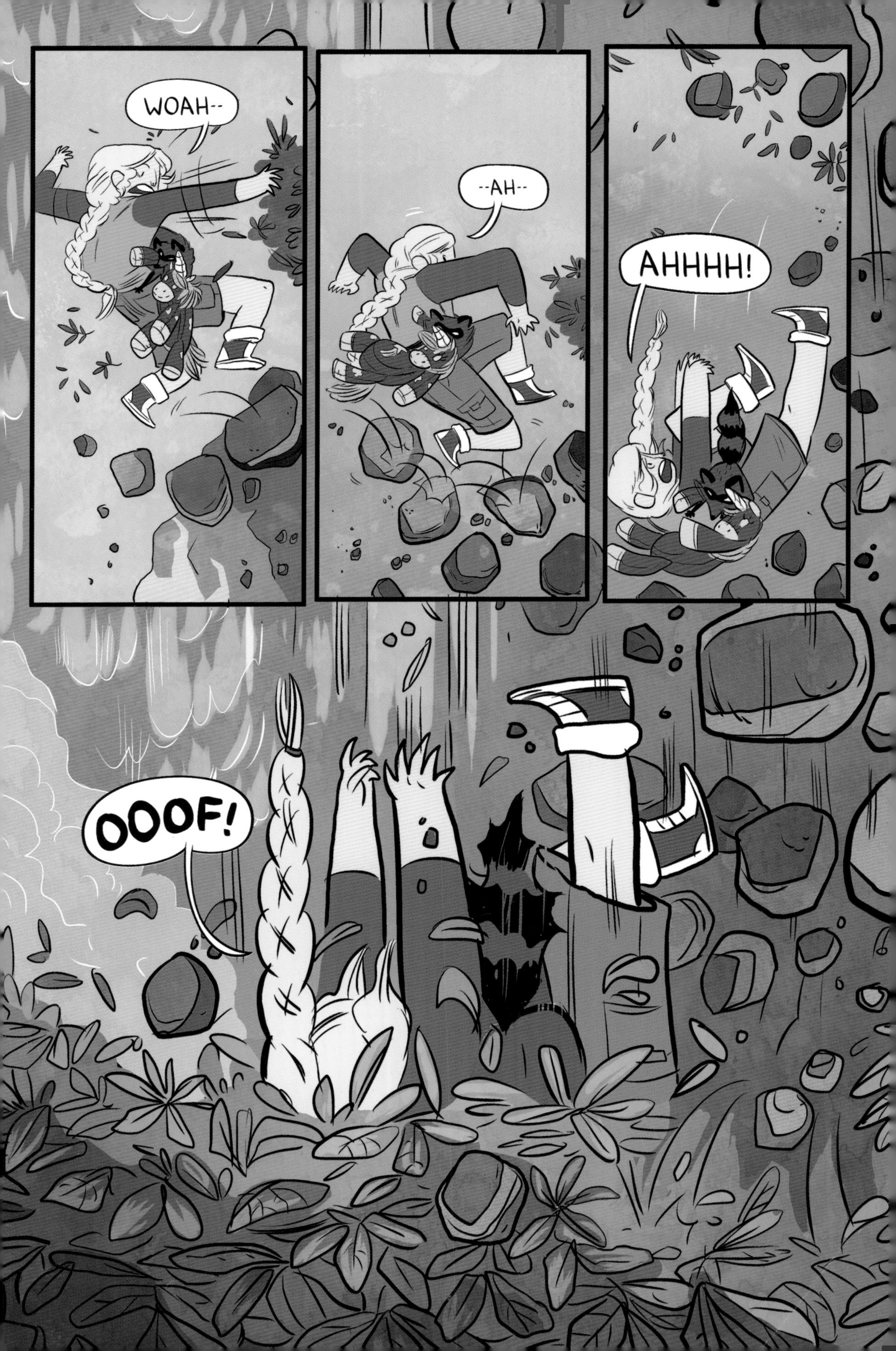
WOAH--
--AH--
AHHHH!
OOOF!

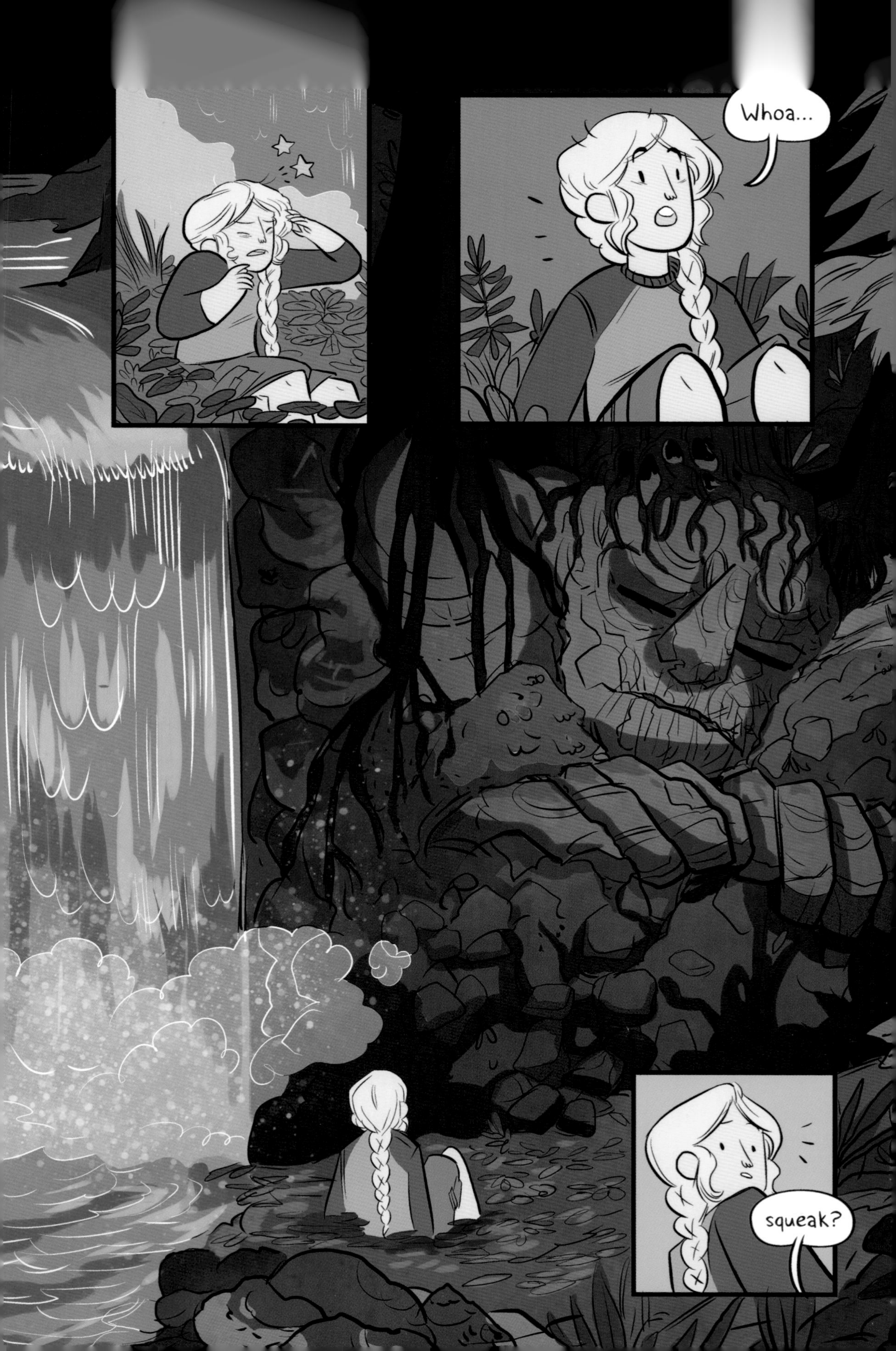
Whoa...
squeak?

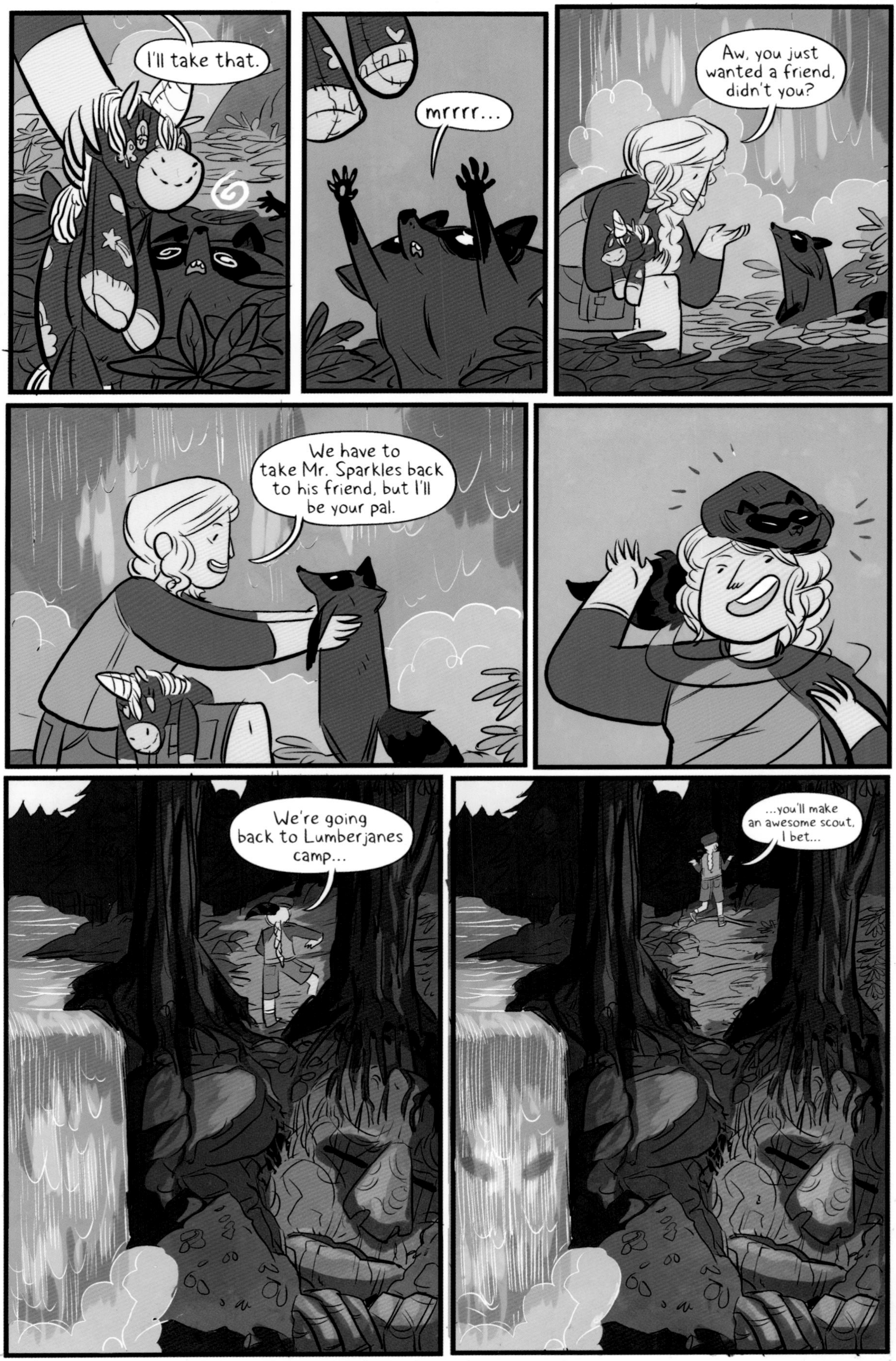
I'll take that.
mrrrr...
Aw, you just wanted a friend, didn't you?
We have to take Mr. Sparkles back to his friend, but I'll be your pal.
We're going back to Lumberjanes camp...
...you'll make an awesome scout, I bet...

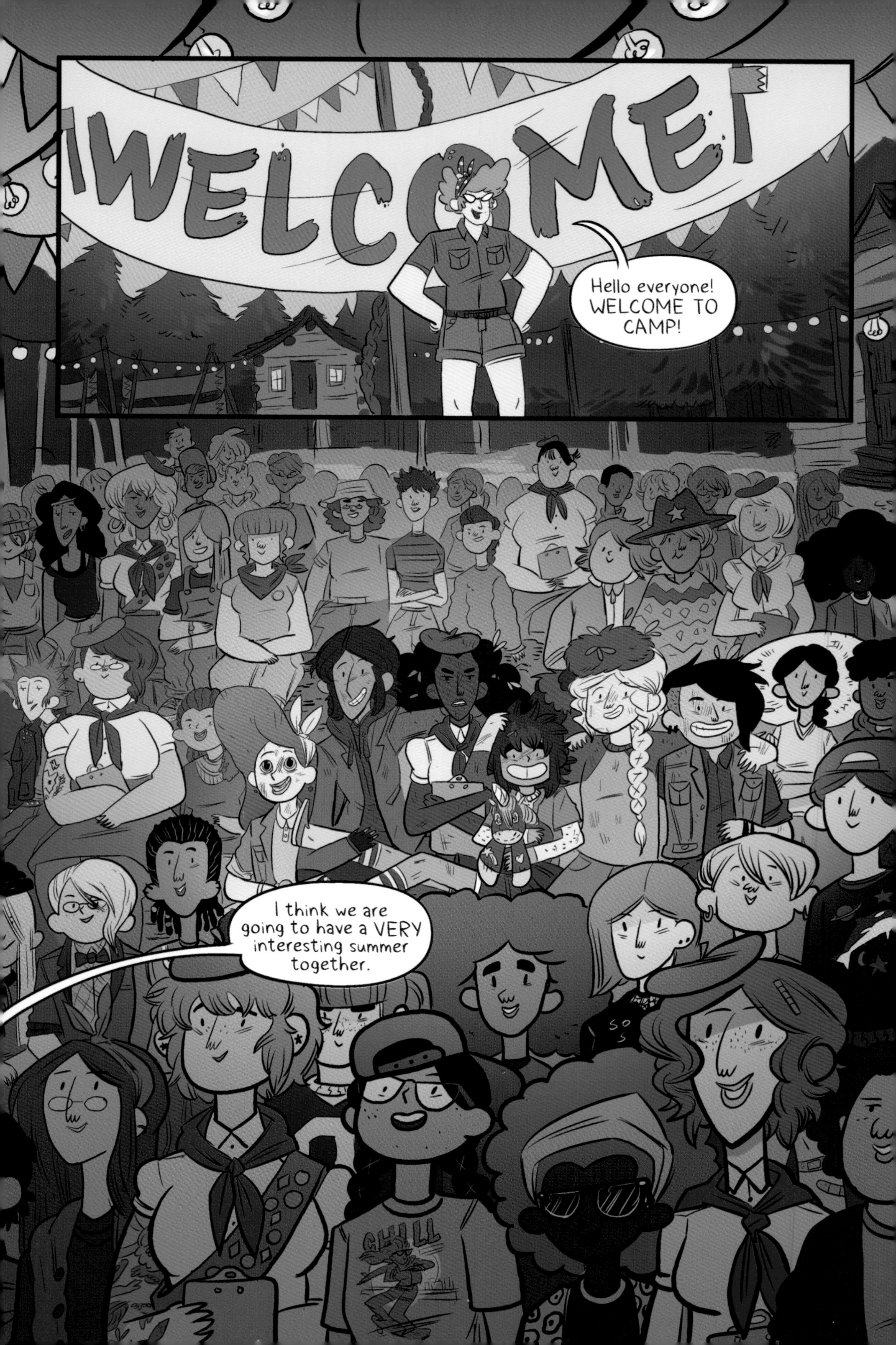
WELCOME!
Hello everyone! WELCOME TO CAMP!
I think we are going to have a VERY interesting summer together.
CHILL

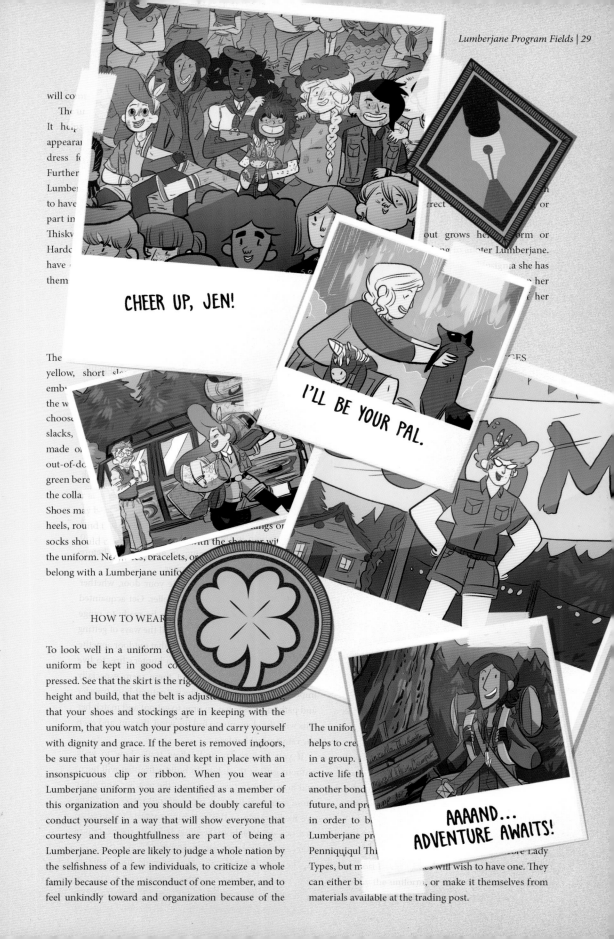

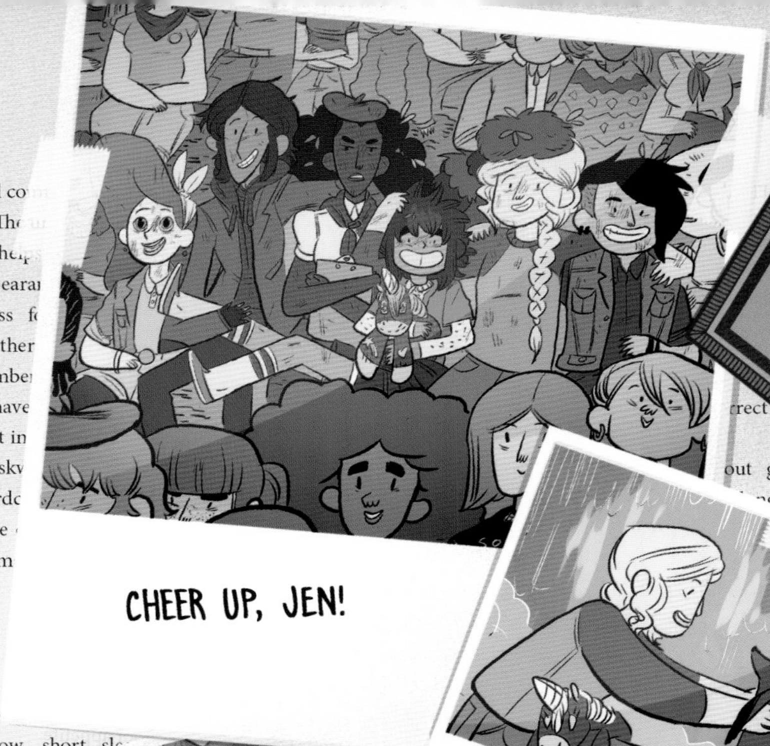
CHEER UP, JEN!

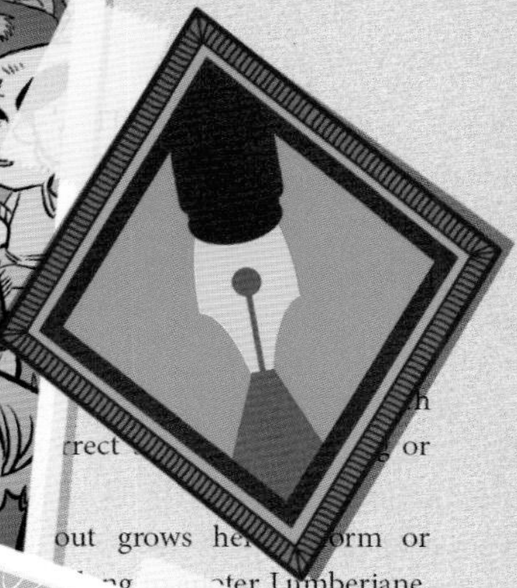

will co

The

It he

appeara

dress f

Further

Lumbe

to have

part in

Thisk

Hard

have

them

out grows he orm or

ter Lumberjane.

a she has

her

her

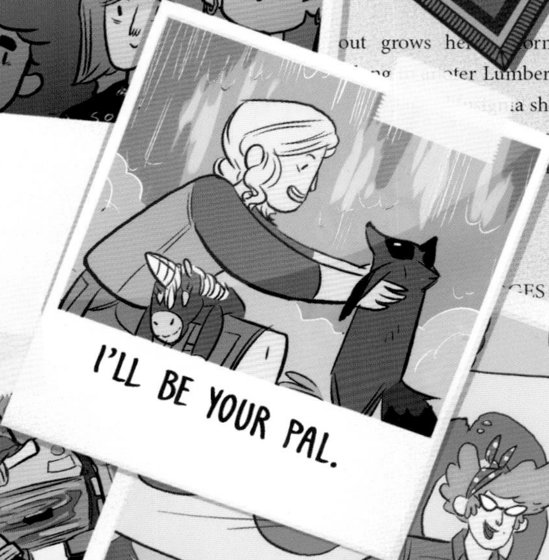
I'LL BE YOUR PAL.

The

yellow, short sl

emb

the w

choos

slacks,

made o

out-of-d

green bere

the colla

Shoes ma

heels, rou ings or

socks shou ith the shoes or wi

the uniform. Ne es, bracelets, or

belong with a Lumberjane unifo

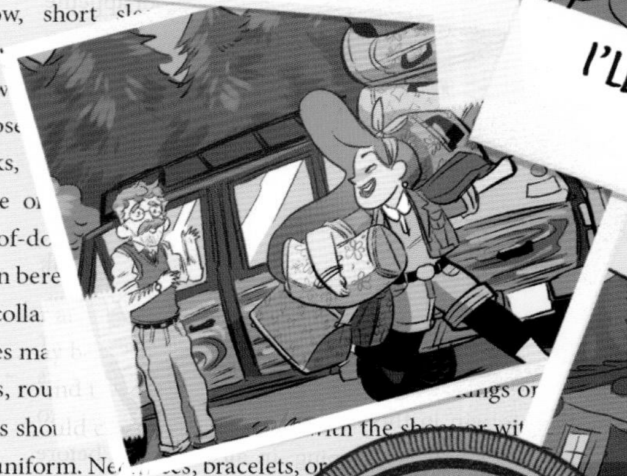

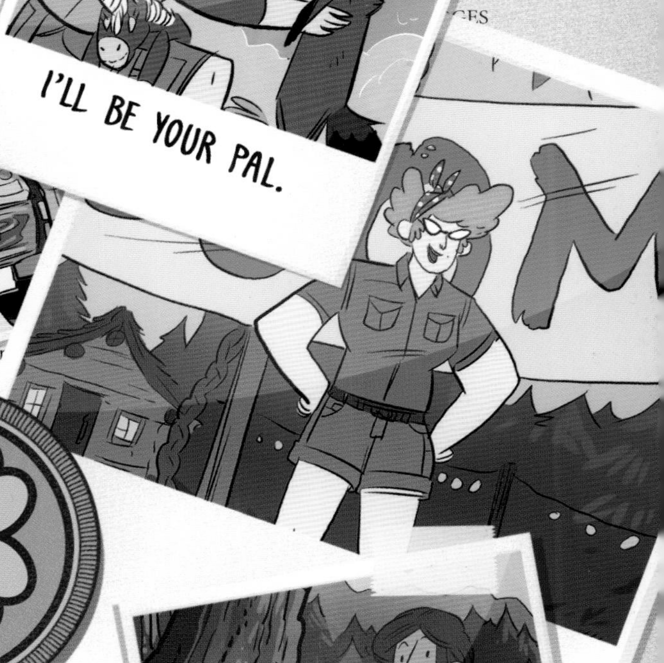

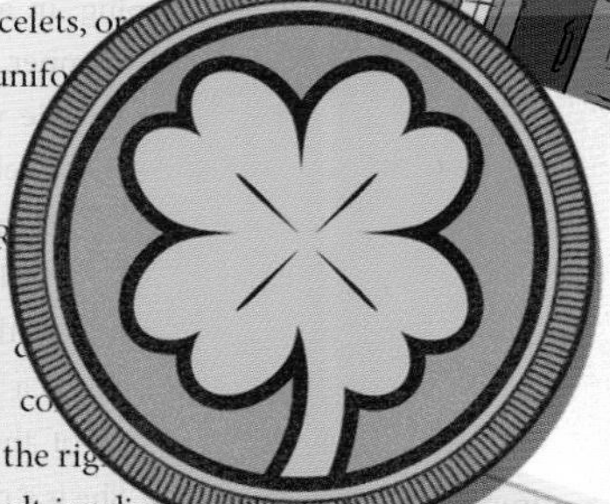

HOW TO WEAR

To look well in a uniform uniform be kept in good co pressed. See that the skirt is the rig height and build, that the belt is adjust that your shoes and stockings are in keeping with the uniform, that you watch your posture and carry yourself with dignity and grace. If the beret is removed indoors, be sure that your hair is neat and kept in place with an insonspicuous clip or ribbon. When you wear a Lumberjane uniform you are identified as a member of this organization and you should be doubly careful to conduct yourself in a way that will show everyone that courtesy and thoughtfullness are part of being a Lumberjane. People are likely to judge a whole nation by the selfishness of a few individuals, to criticize a whole family because of the misconduct of one member, and to feel unkindly toward and organization because of the

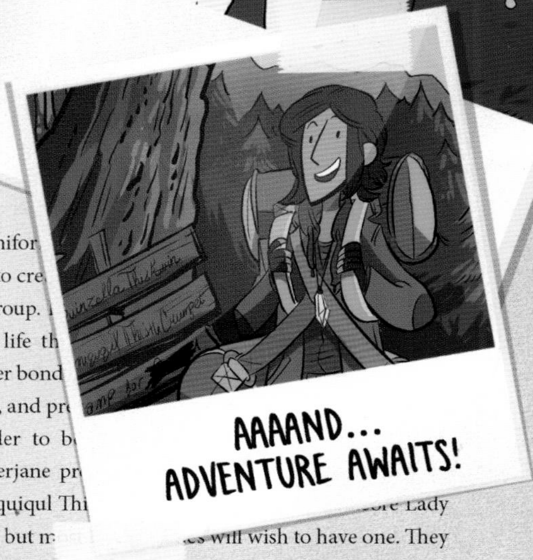
AAAAND...
ADVENTURE AWAITS!

The unifor

helps to cre

in a group.

active life th

another bond

future, and pr

in order to b

Lumberjane pr

Penniquiqul Thi ore Lady

Types, but m es will wish to have one. They

can either bu , or make it themselves from

materials available at the trading post.

LUMBERJANES FIELD MANUAL

CHAPTER EIGHTEEN

Lumberjanes "Literature" Program Field

DRESSIN' FOR SUCCESSIN' BADGE

"Plaid is a good way to go, always."

As a modern Lumberjane, you will be facing new and intriguing things out in the world outside of camp that we can only imagine as we put together this workbook. Time constantly changes, new trials and tribulations will face every Lumberjane, and at the same time, things don't always change. One of the concerns a Lumberjane will have in their day-to-day life from camp and even in the world beyond the camp, is how to represent themselves.

The *Dressin' for Successin'* badge is a point of pride for any Lumberjane, as they learn the importance of not only a functional wardrobe, but how to use every layer to the best of their ability. Does that sweater vest match with the preselected stockings that you brought to camp for a free day with your friends? Can it also serve as a rope and hold the weight of you and your cabin as you decide to climb the neverending tree? Perfect. Clothing looks nice, and there is nothing wrong with wanting to look nice. The best

thing that we can ever teach you at this camp is to be able to dress like you want to dress, and at the end of the day, if bracelets also work as a projectile weapon, then even better.

To obtain the *Dressin' for Successin'* badge a Lumberjane must be able to put together three outfits for a hike through the night. They will come across multiple terrains that cannot be prepared for as the terrains like to move whenever they feel like it and it will be up to the Lumberjane to put together the perfect collection of clothing to help them through any possibility. The only advice that we give our young campers as they prepare to earn this badge would be to dress comfortably, and always know that plaid has never let us down. Once you've obtained the *Dressin' for Successin'* badge, then you'll be able to move on to the next badge with relative ease, depending on your foot wear choice of the day. Keep in mind, friends are always available to help you out when it comes to this badge.

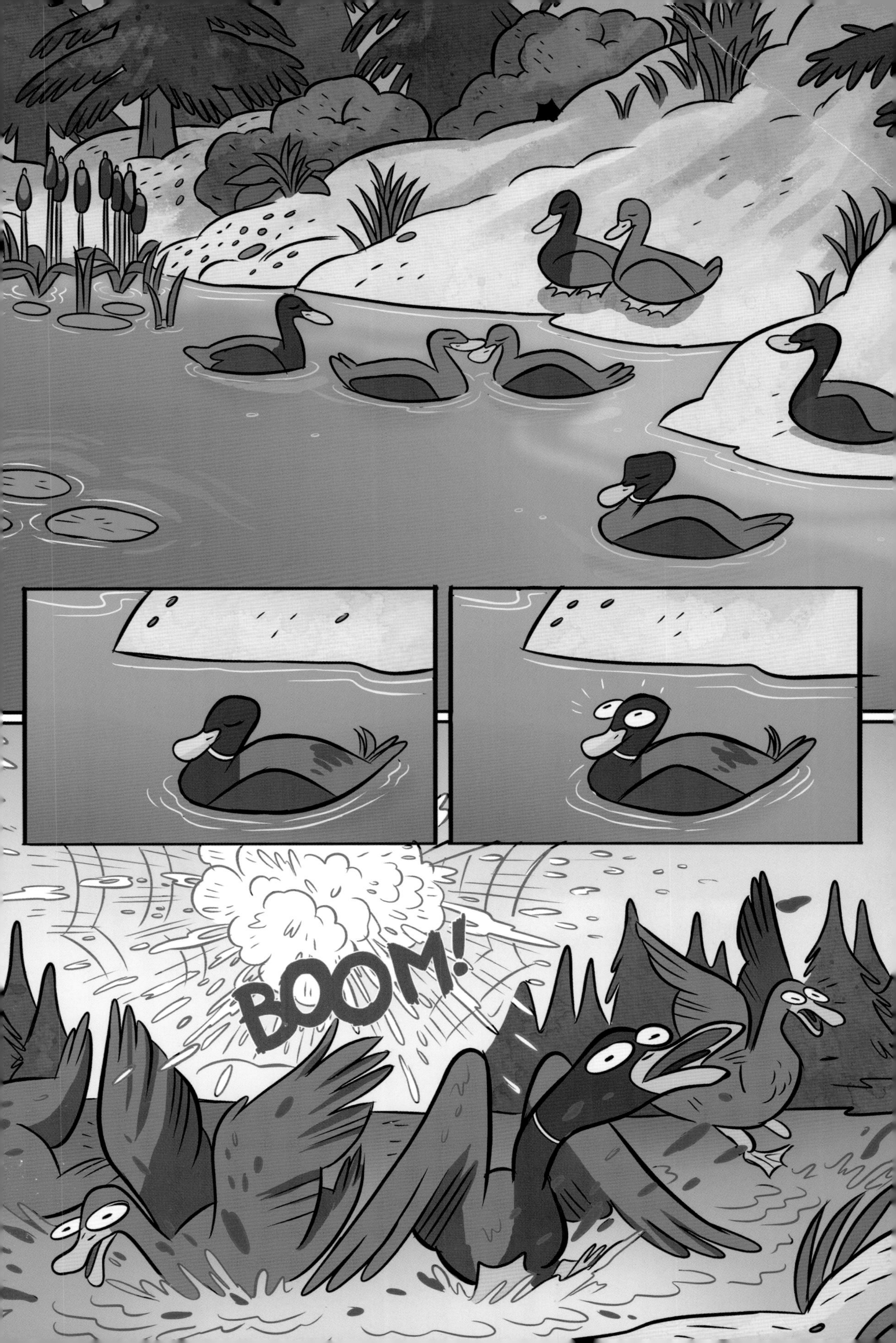
BOOM!

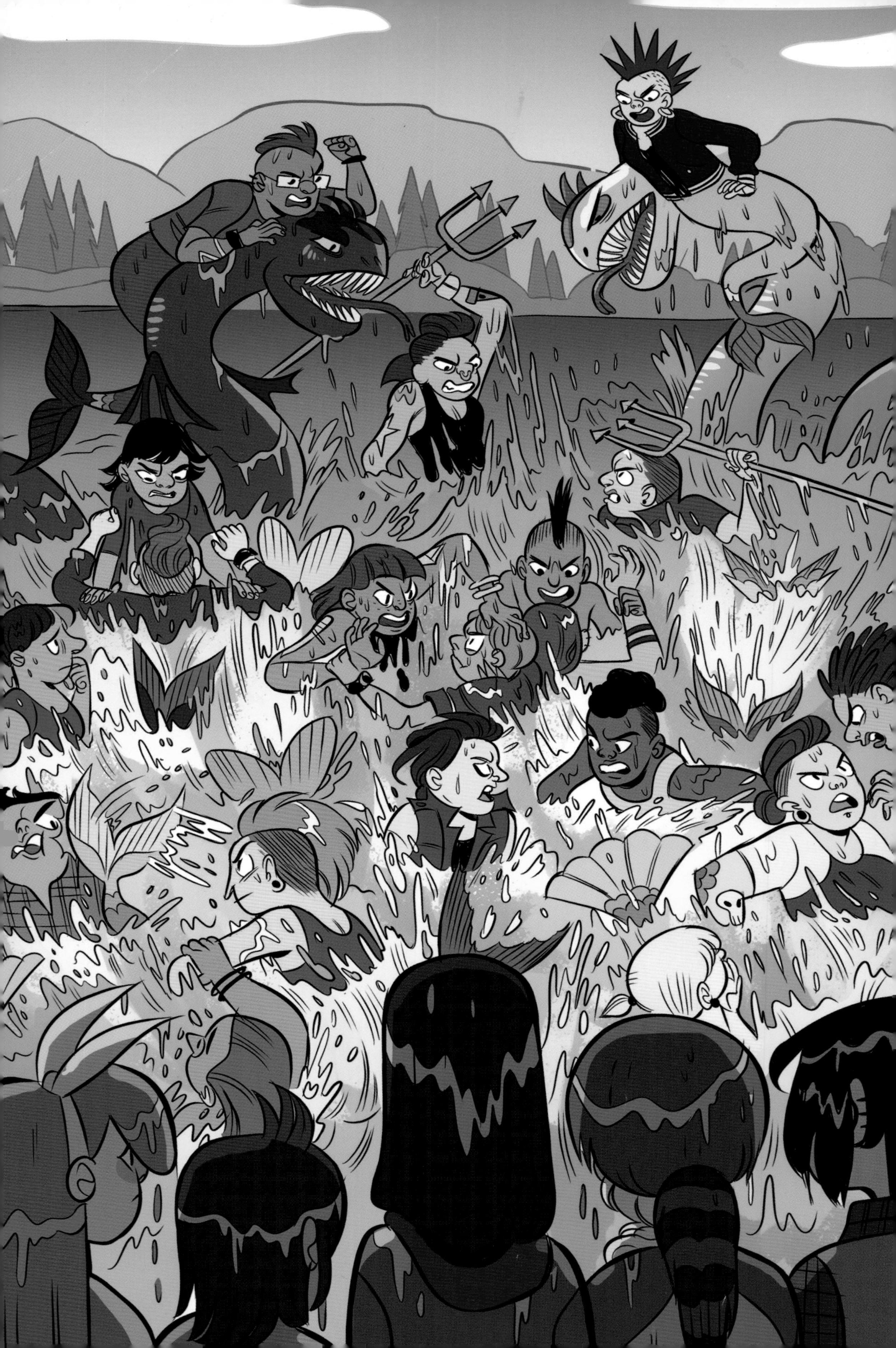

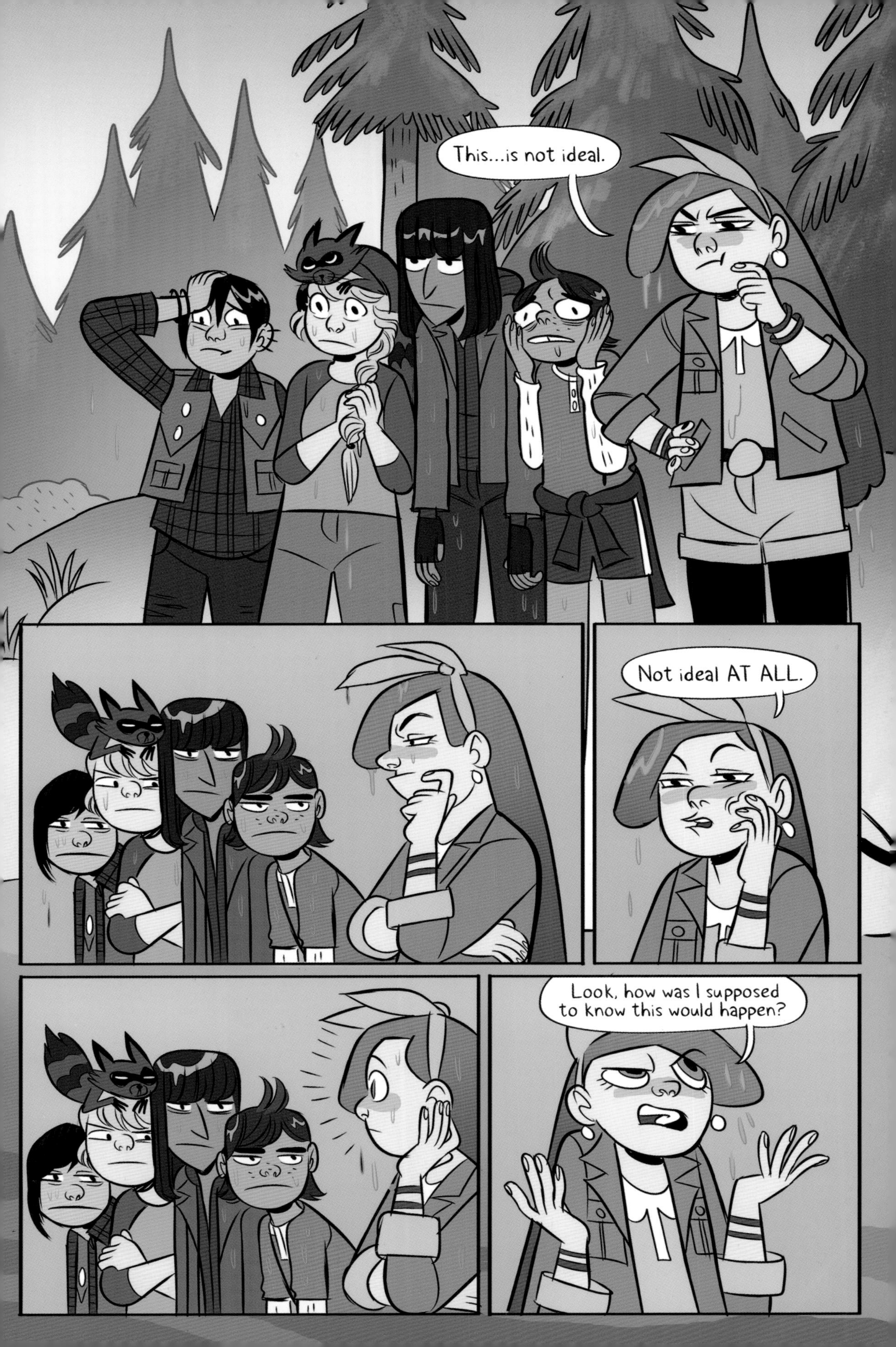
This...is not ideal.
Not ideal AT ALL.
Look, how was I supposed to know this would happen?

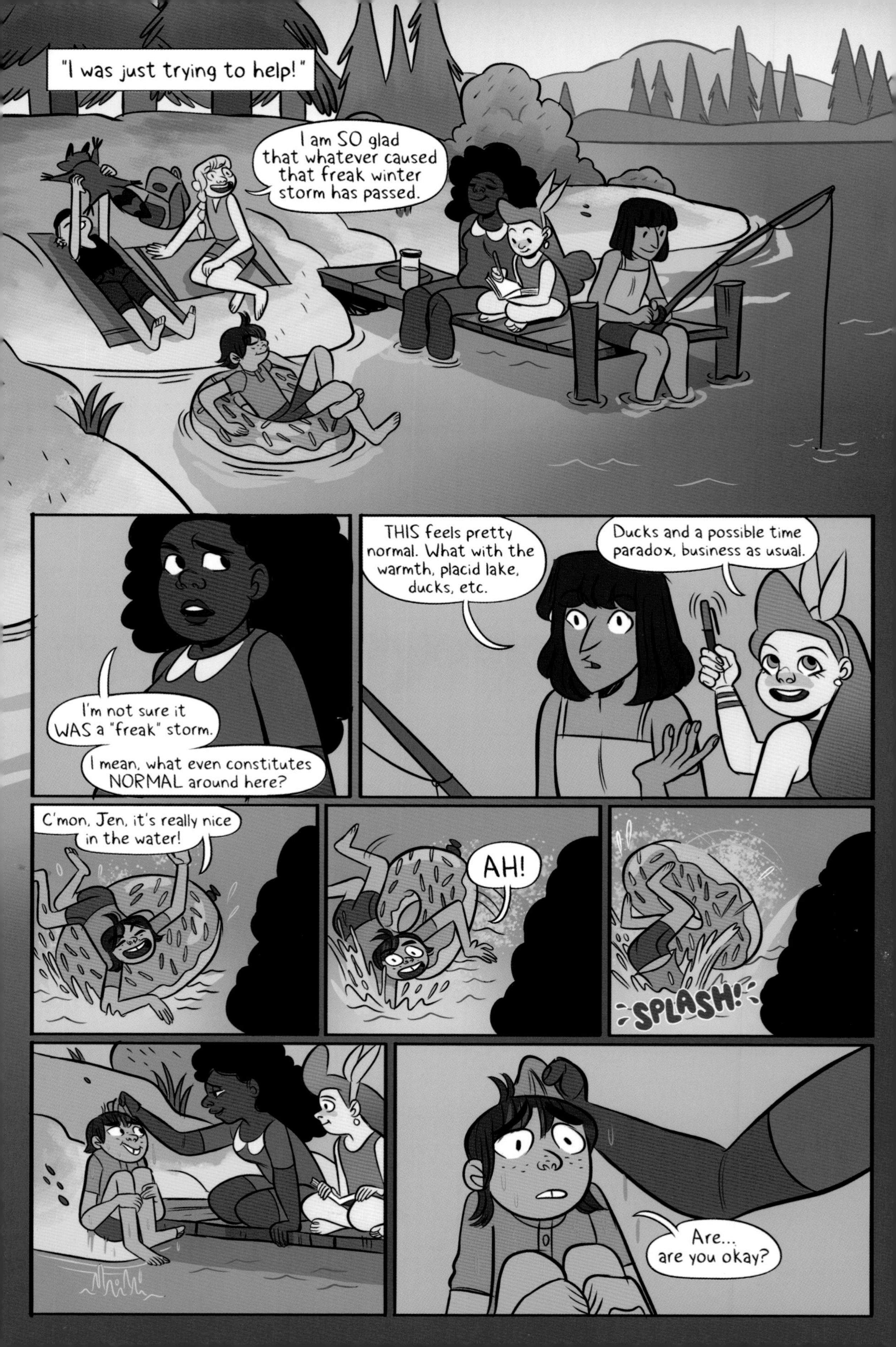
"I was just trying to help!"
I am SO glad that whatever caused that freak winter storm has passed.
I'm not sure it WAS a "freak" storm.
I mean, what even constitutes NORMAL around here?
THIS feels pretty normal. What with the warmth, placid lake, ducks, etc.
Ducks and a possible time paradox, business as usual.
C'mon, Jen, it's really nice in the water!
AH!
SPLASH!
Are... are you okay?

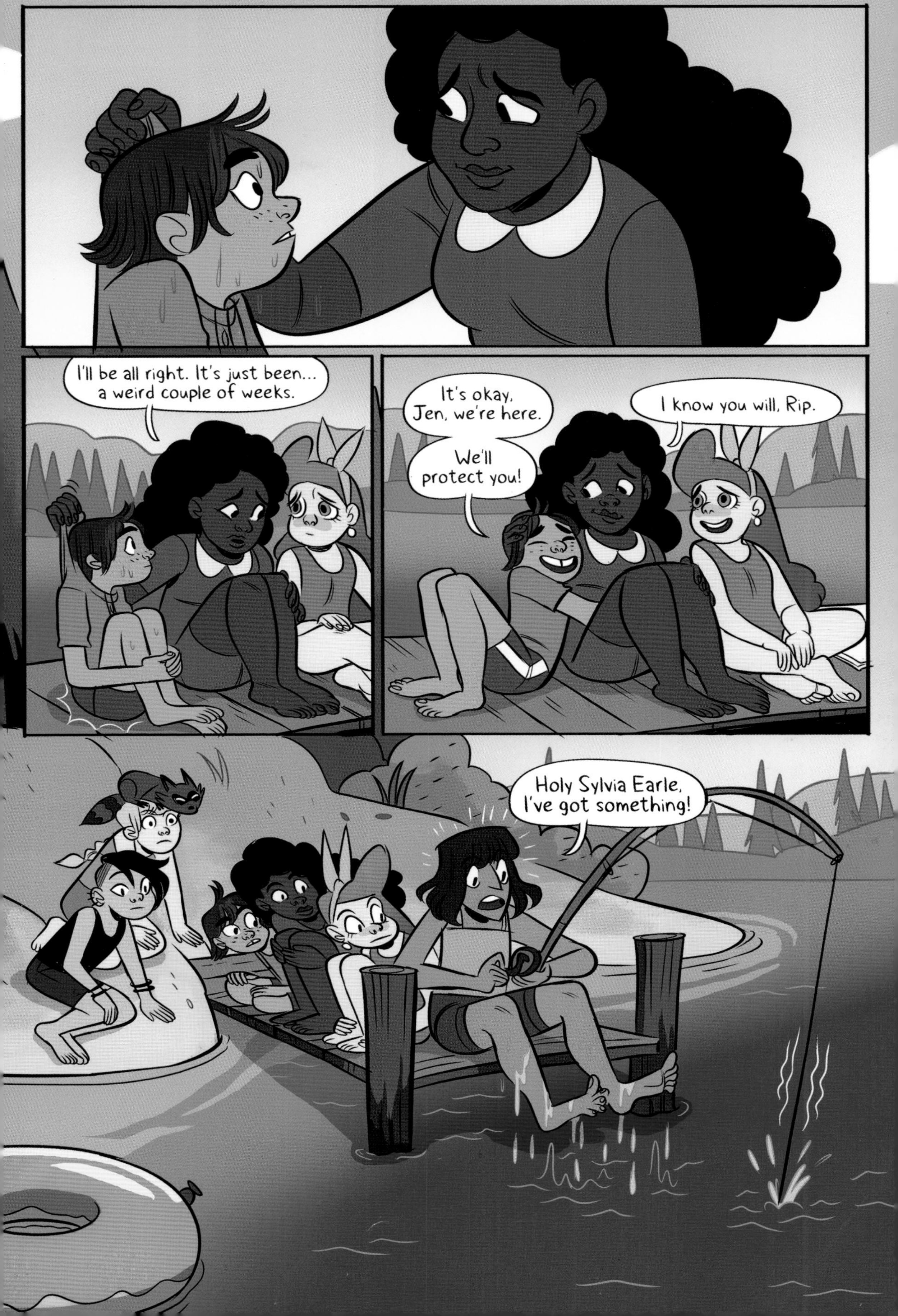
I'll be all right. It's just been... a weird couple of weeks.
It's okay, Jen, we're here.
We'll protect you!
I know you will, Rip.
Holy Sylvia Earle, I've got something!

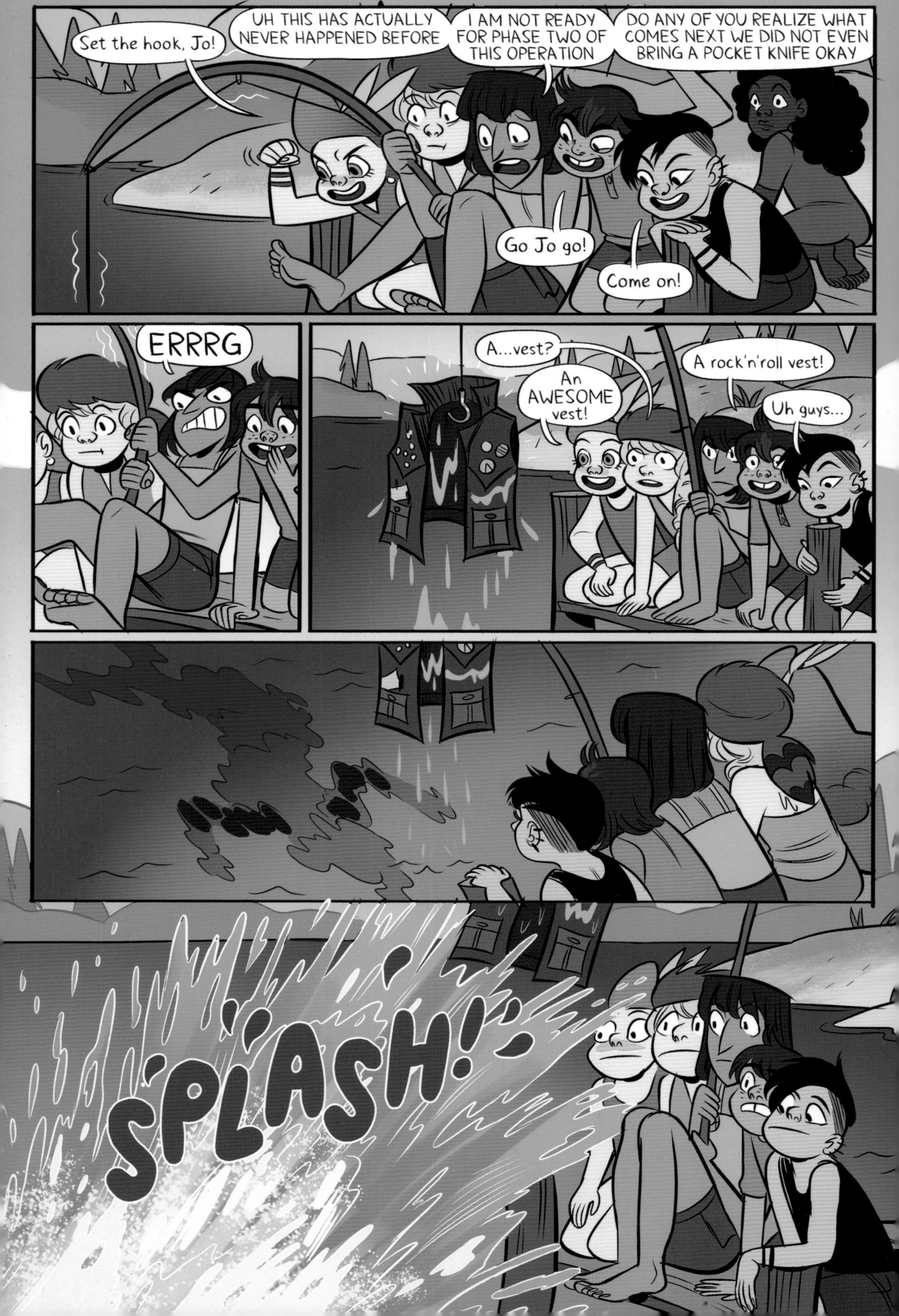
Set the hook, Jo!
UH THIS HAS ACTUALLY NEVER HAPPENED BEFORE
I AM NOT READY FOR PHASE TWO OF THIS OPERATION
DO ANY OF YOU REALIZE WHAT COMES NEXT WE DID NOT EVEN BRING A POCKET KNIFE OKAY
Go Jo go!
Come on!
ERRRG
A...vest?
An AWESOME vest!
A rock'n'roll vest!
Uh guys...
SPLASH!

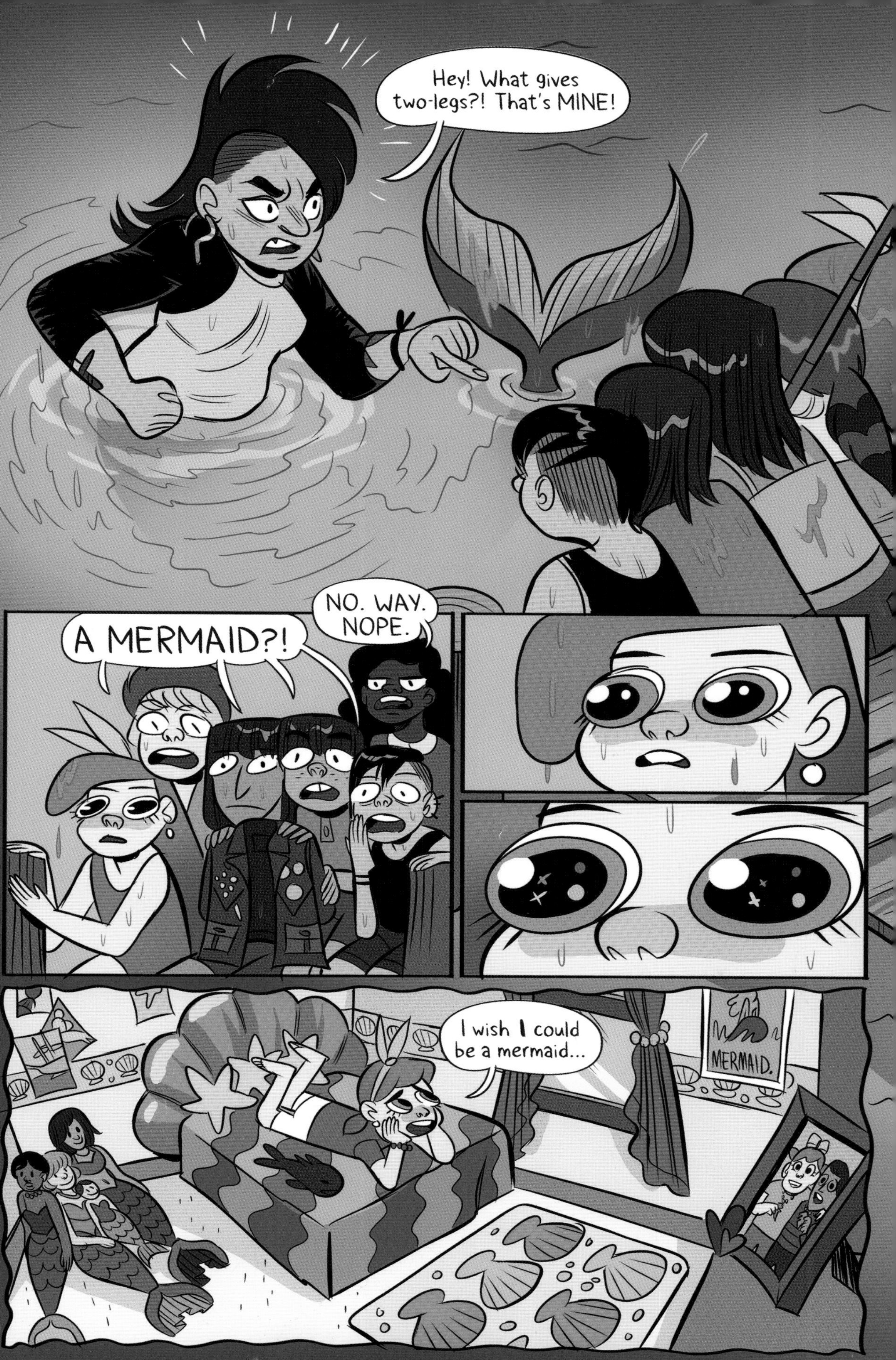
Hey! What gives two-legs?! That's MINE!
A MERMAID?!
NO. WAY. NOPE.
I wish I could be a mermaid...
MERMAID.

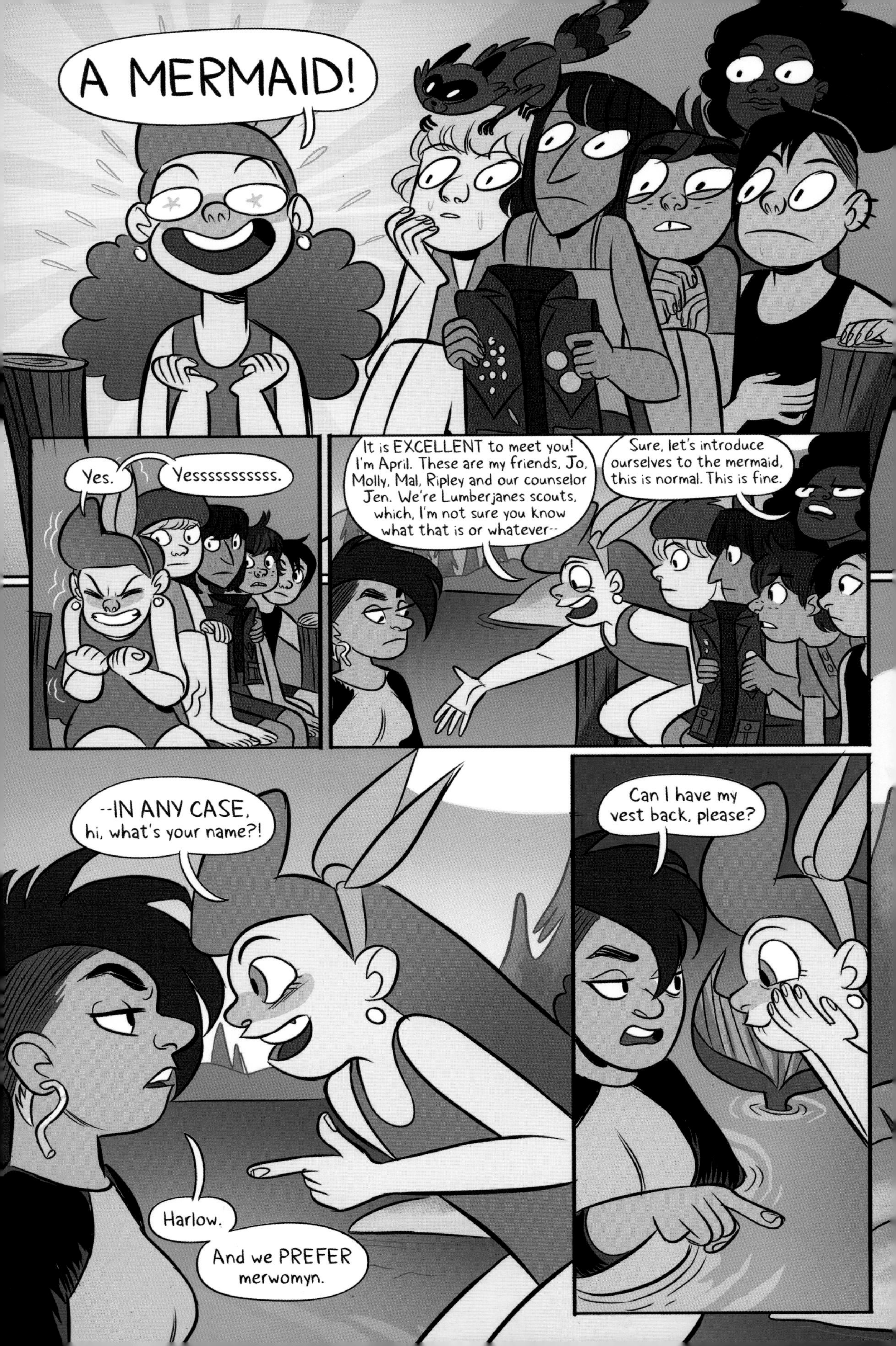
A MERMAID!
Yes.
Yesssssssssss.
It is EXCELLENT to meet you! I'm April. These are my friends, Jo, Molly, Mal, Ripley and our counselor Jen. We're Lumberjanes scouts, which, I'm not sure you know what that is or whatever--
Sure, let's introduce ourselves to the mermaid, this is normal. This is fine.
--IN ANY CASE, hi, what's your name?!
Harlow.
And we PREFER merwomyn.
Can I have my vest back, please?

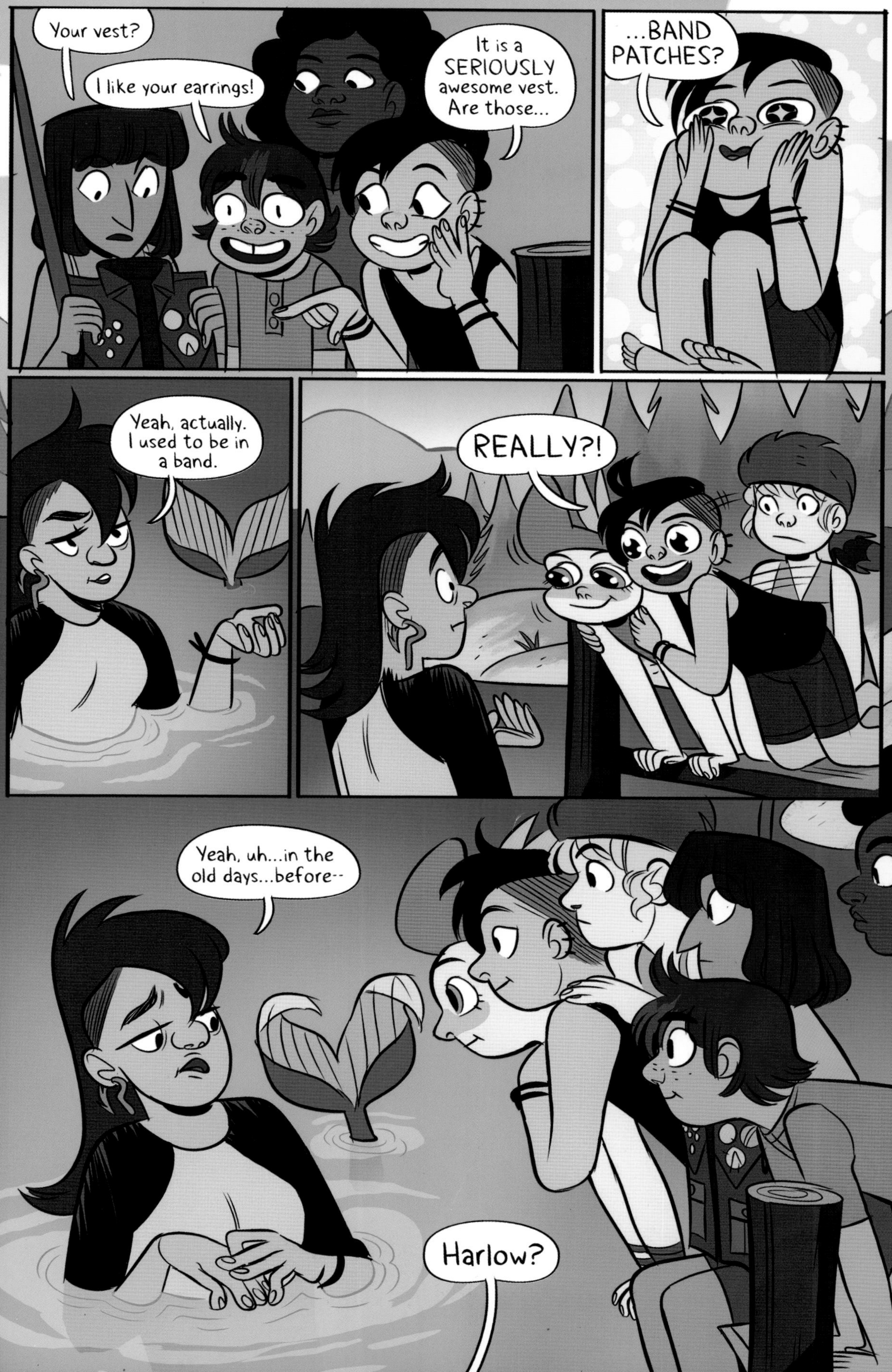

Your vest?
I like your earrings!
It is a SERIOUSLY awesome vest. Are those...
...BAND PATCHES?
Yeah, actually. I used to be in a band.
REALLY?!
Yeah, uh...in the old days...before--
Harlow?

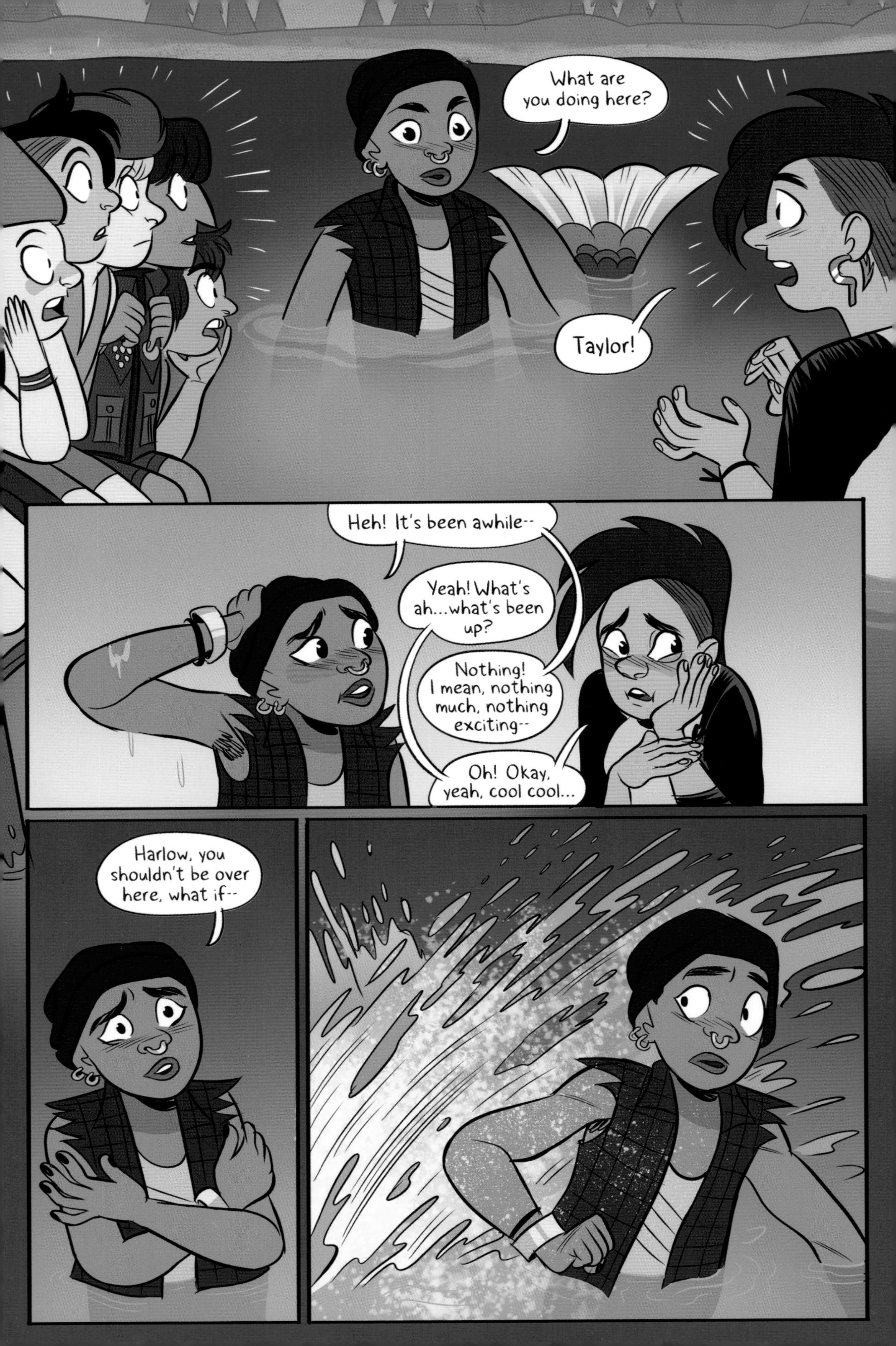
What are you doing here?
Taylor!
Heh! It's been awhile--
Yeah! What's ah...what's been up?
Nothing! I mean, nothing much, nothing exciting--
Oh! Okay, yeah, cool cool...
Harlow, you shouldn't be over here, what if--

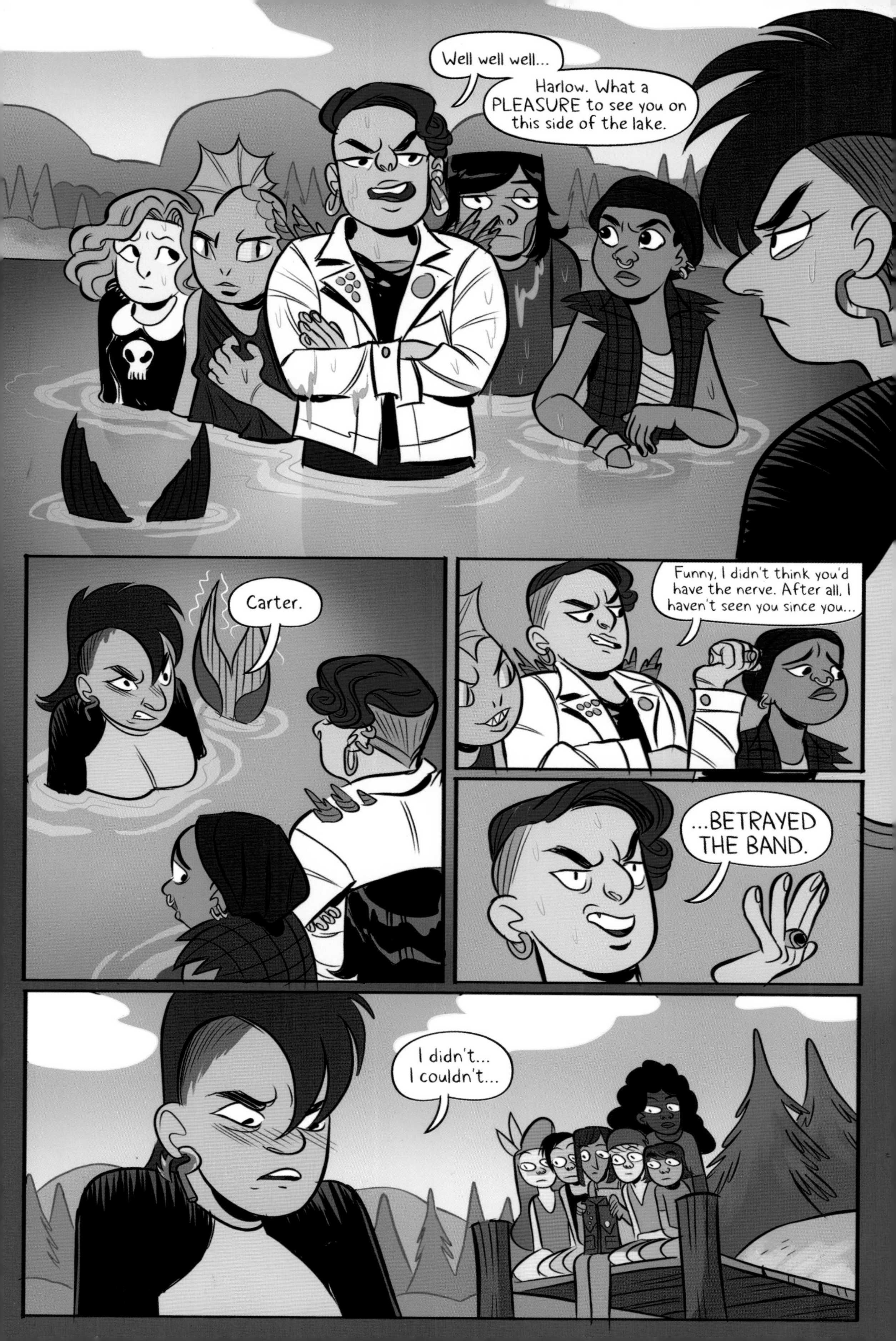
Well well well...
Harlow. What a PLEASURE to see you on this side of the lake.
Carter.
Funny, I didn't think you'd have the nerve. After all, I haven't seen you since you...
...BETRAYED THE BAND.
I didn't... I couldn't...

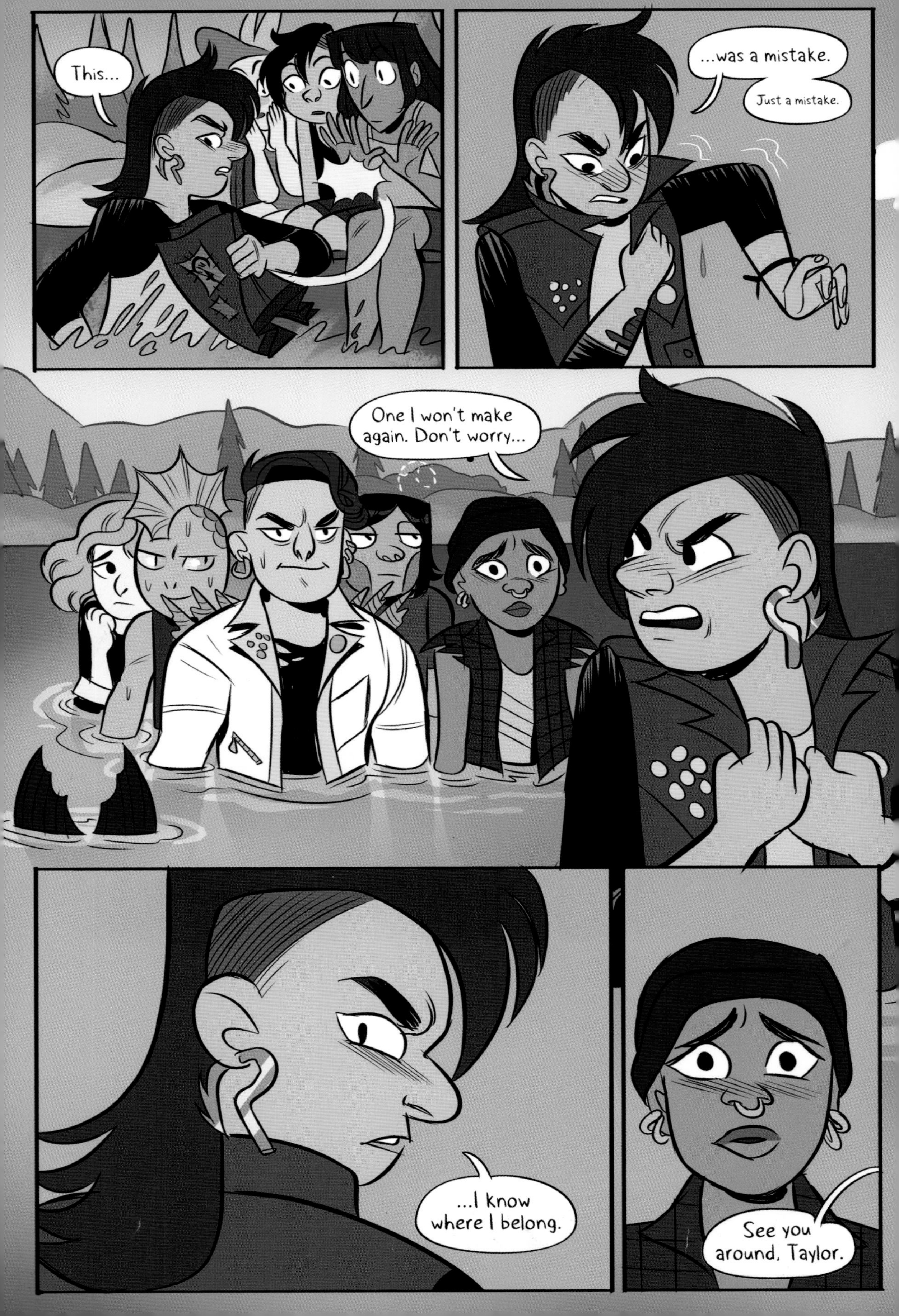
This...
...was a mistake.
Just a mistake.
One I won't make again. Don't worry...
...I know where I belong.
See you around, Taylor.

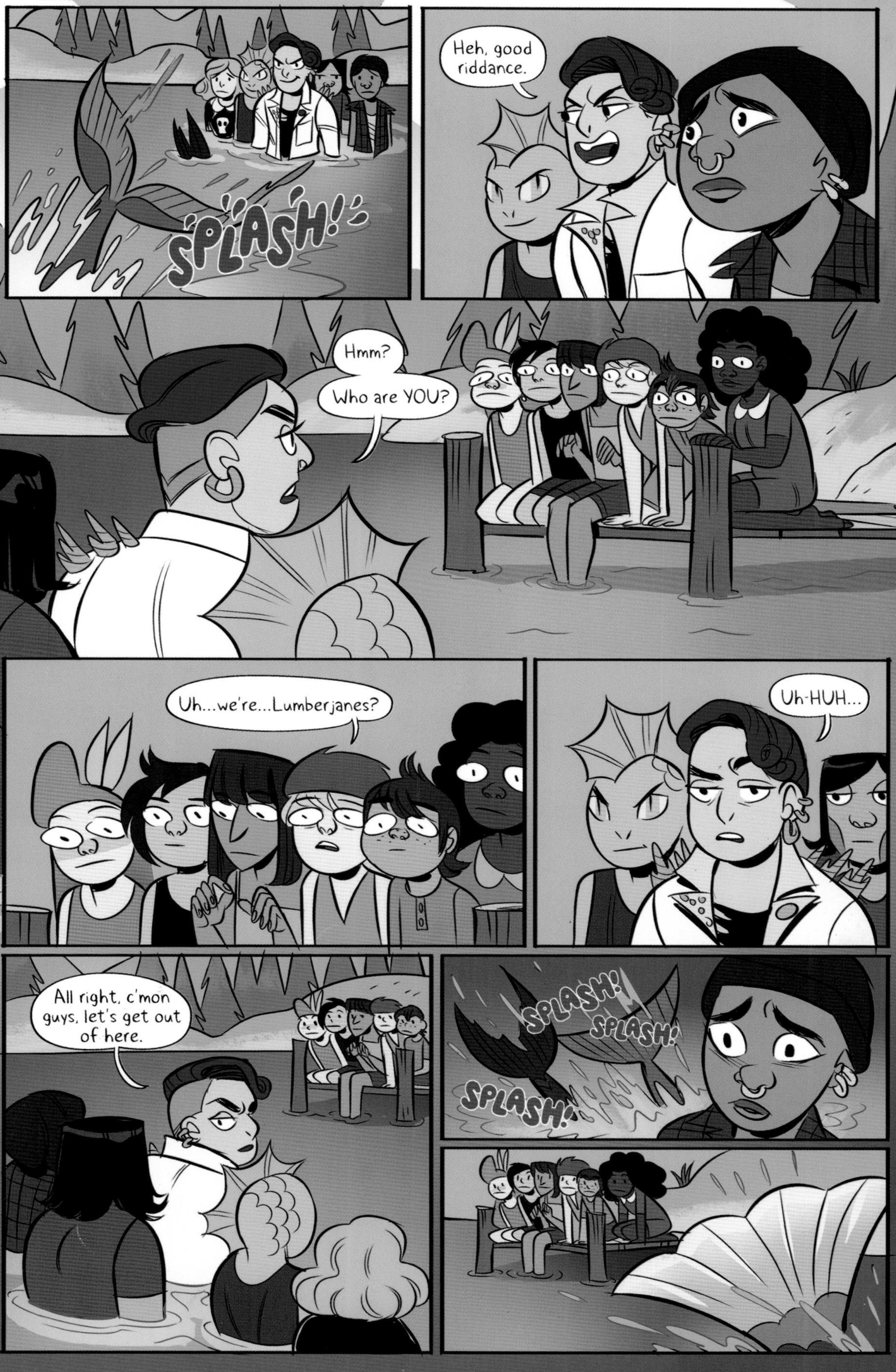
SPLASH!
Heh, good riddance.
Hmm?
Who are YOU?
Uh...we're...Lumberjanes?
Uh-HUH...
All right, c'mon guys, let's get out of here.
SPLASH!
SPLASH!
SPLASH!

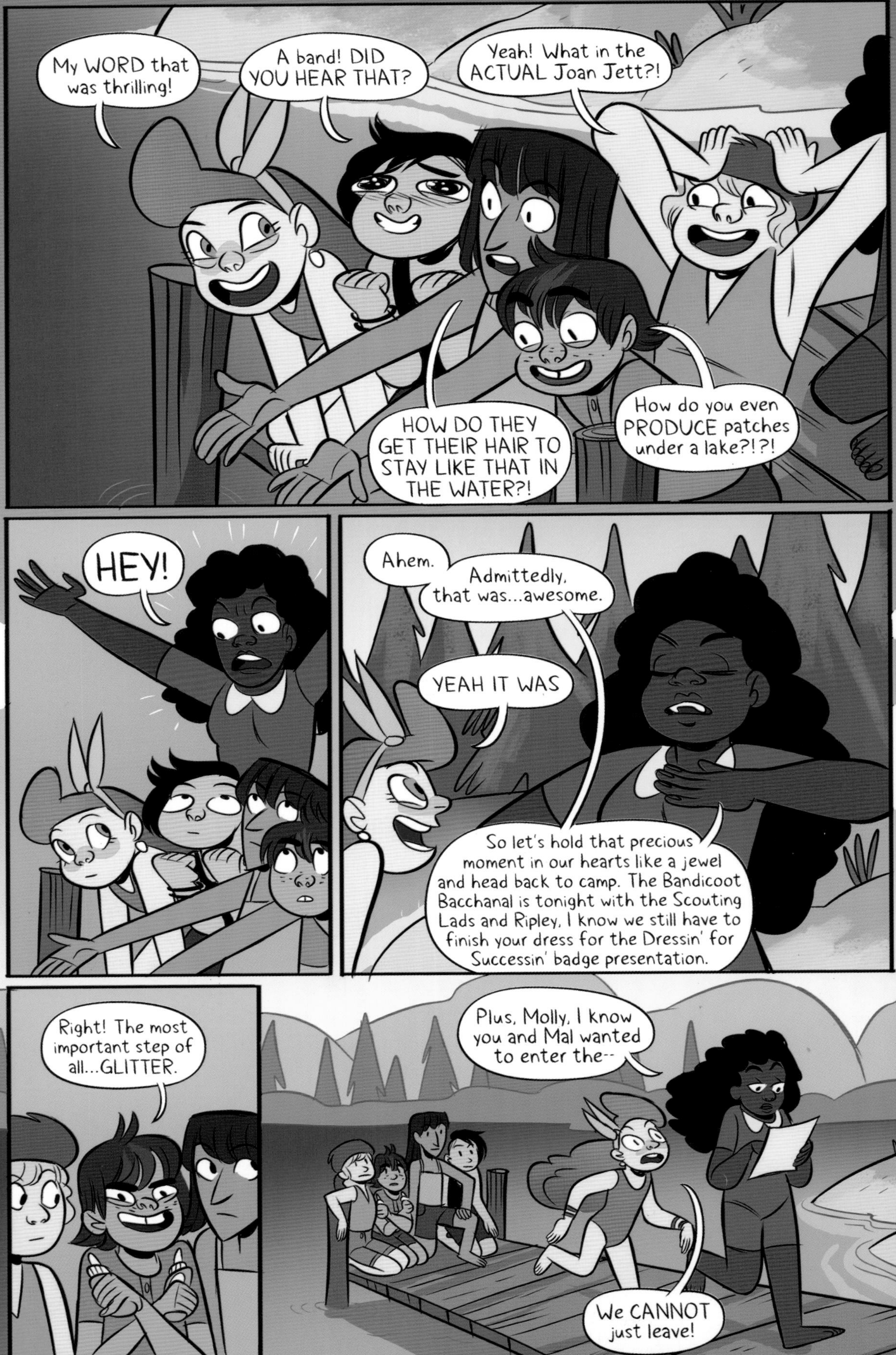
My WORD that was thrilling!
A band! DID YOU HEAR THAT?
Yeah! What in the ACTUAL Joan Jett?!
HOW DO THEY GET THEIR HAIR TO STAY LIKE THAT IN THE WATER?!
How do you even PRODUCE patches under a lake?!?!
HEY!
Ahem.
Admittedly, that was...awesome.
YEAH IT WAS
So let's hold that precious moment in our hearts like a jewel and head back to camp. The Bandicoot Bacchanal is tonight with the Scouting Lads and Ripley, I know we still have to finish your dress for the Dressin' for Successin' badge presentation.
Right! The most important step of all...GLITTER.
Plus, Molly, I know you and Mal wanted to enter the--
We CANNOT just leave!

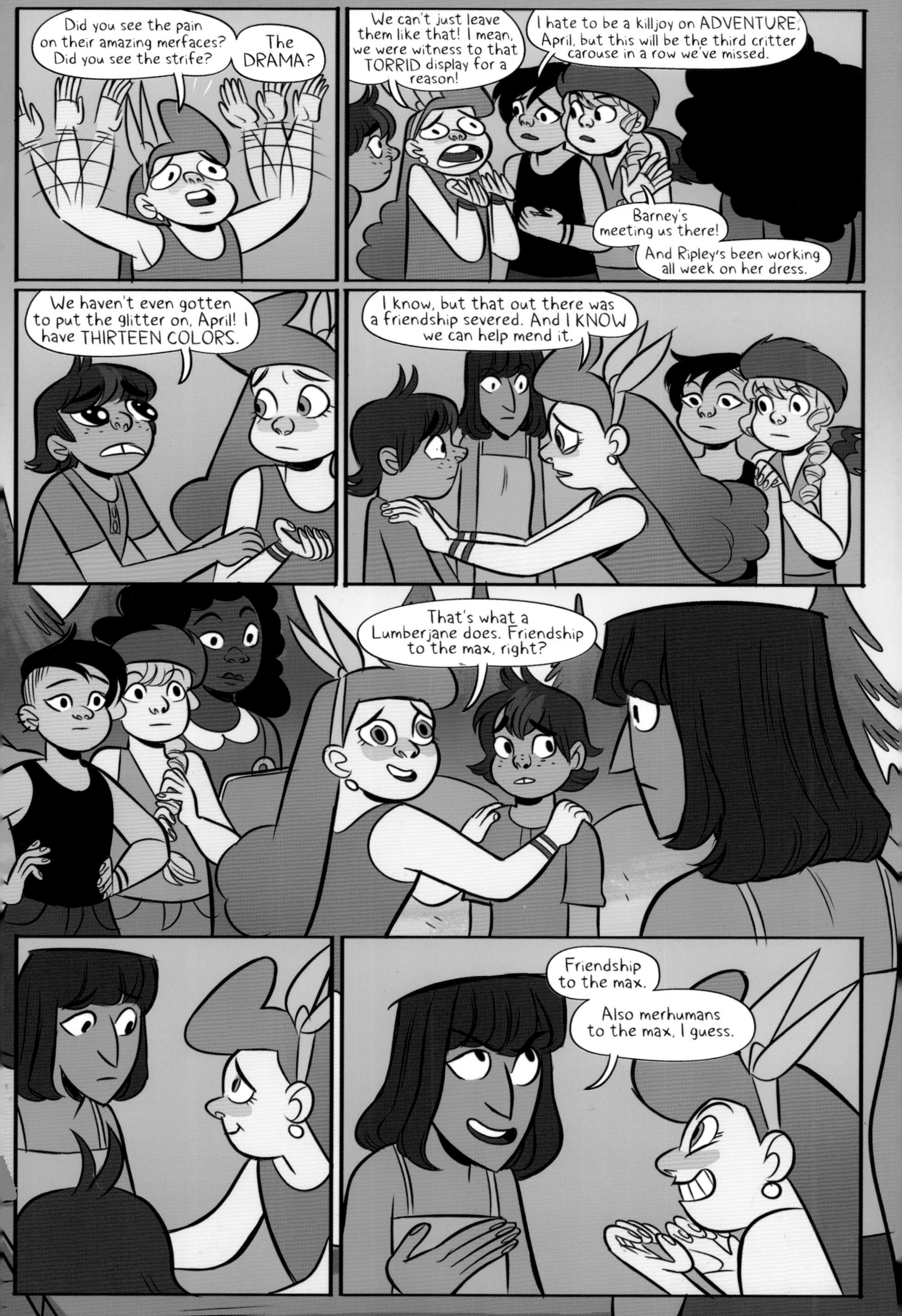
Did you see the pain on their amazing merfaces? Did you see the strife?
The DRAMA?
We can't just leave them like that! I mean, we were witness to that TORRID display for a reason!
I hate to be a killjoy on ADVENTURE, April, but this will be the third critter carouse in a row we've missed.
Barney's meeting us there!
And Ripley's been working all week on her dress.
We haven't even gotten to put the glitter on, April! I have THIRTEEN COLORS.
I know, but that out there was a friendship severed. And I KNOW we can help mend it.
That's what a Lumberjane does. Friendship to the max, right?
Friendship to the max.
Also merhumans to the max, I guess.

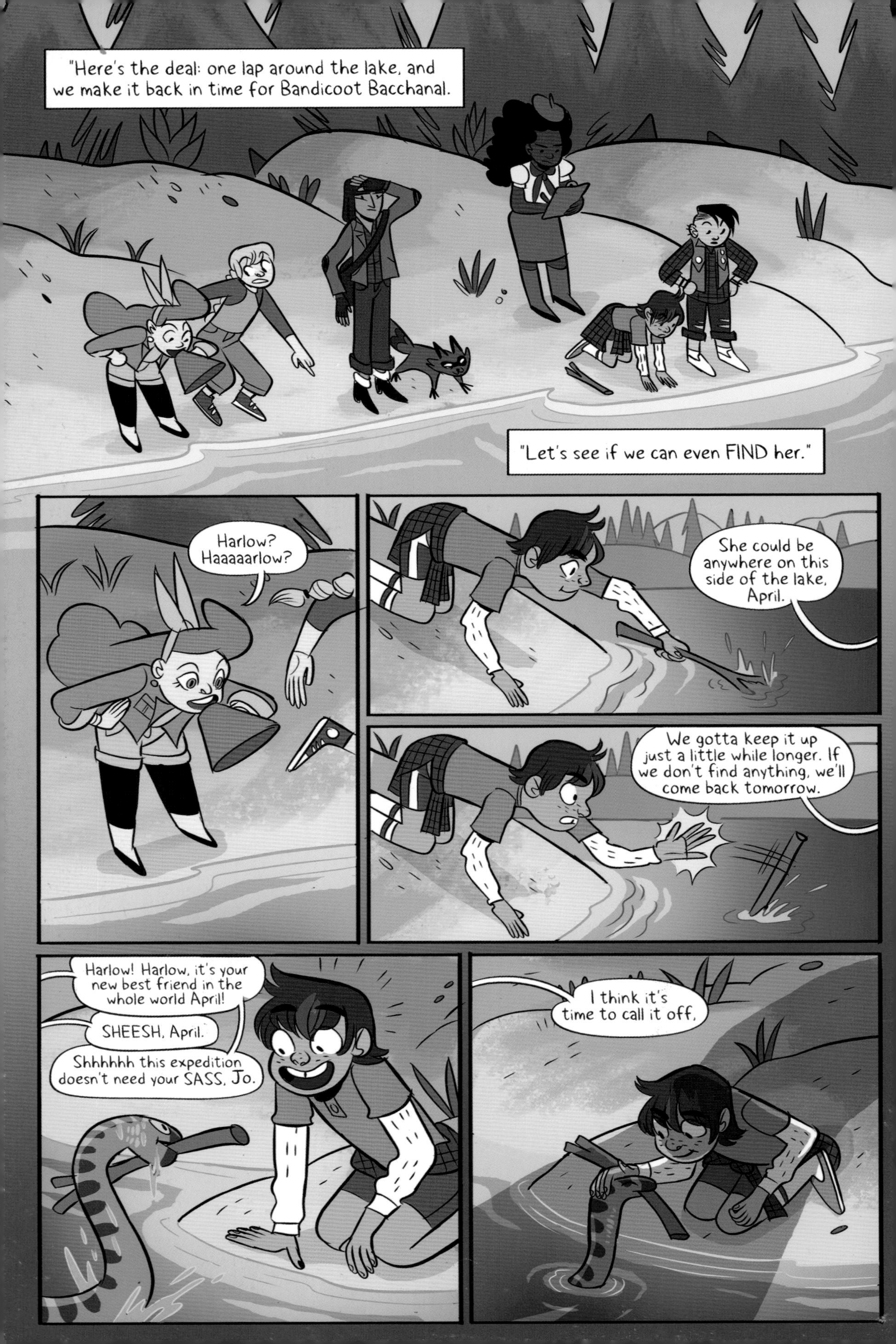
"Here's the deal: one lap around the lake, and we make it back in time for Bandicoot Bacchanal.
"Let's see if we can even FIND her."
Harlow? Haaaaarlow?
She could be anywhere on this side of the lake, April.
We gotta keep it up just a little while longer. If we don't find anything, we'll come back tomorrow.
Harlow! Harlow, it's your new best friend in the whole world April!
SHEESH, April.
Shhhhhh this expedition doesn't need your SASS, Jo.
I think it's time to call it off.

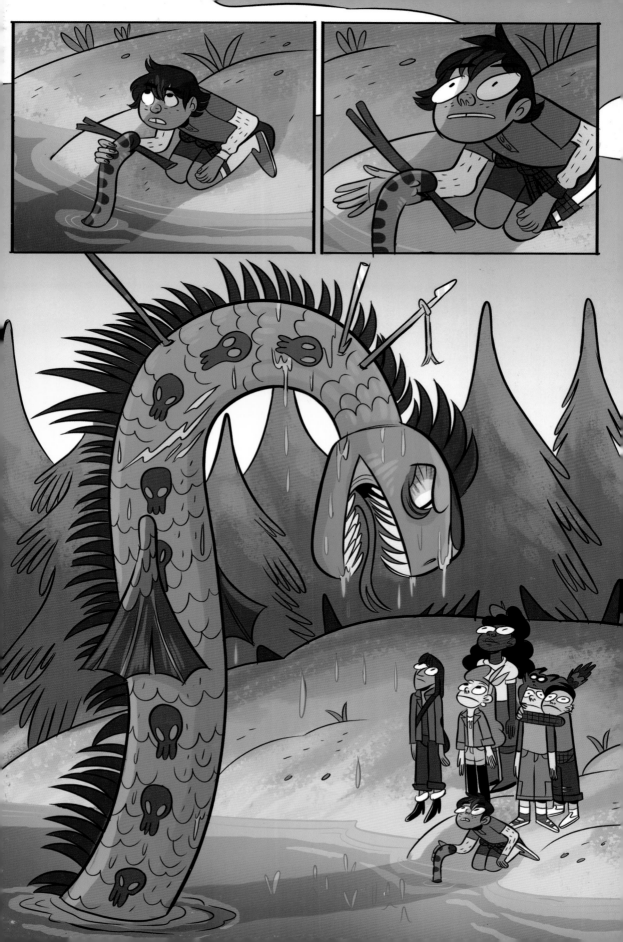

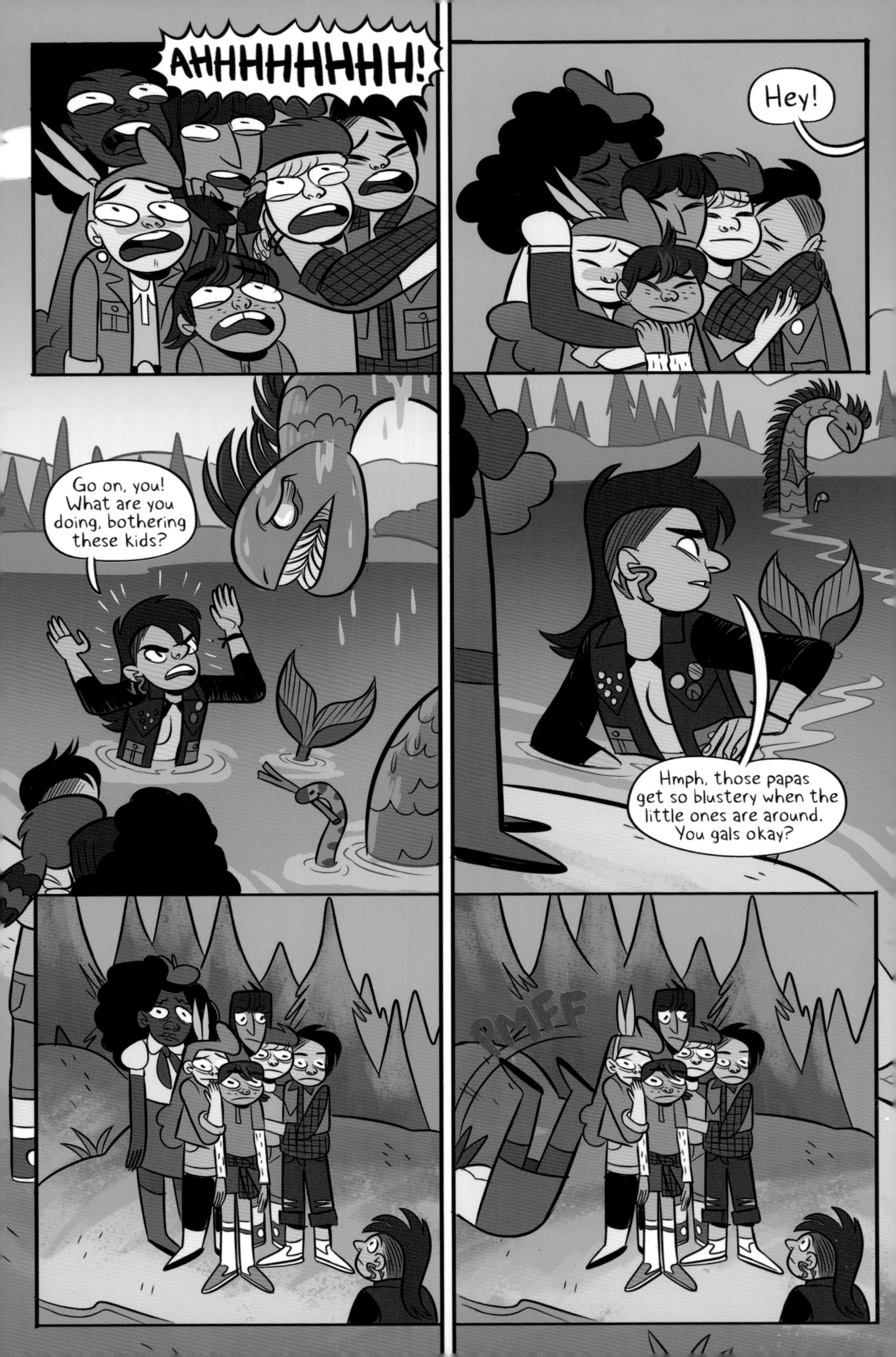
AHHHHHHHH!
Hey!
Go on, you! What are you doing, bothering these kids?
Hmph, those papas get so blustery when the little ones are around. You gals okay?
PMFF

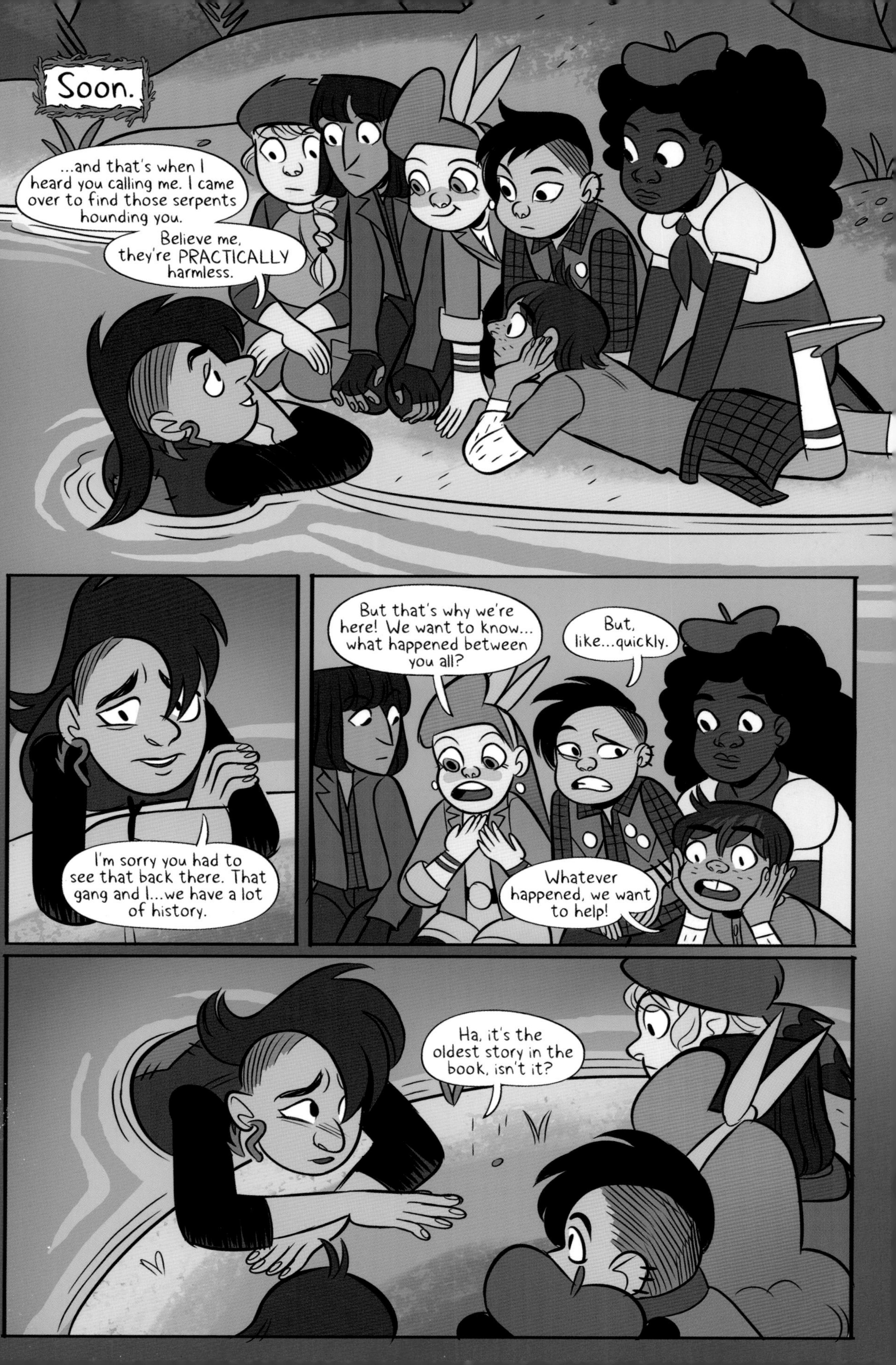

Soon.
...and that's when I heard you calling me. I came over to find those serpents hounding you.
Believe me, they're PRACTICALLY harmless.
I'm sorry you had to see that back there. That gang and I...we have a lot of history.
But that's why we're here! We want to know... what happened between you all?
But, like...quickly.
Whatever happened, we want to help!
Ha, it's the oldest story in the book, isn't it?

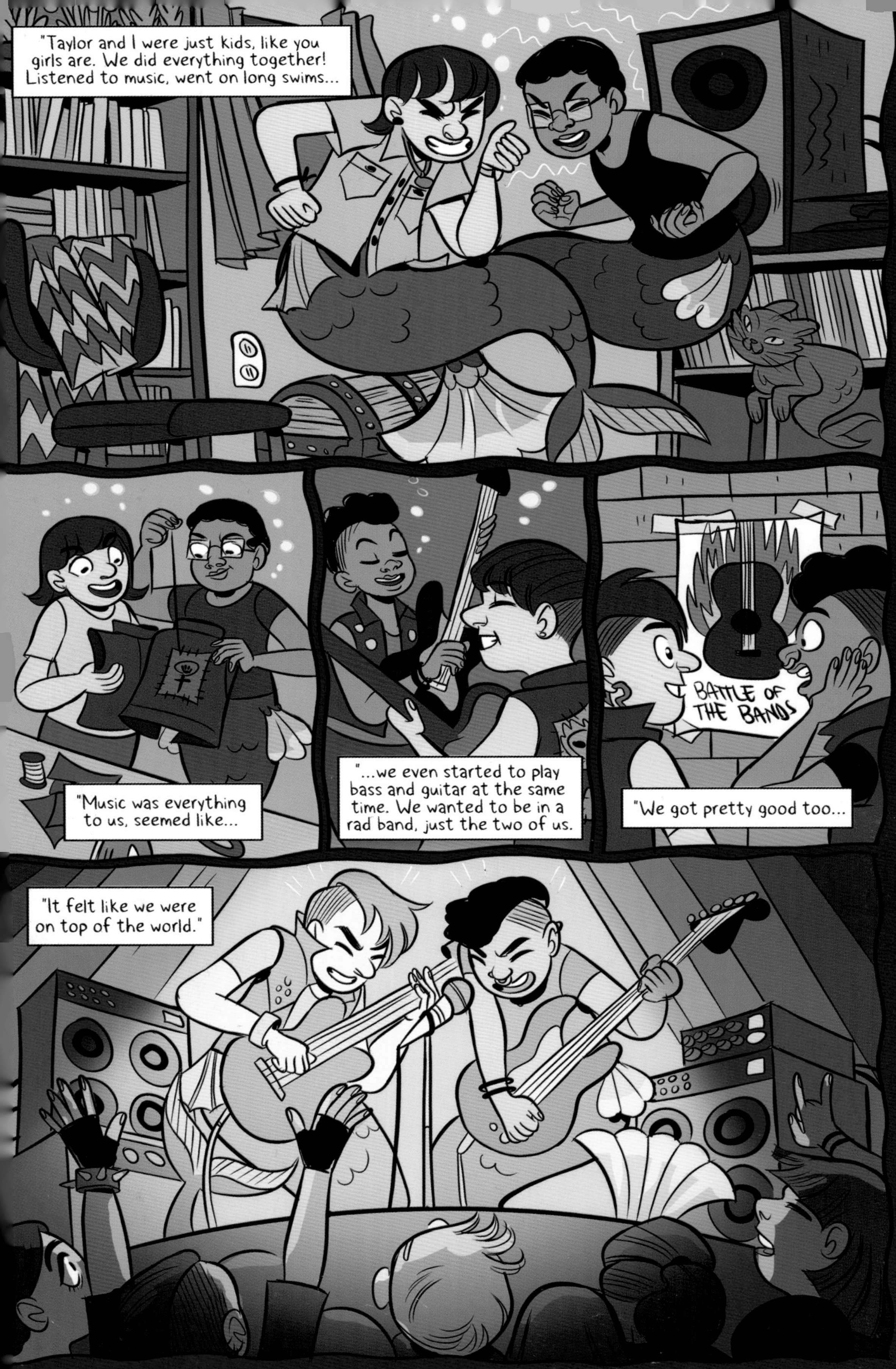
"Taylor and I were just kids, like you girls are. We did everything together! Listened to music, went on long swims...
"Music was everything to us, seemed like...
"...we even started to play bass and guitar at the same time. We wanted to be in a rad band, just the two of us.
BATTLE OF THE BANDS
"We got pretty good too...
"It felt like we were on top of the world."

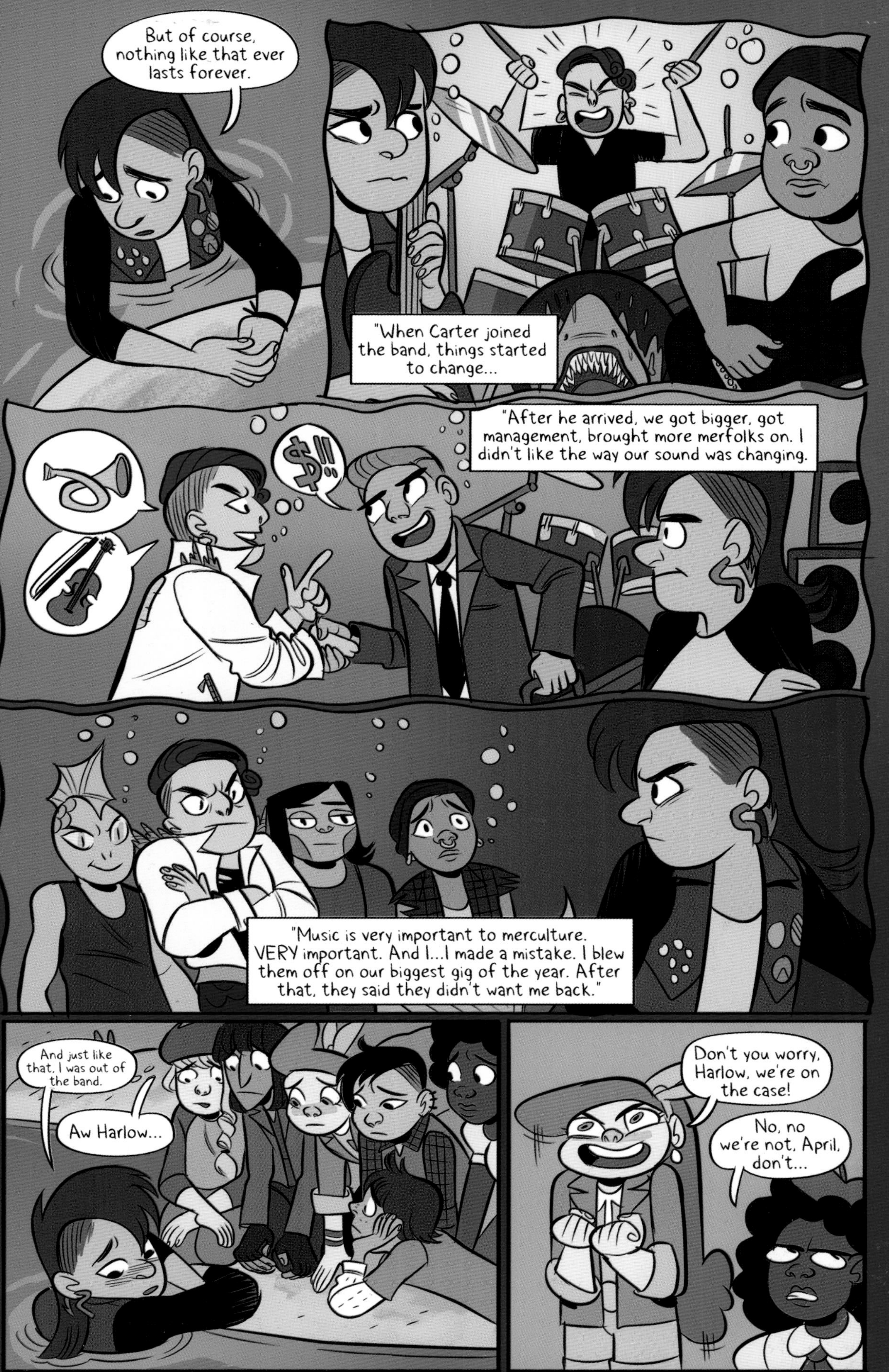

But of course, nothing like that ever lasts forever.
"When Carter joined the band, things started to change...
"After he arrived, we got bigger, got management, brought more merfolks on. I didn't like the way our sound was changing.
$!!
"Music is very important to merculture. VERY important. And I...I made a mistake. I blew them off on our biggest gig of the year. After that, they said they didn't want me back."
And just like that, I was out of the band.
Aw Harlow...
Don't you worry, Harlow, we're on the case!
No, no we're not, April, don't...

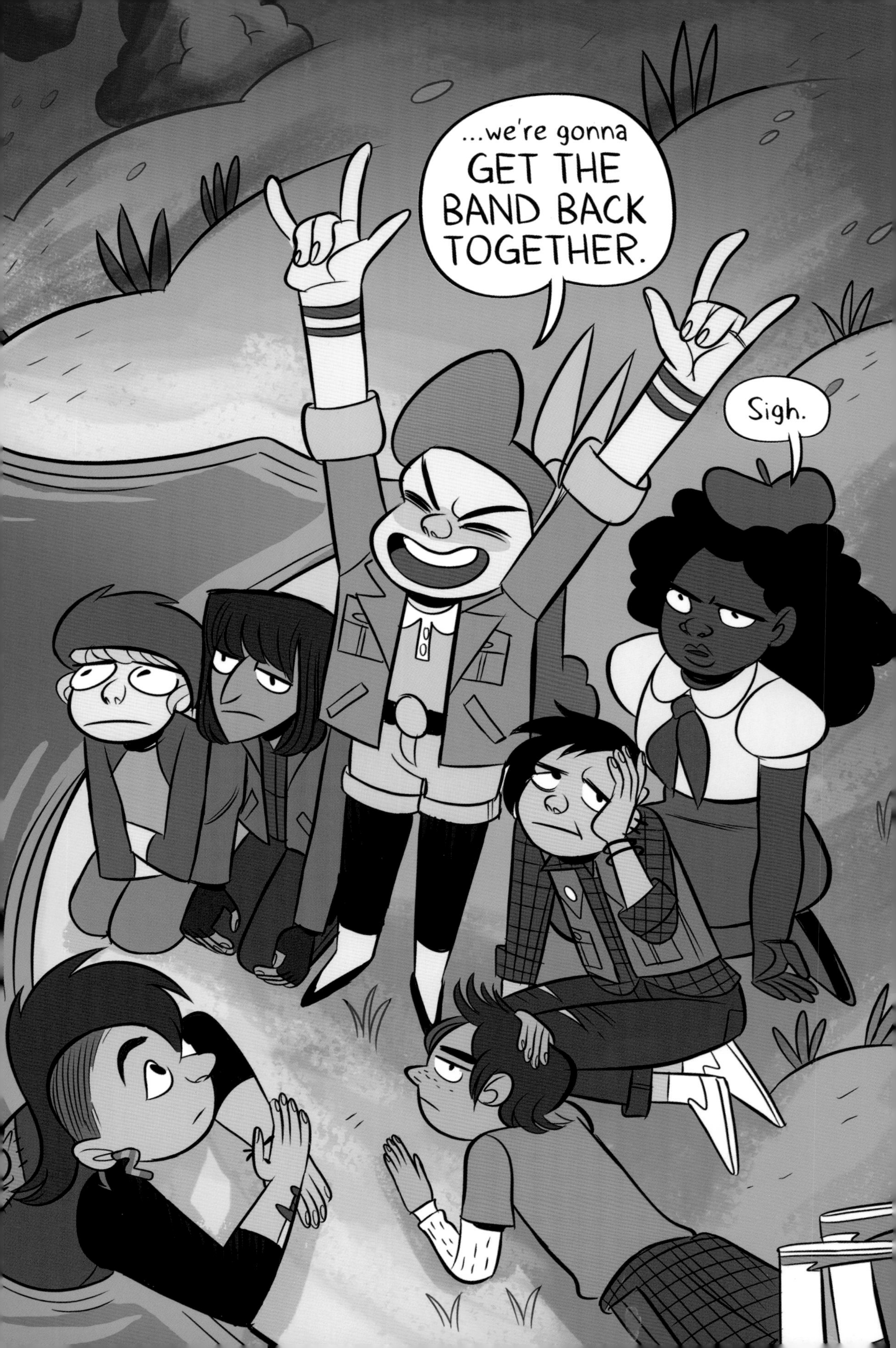
...we're gonna GET THE BAND BACK TOGETHER.
Sigh.

will co...

The...
It help...
appearan...
dress fo...
Further...
Lumber...
to have...
part in...
Thiskw...
Hardc...
have...
them...

OOOOOOOOHH NO.

The...
yellow, short sl...
emb...
the w...
choose...
slacks,...
made o...
out-of-do...
green bere...
the colla...
Shoes may b...
heels, roun...
socks should...
the uniform. Ne...
belong with a Lumberjane uniform.

ARE THOSE...BAND PATCHES?!

HOW TO WEAR THE UNIFOR...

To look well in a uniform dema...
uniform be kept in good condit...
pressed. See that the skirt is the right...
height and build, that the belt is adjus...
that your shoes and stockings are in ke...
uniform, that you watch your posture and...
with dignity and grace. If the beret is remo...
be sure that your hair is neat and kept in pla... with an
insopicuous clip or ribbon. When you wear a
Lumberjane uniform you are identified as a member of
this organization and you should be doubly careful to
conduct yourself in a way that will show everyone that
courtesy and thoughtfullness are part of being a
Lumberjane. People are likely to judge a whole nation by
the selfishness of a few individuals, to criticize a whole
family because of the misconduct of one member, and to
feel unkindly toward and organization because of the

NAMES APRIL, NICE TO MEET YA!

THE UNIFORM

...hould be worn at camp
...events when Lumberjanes
...n may also be worn at other
...ions. It should be worn as a
...the uniform dress with
...rect shoes, and stocking or
...out grows her uniform or
...ter Lumberjane.
...a she has
...her
...her

...ES

The unifor...
helps to cre...
in a group. ...
active life th...
another bond...
future, and pr...
in order to b...
Lumberjane pr...
Penniquiqul Thi...
Types, but m...
can either b... the uniform, or make it themselves from
materials available at the trading post.

LUMBERJANES FIELD MANUAL
CHAPTER NINETEEN

Lumberjanes "Cooking" Program Field

ENSEMBLE ASSEMBLE! BADGE

"Some instructions may be required."

While music is an important subject that should have more focus in schools, a Lumberjane will learn the commonplace use of music in everyday situations, as well as not so everyday, from knowing the proper tone need to help your fellow camp mate out with their song to knowing the proper pitch needed in order to get everyone's attention. A Lumberjane recognizes how basic understanding of music can not only help their understanding of the flow of the world around them but how furthering that knowledge can also lead to a really good time. The human experience can be boiled down to patterns and it is with this understanding that a Lumberjane sees their importance not only in the lives that she directly influences but those outside her known friend group.

To obtain the *Ensemble Assemble!* badge, a Lumberjane must be able to play an instrument. Not only that, a Lumberjanes must be able to gather a group of their fellow campers together to form their own band in order to create unique musical treats as a group. A focus of camp is and will always be the power of friendship and teamwork and this badge is no different. The goal of this badge is to take a variety of campers at different levels in their musical growth and get them to work together to help each other grow while at the same time learning to work in tandem to create a unique sound just for that group.

With an *Ensemble Assemble!* badge, a Lumberjane will be able to read and write music. They will be able to have the basic knowledge of keys and notes, as well as how to handle an instrument of their choosing. More advanced scouts will be allowed to bring their instrument from home and use their knowledge to help their campmates earn this badge. Every cabin will be asked to play one song at the mid-camp festival every term, and each cabin will be judged by their peers. The winning cabin will receive the badge as well as a lesson from the Scout Master.

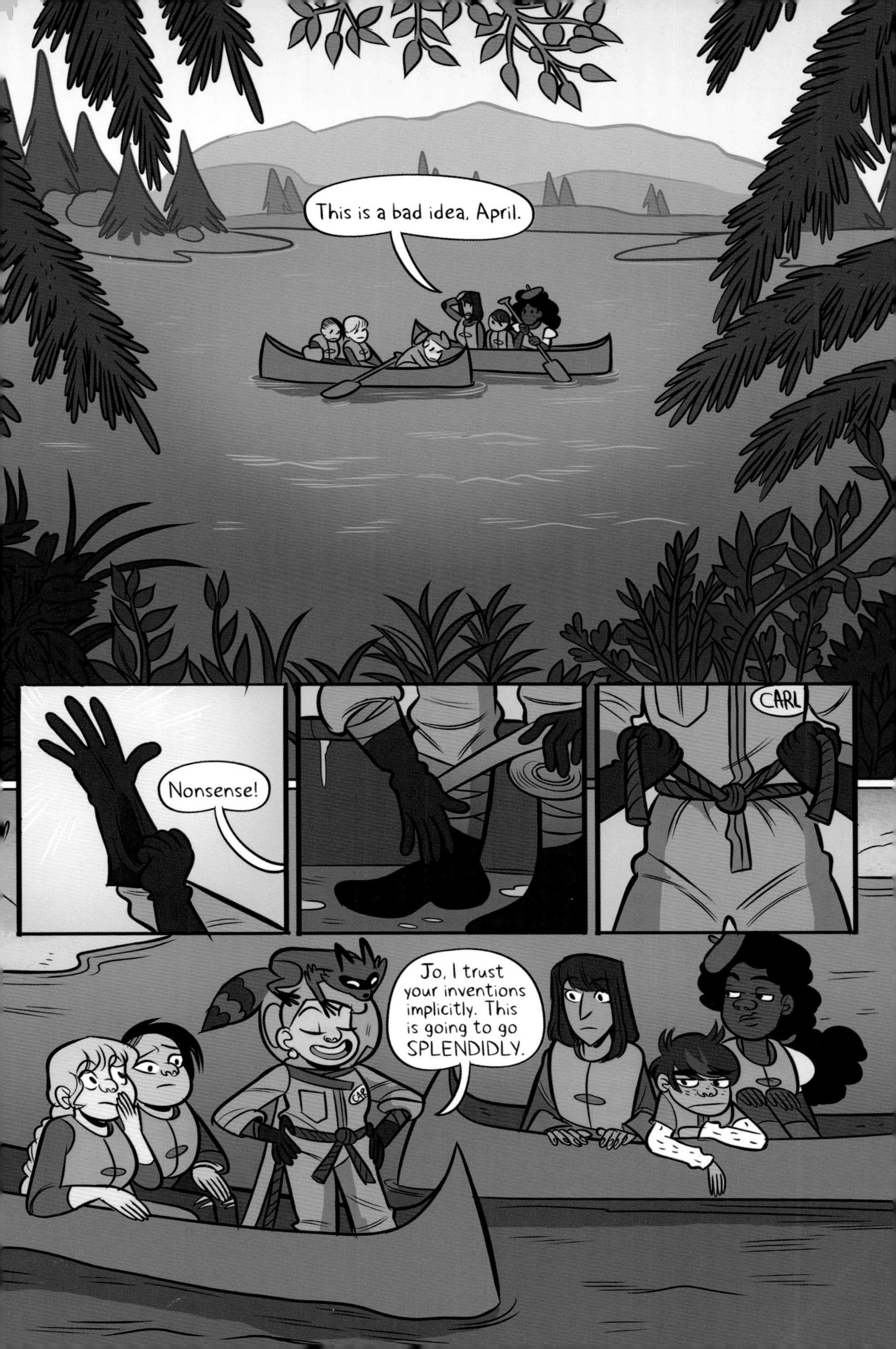
This is a bad idea, April.
Nonsense!
CARL
Jo, I trust your inventions implicitly. This is going to go SPLENDIDLY.

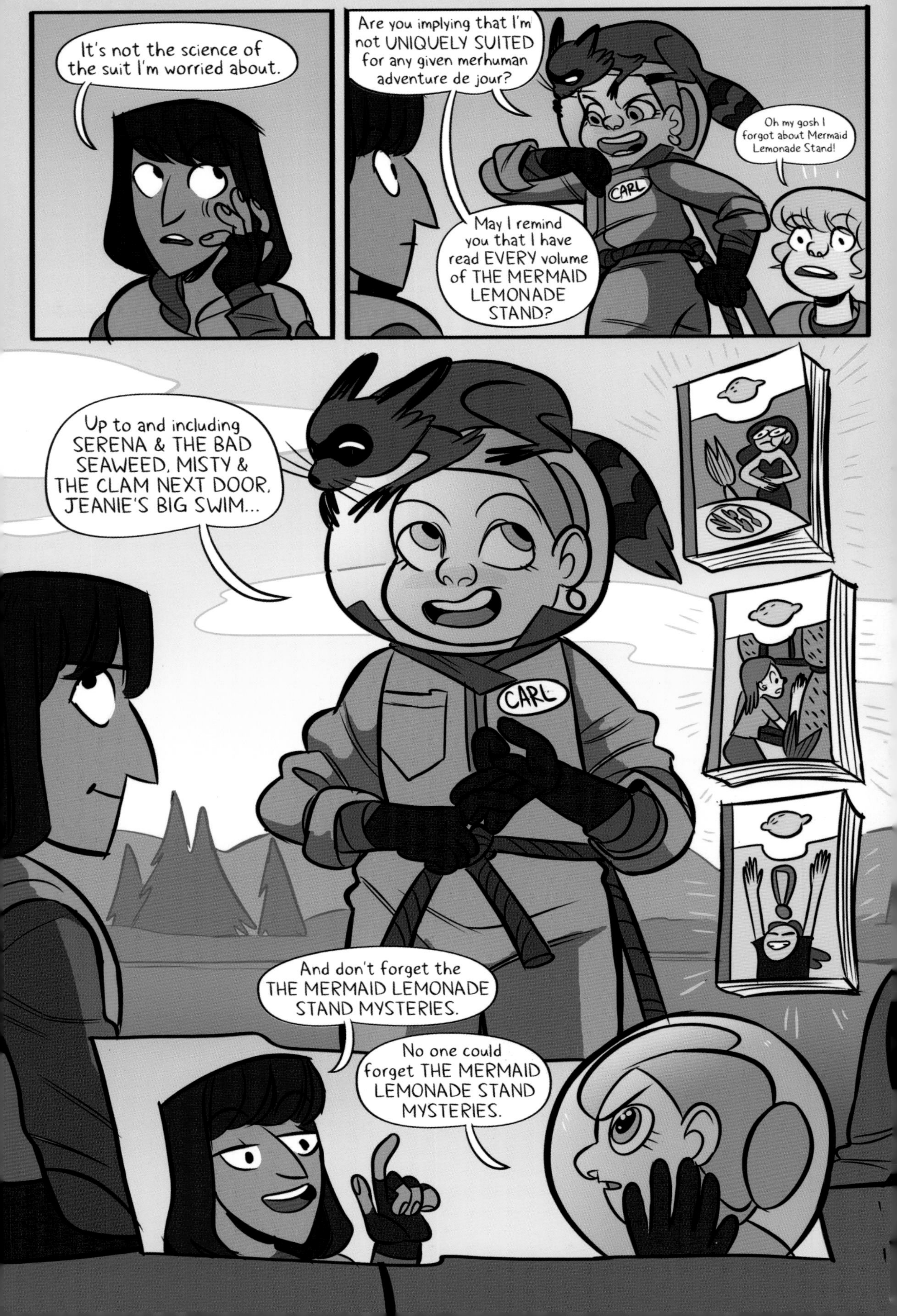
It's not the science of the suit I'm worried about.
Are you implying that I'm not UNIQUELY SUITED for any given merhuman adventure de jour?
May I remind you that I have read EVERY volume of THE MERMAID LEMONADE STAND?
CARL
Oh my gosh I forgot about Mermaid Lemonade Stand!
Up to and including SERENA & THE BAD SEAWEED, MISTY & THE CLAM NEXT DOOR, JEANIE'S BIG SWIM...
CARL
And don't forget the THE MERMAID LEMONADE STAND MYSTERIES.
No one could forget THE MERMAID LEMONADE STAND MYSTERIES.

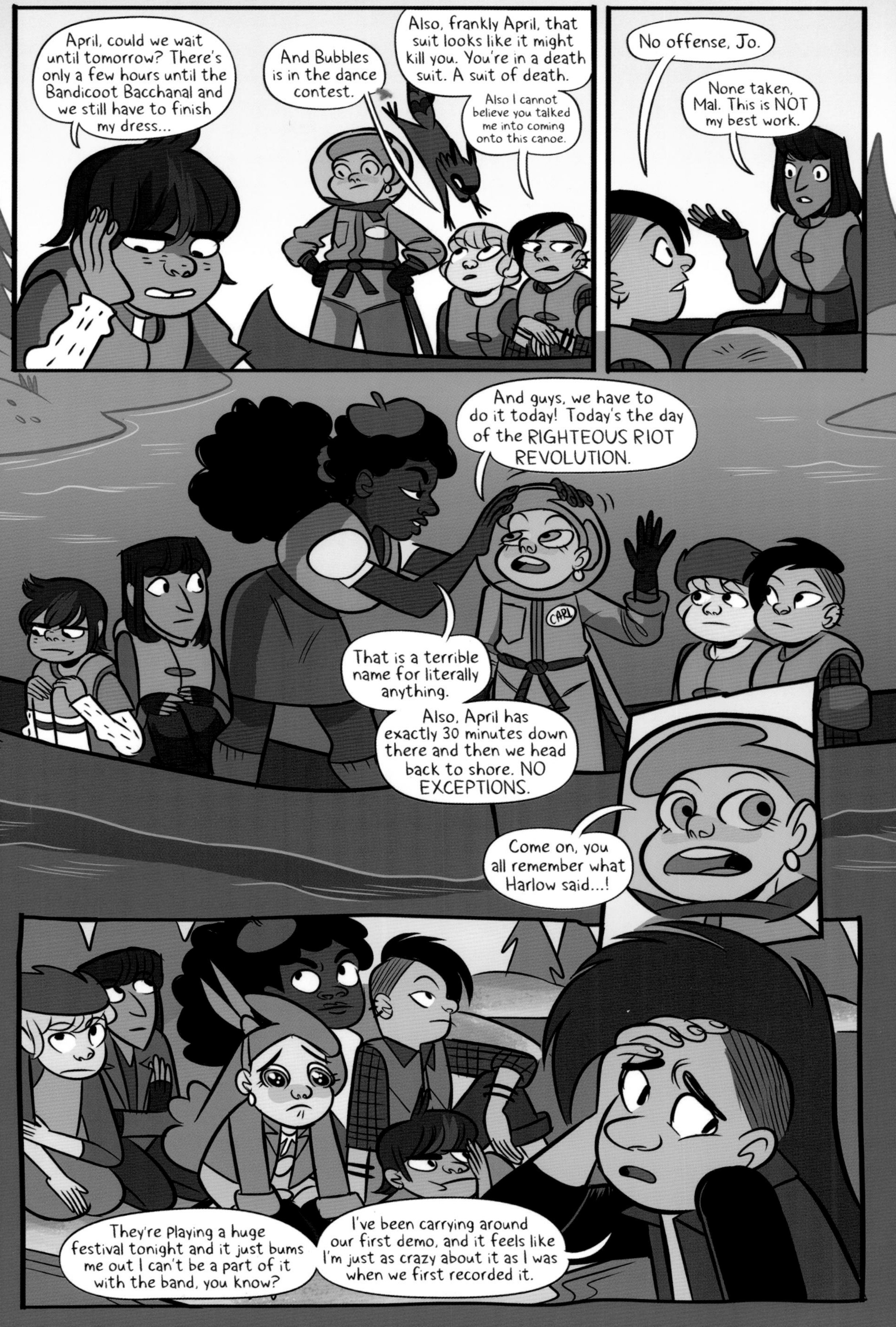
April, could we wait until tomorrow? There's only a few hours until the Bandicoot Bacchanal and we still have to finish my dress...
And Bubbles is in the dance contest.
Also, frankly April, that suit looks like it might kill you. You're in a death suit. A suit of death.
Also I cannot believe you talked me into coming onto this canoe.
No offense, Jo.
None taken, Mal. This is NOT my best work.
And guys, we have to do it today! Today's the day of the RIGHTEOUS RIOT REVOLUTION.
That is a terrible name for literally anything.
Also, April has exactly 30 minutes down there and then we head back to shore. NO EXCEPTIONS.
CARL
Come on, you all remember what Harlow said...!
They're playing a huge festival tonight and it just bums me out I can't be a part of it with the band, you know?
I've been carrying around our first demo, and it feels like I'm just as crazy about it as I was when we first recorded it.

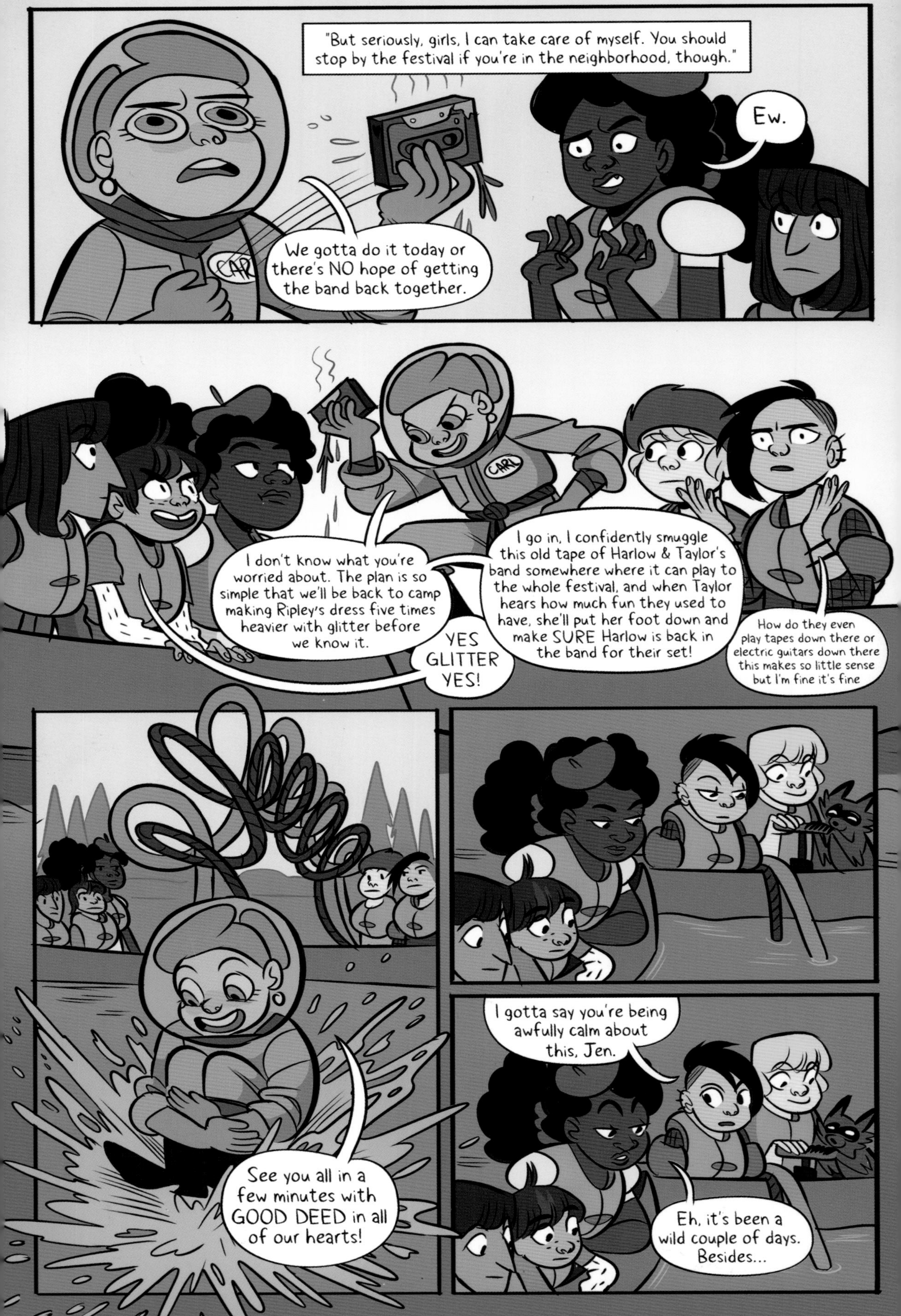
"But seriously, girls, I can take care of myself. You should stop by the festival if you're in the neighborhood, though."
Ew.
We gotta do it today or there's NO hope of getting the band back together.
I don't know what you're worried about. The plan is so simple that we'll be back to camp making Ripley's dress five times heavier with glitter before we know it.
I go in, I confidently smuggle this old tape of Harlow & Taylor's band somewhere where it can play to the whole festival, and when Taylor hears how much fun they used to have, she'll put her foot down and make SURE Harlow is back in the band for their set!
YES GLITTER YES!
How do they even play tapes down there or electric guitars down there this makes so little sense but I'm fine it's fine
See you all in a few minutes with GOOD DEED in all of our hearts!
I gotta say you're being awfully calm about this, Jen.
Eh, it's been a wild couple of days. Besides...

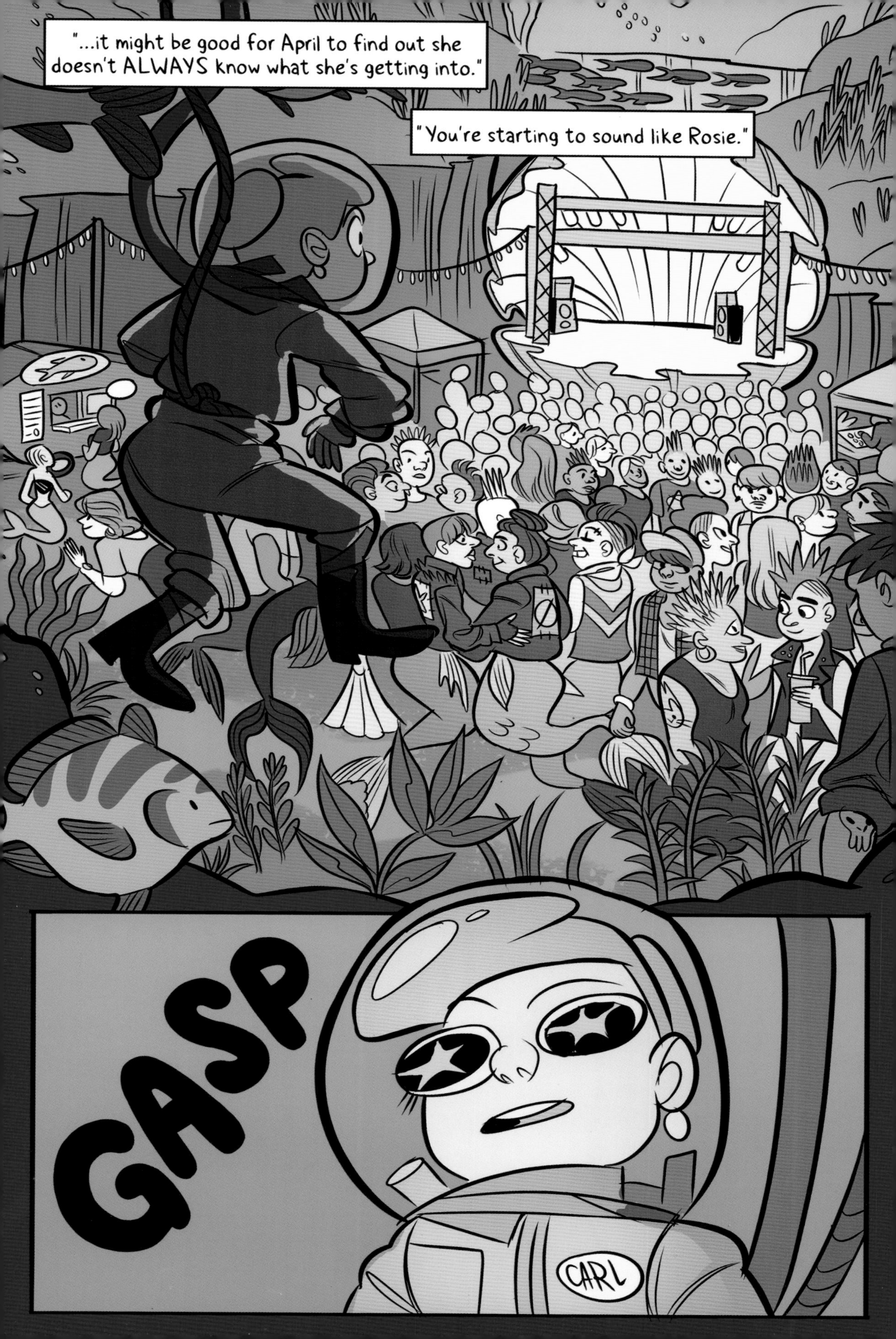
"...it might be good for April to find out she doesn't ALWAYS know what she's getting into."
"You're starting to sound like Rosie."
GASP
CARL

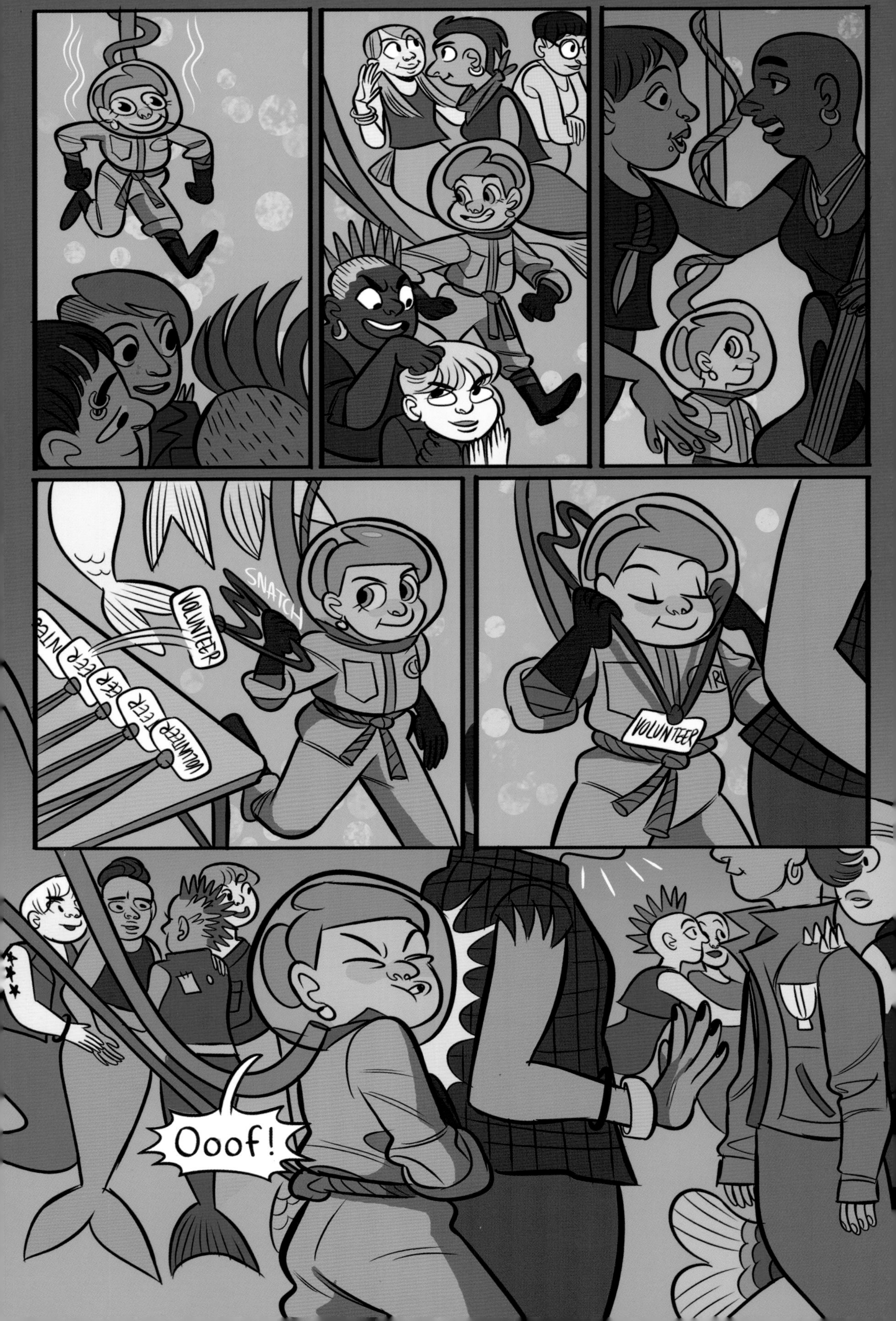
SNATCH
VOLUNTEER
VOLUNTEER
Ooof!

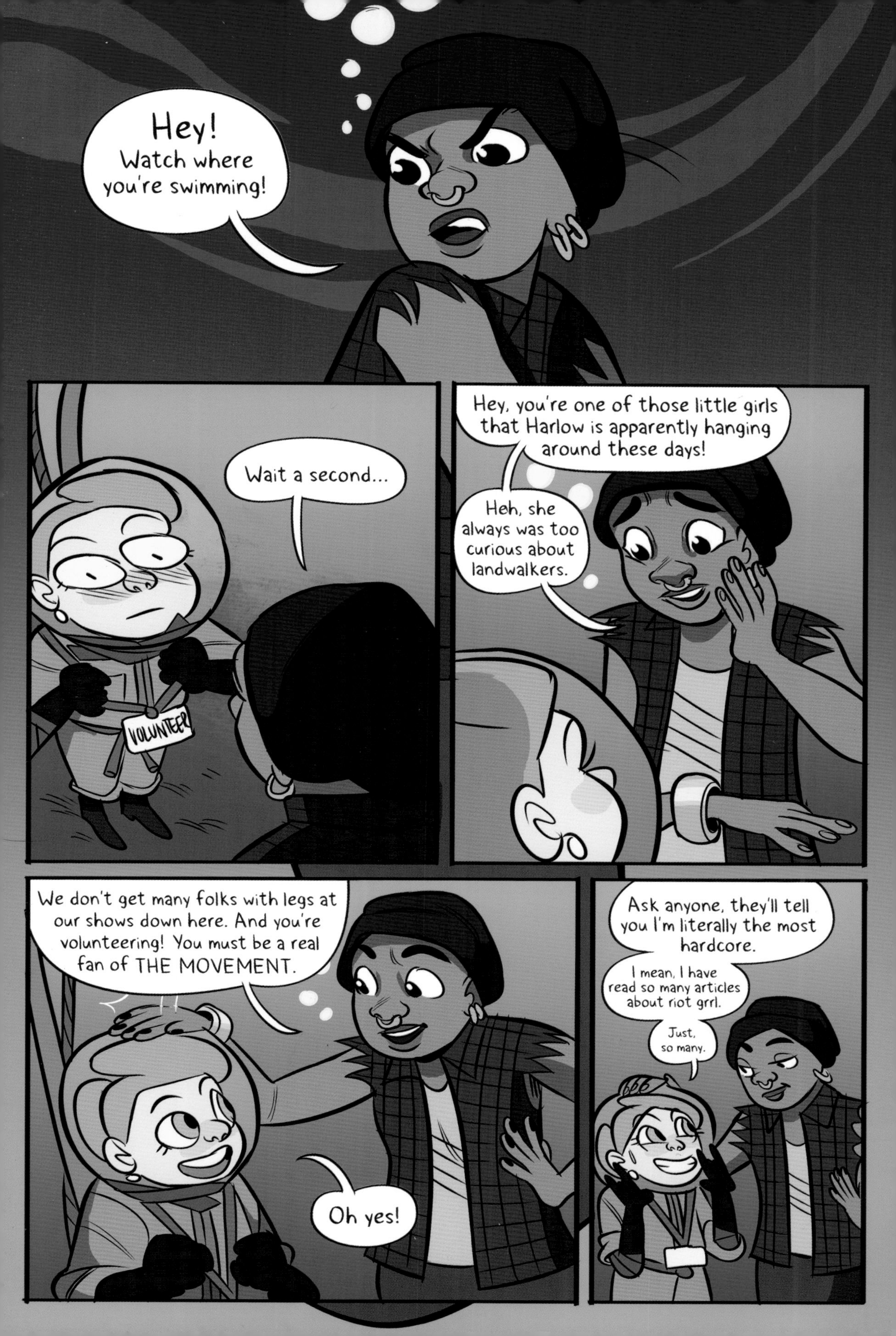
Hey! Watch where you're swimming!
Wait a second...
Hey, you're one of those little girls that Harlow is apparently hanging around these days!
Heh, she always was too curious about landwalkers.
VOLUNTEER
We don't get many folks with legs at our shows down here. And you're volunteering! You must be a real fan of THE MOVEMENT.
Oh yes!
Ask anyone, they'll tell you I'm literally the most hardcore.
I mean, I have read so many articles about riot grrl.
Just, so many.

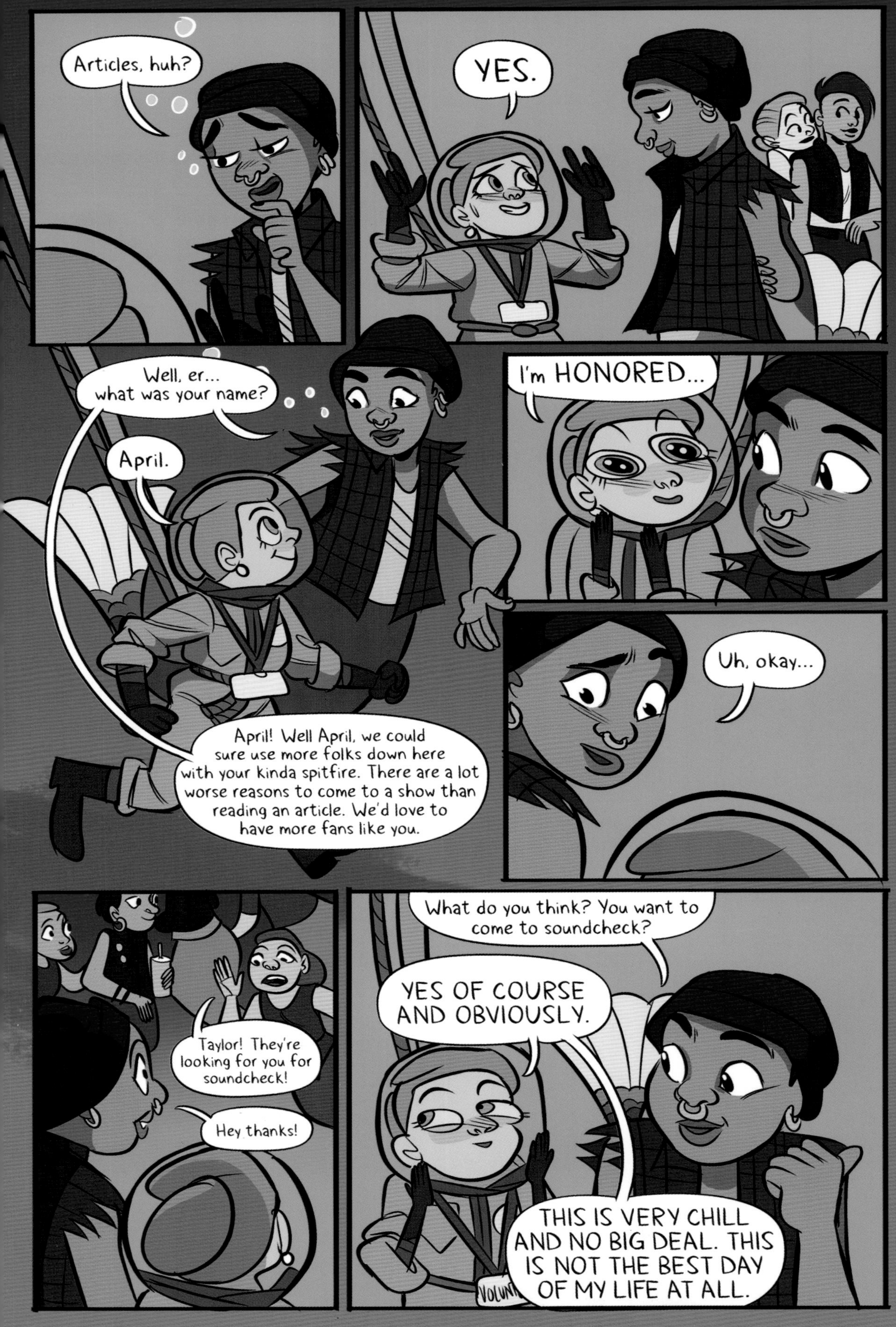
Articles, huh?
YES.
Well, er...
what was your name?
April.
April! Well April, we could sure use more folks down here with your kinda spitfire. There are a lot worse reasons to come to a show than reading an article. We'd love to have more fans like you.
I'm HONORED...
Uh, okay...
Taylor! They're looking for you for soundcheck!
Hey thanks!
What do you think? You want to come to soundcheck?
YES OF COURSE AND OBVIOUSLY.
THIS IS VERY CHILL AND NO BIG DEAL. THIS IS NOT THE BEST DAY OF MY LIFE AT ALL.

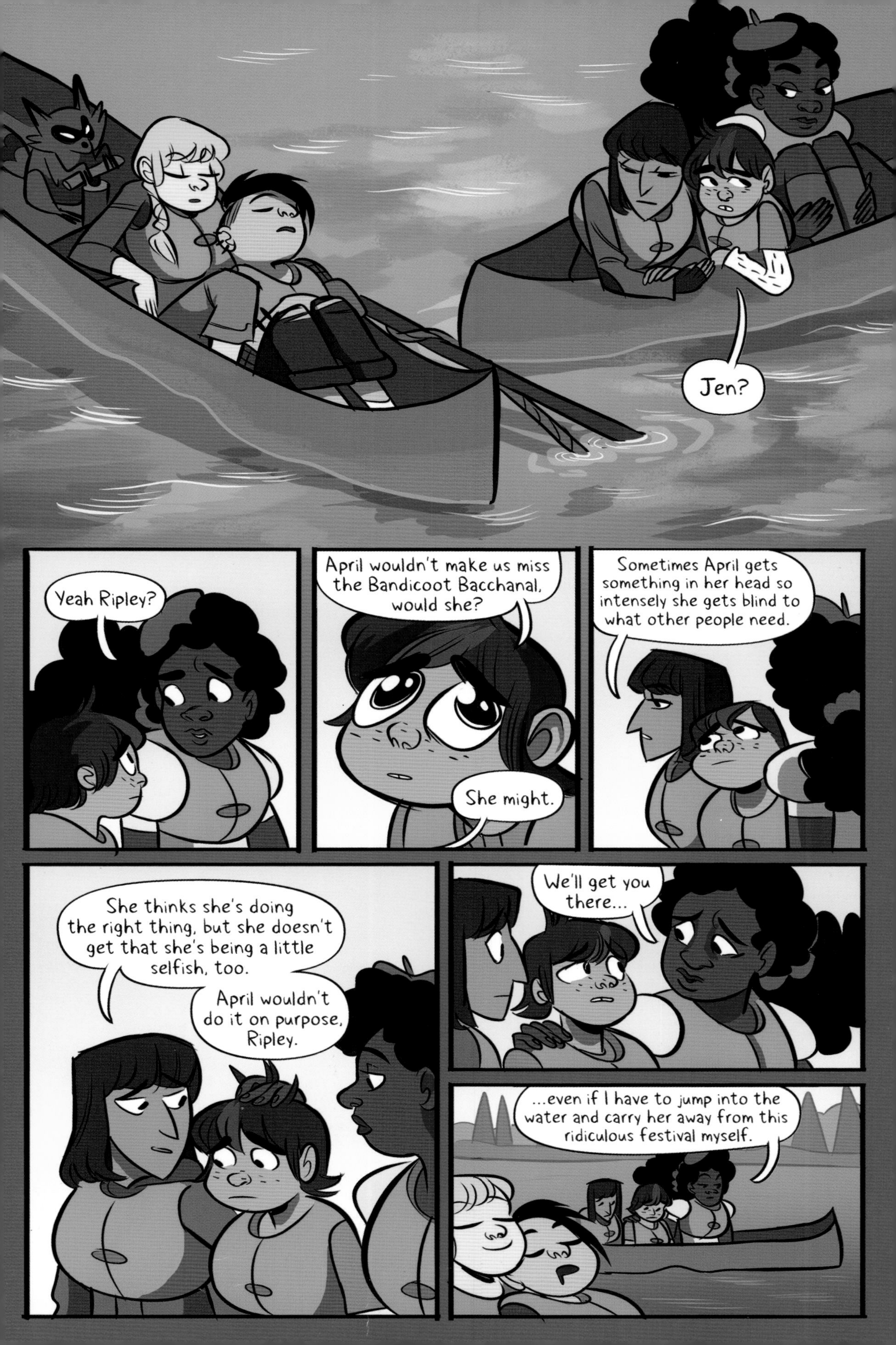
Jen?
Yeah Ripley?
April wouldn't make us miss the Bandicoot Bacchanal, would she?
She might.
Sometimes April gets something in her head so intensely she gets blind to what other people need.
She thinks she's doing the right thing, but she doesn't get that she's being a little selfish, too.
April wouldn't do it on purpose, Ripley.
We'll get you there...
...even if I have to jump into the water and carry her away from this ridiculous festival myself.

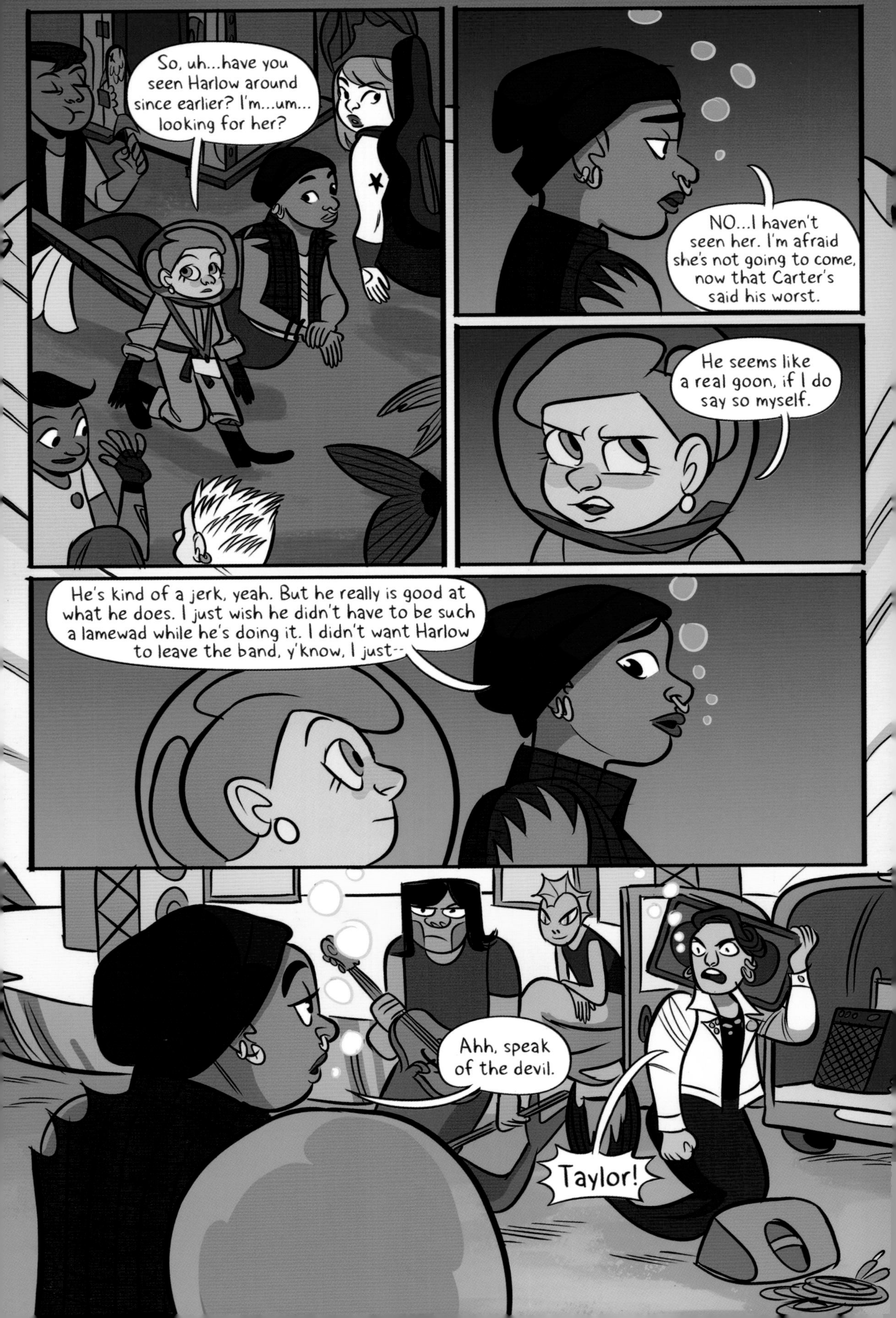
So, uh...have you seen Harlow around since earlier? I'm...um... looking for her?
NO...I haven't seen her. I'm afraid she's not going to come, now that Carter's said his worst.
He seems like a real goon, if I do say so myself.
He's kind of a jerk, yeah. But he really is good at what he does. I just wish he didn't have to be such a lamewad while he's doing it. I didn't want Harlow to leave the band, y'know, I just--
Ahh, speak of the devil.
Taylor!

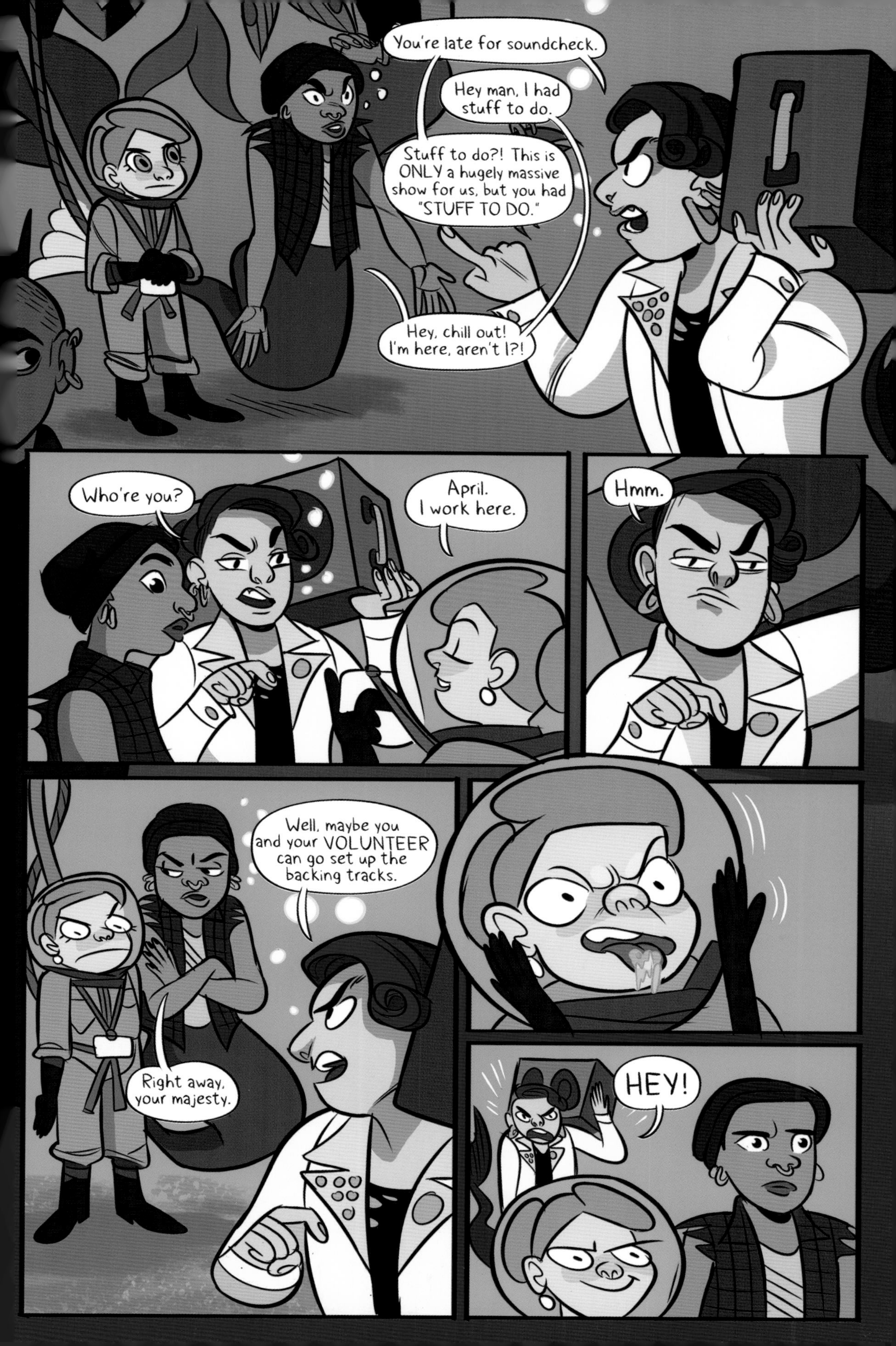
You're late for soundcheck.
Hey man, I had stuff to do.
Stuff to do?! This is ONLY a hugely massive show for us, but you had "STUFF TO DO."
Hey, chill out! I'm here, aren't I?!
Who're you?
April. I work here.
Hmm.
Well, maybe you and your VOLUNTEER can go set up the backing tracks.
Right away, your majesty.
HEY!

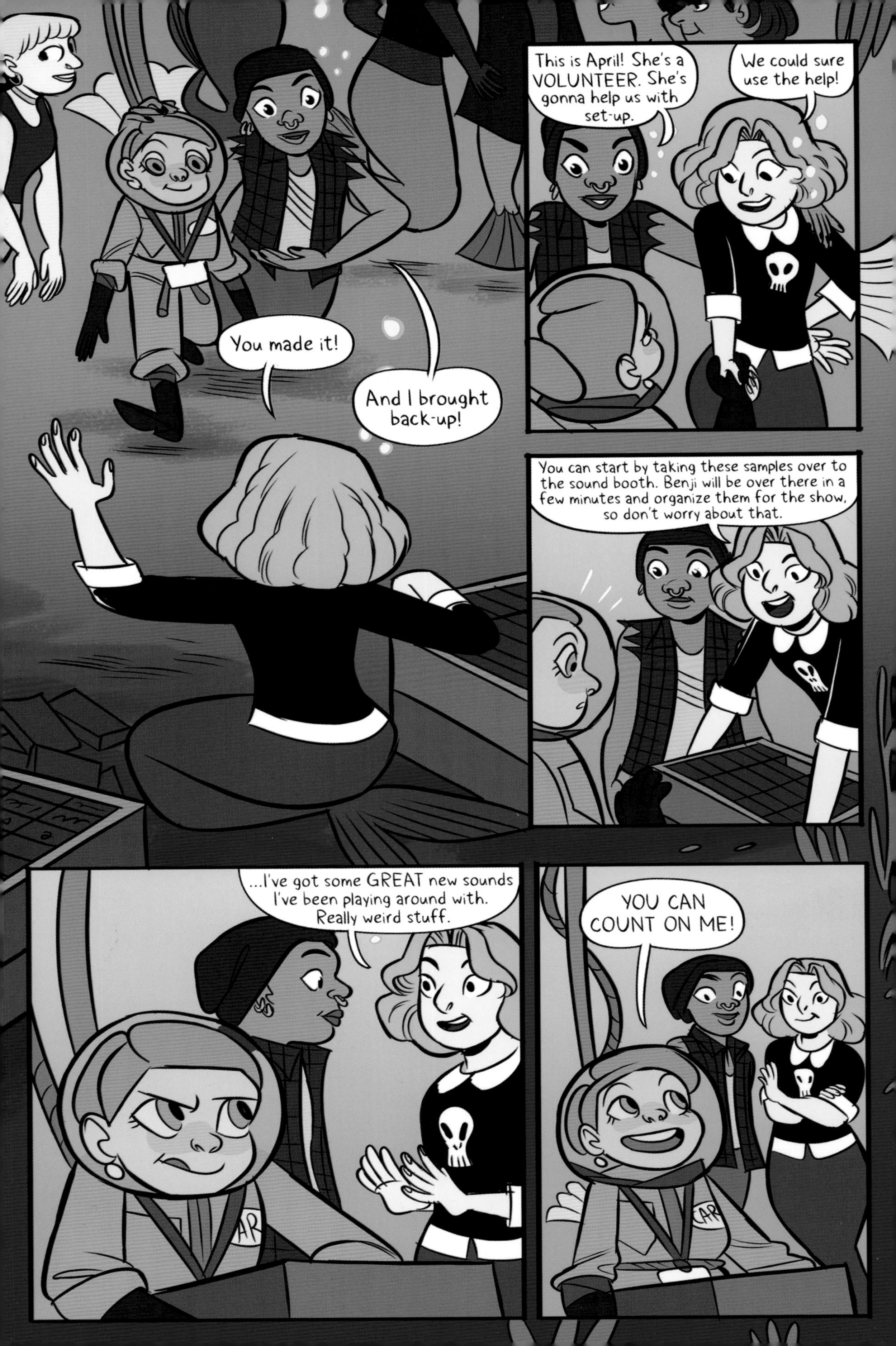
You made it!
And I brought back-up!
This is April! She's a VOLUNTEER. She's gonna help us with set-up.
We could sure use the help!
You can start by taking these samples over to the sound booth. Benji will be over there in a few minutes and organize them for the show, so don't worry about that.
...I've got some GREAT new sounds I've been playing around with. Really weird stuff.
YOU CAN COUNT ON ME!

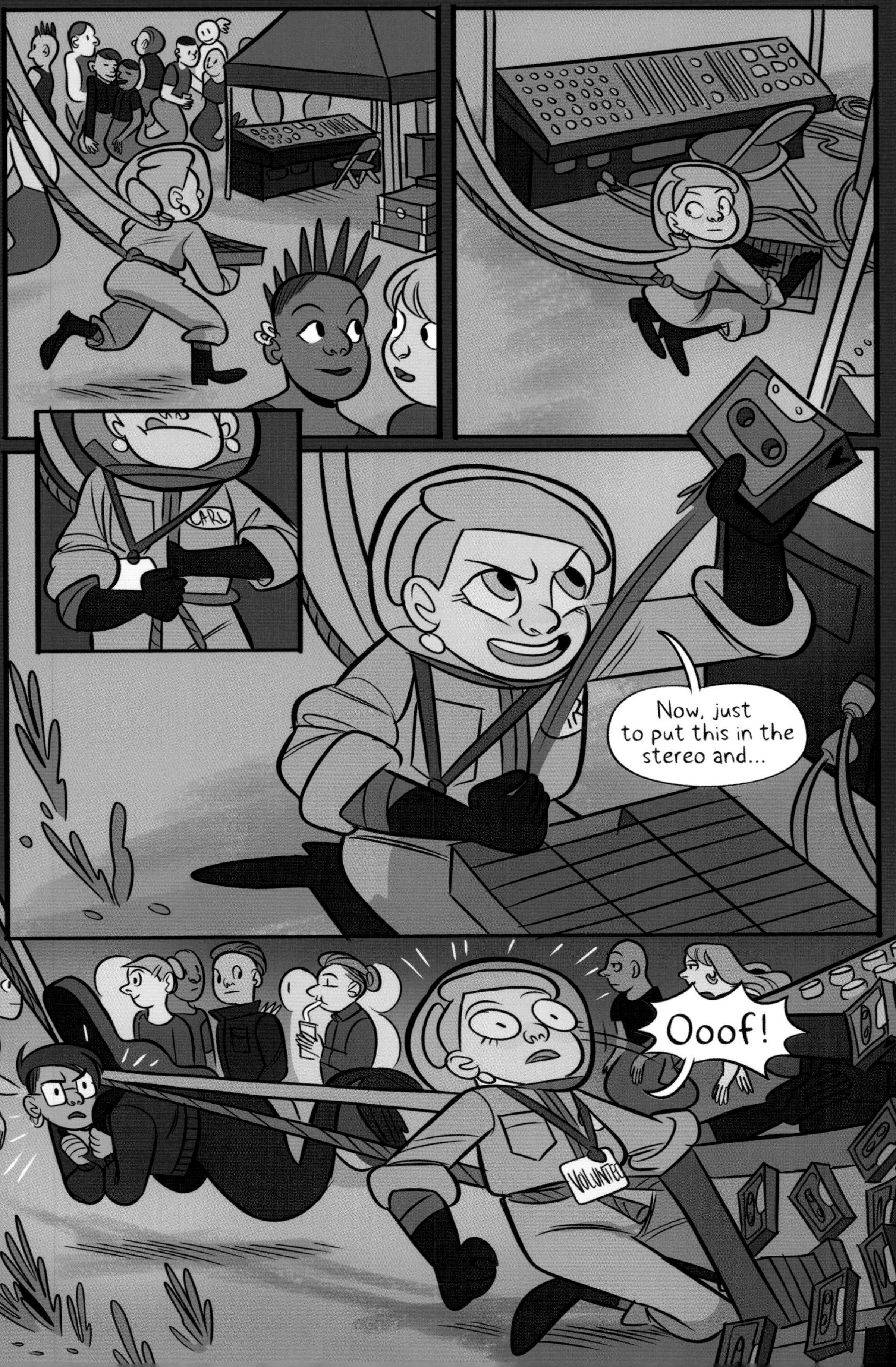
CARL
Now, just to put this in the stereo and...
Ooof!
VOLUNTEE

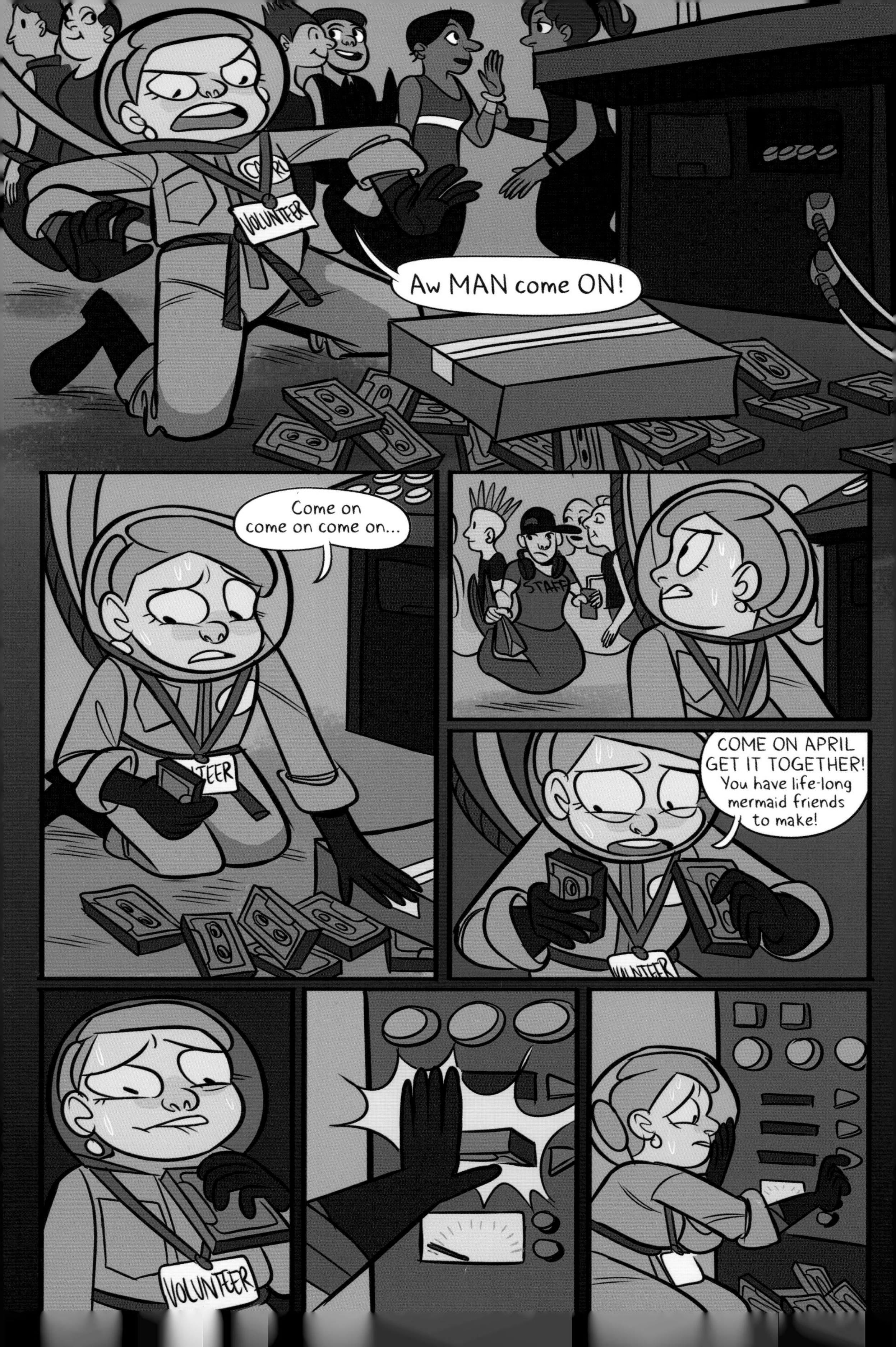
VOLUNTEER
Aw MAN come ON!
Come on
come on come on...
STAFF
COME ON APRIL
GET IT TOGETHER!
You have life-long
mermaid friends
to make!
VOLUNTEER

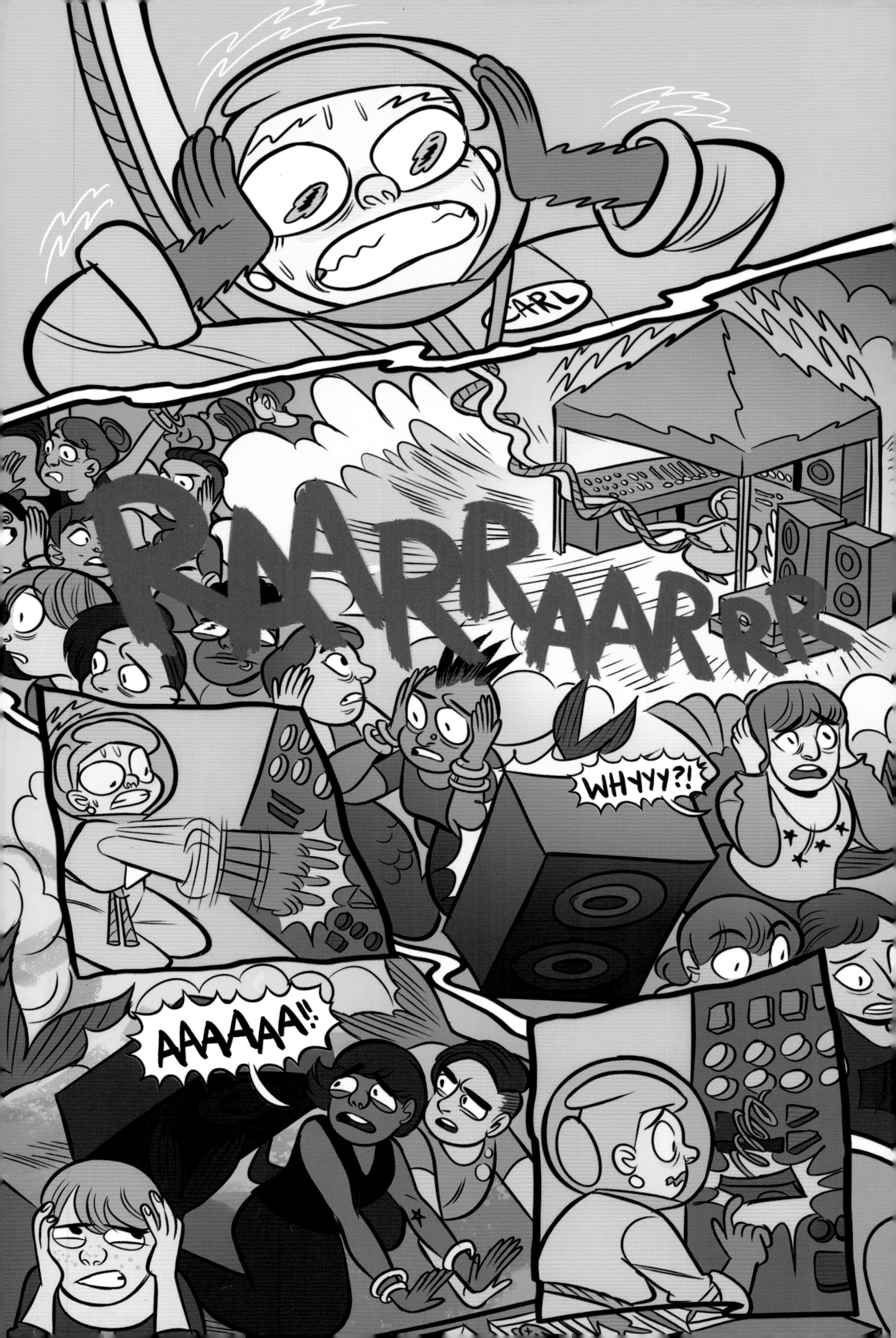
CARL
RRAARRAARRRR
WHYYY?!
AAAAAA!!

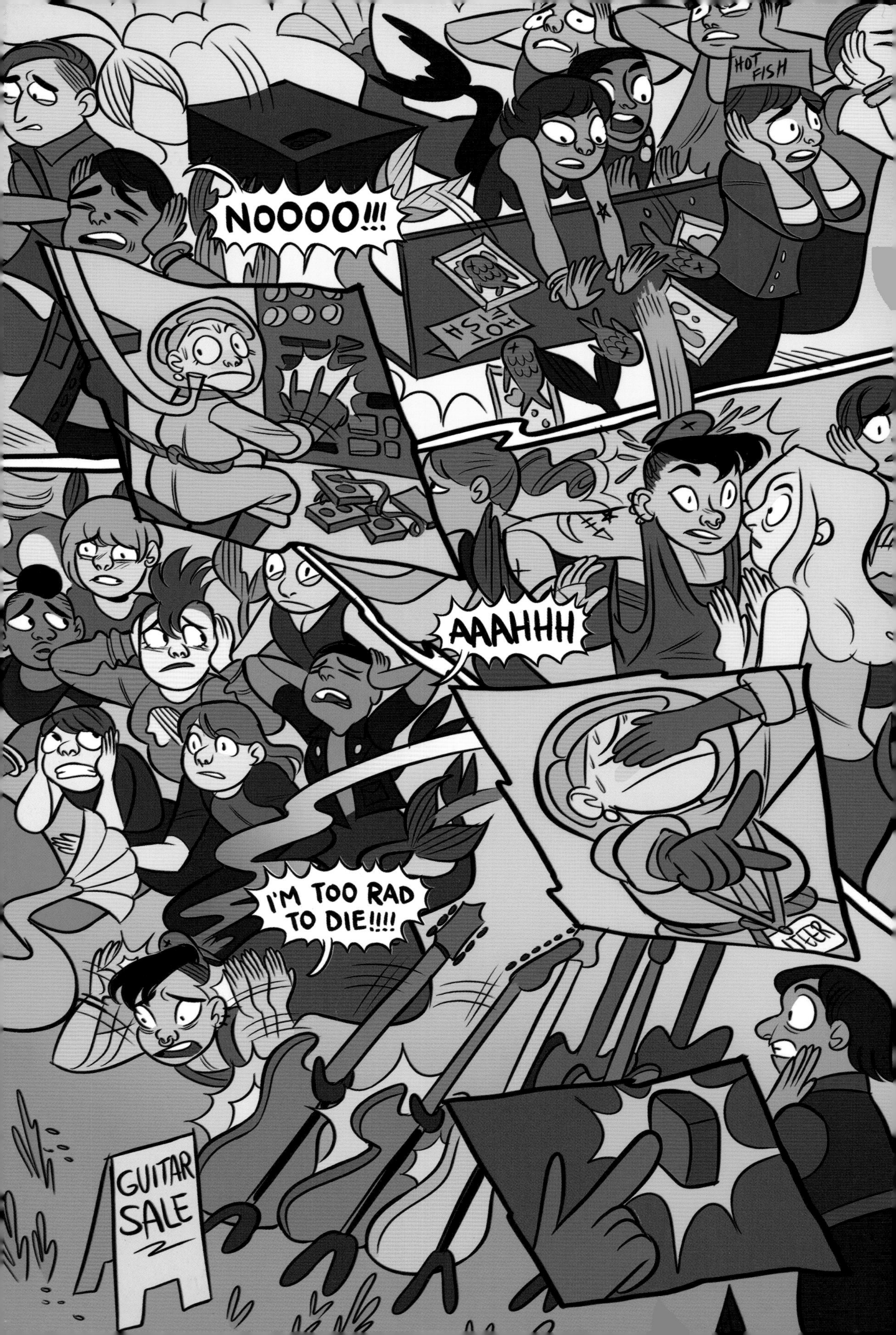
HOT FISH
NOOOO!!!
HOT FISH
AAAHHH
I'M TOO RAD TO DIE!!!!
GUITAR SALE

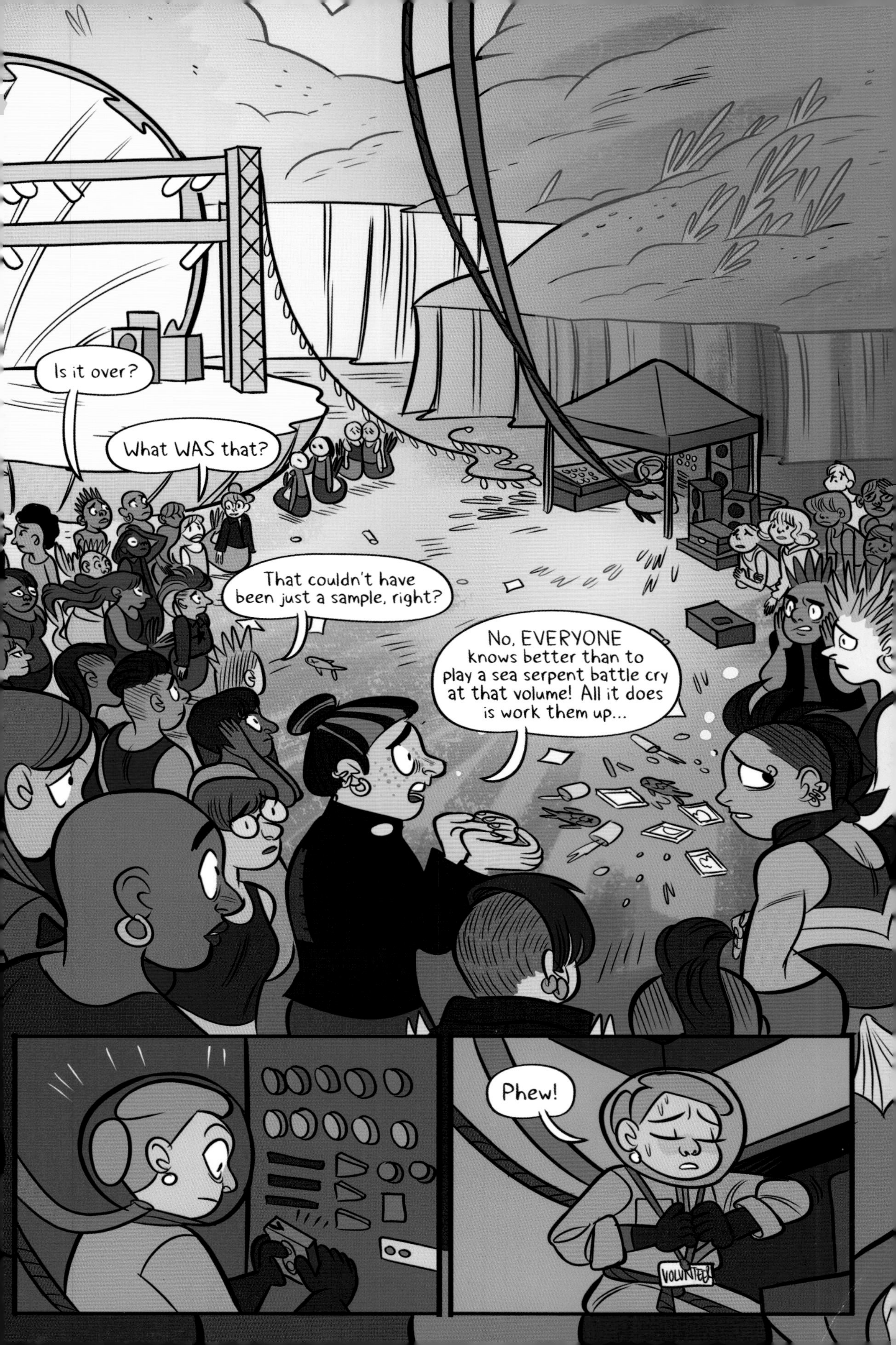

Is it over?
What WAS that?
That couldn't have been just a sample, right?
No, EVERYONE knows better than to play a sea serpent battle cry at that volume! All it does is work them up...
Phew!
VOLUNTEER

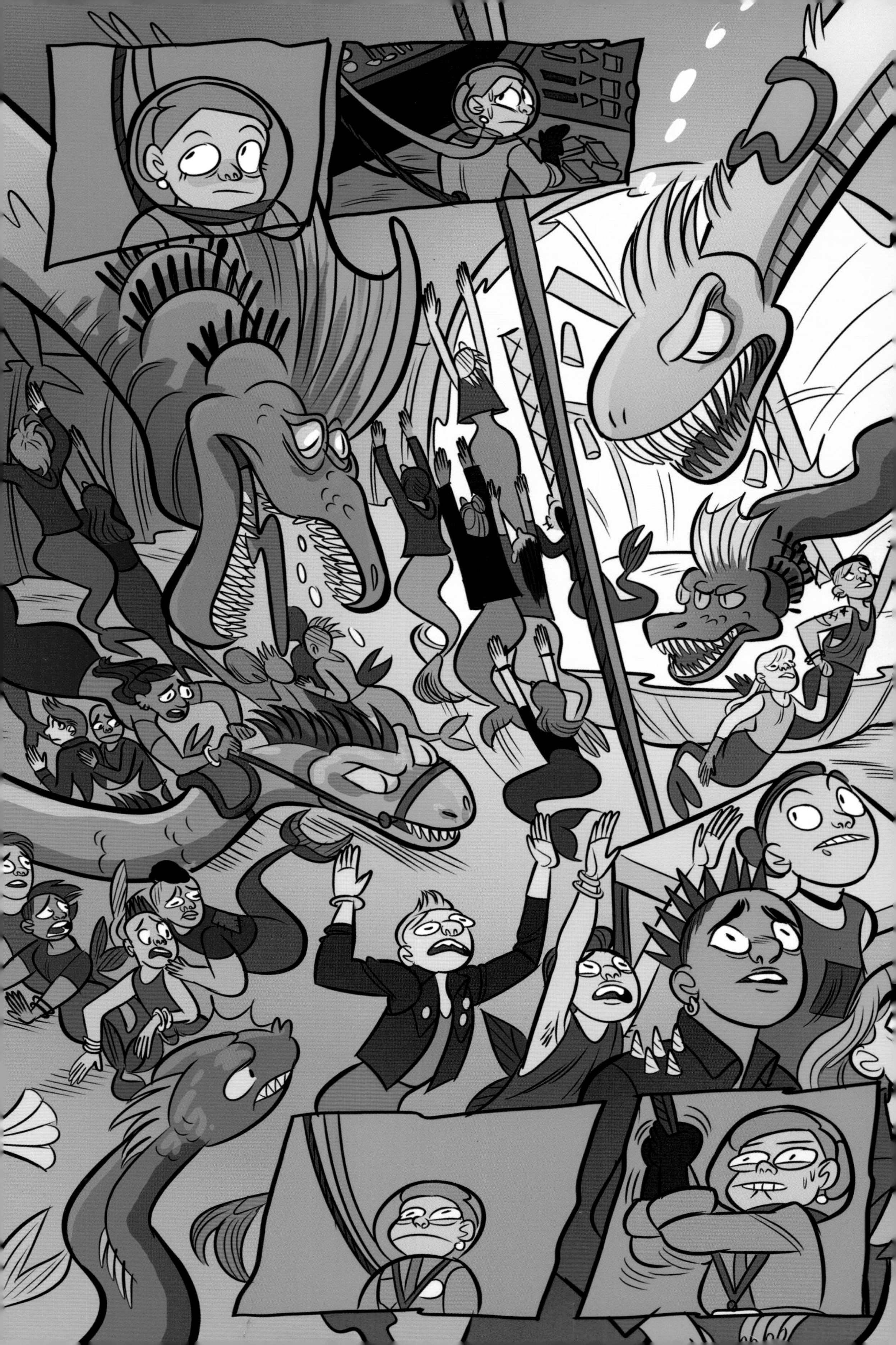

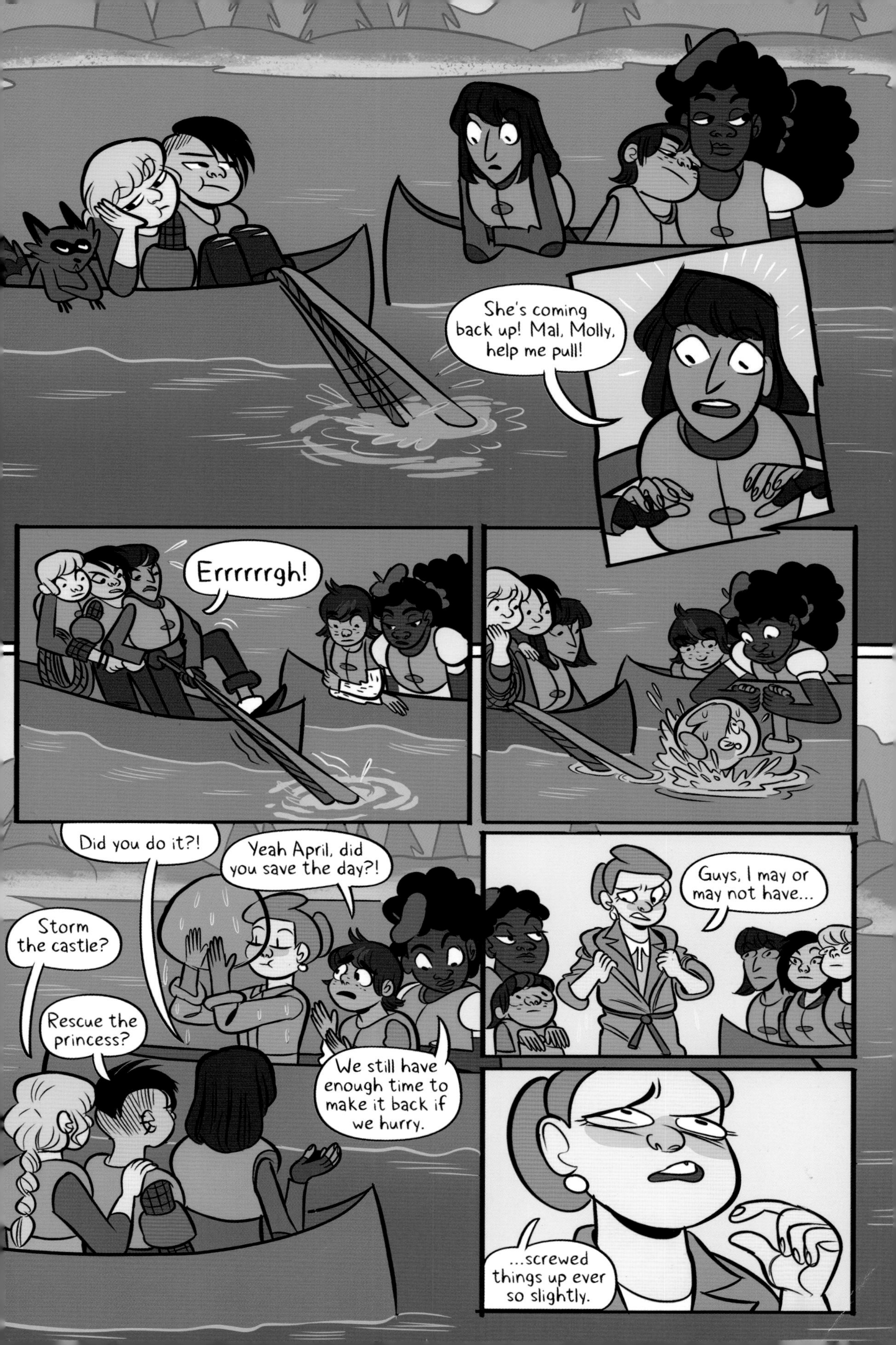
She's coming back up! Mal, Molly, help me pull!
Errrrrrgh!
Did you do it?!
Yeah April, did you save the day?!
Storm the castle?
Rescue the princess?
We still have enough time to make it back if we hurry.
Guys, I may or may not have...
...screwed things up ever so slightly.

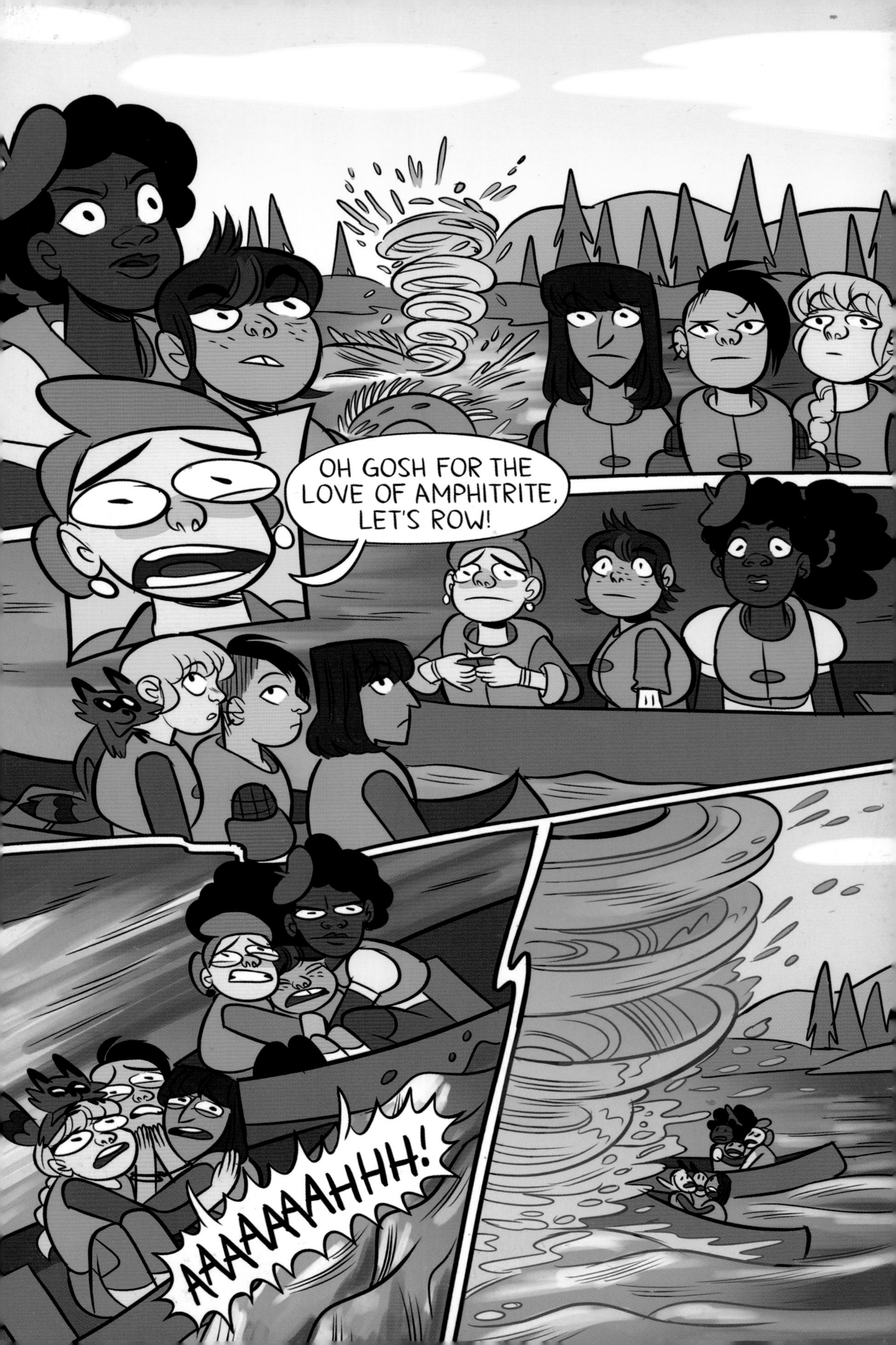
OH GOSH FOR THE LOVE OF AMPHITRITE, LET'S ROW!
AAAAAAHHH!

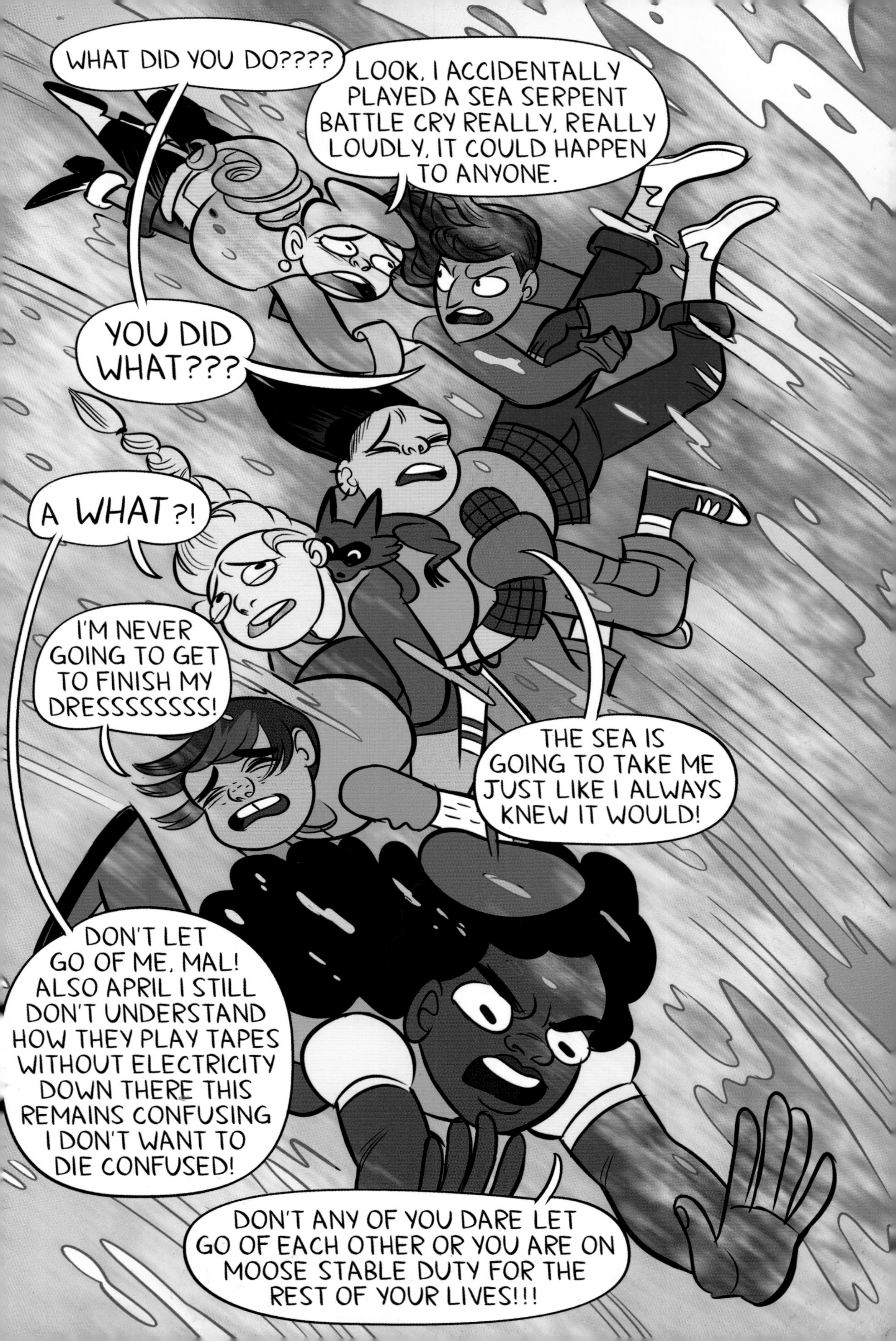
WHAT DID YOU DO????
LOOK, I ACCIDENTALLY PLAYED A SEA SERPENT BATTLE CRY REALLY, REALLY LOUDLY, IT COULD HAPPEN TO ANYONE.
YOU DID WHAT???
A WHAT?!
I'M NEVER GOING TO GET TO FINISH MY DRESSSSSSSS!
THE SEA IS GOING TO TAKE ME JUST LIKE I ALWAYS KNEW IT WOULD!
DON'T LET GO OF ME, MAL! ALSO APRIL I STILL DON'T UNDERSTAND HOW THEY PLAY TAPES WITHOUT ELECTRICITY DOWN THERE THIS REMAINS CONFUSING I DON'T WANT TO DIE CONFUSED!
DON'T ANY OF YOU DARE LET GO OF EACH OTHER OR YOU ARE ON MOOSE STABLE DUTY FOR THE REST OF YOUR LIVES!!!

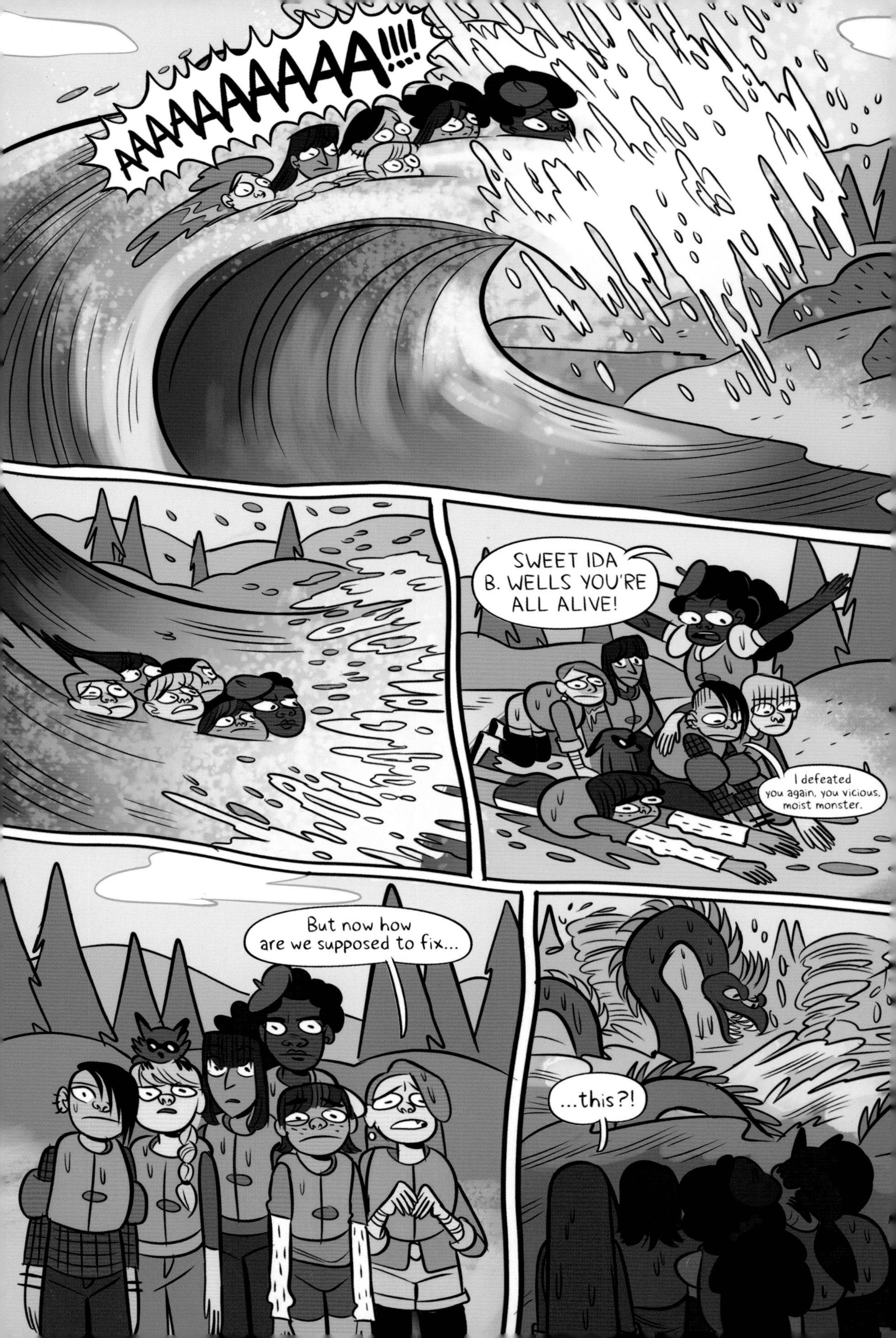
AAAAAAAAAA!!!!
SWEET IDA B. WELLS YOU'RE ALL ALIVE!
I defeated you again, you vicious, moist monster.
But now how are we supposed to fix...
...this?!

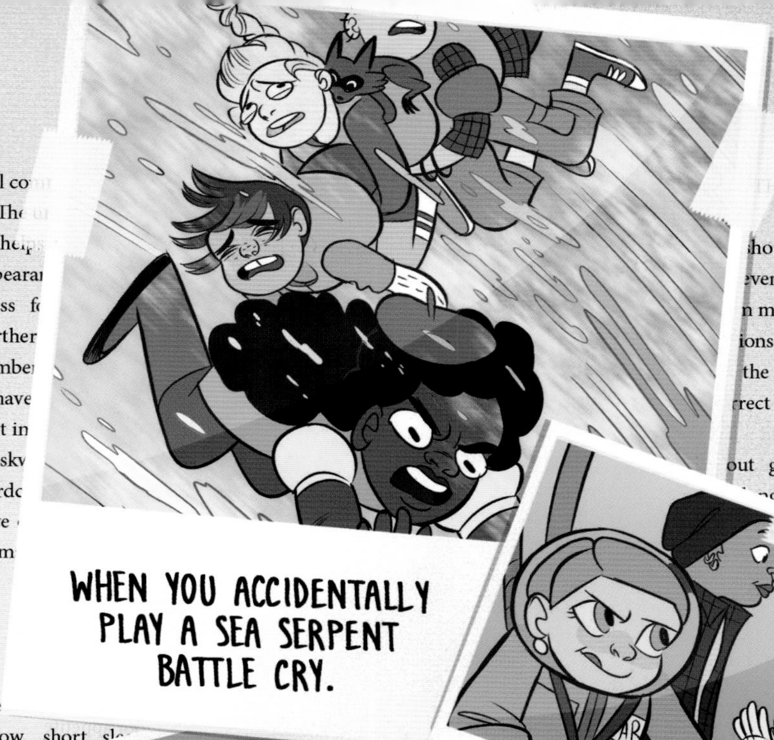
WHEN YOU ACCIDENTALLY PLAY A SEA SERPENT BATTLE CRY.

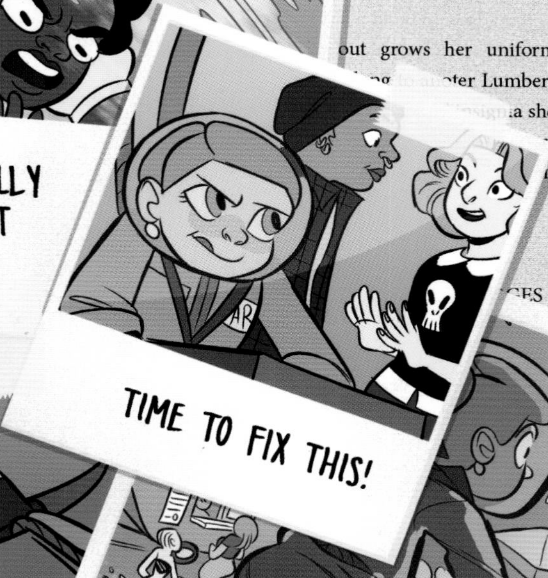
TIME TO FIX THIS!

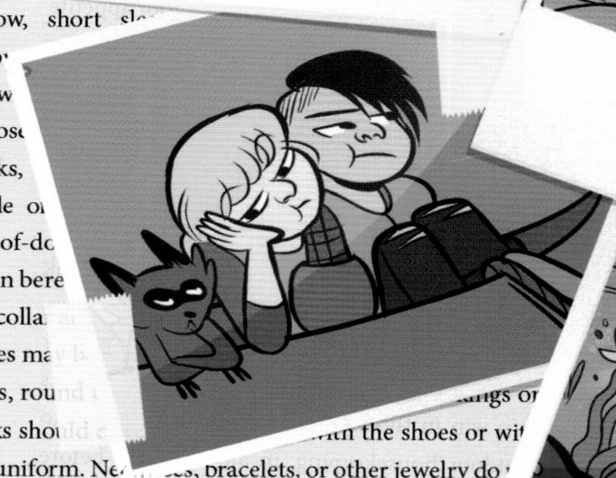

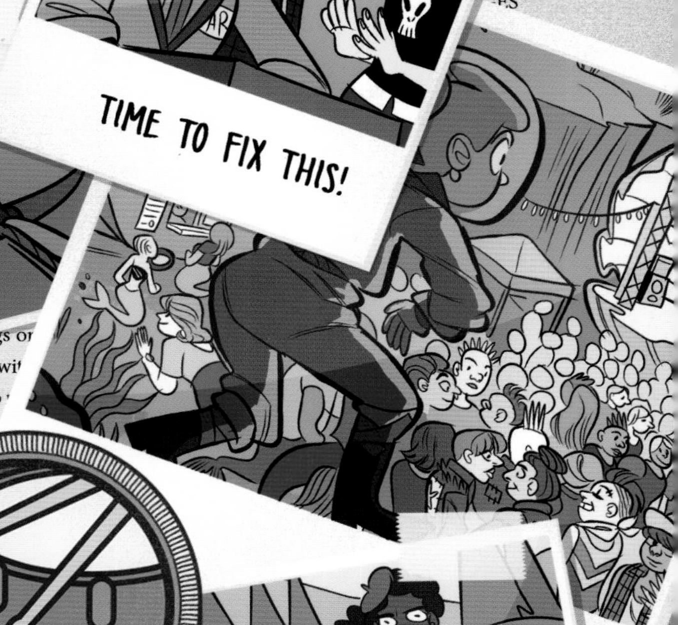

will co

The u

It helps

appearan

dress f

Further

Lumbe

to have

part in

Thiskv

Hardc

have

them

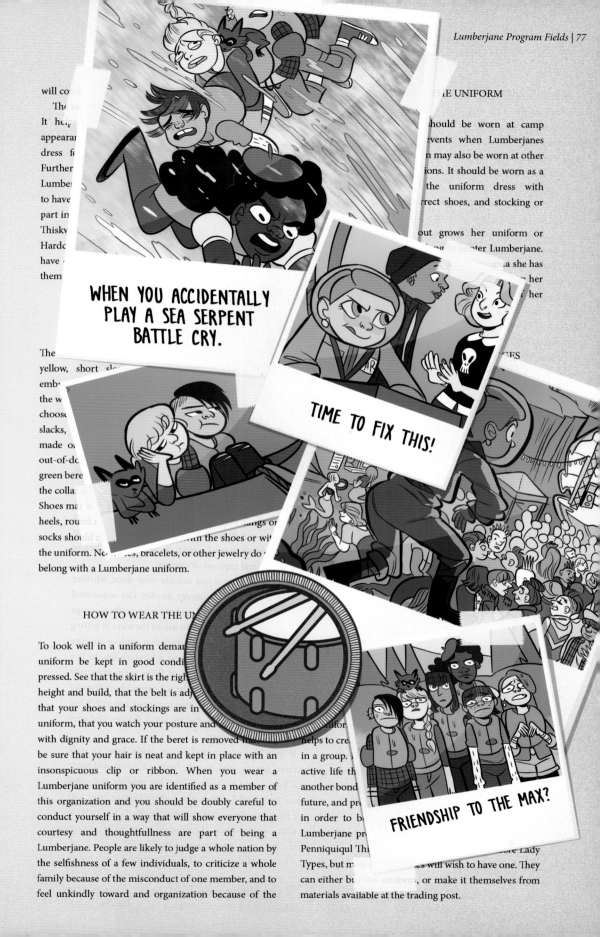

The

yellow, short sl

emb

the w

choose

slacks,

made o

out-of-do

green bere

the colla

Shoes may b

heels, round ... kings or

socks should c ... with the shoes or wit

the uniform. Ne... es, bracelets, or other jewelry do ... belong with a Lumberjane uniform.

HOW TO WEAR THE UN

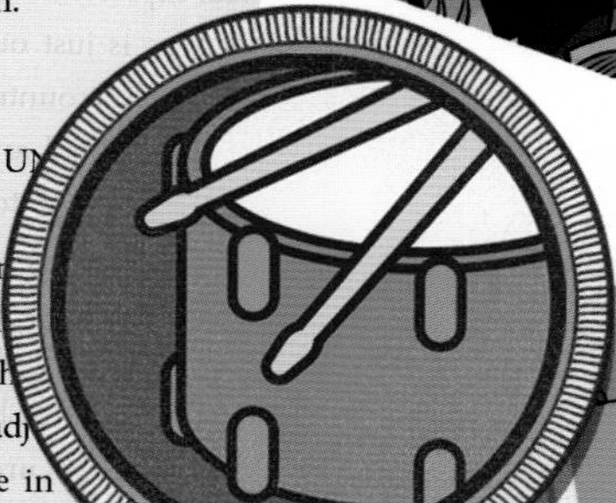

To look well in a uniform deman... uniform be kept in good condi... pressed. See that the skirt is the righ... height and build, that the belt is adj... that your shoes and stockings are in ... uniform, that you watch your posture and ... with dignity and grace. If the beret is removed ... be sure that your hair is neat and kept in place with an insonspicuous clip or ribbon. When you wear a Lumberjane uniform you are identified as a member of this organization and you should be doubly careful to conduct yourself in a way that will show everyone that courtesy and thoughtfullness are part of being a Lumberjane. People are likely to judge a whole nation by the selfishness of a few individuals, to criticize a whole family because of the misconduct of one member, and to feel unkindly toward and organization because of the

...HE UNIFORM

...should be worn at camp ... events when Lumberjanes ... n may also be worn at other ... ions. It should be worn as a ... the uniform dress with ... rrect shoes, and stocking or

... out grows her uniform or ... ter Lumberjane. ... a she has ... her ... her

...GES

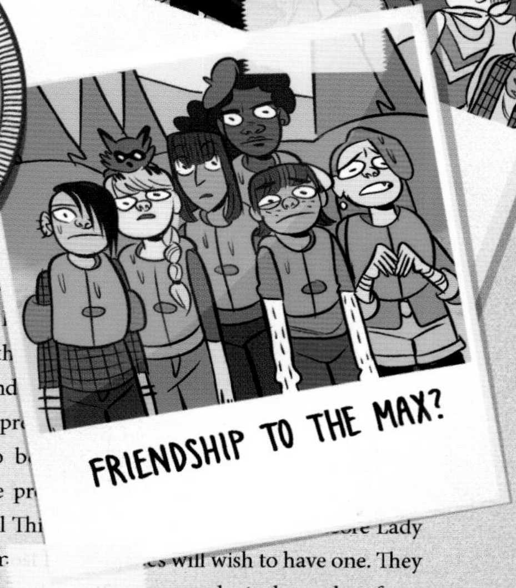
FRIENDSHIP TO THE MAX?

... unifor ... helps to cre ... in a group. ... active life th ... another bond ... future, and pr ... in order to b ... Lumberjane pr ... Penniquiqul Thi ... ore Lady Types, but m... es will wish to have one. They can either b... uniform, or make it themselves from materials available at the trading post.

LUMBERJANES FIELD MANUAL

LUMBERJANES FIELD MANUAL
CHAPTER TWENTY

Lumberjanes "Automotive" Program Field

KEEPIN' IT REEL BADGE

"There is more to life than fish, most of the time."

Fishing, hunting, gathering, all those good things that will be touched on in the basic survival classes are great things to know. At this camp we want to ensure that each and every Lumberjane leaves this camp with a basic understanding of what to do in a blizzard, how to survive in the desert, and what actions are needed with the ring of fire finally activates. We are happy to say that every Lumberjane that comes to this camp will leave with that knowledge and more. But knowledge and skills aren't the only things we want Lumberjanes to leave this camp with, we want Lumberjanes to have a better understand of themselves when they do eventually leave the wooden walls of their lodges.

There are a lot of distractions in the world outside of camp, and some of those distractions will follow every camper here, but to the best of our abilities we want to ensure that this camp is always a safe and welcoming environment for every camp who walks these dirt trails. At camp it is important to understand teamwork and friendship but more importantly, it is vital that you learn acceptance for who you are as a camper and gain a better understanding of that means to you. With the *Keepin' It Reel* badge, each camper is encouraged to be themselves, to find and realize that individuality they have that makes them who they are.

To obtain the *Keepin' It Reel* badge, a Lumberjane must learn the art of meditation and focus. As this is a precursor to many of the badges that need to be earned at this camp, by the time a Lumberjane is ready for the *Keepin' It Reel* badge, meditation is the least of their worries. The Lumberjane, once ready, will then figure out what they need in order to complete this badge by wandering around the camp. They will know what the object is as soon as they come across, remember this badge is all about gut instincts and not actual methods.

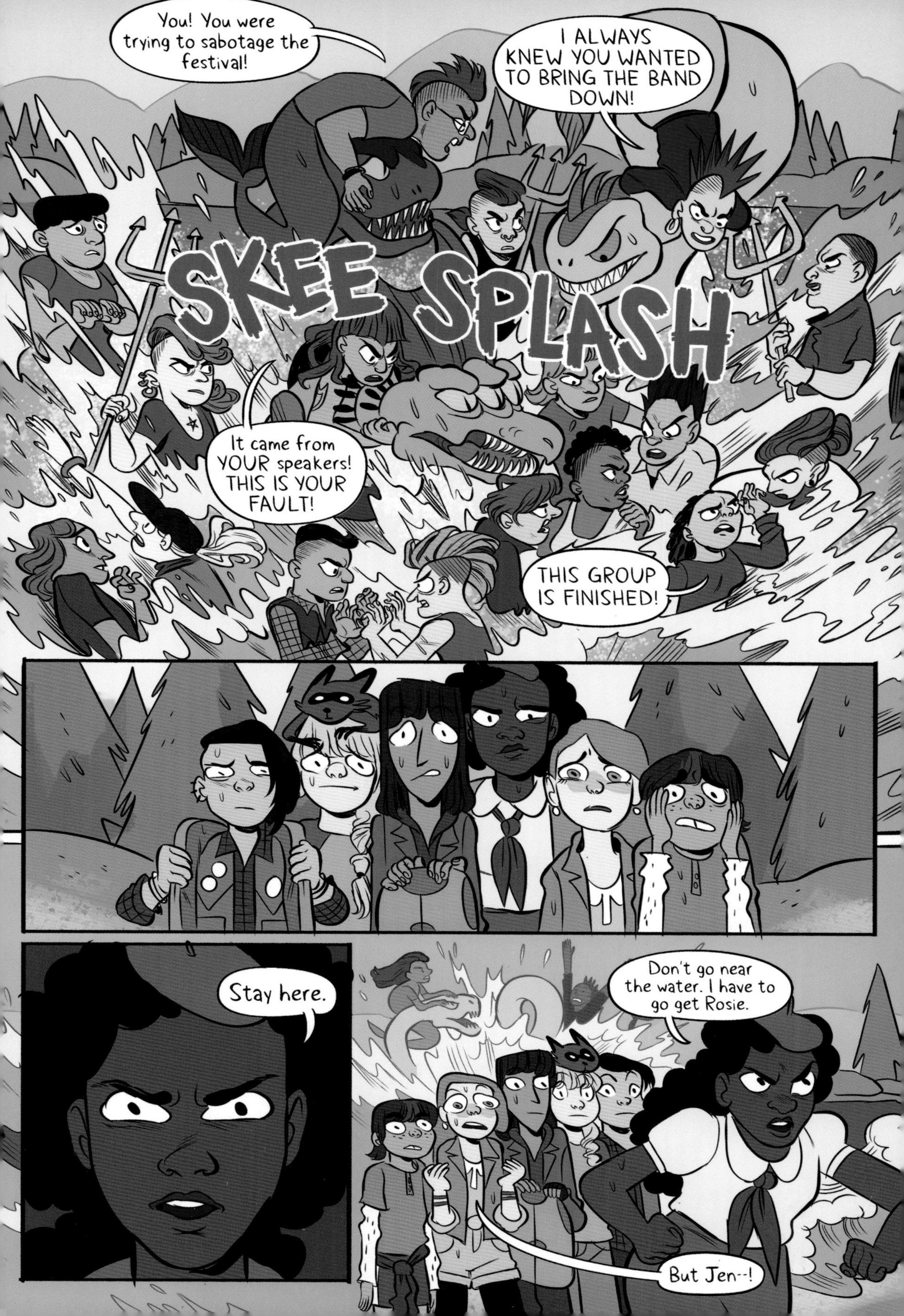
You! You were trying to sabotage the festival!
I ALWAYS KNEW YOU WANTED TO BRING THE BAND DOWN!
SKEE SPLASH
It came from YOUR speakers! THIS IS YOUR FAULT!
THIS GROUP IS FINISHED!
Stay here.
Don't go near the water. I have to go get Rosie.
But Jen--!

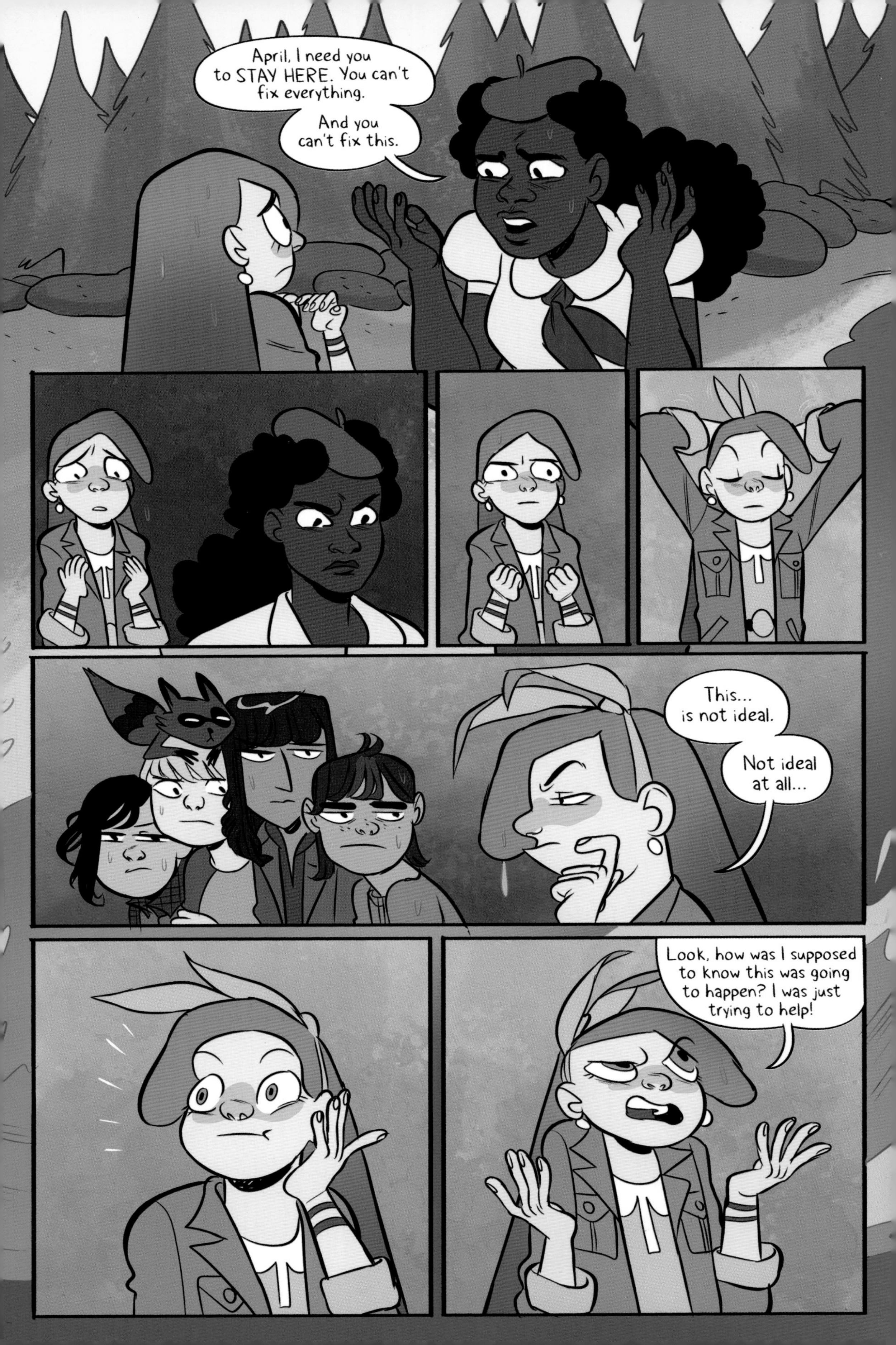
April, I need you to STAY HERE. You can't fix everything.
And you can't fix this.
This... is not ideal.
Not ideal at all...
Look, how was I supposed to know this was going to happen? I was just trying to help!

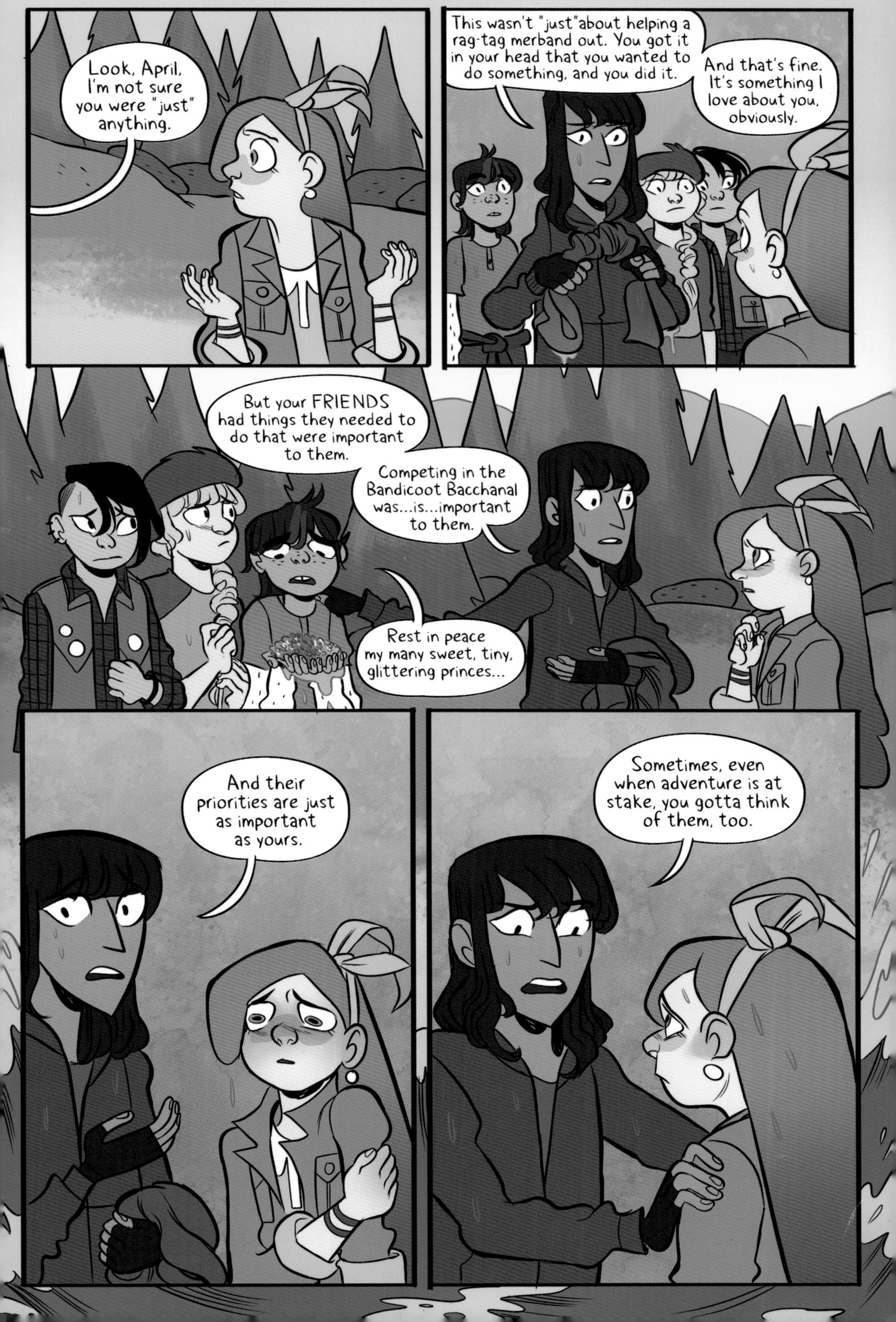
Look, April, I'm not sure you were "just" anything.
This wasn't "just" about helping a rag-tag merband out. You got it in your head that you wanted to do something, and you did it.
And that's fine. It's something I love about you, obviously.
But your FRIENDS had things they needed to do that were important to them.
Competing in the Bandicoot Bacchanal was...is...important to them.
Rest in peace my many sweet, tiny, glittering princes...
And their priorities are just as important as yours.
Sometimes, even when adventure is at stake, you gotta think of them, too.

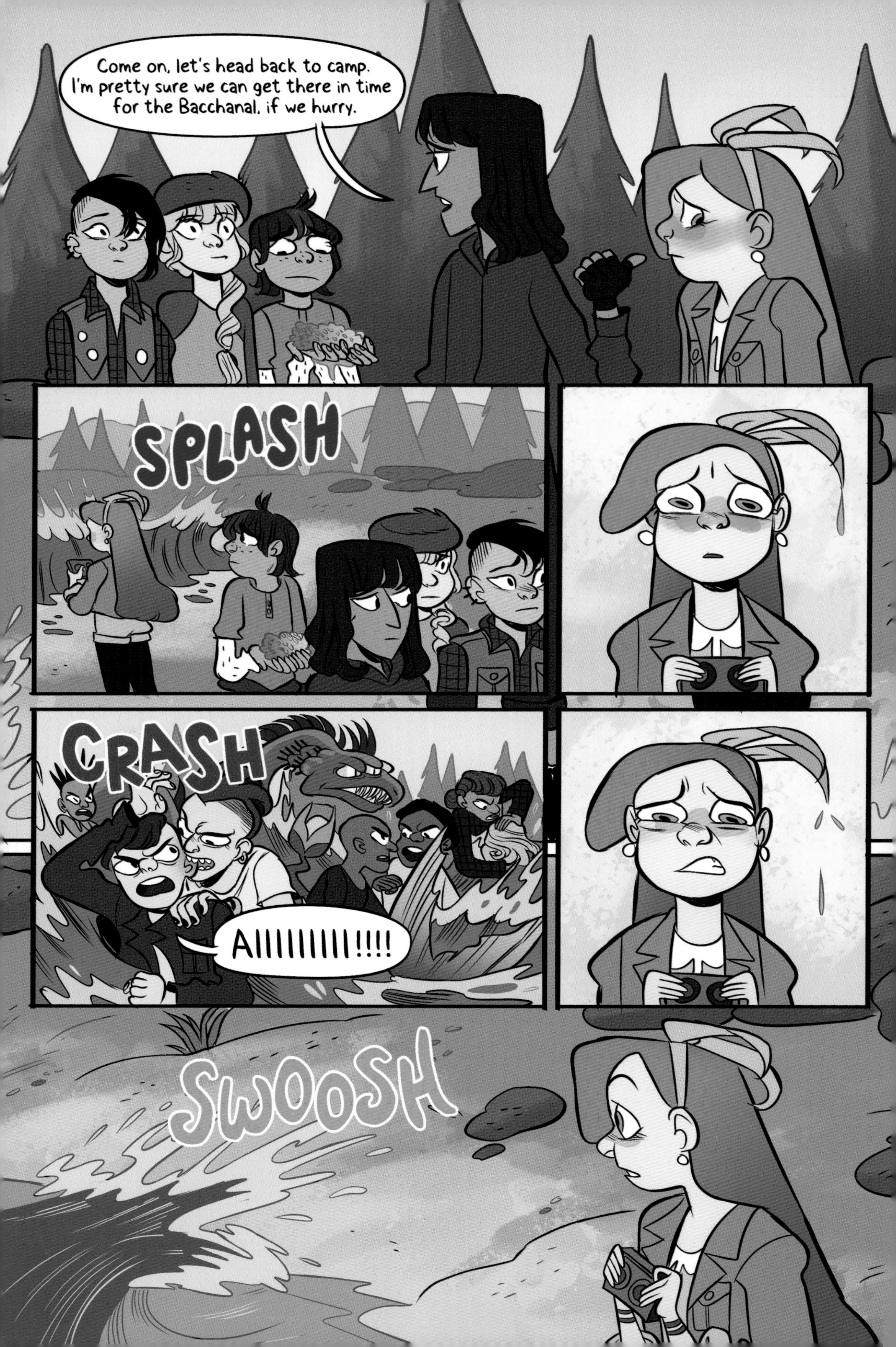
Come on, let's head back to camp. I'm pretty sure we can get there in time for the Bacchanal, if we hurry.
SPLASH
CRASH
AIIIIIIIII!!!!
SWOOSH

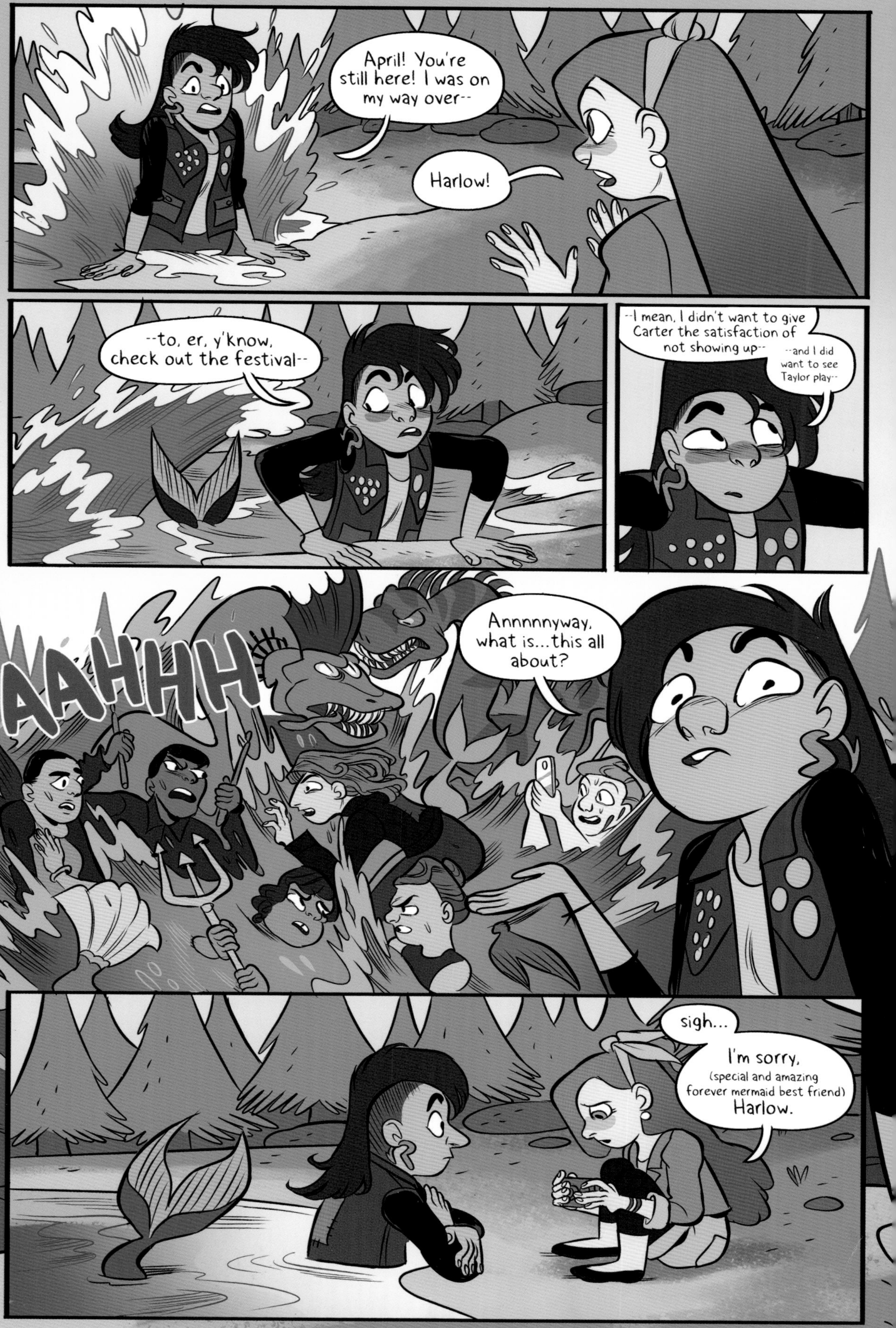
April! You're still here! I was on my way over--
Harlow!
--to, er, y'know, check out the festival--
--I mean, I didn't want to give Carter the satisfaction of not showing up--
--and I did want to see Taylor play--
AAHHH
Annnnnyway, what is...this all about?
sigh...
I'm sorry, (special and amazing forever mermaid best friend) Harlow.

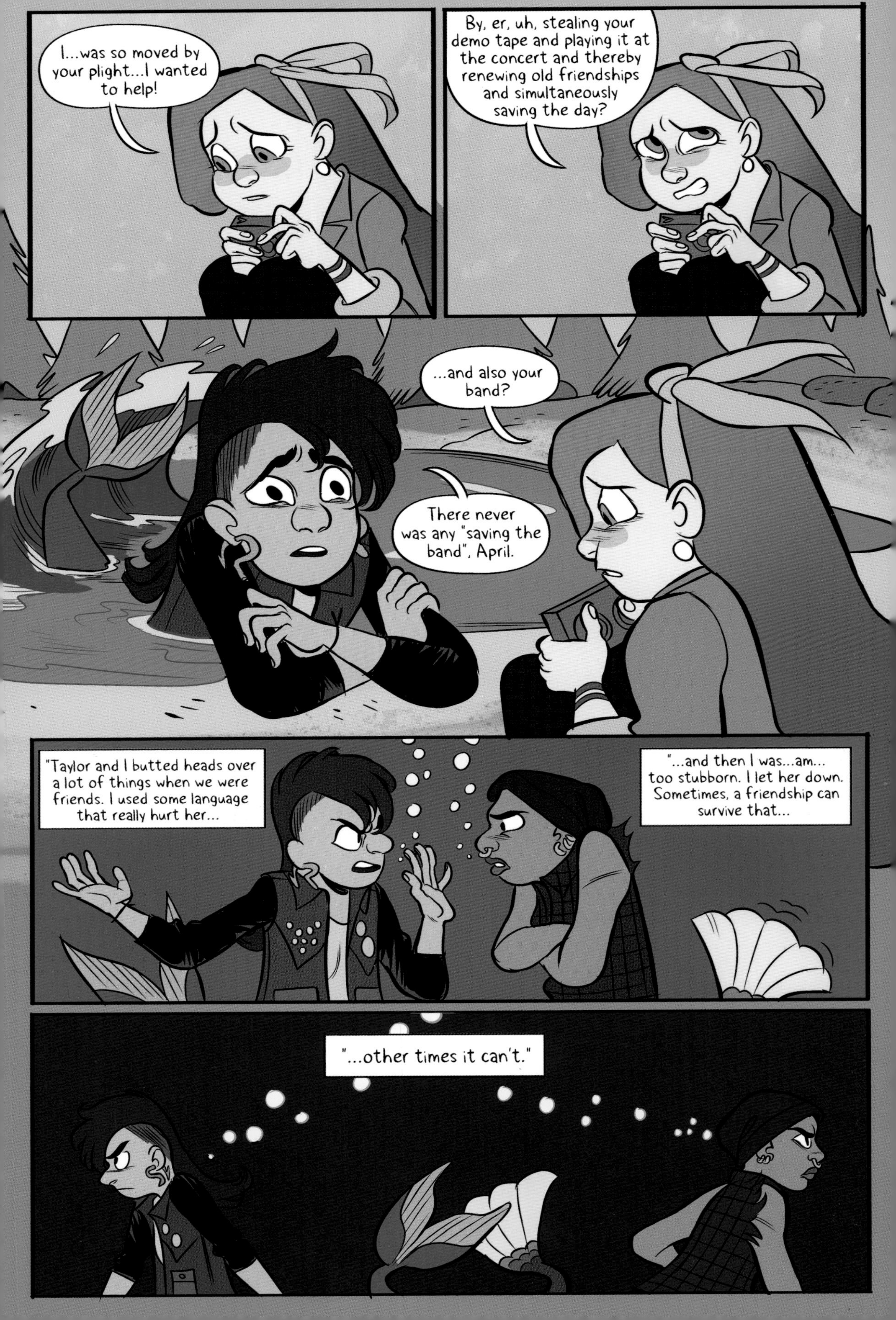
I...was so moved by your plight...I wanted to help!
By, er, uh, stealing your demo tape and playing it at the concert and thereby renewing old friendships and simultaneously saving the day?
...and also your band?
There never was any "saving the band", April.
"Taylor and I butted heads over a lot of things when we were friends. I used some language that really hurt her...
"...and then I was...am... too stubborn. I let her down. Sometimes, a friendship can survive that...
"...other times it can't."

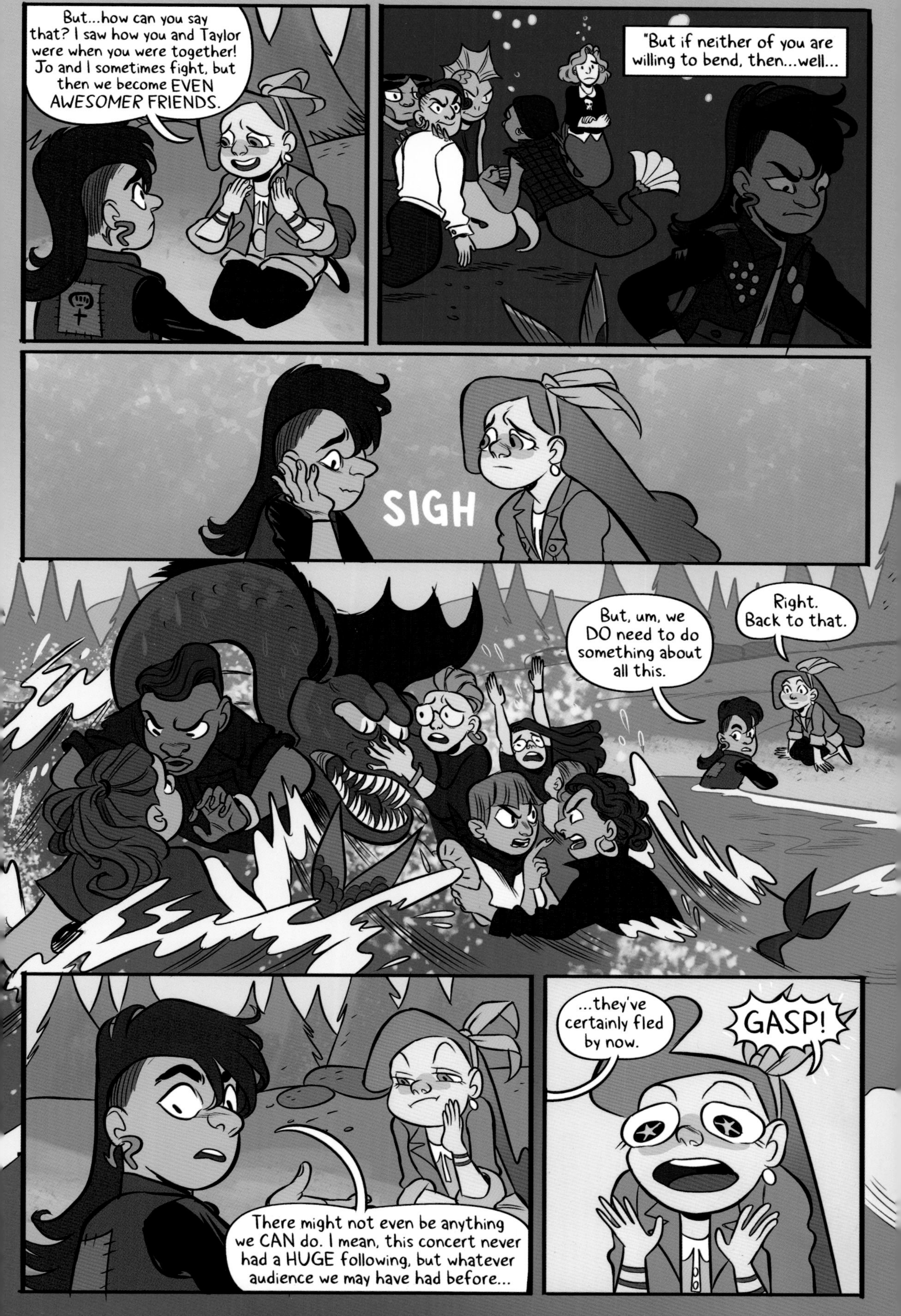
But...how can you say that? I saw how you and Taylor were when you were together! Jo and I sometimes fight, but then we become EVEN AWESOMER FRIENDS.
"But if neither of you are willing to bend, then...well...
SIGH
But, um, we DO need to do something about all this.
Right. Back to that.
There might not even be anything we CAN do. I mean, this concert never had a HUGE following, but whatever audience we may have had before...
...they've certainly fled by now.
GASP!

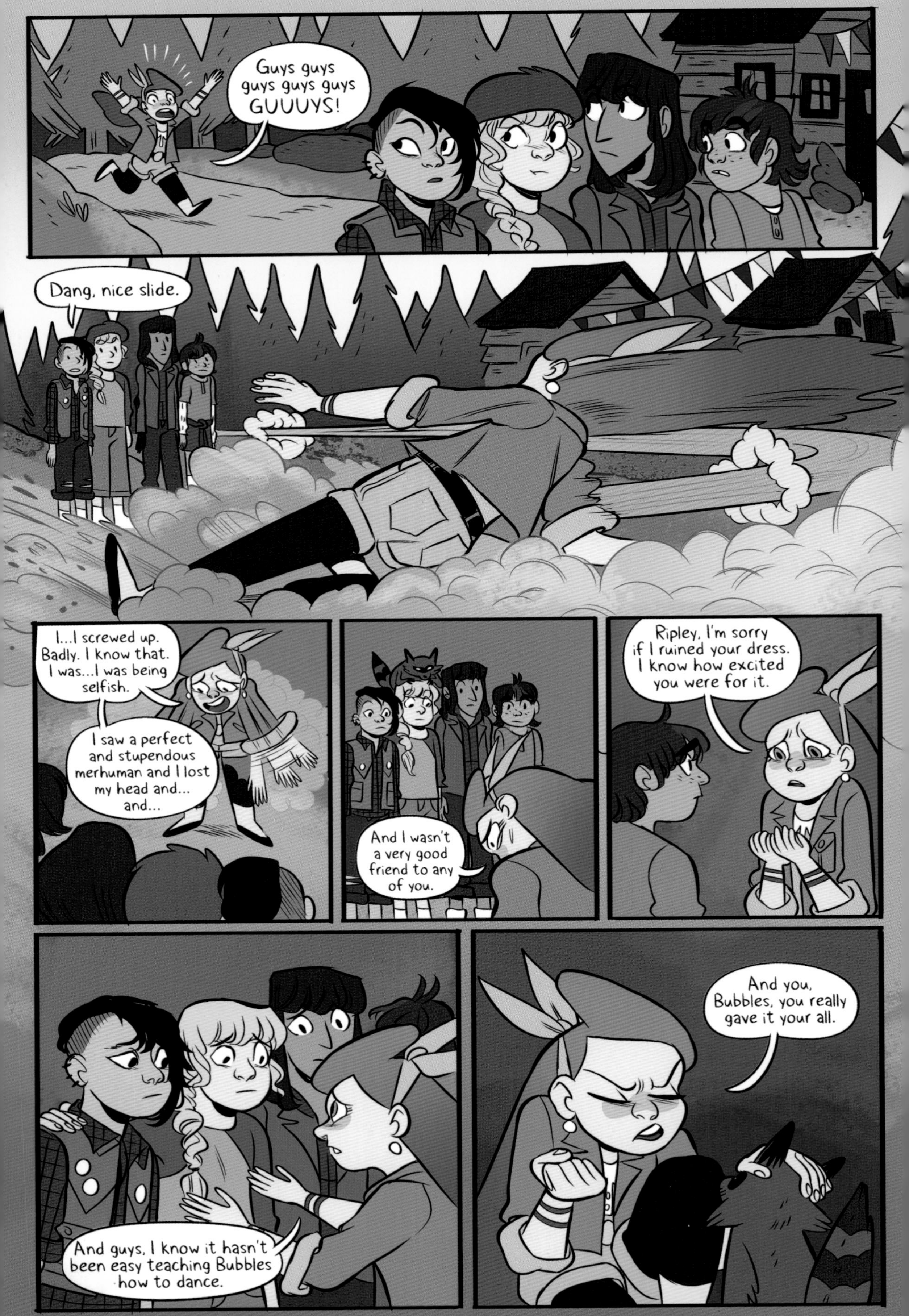
Guys guys guys guys guys GUUUYS!
Dang, nice slide.
I...I screwed up. Badly. I know that. I was...I was being selfish.
I saw a perfect and stupendous merhuman and I lost my head and... and...
And I wasn't a very good friend to any of you.
Ripley, I'm sorry if I ruined your dress. I know how excited you were for it.
And guys, I know it hasn't been easy teaching Bubbles how to dance.
And you, Bubbles, you really gave it your all.

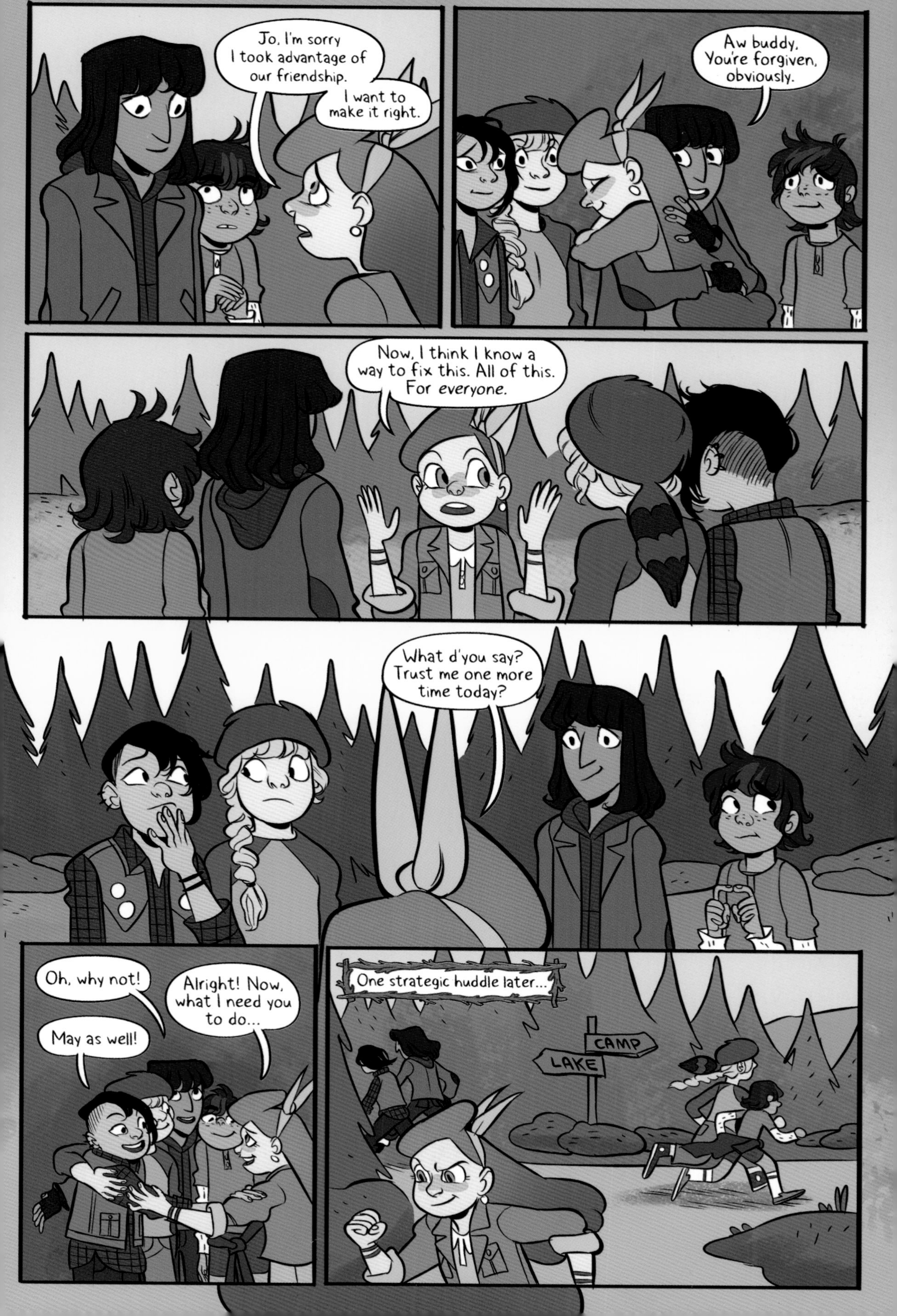
Jo, I'm sorry I took advantage of our friendship.
I want to make it right.
Aw buddy. You're forgiven, obviously.
Now, I think I know a way to fix this. All of this. For everyone.
What d'you say? Trust me one more time today?
Oh, why not!
May as well!
Alright! Now, what I need you to do...
One strategic huddle later...
CAMP
LAKE

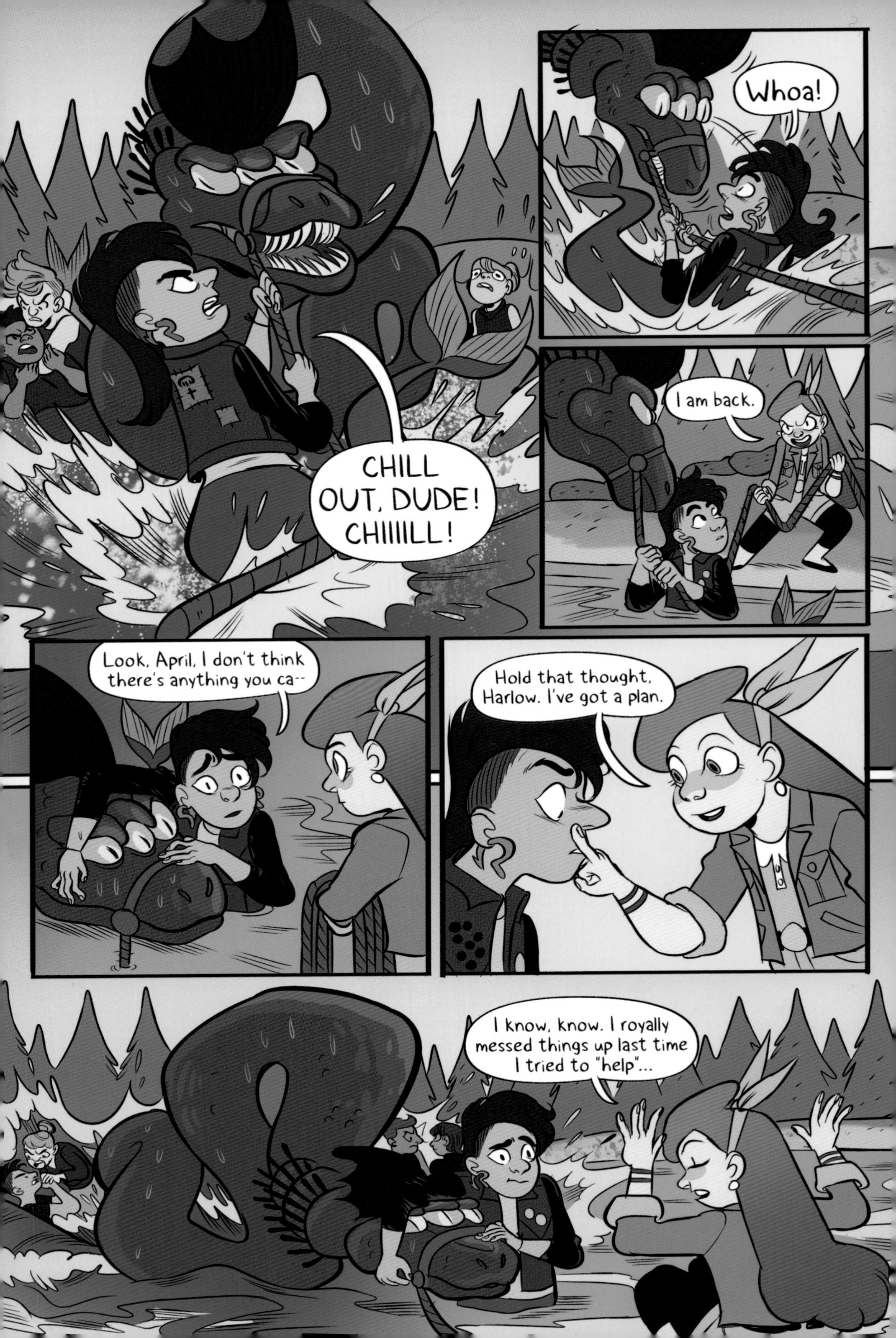
Whoa!
CHILL OUT, DUDE! CHIIIIILL!
I am back.
Look, April, I don't think there's anything you ca--
Hold that thought, Harlow. I've got a plan.
I know, know. I royally messed things up last time I tried to "help"...

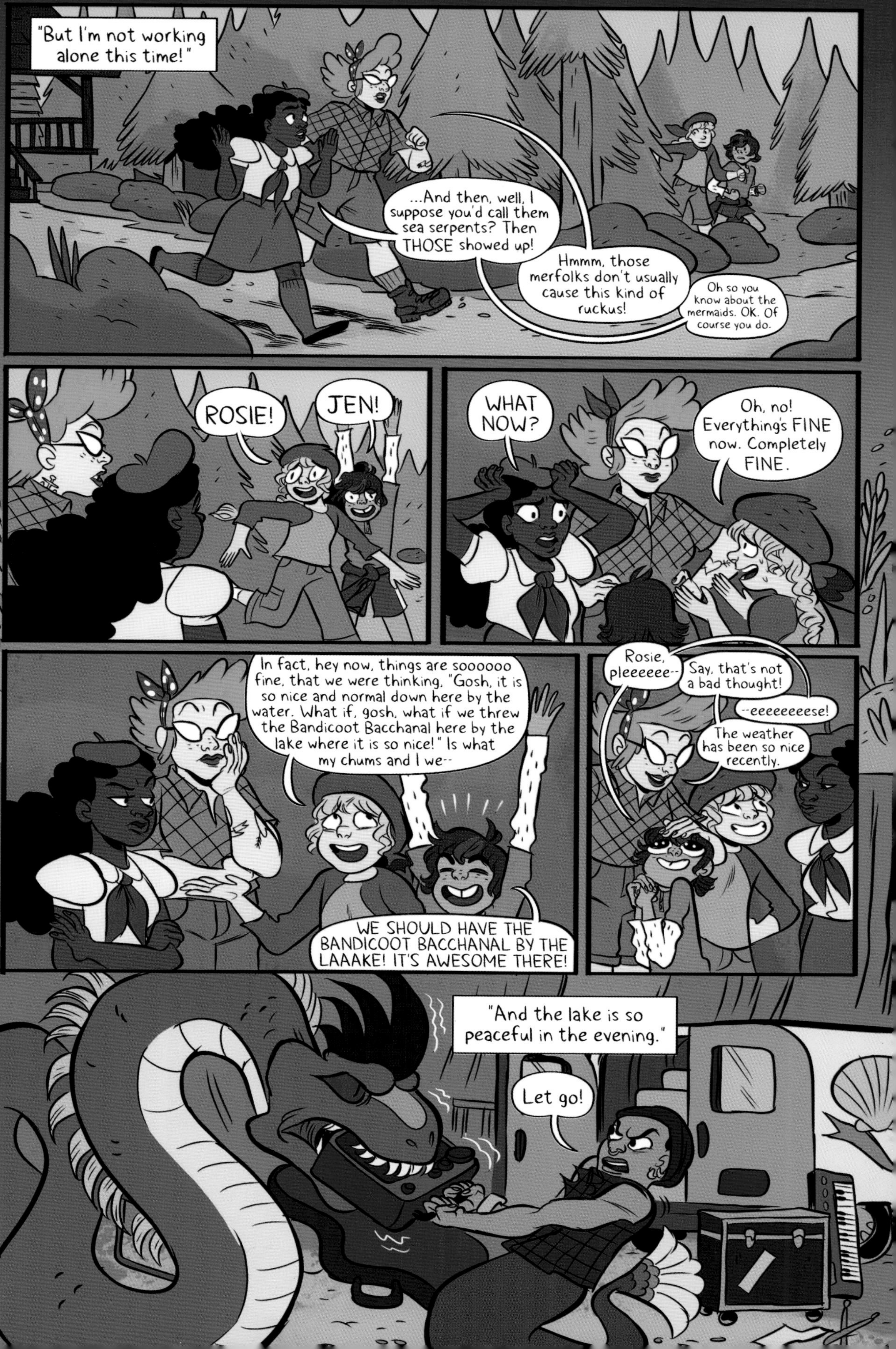
"But I'm not working alone this time!"
...And then, well, I suppose you'd call them sea serpents? Then THOSE showed up!
Hmmm, those merfolks don't usually cause this kind of ruckus!
Oh so you know about the mermaids. OK. Of course you do.
ROSIE!
JEN!
WHAT NOW?
Oh, no! Everything's FINE now. Completely FINE.
In fact, hey now, things are soooooo fine, that we were thinking, "Gosh, it is so nice and normal down here by the water. What if, gosh, what if we threw the Bandicoot Bacchanal here by the lake where it is so nice!" Is what my chums and I we--
WE SHOULD HAVE THE BANDICOOT BACCHANAL BY THE LAAAKE! IT'S AWESOME THERE!
Rosie, pleeeeee--
Say, that's not a bad thought!
--eeeeeeeese!
The weather has been so nice recently.
"And the lake is so peaceful in the evening."
Let go!

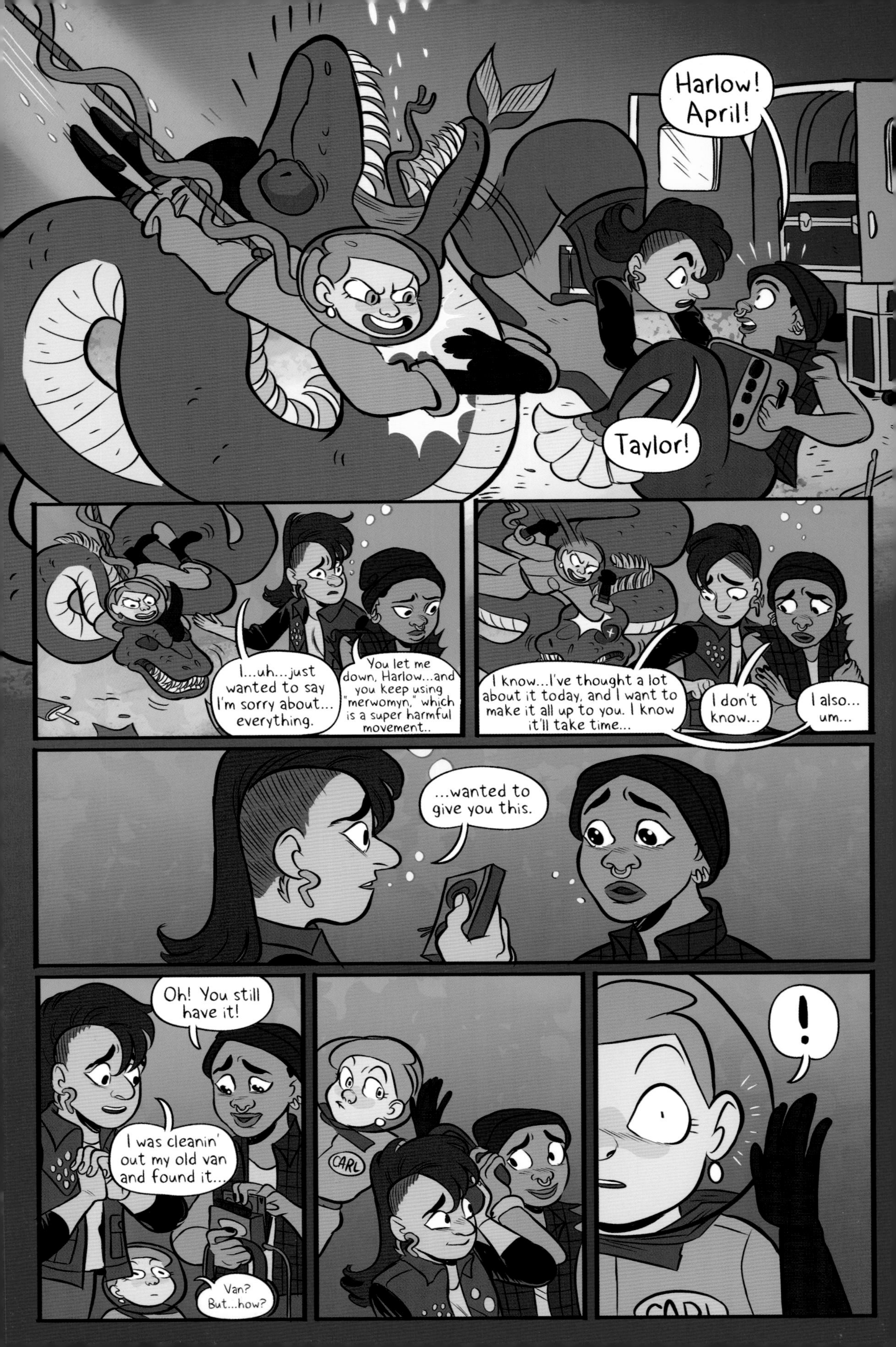
Harlow! April!
Taylor!
I...uh...just wanted to say I'm sorry about... everything.
You let me down, Harlow...and you keep using "merwomyn," which is a super harmful movement..
I know...I've thought a lot about it today, and I want to make it all up to you. I know it'll take time...
I don't know...
I also... um...
...wanted to give you this.
Oh! You still have it!
I was cleanin' out my old van and found it...
Van? But...how?
CARL
!

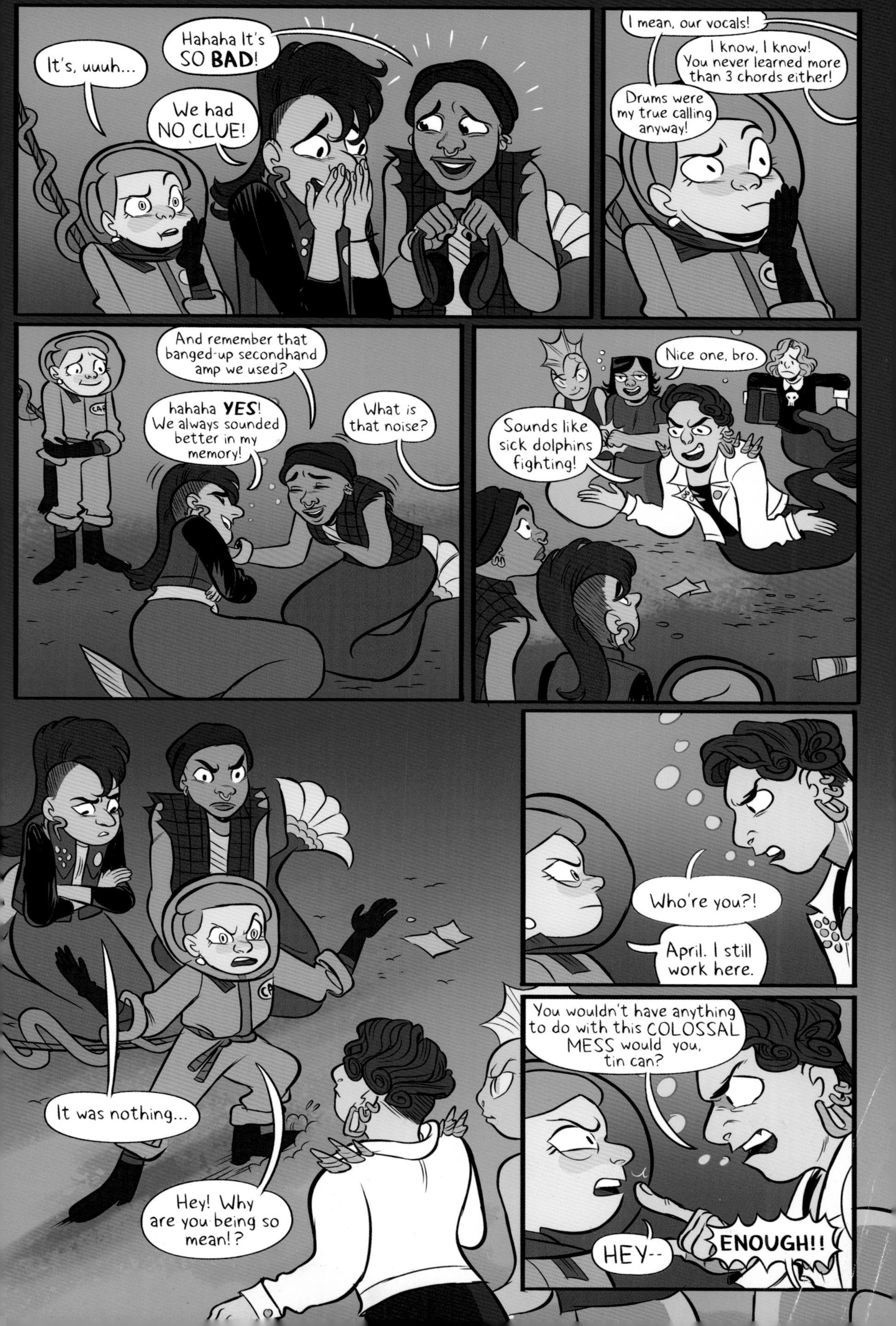
It's, uuuh...
Hahaha It's SO BAD!
We had NO CLUE!
I mean, our vocals!
I know, I know! You never learned more than 3 chords either!
Drums were my true calling anyway!
And remember that banged-up secondhand amp we used?
hahaha YES! We always sounded better in my memory!
What is that noise?
Nice one, bro.
Sounds like sick dolphins fighting!
It was nothing...
Hey! Why are you being so mean!?
Who're you?!
April. I still work here.
You wouldn't have anything to do with this COLOSSAL MESS would you, tin can?
HEY--
ENOUGH!!

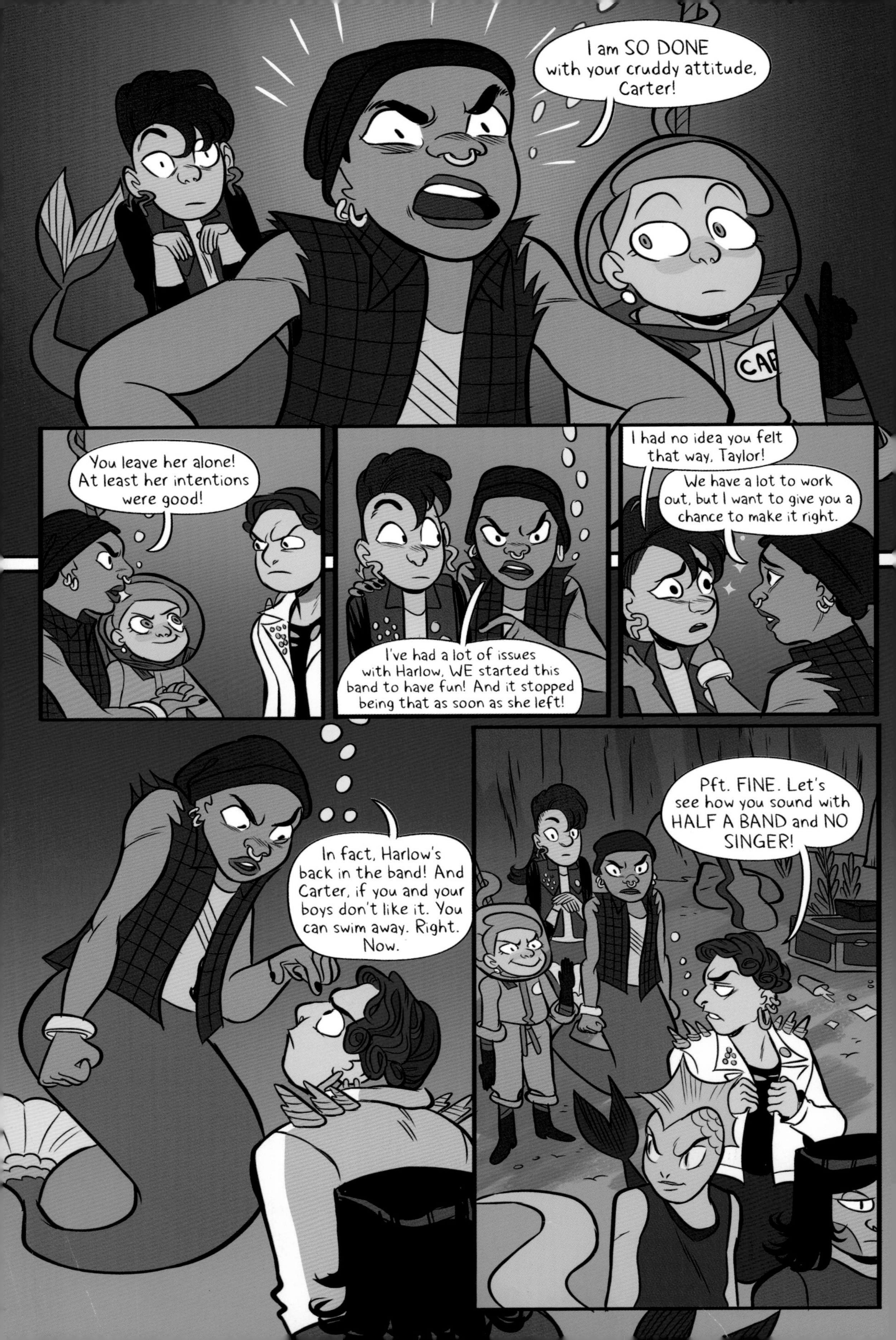
I am SO DONE with your cruddy attitude, Carter!
CAP
You leave her alone! At least her intentions were good!
I've had a lot of issues with Harlow, WE started this band to have fun! And it stopped being that as soon as she left!
I had no idea you felt that way, Taylor!
We have a lot to work out, but I want to give you a chance to make it right.
In fact, Harlow's back in the band! And Carter, if you and your boys don't like it. You can swim away. Right. Now.
Pft. FINE. Let's see how you sound with HALF A BAND and NO SINGER!

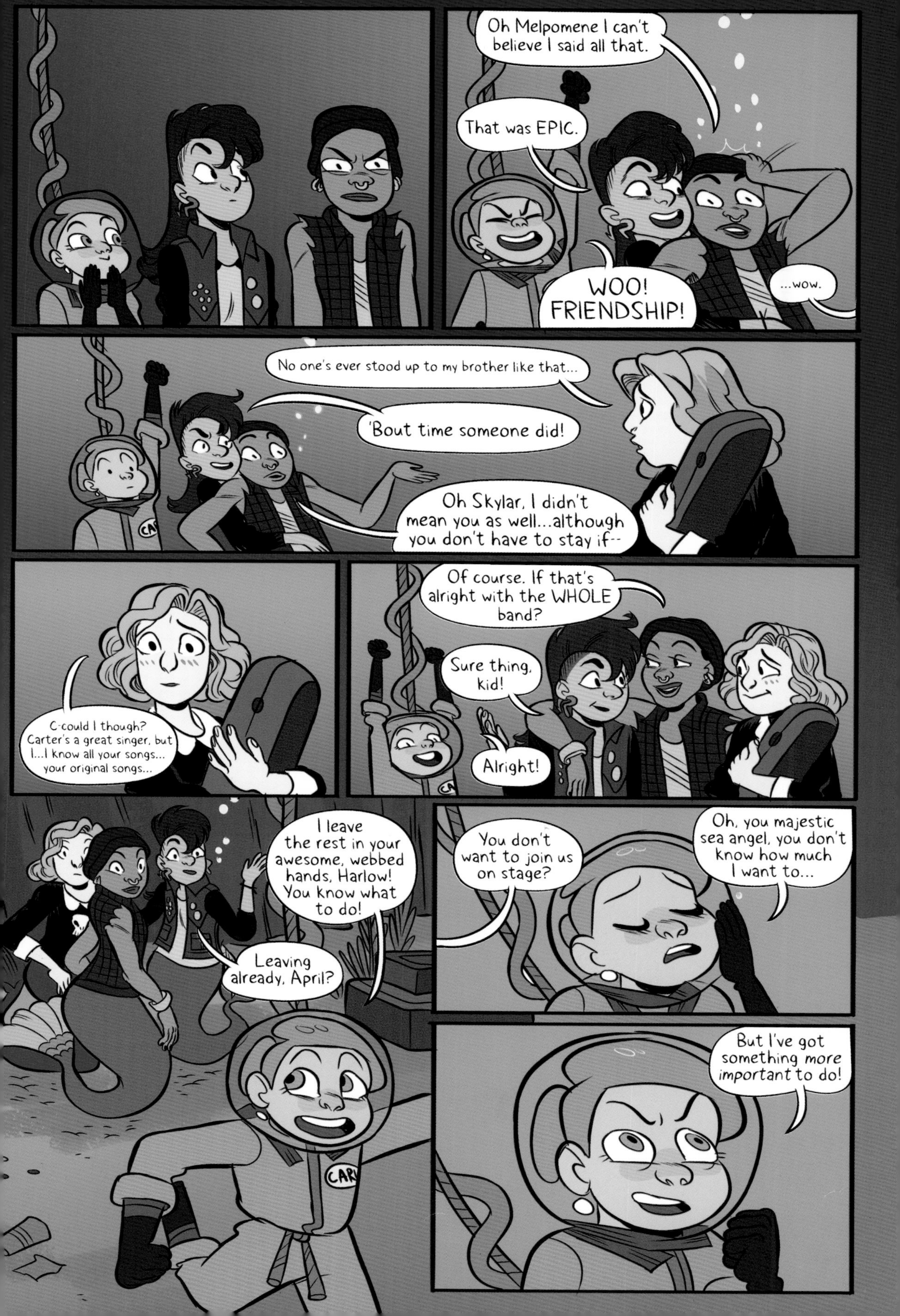

Oh Melpomene I can't believe I said all that.
That was EPIC.
WOO! FRIENDSHIP!
...wow.
No one's ever stood up to my brother like that...
'Bout time someone did!
Oh Skylar, I didn't mean you as well...although you don't have to stay if--
C-could I though? Carter's a great singer, but I...I know all your songs... your original songs...
Of course. If that's alright with the WHOLE band?
Sure thing, kid!
Alright!
I leave the rest in your awesome, webbed hands, Harlow! You know what to do!
Leaving already, April?
You don't want to join us on stage?
Oh, you majestic sea angel, you don't know how much I want to...
But I've got something more important to do!

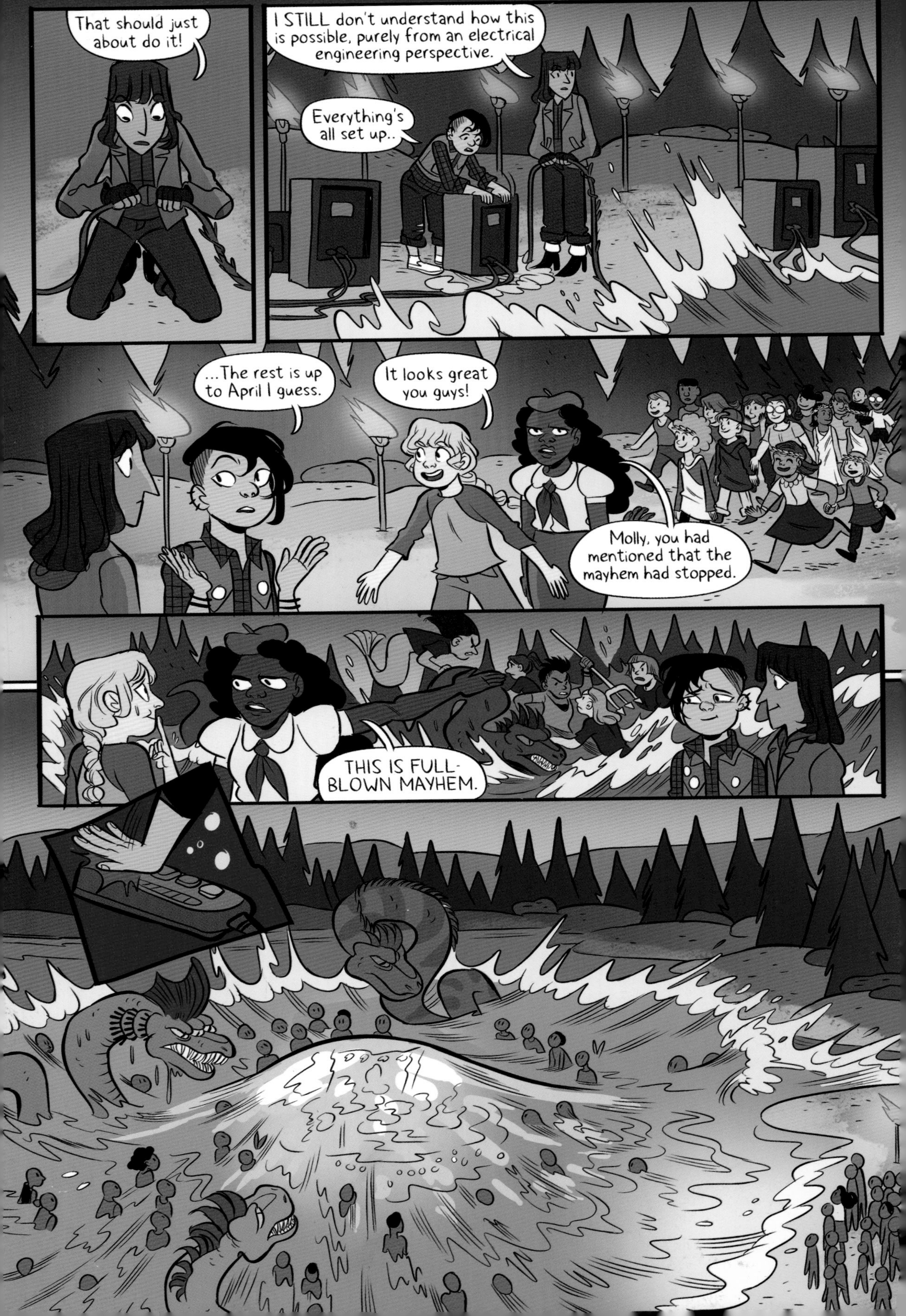
That should just about do it!
I STILL don't understand how this is possible, purely from an electrical engineering perspective.
Everything's all set up..
...The rest is up to April I guess.
It looks great you guys!
Molly, you had mentioned that the mayhem had stopped.
THIS IS FULL-BLOWN MAYHEM.

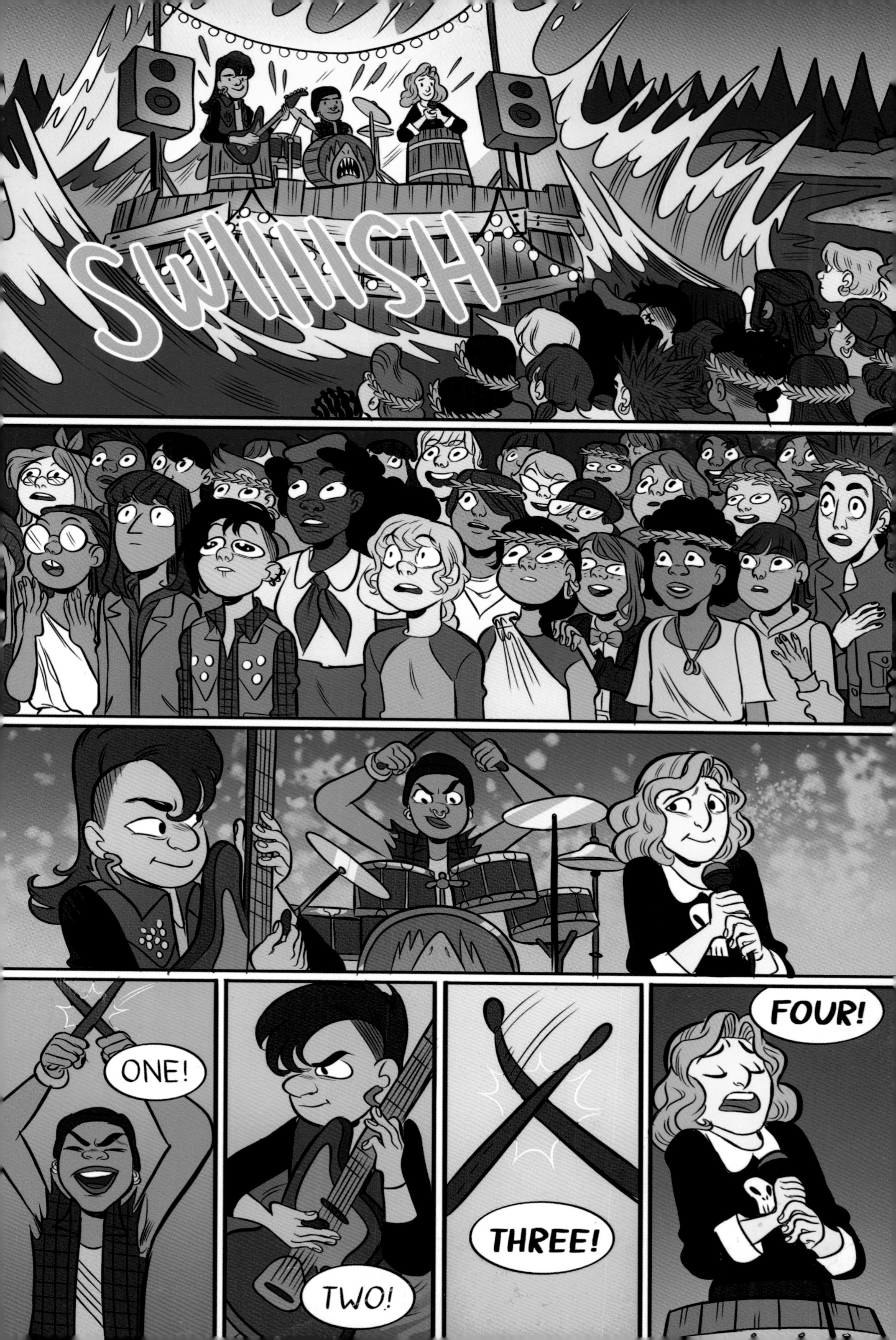
SWIIIISH
ONE!
TWO!
THREE!
FOUR!

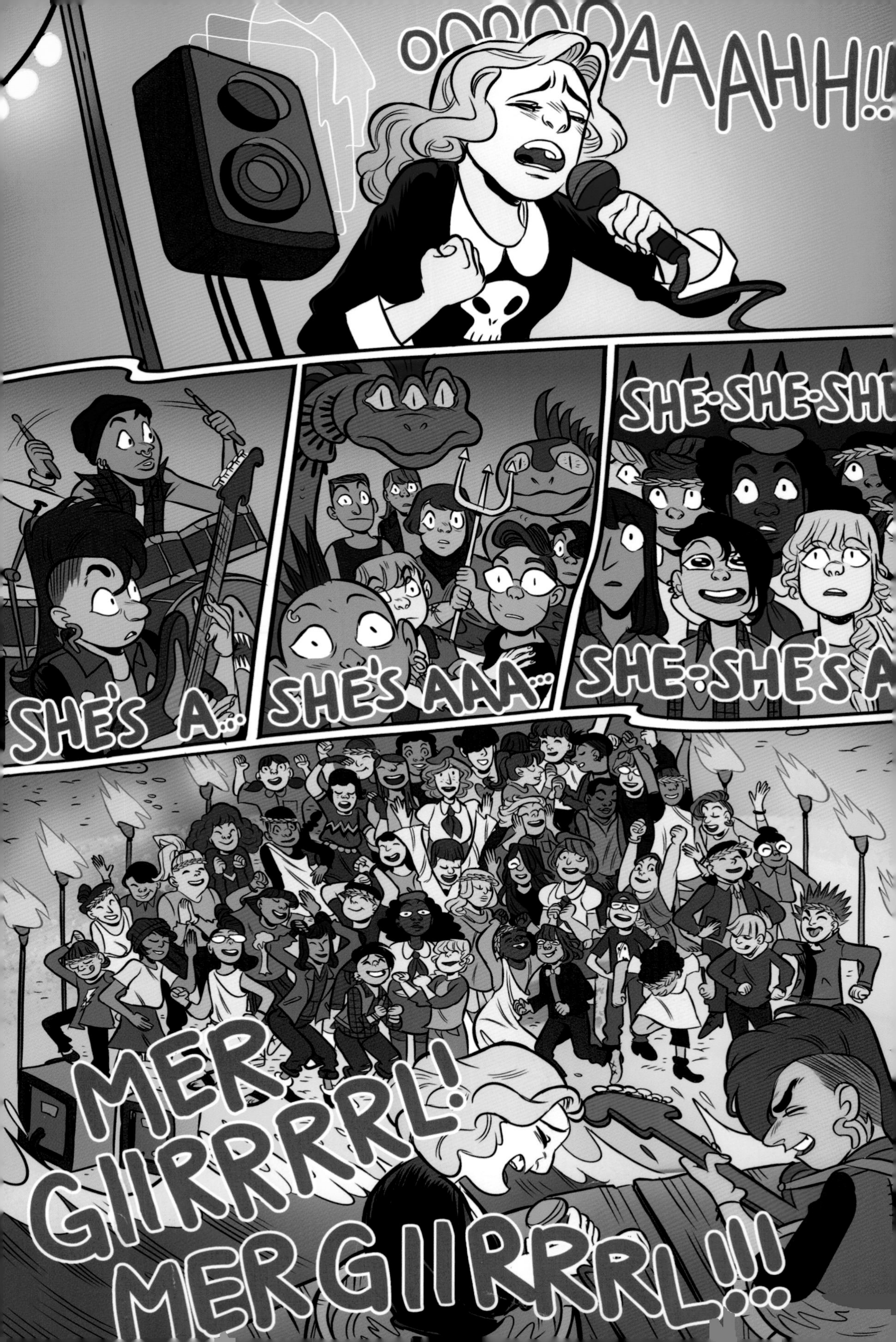
OOOOOOAAAHH!!
SHE'S A...
SHE'S AAA...
SHE-SHE-SHE
SHE-SHE'S A
MER GIIRRRRL!
MERGIIRRRL!!!

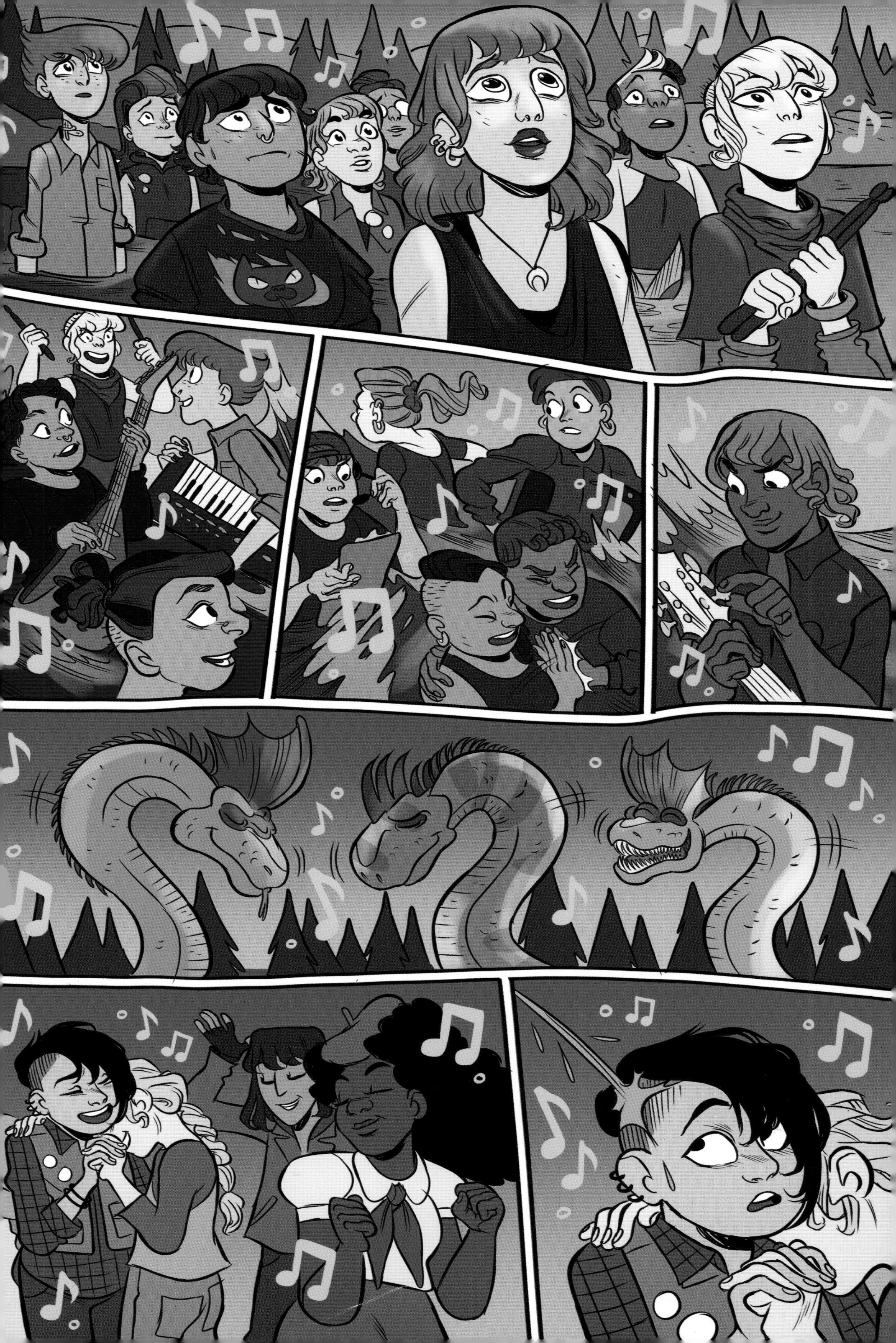

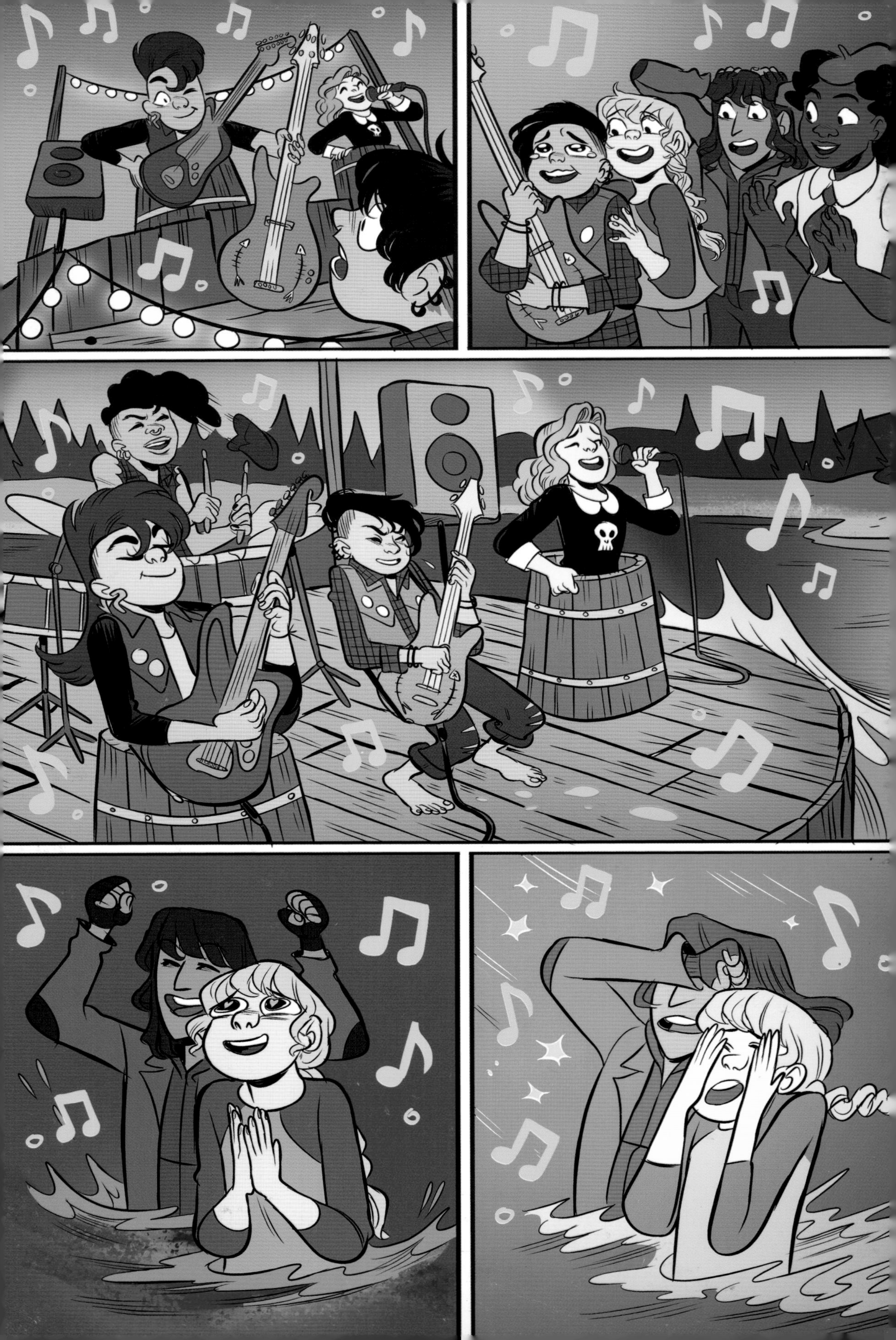

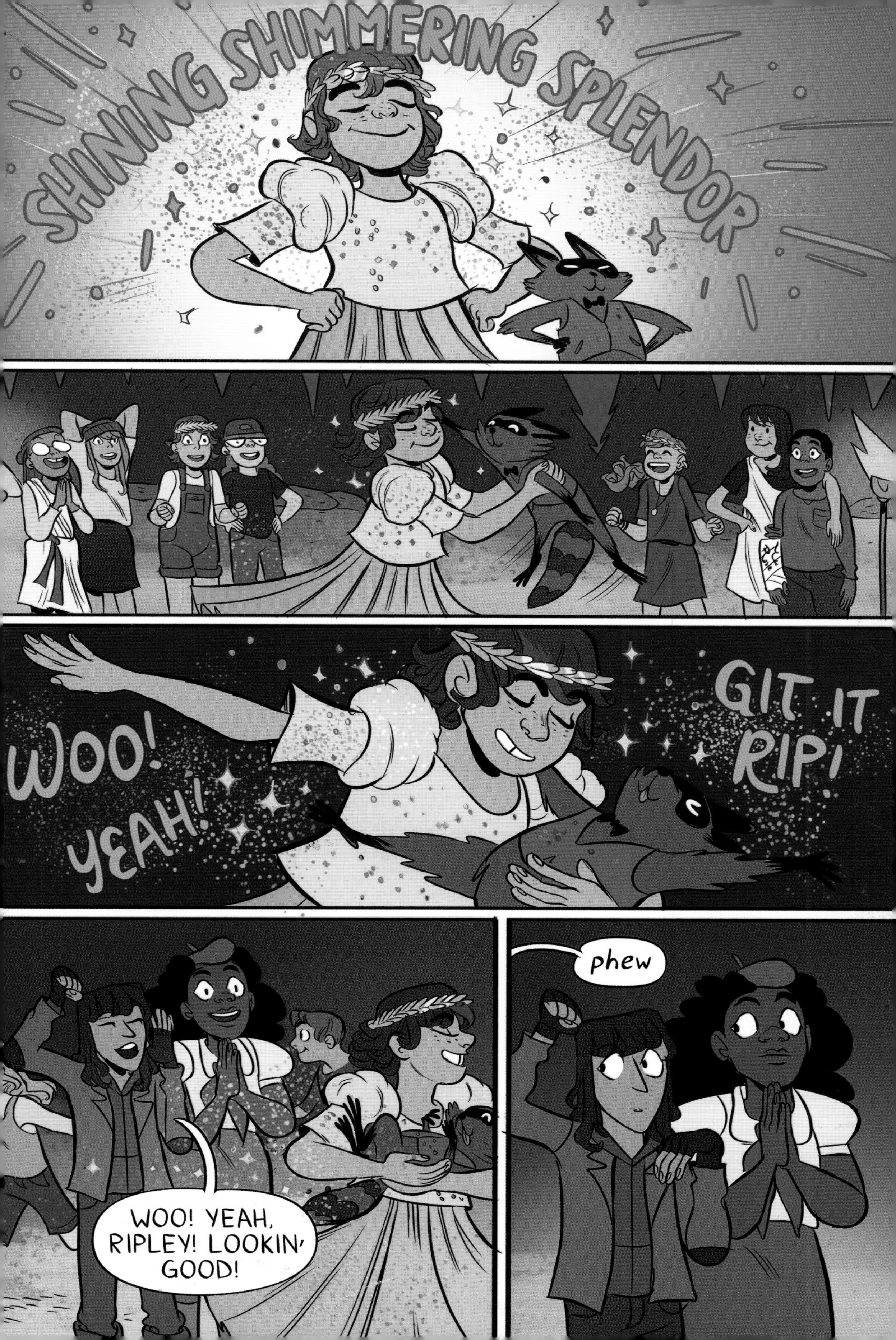
SHINING SHIMMERING SPLENDOR
WOO! YEAH!
GIT IT RIP!
WOO! YEAH, RIPLEY! LOOKIN' GOOD!
phew

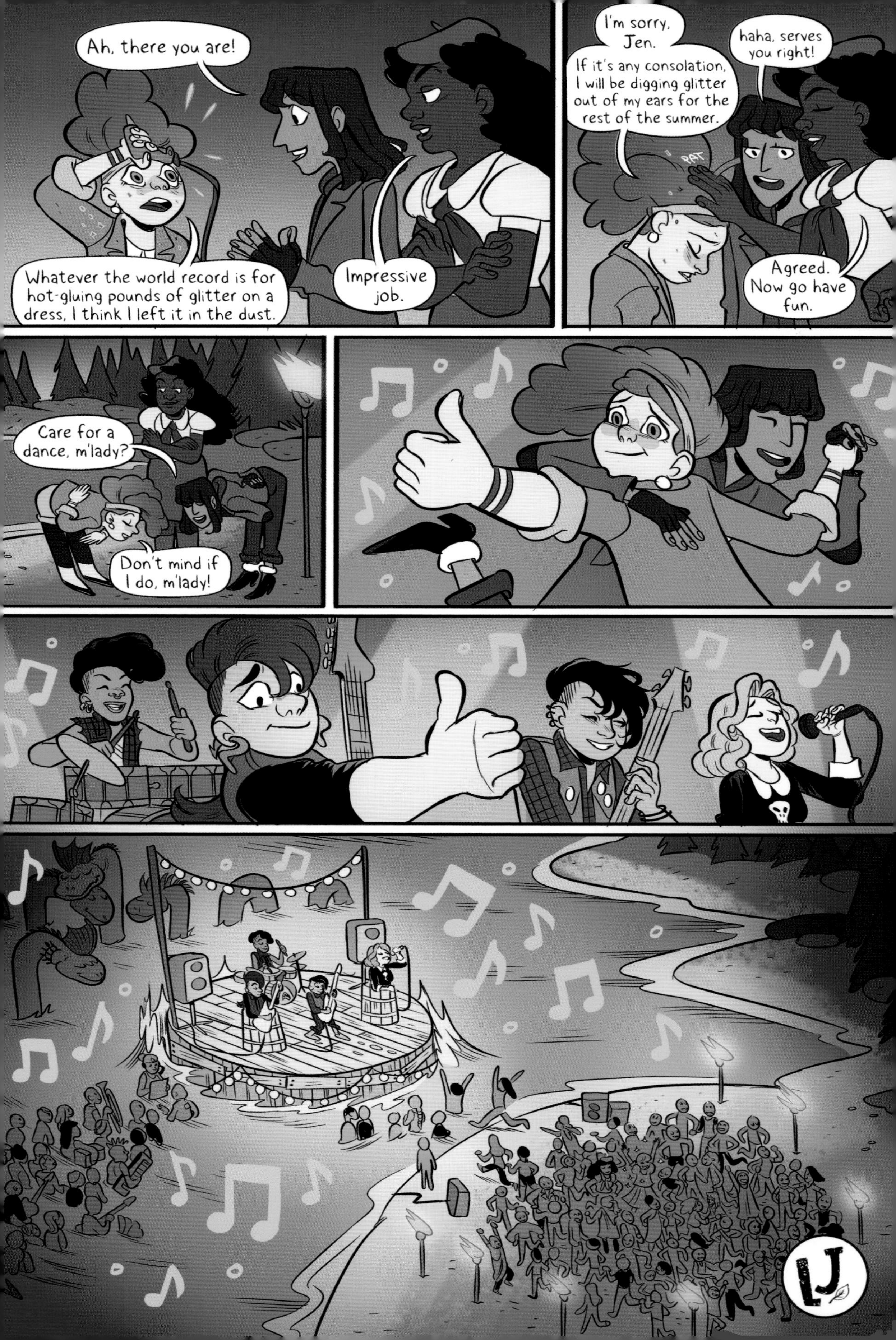

Ah, there you are!
Whatever the world record is for hot-gluing pounds of glitter on a dress, I think I left it in the dust.
Impressive job.
I'm sorry, Jen.
If it's any consolation, I will be digging glitter out of my ears for the rest of the summer.
haha, serves you right!
PAT
Agreed. Now go have fun.
Care for a dance, m'lady?
Don't mind if I do, m'lady!

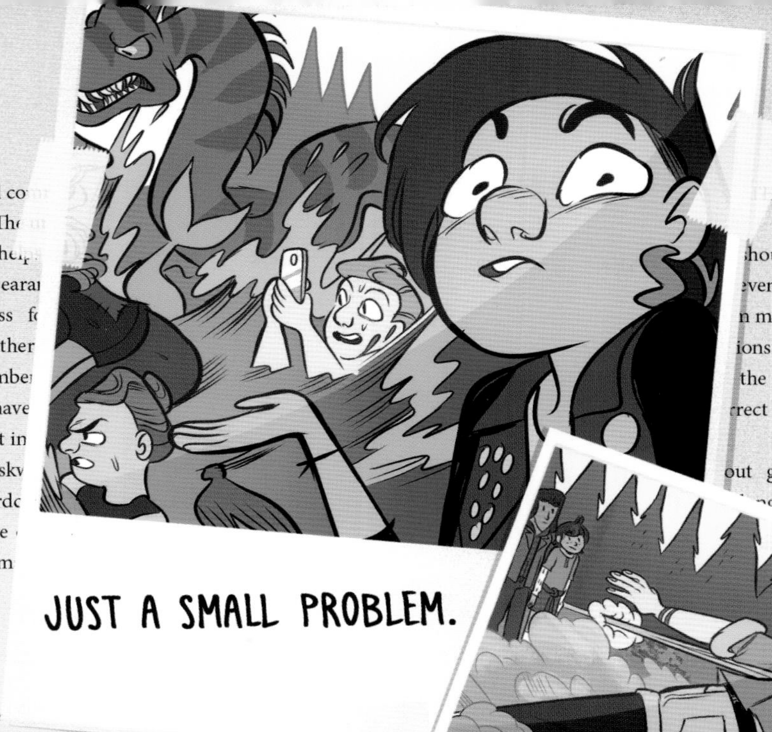
JUST A SMALL PROBLEM.

will co

The

It help

appeara

dress f

Further

Lumbe

to have

part in

Thiskw

Hardc

have

them

HE UNIFORM

should be worn at camp

events when Lumberjanes

n may also be worn at other

ions. It should be worn as a

the uniform dress with

rrect shoes, and stocking or

out grows her uniform or

ter Lumberjane.

a she has

her

her

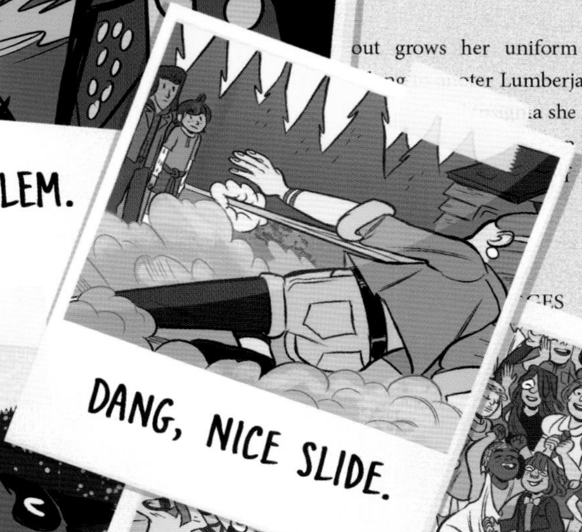
DANG, NICE SLIDE.

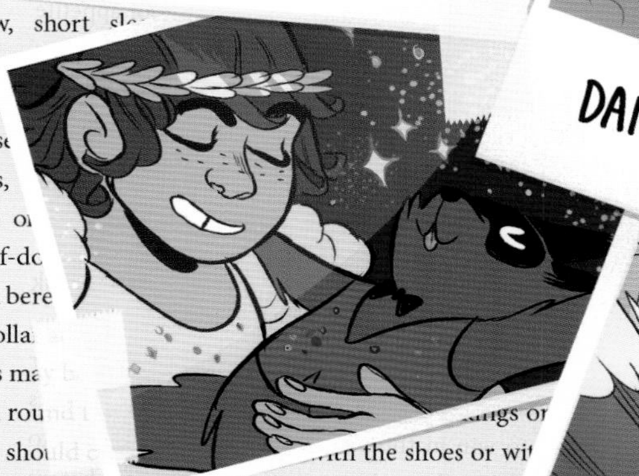

The

yellow, short sl

emb

the w

choose

slacks,

made o

out-of-do

green bere

the colla

Shoes ma

heels, rou ... kings or

socks shou ... with the shoes or wit

the uniform. Ne... es, bracelets, or other jewelry do

belong with a Lumberjane uniform.

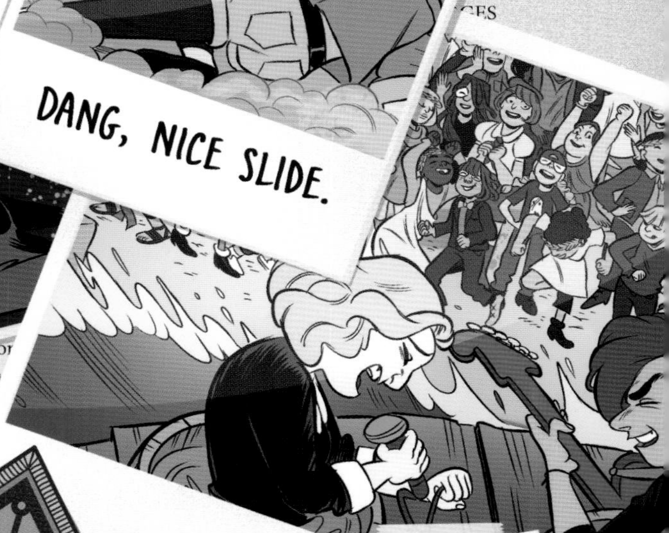

HOW TO WEAR THE UNIFOR

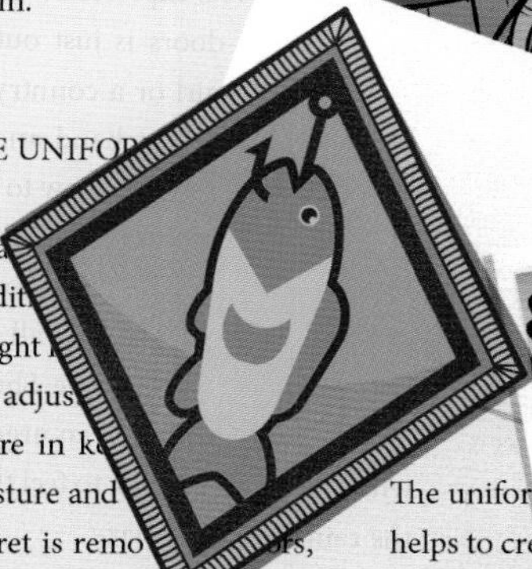

To look well in a uniform dema

uniform be kept in good conditi

pressed. See that the skirt is the right

height and build, that the belt is adjus

that your shoes and stockings are in k

uniform, that you watch your posture and

with dignity and grace. If the beret is remo ... rs,

be sure that your hair is neat and kept in place with an insonspicuous clip or ribbon. When you wear a Lumberjane uniform you are identified as a member of this organization and you should be doubly careful to conduct yourself in a way that will show everyone that courtesy and thoughtfullness are part of being a Lumberjane. People are likely to judge a whole nation by the selfishness of a few individuals, to criticize a whole family because of the misconduct of one member, and to feel unkindly toward and organization because of the

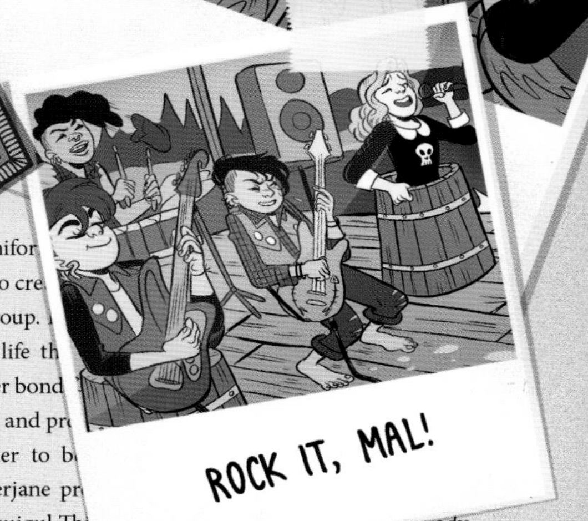
ROCK IT, MAL!

The unifor

helps to cre

in a group.

active life th

another bond

future, and pr

in order to b

Lumberjane pr

Penniquiqul Thi ... ore Lady

Types, but m... s will wish to have one. They can either bu... the uniform, or make it themselves from materials available at the trading post.

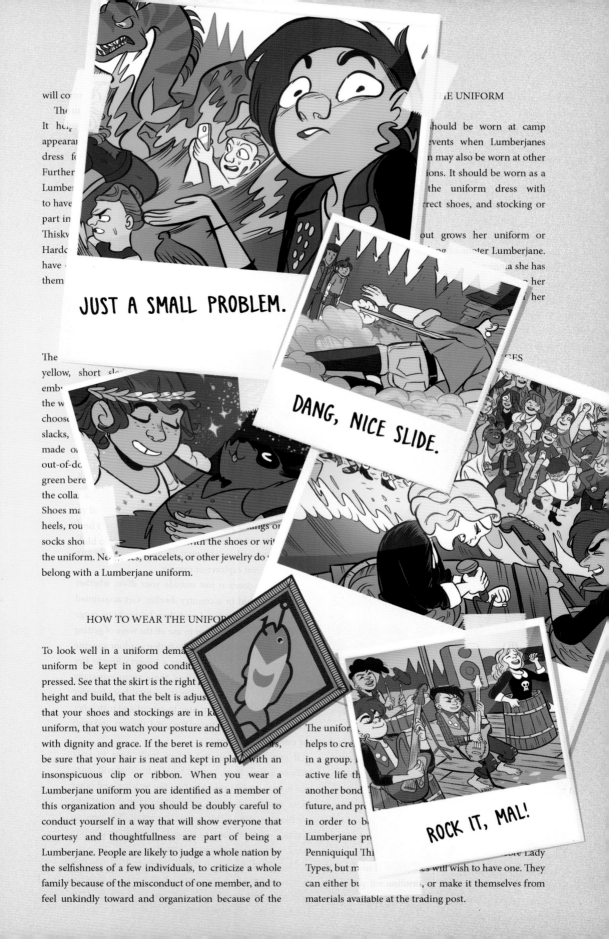

LUMBERJANES FIELD MANUAL

CHAPTER TWENTY-ONE

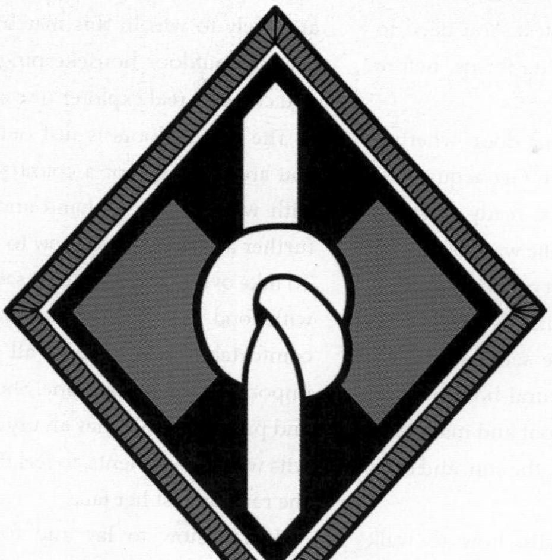

Lumberjanes "Out-of-Doors" Program Field

ALL FOR KNOT BADGE

"An easy-going bonding activity."

Everyday at camp comes with its own obstacles, some of those are the same everyday issues that we face regardless of where we are. The other obstacles, the ones that surprise us, those are the problems that we need our friends for. We need our community and we need our friends to help us out of these problems. They aren't frequent, and they often show up out of the blue, but that is why we work so hard at building such a tight-knit community here at camp. As a Lumberjane, you will need to know how to respond to these kinds of problems, regardless if they are your own or if they are from another member of this camp.

The *All For Knot* badge is meant to be a bonding activity, not only between the different types of rope that your counselor has given you, but between the campers who decide to earn this badge together. The *All For Knot* badge is one of the most unique badges at this camp because this is a badge that must be earned as a team. Every member of the team will need to show off their mastery of rope and knot tying to earn this badge.

To obtain the *All For Knot* badge, the campers must first take the basic knot tying courses that are required of all campers. They must learn mastery over rope and gain the knowledge that is needed for basic tying around camp. Rope is commonplace at camp, whether it's from pitching tents or tying boats to the dock, they can be found to have many uses. When a group of campers feels they are ready to earn the *All For Knot* badge, they will approach the appropriate counselor and start the test. Every member of the team will need to tie the knot that their counselor asks for, and if one member of the team fails to complete the task, then every member of the team fails the test. They are allowed to come back and test for the badge the following day, but may not change their team and may not take the task more than once a day.

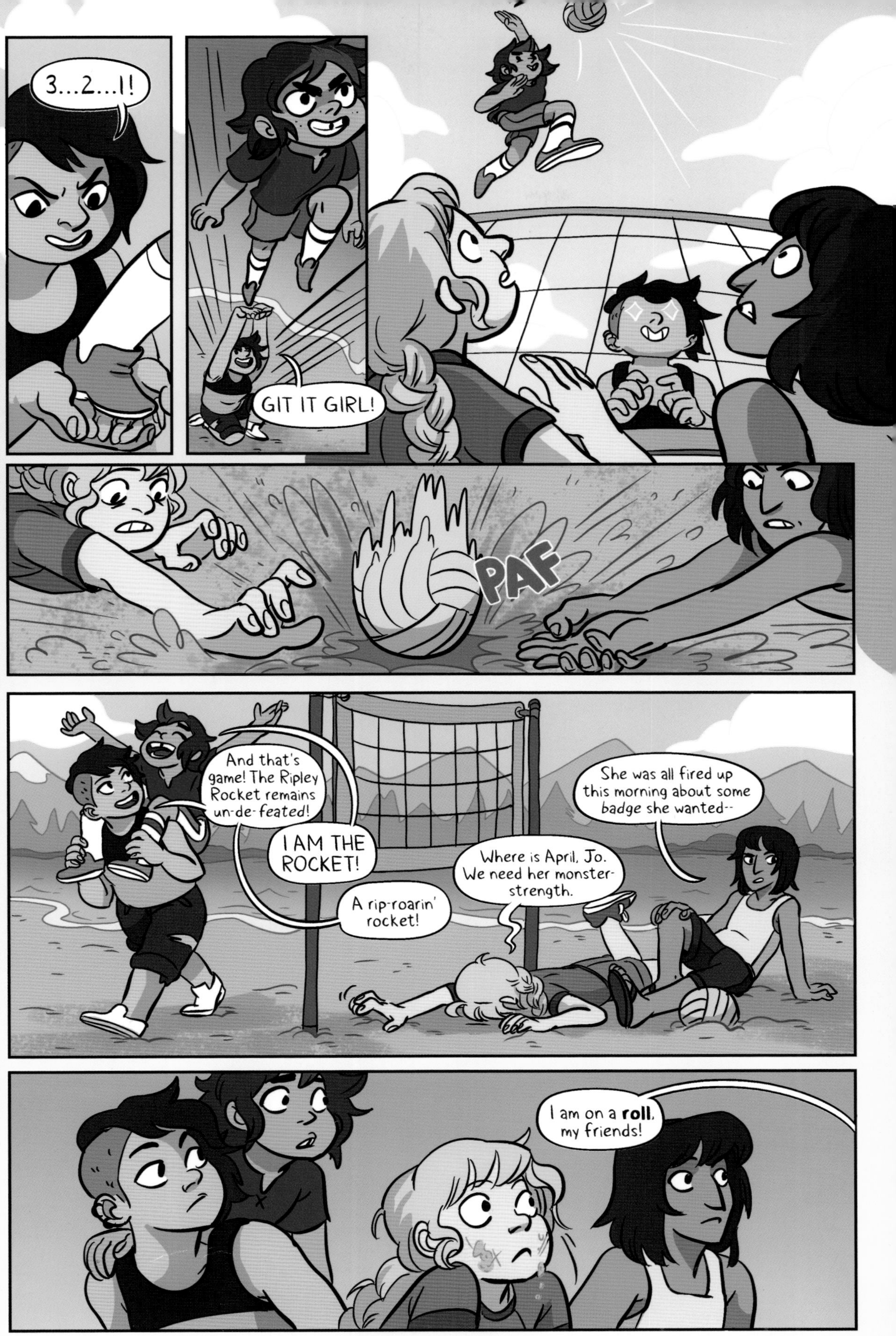

3...2...1!
GIT IT GIRL!
PAF
And that's game! The Ripley Rocket remains un-de-feated!
I AM THE ROCKET!
A rip-roarin' rocket!
Where is April, Jo. We need her monster-strength.
She was all fired up this morning about some *badge* she wanted--
I am on a **roll**, my friends!

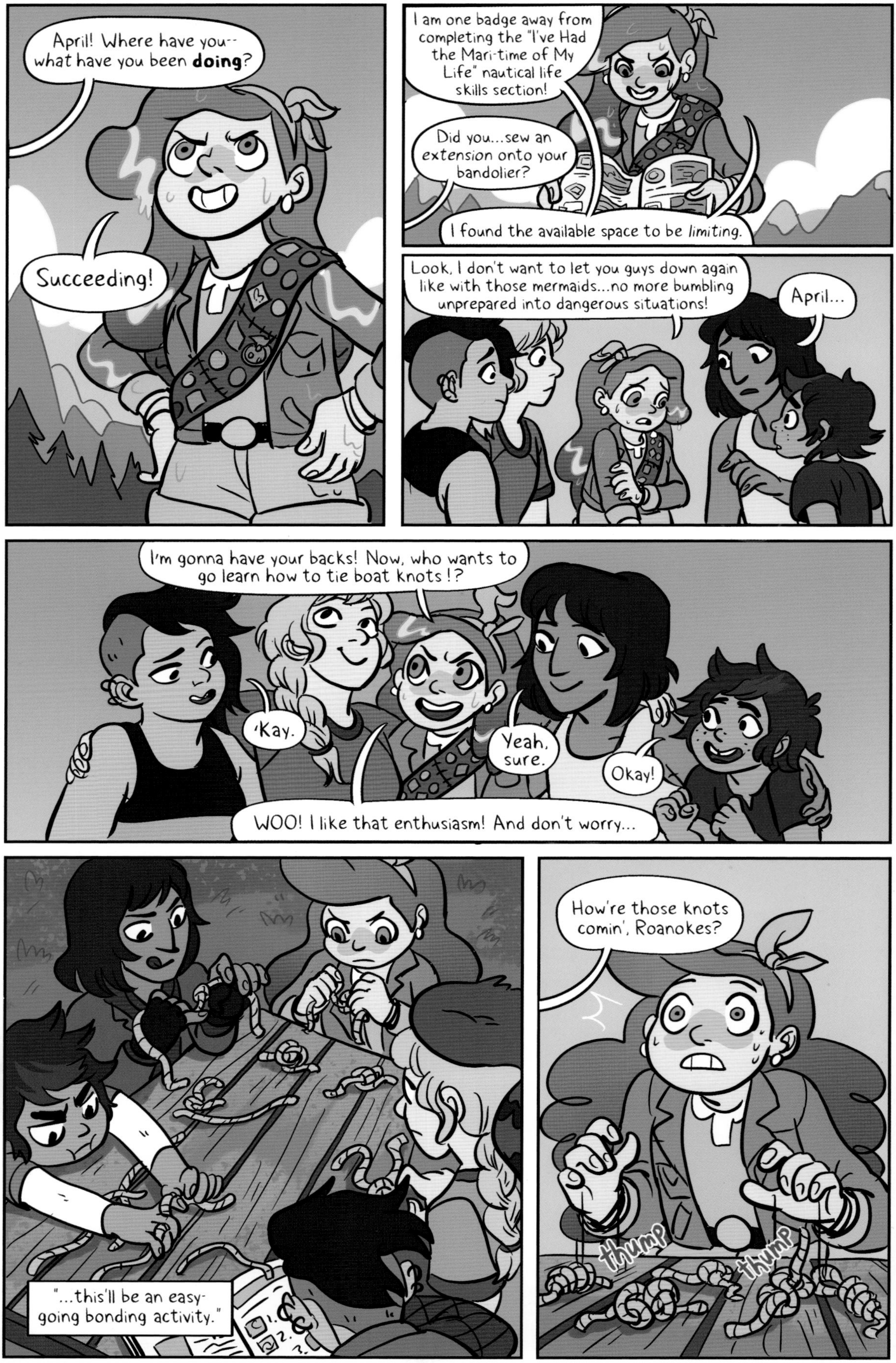

April! Where have you--what have you been **doing**?
Succeeding!
I am one badge away from completing the "I've Had the Mari-time of My Life" nautical life skills section!
Did you...sew an extension onto your bandolier?
I found the available space to be *limiting*.
Look, I don't want to let you guys down again like with those mermaids...no more bumbling unprepared into dangerous situations!
April...
I'm gonna have your backs! Now, who wants to go learn how to tie boat knots!?
'Kay.
Yeah, sure.
Okay!
WOO! I like that enthusiasm! And don't worry...
"...this'll be an easy-going bonding activity."
How're those knots comin', Roanokes?
thump
thump

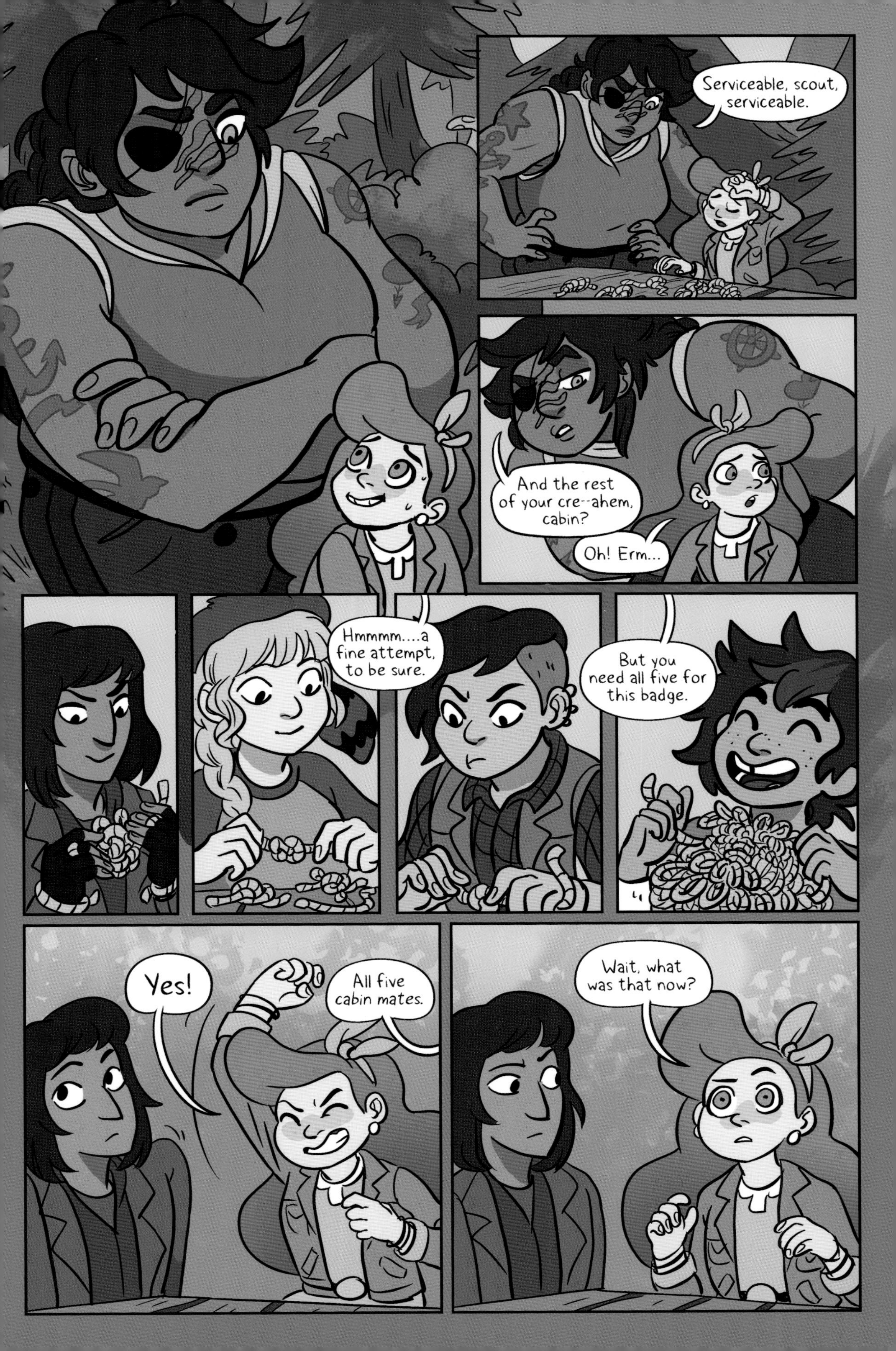
Serviceable, scout, serviceable.
And the rest of your cre--ahem, cabin?
Oh! Erm...
Hmmmm....a fine attempt, to be sure.
But you need all five for this badge.
Yes!
All five cabin mates.
Wait, what was that now?

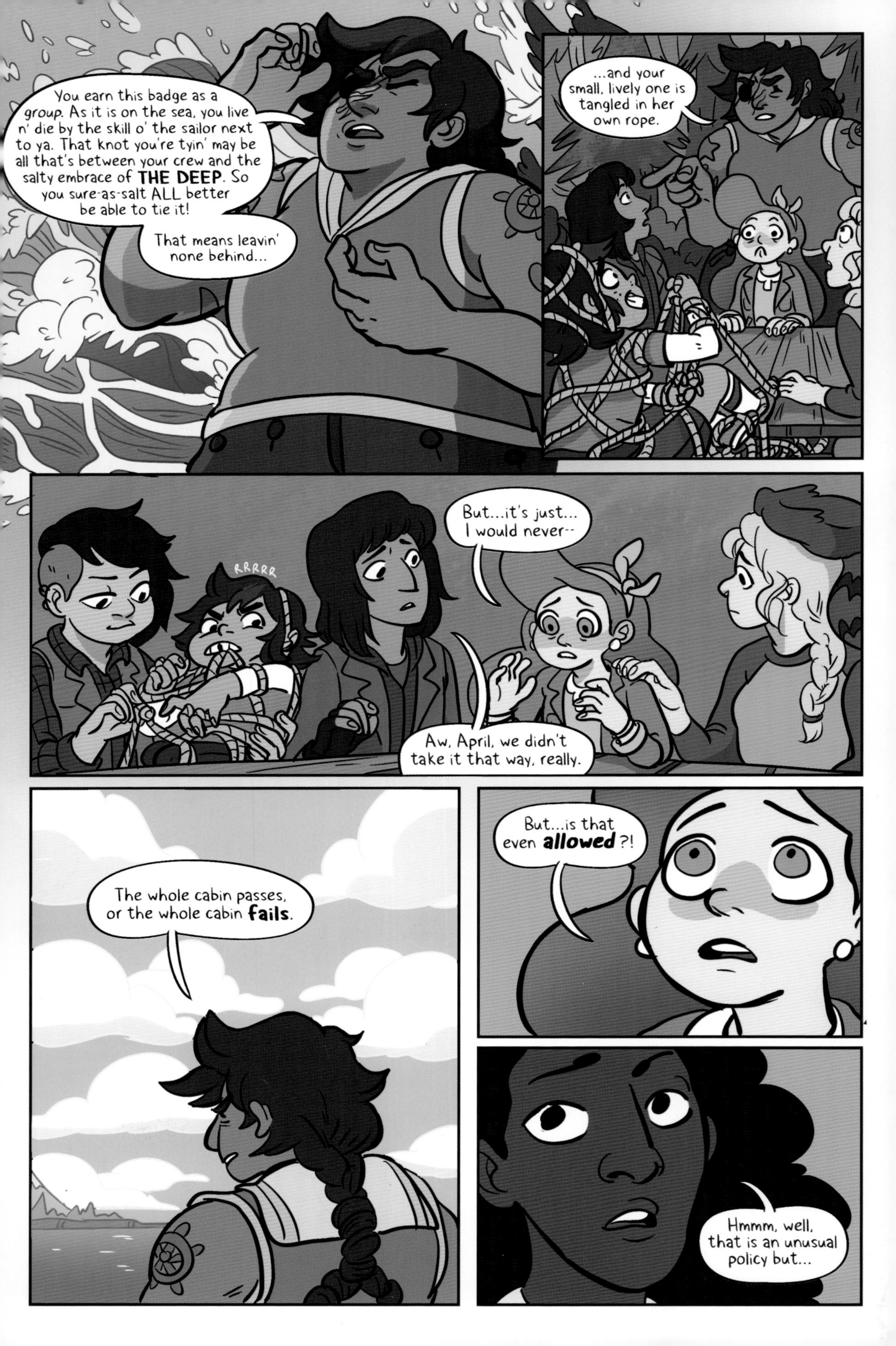
You earn this badge as a group. As it is on the sea, you live n' die by the skill o' the sailor next to ya. That knot you're tyin' may be all that's between your crew and the salty embrace of THE DEEP. So you sure-as-salt ALL better be able to tie it!
That means leavin' none behind...
...and your small, lively one is tangled in her own rope.
RRRRR
But...it's just... I would never--
Aw, April, we didn't take it that way, really.
The whole cabin passes, or the whole cabin fails.
But...is that even allowed?!
Hmmm, well, that is an unusual policy but...

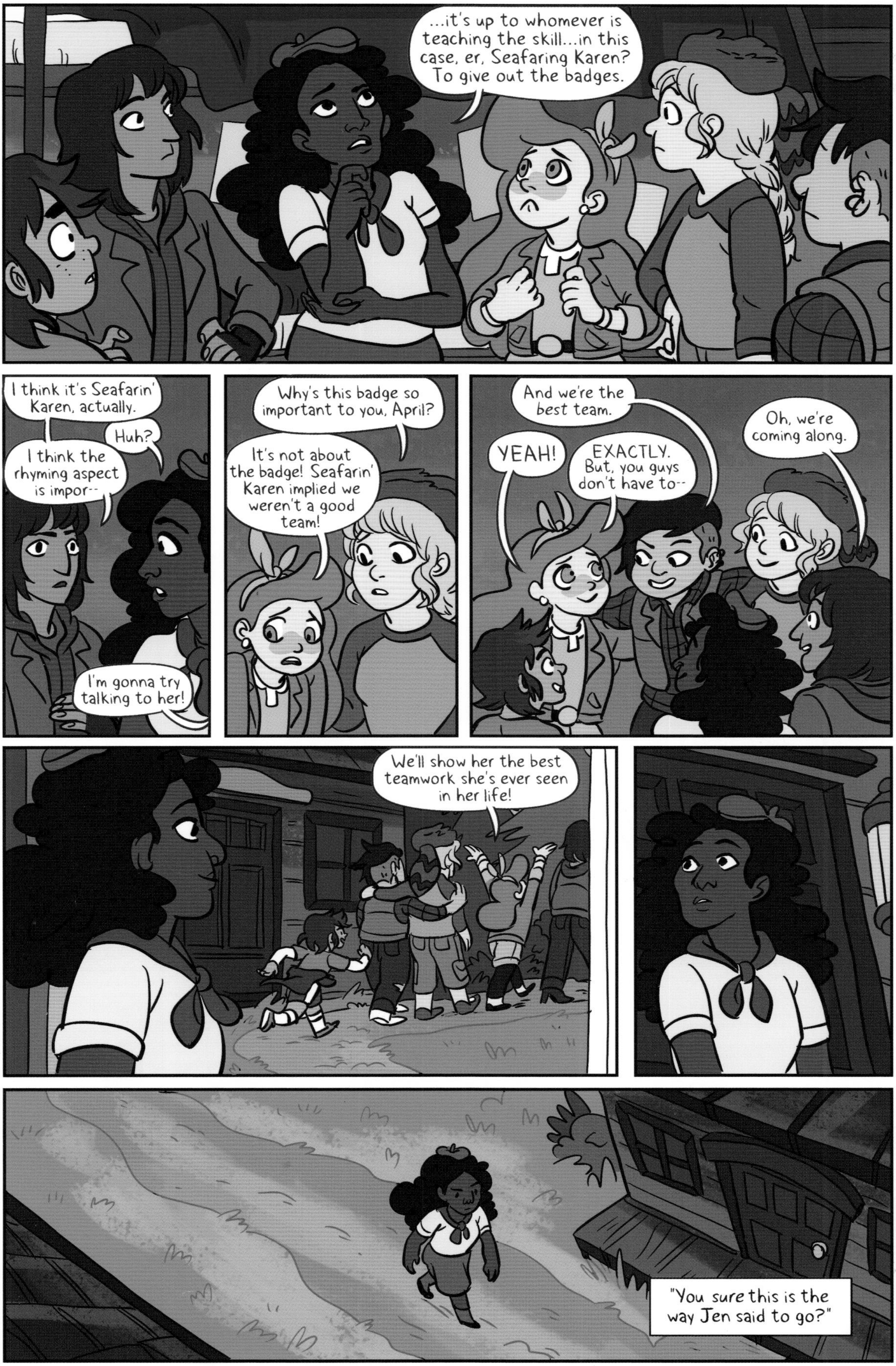
...it's up to whomever is teaching the skill...in this case, er, Seafaring Karen? To give out the badges.
I think it's Seafarin' Karen, actually.
Huh?
I think the rhyming aspect is impor--
I'm gonna try talking to her!
Why's this badge so important to you, April?
It's not about the badge! Seafarin' Karen implied we weren't a good team!
And we're the *best* team.
YEAH!
EXACTLY. But, you guys don't have to--
Oh, we're coming along.
We'll show her the best teamwork she's ever seen in her life!
"You *sure* this is the way Jen said to go?"

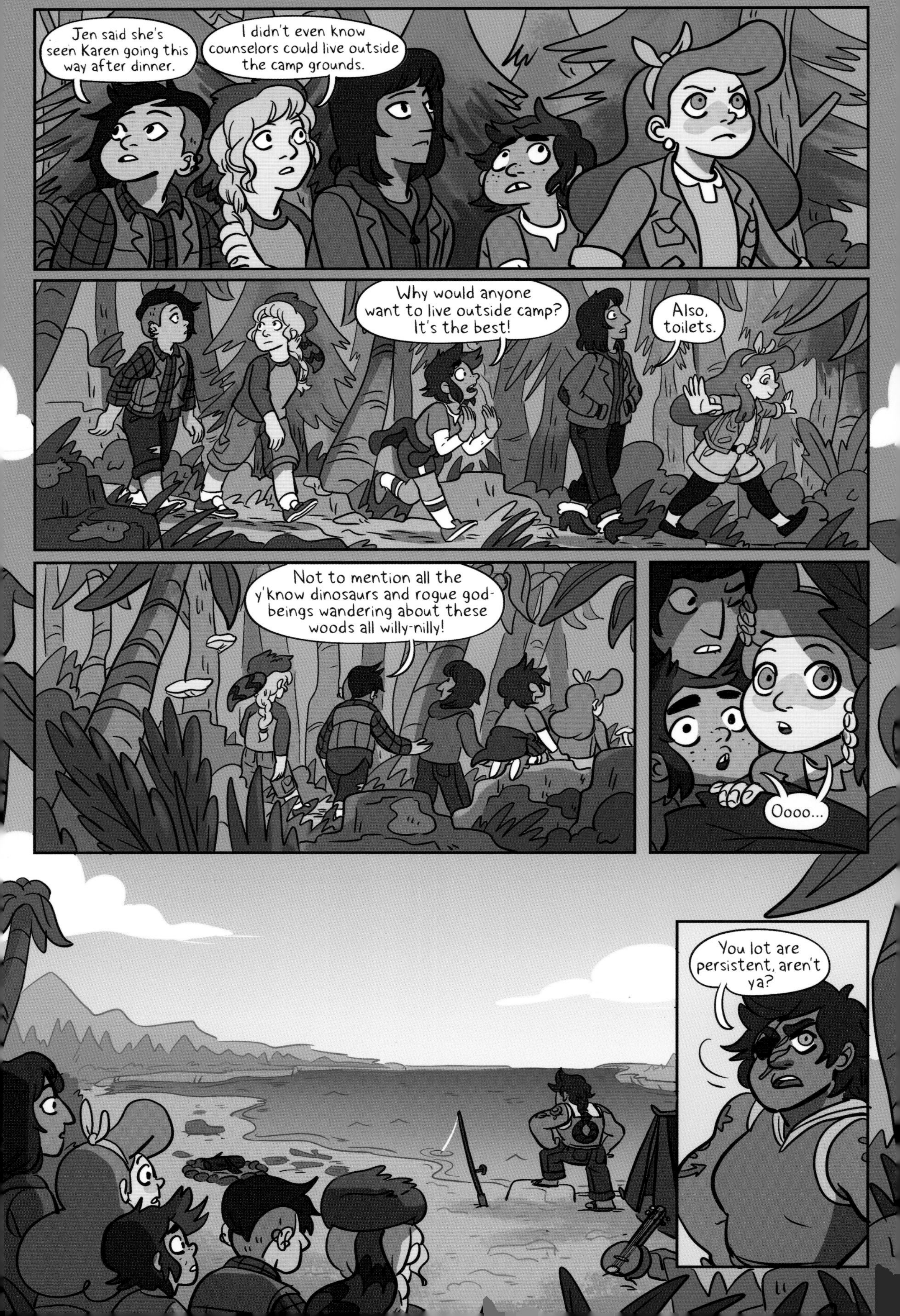
Jen said she's seen Karen going this way after dinner.
I didn't even know counselors could live outside the camp grounds.
Why would anyone want to live outside camp? It's the best!
Also, toilets.
Not to mention all the y'know dinosaurs and rogue god-beings wandering about these woods all willy-nilly!
Oooo...
You lot are persistent, aren't ya?

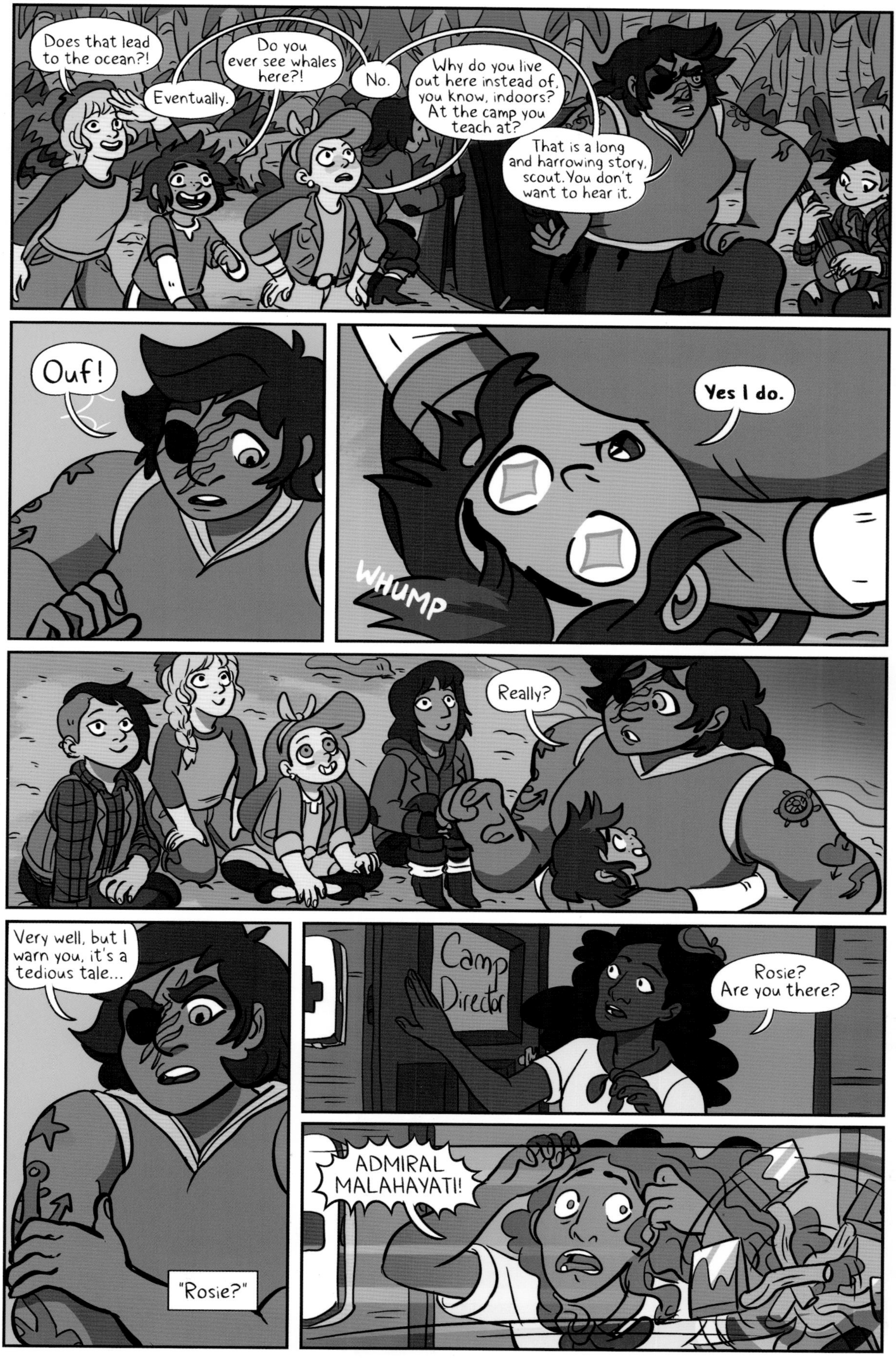
Does that lead to the ocean?!
Eventually.
Do you ever see whales here?!
No.
Why do you live out here instead of, you know, indoors? At the camp you teach at?
That is a long and harrowing story, scout. You don't want to hear it.
Ouf!
Yes I do.
WHUMP
Really?
Very well, but I warn you, it's a tedious tale...
"Rosie?"
Camp Director
Rosie? Are you there?
ADMIRAL MALAHAYATI!

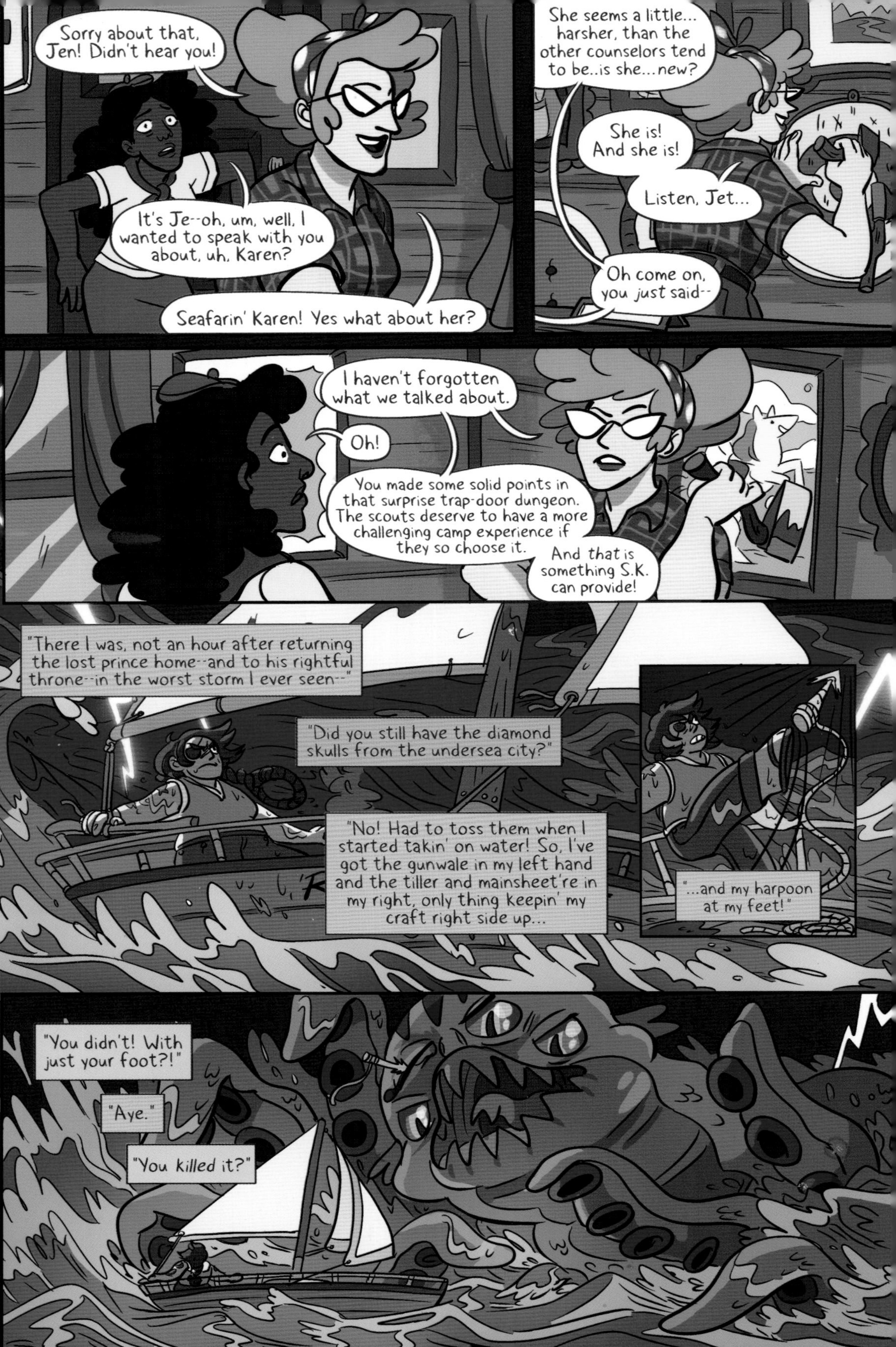
Sorry about that, Jen! Didn't hear you!
It's Je--oh, um, well, I wanted to speak with you about, uh, Karen?
Seafarin' Karen! Yes what about her?
She seems a little... harsher, than the other counselors tend to be..is she...new?
She is! And she is!
Listen, Jet...
Oh come on, you just said--
I haven't forgotten what we talked about.
Oh!
You made some solid points in that surprise trap-door dungeon. The scouts deserve to have a more challenging camp experience if they so choose it.
And that is something S.K. can provide!
"There I was, not an hour after returning the lost prince home--and to his rightful throne--in the worst storm I ever seen--"
"Did you still have the diamond skulls from the undersea city?"
"No! Had to toss them when I started takin' on water! So, I've got the gunwale in my left hand and the tiller and mainsheet're in my right, only thing keepin' my craft right side up...
"...and my harpoon at my feet!"
"You didn't! With just your foot?!"
"Aye."
"You killed it?"

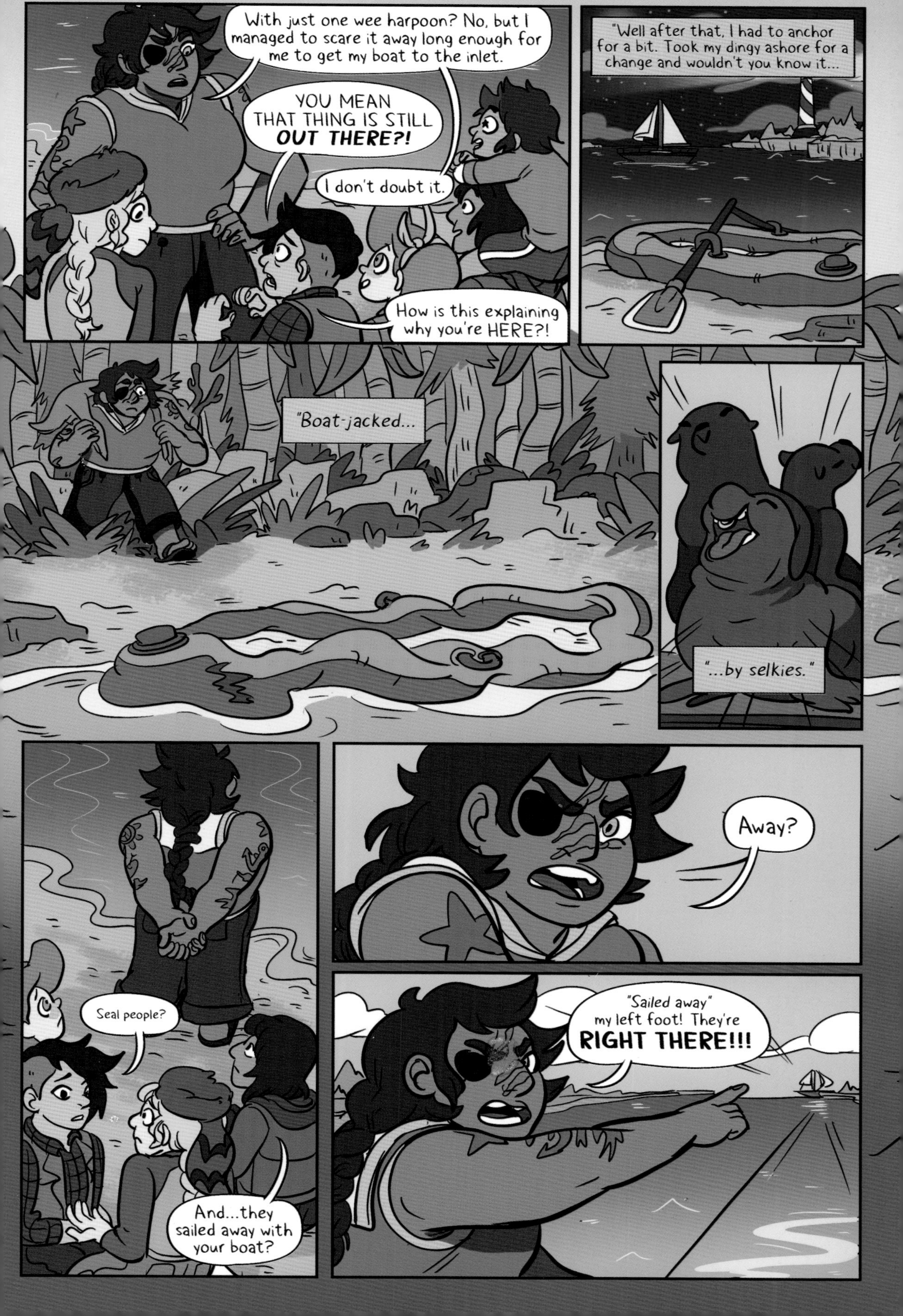
With just one wee harpoon? No, but I managed to scare it away long enough for me to get my boat to the inlet.
YOU MEAN THAT THING IS STILL **OUT THERE?!**
I don't doubt it.
How is this explaining why you're HERE?!
"Well after that, I had to anchor for a bit. Took my dingy ashore for a change and wouldn't you know it...
"Boat-jacked...
"...by selkies."
Seal people?
And...they sailed away with your boat?
Away?
"Sailed away" my left foot! They're **RIGHT THERE!!!**

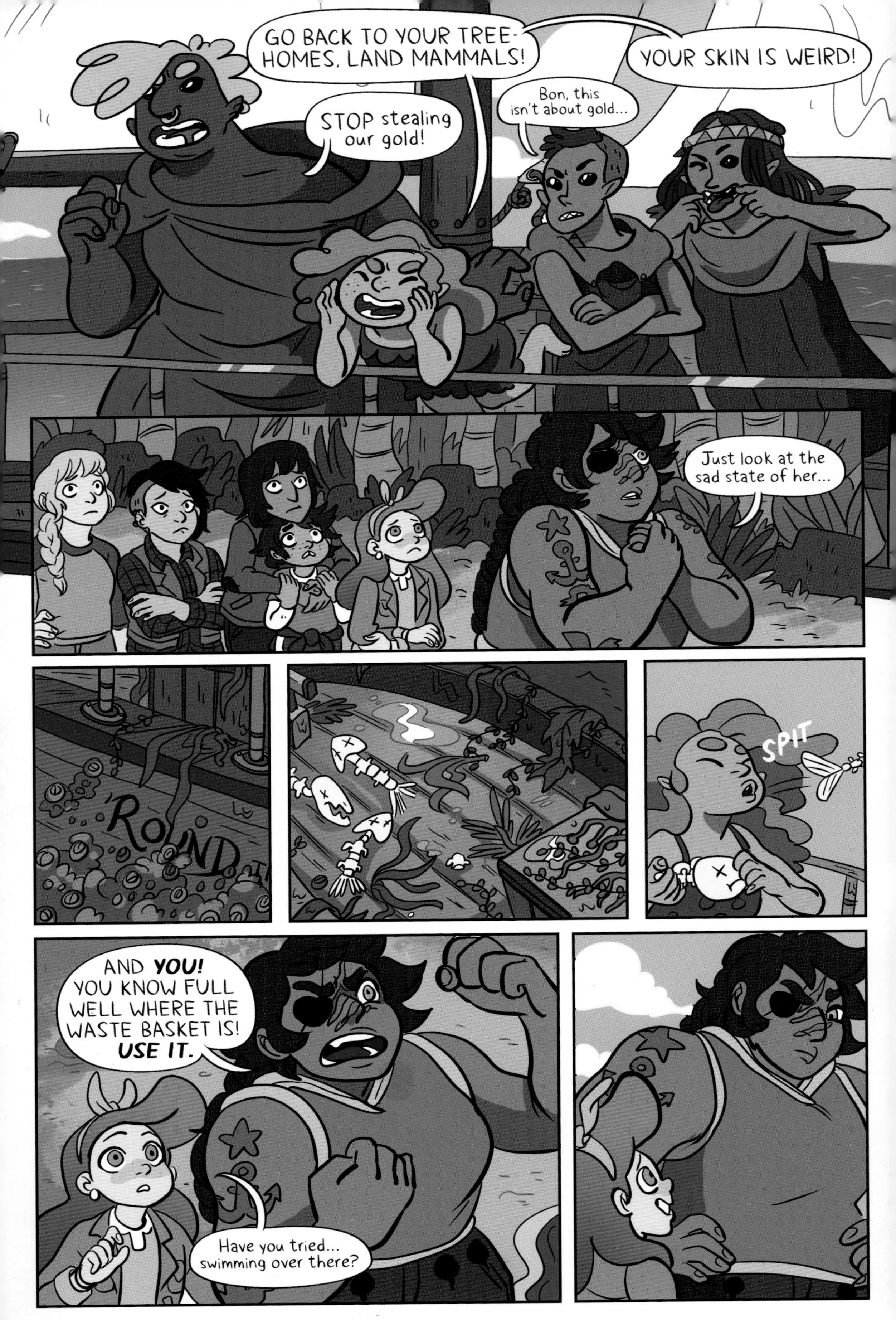
GO BACK TO YOUR TREE-HOMES, LAND MAMMALS!
YOUR SKIN IS WEIRD!
STOP stealing our gold!
Bon, this isn't about gold...
Just look at the sad state of her...
ROUND
SPIT
AND **YOU!** YOU KNOW FULL WELL WHERE THE WASTE BASKET IS! ***USE IT.***
Have you tried... swimming over there?

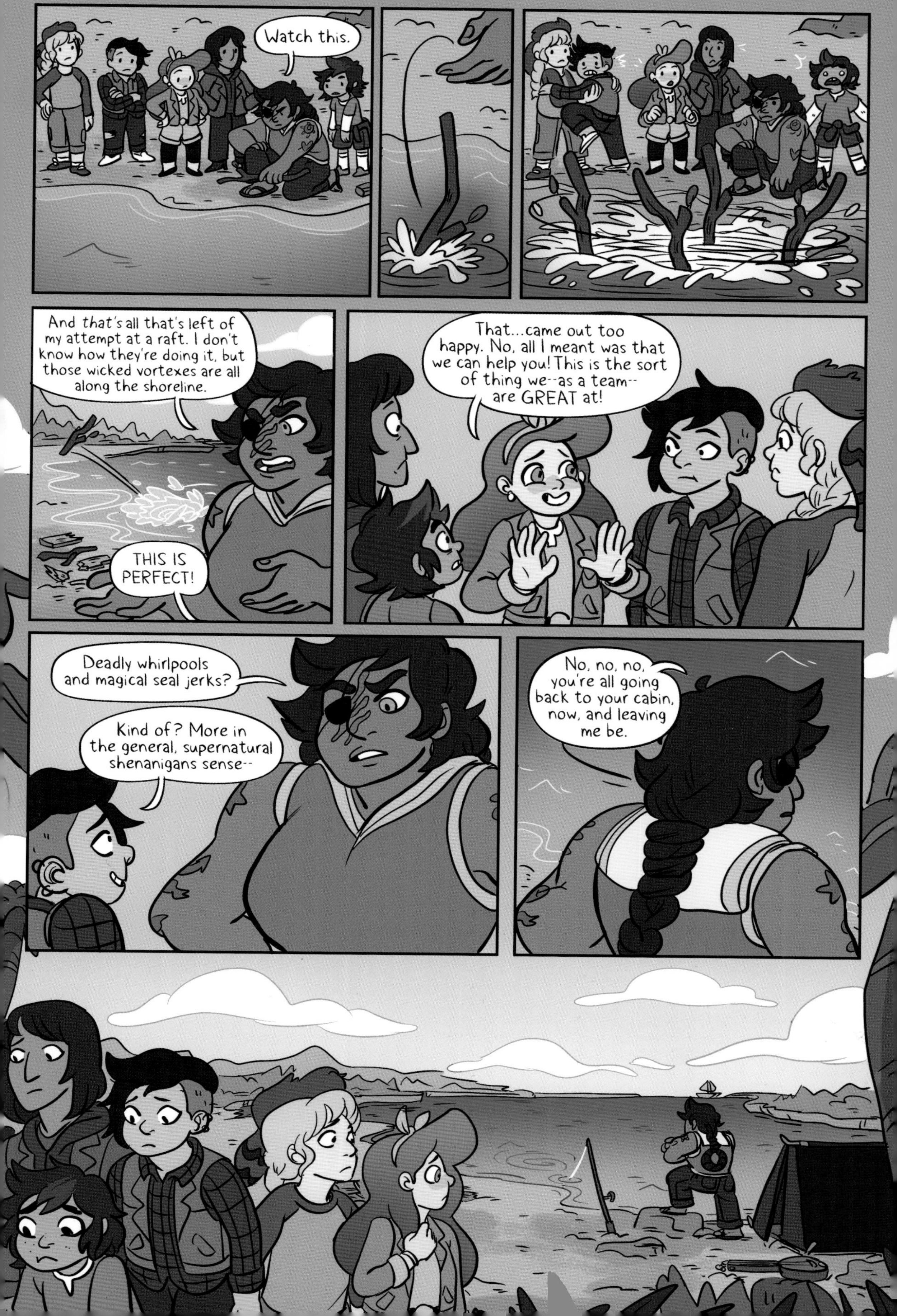
Watch this.
And *that's* all that's left of my attempt at a raft. I don't know how they're doing it, but those wicked vortexes are all along the shoreline.
THIS IS PERFECT!
That...came out too happy. No, all I meant was that we can help you! This is the sort of thing we--as a team--are GREAT at!
Deadly whirlpools and magical seal jerks?
Kind of? More in the general, supernatural shenanigans sense--
No, no, no, you're all going back to your cabin, now, and leaving me be.

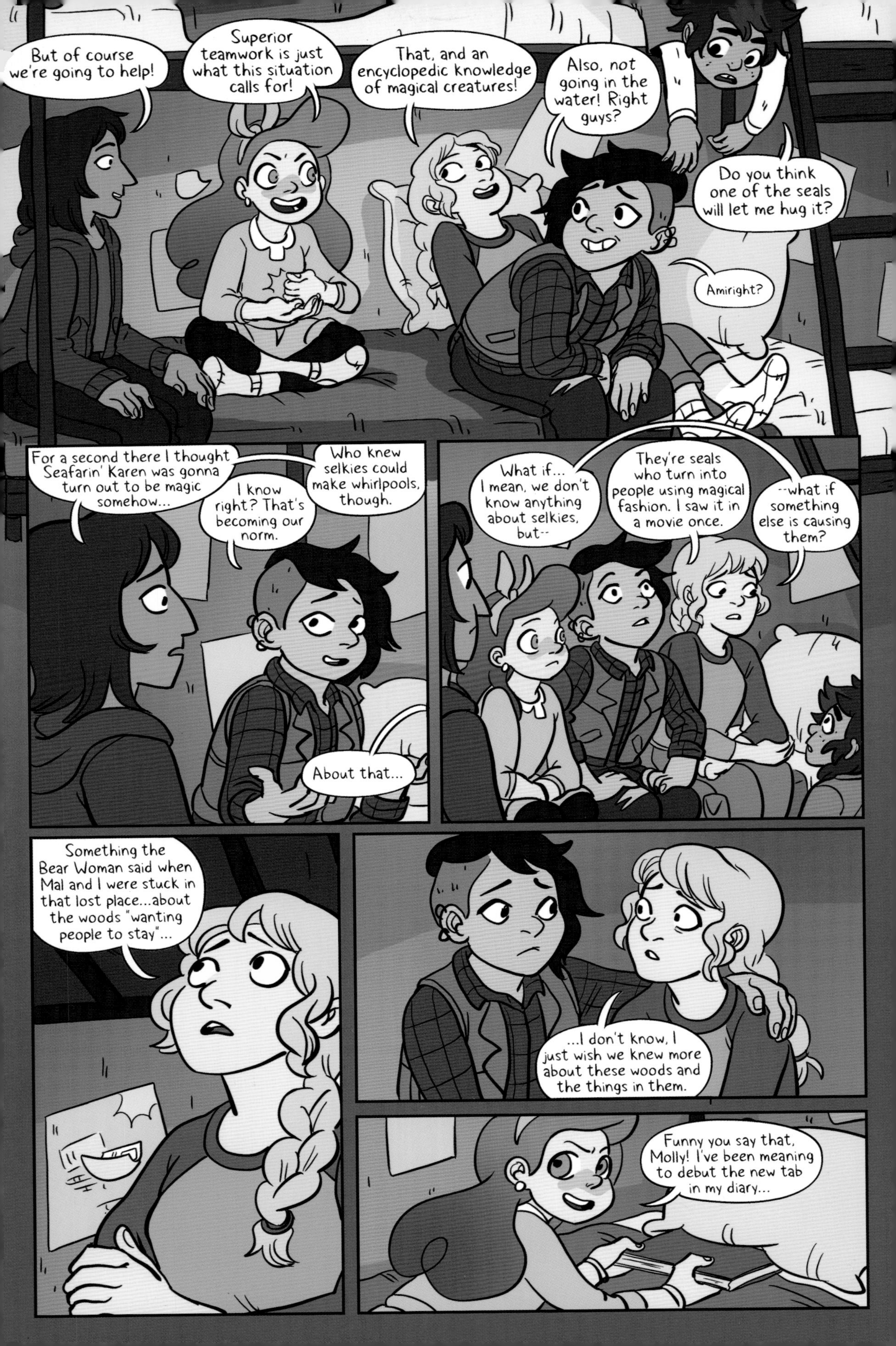
But of course we're going to help!
Superior teamwork is just what this situation calls for!
That, and an encyclopedic knowledge of magical creatures!
Also, not going in the water! Right guys?
Do you think one of the seals will let me hug it?
Amiright?
For a second there I thought Seafarin' Karen was gonna turn out to be magic somehow...
Who knew selkies could make whirlpools, though.
I know right? That's becoming our norm.
About that...
What if... I mean, we don't know anything about selkies, but--
They're seals who turn into people using magical fashion. I saw it in a movie once.
--what if something else is causing them?
Something the Bear Woman said when Mal and I were stuck in that lost place...about the woods "wanting people to stay"...
...I don't know, I just wish we knew more about these woods and the things in them.
Funny you say that, Molly! I've been meaning to debut the new tab in my diary...

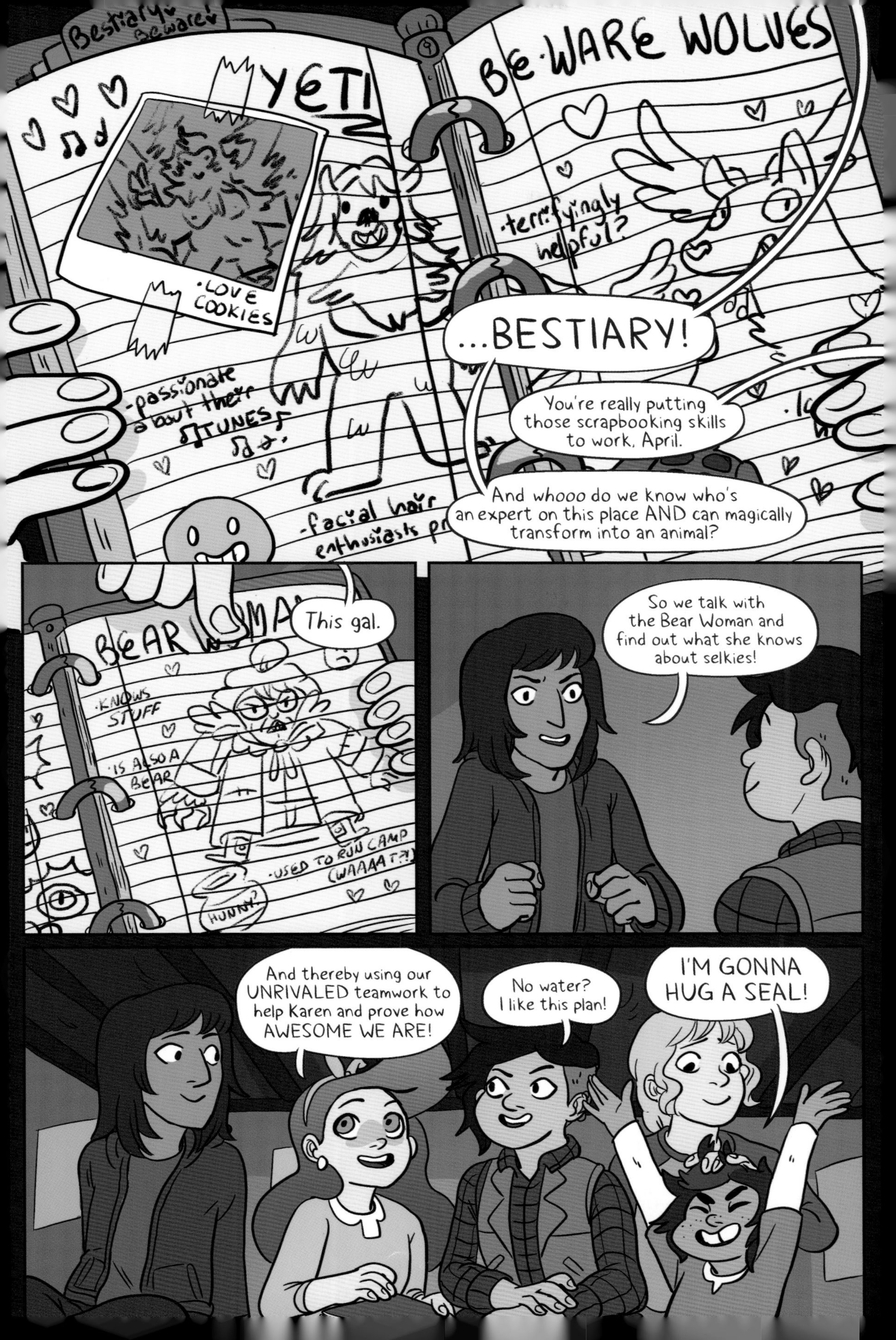
Bestiary♥ Beware♥
YETI
·LOVE COOKIES
-passionate about their TUNES
-facial hair enthusiasts
BE·WARE WOLVES
·terrifyingly helpful?
...BESTIARY!
You're really putting those scrapbooking skills to work, April.
And whooo do we know who's an expert on this place AND can magically transform into an animal?
This gal.
·KNOWS STUFF
·IS ALSO A BEAR
·USED TO RUN CAMP (WAAAAT?!)
HUNNY?
So we talk with the Bear Woman and find out what she knows about selkies!
And thereby using our UNRIVALED teamwork to help Karen and prove how AWESOME WE ARE!
No water? I like this plan!
I'M GONNA HUG A SEAL!

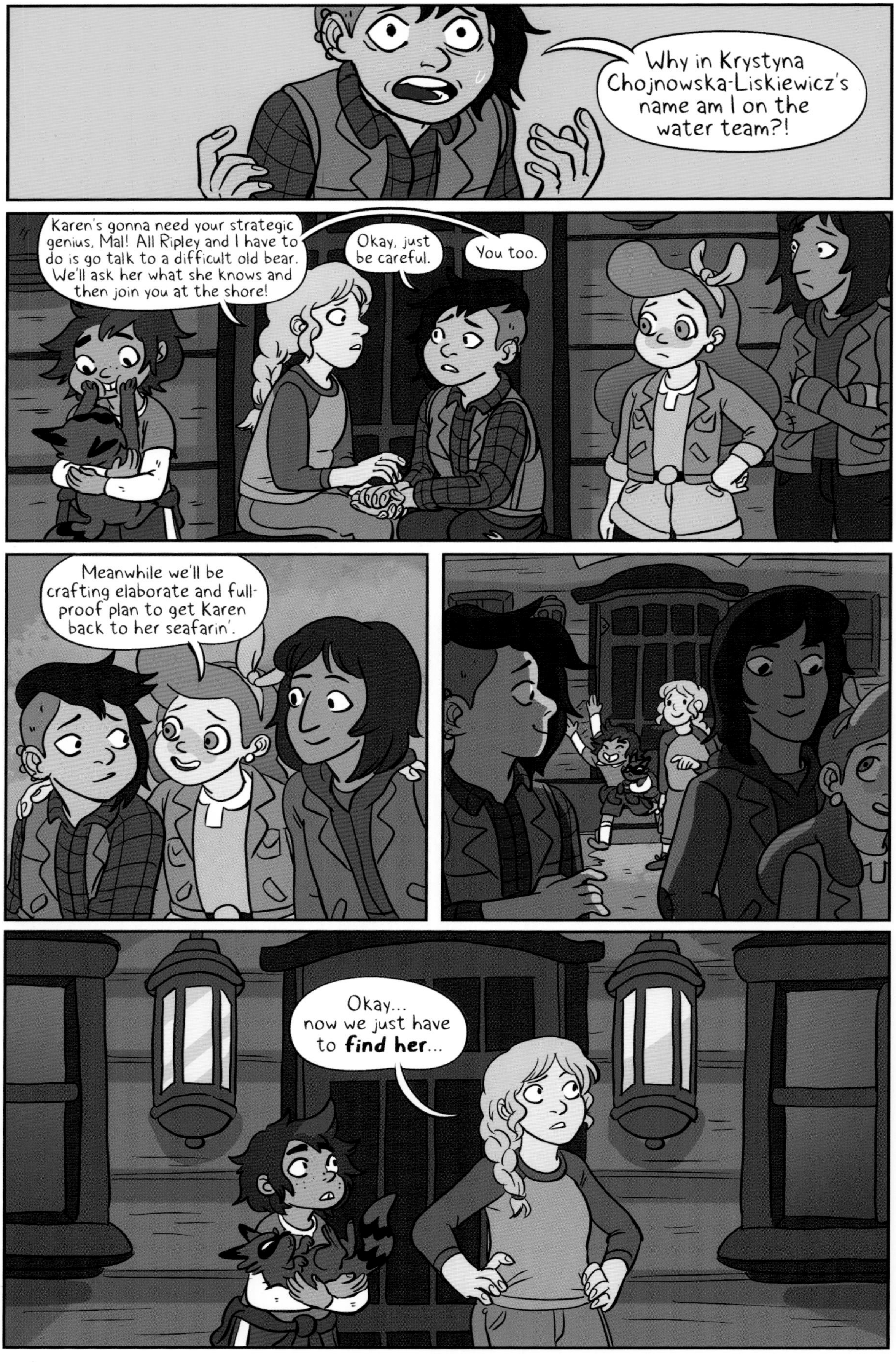
Why in Krystyna Chojnowska-Liskiewicz's name am I on the water team?!
Karen's gonna need your strategic genius, Mal! All Ripley and I have to do is go talk to a difficult old bear. We'll ask her what she knows and then join you at the shore!
Okay, just be careful.
You too.
Meanwhile we'll be crafting elaborate and full-proof plan to get Karen back to her seafarin'.
Okay... now we just have to **find her**...

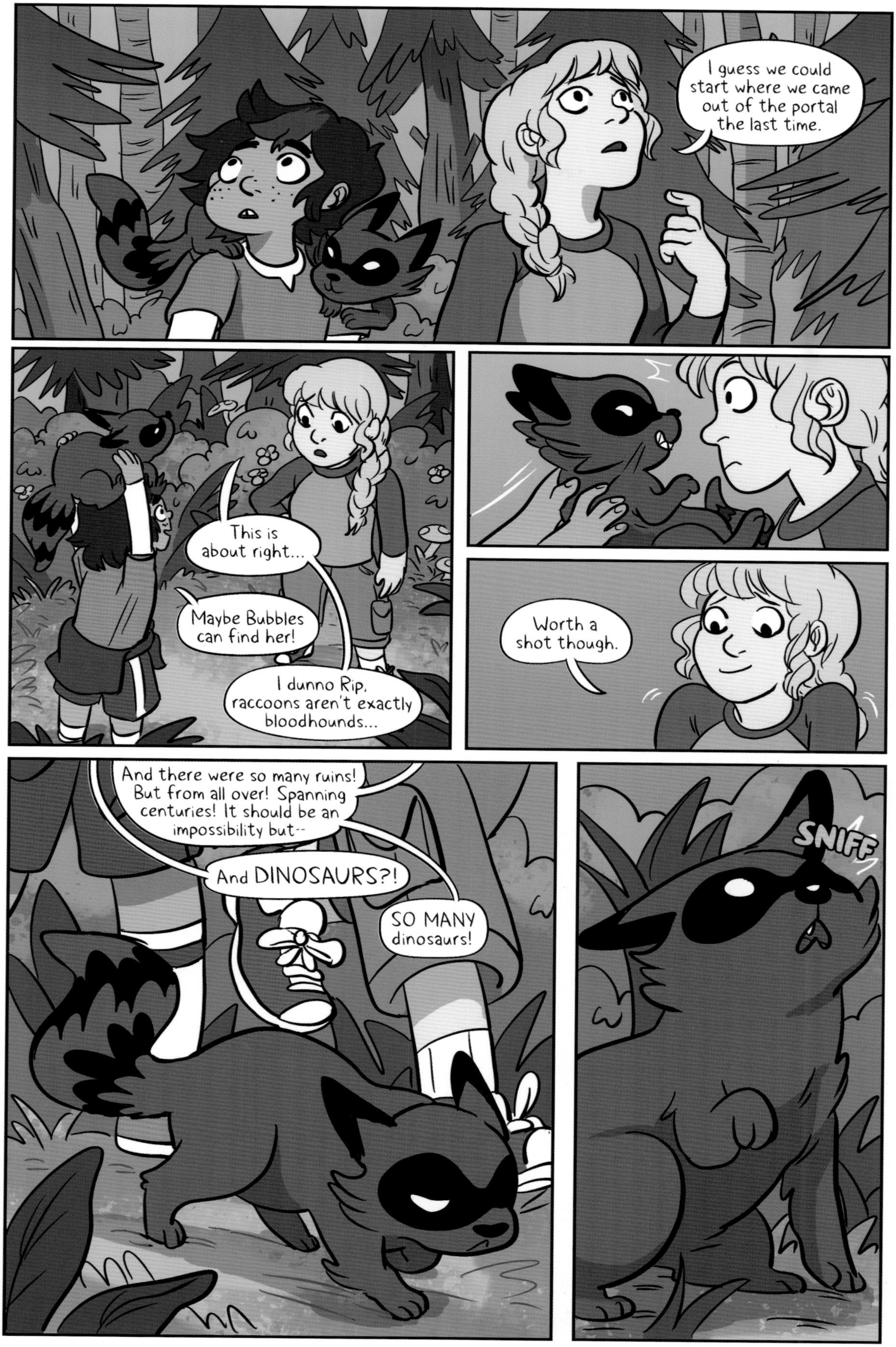
I guess we could start where we came out of the portal the last time.
This is about right...
Maybe Bubbles can find her!
I dunno Rip, raccoons aren't exactly bloodhounds...
Worth a shot though.
And there were so many ruins! But from all over! Spanning centuries! It should be an impossibility but--
And DINOSAURS?!
SO MANY dinosaurs!
SNIFF

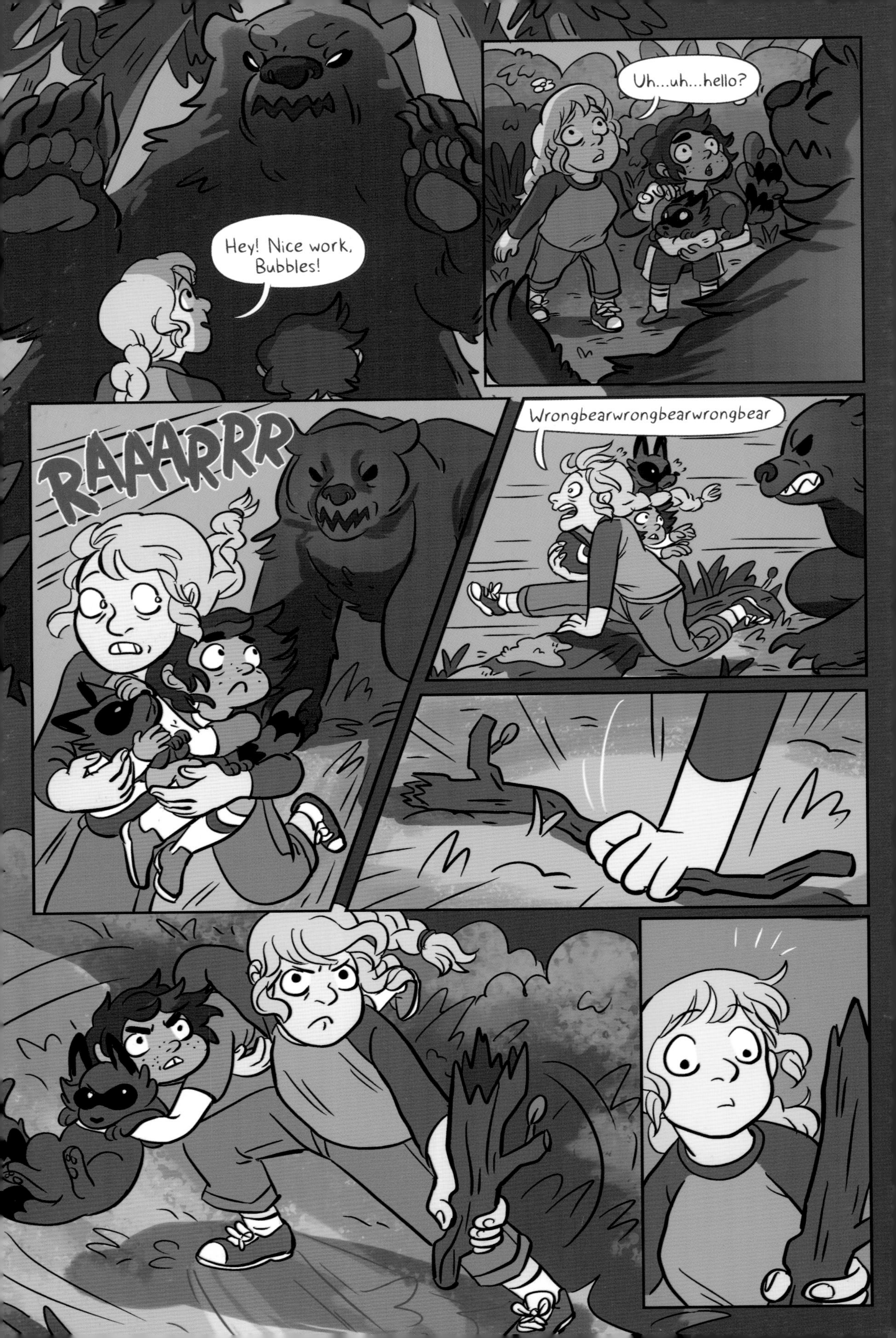
Hey! Nice work, Bubbles!
Uh...uh...hello?
RAAARRR
Wrongbearwrongbearwrongbear

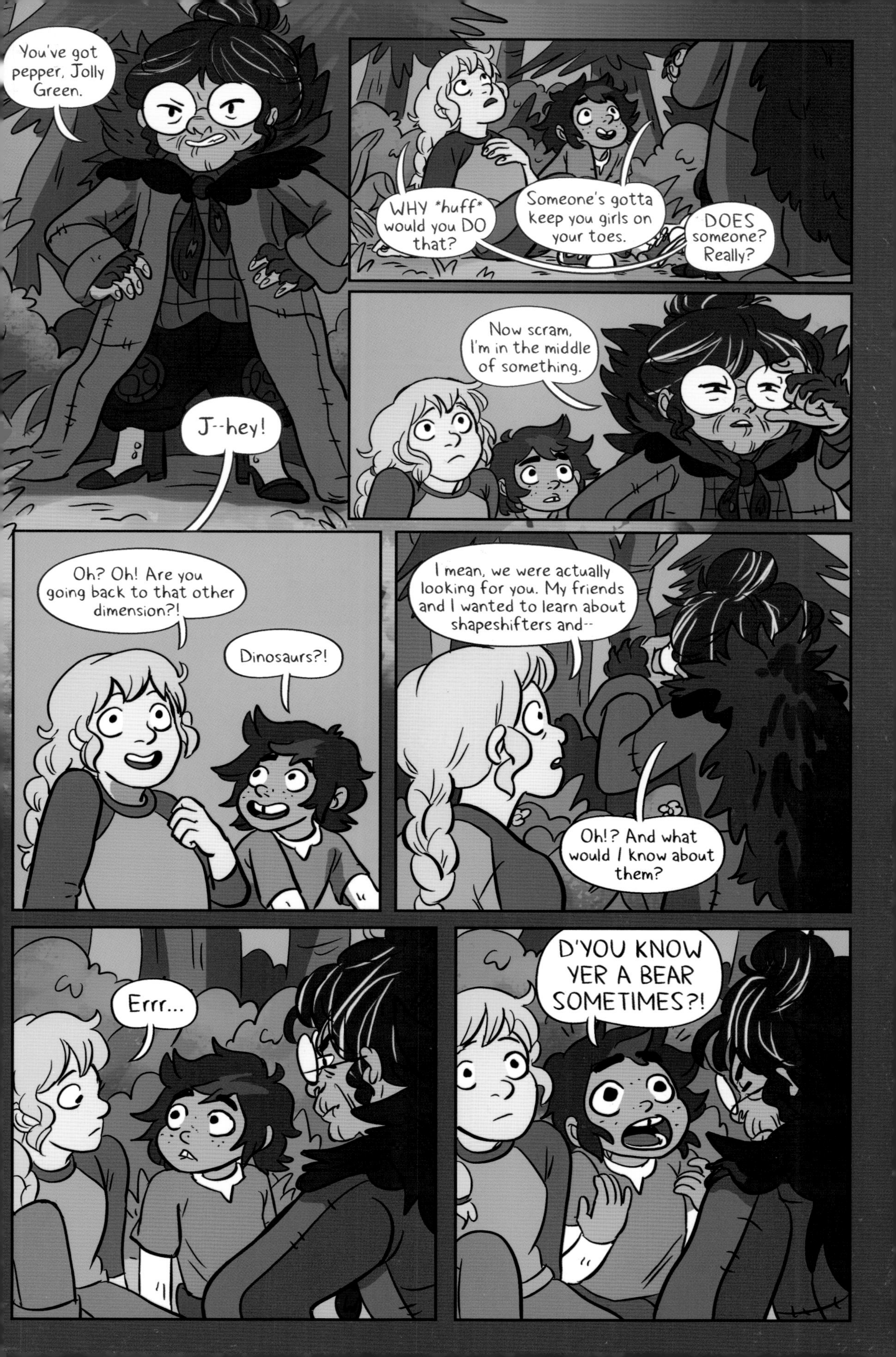
You've got pepper, Jolly Green.
J--hey!
WHY *huff* would you DO that?
Someone's gotta keep you girls on your toes.
DOES someone? Really?
Now scram, I'm in the middle of something.
Oh? Oh! Are you going back to that other dimension?!
Dinosaurs?!
I mean, we were actually looking for you. My friends and I wanted to learn about shapeshifters and--
Oh!? And what would I know about them?
Errr...
D'YOU KNOW YER A BEAR SOMETIMES?!

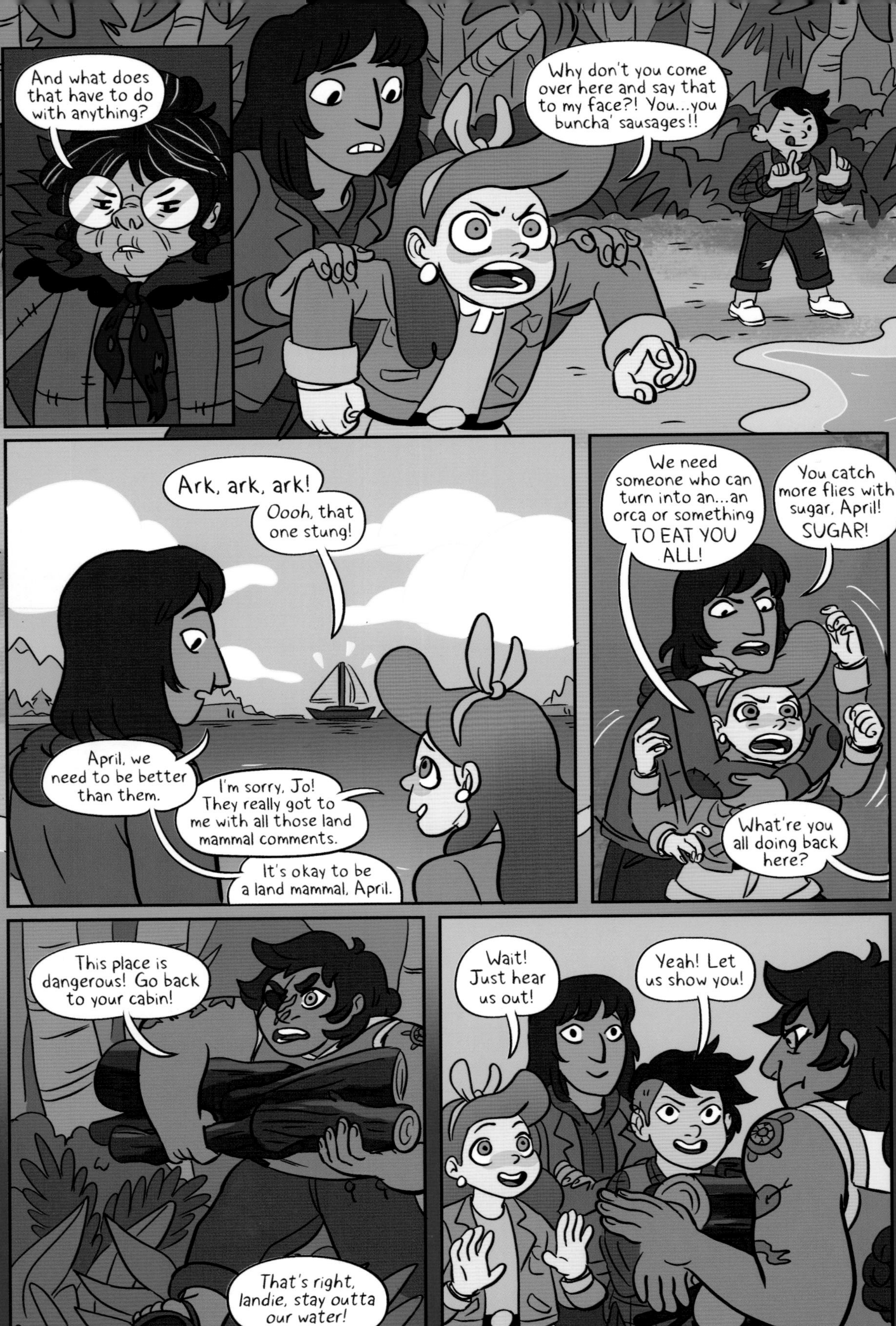
And what does that have to do with anything?
Why don't you come over here and say that to my face?! You...you buncha' sausages!!
Ark, ark, ark!
Oooh, that one stung!
April, we need to be better than them.
I'm sorry, Jo! They really got to me with all those land mammal comments.
It's okay to be a land mammal, April.
We need someone who can turn into an...an orca or something TO EAT YOU ALL!
You catch more flies with sugar, April! SUGAR!
What're you all doing back here?
This place is dangerous! Go back to your cabin!
That's right, landie, stay outta our water!
Wait! Just hear us out!
Yeah! Let us show you!

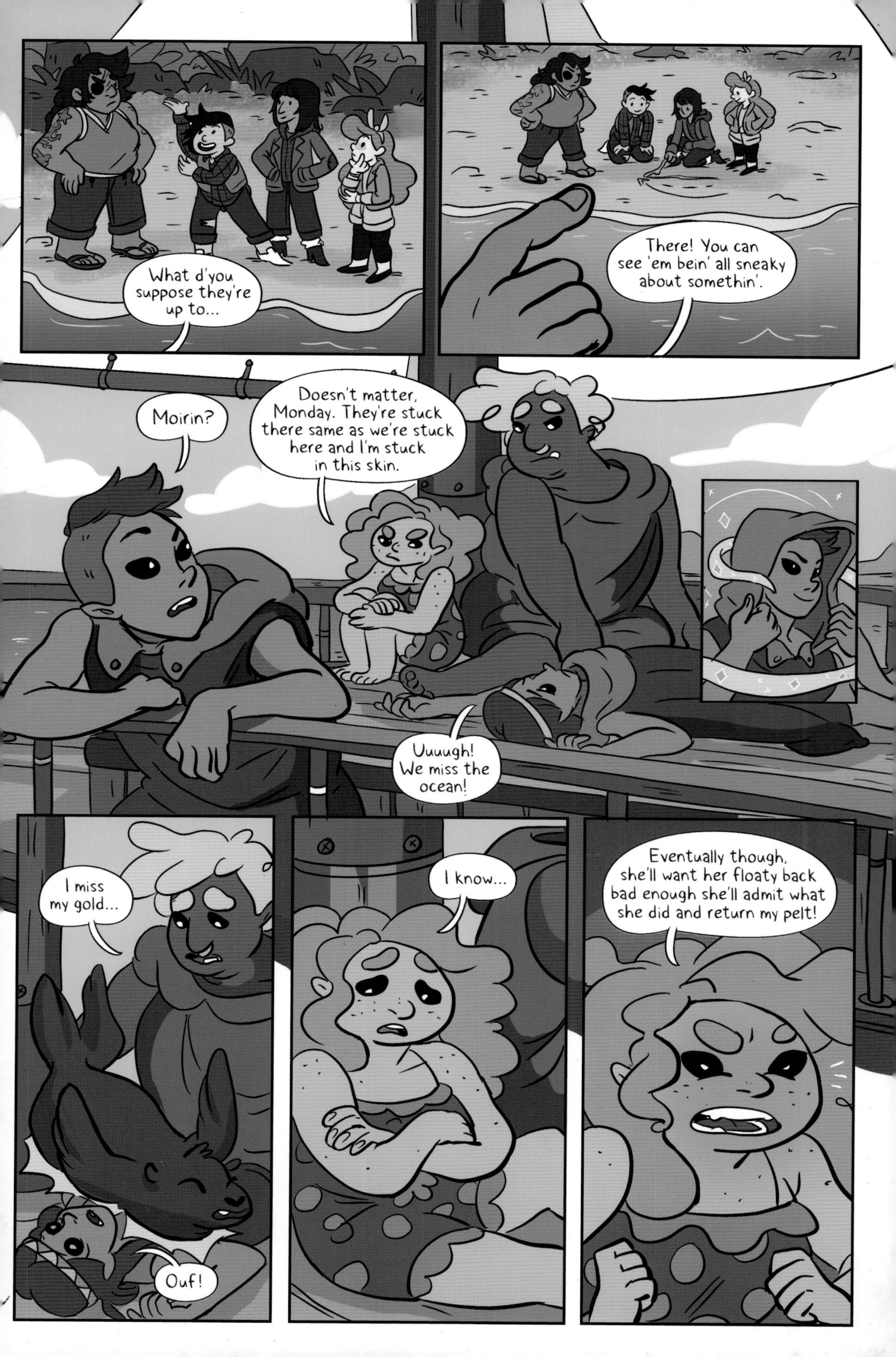
What d'you suppose they're up to...
There! You can see 'em bein' all sneaky about somethin'.
Moirin?
Doesn't matter, Monday. They're stuck there same as we're stuck here and I'm stuck in this skin.
Uuuugh! We miss the ocean!
I miss my gold...
Ouf!
I know...
Eventually though, she'll want her floaty back bad enough she'll admit what she did and return my pelt!

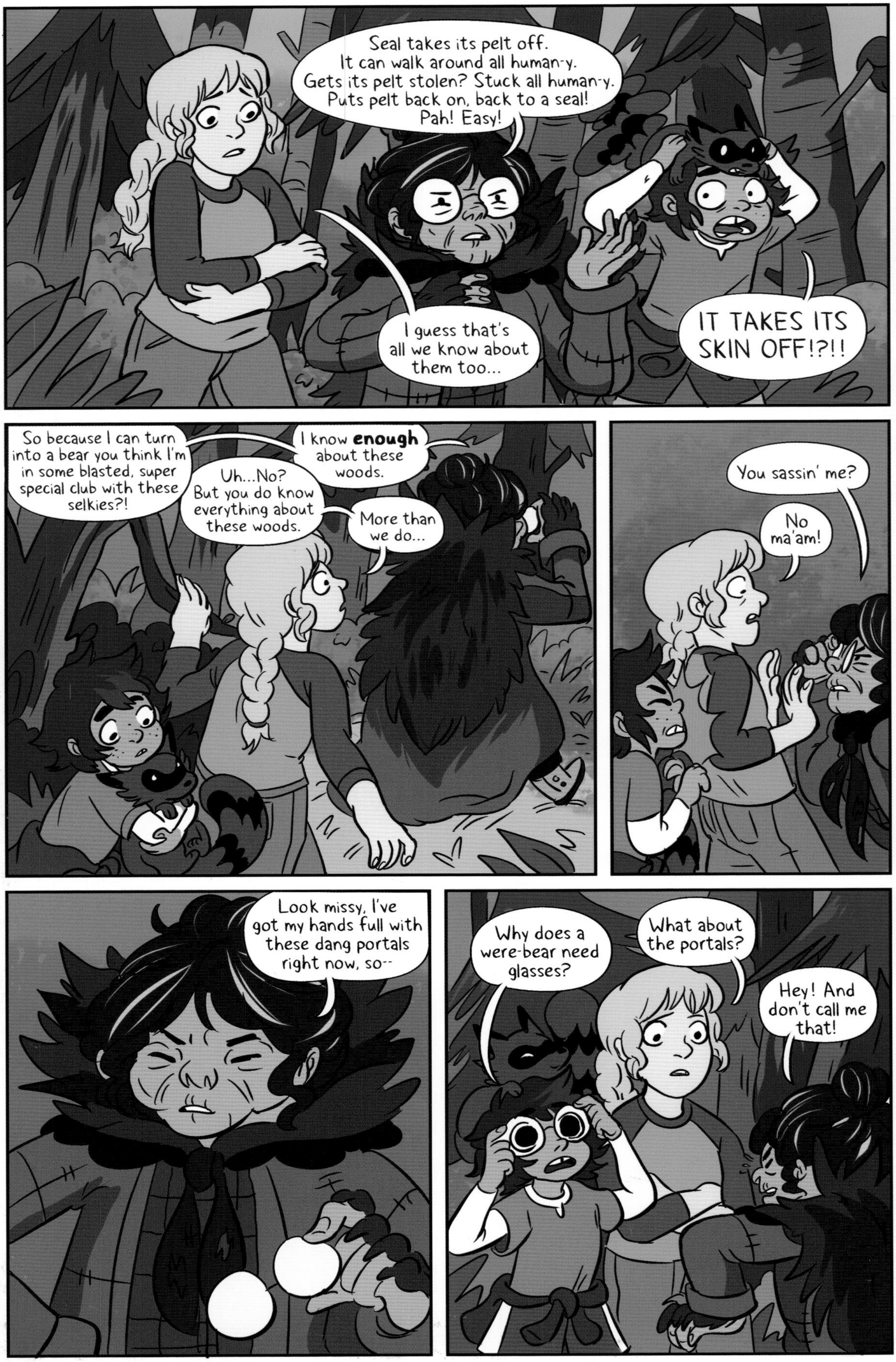

Seal takes its pelt off. It can walk around all human-y. Gets its pelt stolen? Stuck all human-y. Puts pelt back on, back to a seal! Pah! Easy!
I guess that's all we know about them too...
IT TAKES ITS SKIN OFF!?!!
So because I can turn into a bear you think I'm in some blasted, super special club with these selkies?!
I know **enough** about these woods.
Uh...No? But you do know everything about these woods.
More than we do...
You sassin' me?
No ma'am!
Look missy, I've got my hands full with these dang portals right now, so--
Why does a were-bear need glasses?
What about the portals?
Hey! And don't call me that!

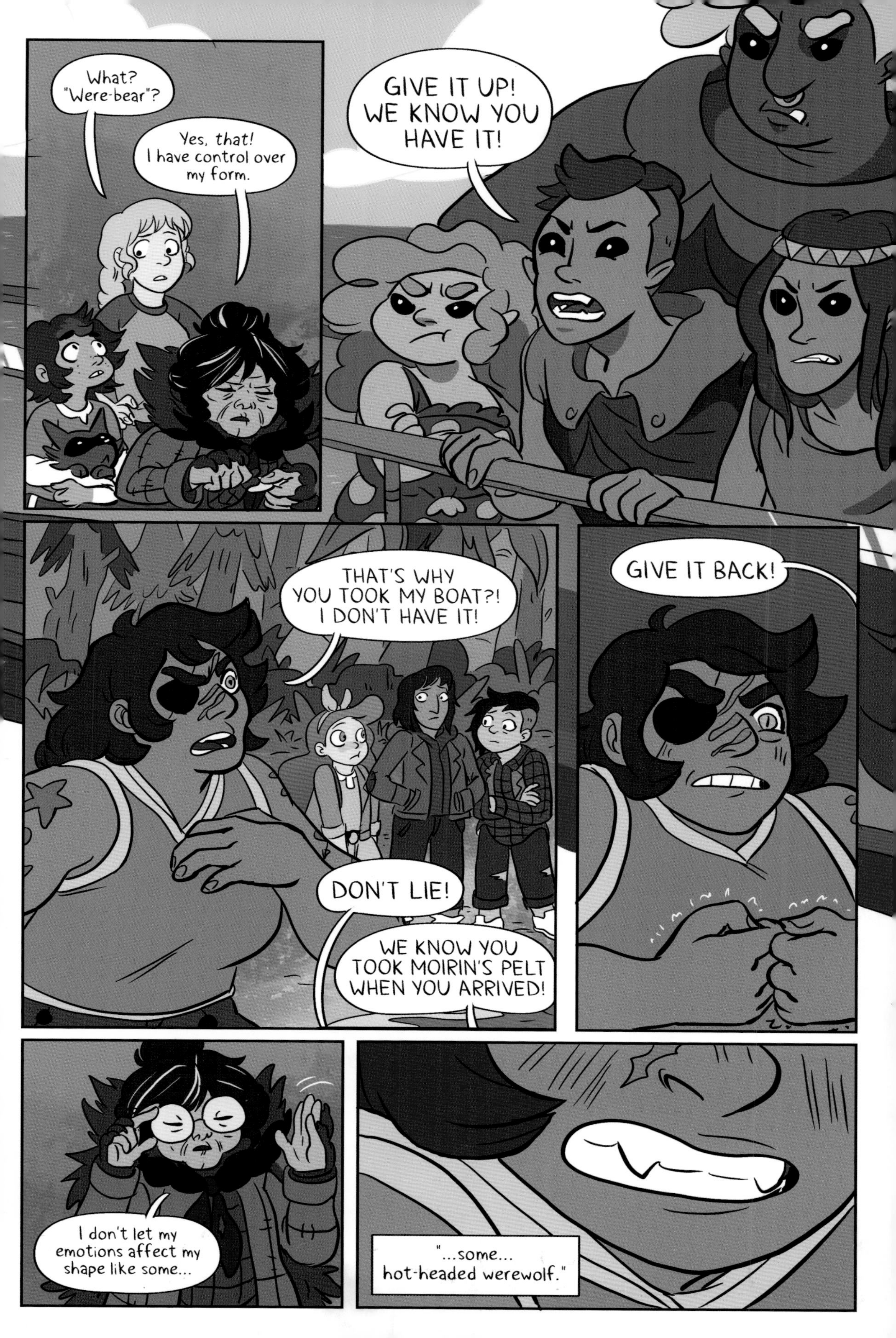
What? "Were-bear"?
Yes, that! I have control over my form.
GIVE IT UP! WE KNOW YOU HAVE IT!
THAT'S WHY YOU TOOK MY BOAT?! I DON'T HAVE IT!
DON'T LIE!
WE KNOW YOU TOOK MOIRIN'S PELT WHEN YOU ARRIVED!
GIVE IT BACK!
I don't let my emotions affect my shape like some...
"...some... hot-headed werewolf."

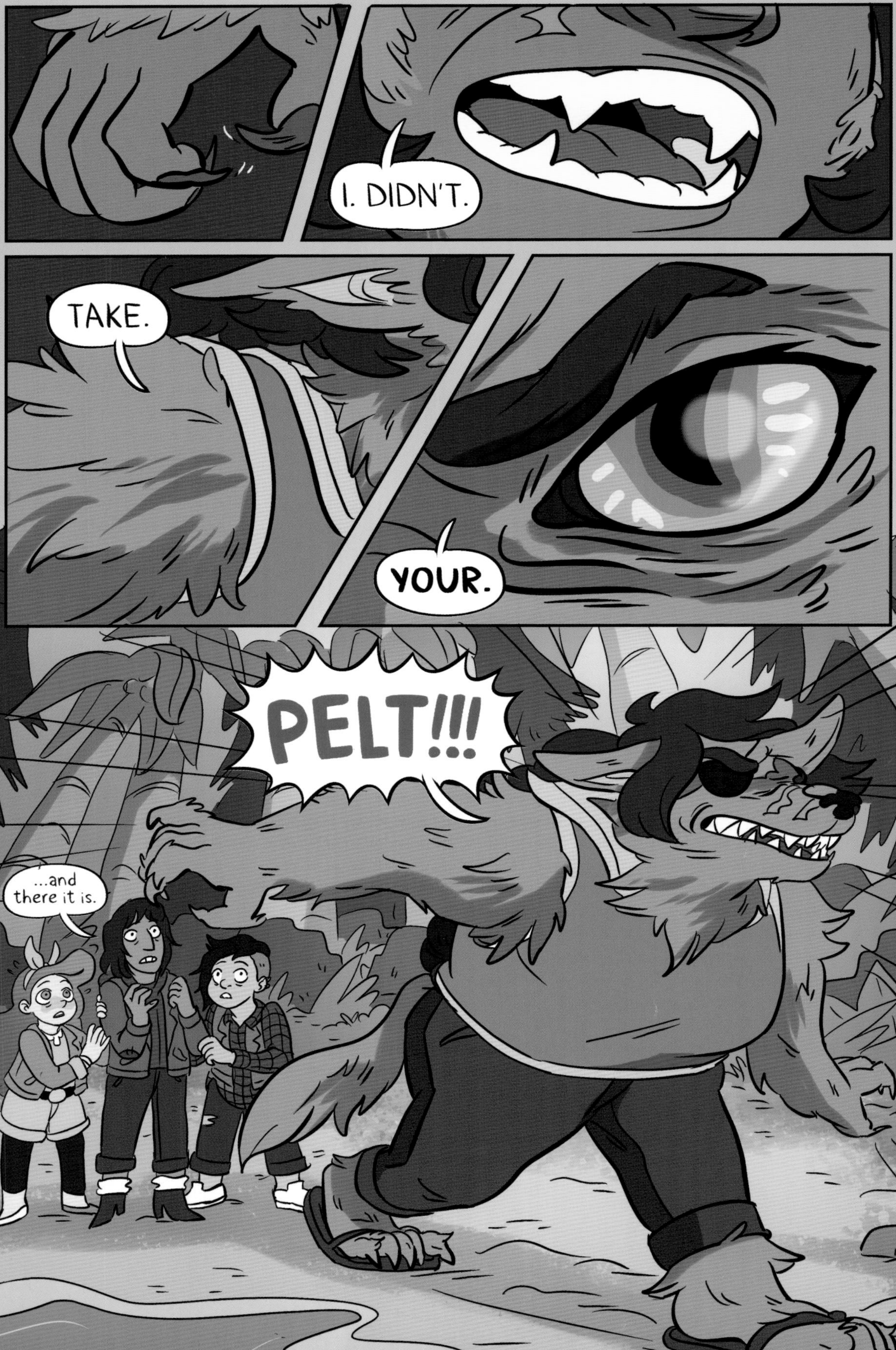
I. DIDN'T.
TAKE.
YOUR.
PELT!!!
...and there it is.

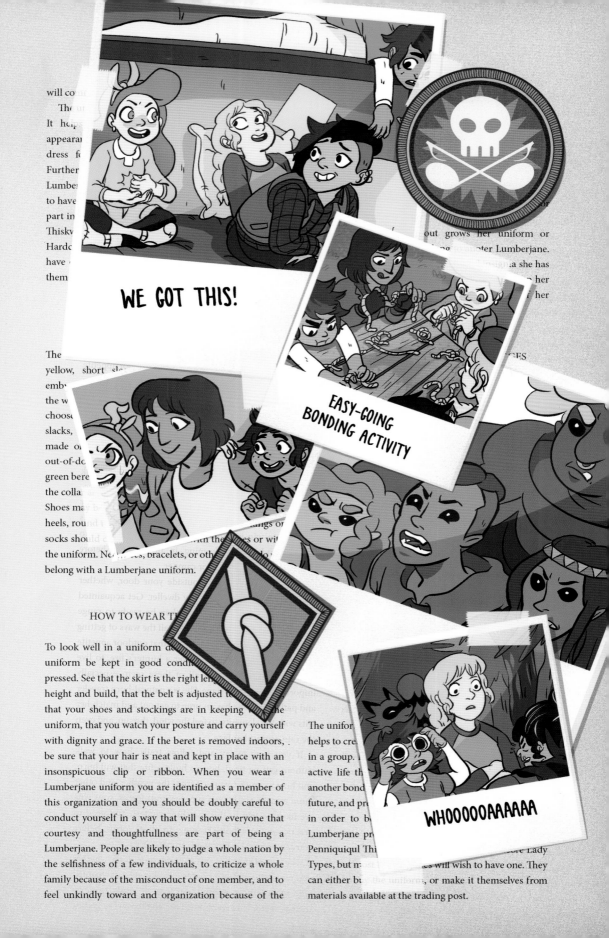

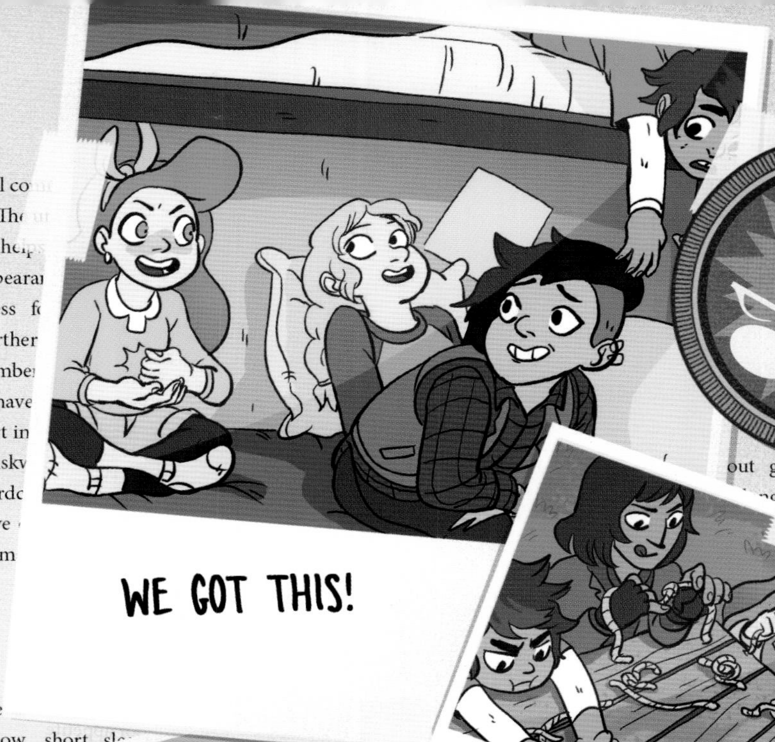
WE GOT THIS!

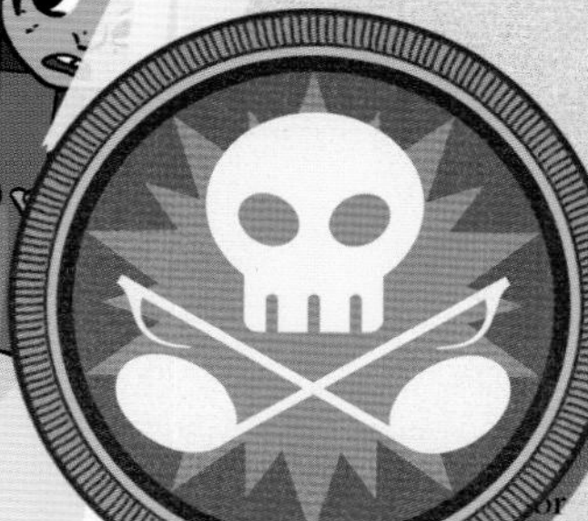

will co…

The u… It helps… appearan… dress f… Further… Lumbe… to have… part in… Thiskv… Hardc… have… them… out grows her uniform or …g to another Lumberjane. …insignia she has … her … her

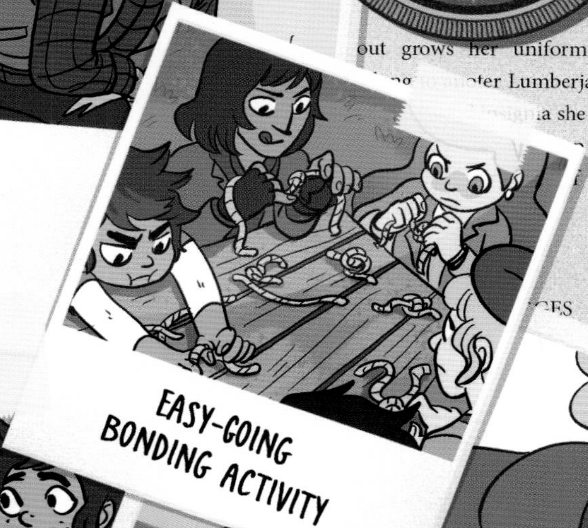
EASY-GOING
BONDING ACTIVITY

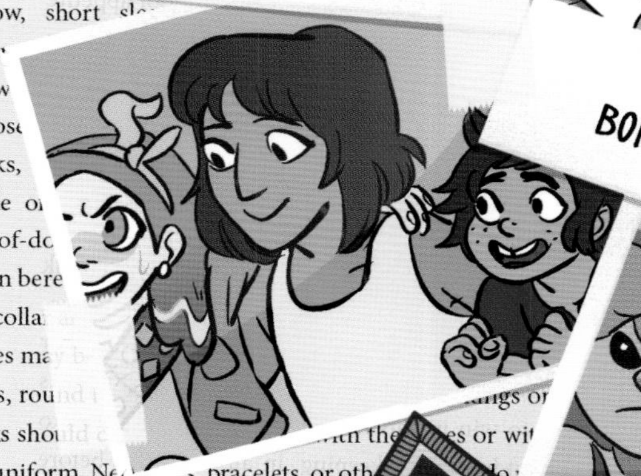

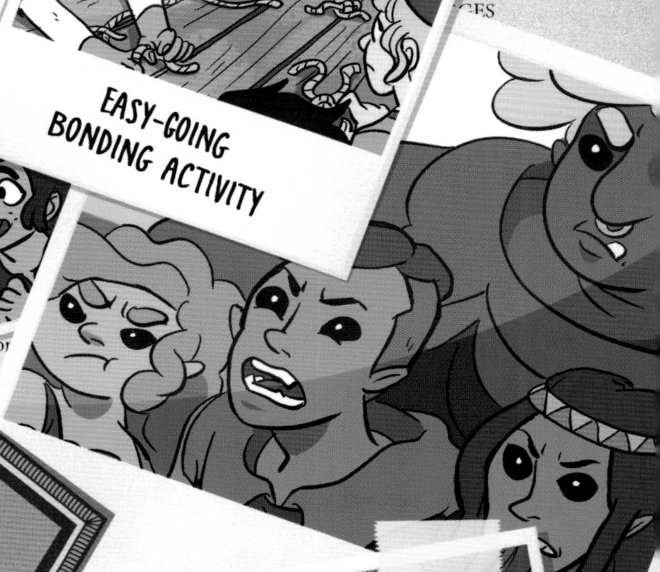

The … yellow, short sl… emb… the w… choose… slacks, … made o… out-of-do… green bere… the colla… Shoes may… heels, rou… …kings or socks shou… with the…es or wit… the uniform. Ne…ces, bracelets, or othe… do… belong with a Lumberjane uniform.

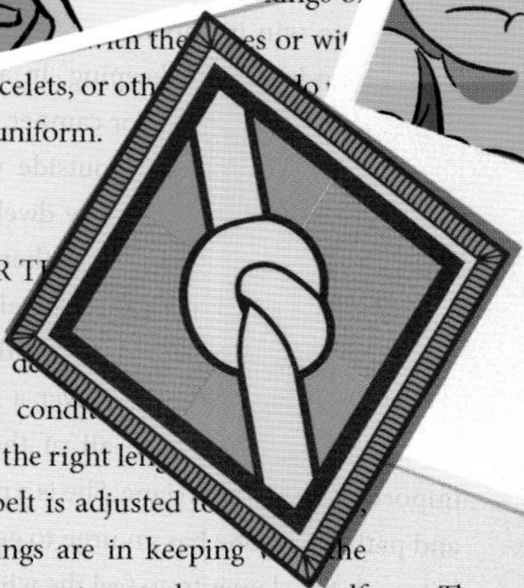

HOW TO WEAR T…

To look well in a uniform d… uniform be kept in good condi… pressed. See that the skirt is the right len… height and build, that the belt is adjusted t… that your shoes and stockings are in keeping … the uniform, that you watch your posture and carry yourself with dignity and grace. If the beret is removed indoors, be sure that your hair is neat and kept in place with an insonspicuous clip or ribbon. When you wear a Lumberjane uniform you are identified as a member of this organization and you should be doubly careful to conduct yourself in a way that will show everyone that courtesy and thoughtfullness are part of being a Lumberjane. People are likely to judge a whole nation by the selfishness of a few individuals, to criticize a whole family because of the misconduct of one member, and to feel unkindly toward and organization because of the

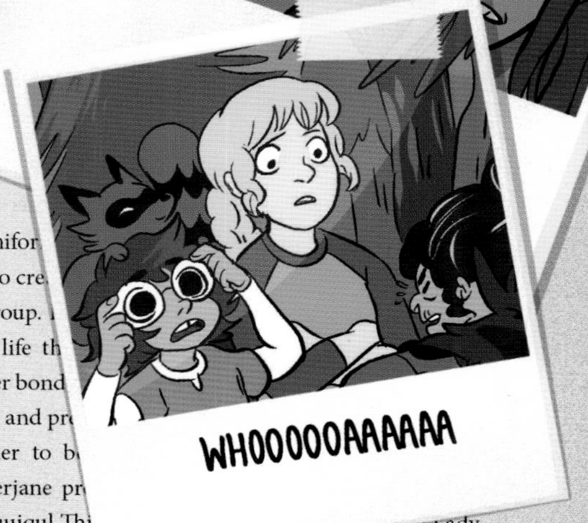
WHOOOOOAAAAAA

The unifor… helps to cre… in a group. … active life th… another bond… future, and pr… in order to b… Lumberjane pr… Penniquiqul Thi… …ore Lady Types, but m… …es will wish to have one. They can either bu… the uniform, or make it themselves from materials available at the trading post.

LUMBERJANES FIELD MANUAL

CHAPTER TWENTY-TWO

Lumberjanes "Out-of-Doors" Program Field

SEAS THE DAY BADGE

"Carp-ay Diem and all that noise."

It's important for every camper at our camp for hardcore lady-types feel like they are getting the most out of their day. If a camper is ever bored, then it's up to that camper, and the friends that they've collected at this camp, to solve the issue of their boredom by challenging themselves to something exciting and new. We pride ourselves with the challenging tasks that we have at our camp, and know that we are able to push every camper to their limits so that they grow to the best versions of themselves, no matter where they are in their lives.

Every Lumberjane will have their favorite badge when they eventually leave camp, and this is a personal favorite of some members of the High Council. The *Seas The Day* badge is about making sure you get the most you can out of every hour, minute, and second of the day. Every day that you are given is a unique opportunity for campers to change a life, whether it's the life of another camper, of a passing forest

creature that they might find in the forest, or maybe the life they change is their own. Either way, the goal of this badge is for our campers to take a look at their day and understand how they can live life to the fullest before time resets itself as the sun sets. Living life to the fullest is the ground work to a happy and fulfilled life that we want every camper to have.

There are many ways to obtain the *Seas The Day* badge. The main point to the badge is the action that the camper takes to make sure they are using their day to the fullest. The *Seas The Day* badge needs a full 24 hours to complete, and in order for the camper to be eligible to receive the badge, they must start at sunrise before they begin their actions for the rest of the day. They will have two check points throughout the day: sunrise with their counselor to start off the task to earn the badge and then at dinner they must check in with their counselor again to go over every task they've completed so far.

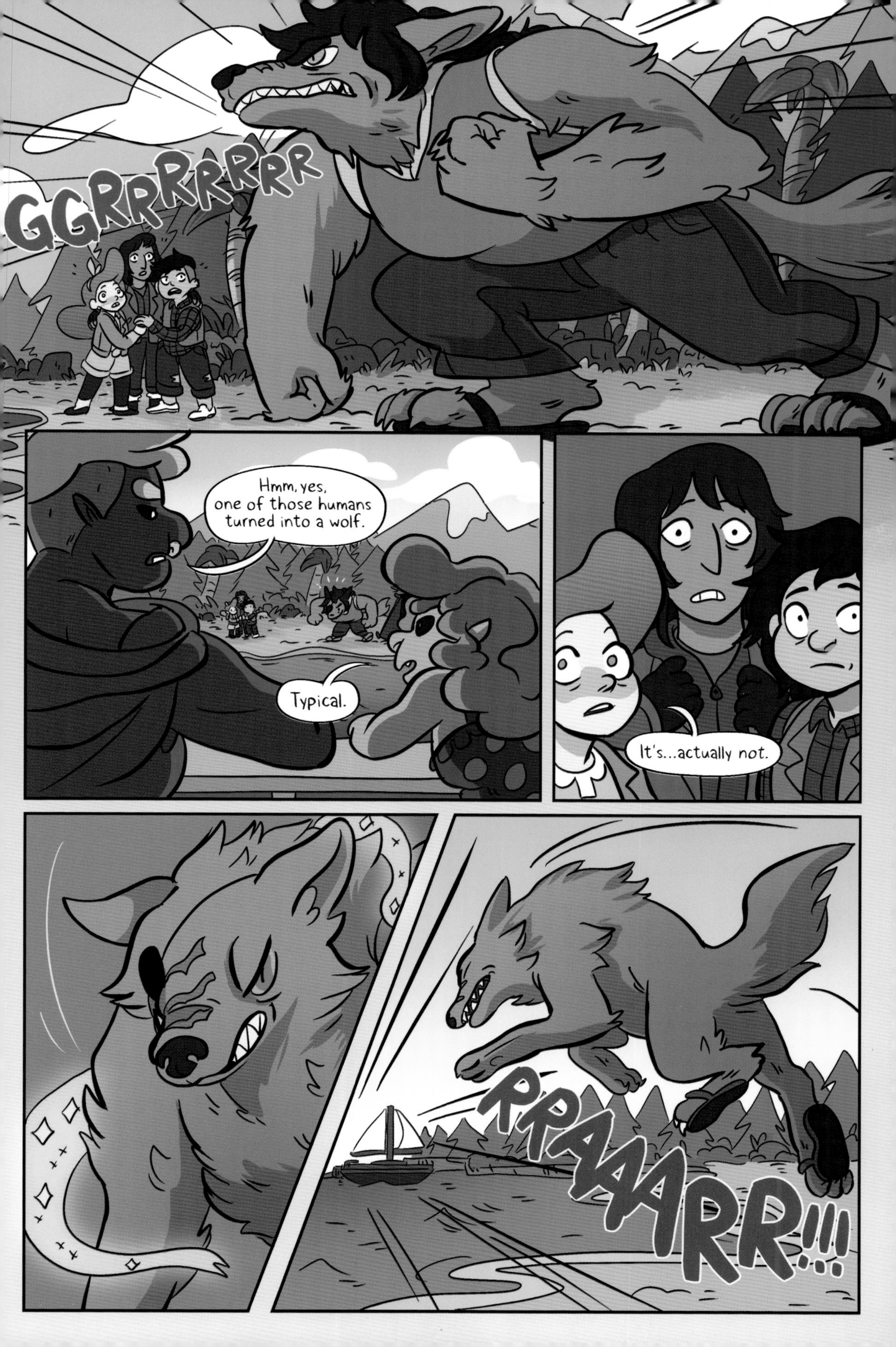
GGRRRRRRR
Hmm, yes, one of those humans turned into a wolf.
Typical.
It's...actually not.
RRAAAARR!!!

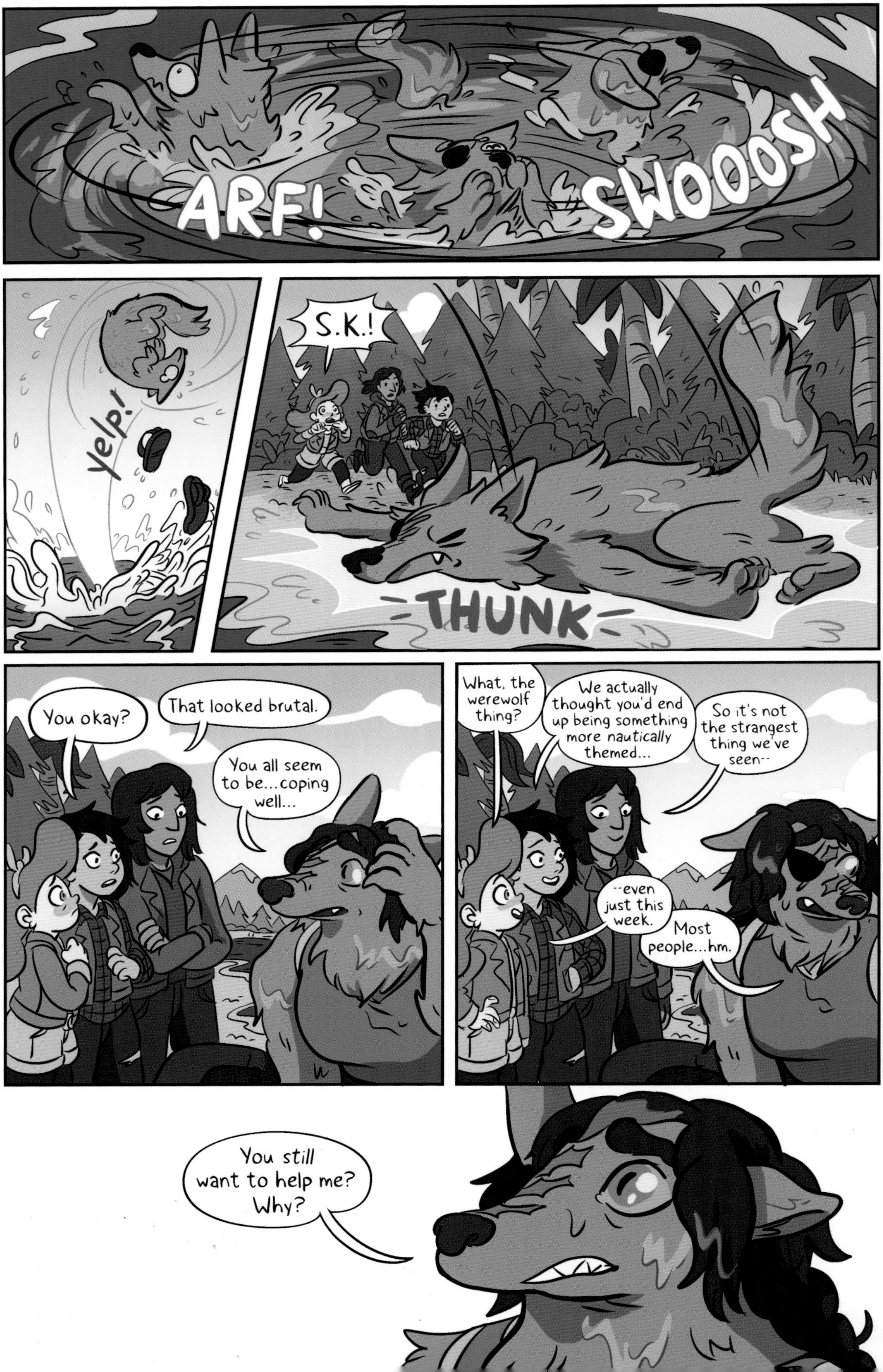
ARF!
SWOOOSH
yelp!
S.K.!
THUNK
You okay?
That looked brutal.
You all seem to be...coping well...
What, the werewolf thing?
We actually thought you'd end up being something more nautically themed...
So it's not the strangest thing we've seen--
--even just this week.
Most people...hm.
You still want to help me? Why?

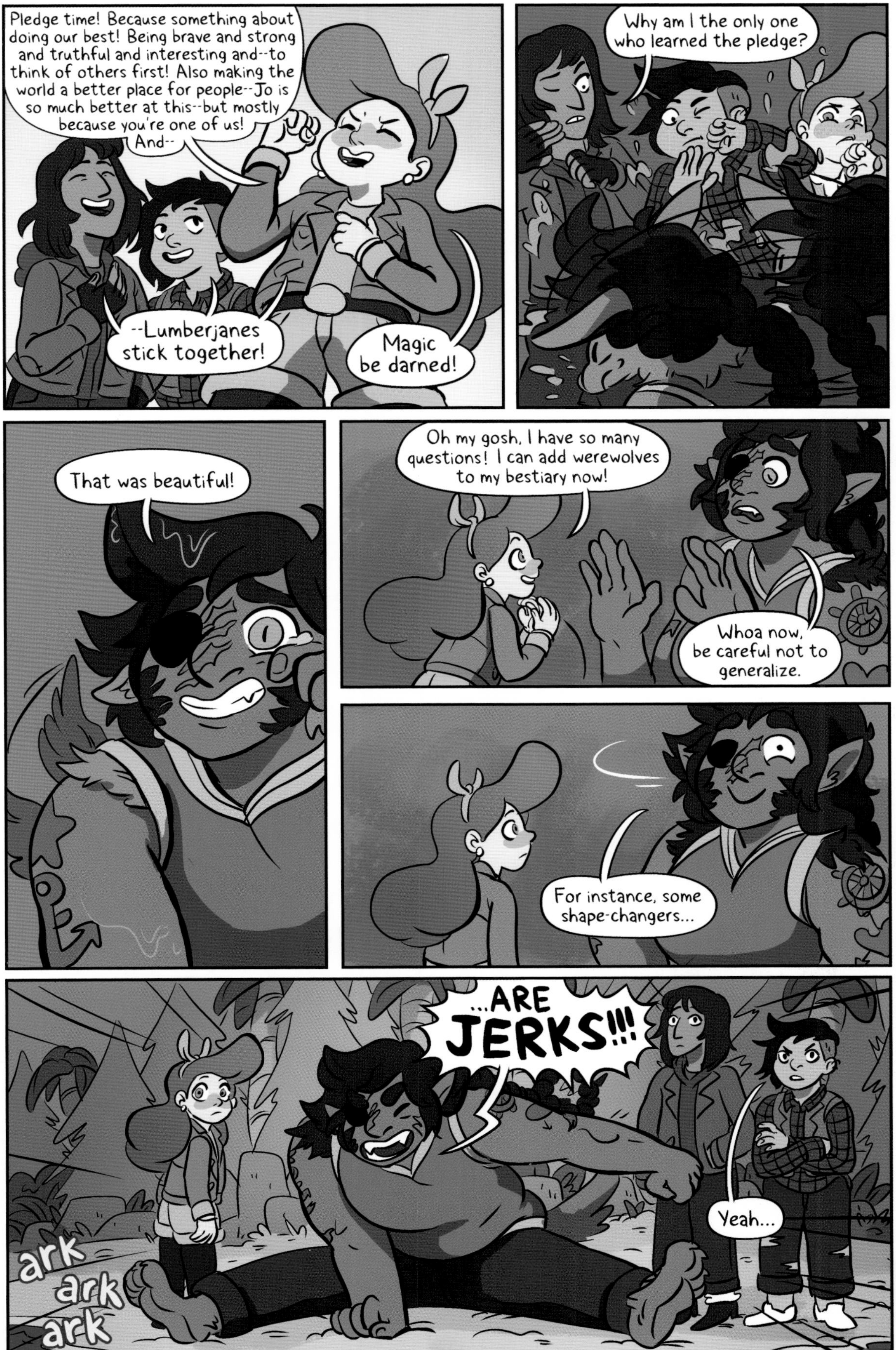

Pledge time! Because something about doing our best! Being brave and strong and truthful and interesting and--to think of others first! Also making the world a better place for people--Jo is so much better at this--but mostly because you're one of us! And--
--Lumberjanes stick together!
Magic be darned!
Why am I the only one who learned the pledge?
That was beautiful!
Oh my gosh, I have so many questions! I can add werewolves to my bestiary now!
Whoa now, be careful not to generalize.
For instance, some shape-changers...
...ARE JERKS!!!
Yeah...
ark ark ark

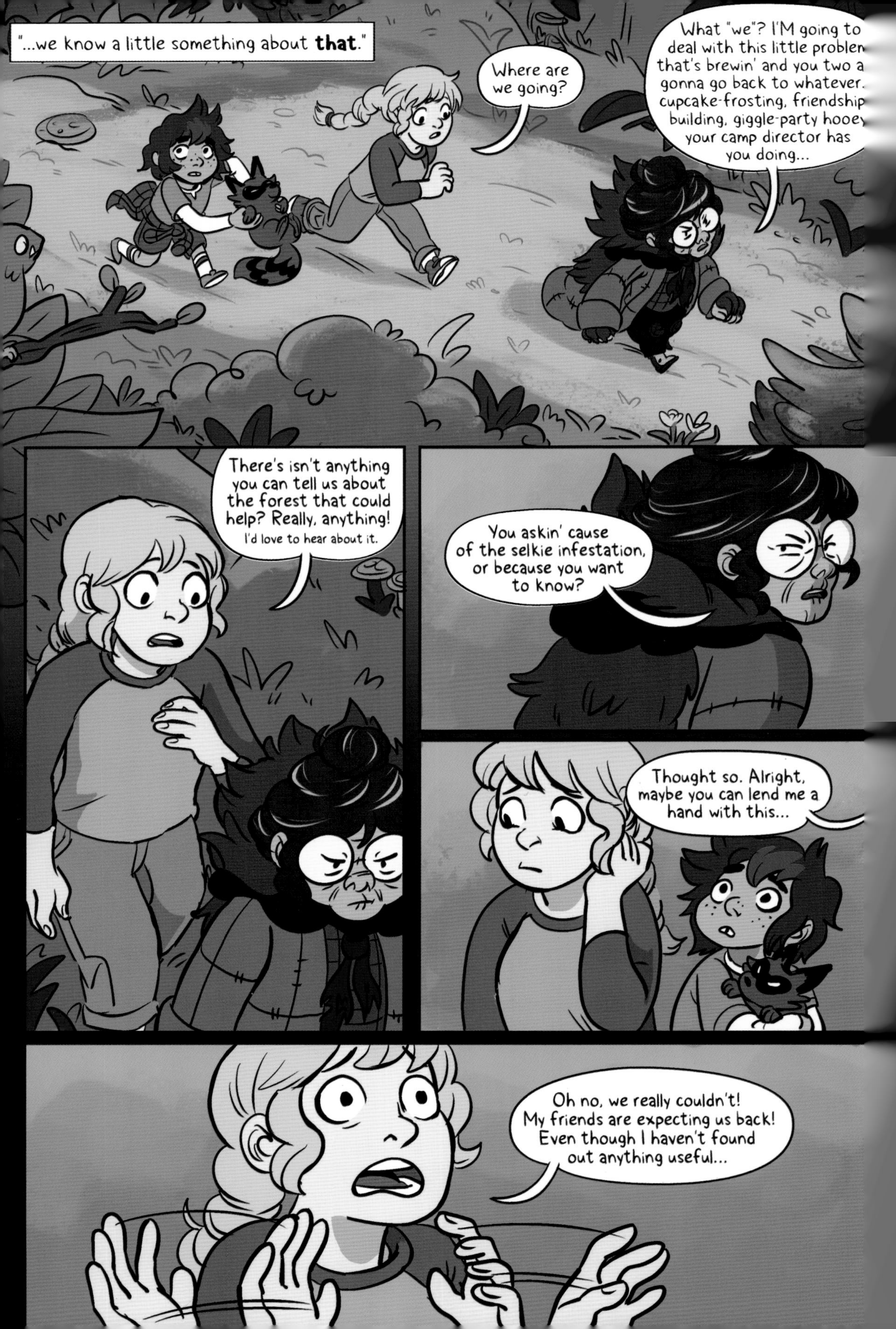
"...we know a little something about **that**."
Where are we going?
What "we"? I'M going to deal with this little problen that's brewin' and you two a gonna go back to whatever. cupcake-frosting, friendship building, giggle-party hooey your camp director has you doing...
There's isn't anything you can tell us about the forest that could help? Really, anything! I'd love to hear about it.
You askin' cause of the selkie infestation, or because you want to know?
Thought so. Alright, maybe you can lend me a hand with this...
Oh no, we really couldn't! My friends are expecting us back! Even though I haven't found out anything useful...

Time moves quicker in that other place, don't it? That's where we're going. Your friends won't even notice.

Hmm, well...

What do you think, Rip? Quick trip to an impossible parallel dimension of lost things?

Dinosaurs?

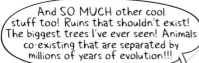

And SO MUCH other cool stuff too! Ruins that shouldn't exist! The biggest trees I've ever seen! Animals co-existing that are separated by millions of years of evolution!!!

...and by that I mean dinosaurs!

EEEEE!

Yes, yes, all that crud. We'll just need to stop off at my place first...

The others will really be okay without us?

Just wait, time will pass quicker for us and we'll be back before they have a chance to miss us!

Missing Molly?

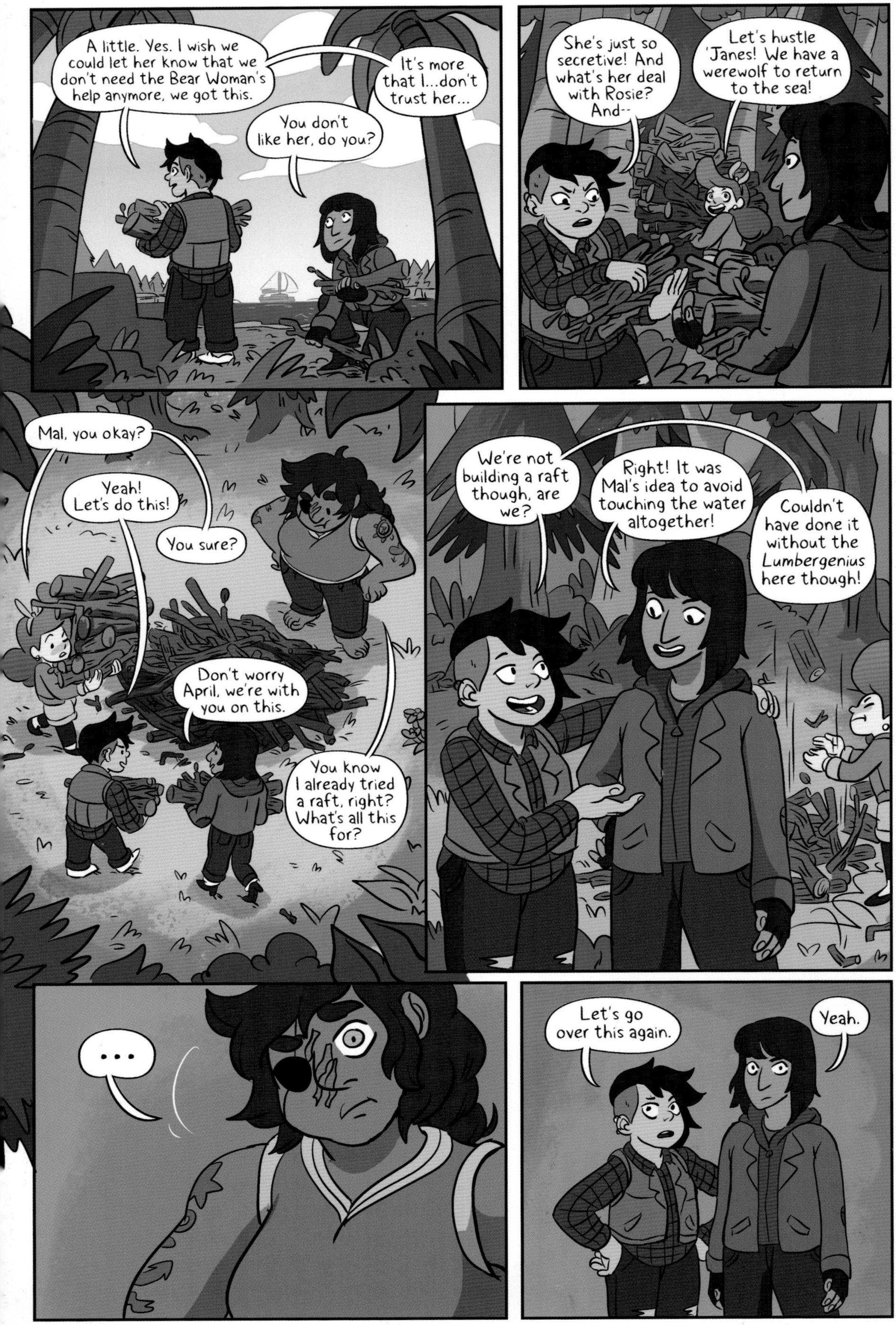
A little. Yes. I wish we could let her know that we don't need the Bear Woman's help anymore, we got this.
You don't like her, do you?
It's more that I...don't trust her...
She's just so secretive! And what's her deal with Rosie? And--
Let's hustle 'Janes! We have a werewolf to return to the sea!
Mal, you okay?
Yeah! Let's do this!
You sure?
Don't worry April, we're with you on this.
You know I already tried a raft, right? What's all this for?
We're not building a raft though, are we?
Right! It was Mal's idea to avoid touching the water altogether!
Couldn't have done it without the *Lumbergenius* here though!
...
Let's go over this again.
Yeah.

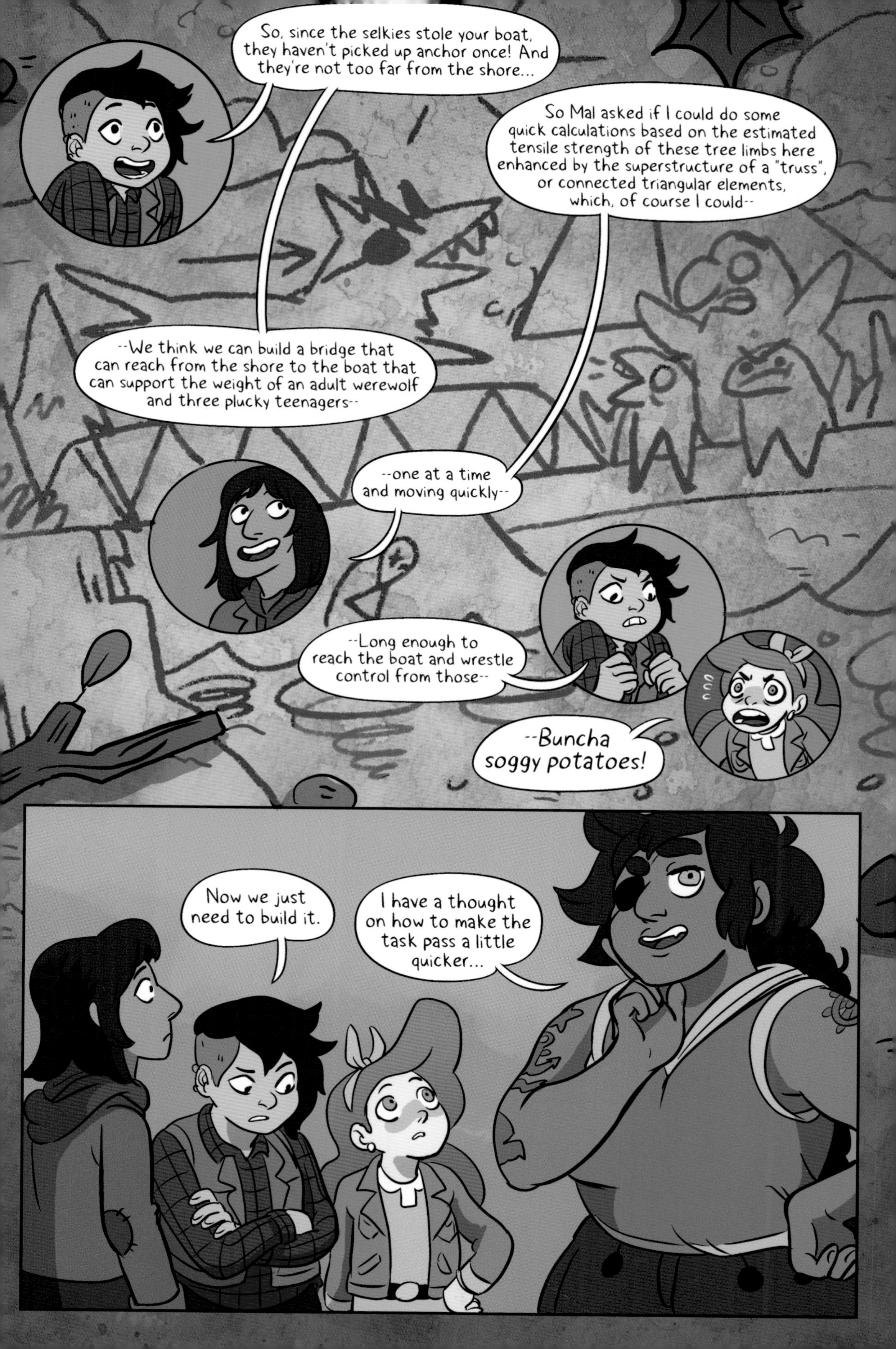

So, since the selkies stole your boat, they haven't picked up anchor once! And they're not too far from the shore...
So Mal asked if I could do some quick calculations based on the estimated tensile strength of these tree limbs here enhanced by the superstructure of a "truss", or connected triangular elements, which, of course I could--
--We think we can build a bridge that can reach from the shore to the boat that can support the weight of an adult werewolf and three plucky teenagers--
--one at a time and moving quickly--
--Long enough to reach the boat and wrestle control from those--
--Buncha soggy potatoes!
Now we just need to build it.
I have a thought on how to make the task pass a little quicker...

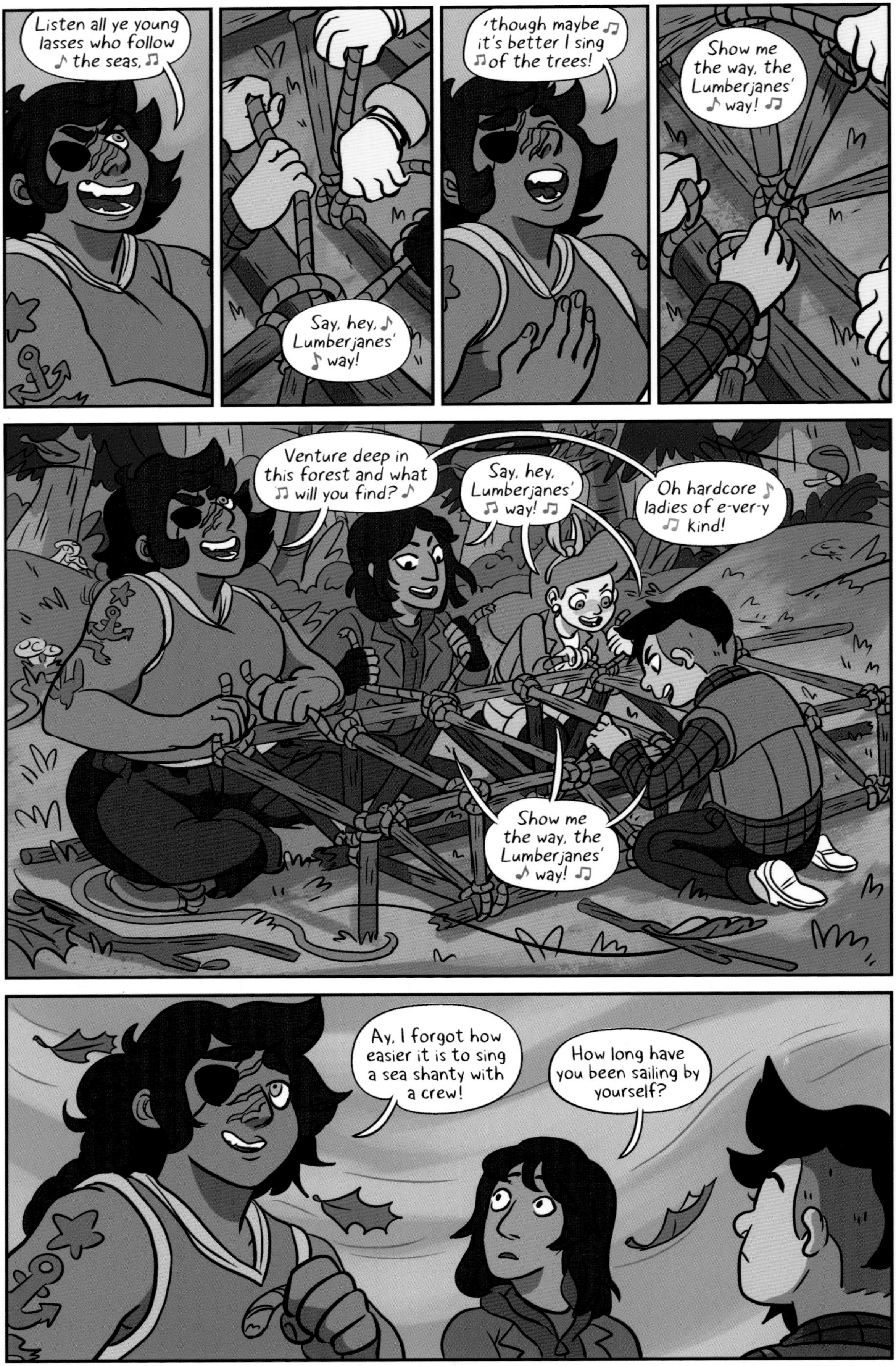

Listen all ye young lasses who follow ♪ the seas, ♫
Say, hey, ♪ Lumberjanes' ♪ way!
'though maybe ♫ it's better I sing ♫ of the trees!
Show me the way, the Lumberjanes' ♪ way! ♫
Venture deep in this forest and what ♫ will you find? ♪
Say, hey, Lumberjanes' ♫ way! ♫
Oh hardcore ♪ ladies of e-ver-y ♫ kind!
Show me the way, the Lumberjanes' ♪ way! ♫
Ay, I forgot how easier it is to sing a sea shanty with a crew!
How long have you been sailing by yourself?

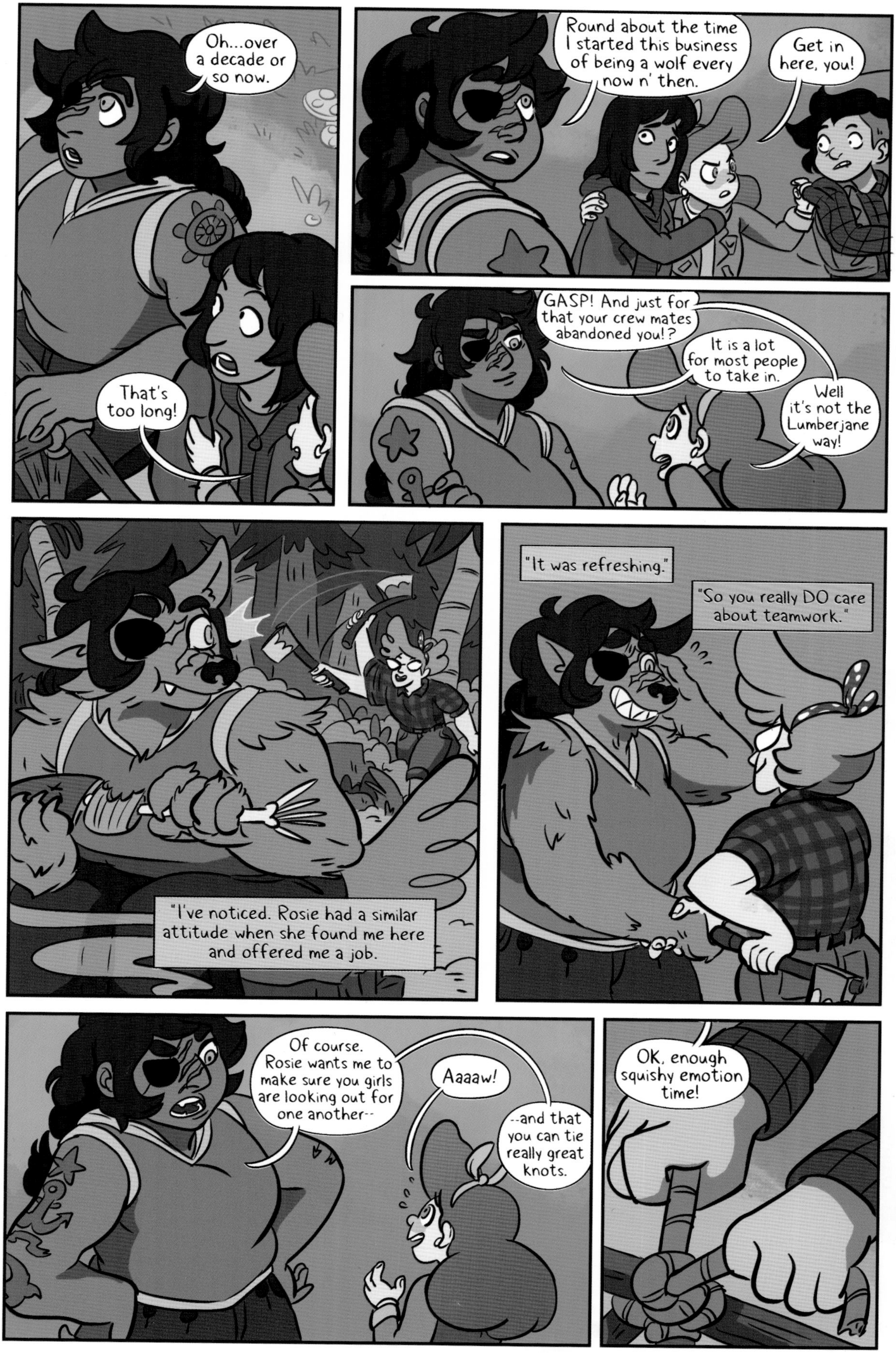
Oh...over a decade or so now.
That's too long!
Round about the time I started this business of being a wolf every now n' then.
Get in here, you!
GASP! And just for that your crew mates abandoned you!?
It is a lot for most people to take in.
Well it's not the Lumberjane way!
"I've noticed. Rosie had a similar attitude when she found me here and offered me a job.
"It was refreshing."
"So you really DO care about teamwork."
Of course. Rosie wants me to make sure you girls are looking out for one another--
Aaaaw!
--and that you can tie really great knots.
OK, enough squishy emotion time!

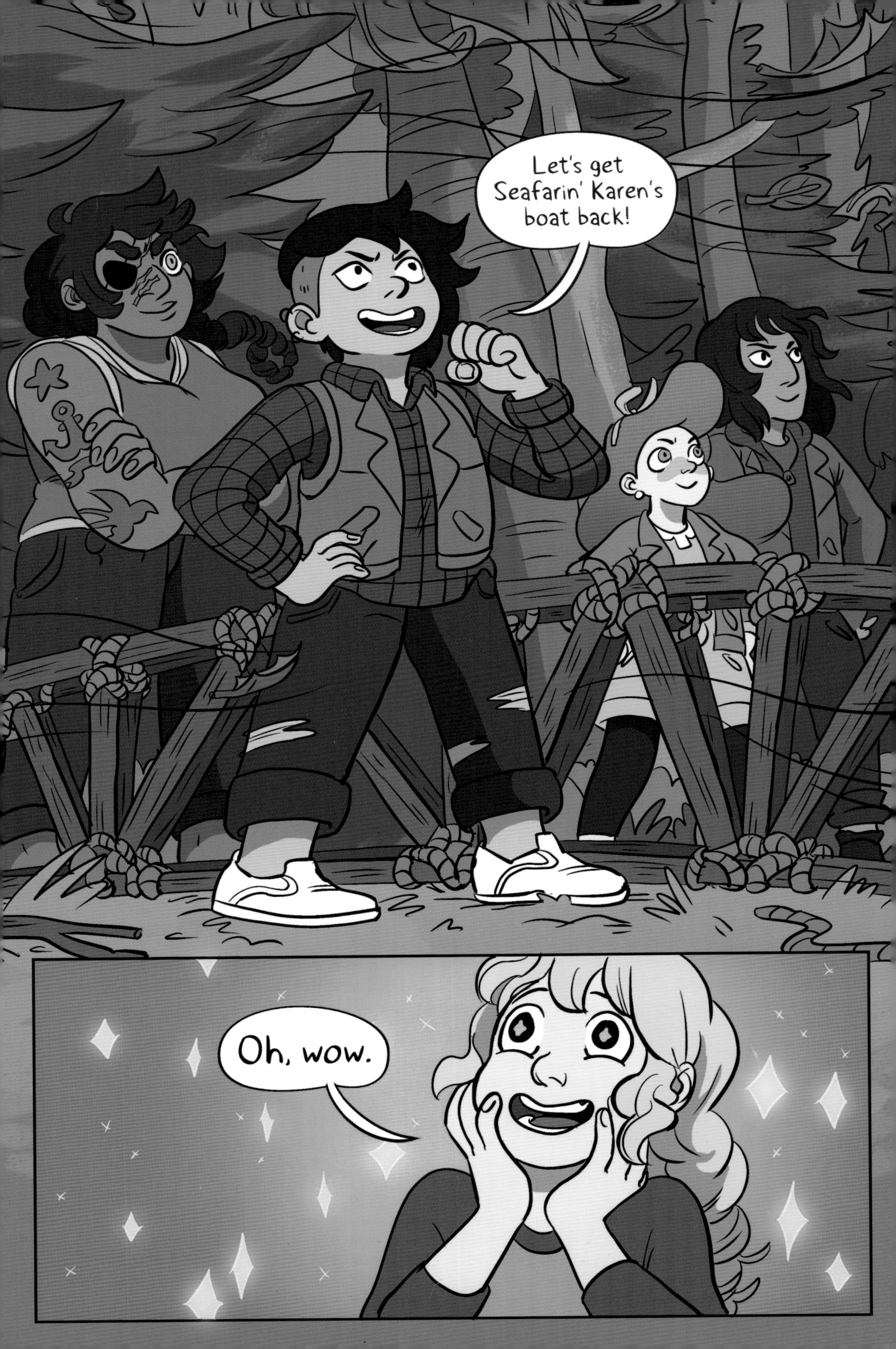

Let's get Seafarin' Karen's boat back!
Oh, wow.

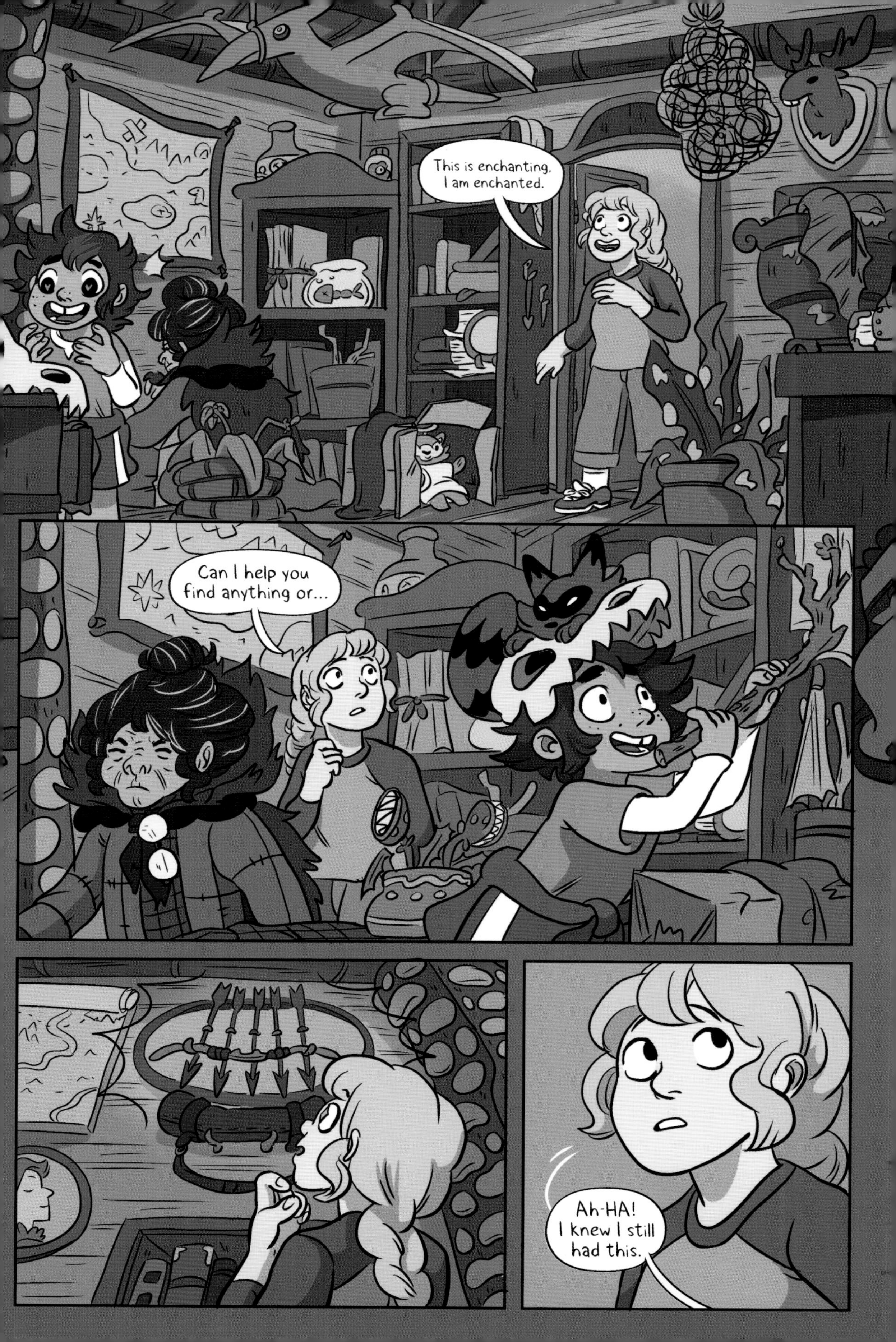
This is enchanting, I am enchanted.
Can I help you find anything or...
Ah-HA! I knew I still had this.

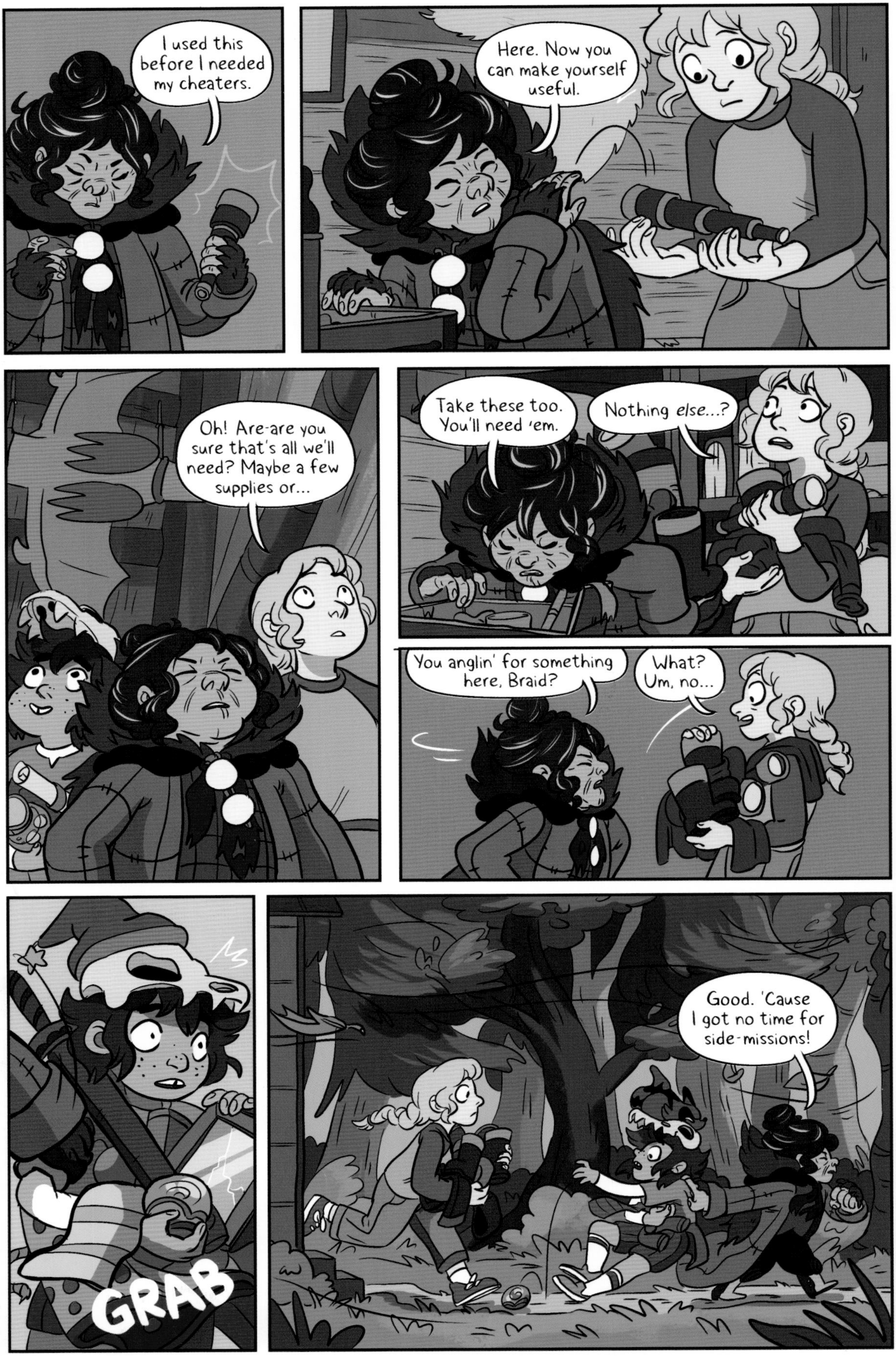

I used this before I needed my cheaters.
Here. Now you can make yourself useful.
Oh! Are-are you sure that's all we'll need? Maybe a few supplies or...
Take these too. You'll need 'em.
Nothing *else*...?
You anglin' for something here, Braid?
What? Um, no...
GRAB
Good. 'Cause I got no time for side-missions!

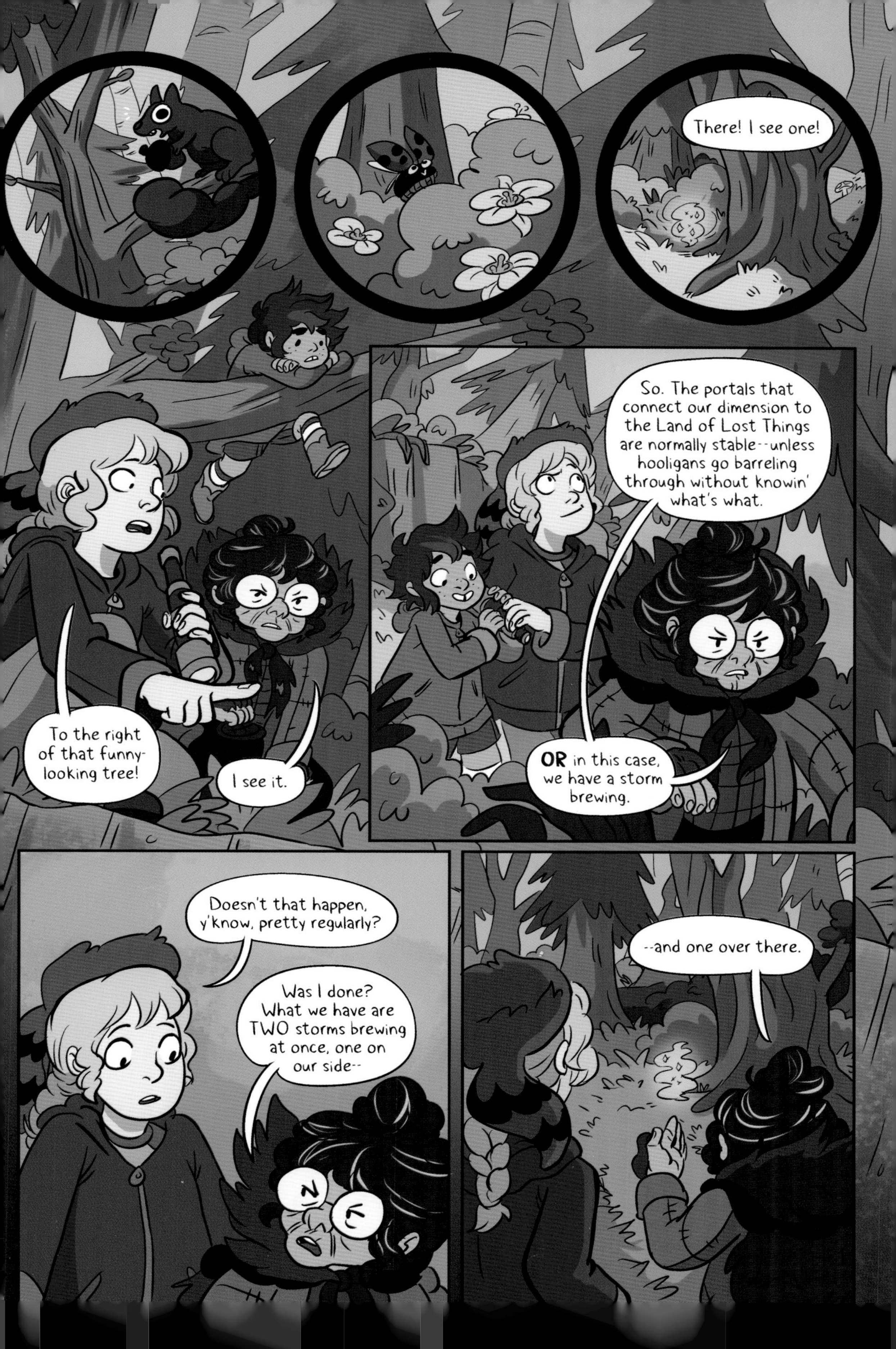
There! I see one!
To the right of that funny-looking tree!
I see it.
So. The portals that connect our dimension to the Land of Lost Things are normally stable--unless hooligans go barreling through without knowin' what's what.
OR in this case, we have a storm brewing.
Doesn't that happen, y'know, pretty regularly?
Was I done? What we have are TWO storms brewing at once, one on our side--
--and one over there.

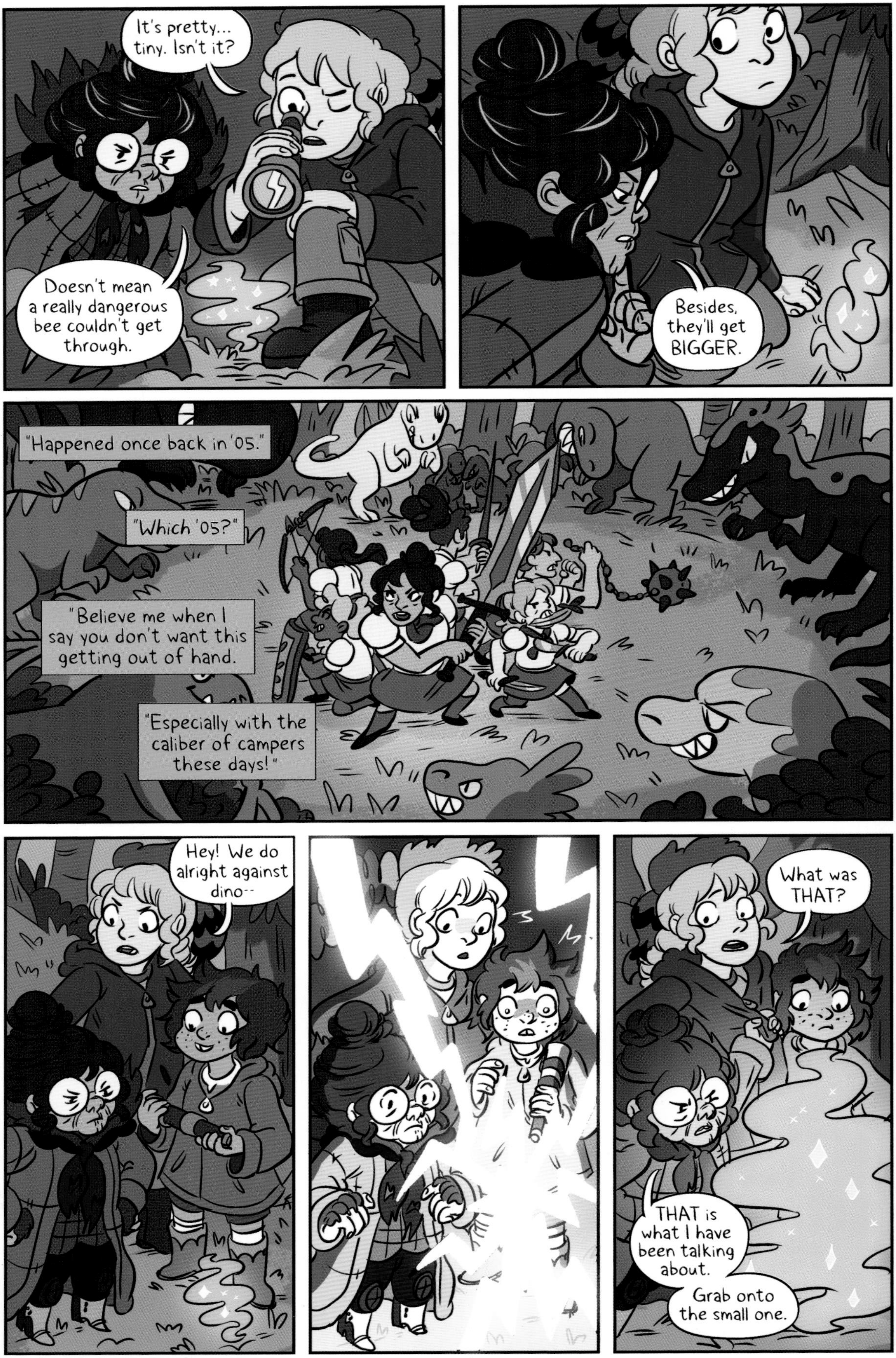
It's pretty... tiny. Isn't it?
Doesn't mean a really dangerous bee couldn't get through.
Besides, they'll get BIGGER.
"Happened once back in '05."
"Which '05?"
"Believe me when I say you don't want this getting out of hand.
"Especially with the caliber of campers these days!"
Hey! We do alright against dino--
What was THAT?
THAT is what I have been talking about.
Grab onto the small one.

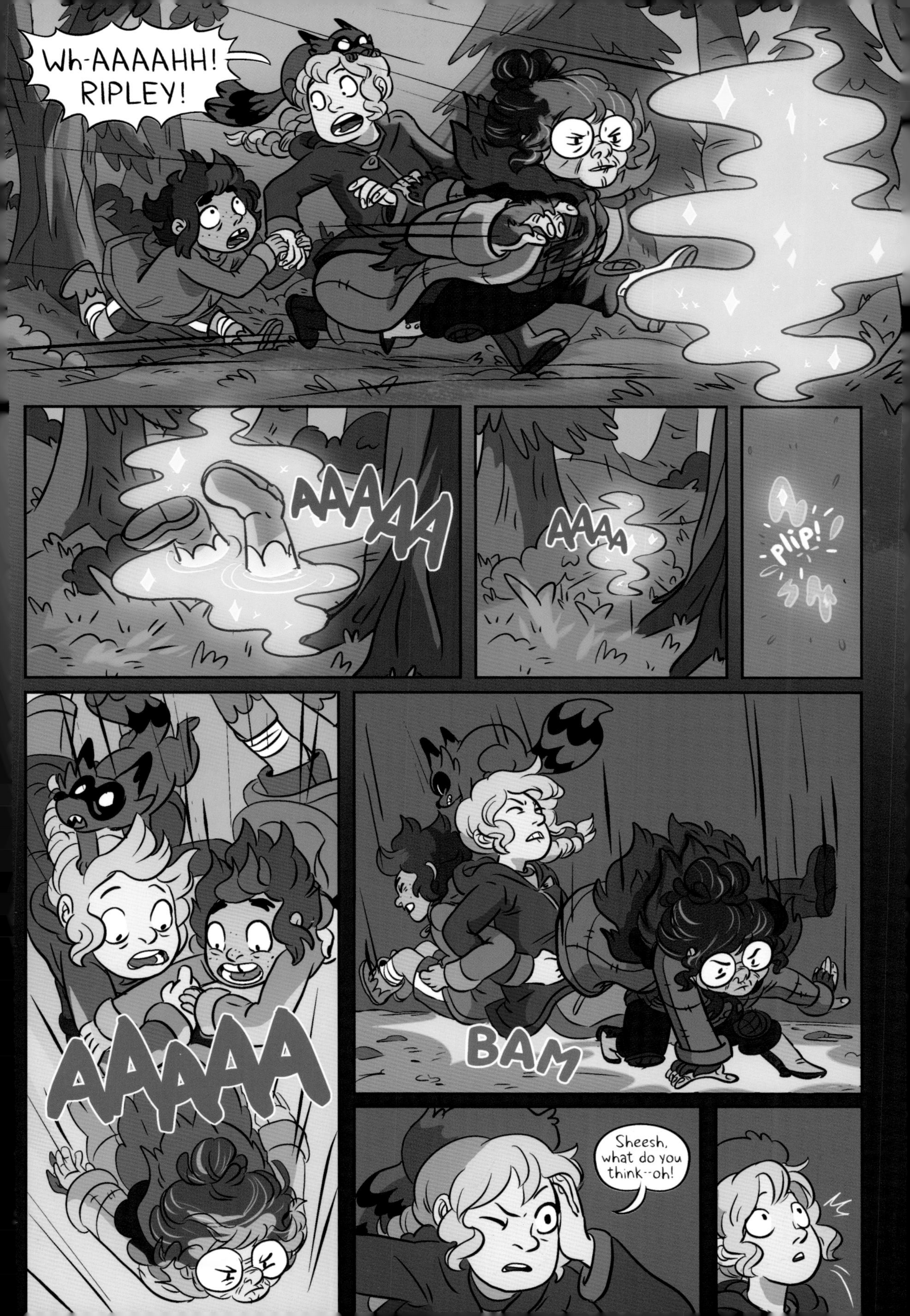
Wh-AAAAHH! RIPLEY!
AAAAAA
AAAA
plip!
AAAAA
BAM
Sheesh, what do you think--oh!

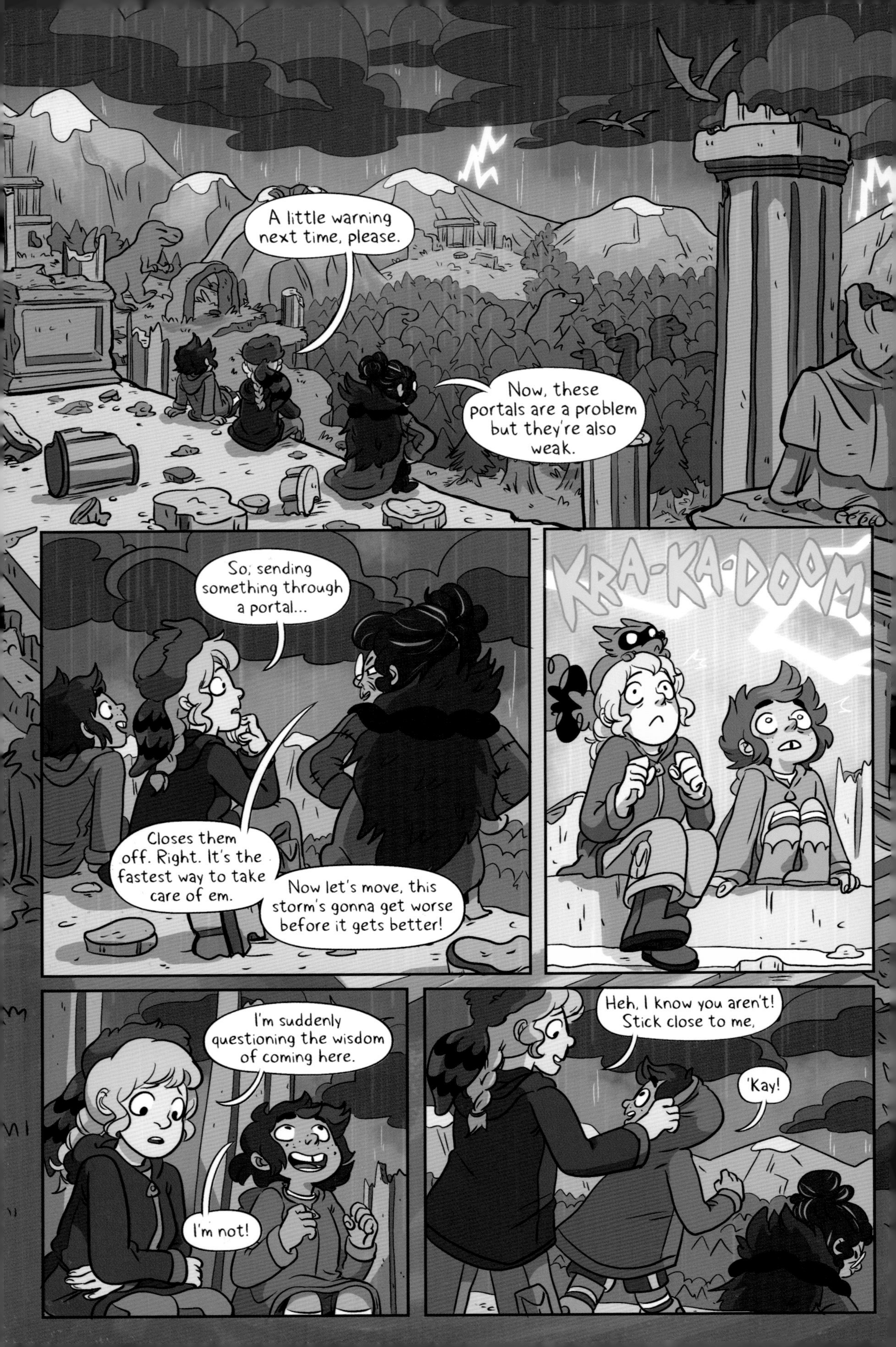

A little warning next time, please.
Now, these portals are a problem but they're also weak.
So; sending something through a portal...
Closes them off. Right. It's the fastest way to take care of em.
Now let's move, this storm's gonna get worse before it gets better!
KRA-KA-DOOM
I'm suddenly questioning the wisdom of coming here.
I'm not!
Heh, I know you aren't! Stick close to me,
'Kay!

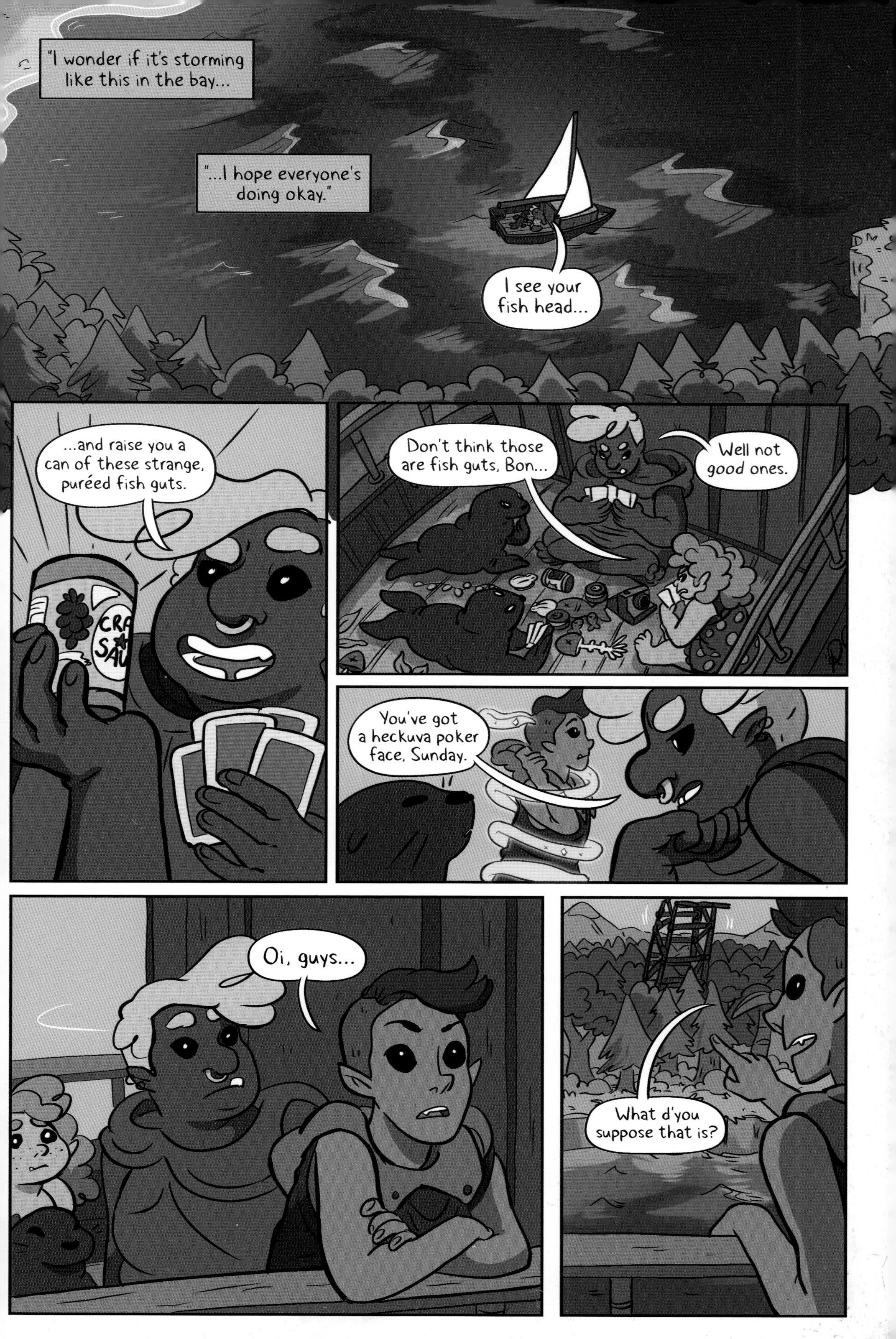
"I wonder if it's storming like this in the bay...
"...I hope everyone's doing okay."
I see your fish head...
...and raise you a can of these strange, puréed fish guts.
Don't think those are fish guts, Bon...
Well not good ones.
You've got a heckuva poker face, Sunday.
Oi, guys...
What d'you suppose that is?

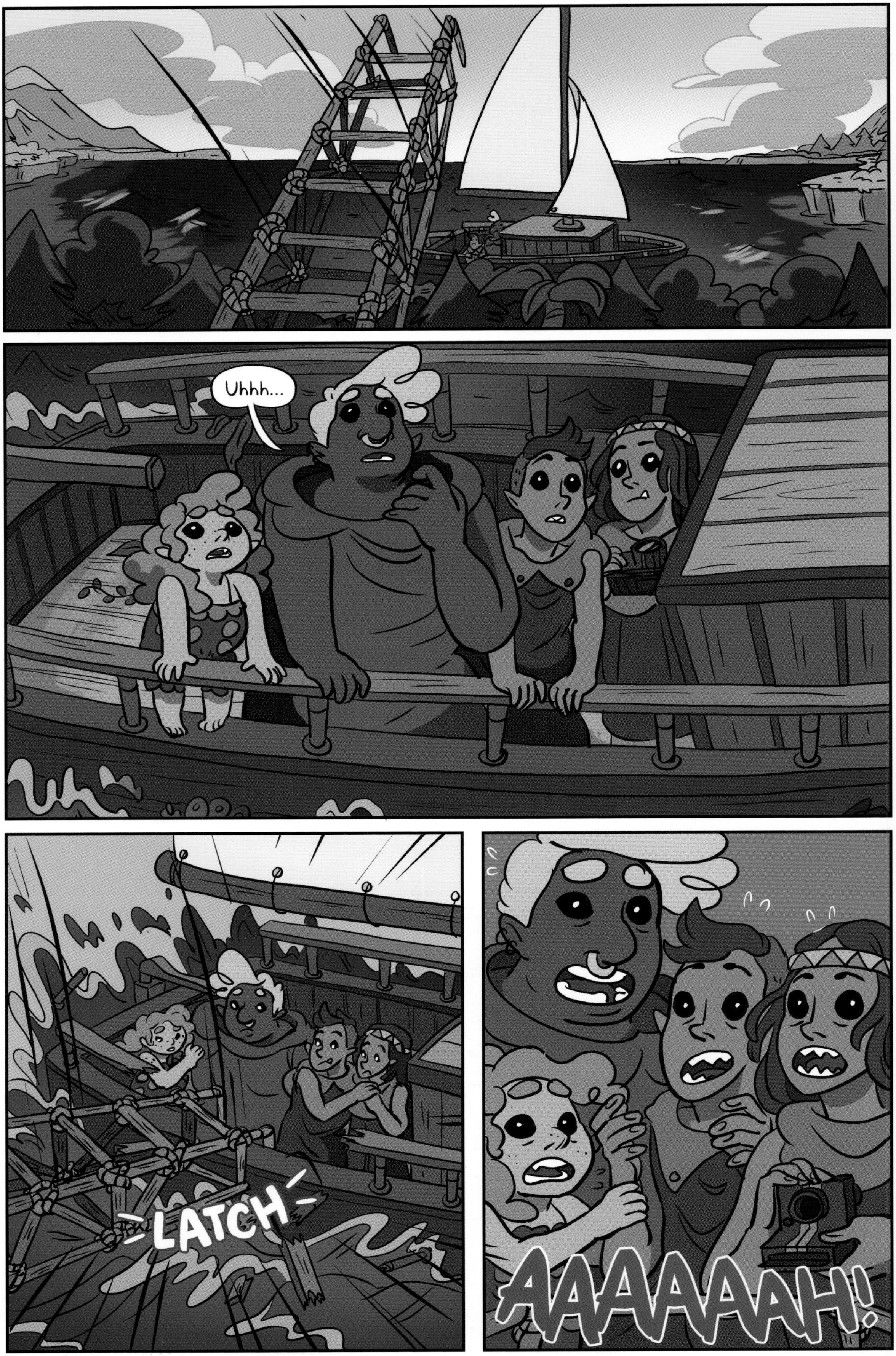
Uhhh...
LATCH
AAAAAAH!

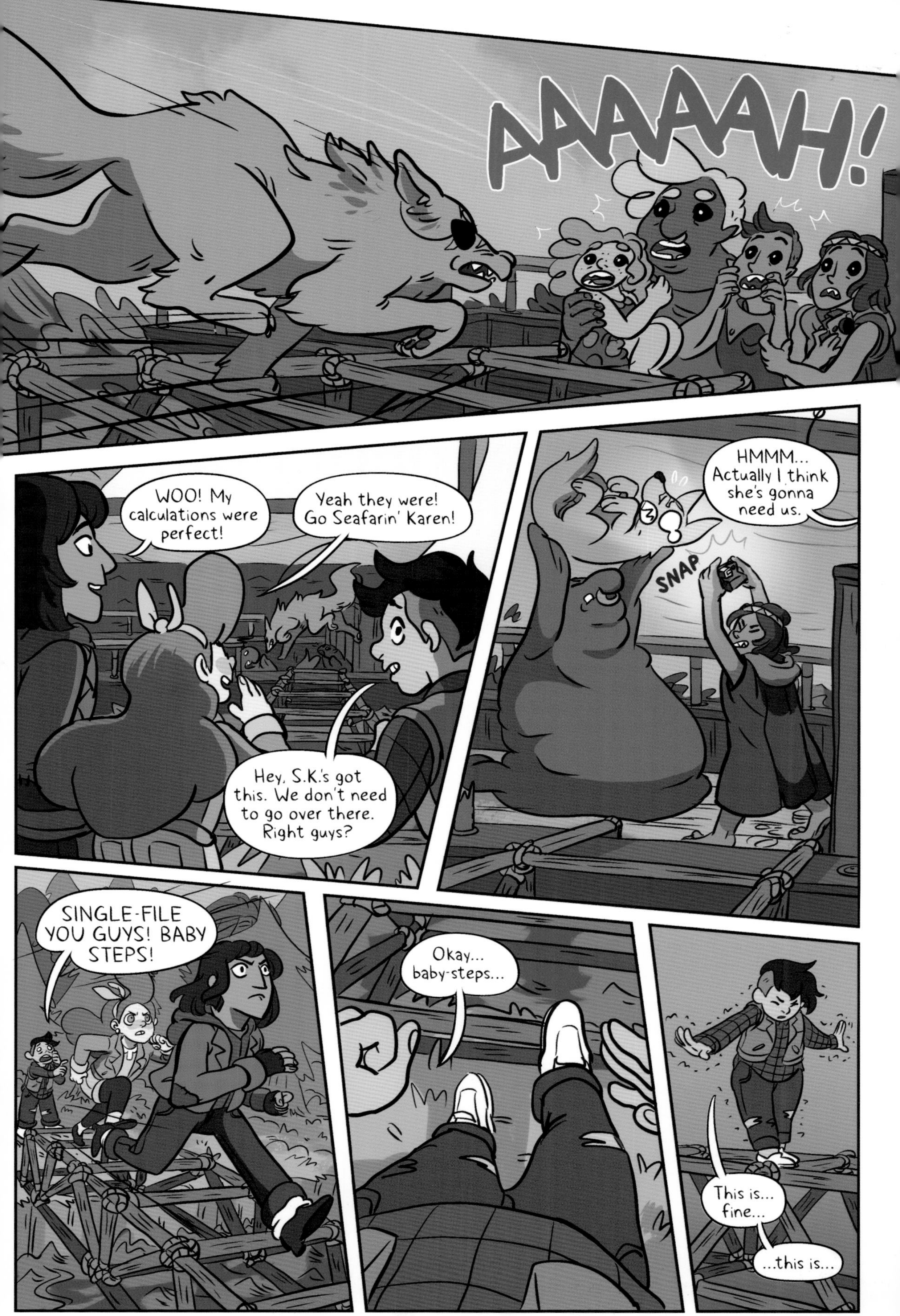
AAAAAH!
WOO! My calculations were perfect!
Yeah they were! Go Seafarin' Karen!
Hey, S.K.'s got this. We don't need to go over there. Right guys?
HMMM... Actually I think she's gonna need us.
SNAP
SINGLE-FILE YOU GUYS! BABY STEPS!
Okay... baby-steps...
This is... fine...
...this is...

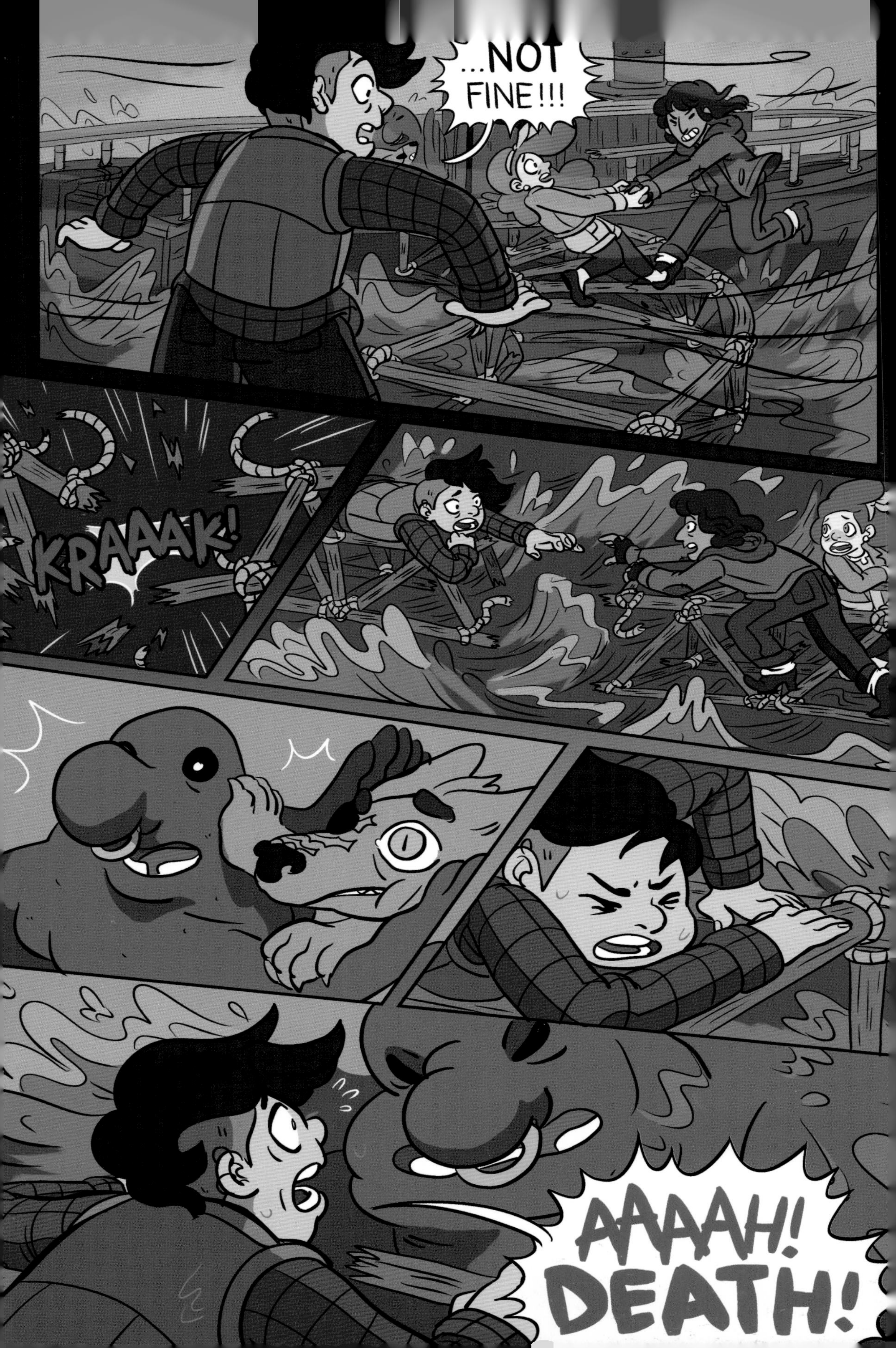
...NOT FINE!!!
KRAAAK!
AAAAH! DEATH!

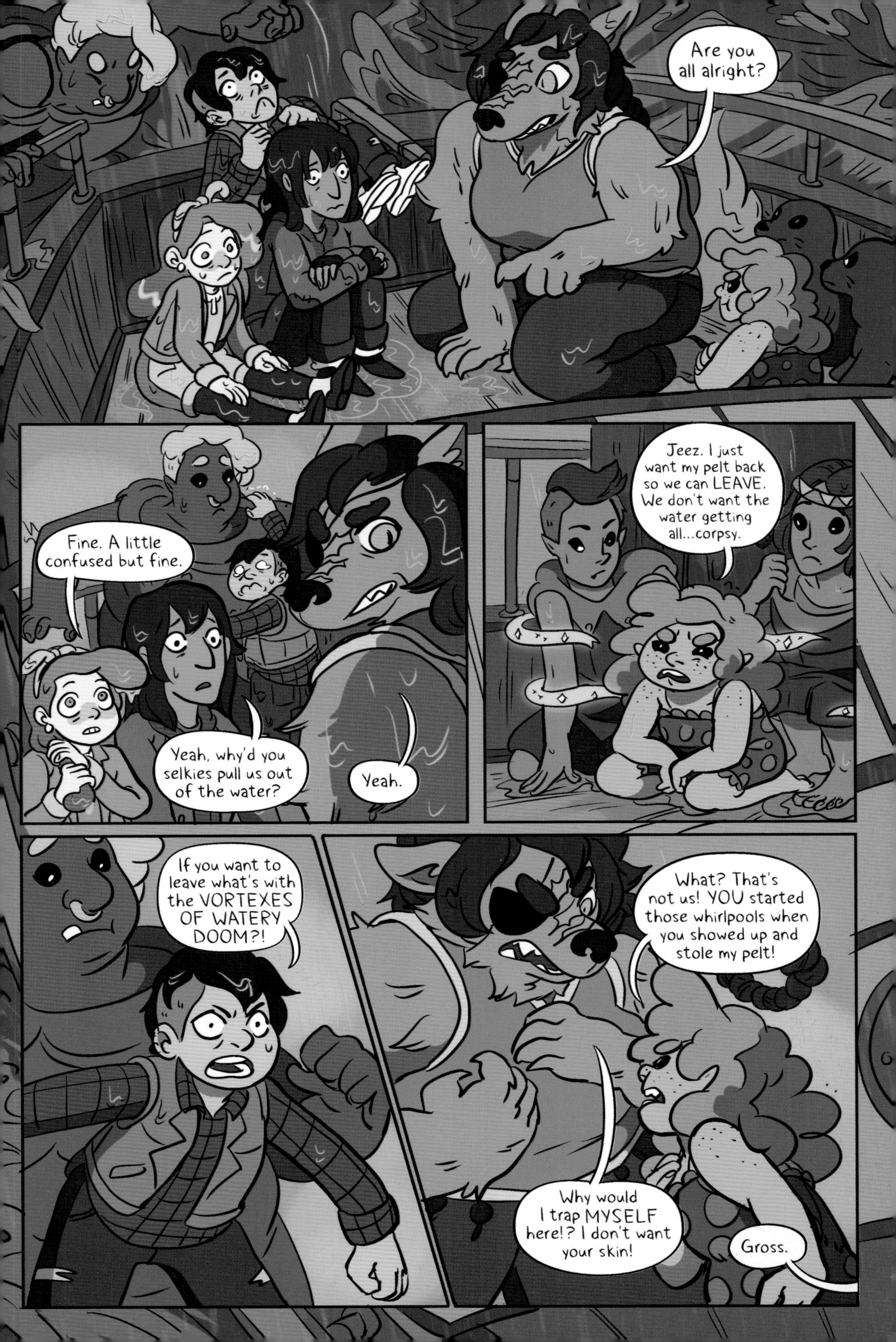
Are you all alright?
Fine. A little confused but fine.
Yeah, why'd you selkies pull us out of the water?
Yeah.
Jeez. I just want my pelt back so we can LEAVE. We don't want the water getting all...corpsy.
If you want to leave what's with the VORTEXES OF WATERY DOOM?!
What? That's not us! YOU started those whirlpools when you showed up and stole my pelt!
Why would I trap MYSELF here!? I don't want your skin!
Gross.

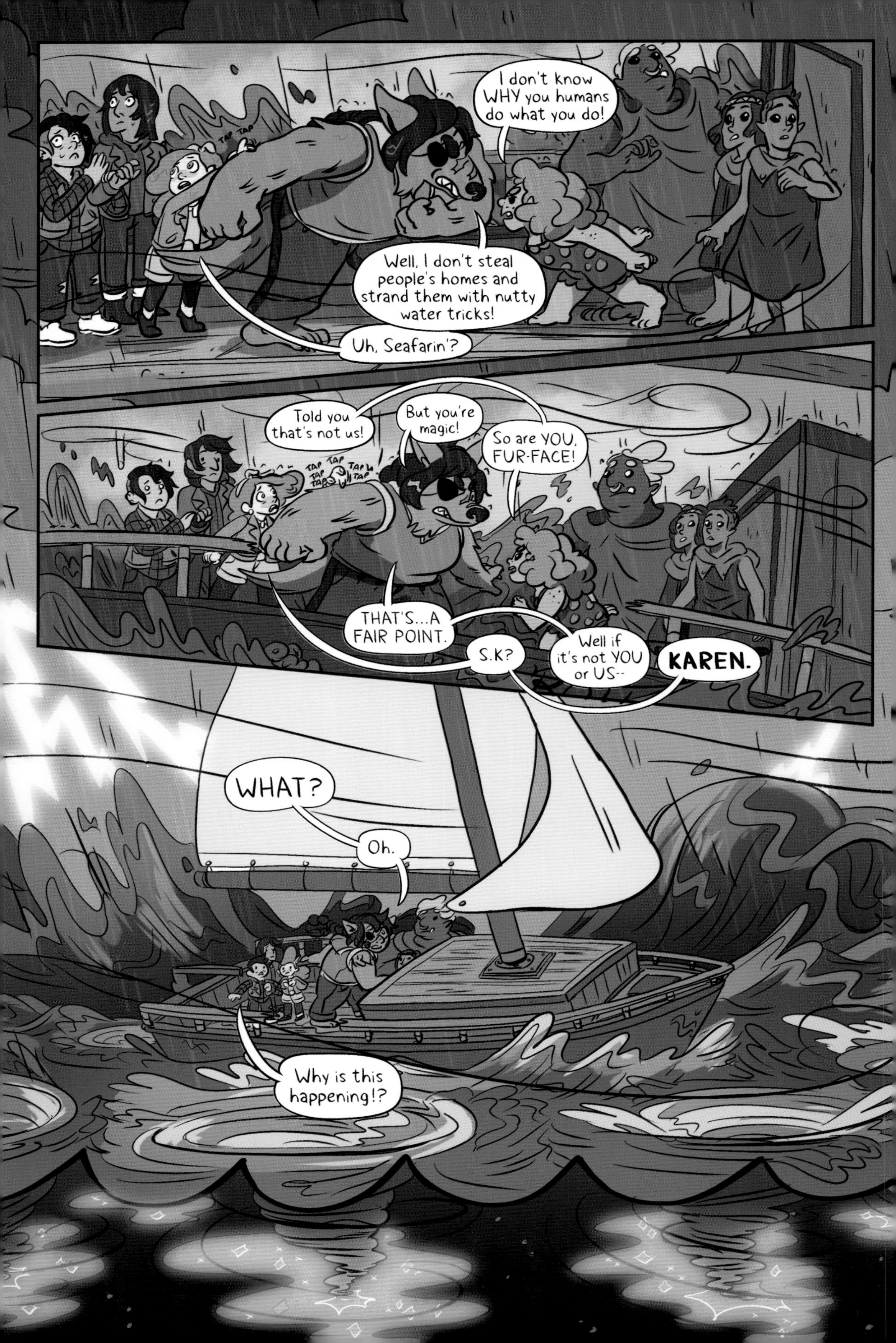

I don't know WHY you humans do what you do!
Well, I don't steal people's homes and strand them with nutty water tricks!
TAP TAP
Uh, Seafarin'?
Told you that's not us!
But you're magic!
So are YOU, FUR-FACE!
TAP TAP TAP TAP TAP TAP TAP
THAT'S...A FAIR POINT.
S.K?
Well if it's not YOU or US--
KAREN.
WHAT?
Oh.
Why is this happening!?

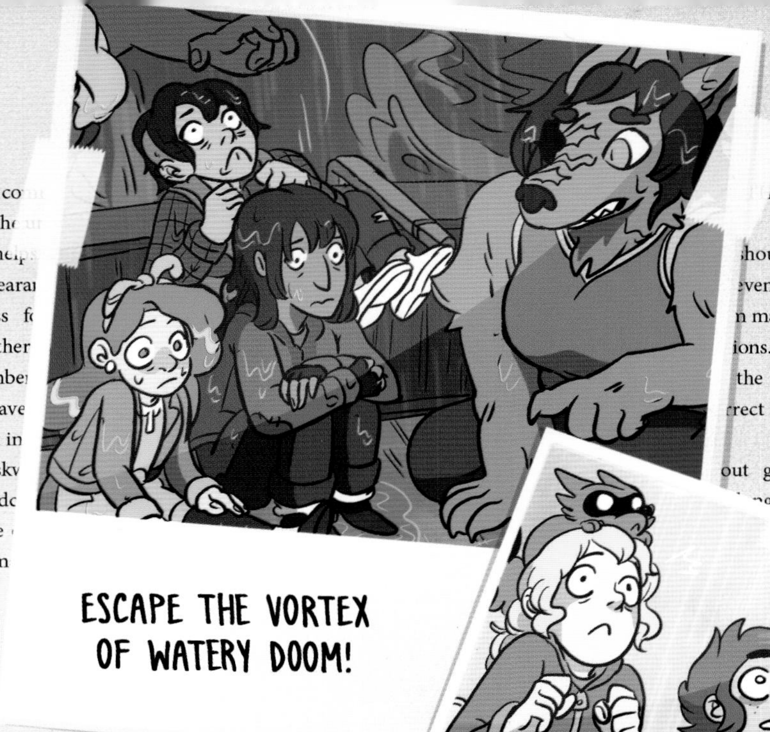
ESCAPE THE VORTEX
OF WATERY DOOM!

will co...

The ...
It help...
appearan...
dress fo...
Further...
Lumber...
to have...
part in...
Thiskv...
Hardc...
have ...
them...

...HE UNIFORM

...should be worn at camp ...events when Lumberjanes ...n may also be worn at other ...ions. It should be worn as a ... the uniform dress with ...rrect shoes, and stocking or

...out grows her uniform or ...g to another Lumberjane. ...signia she has ... her ... her

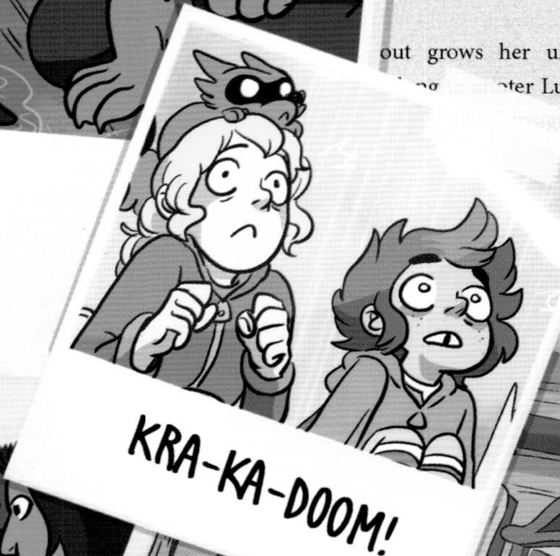
KRA-KA-DOOM!

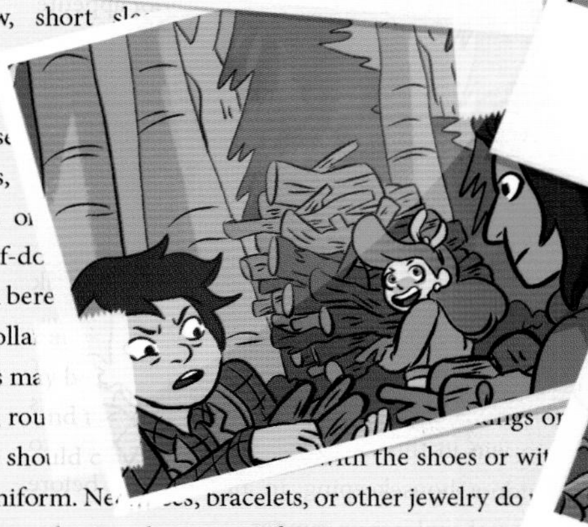

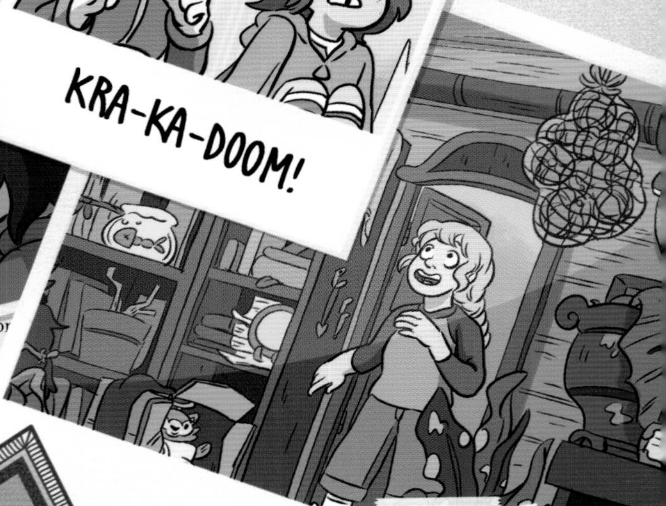

The ...
yellow, short sl...
emb...
the w...
choose...
slacks, ...
made o...
out-of-do...
green bere...
the colla...
Shoes ma...
heels, rou... ...kings or
socks shou... ...ith the shoes or wi...
the uniform. Ne... ...s, bracelets, or other jewelry do ...
belong with a Lumberjane uniform.

HOW TO WEAR THE UNIFOR...

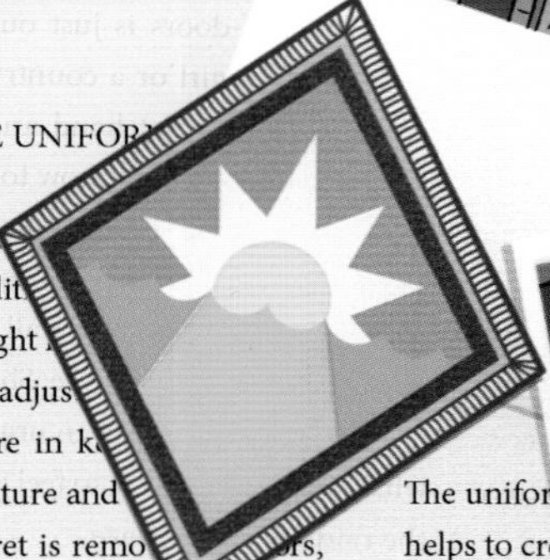

To look well in a uniform dema... uniform be kept in good conditi... pressed. See that the skirt is the right ... height and build, that the belt is adjus... that your shoes and stockings are in k... uniform, that you watch your posture and ... with dignity and grace. If the beret is remo... ...rs, be sure that your hair is neat and kept in pla... with an insonspicuous clip or ribbon. When you wear a Lumberjane uniform you are identified as a member of this organization and you should be doubly careful to conduct yourself in a way that will show everyone that courtesy and thoughtfullness are part of being a Lumberjane. People are likely to judge a whole nation by the selfishness of a few individuals, to criticize a whole family because of the misconduct of one member, and to feel unkindly toward and organization because of the

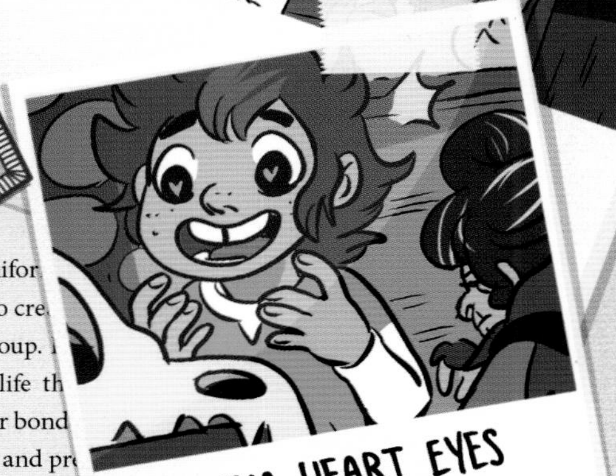
HECKA HEART EYES

The unifor... helps to cre... in a group. ... active life th... another bond... future, and pr... in order to b... Lumberjane pr... Penniquiqul Thi... ...ore Lady Types, but m... ...s will wish to have one. They can either bu... ...niform, or make it themselves from materials available at the trading post.

LUMBERJANES FIELD MANUAL
CHAPTER TWENTY-THREE

Lumberjanes "Out-of-Doors" Program Field

FOR THE HALIBUT BADGE

"Jumping in head first is always the best solution."

Life is a collection of choices. These choices help create who we become as individuals, and while everyone will have something that they might wish they could go back in time to change, we must learn to accept the events that have already happened and learn to embrace the future that we've made for ourselves. Not everything will be a choice that we're ready to make, and some of these decisions might be based on a reaction to someone else, but as a Lumberjane, we hope that every step that we take is the best one. It might not always be the case, but we have to learn to think on our feet and deal with the consequences regardless if they are positive or otherwise. *For The Halibut* badge is about making decisions without any forethought. This badge is about jumping into a situation with no knowledge of what you might find on the other end and learning how to not only make

the best of the situation, but learn how to think on your feet. Life outside of camp, and even inside of camp, might not be as forgiving as we hope it is, but we want to make sure that everyone learns how to make those split-second decisions and how to hone your instincts in order to get more positive outcomes out of every situation.

There are a few ways to obtain the *For The Halibut* badge, and they all deal with water. It is important to have already earned the basic water safety badges before you will be able to earn the *For The Halibut* badge. The first task for this badge will be up to your counselor, as they will do their best to find a challenge for you that not only meets your level of difficulty but creates a problem that has several possible answers. It will be up to you to jump into the challenge with no forewarning and solve it with the best solution. Your counselor will evaluate your task and if they need to they will

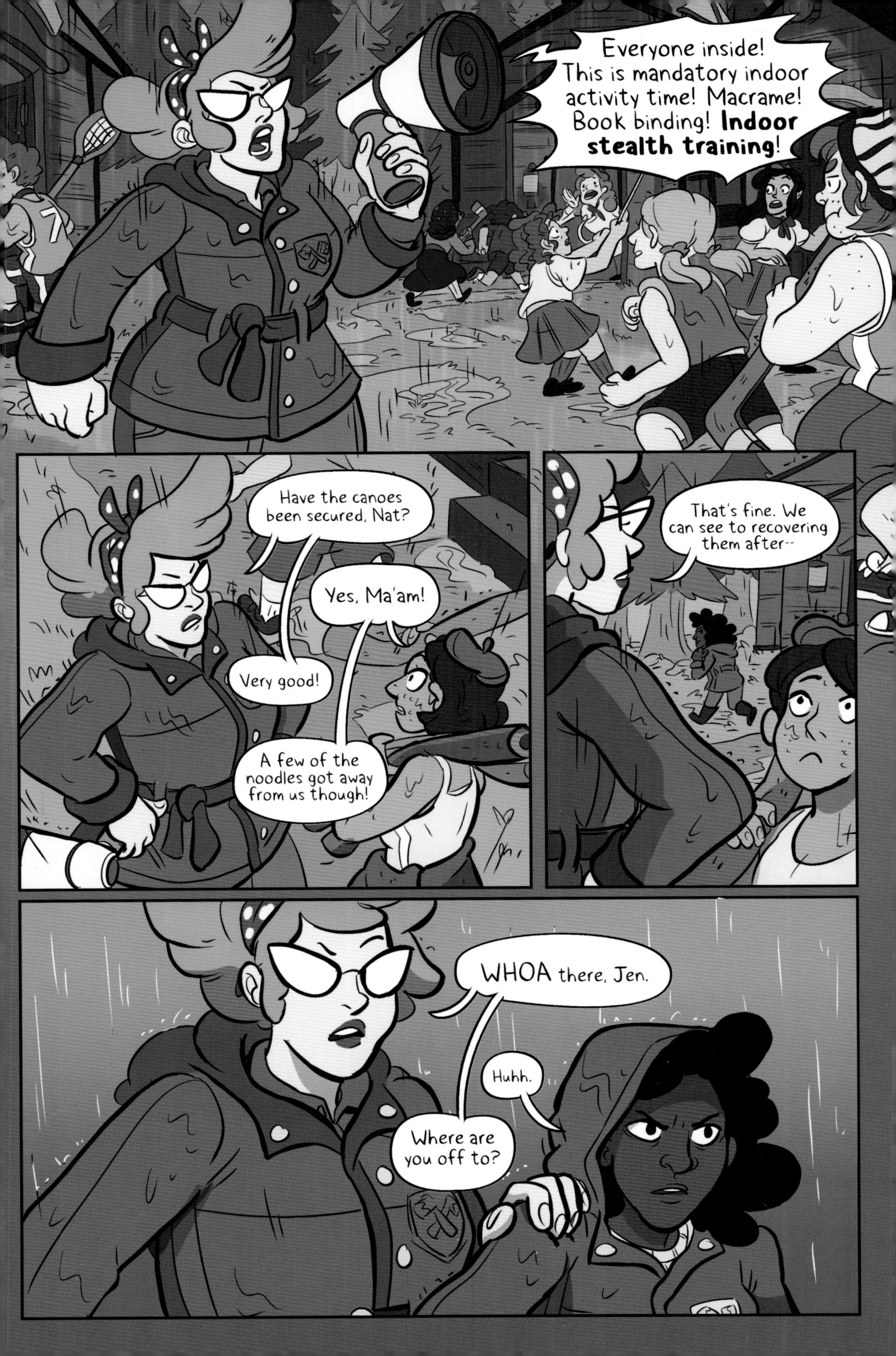
Everyone inside! This is mandatory indoor activity time! Macrame! Book binding! **Indoor stealth training**!
Have the canoes been secured, Nat?
Yes, Ma'am!
Very good!
A few of the noodles got away from us though!
That's fine. We can see to recovering them after--
WHOA there, Jen.
Huhh.
Where are you off to?

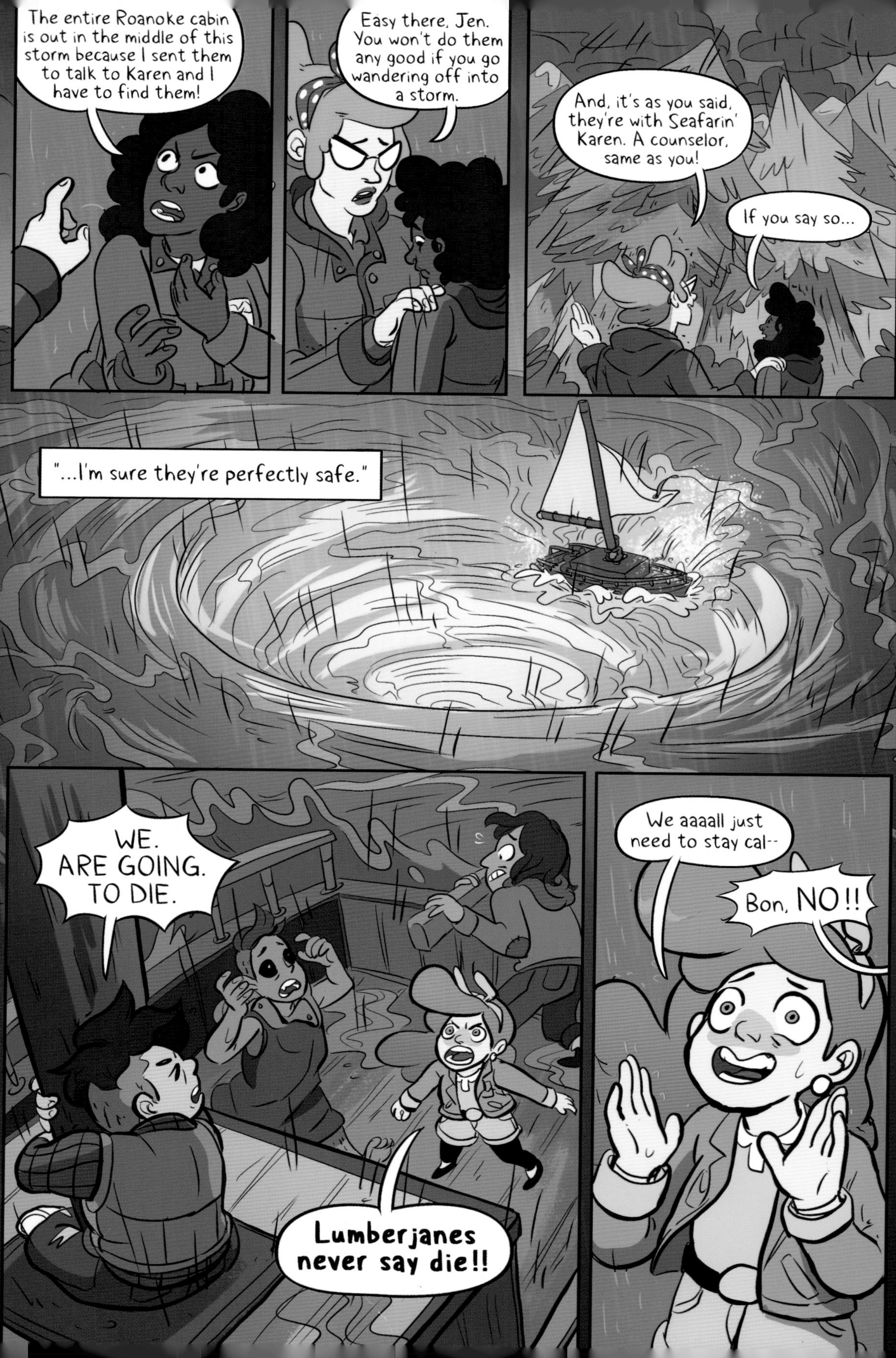
The entire Roanoke cabin is out in the middle of this storm because I sent them to talk to Karen and I have to find them!
Easy there, Jen. You won't do them any good if you go wandering off into a storm.
And, it's as you said, they're with Seafarin' Karen. A counselor, same as you!
If you say so...
"...I'm sure they're perfectly safe."
WE. ARE GOING. TO DIE.
Lumberjanes never say die!!
We aaaall just need to stay cal--
Bon, NO!!

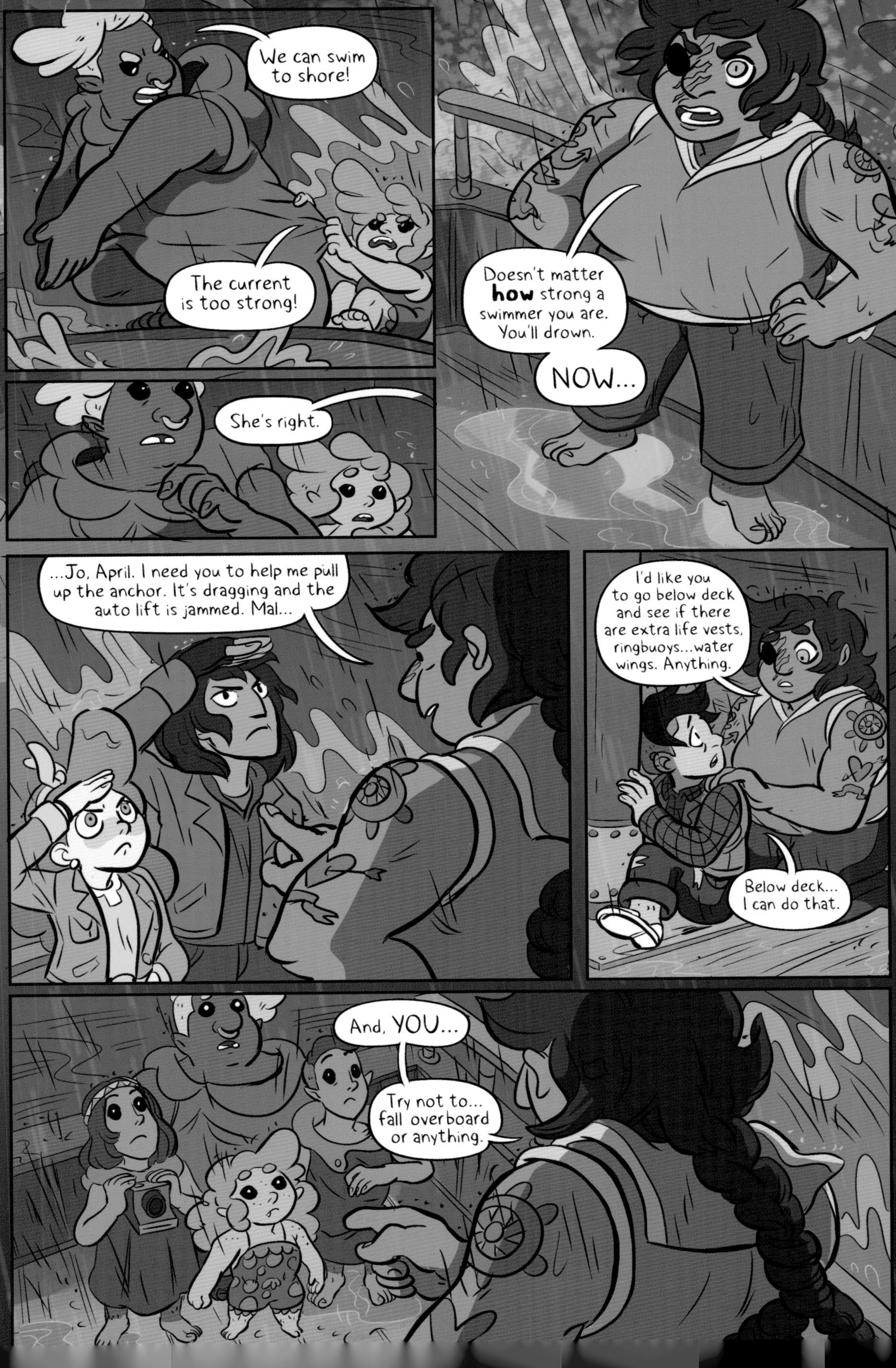
We can swim to shore!
The current is too strong!
Doesn't matter **how** strong a swimmer you are. You'll drown.
NOW...
She's right.
...Jo, April. I need you to help me pull up the anchor. It's dragging and the auto lift is jammed. Mal...
I'd like you to go below deck and see if there are extra life vests, ringbuoys...water wings. Anything.
Below deck... I can do that.
And, YOU...
Try not to... fall overboard or anything.

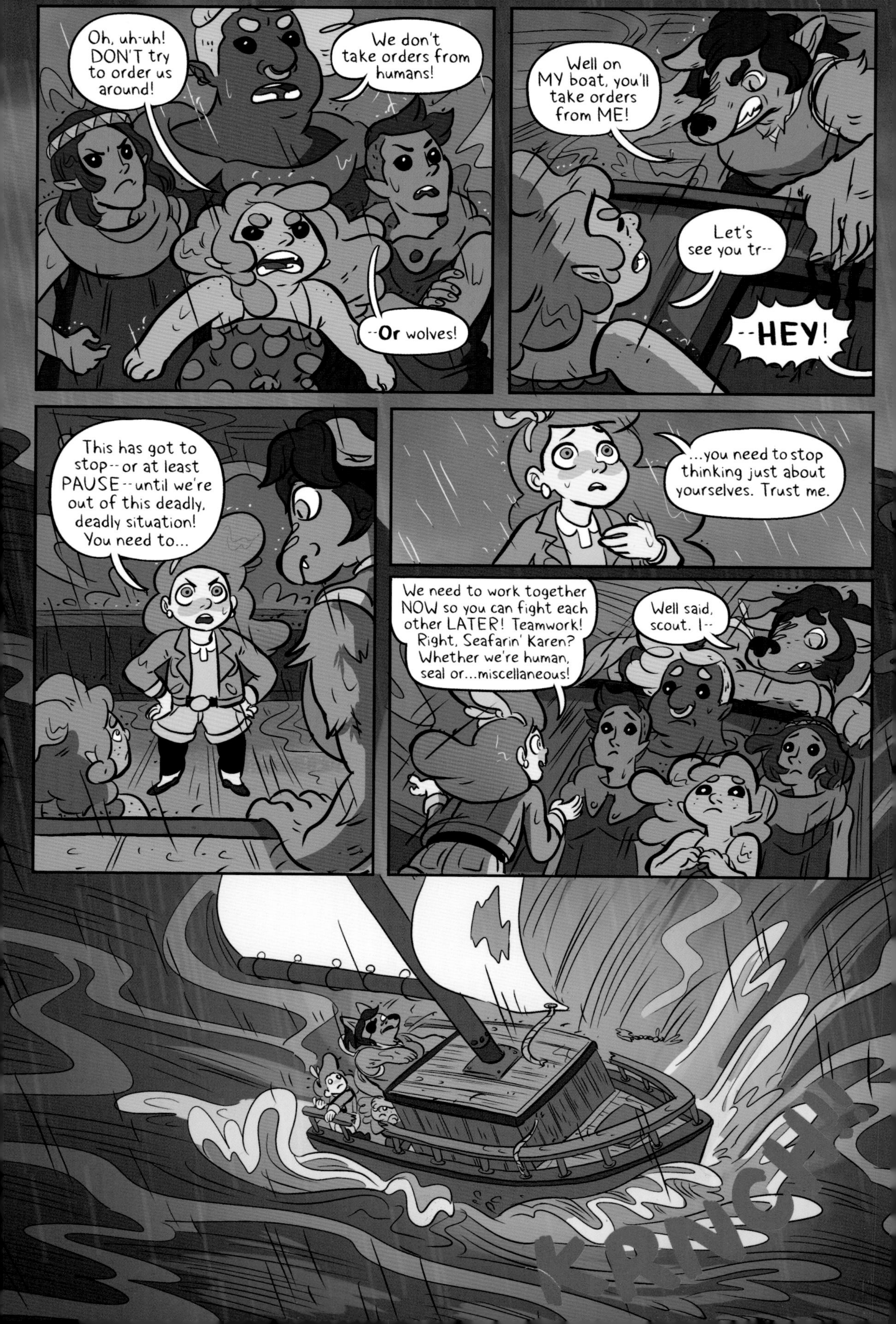
Oh, uh-uh! DON'T try to order us around!
We don't take orders from humans!
--Or wolves!
Well on MY boat, you'll take orders from ME!
Let's see you tr--
--HEY!
This has got to stop--or at least PAUSE--until we're out of this deadly, deadly situation! You need to...
...you need to stop thinking just about yourselves. Trust me.
We need to work together NOW so you can fight each other LATER! Teamwork! Right, Seafarin' Karen? Whether we're human, seal or...miscellaneous!
Well said, scout. I--
KRNCH!!

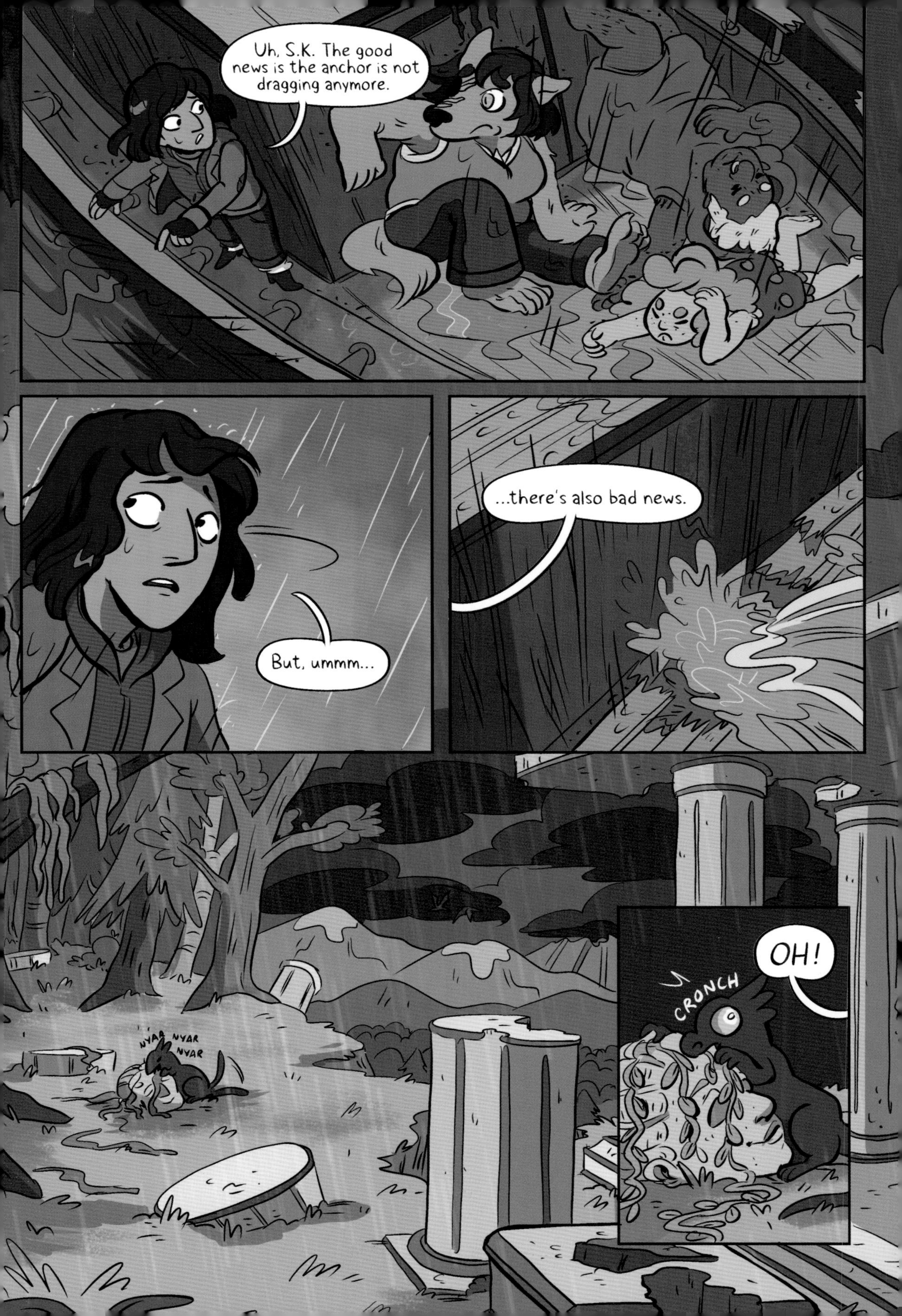

Uh, S.K. The good news is the anchor is not dragging anymore.
But, ummm...
...there's also bad news.
NYAR NYAR NYAR
CRONCH
OH!

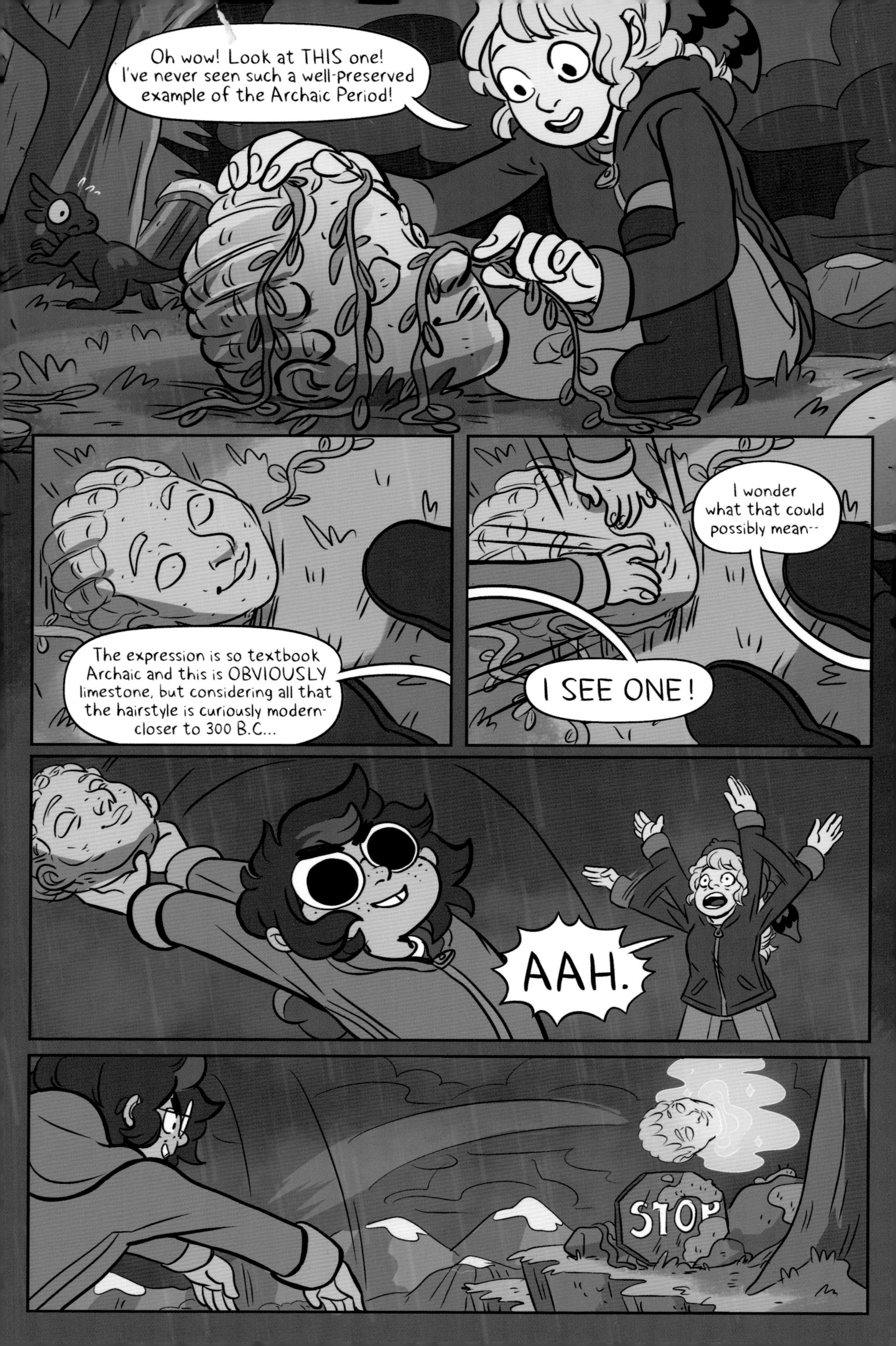
Oh wow! Look at THIS one!
I've never seen such a well-preserved
example of the Archaic Period!
The expression is so textbook
Archaic and this is OBVIOUSLY
limestone, but considering all that
the hairstyle is curiously modern-
closer to 300 B.C...
I wonder
what that could
possibly mean--
I SEE ONE!
AAH.
STOP

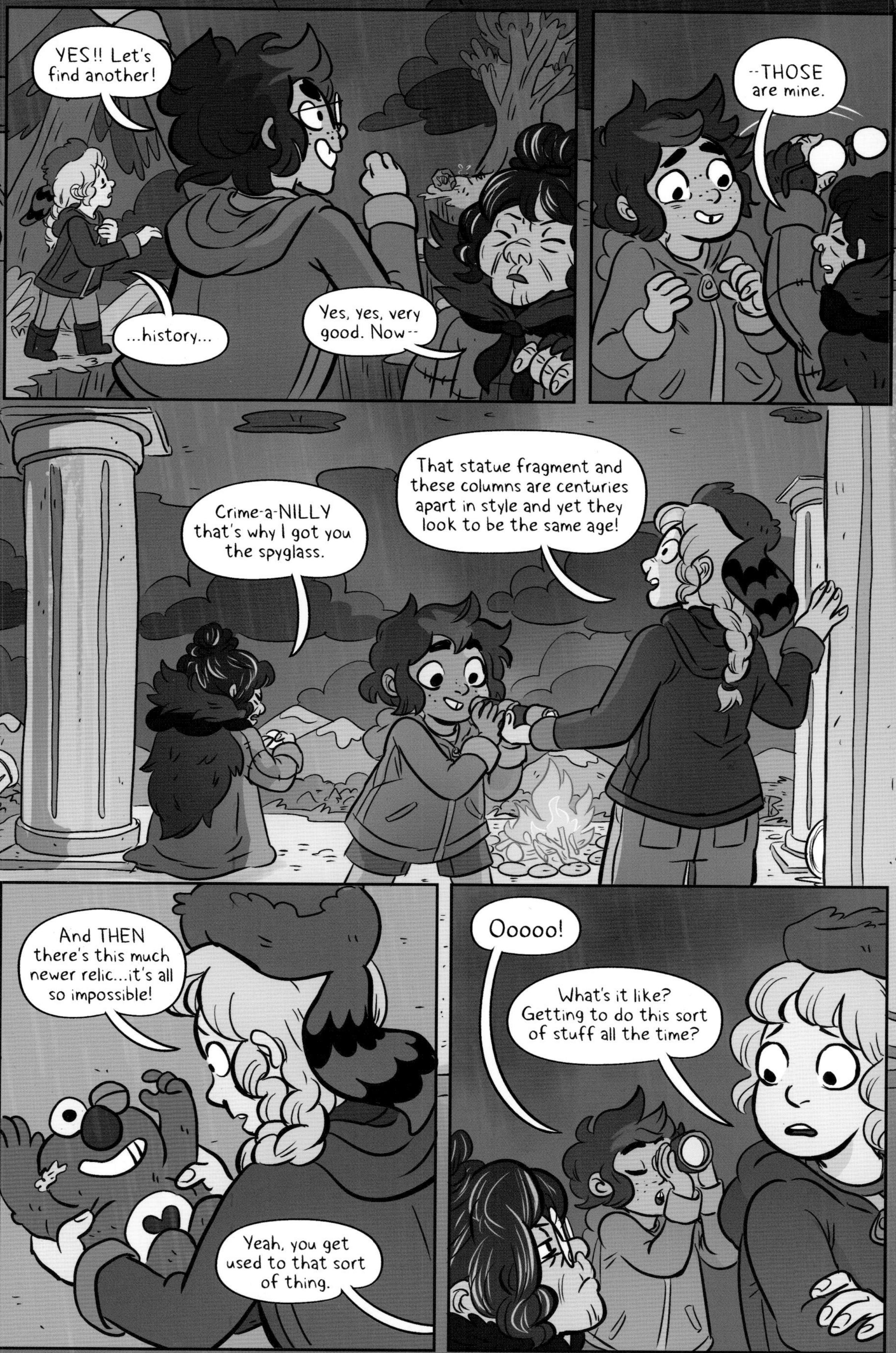
YES!! Let's find another!
...history...
Yes, yes, very good. Now--
--THOSE are mine.
Crime-a-NILLY that's why I got you the spyglass.
That statue fragment and these columns are centuries apart in style and yet they look to be the same age!
And THEN there's this much newer relic...it's all so impossible!
Yeah, you get used to that sort of thing.
Ooooo!
What's it like? Getting to do this sort of stuff all the time?

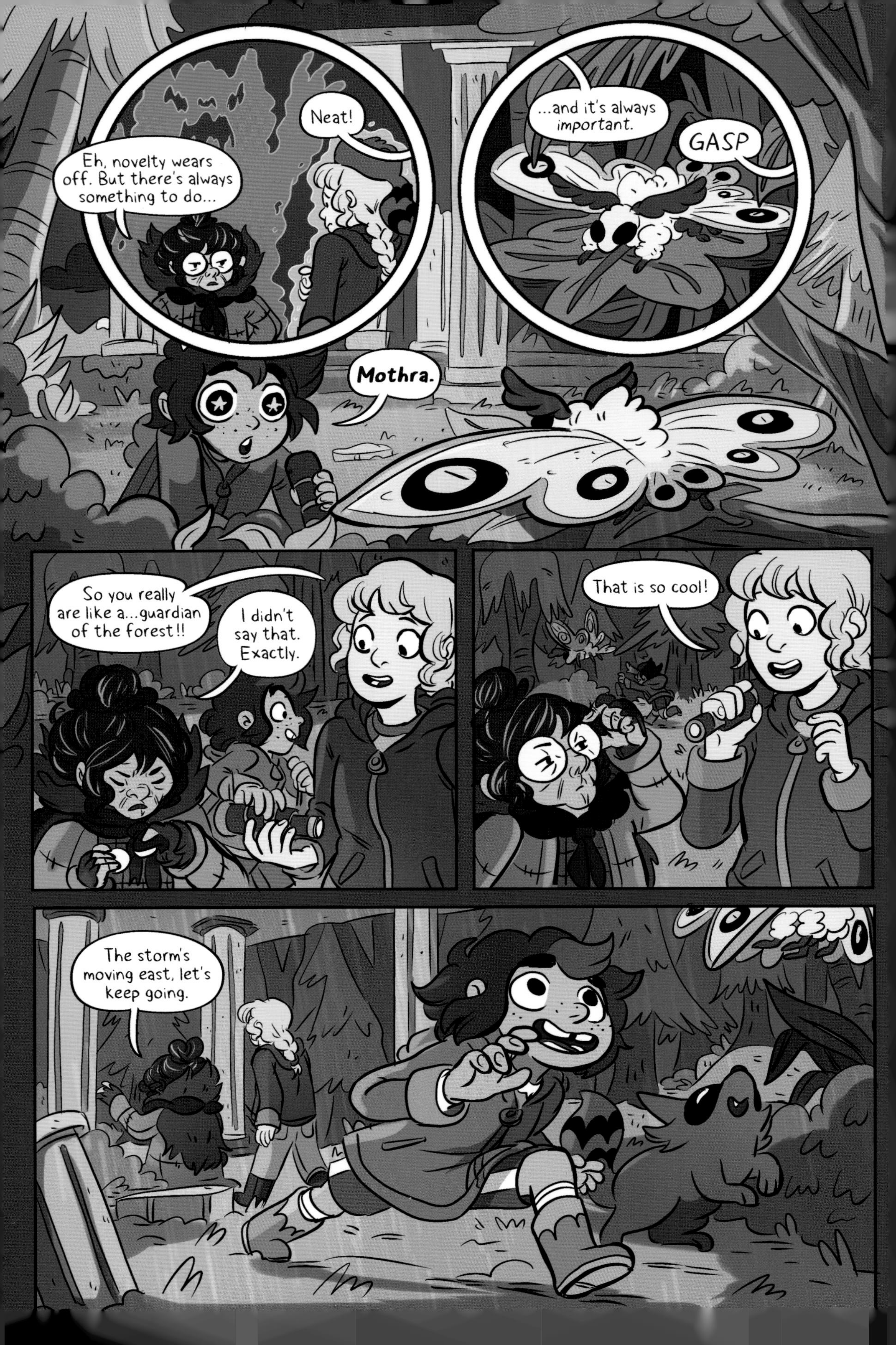
Eh, novelty wears off. But there's always something to do...
Neat!
...and it's always important.
GASP
Mothra.
So you really are like a...guardian of the forest!!
I didn't say that. Exactly.
That is so cool!
The storm's moving east, let's keep going.

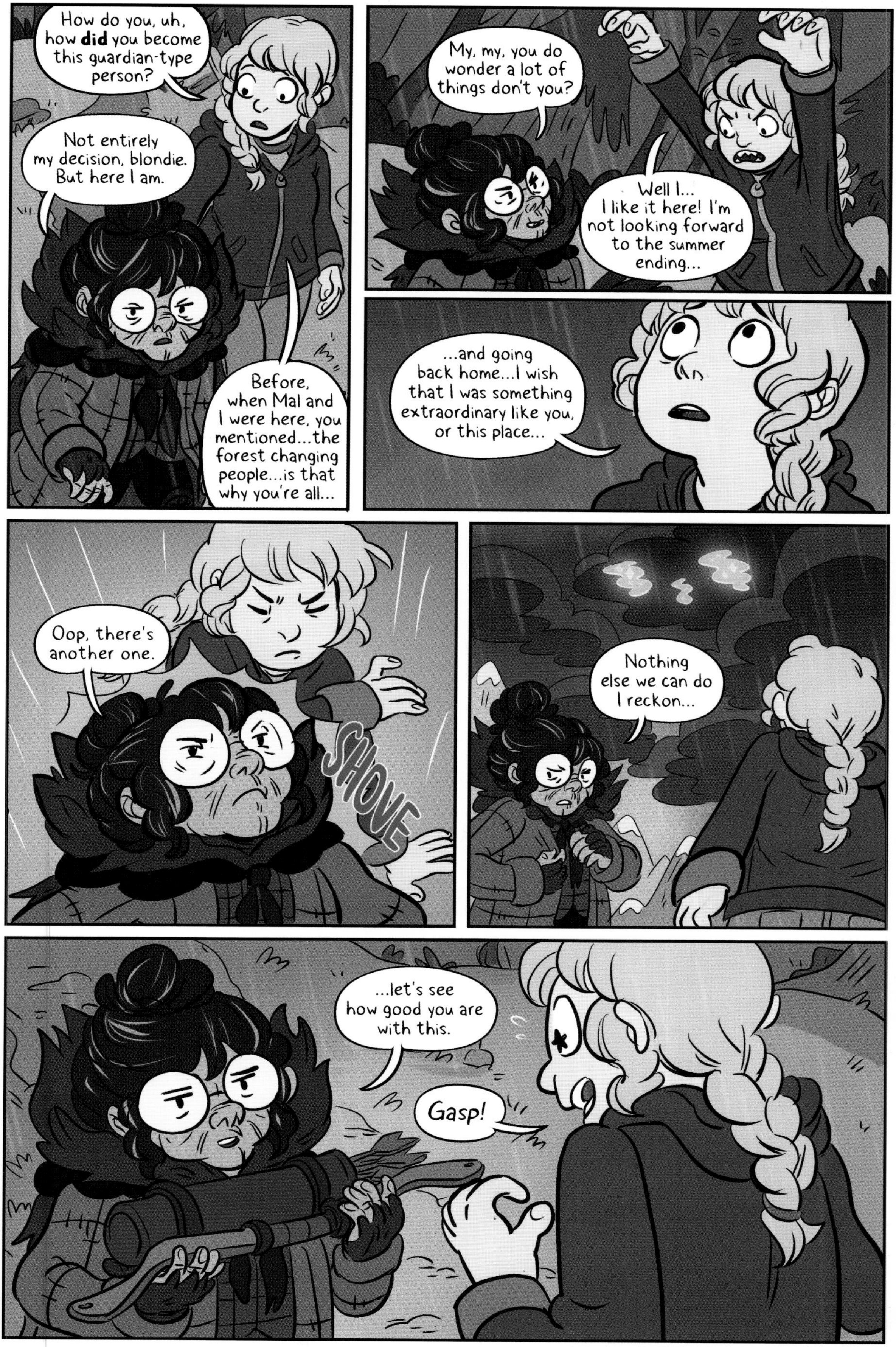
How do you, uh, how **did** you become this guardian-type person?
Not entirely my decision, blondie. But here I am.
Before, when Mal and I were here, you mentioned...the forest changing people...is that why you're all...
My, my, you do wonder a lot of things don't you?
Well I... I like it here! I'm not looking forward to the summer ending...
...and going back home...I wish that I was something extraordinary like you, or this place...
Oop, there's another one.
SHOVE
Nothing else we can do I reckon...
...let's see how good you are with this.
Gasp!

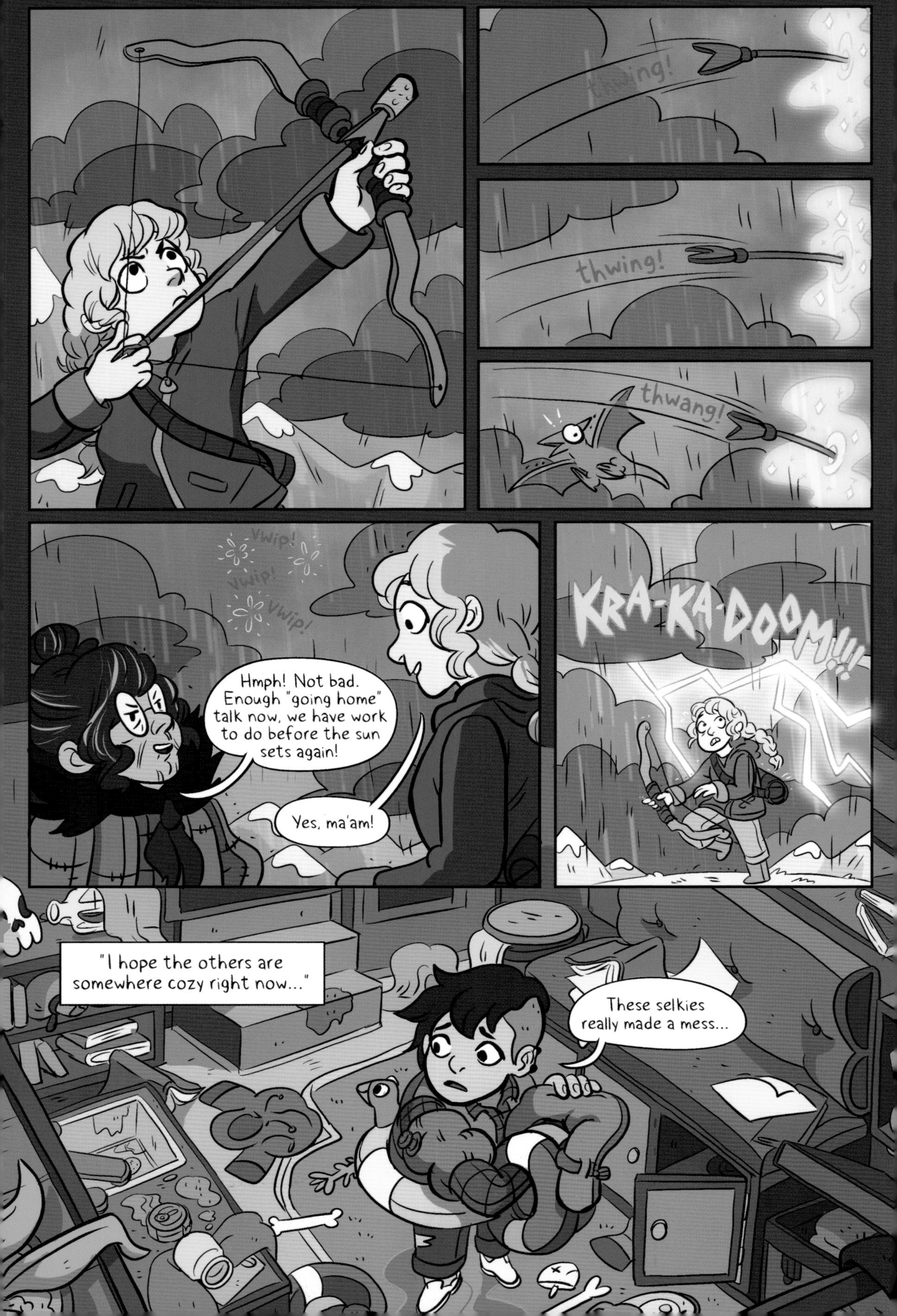
thwing!
thwing!
thwang!
vwip!
vwip!
vwip!
Hmph! Not bad. Enough "going home" talk now, we have work to do before the sun sets again!
Yes, ma'am!
KRA-KA-DOOM!!!
"I hope the others are somewhere cozy right now..."
These selkies really made a mess...

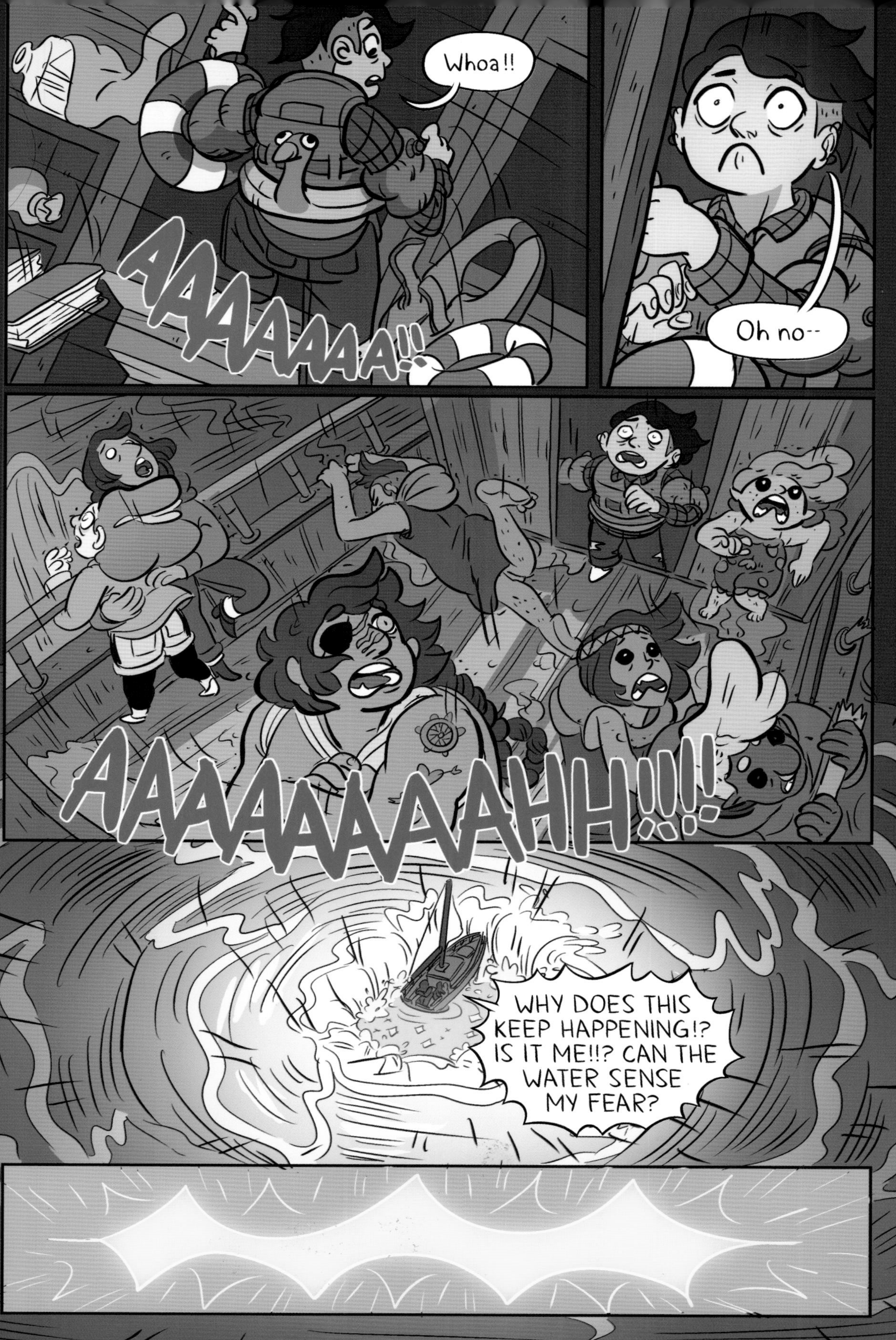
Whoa!!
AAAAAAAA!!
Oh no--
AAAAAAAAAHH!!!!
WHY DOES THIS KEEP HAPPENING!? IS IT ME!!? CAN THE WATER SENSE MY FEAR?

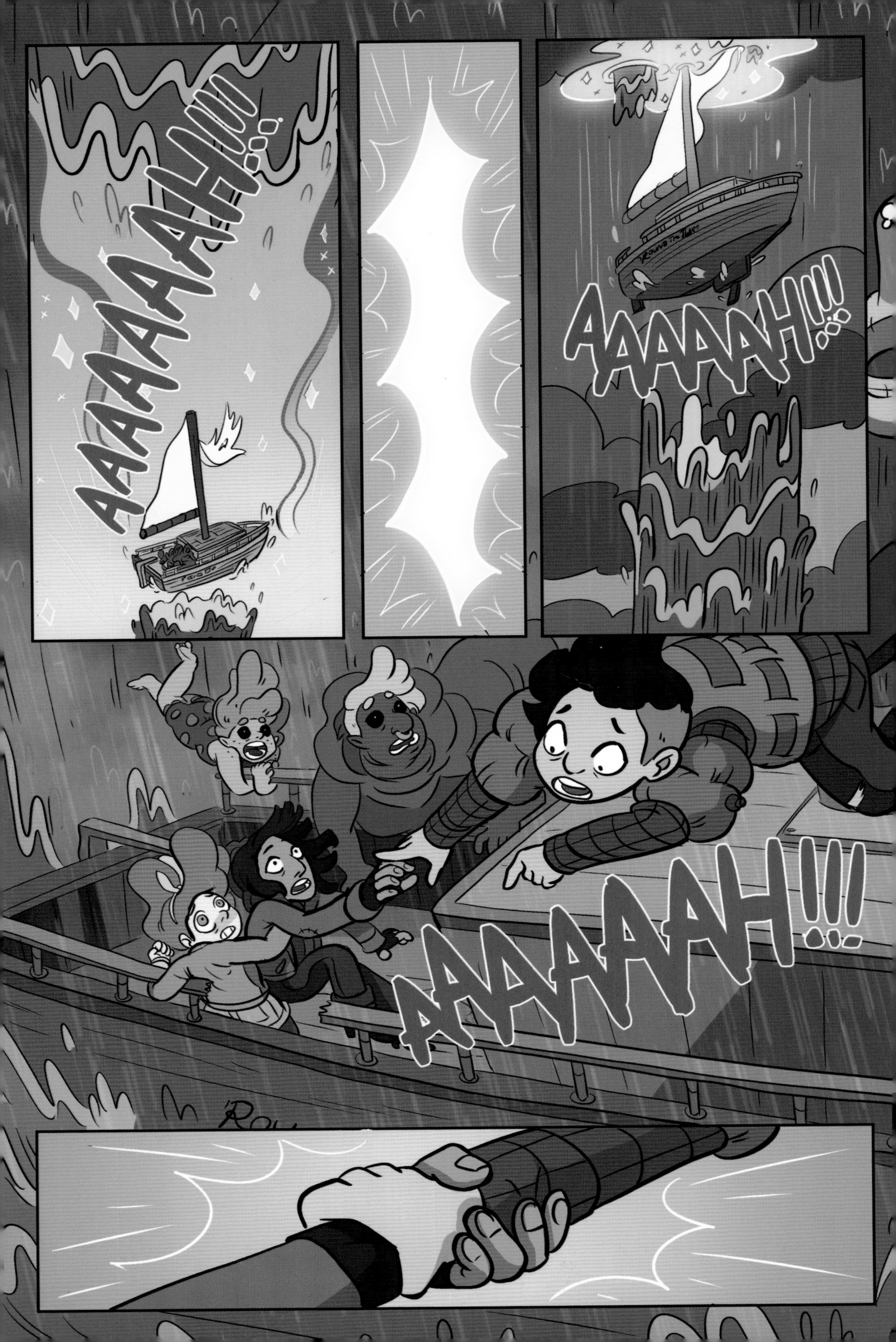
AAAAAAH!!!
AAAAAH!!!
AAAAAAH!!!

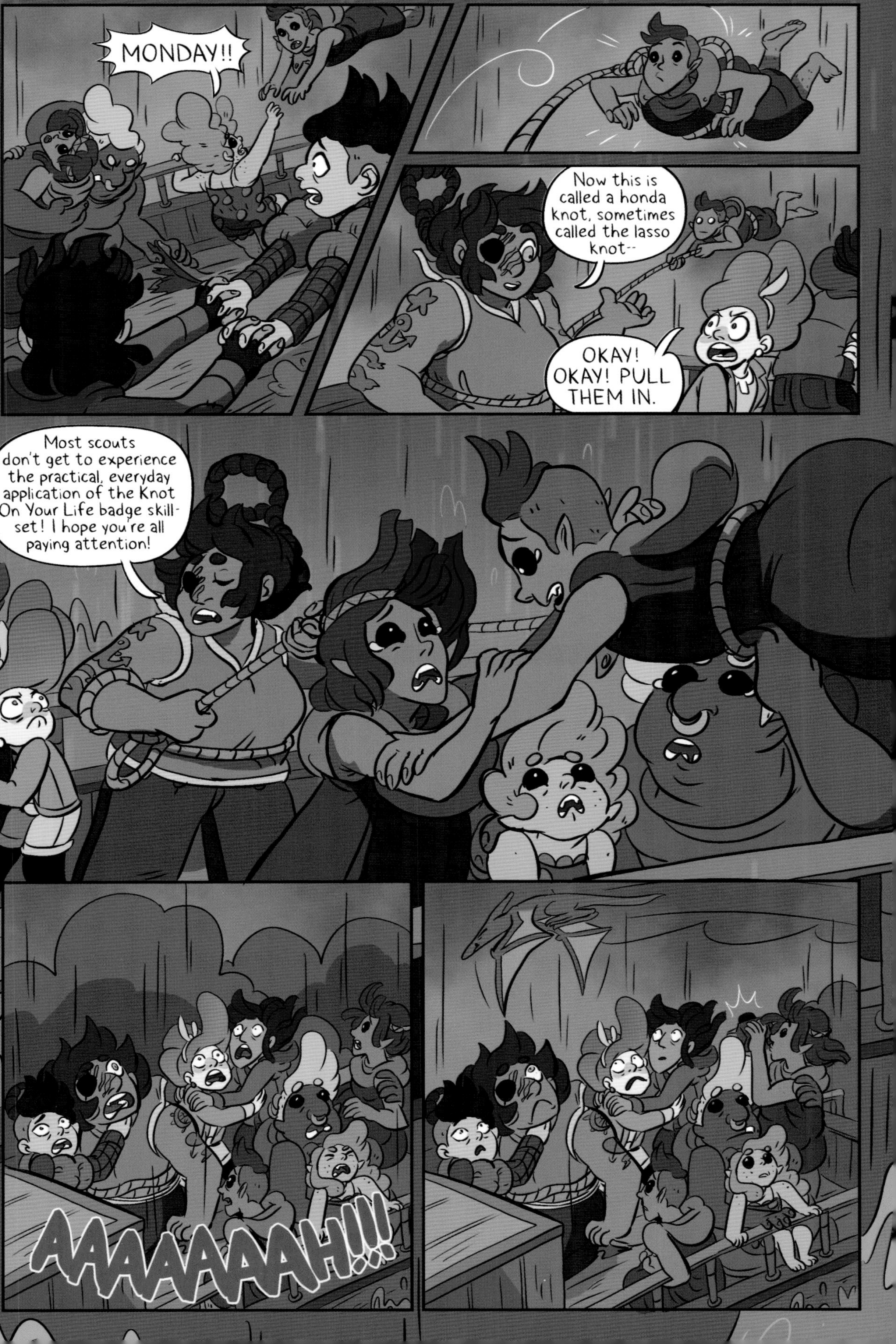
MONDAY!!
Now this is called a honda knot, sometimes called the lasso knot--
OKAY! OKAY! PULL THEM IN.
Most scouts don't get to experience the practical, everyday application of the Knot On Your Life badge skill-set! I hope you're all paying attention!
AAAAAAAAH!!!

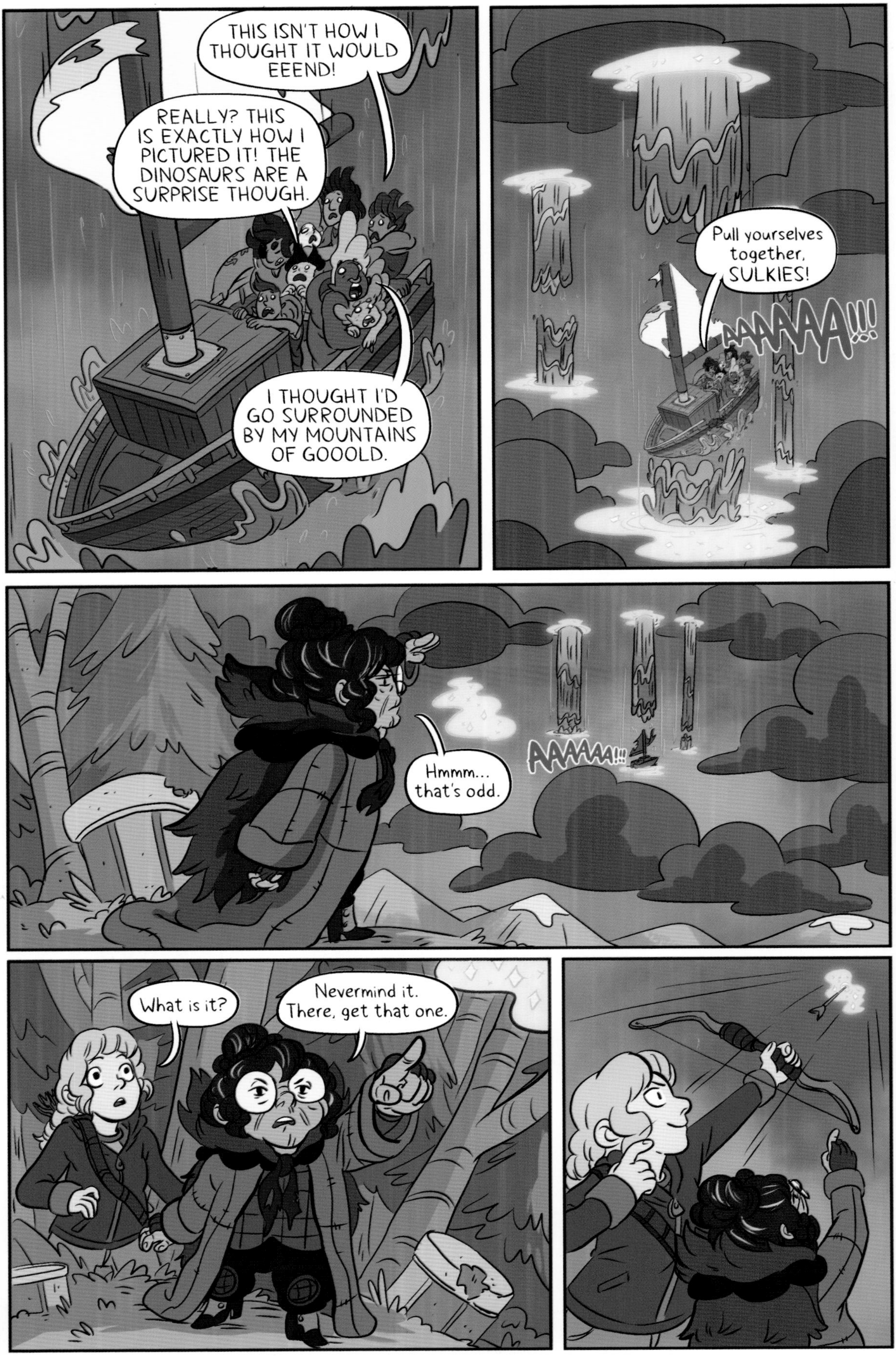
THIS ISN'T HOW I THOUGHT IT WOULD EEEND!
REALLY? THIS IS EXACTLY HOW I PICTURED IT! THE DINOSAURS ARE A SURPRISE THOUGH.
I THOUGHT I'D GO SURROUNDED BY MY MOUNTAINS OF GOOOLD.
Pull yourselves together, SULKIES!
AAAAAA!!!
AAAAAA!!!
Hmmm... that's odd.
What is it?
Nevermind it. There, get that one.

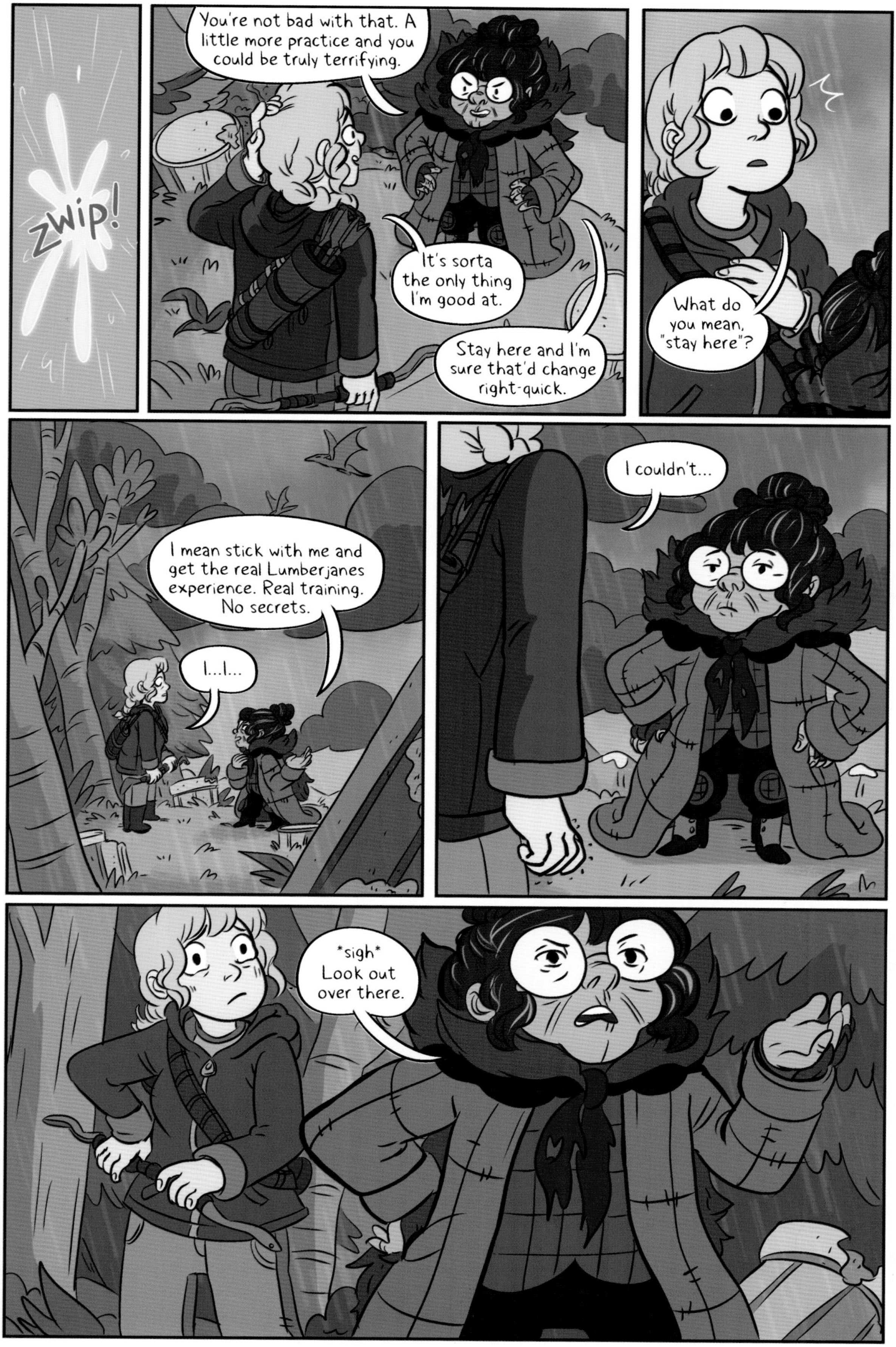
ZWIP!
You're not bad with that. A little more practice and you could be truly terrifying.
It's sorta the only thing I'm good at.
Stay here and I'm sure that'd change right-quick.
What do you mean, "stay here"?
I mean stick with me and get the real Lumberjanes experience. Real training. No secrets.
I...I...
I couldn't...
sigh Look out over there.

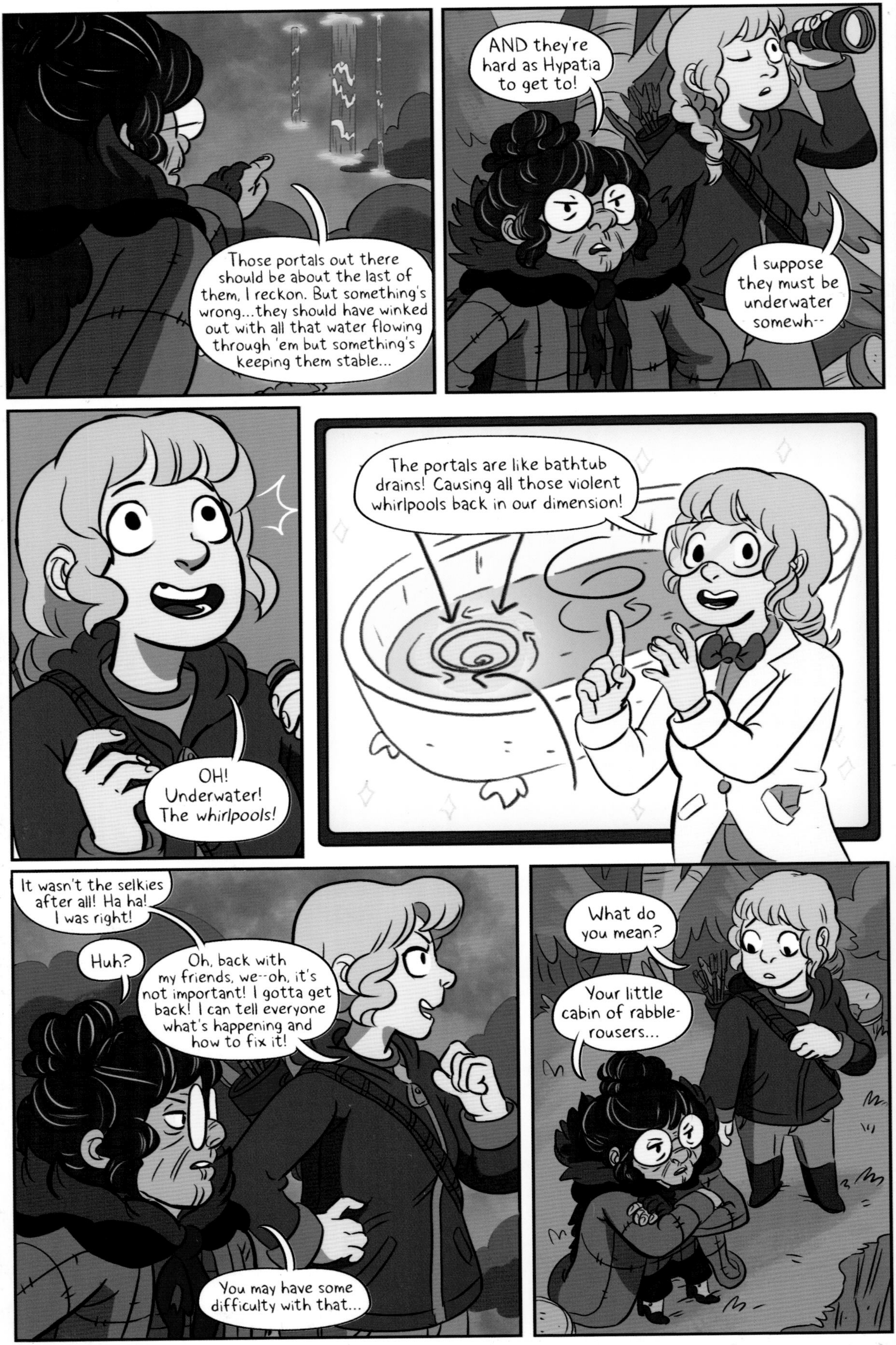
Those portals out there should be about the last of them, I reckon. But something's wrong...they should have winked out with all that water flowing through 'em but something's keeping them stable...
AND they're hard as Hypatia to get to!
I suppose they must be underwater somewh--
OH! Underwater! The whirlpools!
The portals are like bathtub drains! Causing all those violent whirlpools back in our dimension!
It wasn't the selkies after all! Ha ha! I was right!
Huh?
Oh, back with my friends, we--oh, it's not important! I gotta get back! I can tell everyone what's happening and how to fix it!
You may have some difficulty with that...
What do you mean?
Your little cabin of rabble-rousers...

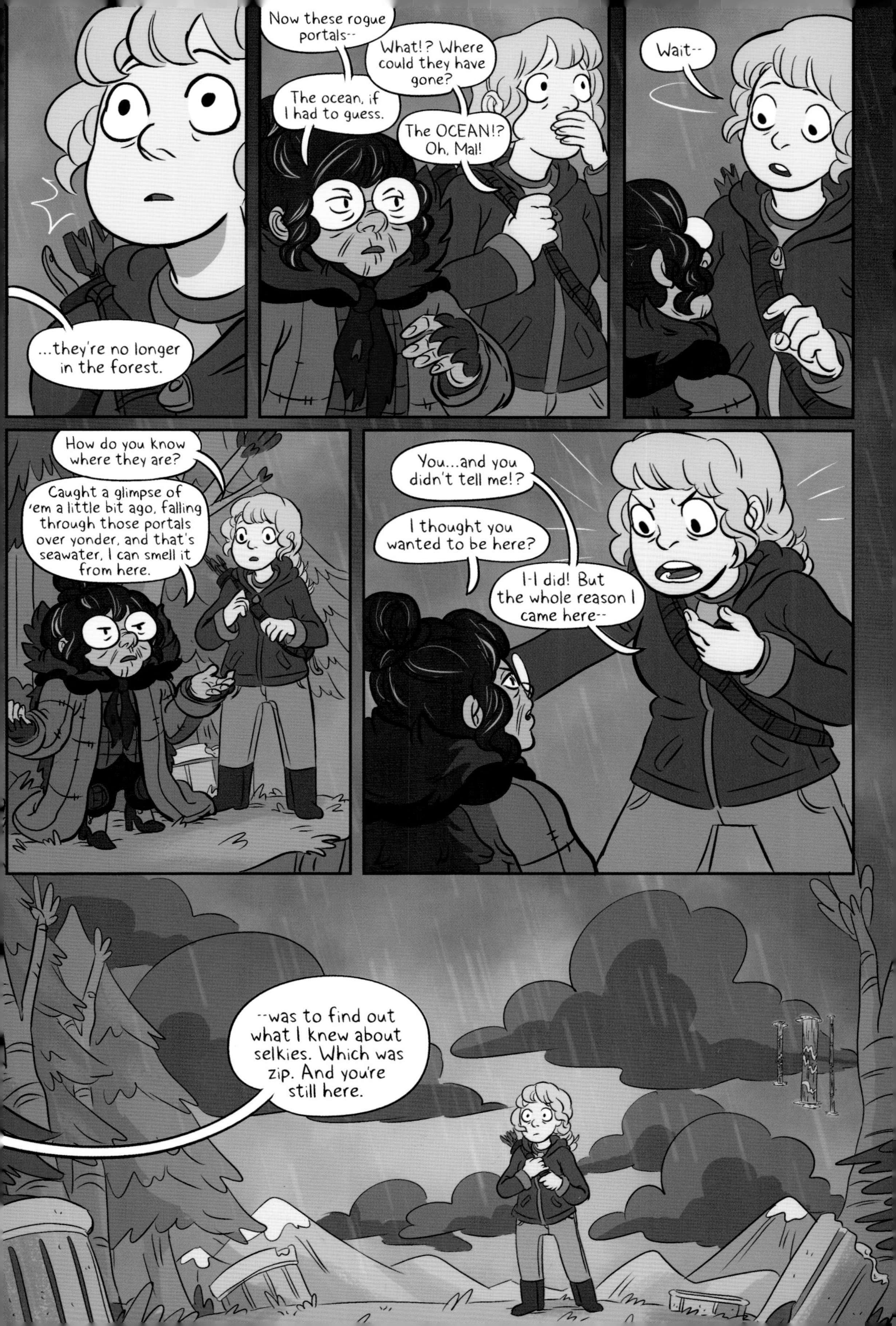
...they're no longer in the forest.
Now these rogue portals--
The ocean, if I had to guess.
What!? Where could they have gone?
The OCEAN!? Oh, Mal!
Wait--
How do you know where they are?
Caught a glimpse of 'em a little bit ago, falling through those portals over yonder, and that's seawater, I can smell it from here.
You...and you didn't tell me!?
I thought you wanted to be here?
I-I did! But the whole reason I came here--
--was to find out what I knew about selkies. Which was zip. And you're still here.

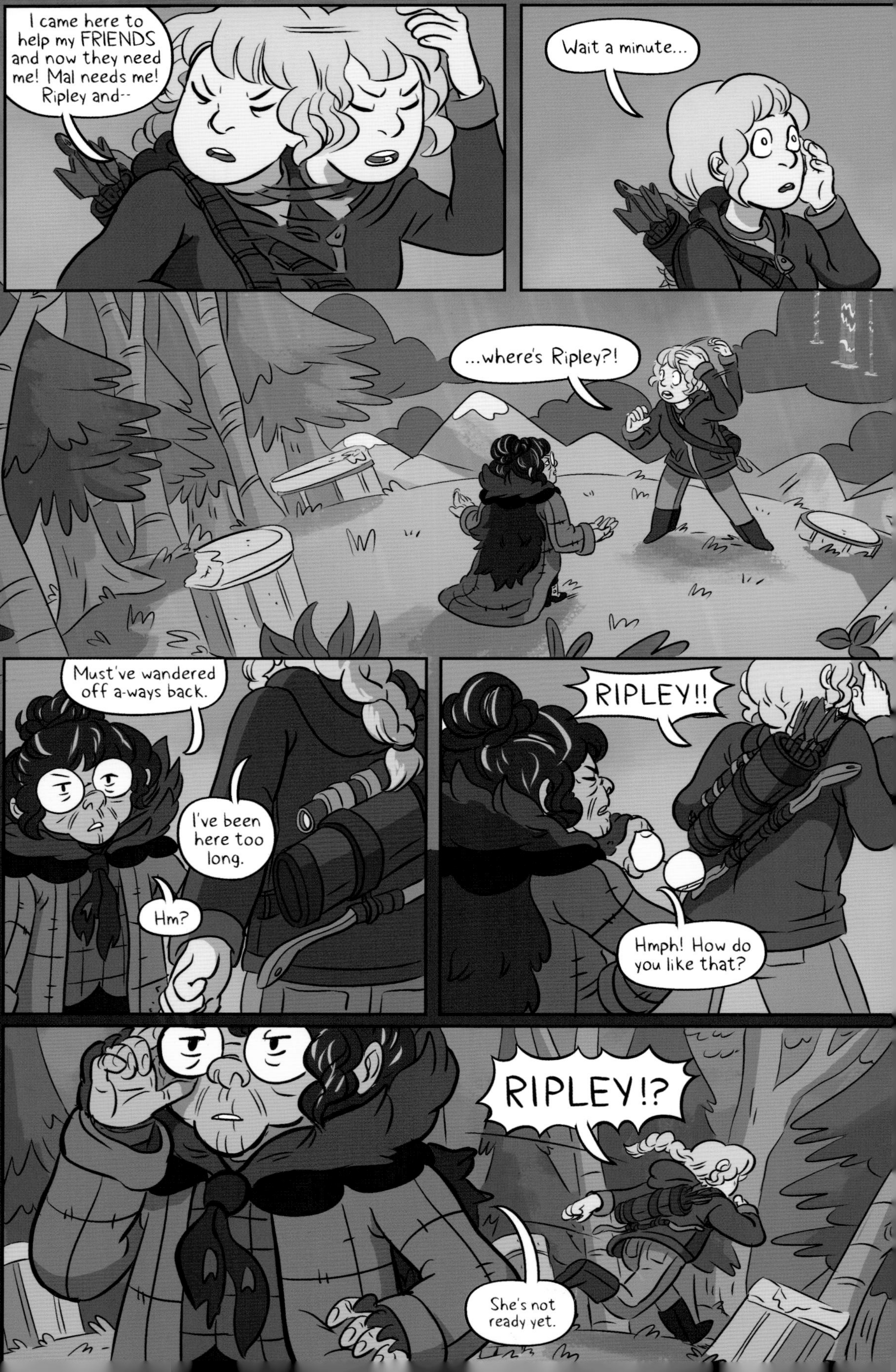
I came here to help my FRIENDS and now they need me! Mal needs me! Ripley and--
Wait a minute...
...where's Ripley?!
Must've wandered off a-ways back.
I've been here too long.
Hm?
RIPLEY!!
Hmph! How do you like that?
RIPLEY!?
She's not ready yet.

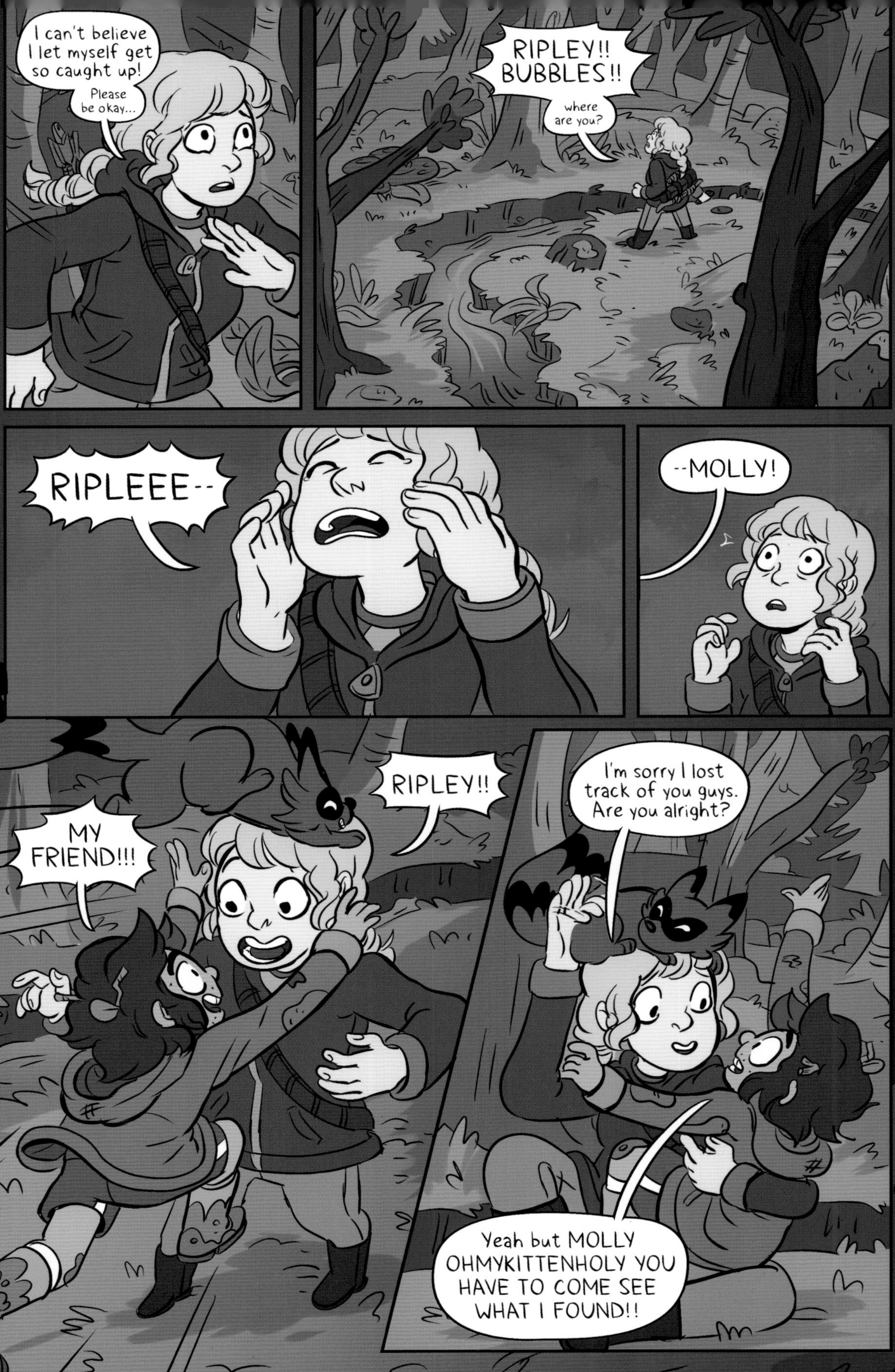
I can't believe I let myself get so caught up!
Please be okay...
RIPLEY!! BUBBLES!!
where are you?
RIPLEEE--
--MOLLY!
MY FRIEND!!!
RIPLEY!!
I'm sorry I lost track of you guys. Are you alright?
Yeah but MOLLY OHMYKITTENHOLY YOU HAVE TO COME SEE WHAT I FOUND!!

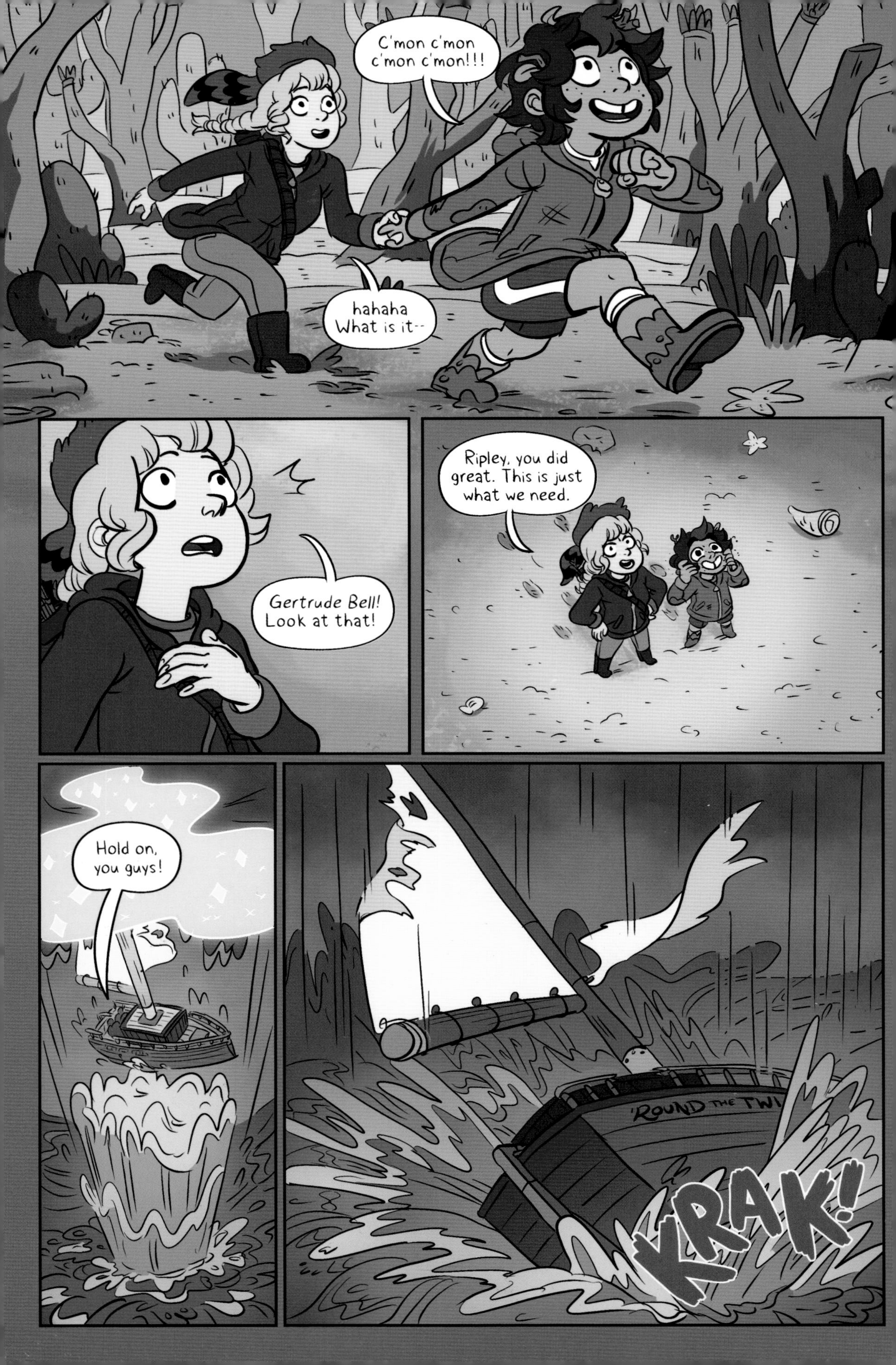
C'mon c'mon
c'mon c'mon!!!
hahaha
What is it--
Gertrude Bell!
Look at that!
Ripley, you did great. This is just what we need.
Hold on, you guys!
'ROUND THE TWI
KRAK!

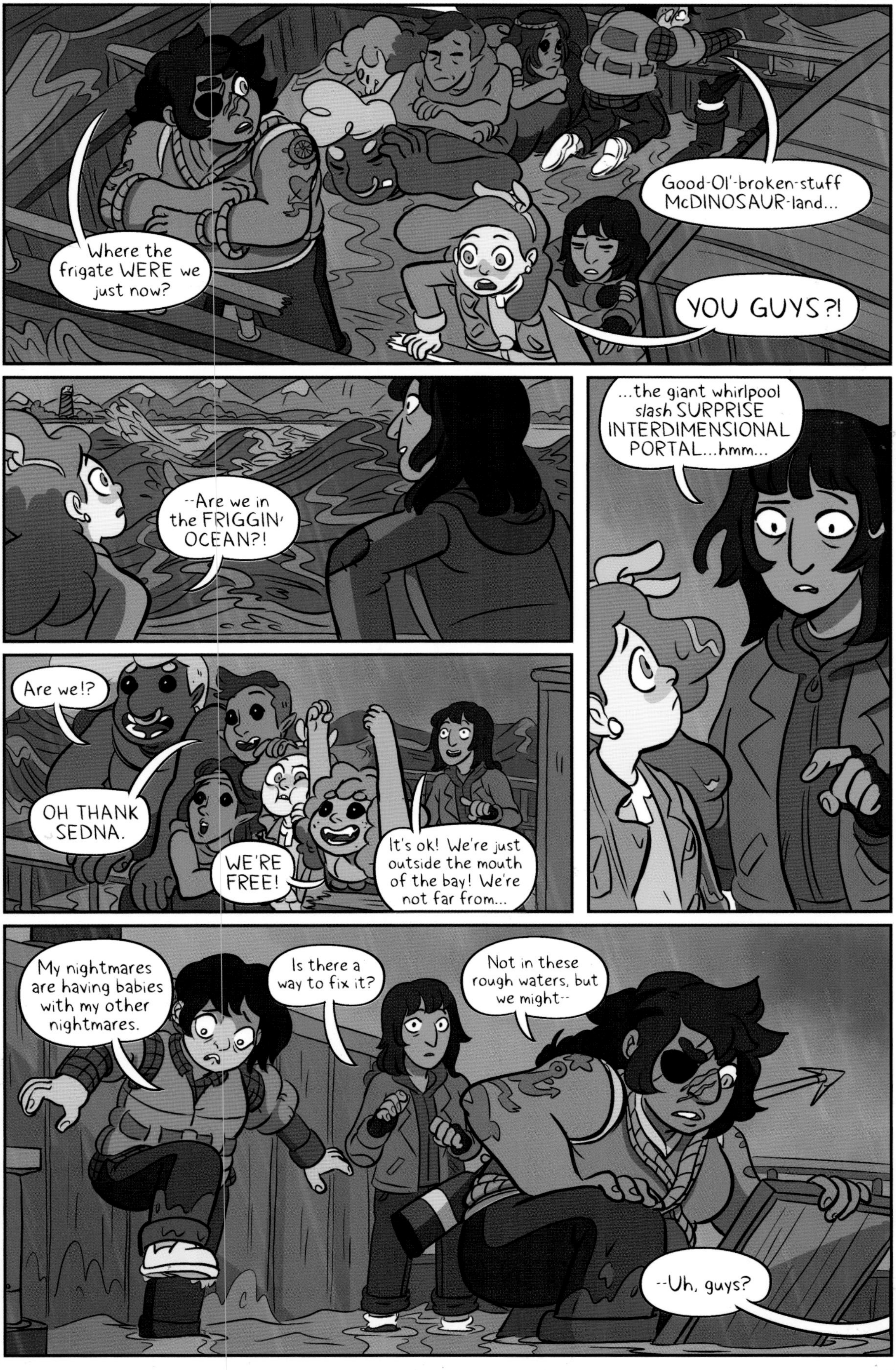
Where the frigate WERE we just now?
Good-Ol'-broken-stuff McDINOSAUR-land...
YOU GUYS?!
--Are we in the FRIGGIN' OCEAN?!
...the giant whirlpool slash SURPRISE INTERDIMENSIONAL PORTAL...hmm...
Are we!?
OH THANK SEDNA.
WE'RE FREE!
It's ok! We're just outside the mouth of the bay! We're not far from...
My nightmares are having babies with my other nightmares.
Is there a way to fix it?
Not in these rough waters, but we might--
--Uh, guys?

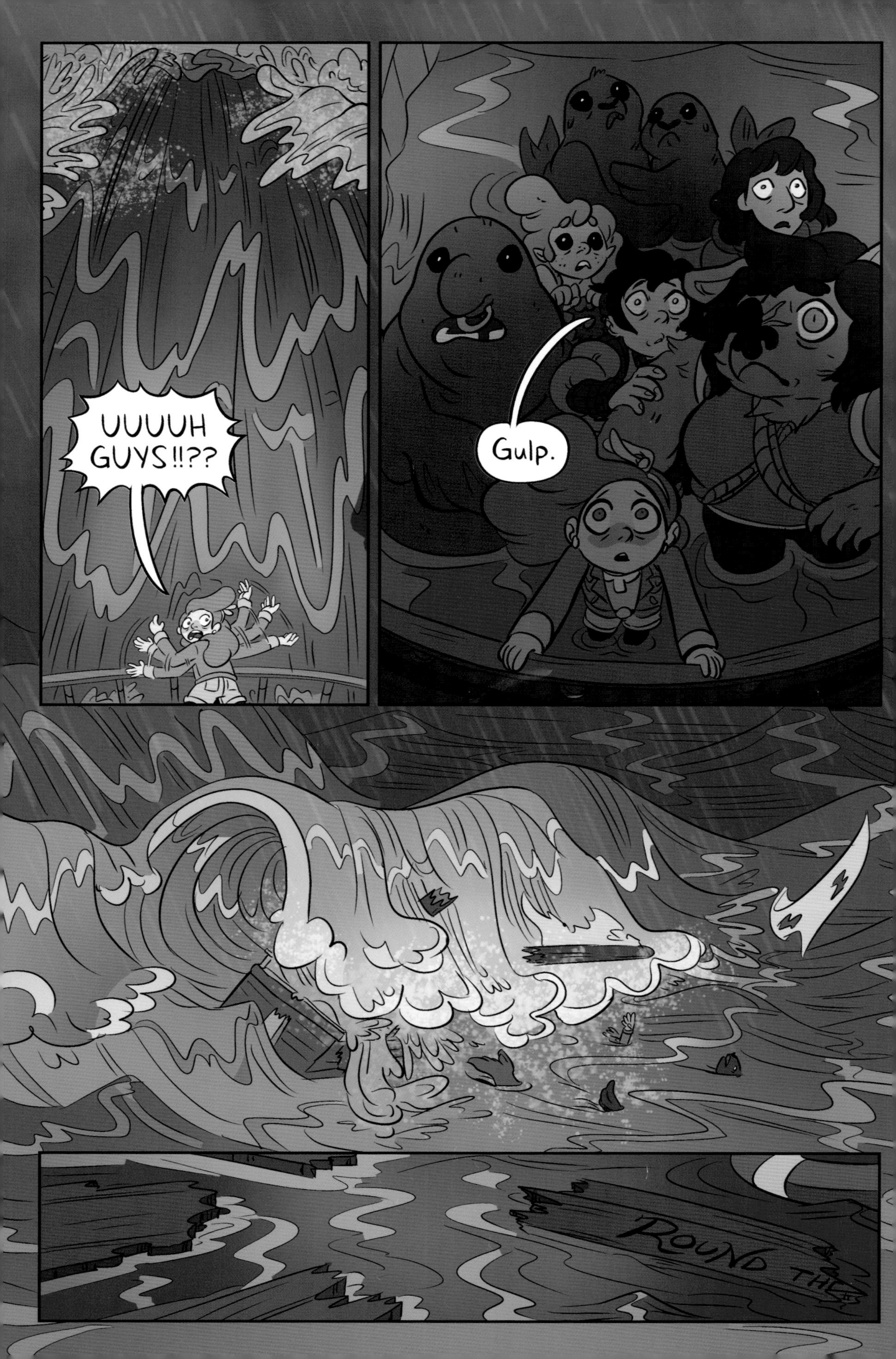
UUUUH GUYS!!??
Gulp.
ROUND THE

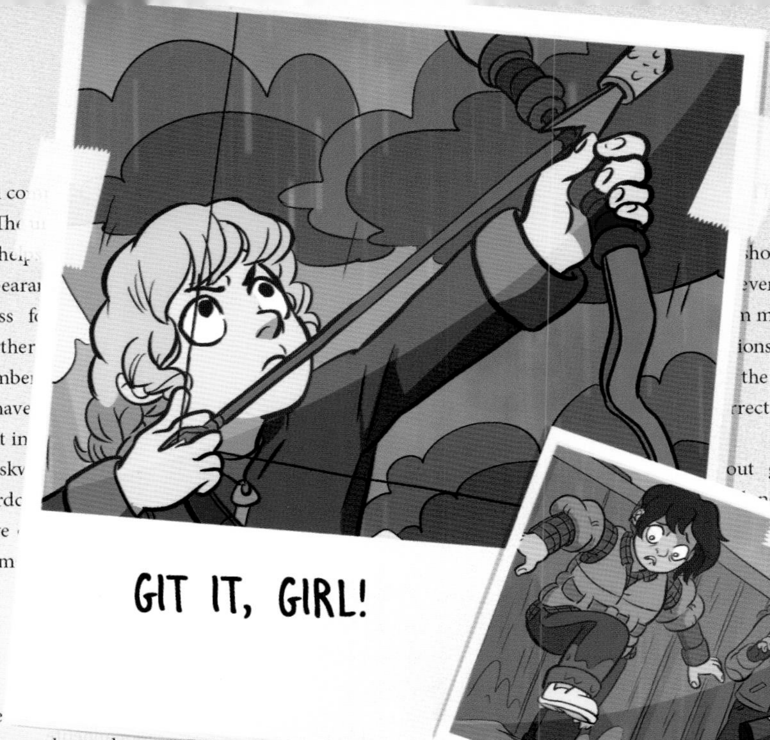
GIT IT, GIRL!

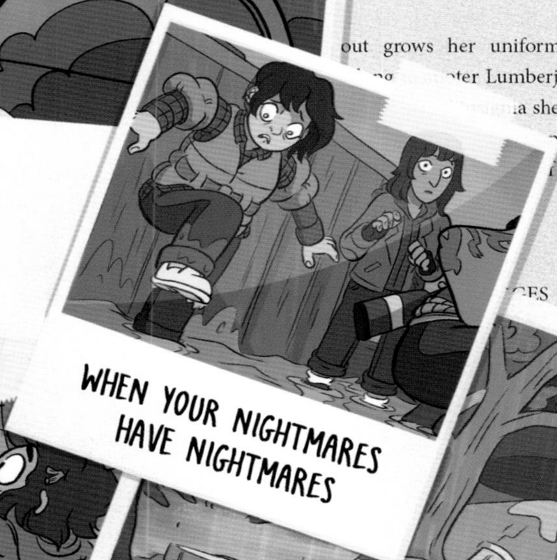
WHEN YOUR NIGHTMARES
HAVE NIGHTMARES

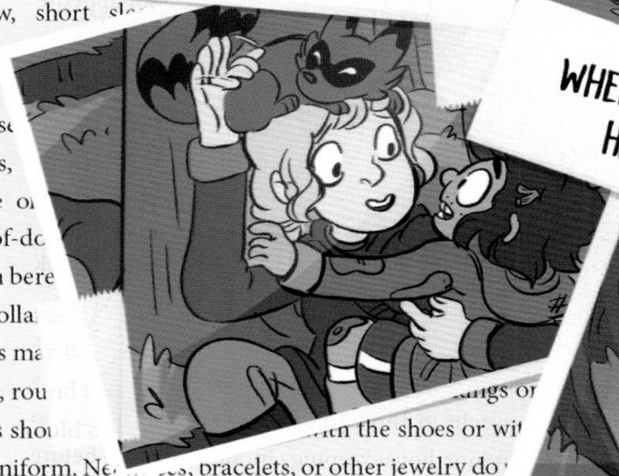

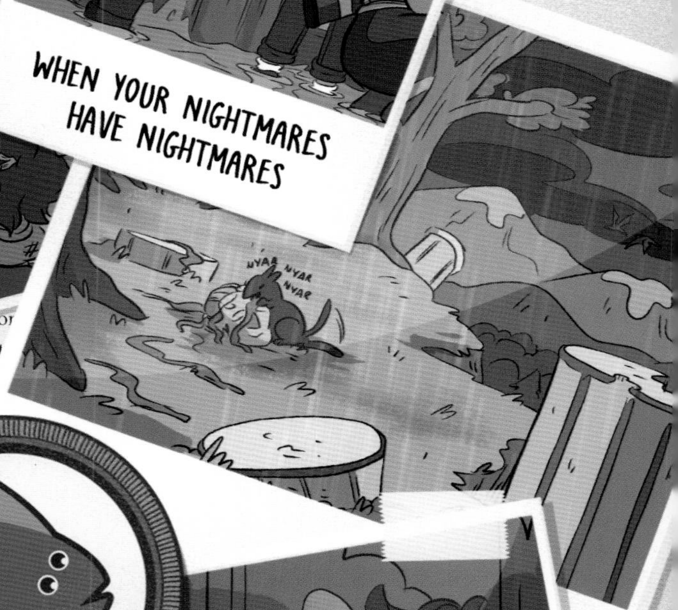
NYAR NYAR
NYAR

will co…

The… It hel… appeara… dress f… Further… Lumbe… to have… part in… Thiskv… Hardc… have… them…

…IE UNIFORM

…should be worn at camp …events when Lumberjanes …n may also be worn at other …ions. It should be worn as a … the uniform dress with …rrect shoes, and stocking or

…out grows her uniform or …ter Lumberjane. …a she has … her … her

…GES

The… yellow, short sl… emb… the w… choose… slacks, … made o… out-of-dc… green bere… the colla… Shoes ma… heels, rou… …kings or socks should … with the shoes or wit… the uniform. Ne… …es, bracelets, or other jewelry do … belong with a Lumberjane uniform.

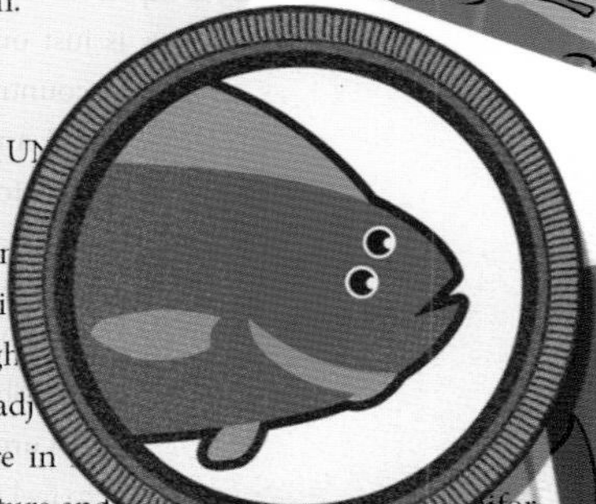

HOW TO WEAR THE UN…

To look well in a uniform demar… uniform be kept in good condi… pressed. See that the skirt is the righ… height and build, that the belt is adj… that your shoes and stockings are in … uniform, that you watch your posture and … with dignity and grace. If the beret is removed … be sure that your hair is neat and kept in place with an insonspicuous clip or ribbon. When you wear a Lumberjane uniform you are identified as a member of this organization and you should be doubly careful to conduct yourself in a way that will show everyone that courtesy and thoughtfullness are part of being a Lumberjane. People are likely to judge a whole nation by the selfishness of a few individuals, to criticize a whole family because of the misconduct of one member, and to feel unkindly toward and organization because of the

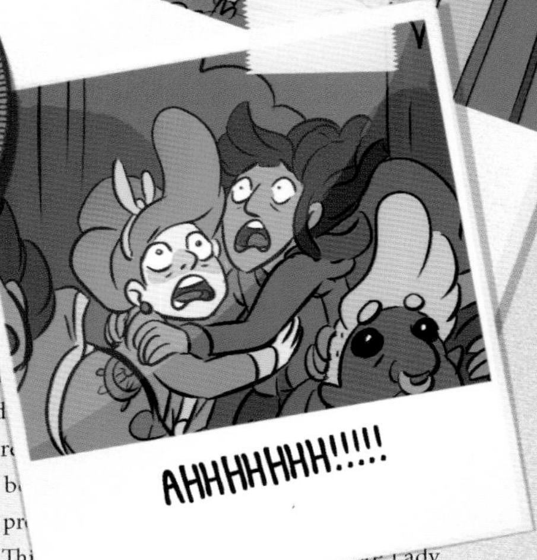
AHHHHHHH!!!!!

…unifor… helps to cre… in a group. … active life th… another bond … future, and pr… in order to b… Lumberjane pr… Penniquiqul Thi… …ore Lady Types, but m… …es will wish to have one. They can either bu… …uniform, or make it themselves from materials available at the trading post.

LUMBERJANES FIELD MANUAL

CHAPTER TWENTY-FOUR

Lumberjanes "Out-of-Doors" Program Field

SEAL OF APPROVAL BADGE

"Criticism and approval often come hand in hand."

There are many things in life that we are grateful for, even if we don't realize it at the time. There is one thing in life that we are constantly searching for, and even if it can come from a variety of sources, most often the harder we work for it, the more satisfying it is to finally receive it. Approval drives all of us, and on some level, it is something we need just as much as security. Lumberjanes will find approval at this camp. They will find acceptance for who they are and they will find a community that has been built on love and was created as a home for anyone who feels that they are a hardcore lady-type.

This badge, the *Seal Of Approval* badge, is about learning to accept criticism and approval together. Learning that some words, while not the words that we might want to hear, are a different form of approval. The *Seal Of Approval* badge is different from other Lumberjane badges as it is not actions that are needed to complete this badge but more the understanding of words, and the

power behind every language, spoken or written. This badge is considered one of the more obscure badges at camp, and while some find it easy to earn, some find it hard. But at the end of the day, every Lumberjane will earn this badge regardless if they have realized it or not.

Obtaining the *Seal Of Approval* badge is a closely guarded secret among the High Council. Every head counselor will know the needed steps that must be taken to earn this badge and will relay them to the counselors at the beginning of camp so that every counselor will know what to look for. Lumberjanes will earn this badge when they have completed the steps necessary, on their own and without any guidance. The advice that we offer to all of the campers is that when they start their tenure at camp this summer, they enter with an open mind and a love for their fellow campers. That they are kind, and honest, in any advice or recognition that they pass along.

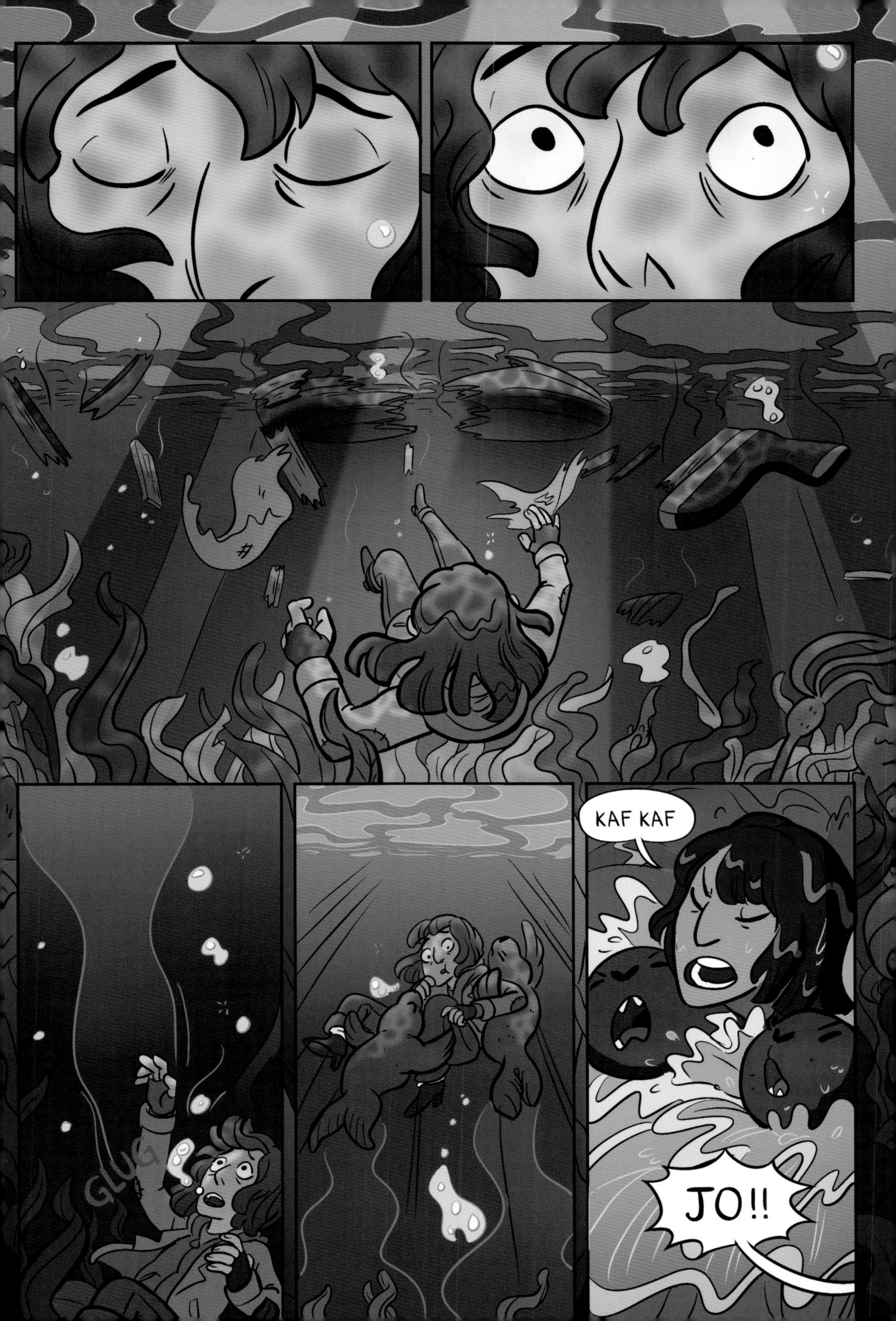
GLUG
KAF KAF
JO!!

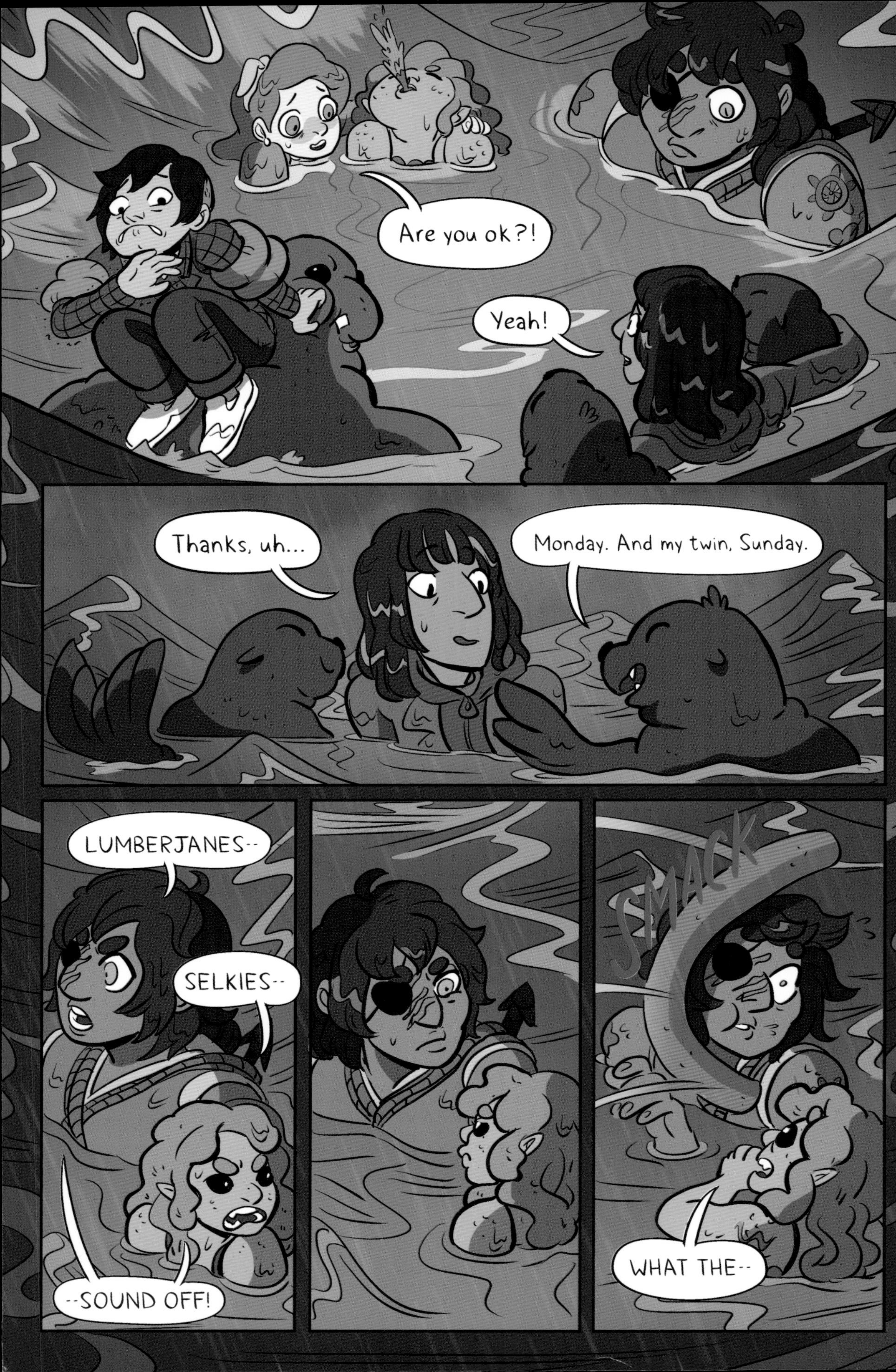
Are you ok?!
Yeah!
Thanks, uh...
Monday. And my twin, Sunday.
LUMBERJANES--
SELKIES--
--SOUND OFF!
SMACK
WHAT THE--

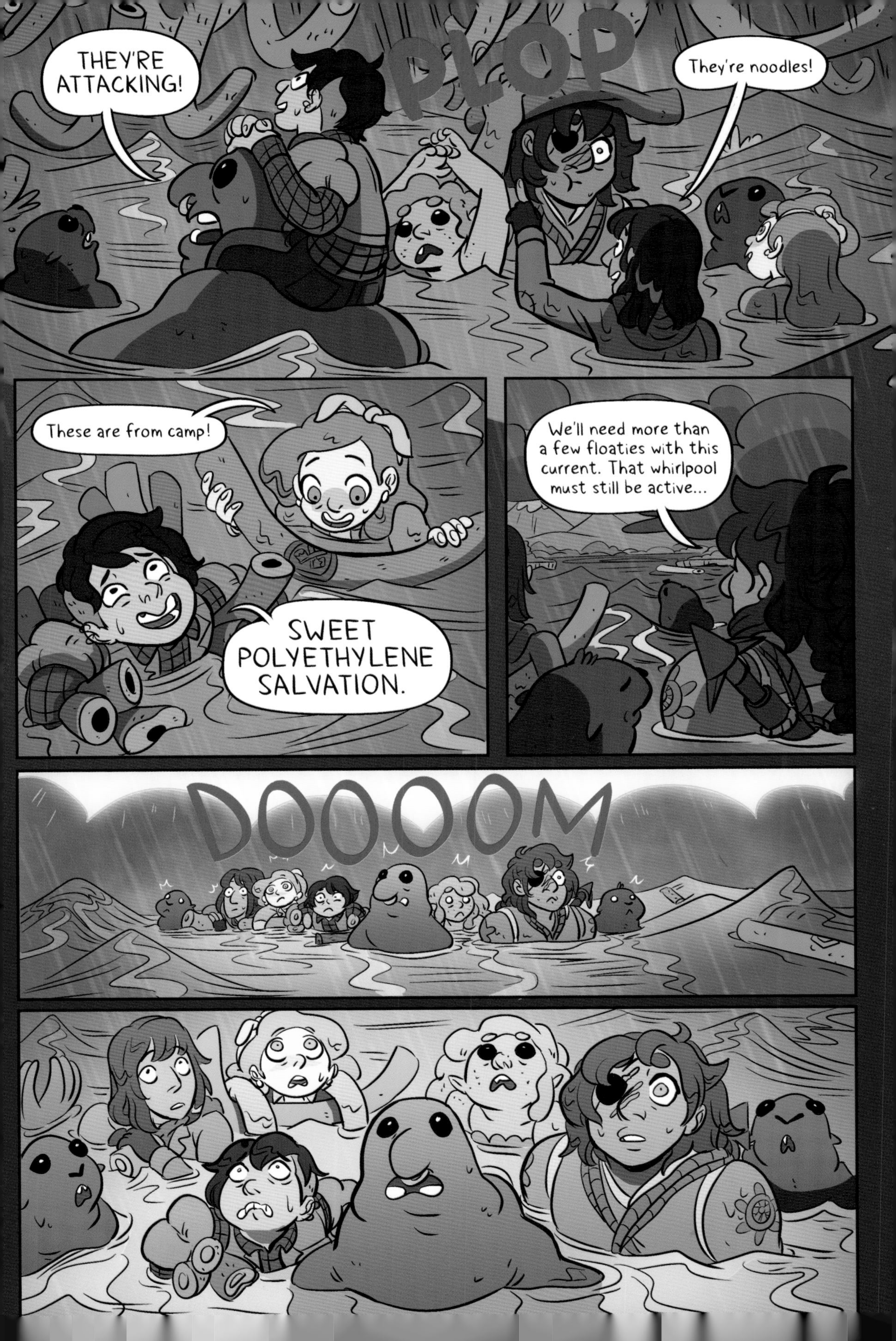
THEY'RE ATTACKING!
PLOP
They're noodles!
These are from camp!
SWEET POLYETHYLENE SALVATION.
We'll need more than a few floaties with this current. That whirlpool must still be active...
DOOOOM

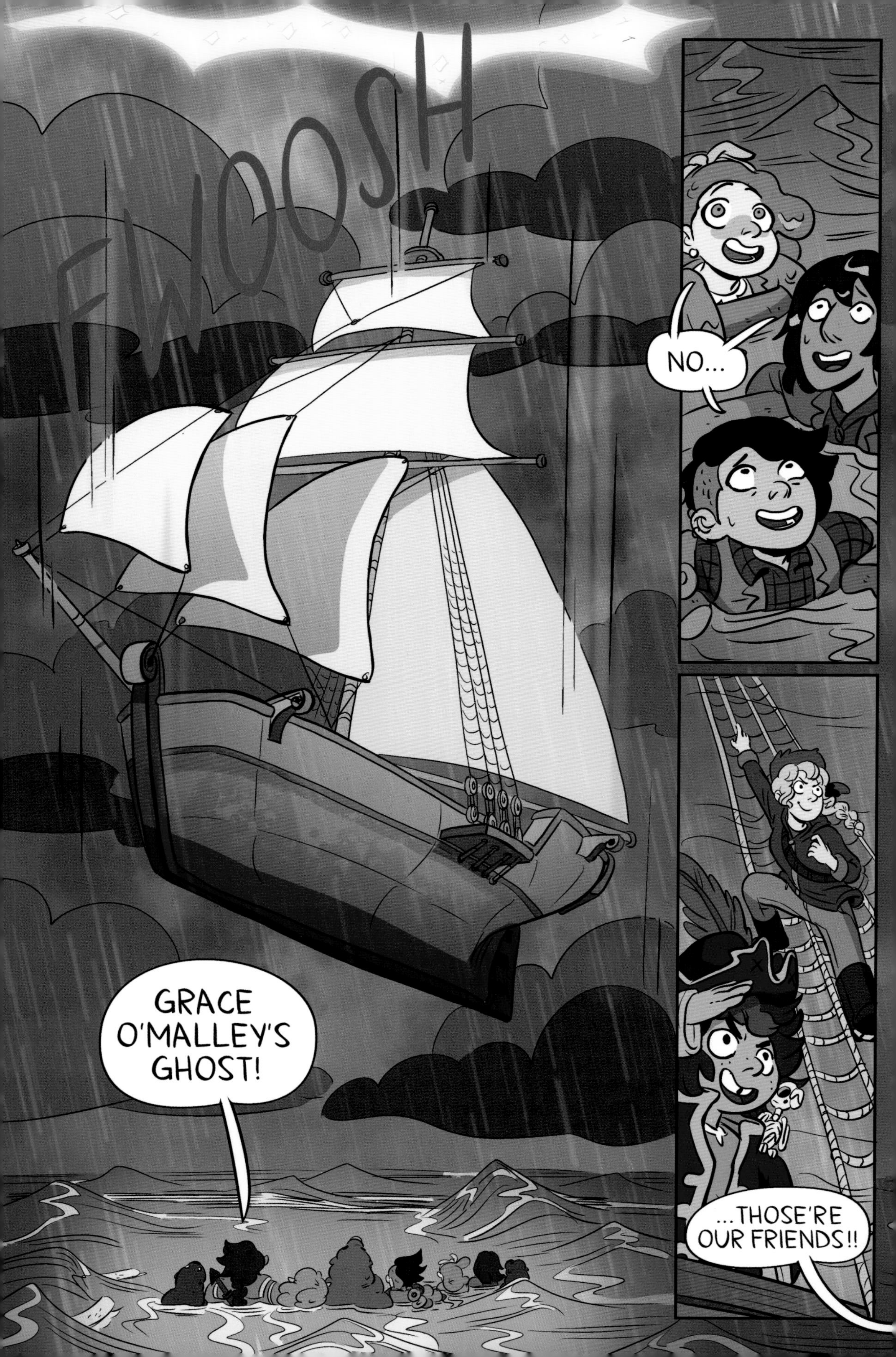
FWOOSH
NO...
GRACE O'MALLEY'S GHOST!
...THOSE'RE OUR FRIENDS!!

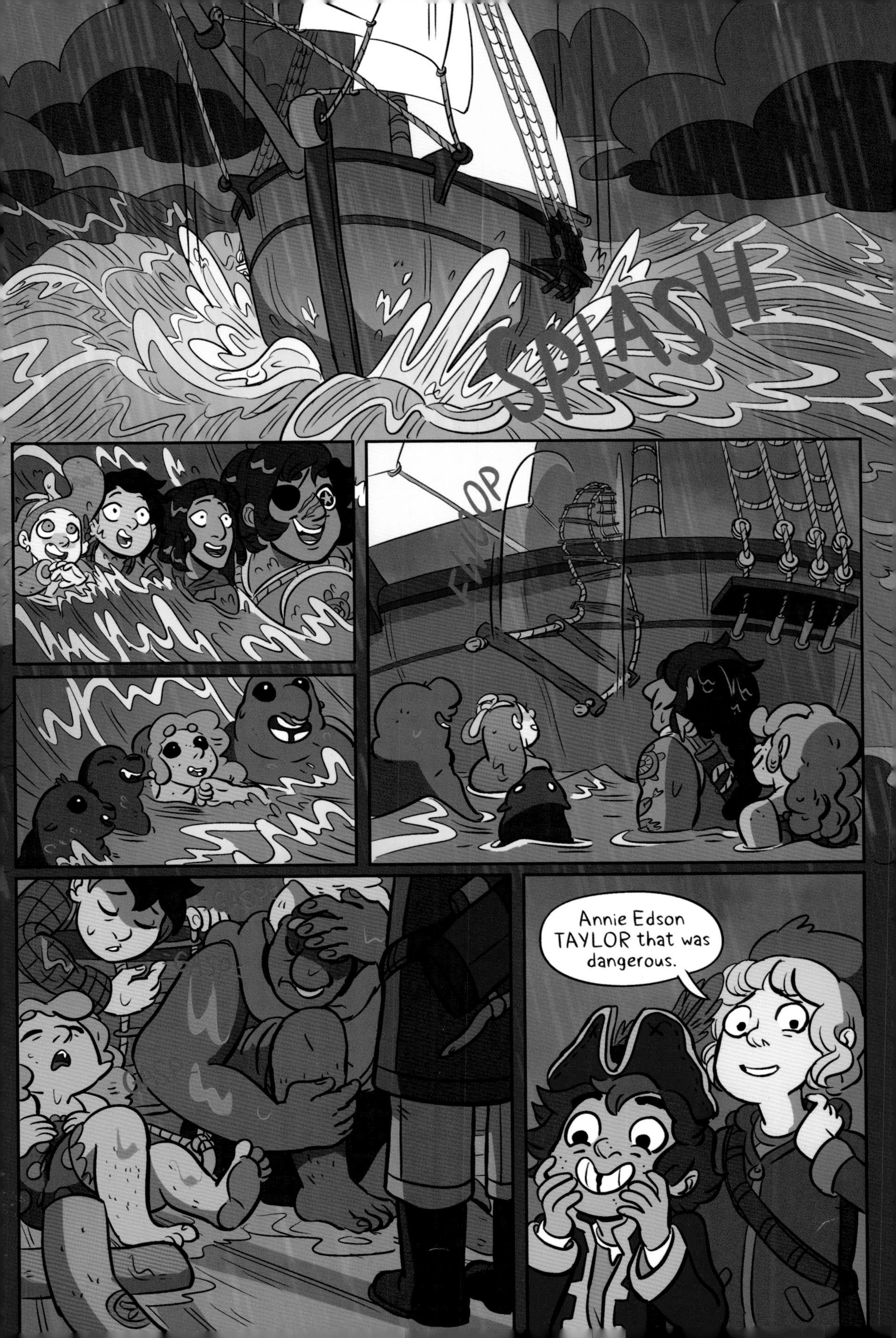
SPLASH
FWOOP
Annie Edson TAYLOR that was dangerous.

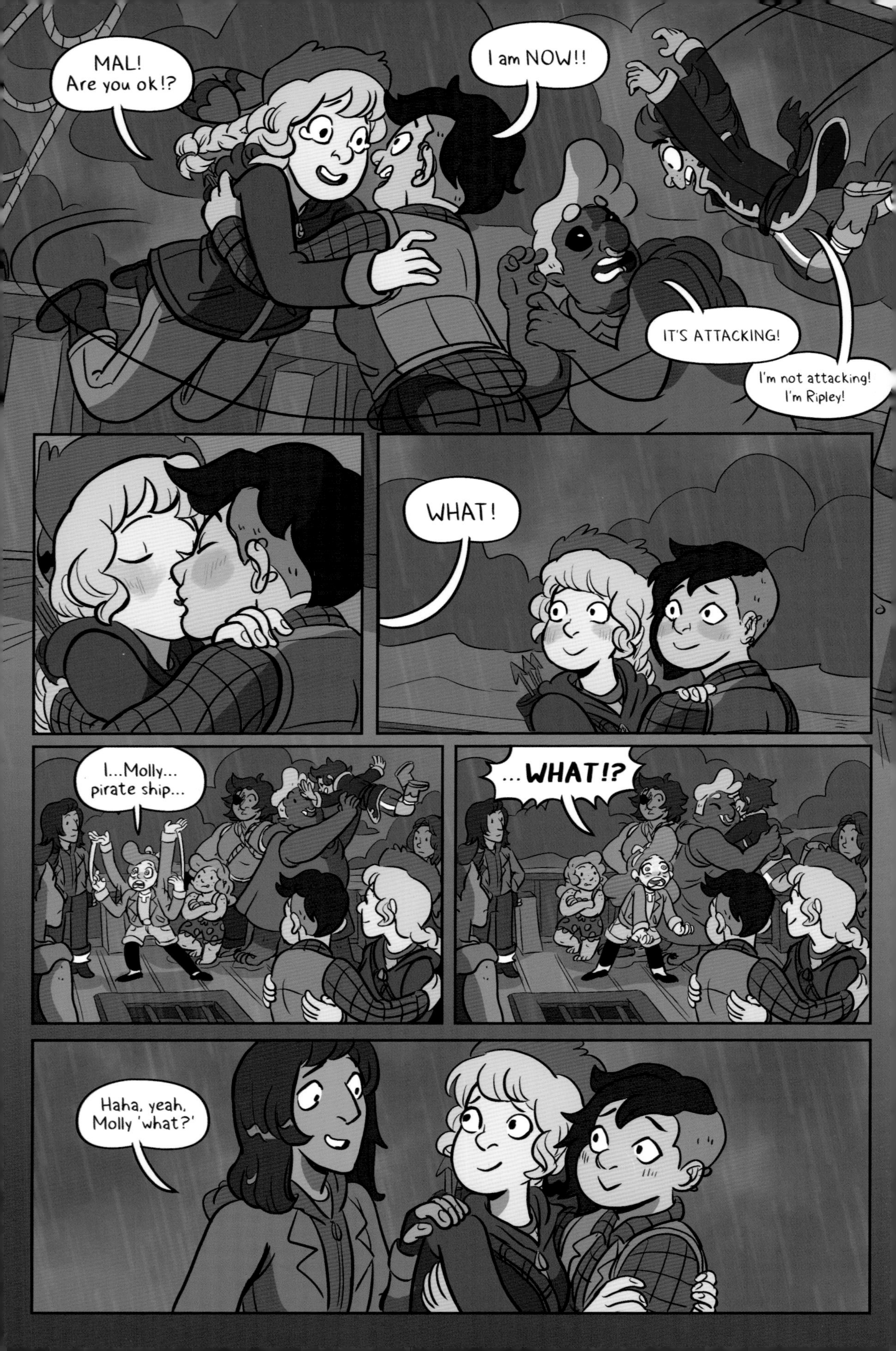
MAL! Are you ok!?
I am NOW!!
IT'S ATTACKING!
I'm not attacking! I'm Ripley!
WHAT!
I...Molly... pirate ship...
...WHAT!?
Haha, yeah, Molly 'what?'

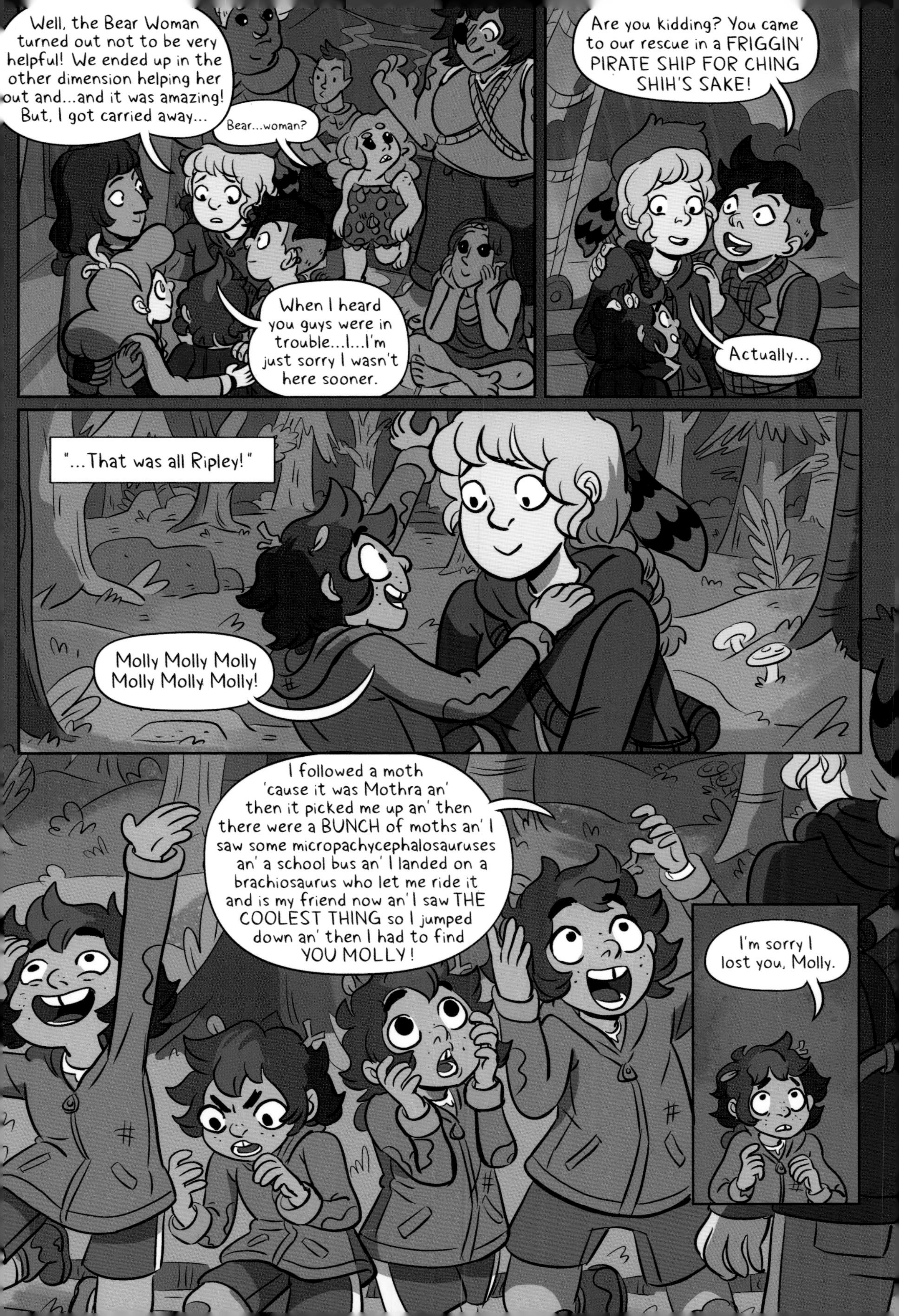
Well, the Bear Woman turned out not to be very helpful! We ended up in the other dimension helping her out and...and it was amazing! But, I got carried away...
Bear...woman?
When I heard you guys were in trouble...I...I'm just sorry I wasn't here sooner.
Are you kidding? You came to our rescue in a FRIGGIN' PIRATE SHIP FOR CHING SHIH'S SAKE!
Actually...
"...That was all Ripley!"
Molly Molly Molly Molly Molly Molly!
I followed a moth 'cause it was Mothra an' then it picked me up an' then there were a BUNCH of moths an' I saw some micropachycephalosauruses an' a school bus an' I landed on a brachiosaurus who let me ride it and is my friend now an' I saw THE COOLEST THING so I jumped down an' then I had to find YOU MOLLY!
I'm sorry I lost you, Molly.

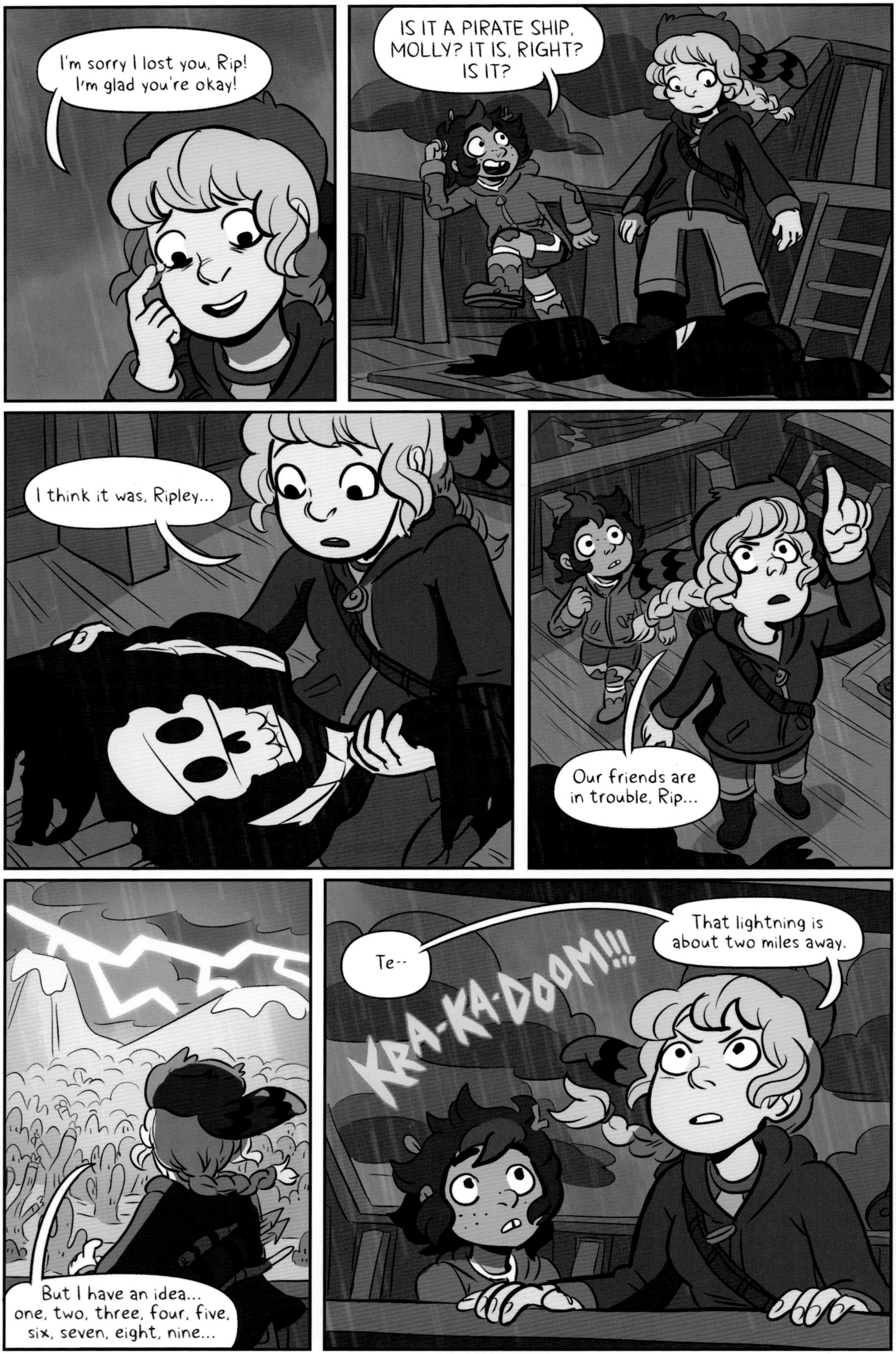
I'm sorry I lost you, Rip! I'm glad you're okay!
IS IT A PIRATE SHIP, MOLLY? IT IS, RIGHT? IS IT?
I think it was, Ripley...
Our friends are in trouble, Rip...
But I have an idea... one, two, three, four, five, six, seven, eight, nine...
Te--
That lightning is about two miles away.
KRA-KA-DOOM!!!

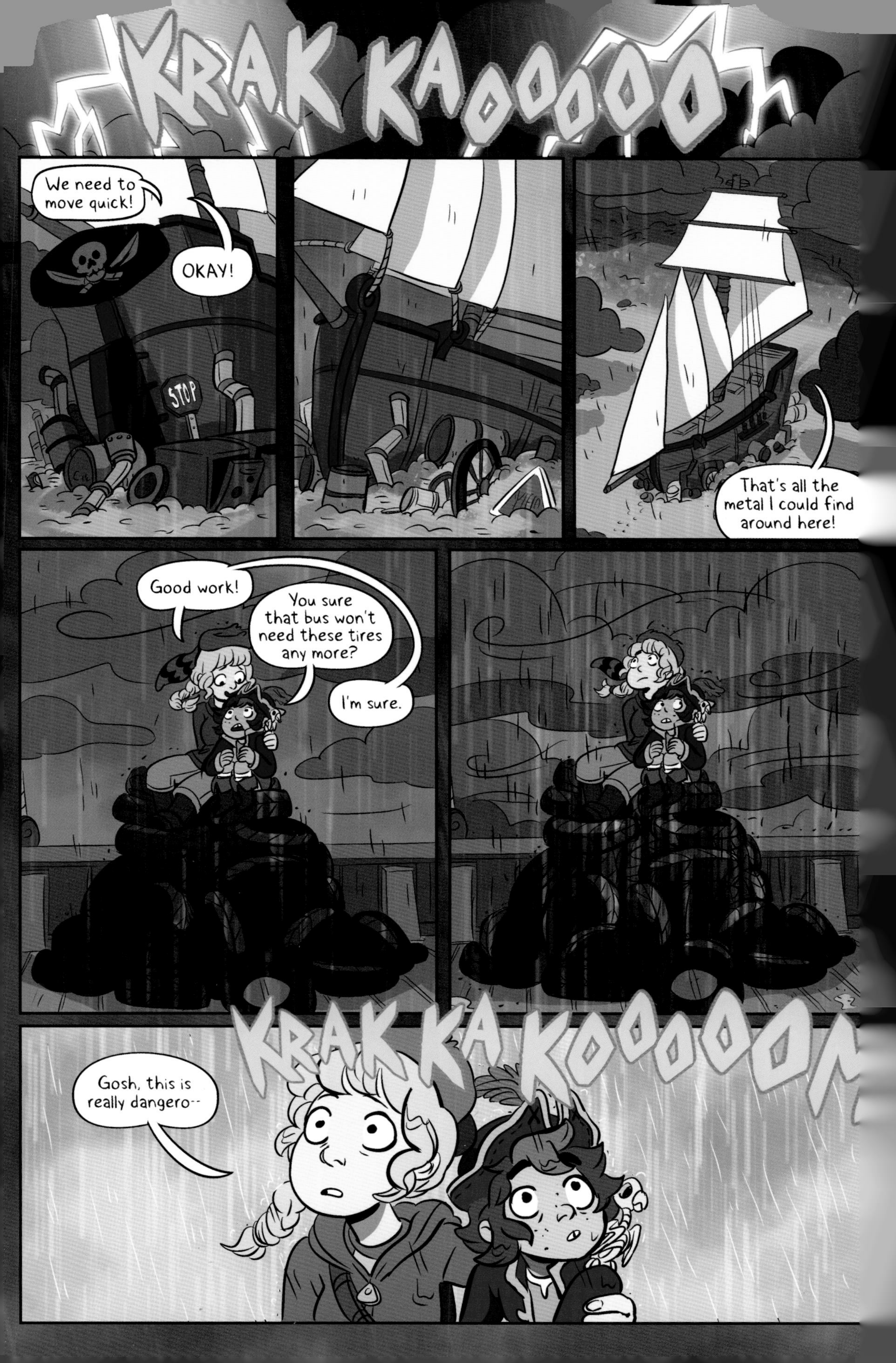
KRAK KAOOOOO
We need to move quick!
OKAY!
STOP
That's all the metal I could find around here!
Good work!
You sure that bus won't need these tires any more?
I'm sure.
KRAK KA KOOOOOM
Gosh, this is really dangero--

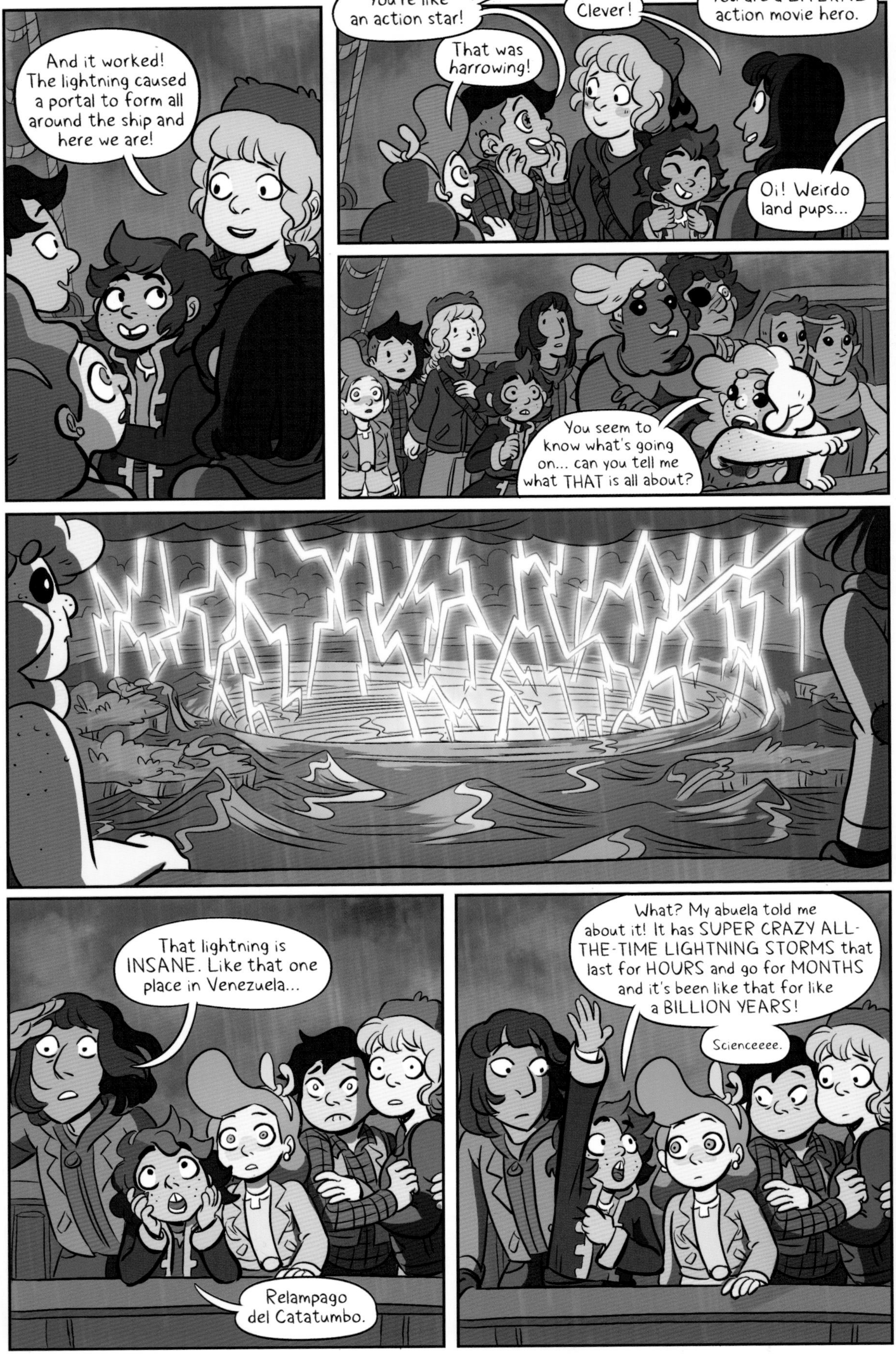
And it worked! The lightning caused a portal to form all around the ship and here we are!
You're like an action star!
Clever!
You are a LITERAL action movie hero.
That was harrowing!
Oi! Weirdo land pups...
You seem to know what's going on... can you tell me what THAT is all about?
That lightning is INSANE. Like that one place in Venezuela...
Relampago del Catatumbo.
What? My abuela told me about it! It has SUPER CRAZY ALL-THE-TIME LIGHTNING STORMS that last for HOURS and go for MONTHS and it's been like that for like a BILLION YEARS!
Scienceeee.

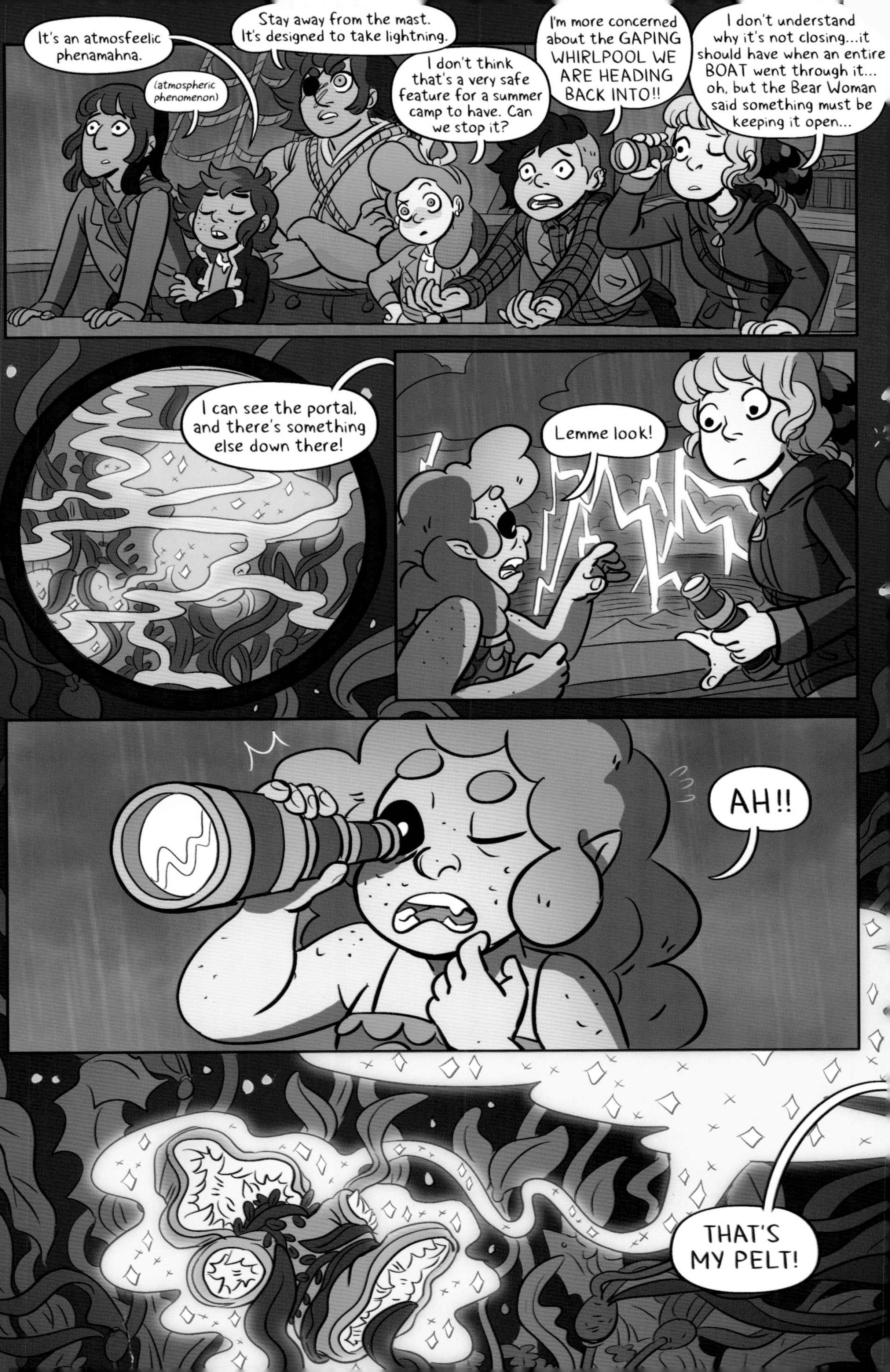
It's an atmosfeelic phenamahna.
(atmospheric phenomenon)
Stay away from the mast. It's designed to take lightning.
I don't think that's a very safe feature for a summer camp to have. Can we stop it?
I'm more concerned about the GAPING WHIRLPOOL WE ARE HEADING BACK INTO!!
I don't understand why it's not closing...it should have when an entire BOAT went through it... oh, but the Bear Woman said something must be keeping it open...
I can see the portal, and there's something else down there!
Lemme look!
AH!!
THAT'S MY PELT!

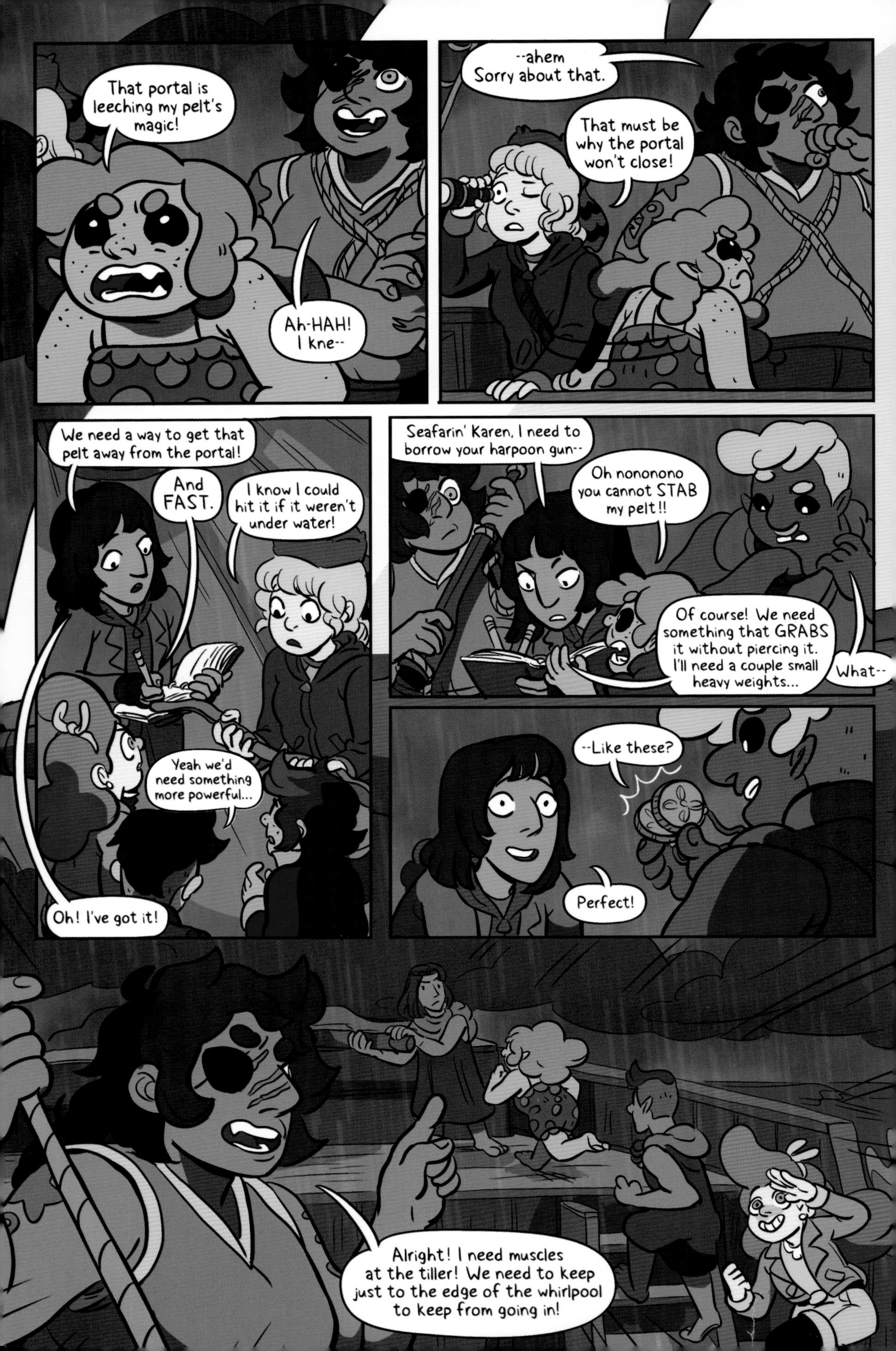
That portal is leeching my pelt's magic!
Ah-HAH! I kne--
--ahem Sorry about that.
That must be why the portal won't close!
We need a way to get that pelt away from the portal!
And FAST.
I know I could hit it if it weren't under water!
Yeah we'd need something more powerful...
Oh! I've got it!
Seafarin' Karen, I need to borrow your harpoon gun--
Oh nononono you cannot STAB my pelt!!
Of course! We need something that GRABS it without piercing it. I'll need a couple small heavy weights...
What--
--Like these?
Perfect!
Alright! I need muscles at the tiller! We need to keep just to the edge of the whirlpool to keep from going in!

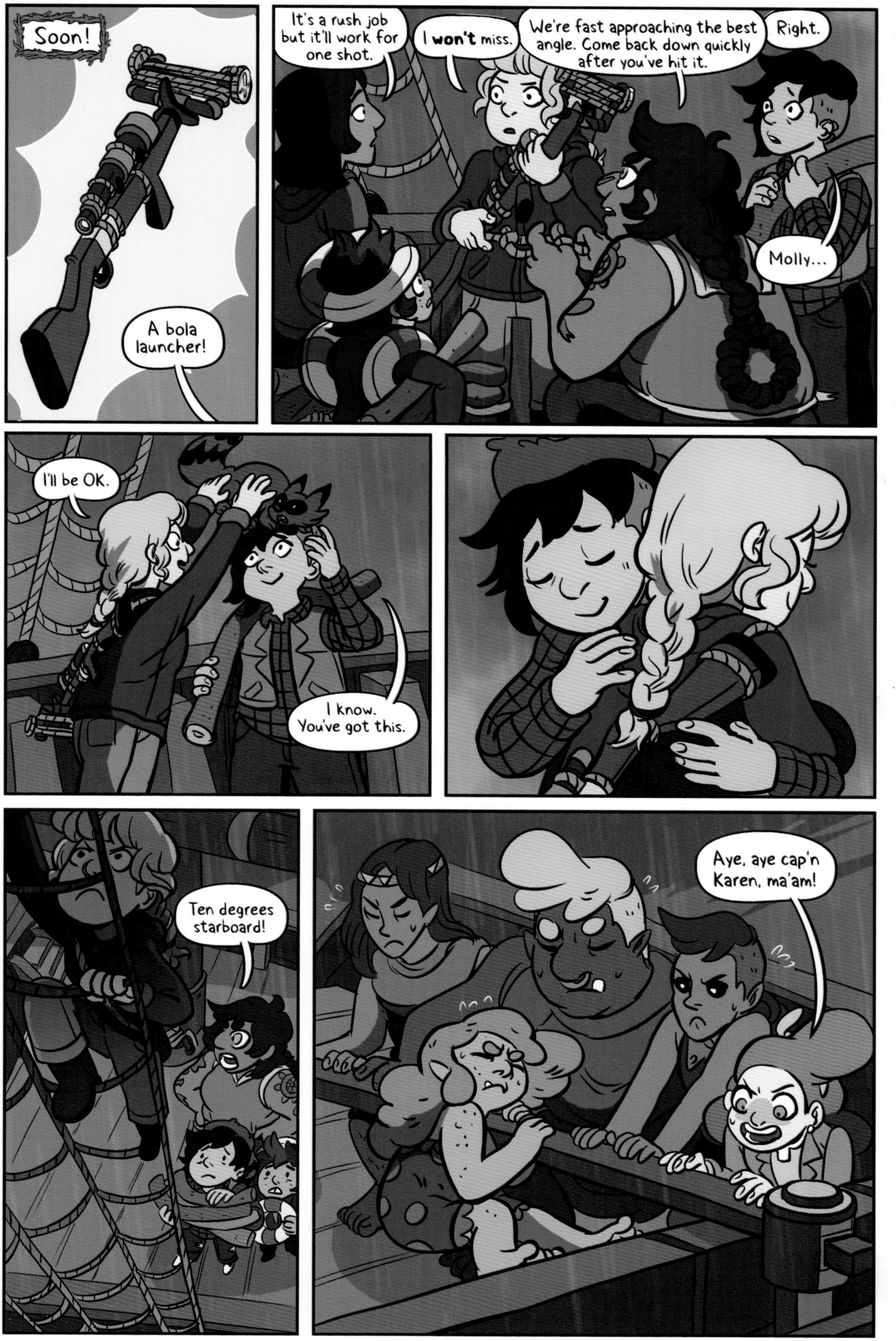
Soon!
A bola launcher!
It's a rush job but it'll work for one shot.
I **won't** miss.
We're fast approaching the best angle. Come back down quickly after you've hit it.
Right.
Molly...
I'll be OK.
I know. You've got this.
Ten degrees starboard!
Aye, aye cap'n Karen, ma'am!

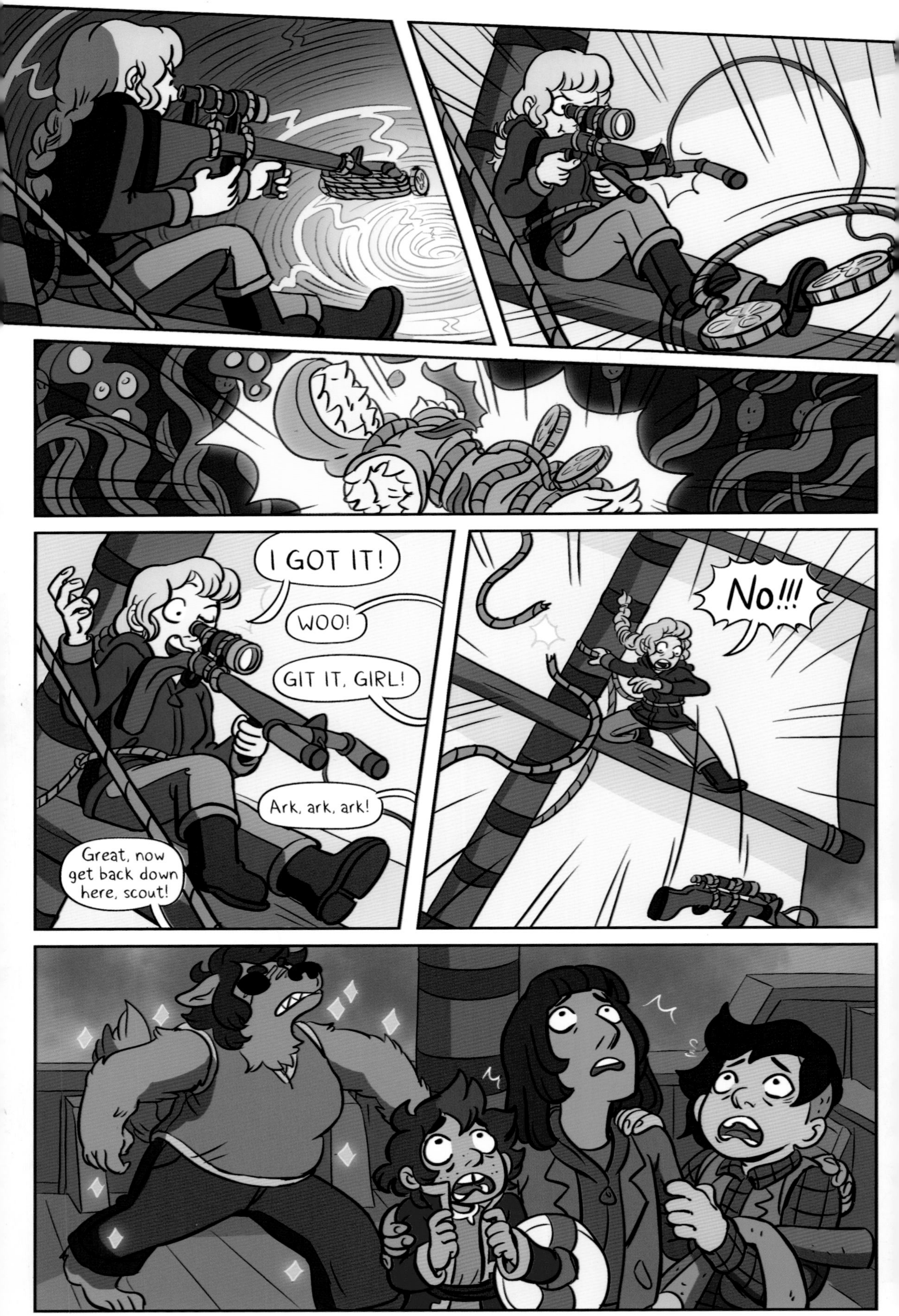
I GOT IT!
WOO!
GIT IT, GIRL!
Ark, ark, ark!
Great, now get back down here, scout!
No!!!

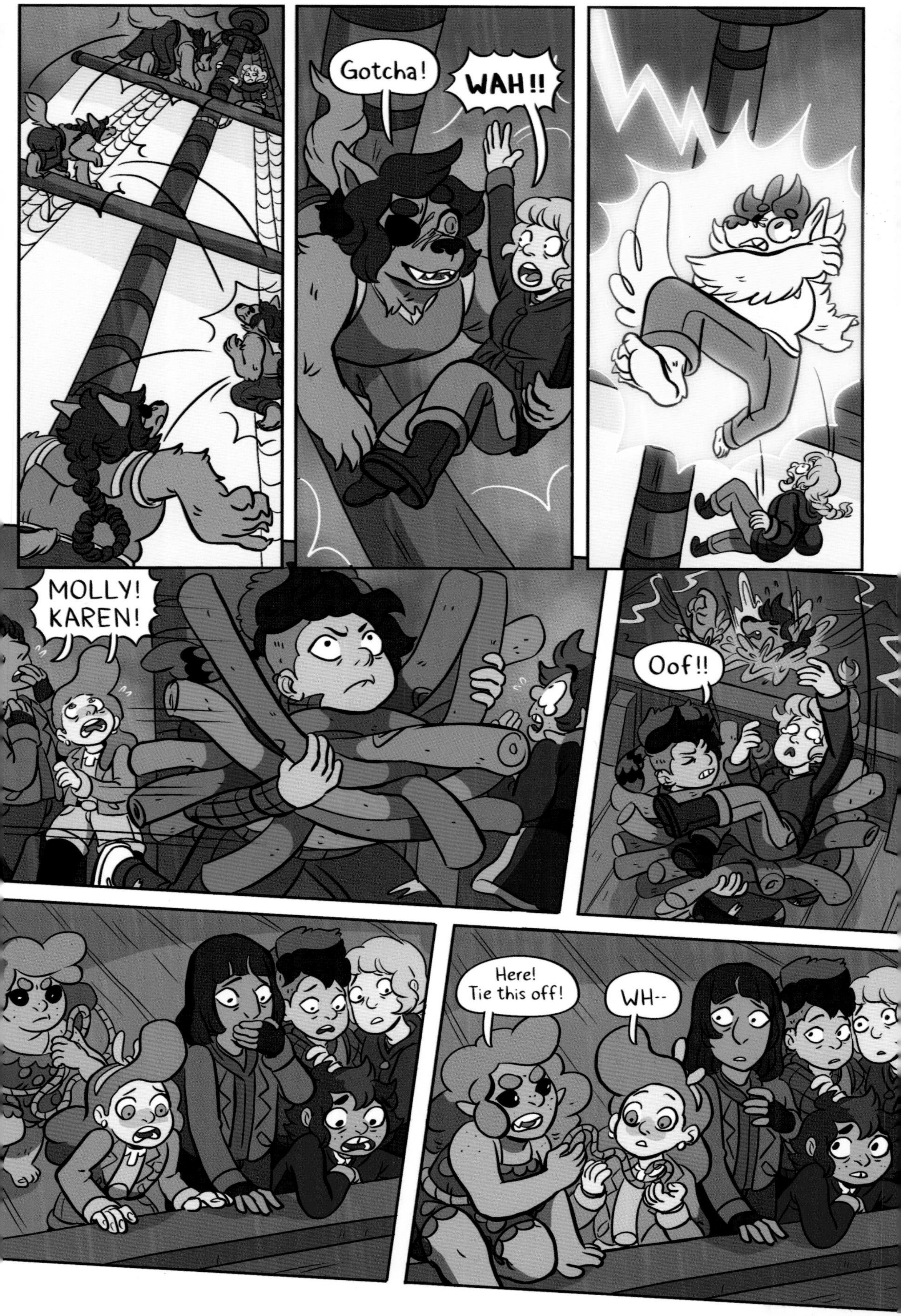
Gotcha!
WAH!!
MOLLY! KAREN!
Oof!!
Here! Tie this off!
WH--

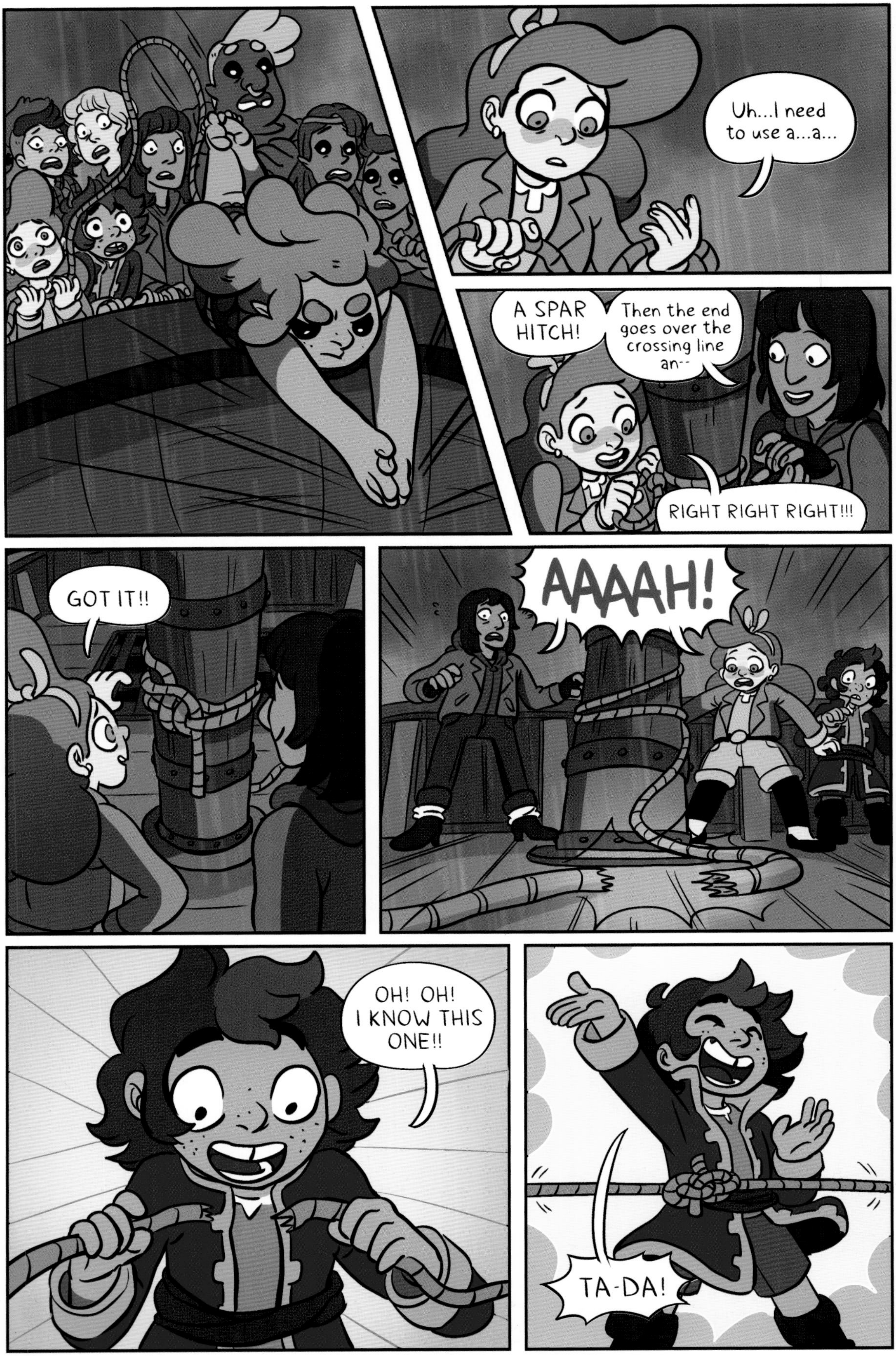
Uh...I need to use a...a...
A SPAR HITCH!
Then the end goes over the crossing line an--
RIGHT RIGHT RIGHT!!!
GOT IT!!
AAAAH!
OH! OH! I KNOW THIS ONE!!
TA-DA!

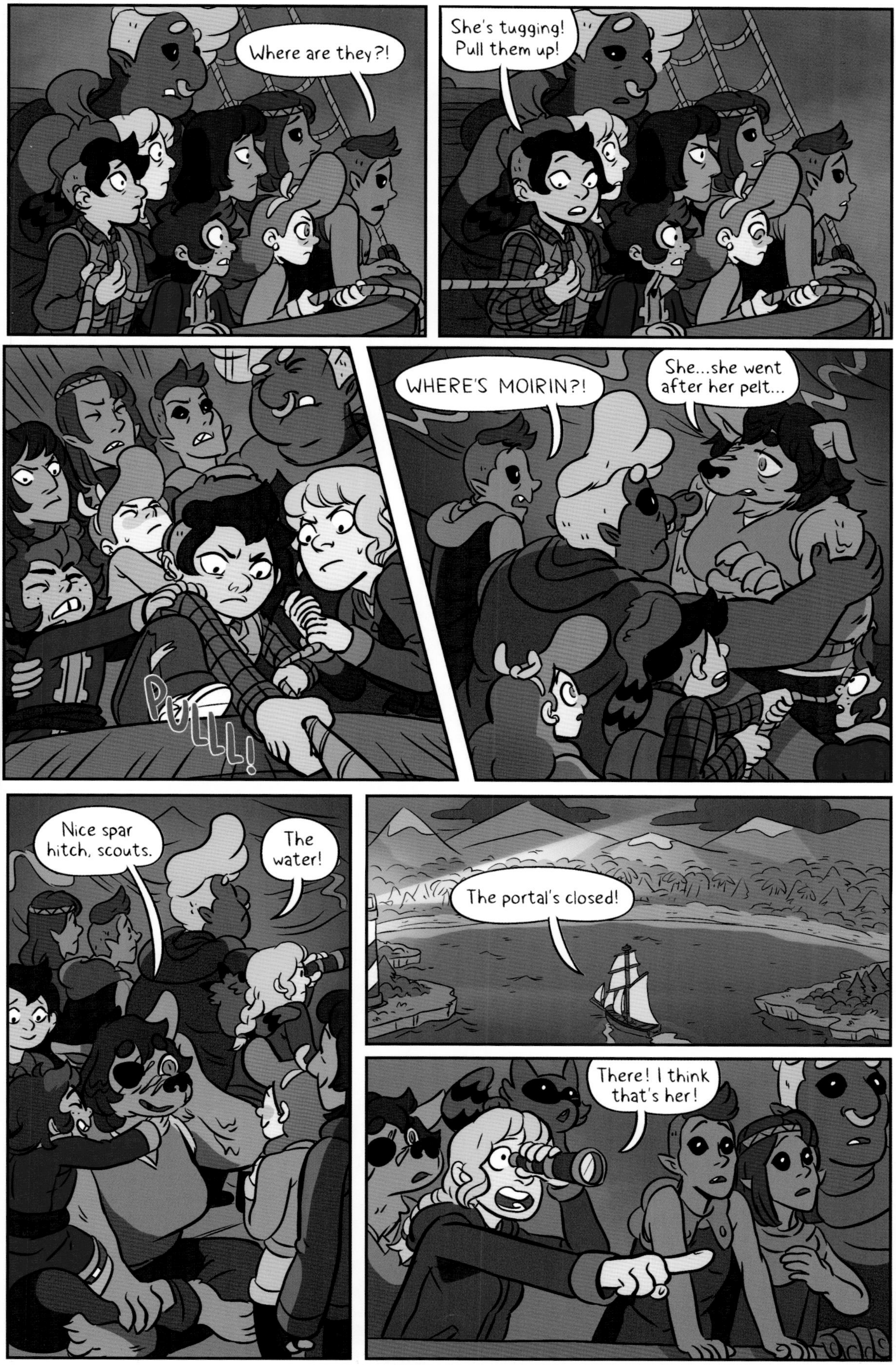
Where are they?!
She's tugging! Pull them up!
PULLL!
WHERE'S MOIRIN?!
She...she went after her pelt...
Nice spar hitch, scouts.
The water!
The portal's closed!
There! I think that's her!

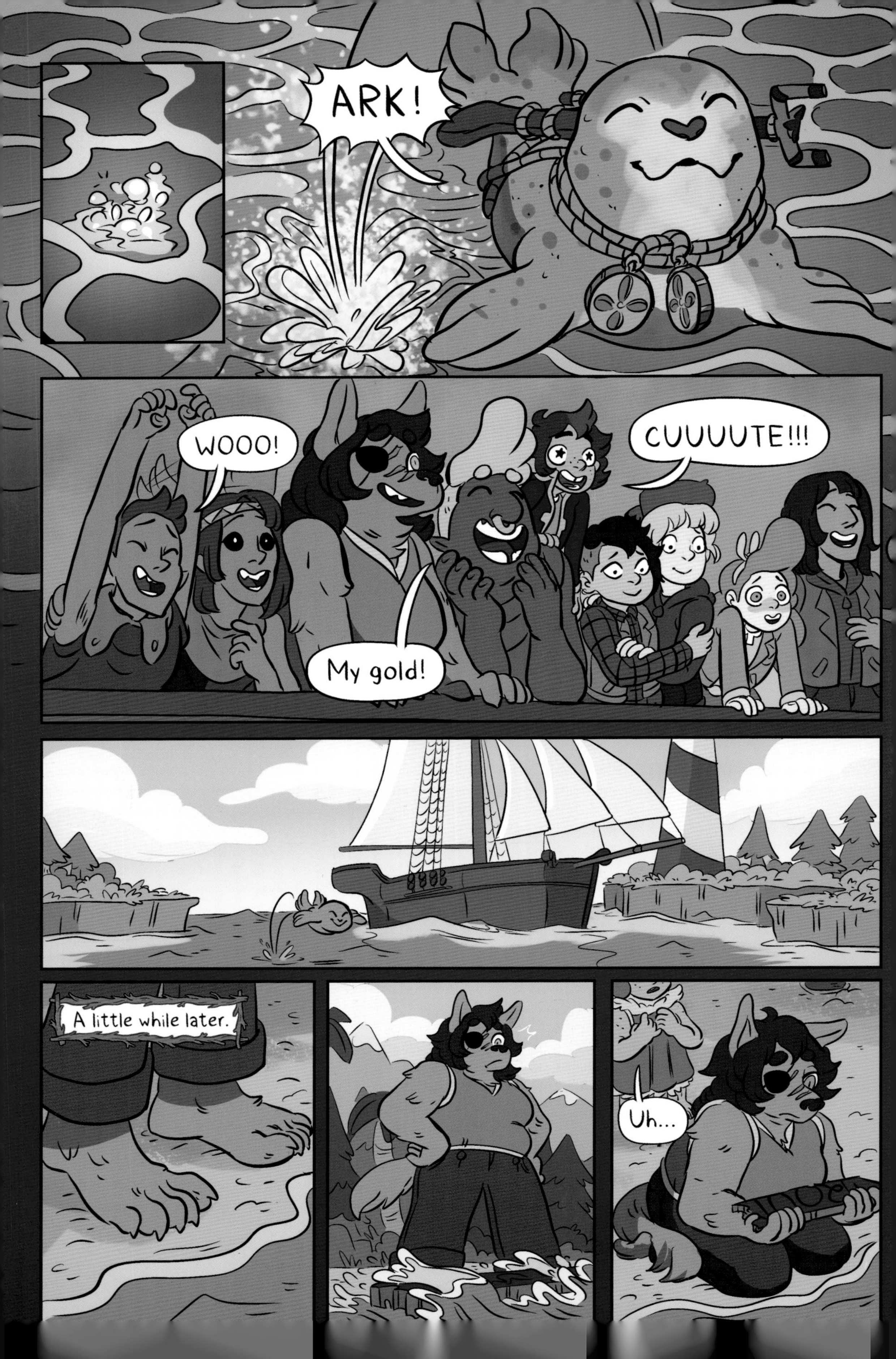
ARK!
WOOO!
My gold!
CUUUUTE!!!
A little while later.
Uh...

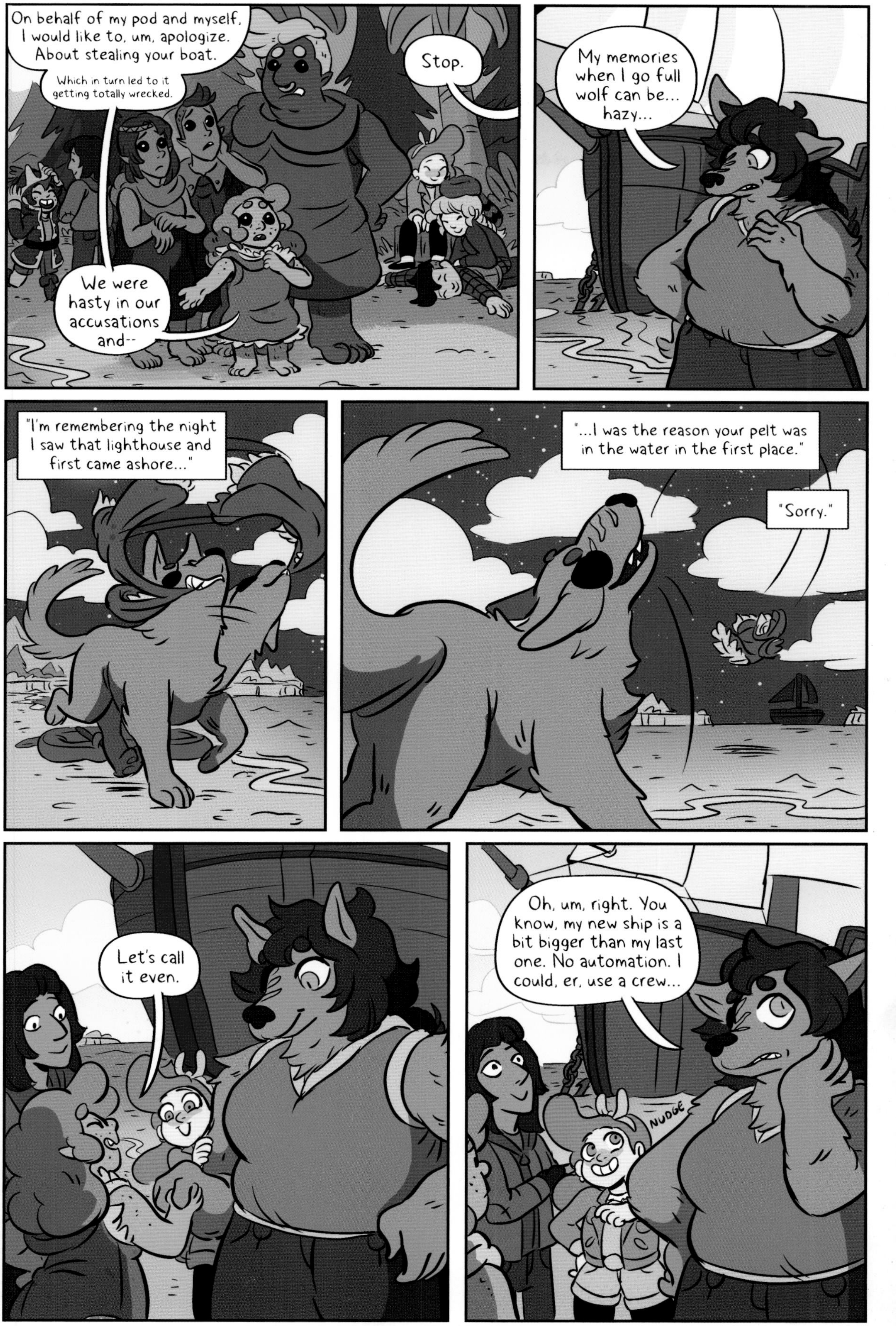
On behalf of my pod and myself, I would like to, um, apologize. About stealing your boat.
Which in turn led to it getting totally wrecked.
We were hasty in our accusations and--
Stop.
My memories when I go full wolf can be... hazy...
"I'm remembering the night I saw that lighthouse and first came ashore..."
"...I was the reason your pelt was in the water in the first place."
"Sorry."
Let's call it even.
Oh, um, right. You know, my new ship is a bit bigger than my last one. No automation. I could, er, use a crew...
NUDGE

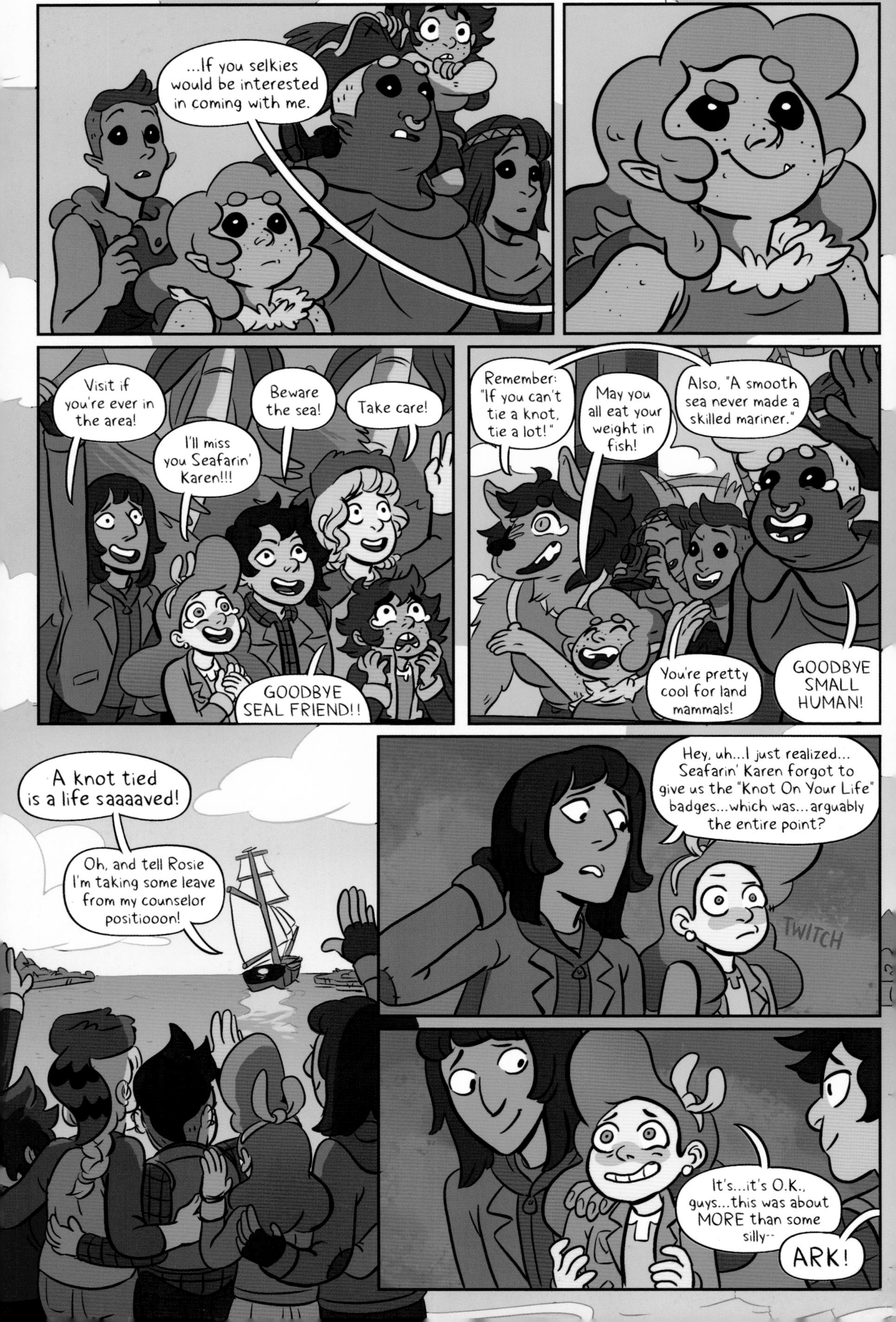
...If you selkies would be interested in coming with me.
Visit if you're ever in the area!
I'll miss you Seafarin' Karen!!!
Beware the sea!
Take care!
GOODBYE SEAL FRIEND!!
Remember: "If you can't tie a knot, tie a lot!"
May you all eat your weight in fish!
Also, "A smooth sea never made a skilled mariner."
You're pretty cool for land mammals!
GOODBYE SMALL HUMAN!
A knot tied is a life saaaaved!
Oh, and tell Rosie I'm taking some leave from my counselor positiooon!
Hey, uh...I just realized... Seafarin' Karen forgot to give us the "Knot On Your Life" badges...which was...arguably the entire point?
TWITCH
It's...it's O.K., guys...this was about MORE than some silly--
ARK!

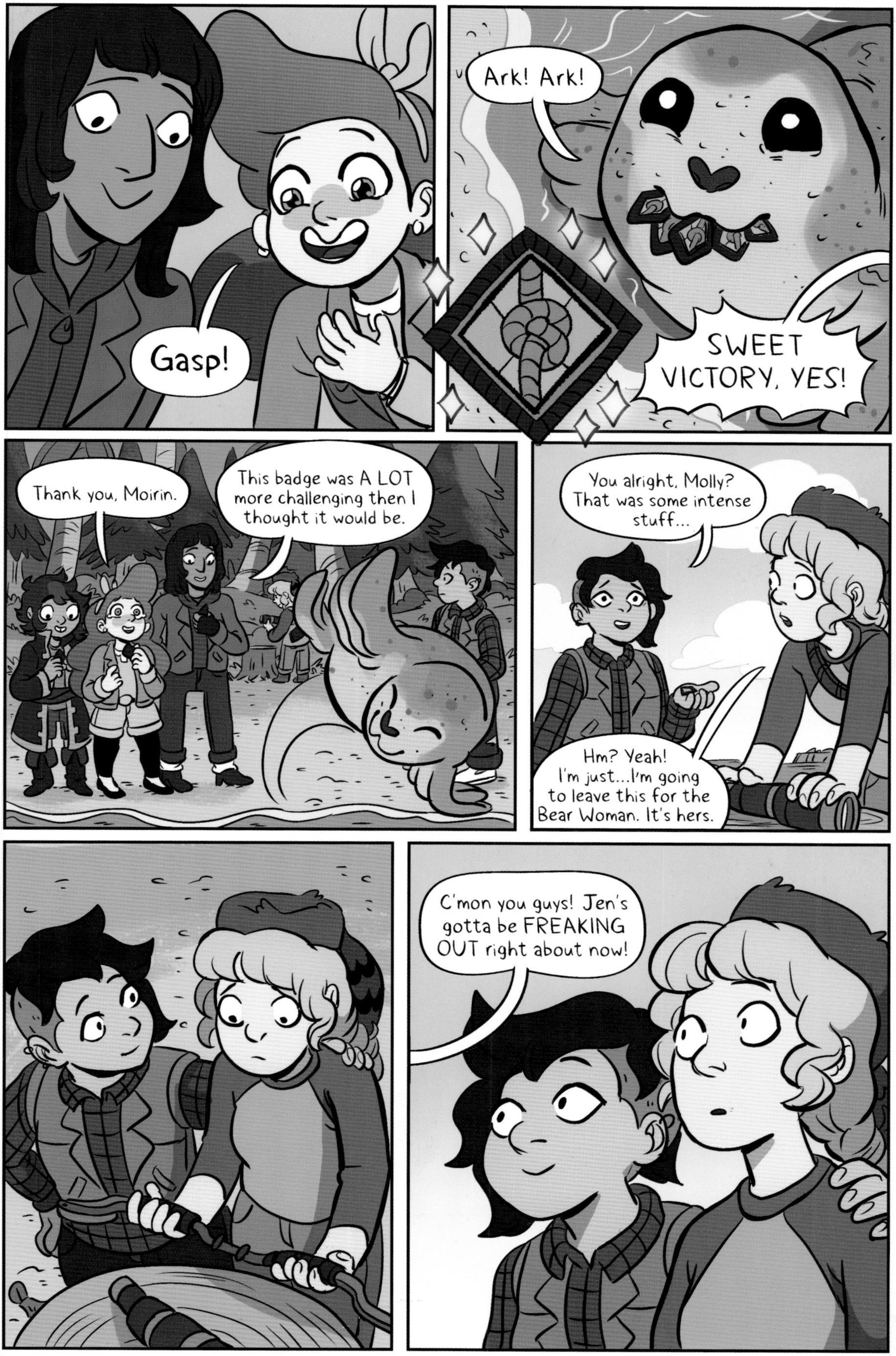
Gasp!
Ark! Ark!
SWEET VICTORY, YES!
Thank you, Moirin.
This badge was A LOT more challenging then I thought it would be.
You alright, Molly? That was some intense stuff...
Hm? Yeah! I'm just...I'm going to leave this for the Bear Woman. It's hers.
C'mon you guys! Jen's gotta be FREAKING OUT right about now!

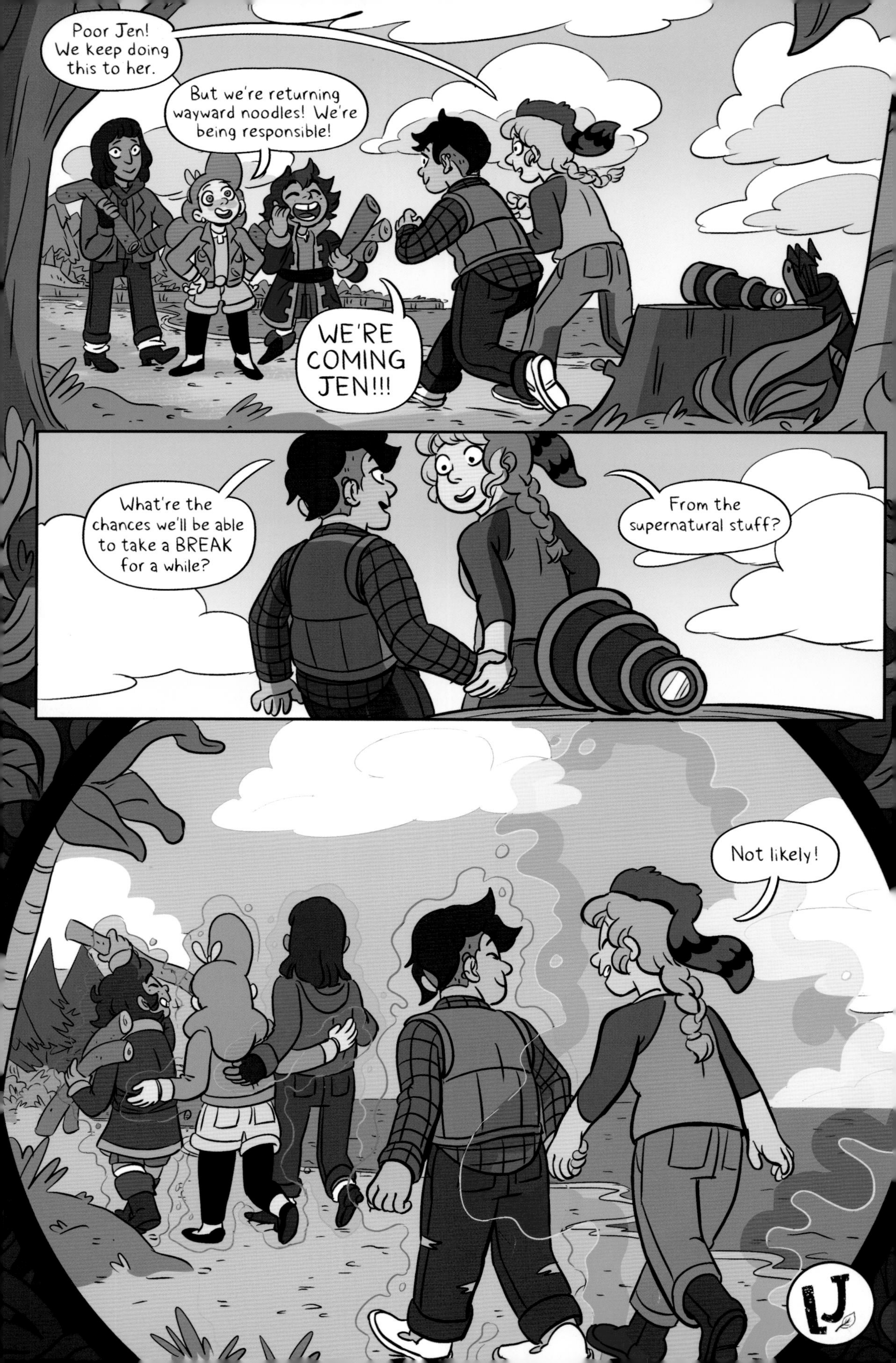
Poor Jen! We keep doing this to her.
But we're returning wayward noodles! We're being responsible!
WE'RE COMING JEN!!!
What're the chances we'll be able to take a BREAK for a while?
From the supernatural stuff?
Not likely!

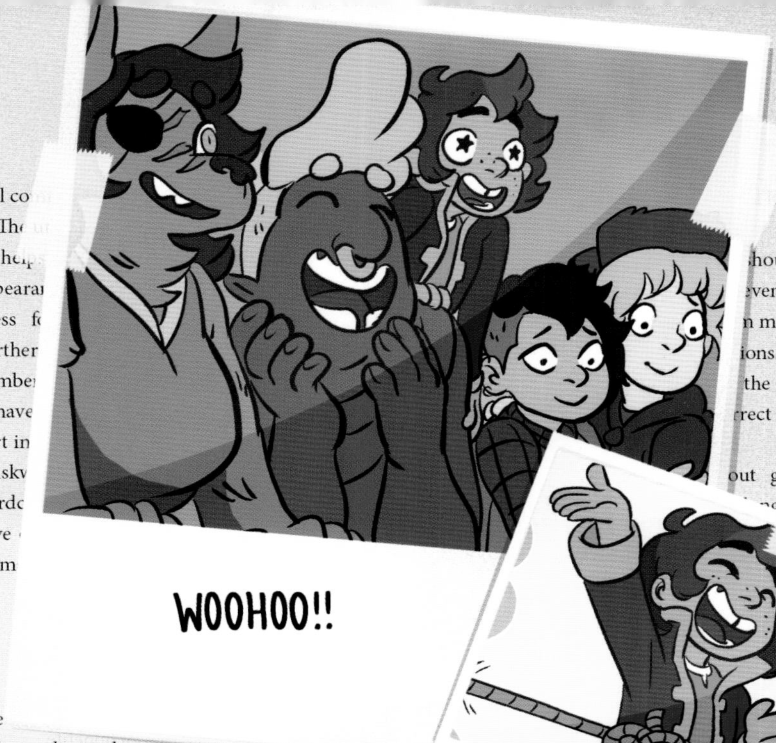
WOOHOO!!

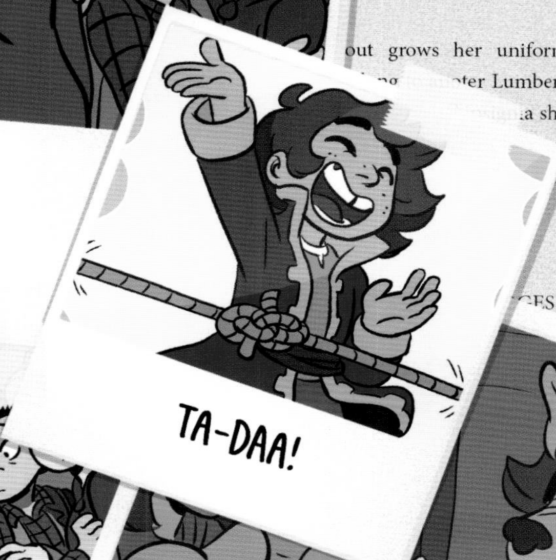
TA-DAA!

will co

The u
It help
appeara
dress fo
Further
Lumbe
to have
part in
Thiskv
Hardc
have
them

HE UNIFORM

should be worn at camp
events when Lumberjanes
n may also be worn at other
ions. It should be worn as a
the uniform dress with
rrect shoes, and stocking or

out grows her uniform or
ter Lumberjane.
a she has
her
her

The
yellow, short sl
emb
the w
choose
slacks,
made o
out-of-dc
green bere
the colla
Shoes ma
heels, rou
socks shou
the uniform. Ne
belong with a Lumberjane uniform.

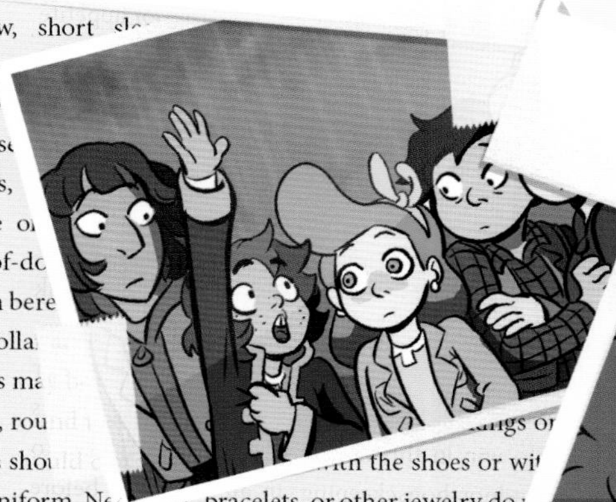

GES

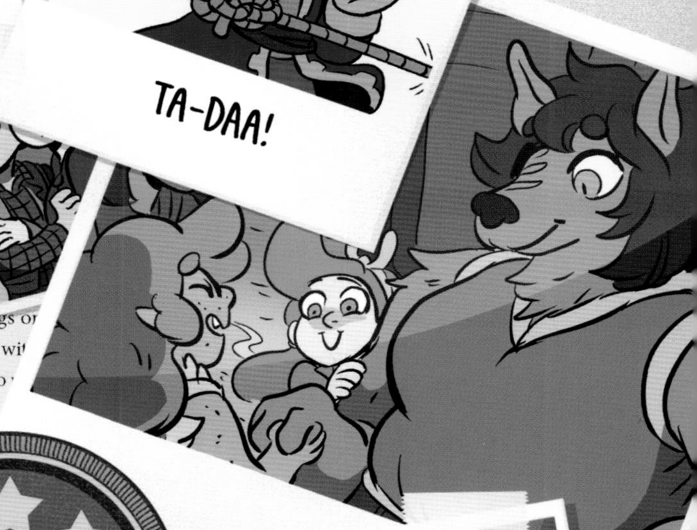

kings or
the shoes or wit
bracelets, or other jewelry do

HOW TO WEAR THE U

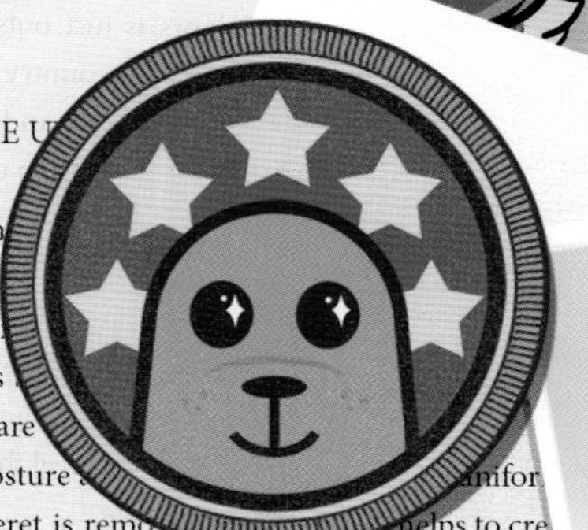

To look well in a uniform dem
uniform be kept in good con
pressed. See that the skirt is the r
height and build, that the belt is
that your shoes and stockings are
uniform, that you watch your posture
with dignity and grace. If the beret is remo
be sure that your hair is neat and kept in place with an insonspicuous clip or ribbon. When you wear a Lumberjane uniform you are identified as a member of this organization and you should be doubly careful to conduct yourself in a way that will show everyone that courtesy and thoughtfullness are part of being a Lumberjane. People are likely to judge a whole nation by the selfishness of a few individuals, to criticize a whole family because of the misconduct of one member, and to feel unkindly toward and organization because of the

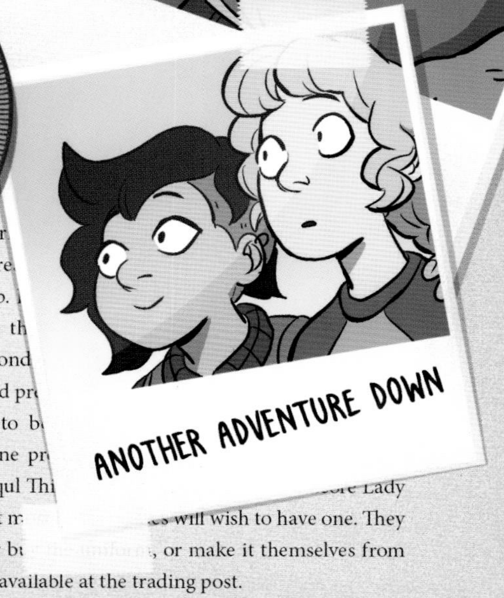
ANOTHER ADVENTURE DOWN

unifor
helps to cre
in a group.
active life th
another bond
future, and pr
in order to b
Lumberjane pr
Penniquiqul Thi
Types, but m
will wish to have one. They
can either bu
or make it themselves from
materials available at the trading post.

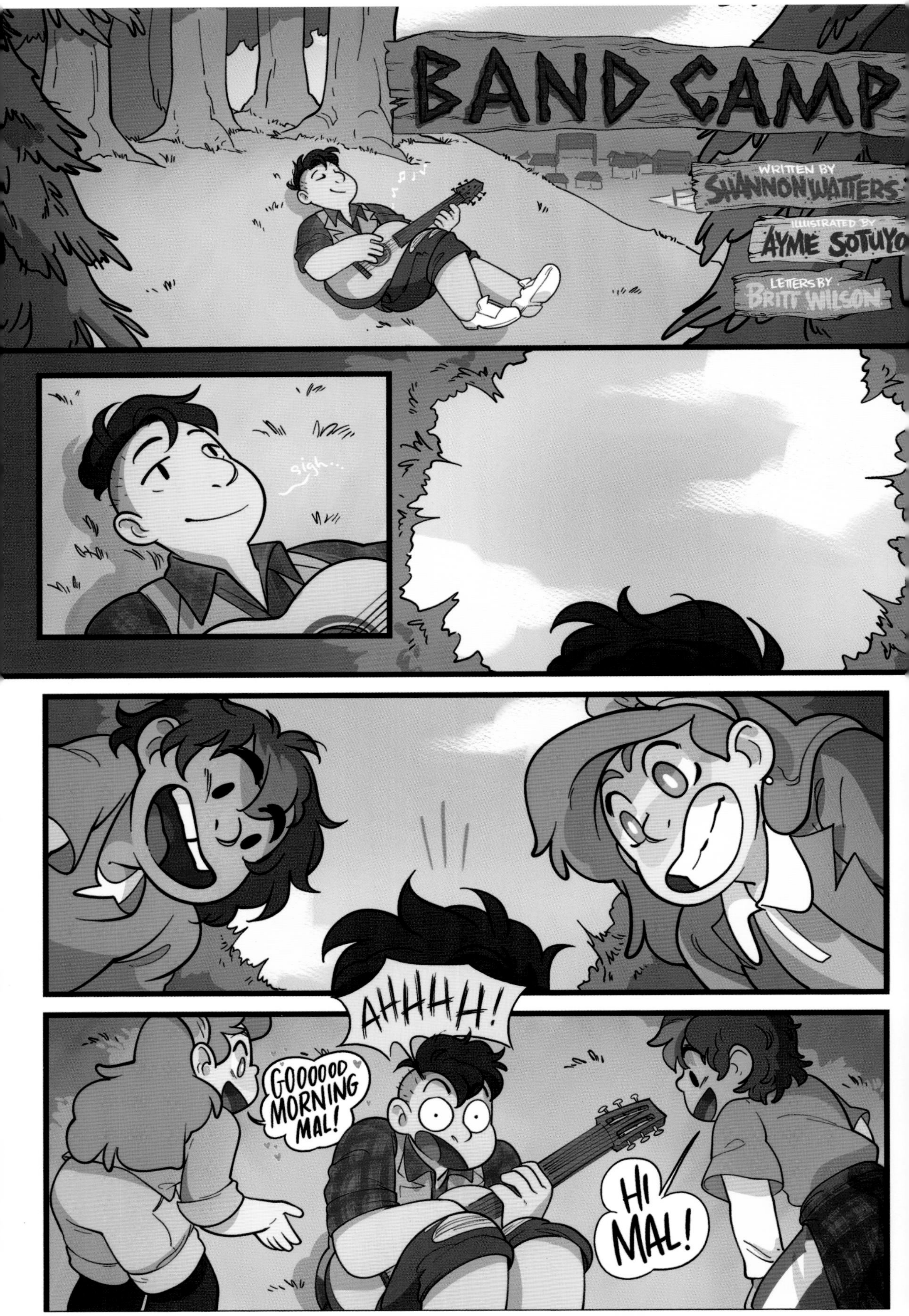
BAND CAMP
WRITTEN BY
SHANNON WATTERS
ILLUSTRATED BY
AYME SOTUYO
LETTERS BY
BRITT WILSON
sigh...
AHHHH!
GOOOOOD MORNING MAL!
HI MAL!

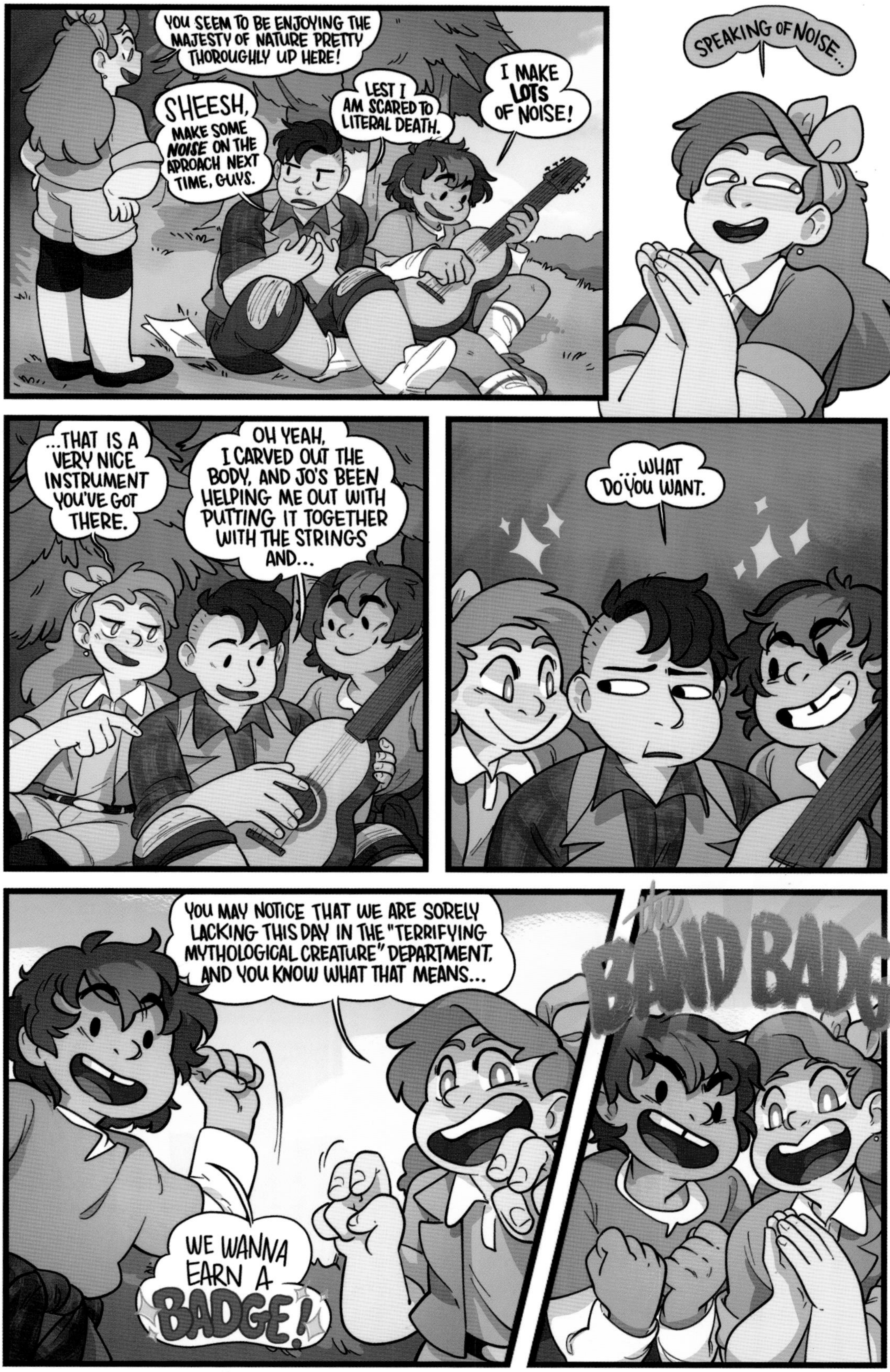
YOU SEEM TO BE ENJOYING THE MAJESTY OF NATURE PRETTY THOROUGHLY UP HERE!
SHEESH, MAKE SOME NOISE ON THE APROACH NEXT TIME, GUYS.
LEST I AM SCARED TO LITERAL DEATH.
I MAKE LOTS OF NOISE!
SPEAKING OF NOISE...
...THAT IS A VERY NICE INSTRUMENT YOU'VE GOT THERE.
OH YEAH, I CARVED OUT THE BODY, AND JO'S BEEN HELPING ME OUT WITH PUTTING IT TOGETHER WITH THE STRINGS AND...
...WHAT DO YOU WANT.
YOU MAY NOTICE THAT WE ARE SORELY LACKING THIS DAY IN THE "TERRIFYING MYTHOLOGICAL CREATURE" DEPARTMENT, AND YOU KNOW WHAT THAT MEANS...
WE WANNA EARN A BADGE!
the BAND BADGE

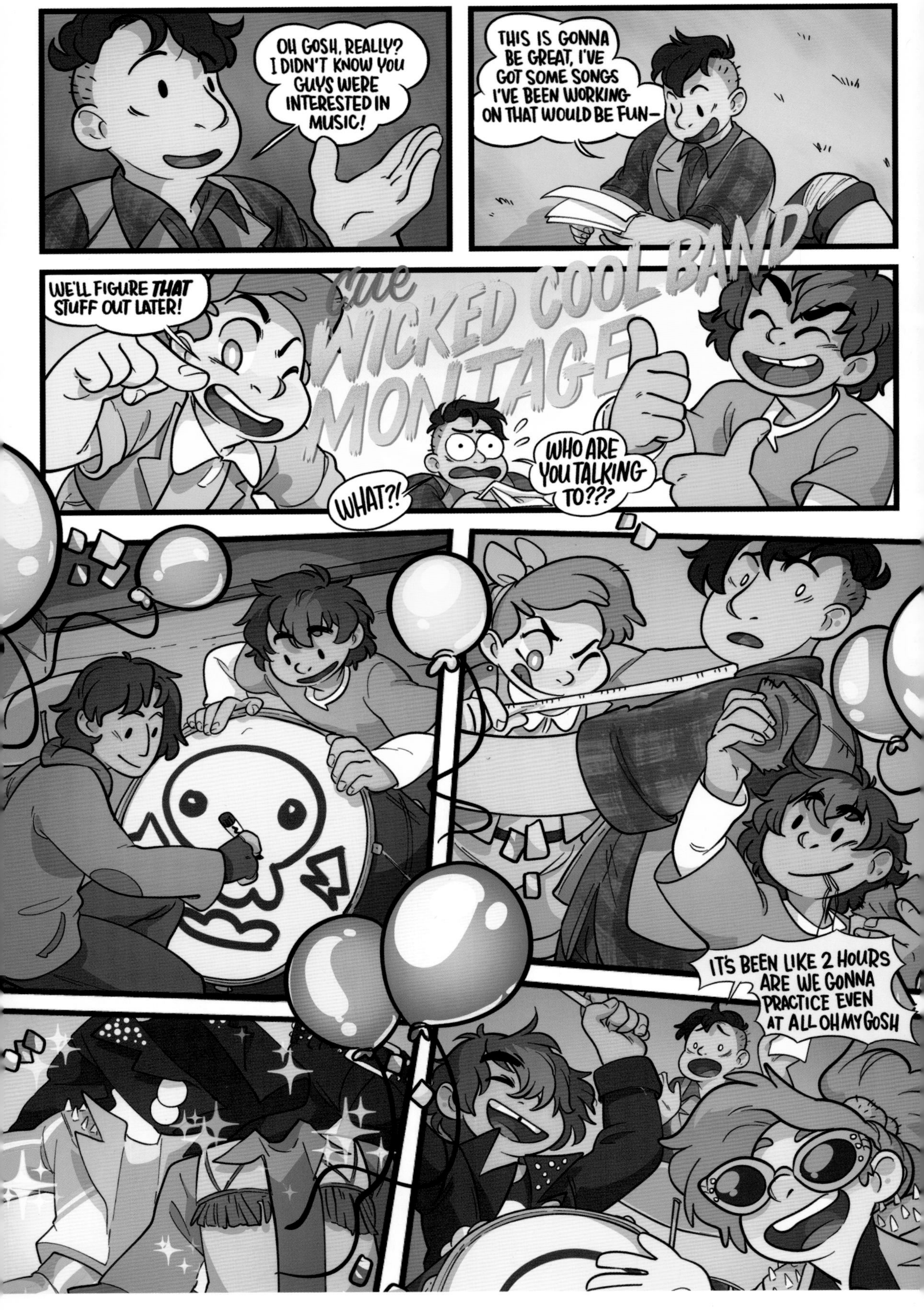

OH GOSH, REALLY? I DIDN'T KNOW YOU GUYS WERE INTERESTED IN MUSIC!
THIS IS GONNA BE GREAT, I'VE GOT SOME SONGS I'VE BEEN WORKING ON THAT WOULD BE FUN–
WE'LL FIGURE THAT STUFF OUT LATER!
Cue WICKED COOL BAND MONTAGE
WHAT?!
WHO ARE YOU TALKING TO???
IT'S BEEN LIKE 2 HOURS ARE WE GONNA PRACTICE EVEN AT ALL OH MY GOSH

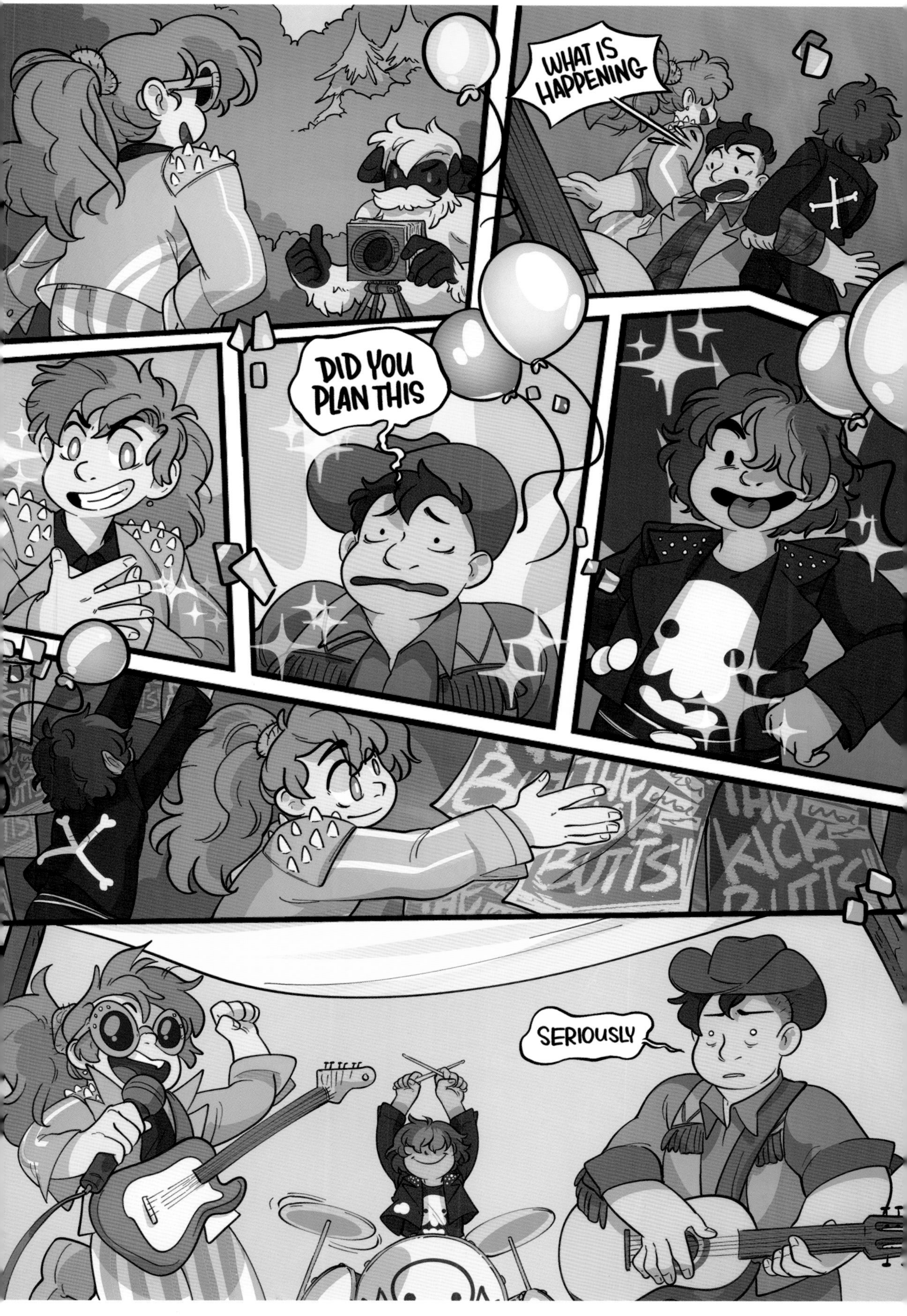
WHAT IS HAPPENING
DID YOU PLAN THIS
SERIOUSLY

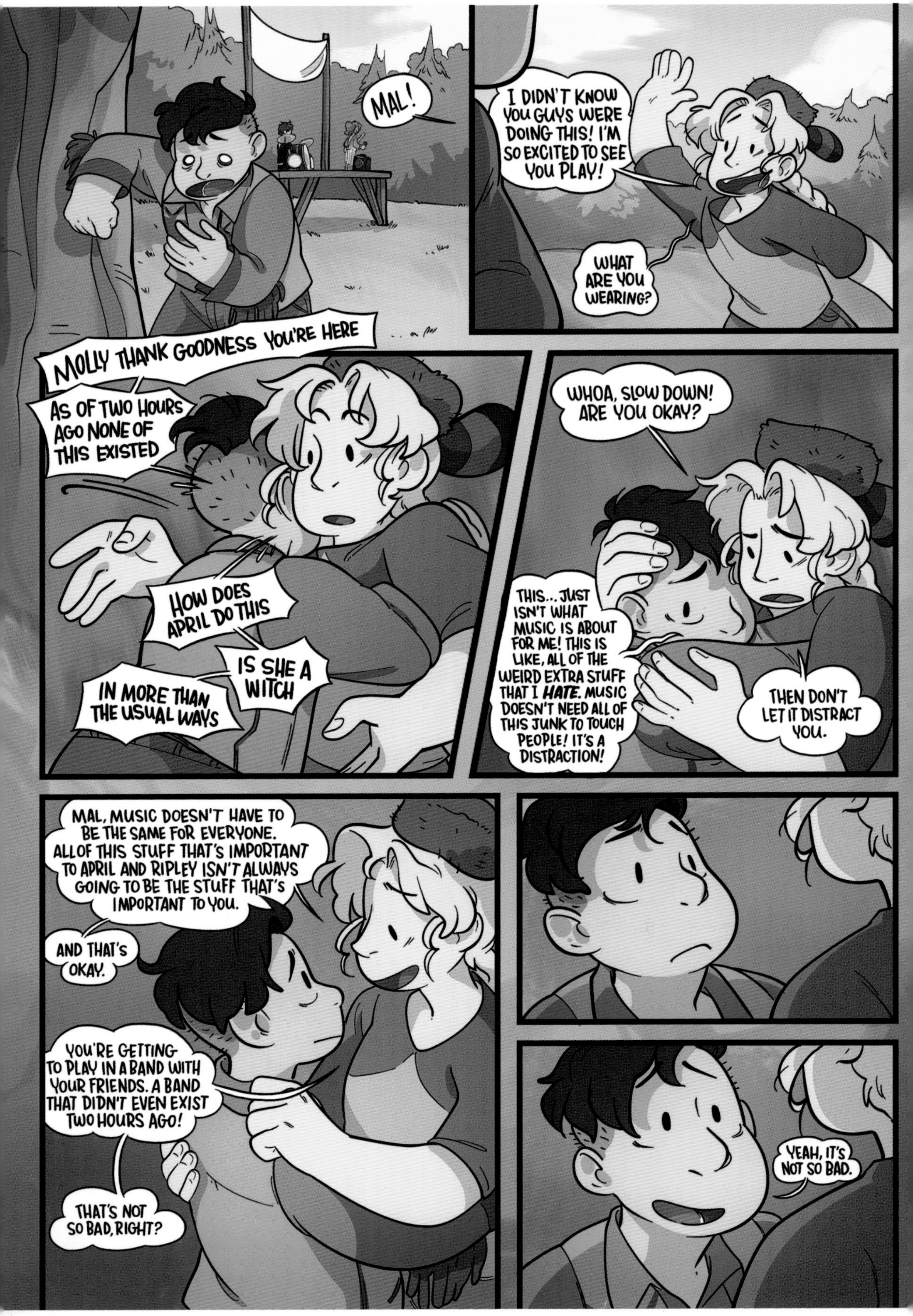
MAL!
I DIDN'T KNOW YOU GUYS WERE DOING THIS! I'M SO EXCITED TO SEE YOU PLAY!
WHAT ARE YOU WEARING?
MOLLY THANK GOODNESS YOU'RE HERE
AS OF TWO HOURS AGO NONE OF THIS EXISTED
HOW DOES APRIL DO THIS
IS SHE A WITCH
IN MORE THAN THE USUAL WAYS
WHOA, SLOW DOWN! ARE YOU OKAY?
THIS... JUST ISN'T WHAT MUSIC IS ABOUT FOR ME! THIS IS LIKE, ALL OF THE WEIRD EXTRA STUFF THAT I **HATE**. MUSIC DOESN'T NEED ALL OF THIS JUNK TO TOUCH PEOPLE! IT'S A DISTRACTION!
THEN DON'T LET IT DISTRACT YOU.
MAL, MUSIC DOESN'T HAVE TO BE THE SAME FOR EVERYONE. ALL OF THIS STUFF THAT'S IMPORTANT TO APRIL AND RIPLEY ISN'T ALWAYS GOING TO BE THE STUFF THAT'S IMPORTANT TO YOU.
AND THAT'S OKAY.
YOU'RE GETTING TO PLAY IN A BAND WITH YOUR FRIENDS. A BAND THAT DIDN'T EVEN EXIST TWO HOURS AGO!
THAT'S NOT SO BAD, RIGHT?
YEAH, IT'S NOT SO BAD.

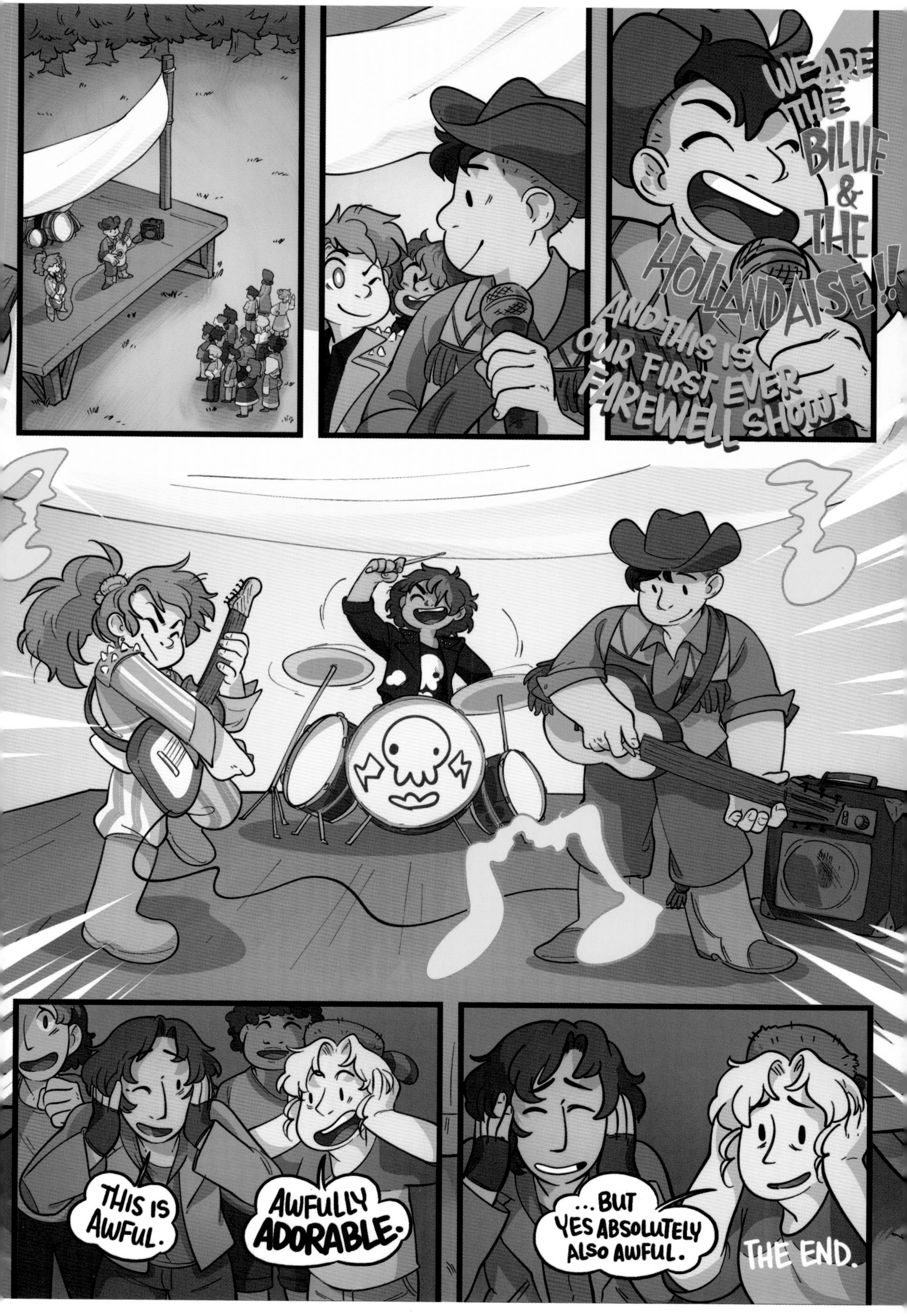
WE ARE THE BILLIE & THE HOLLANDAISE!!
AND THIS IS OUR FIRST EVER FAREWELL SHOW!
THIS IS AWFUL.
AWFULLY ADORABLE.
...BUT YES ABSOLUTELY ALSO AWFUL.
THE END.

BROOKE a ALLEN

LUMBERJANES FIELD MANUAL

AFTERWORD

I joined the *Lumberjanes* team at issue 18 as co-writer. And it was daunting. I would be joining a book that was already well underway and LOVED by so many—myself included. It was my first job as writer for an on-going series AND I was taking the place of someone as talented as Noelle. I didn't want to screw up.

There was no need to worry. Like so many others, this story about enthusiastic, diverse, queer, and capable girls in a magical forest feels so RIGHT to me. I can think back to when I was a kid and write the stories that I would have loved and didn't even know I was missing at the time. I needed characters like these and I know all of you do as well. This is reaffirmed every time I get to meet a lovely fan and hear what this book means to them. There's no end to what these girls can do! And I grow to understand them more with every arc.

I didn't only have a great story and characters to work with. As I said before, I joined the Lumberjanes TEAM. Shannon and I went over all the characters to the point where I felt I knew them all as well as my own. And Whitney and Dafna are endlessly encouraging and supportive. Every comic I had ever written before I had also drawn, so it has been absolutely magical to see my writing brought to life by such an incredible group of artists—Maarta, Aubrey, Carolyn, and Carey! They took the first few scripts Shannon and I wrote and turned them into the lovely book you're holding now!

This book is powered by amazing women, and I'm fortunate to be a part of that group.

I love that those of you reading this have stuck with us so far. Little else is as encouraging as knowing people out there are enjoying the book you enjoy making, and I can't wait for you to see what's next!

KAT LEYH
co-wrtier, cover artist, and PUNgineer

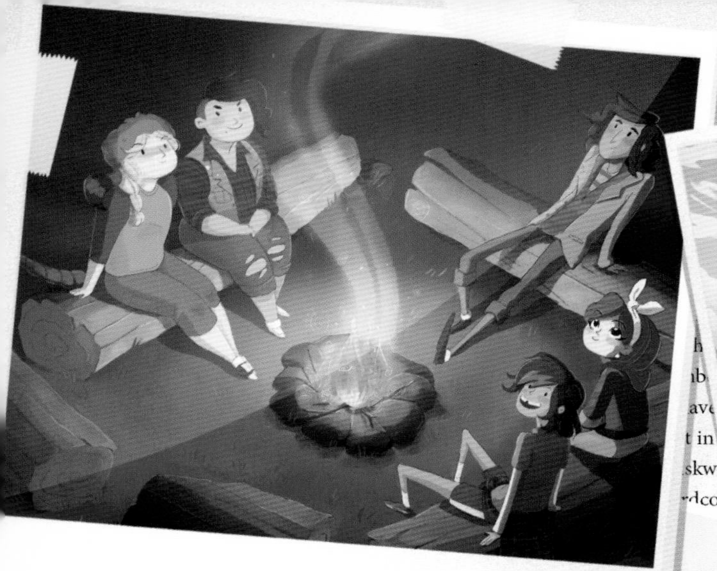

A LITTLE TIME AROUND THE FIRE

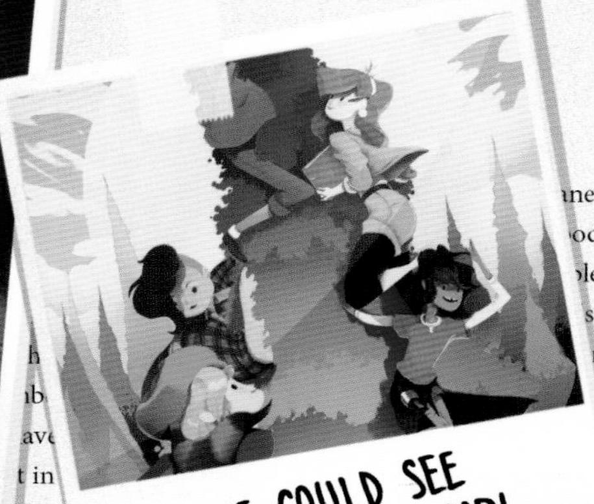

WE COULD SEE THE WHOLE CAMP!

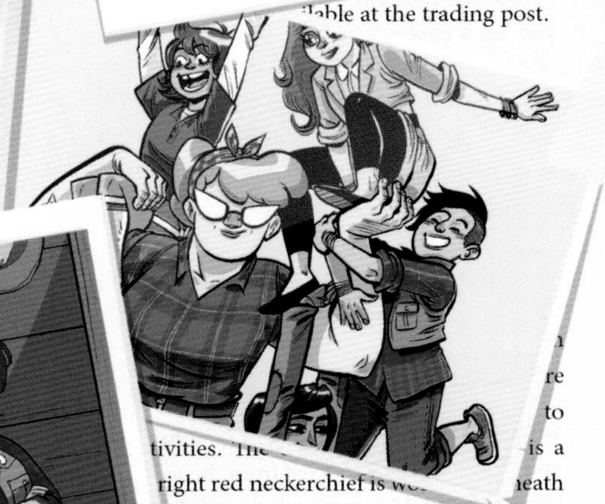

The Lumberjane uniform

meeting

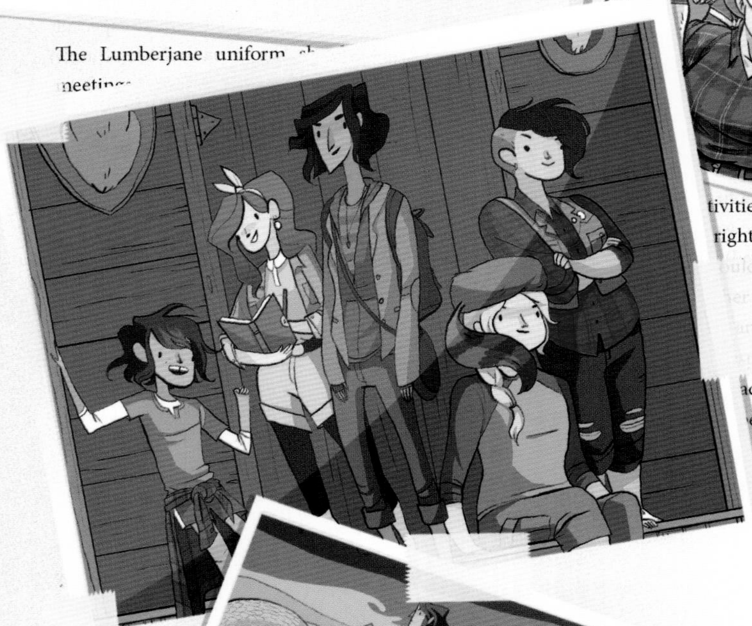

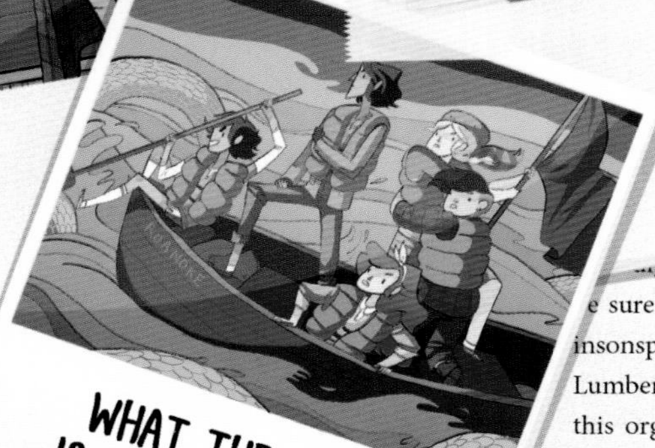

WHAT THE JUNK IS IN THE WATER?!

The

helps

in a g

active

another

future

in or

Lumberjane p

Penniquiqul Thistle Cr

Types, but most Lumberjanes wi ey

can either buy the uniform, or make it the rom

materials available at the trading post.

ane.

od

le

s.

h r

ib

ave

t in

skwi

rdcor

, or make it

lable at the trading post.

n

re

to

tivities. The is a

right red neckerchief is wo neath

ould be tied in a simple friendship knot.

lack or brown and should have flat

a straight inner line. Stockings or

nd in color with the shoes or with

aces, bracelets, or other jewelry do not

erjane uniform.

WEAR THE UNIFORM

orm demans first of all that the

ood condition—clean and well

t is the right length for your own

e belt is adjusted to your waist,

kings are in keeping with the

our posture and carry yourself

dignity and grace. If the beret is removed indoors, e sure that your hair is neat and kept in place with an insonspicuous clip or ribbon. When you wear a Lumberjane uniform you are identified as a member of this organization and you should be doubly careful to conduct yourself in a way that will show everyone that courtesy and thoughtfullness are part of being a Lumberjane. People are likely to judge a whole nation by the selfishness of a few individuals, to criticize a whole family because of the misconduct of one member, and to feel unkindly toward and organization because of the

COVER GALLERY

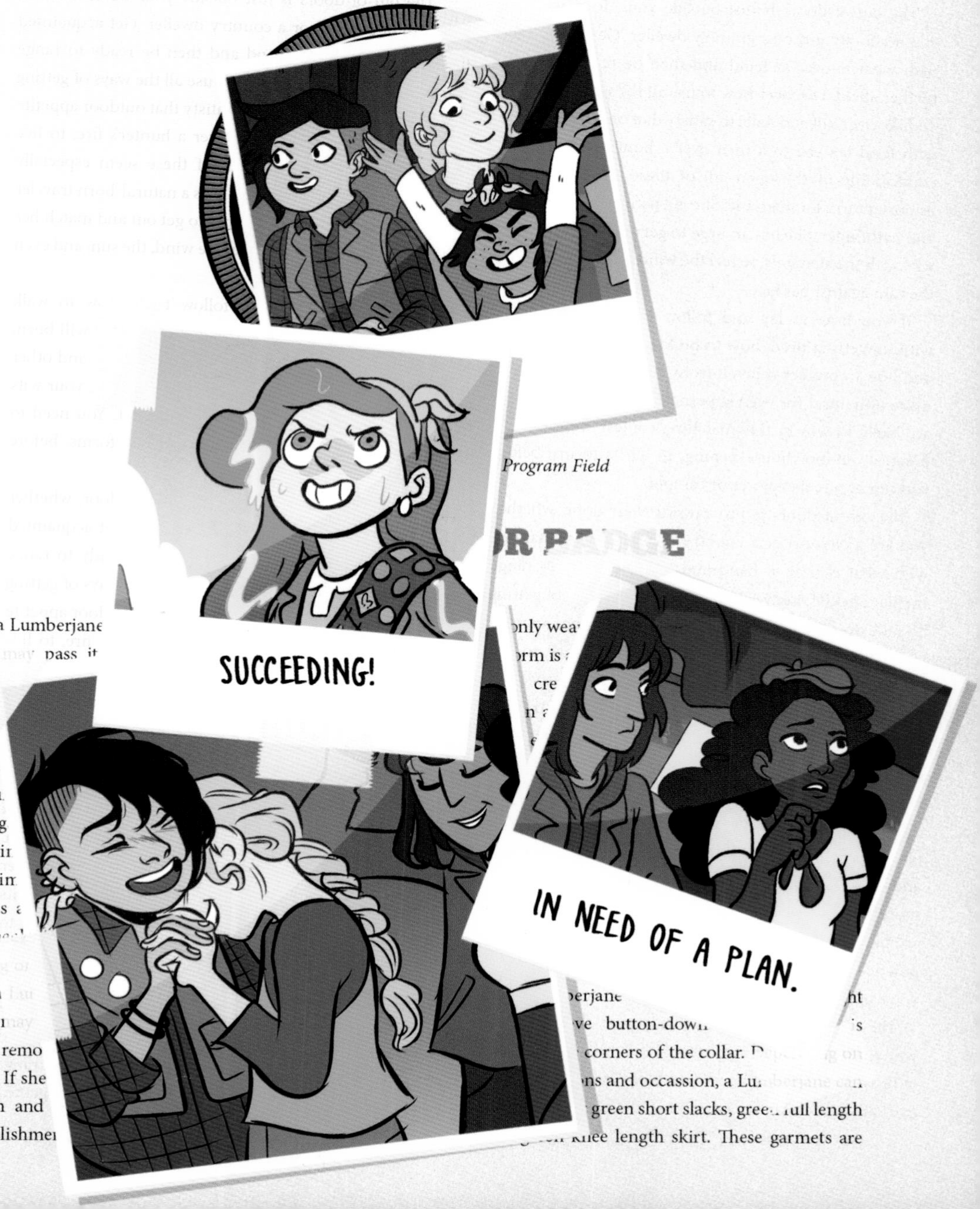
SUCCEEDING!
IN NEED OF A PLAN.

Issue Thirteen
BROOKE ALLEN

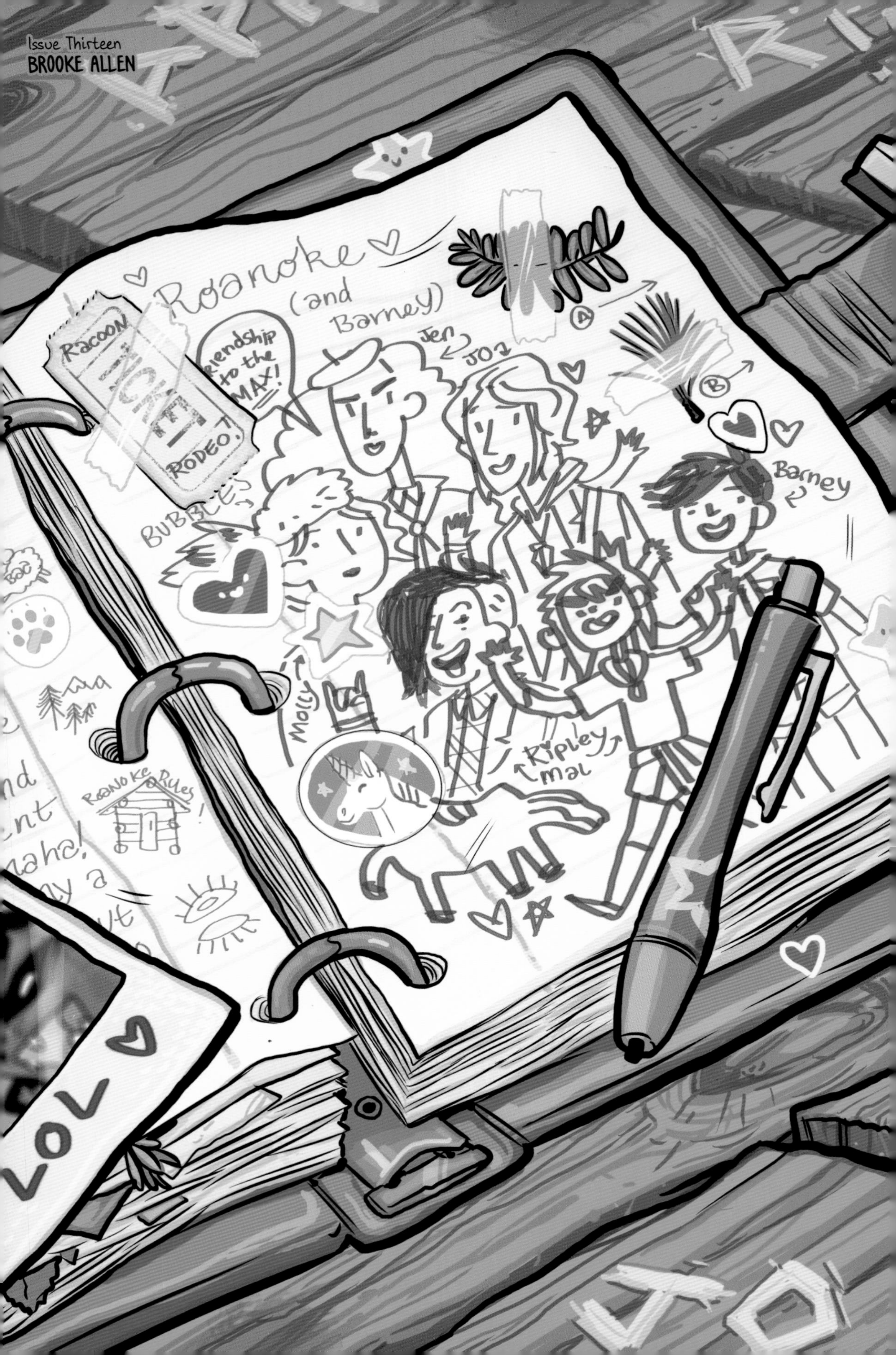

Roanoke
(and Barney)
Jen
Jo
Friendship to the MAX!
RACOON RODEO TICKET
BUBBLES
Barney
Molly
Ripley
Mal
Roanoke Rules

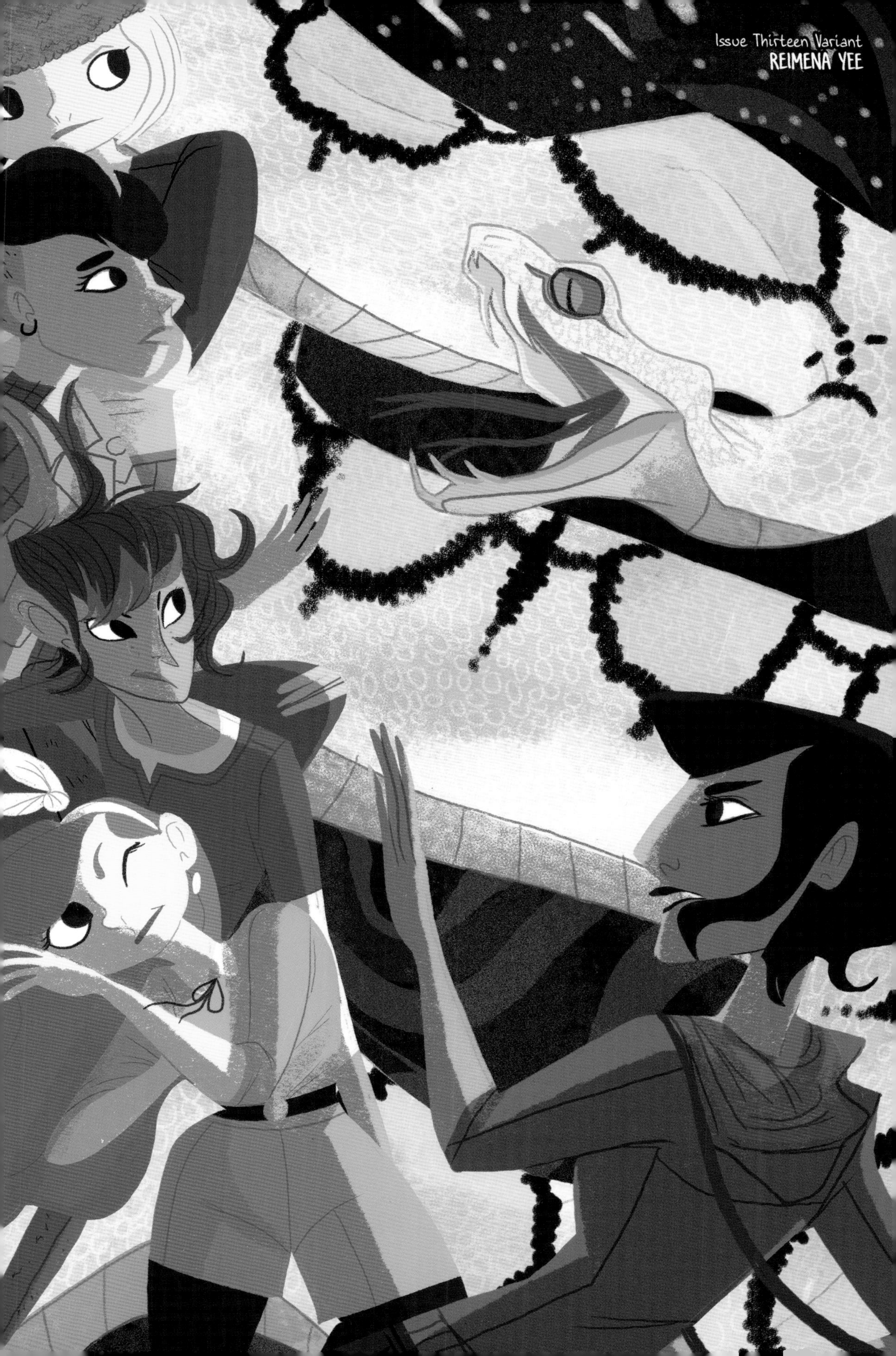

Issue Thirteen Variant
REIMENA YEE

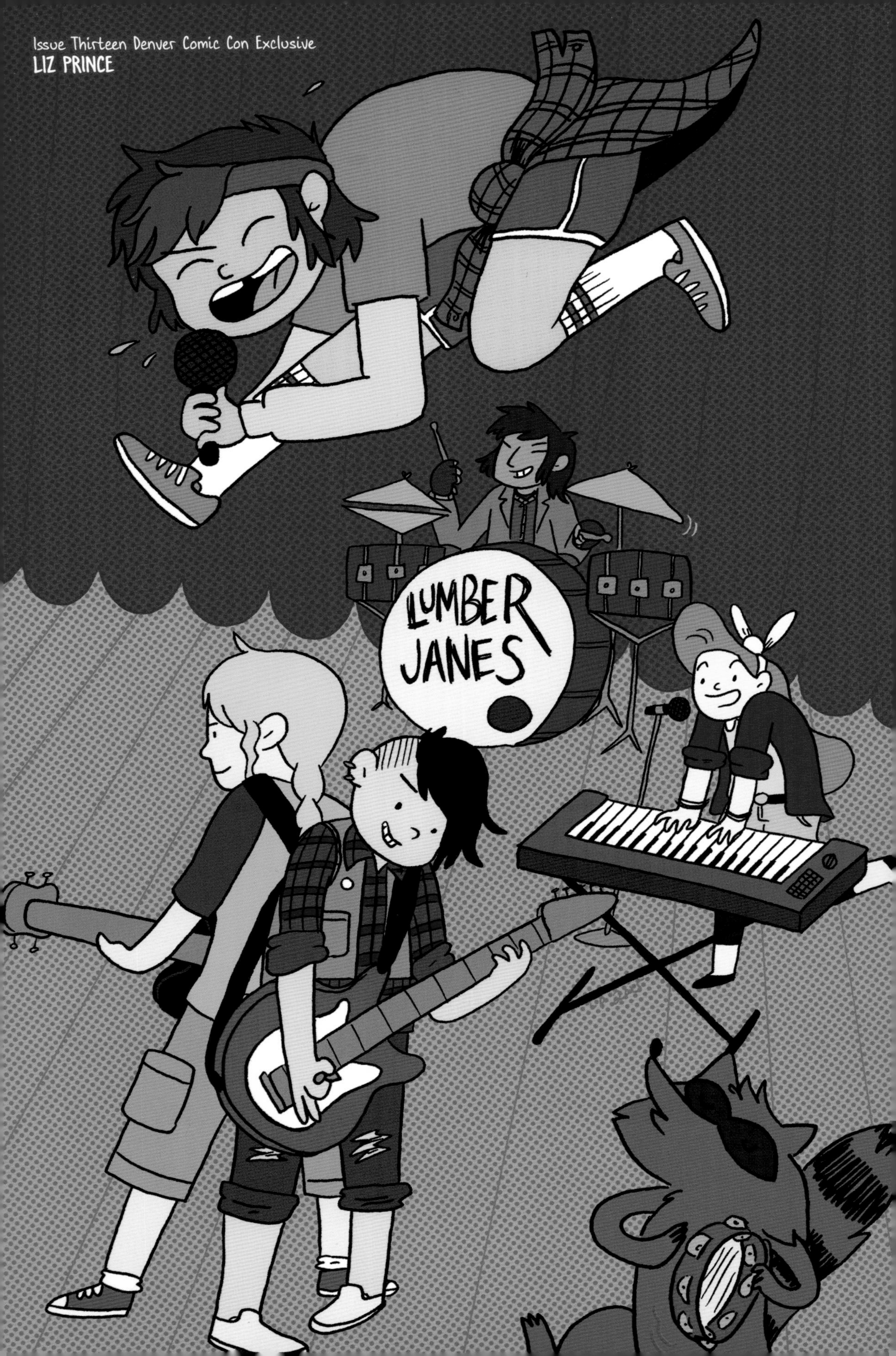
Issue Thirteen Denver Comic Con Exclusive
LIZ PRINCE
LUMBER
JANES

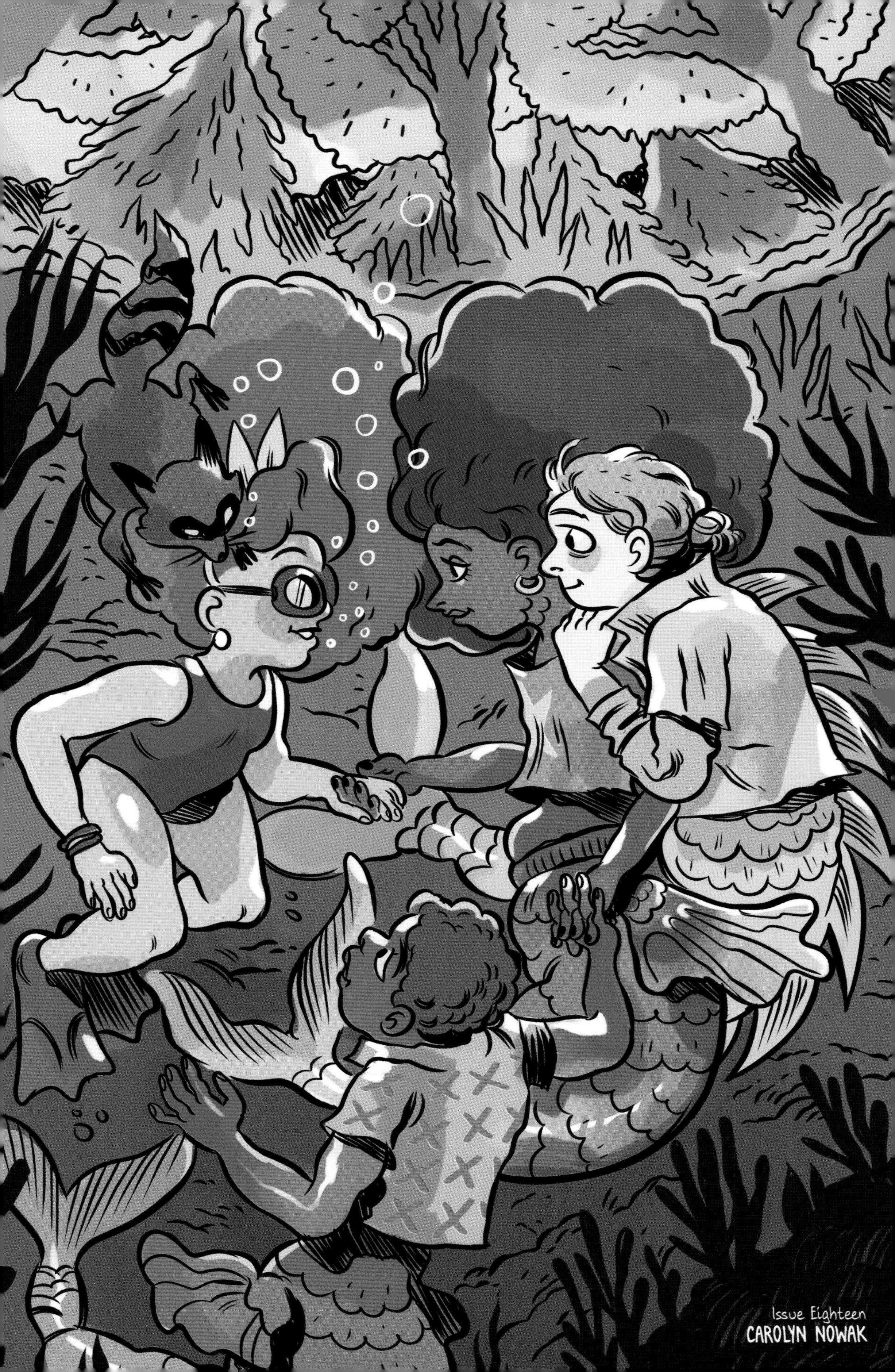
Issue Eighteen
CAROLYN NOWAK

Issue Eighteen Variant
LAUREN DAWSON

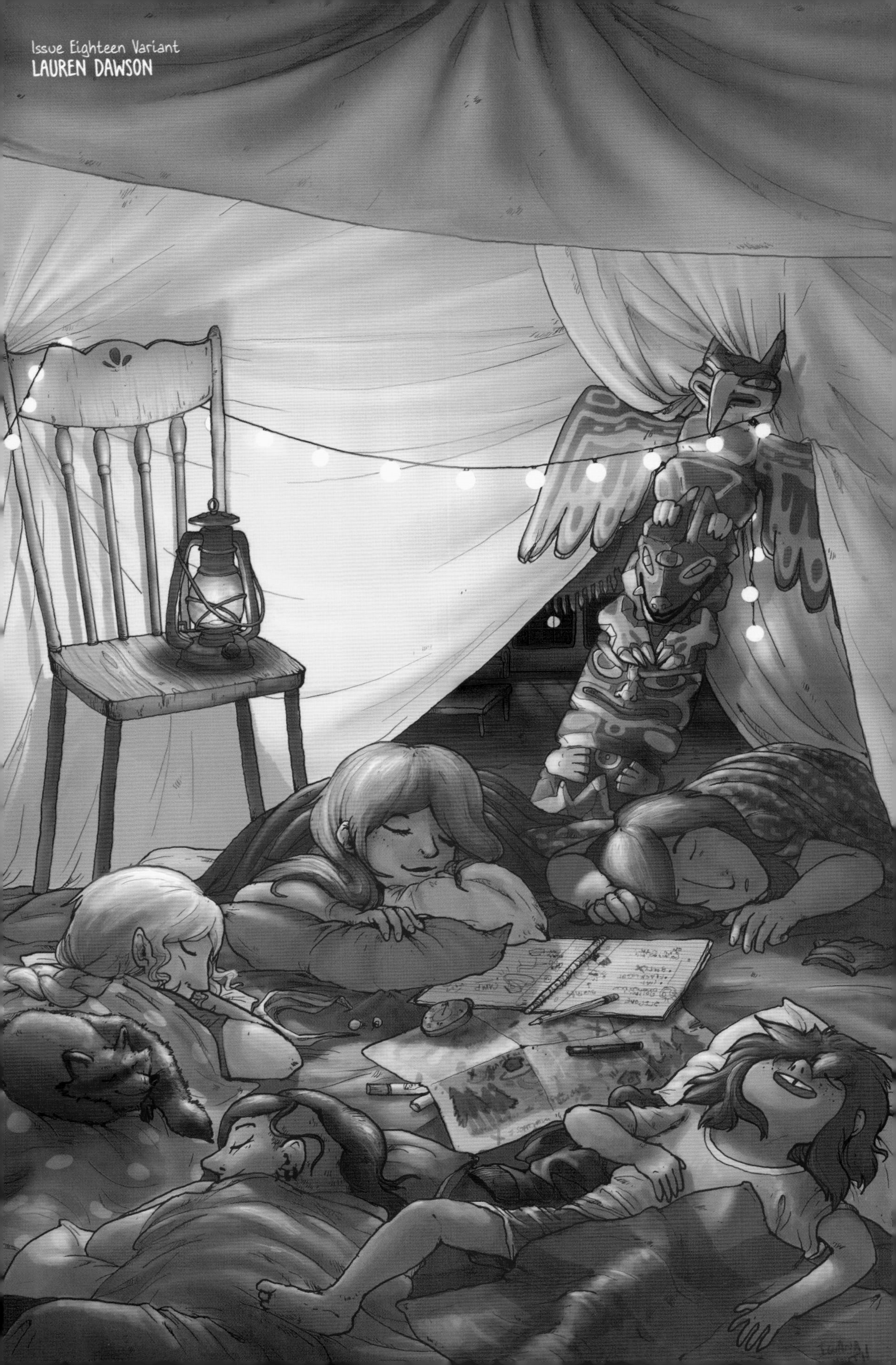

Issue Eighteen CAB Comics Exclusive
RACHEL DUKES

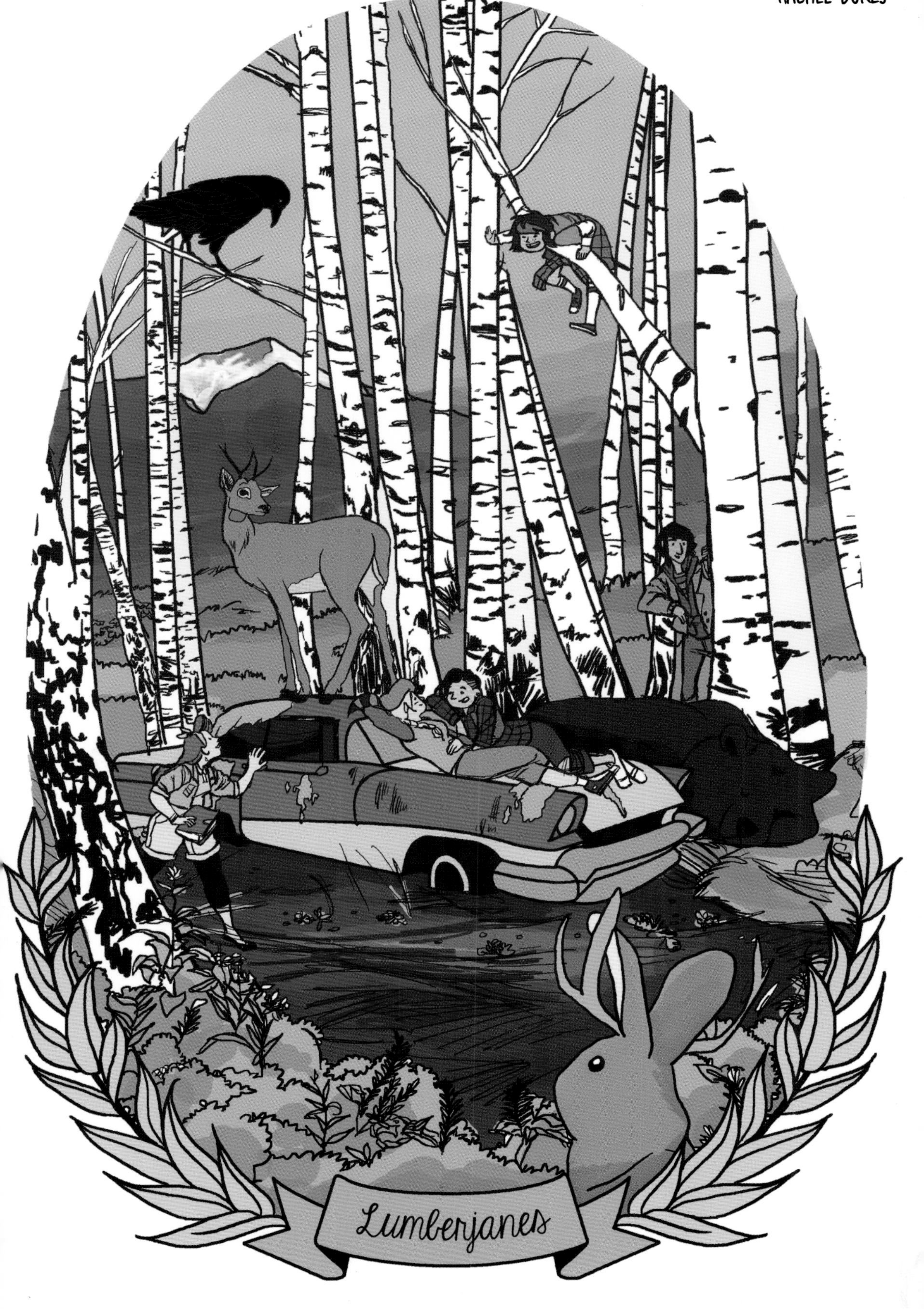
Lumberjanes

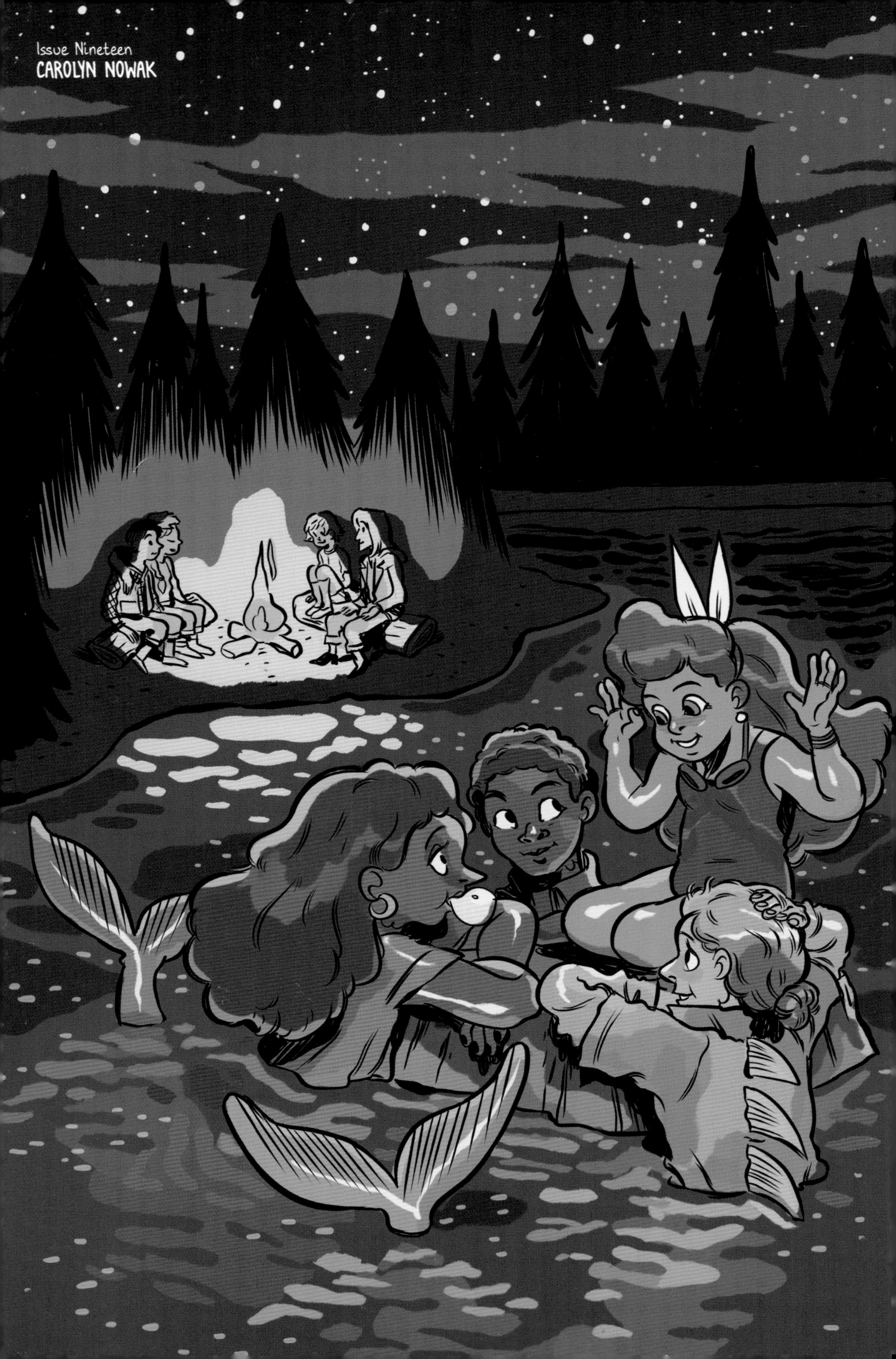
Issue Nineteen
CAROLYN NOWAK

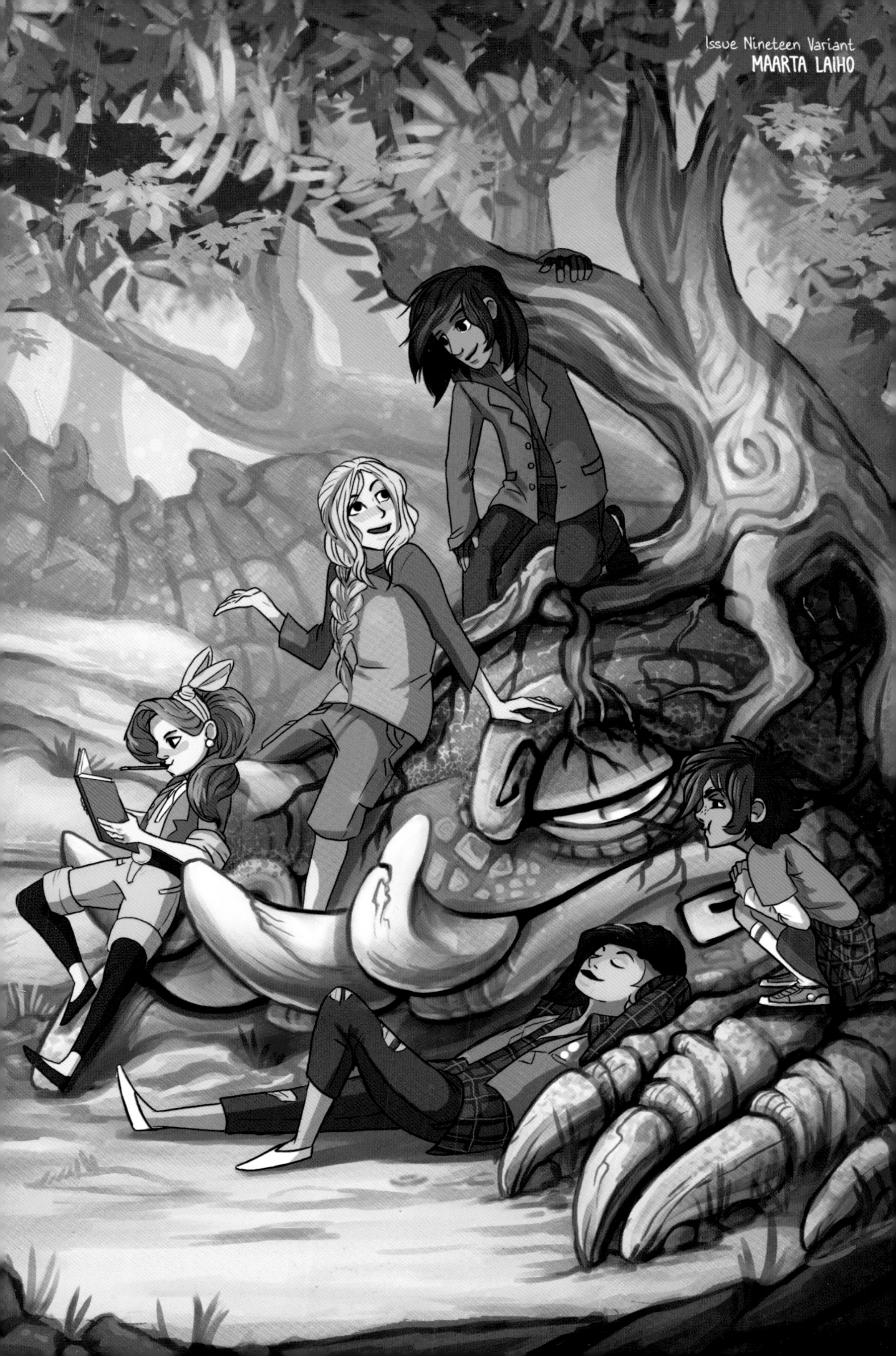
Issue Nineteen Variant
MAARTA LAIHO

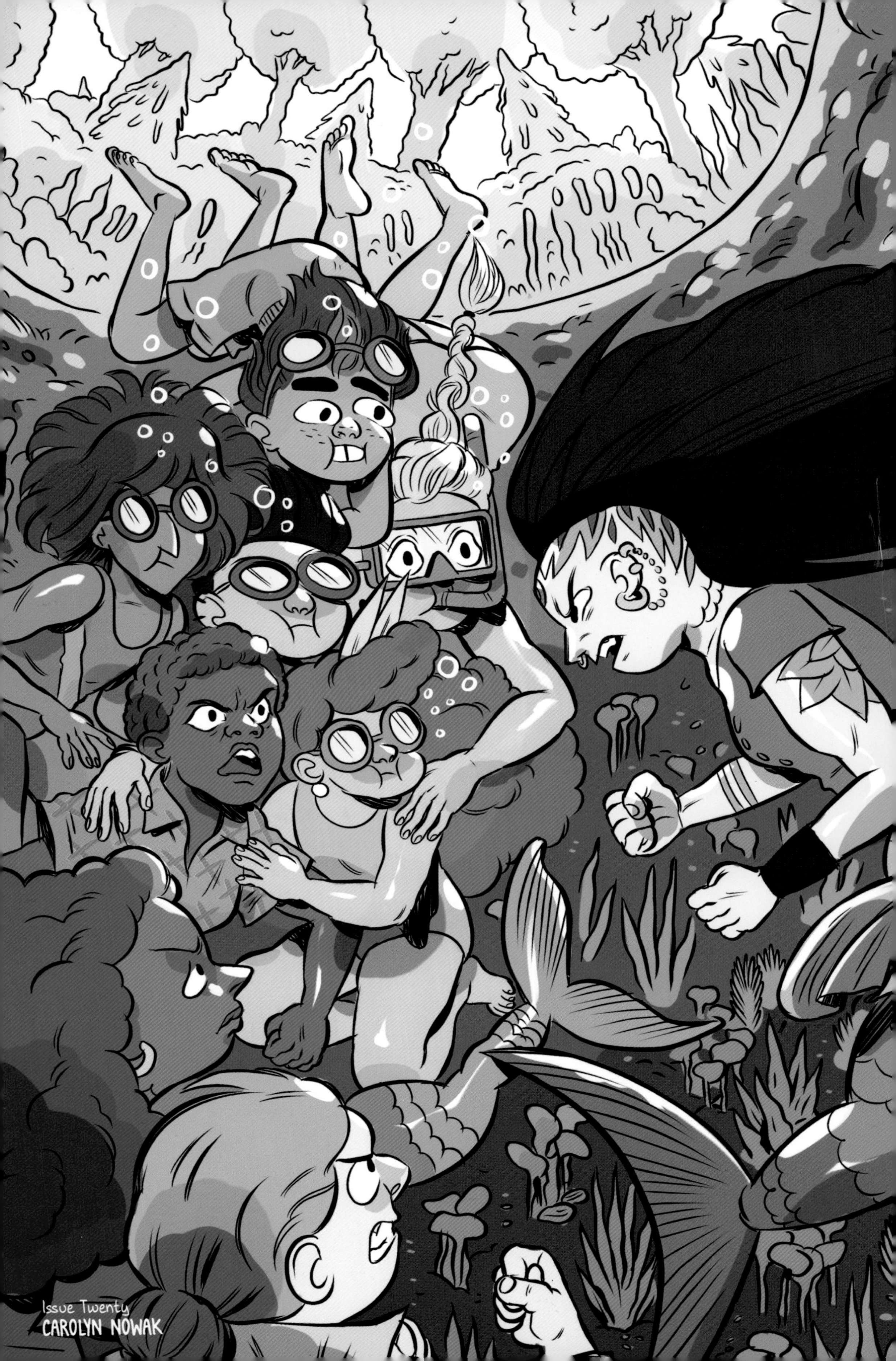
Issue Twenty
CAROLYN NOWAK

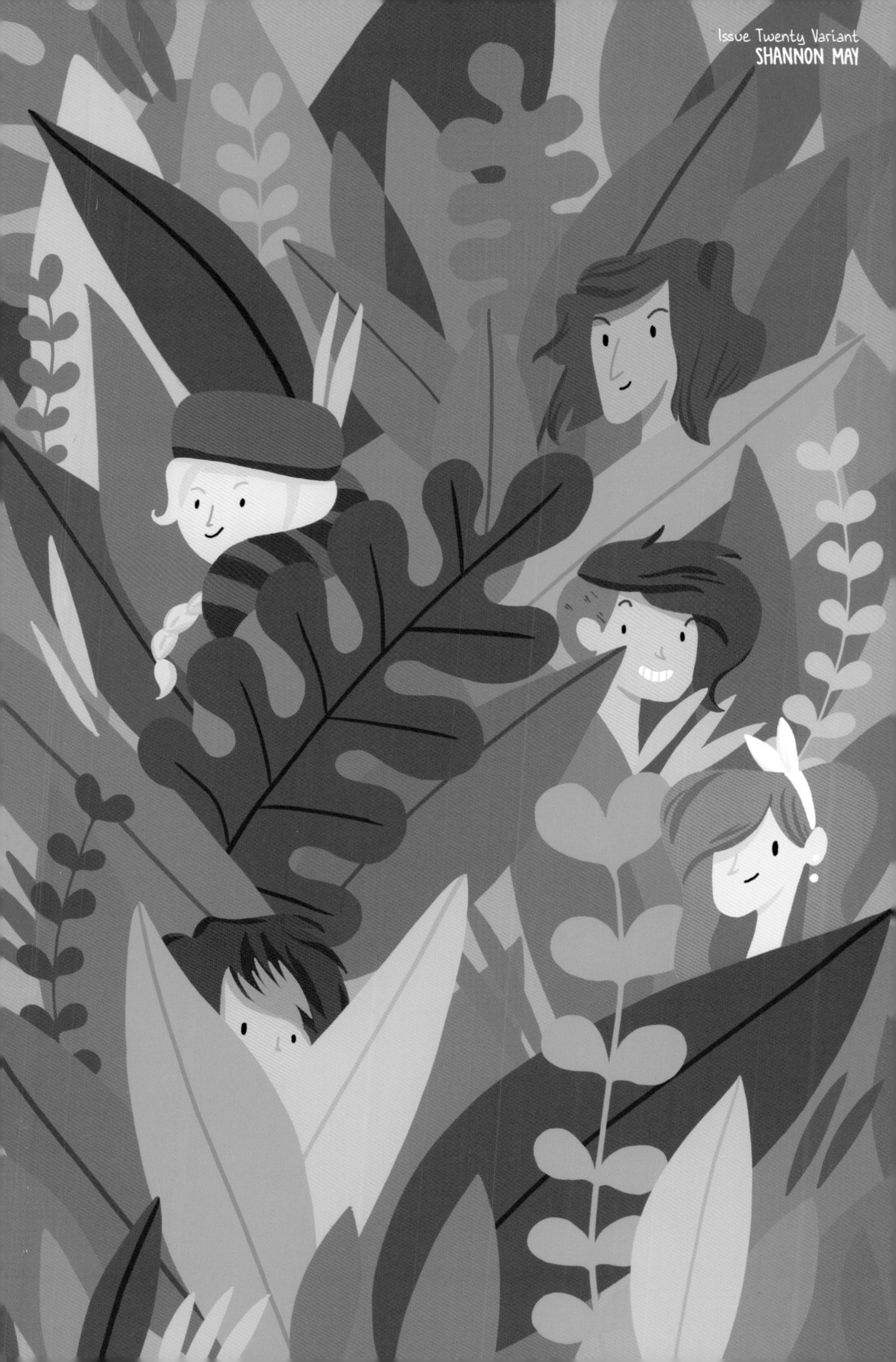

Issue Twenty Variant
SHANNON MAY

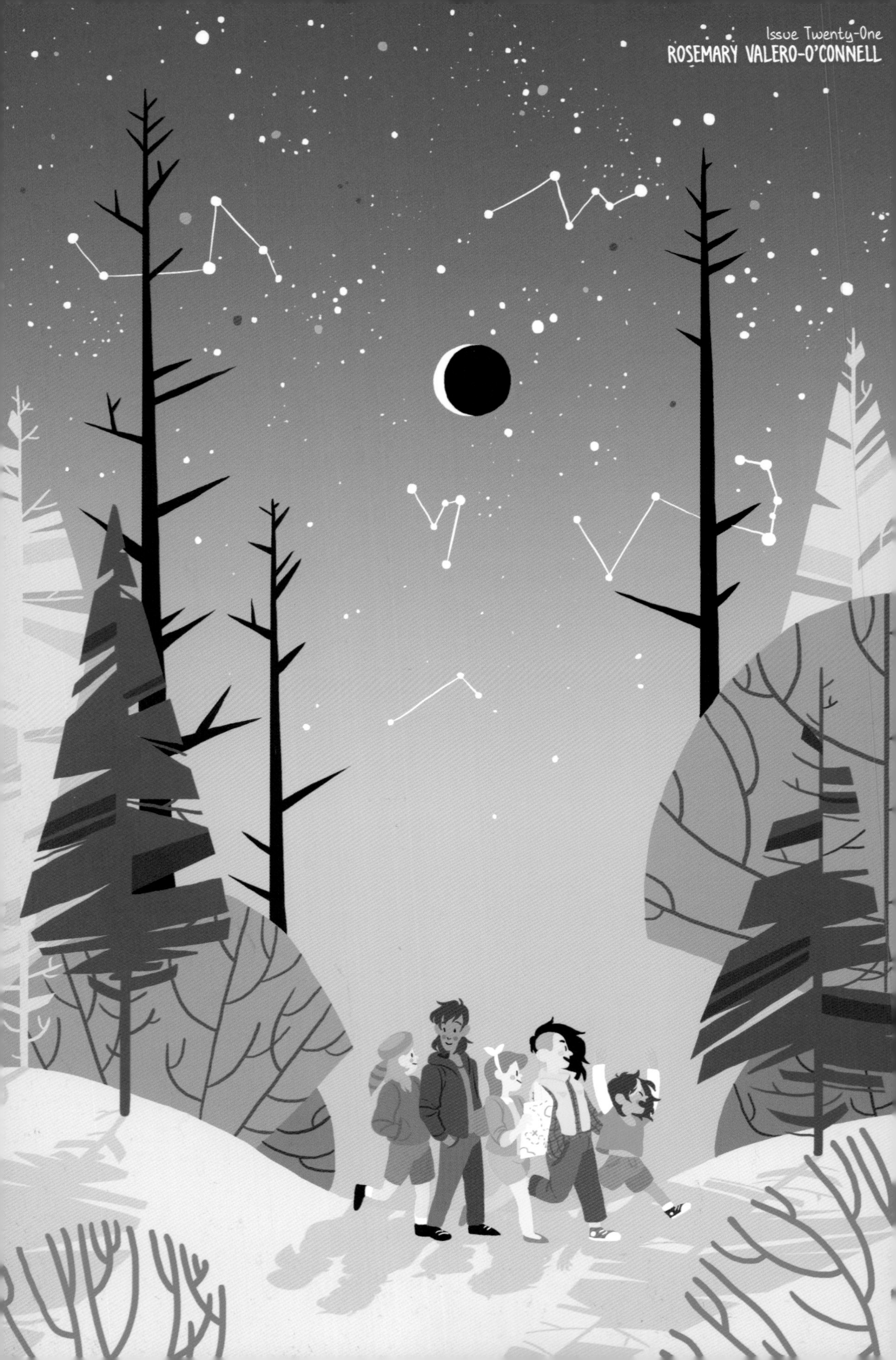
Issue Twenty-One
ROSEMARY VALERO-O'CONNELL

ssue Twenty-One Variant
MELANIE GILLMAN

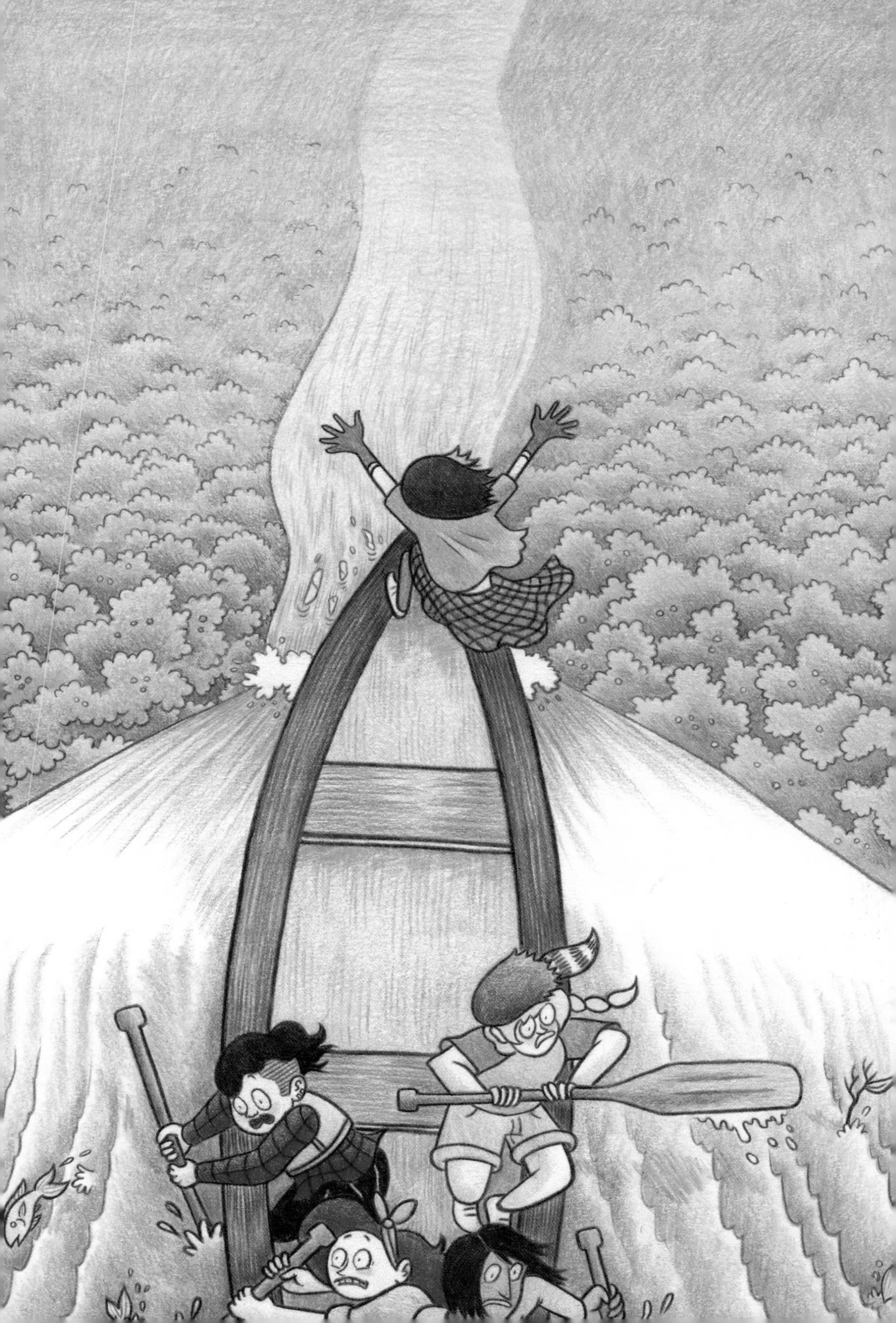

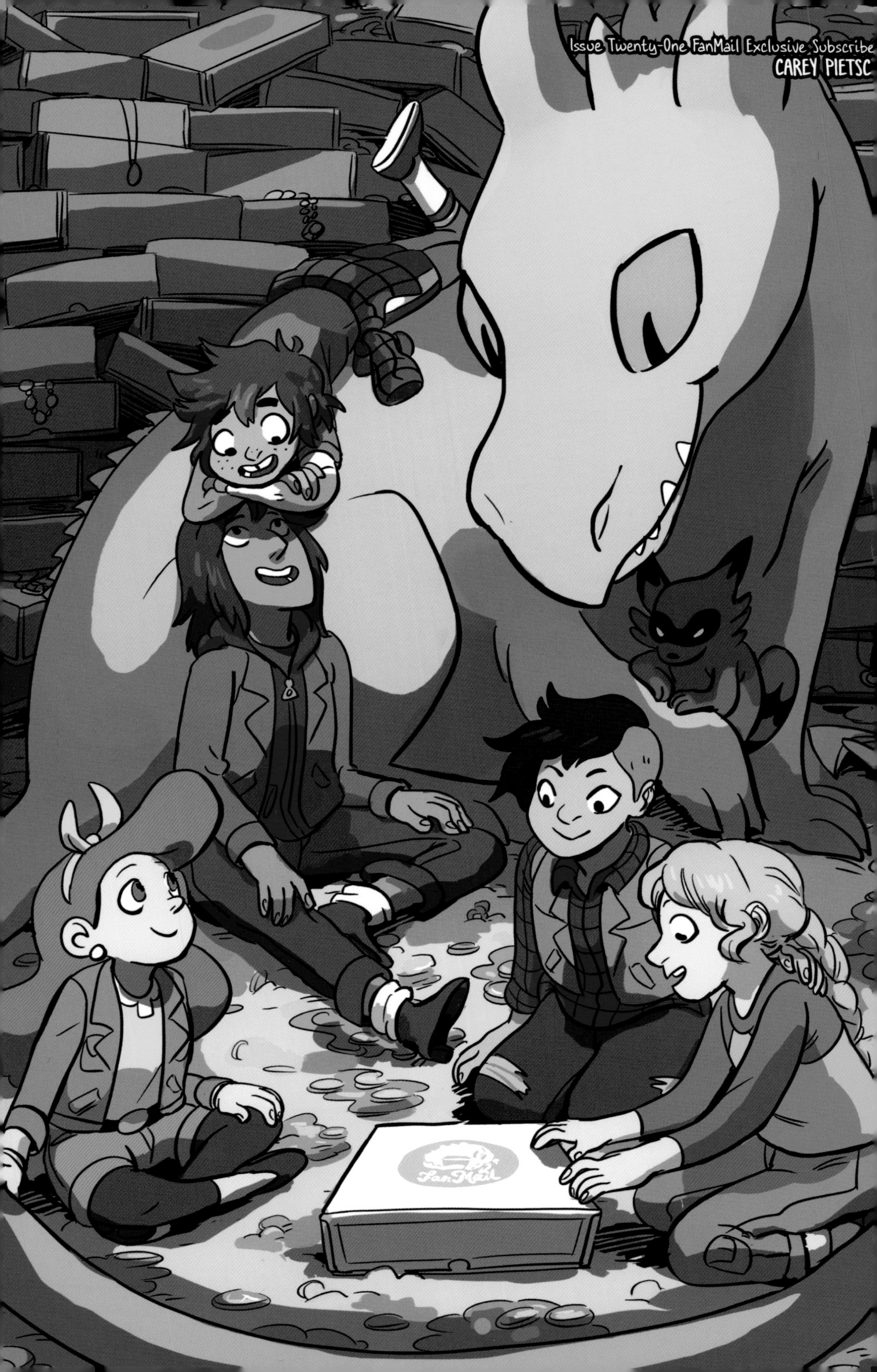
Issue Twenty-One FanMail Exclusive Subscribe
CAREY PIETSC
FanMail

Issue Twenty-Two
ROSEMARY VALERO-O'CONNELL

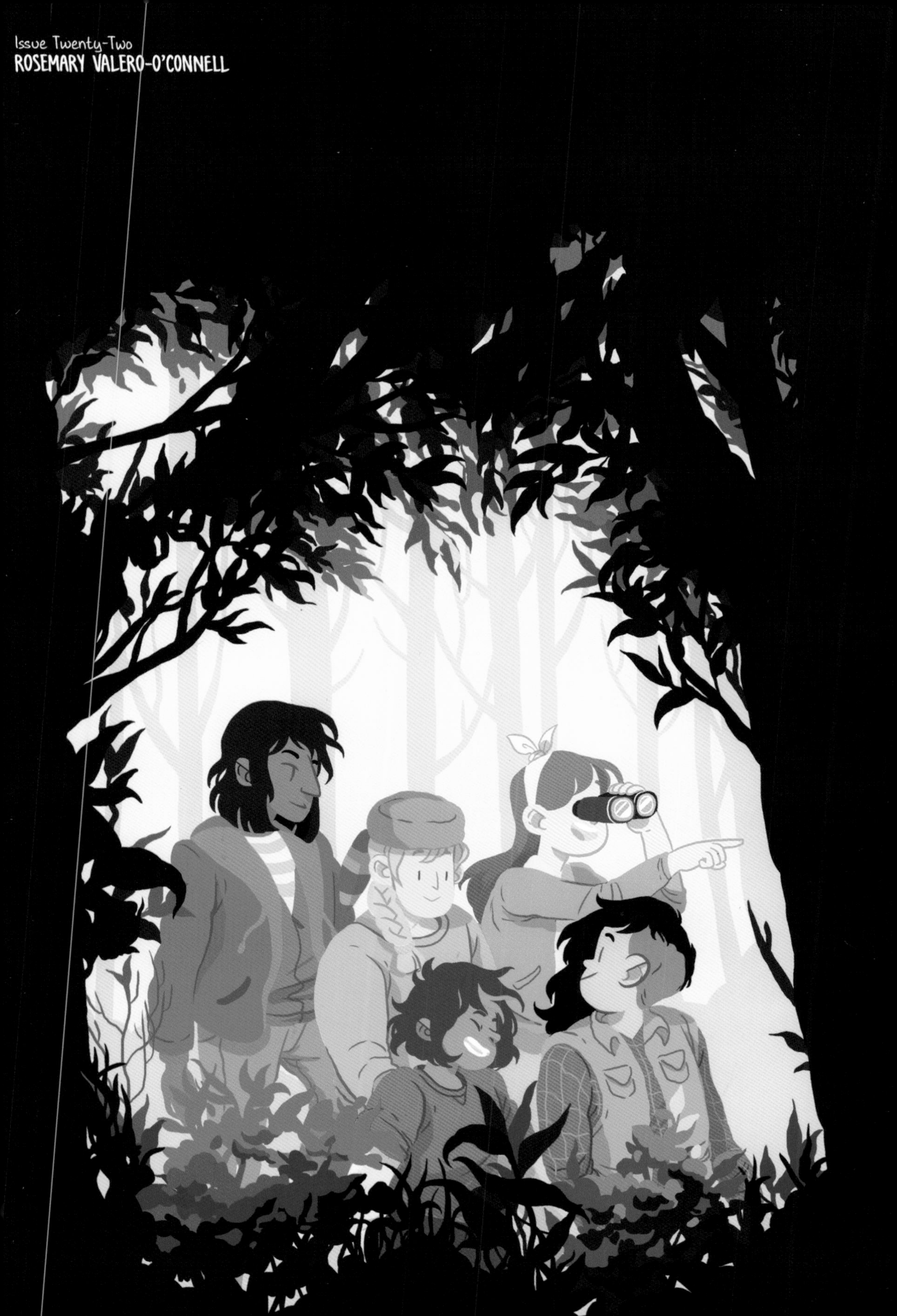

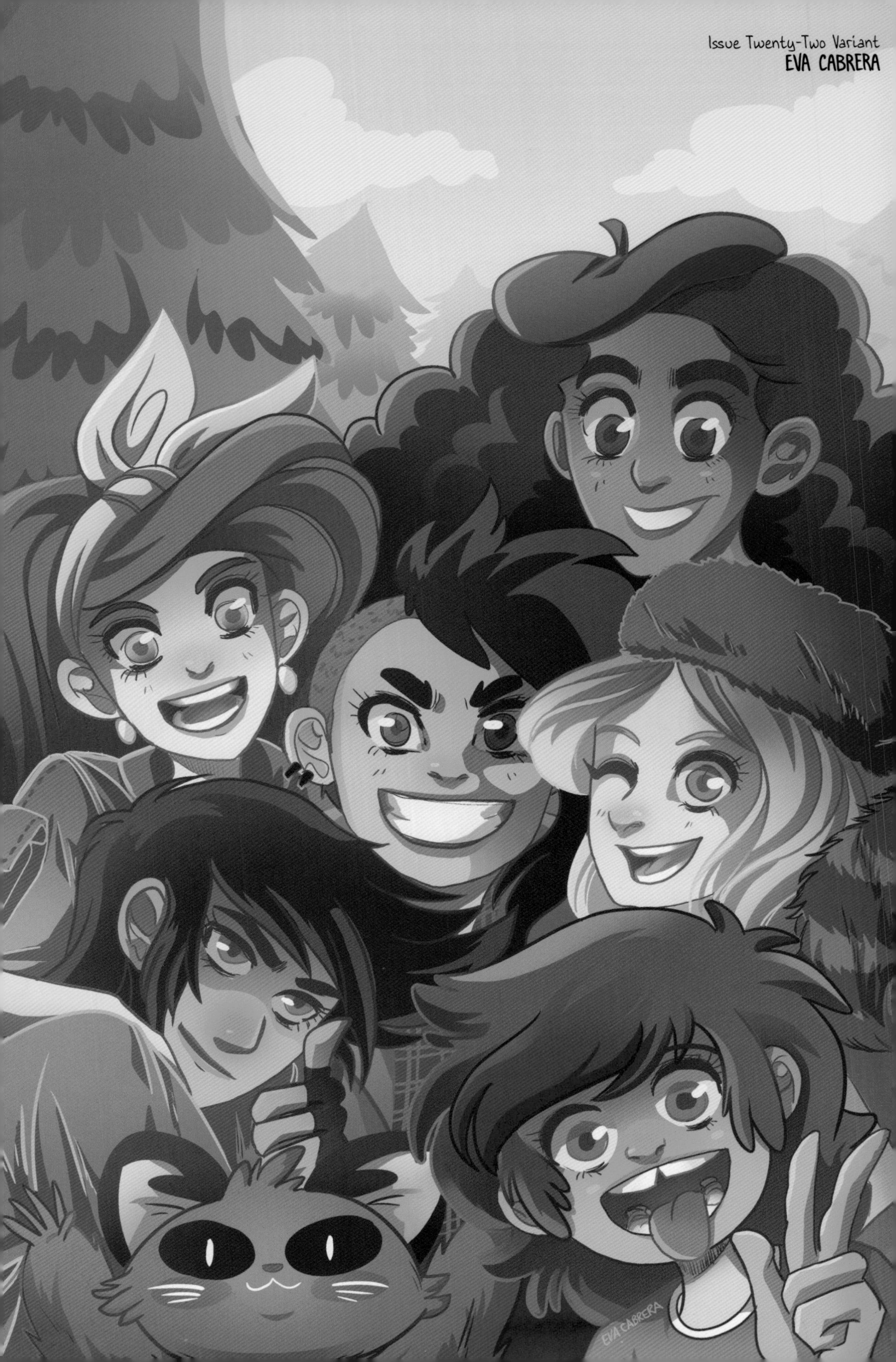
EVA CABRERA
Issue Twenty-Two Variant
EVA CABRERA

Issue Twenty-Three
ROSEMARY VALERO-O'CONNELL

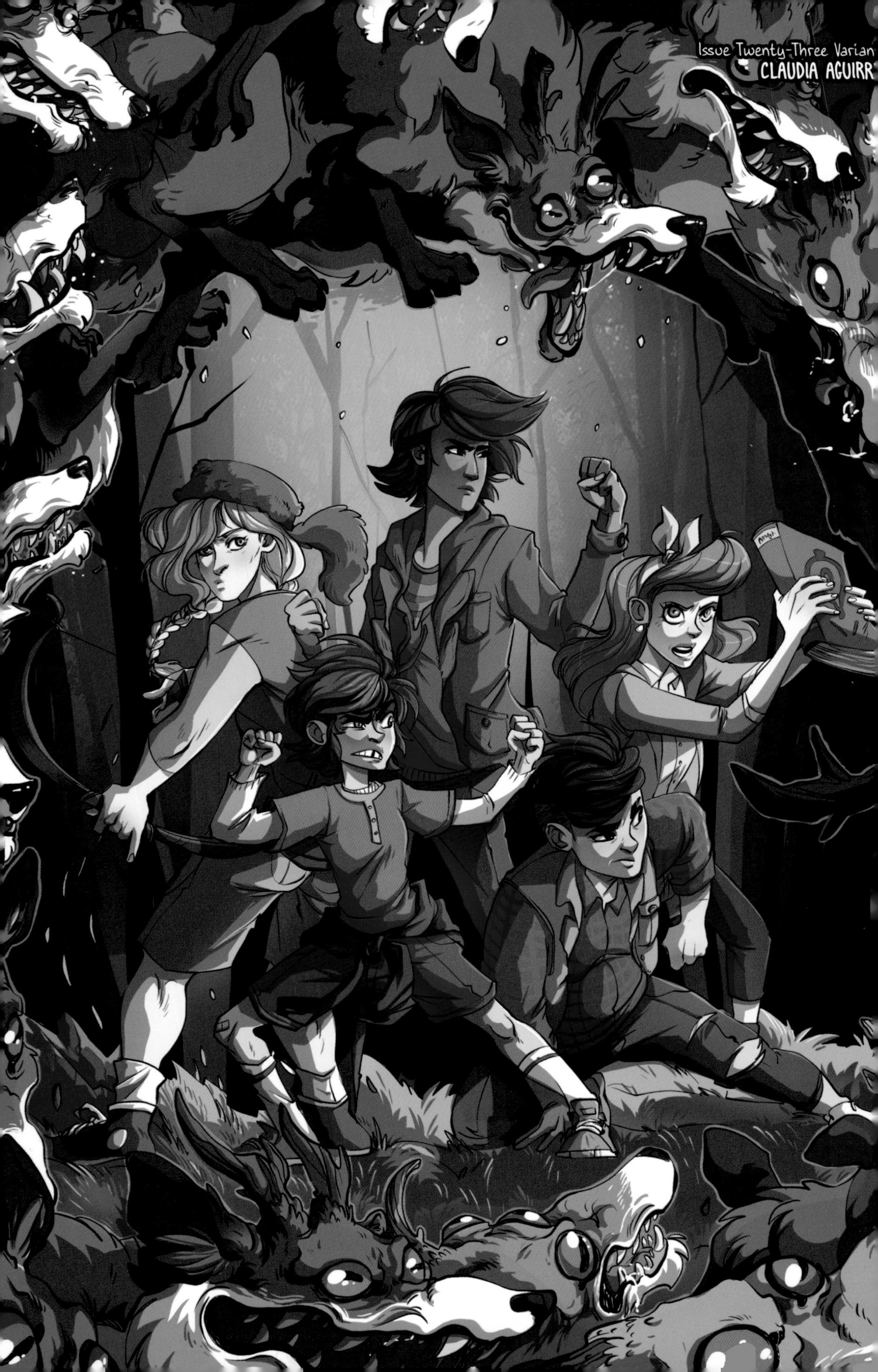
Issue Twenty-Three Varian
CLAUDIA AGUIRR

Issue Twenty-Four
KAT LEYH

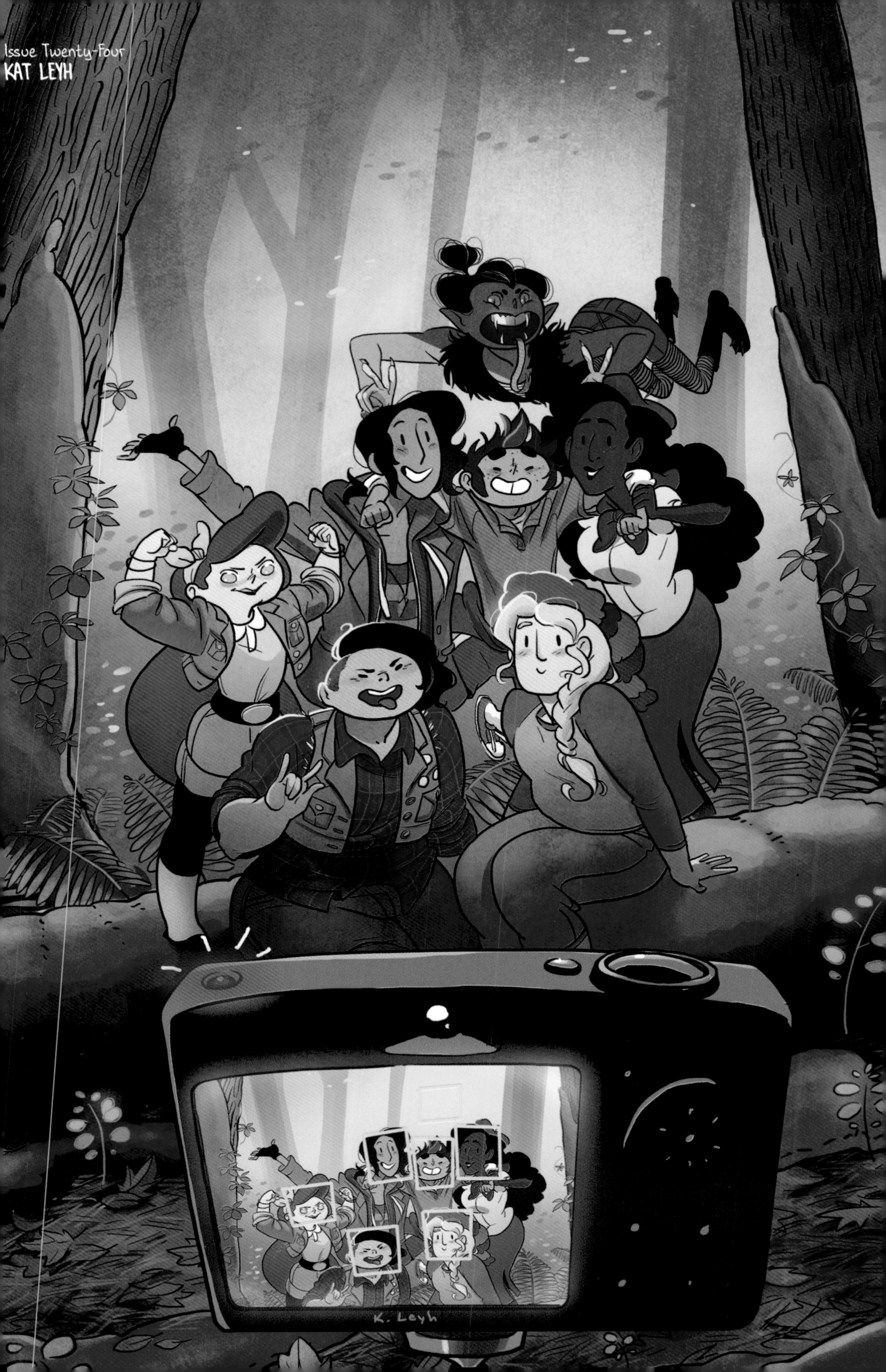
K. Leyh

Issue Twenty-Four Variant
KELSEY SHORT

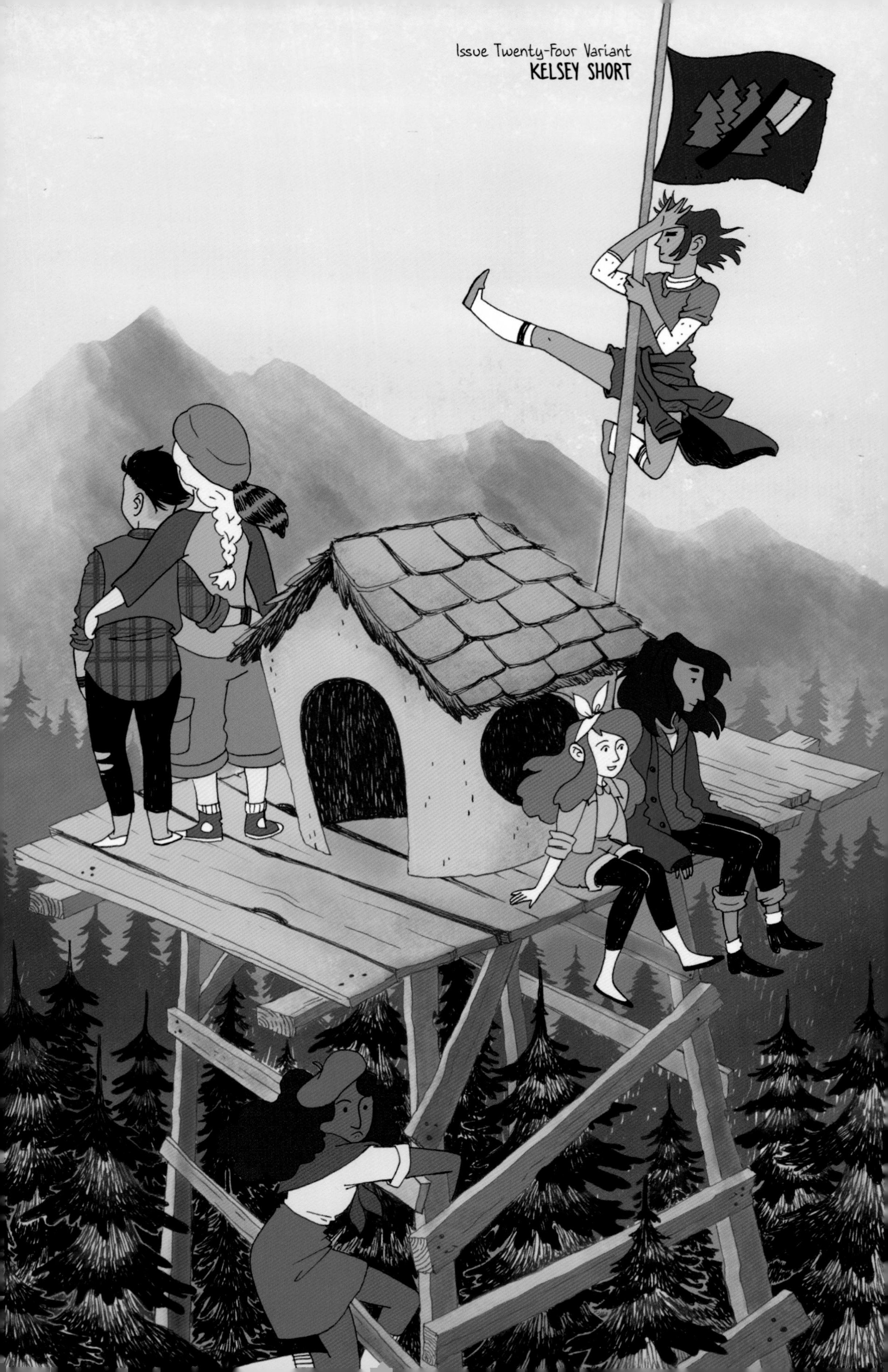

will con...
The ur...
It he...
appearan...
dress fo...
Further...
Lumber...
to have...
part in...
Thiskw...
Hardc...
have...
thems...

...LE UNIFORM

...hould be worn at camp
...vents when Lumberjanes
...a may also be worn at other
...ions. It should be worn as a
...the uniform dress with
...rect shoes, and stocking or

...ut grows her uniform or
...ng...ater Lumberjane.
...a she has
...her
...her

The...
yellow, short sl...
emb...
the w...
choose...
slacks, ...
made of...
out-of-do...
green bere...
the collar...
Shoes ma...
heels, rou...
socks should...
the uniform. Ne... ...es, bracelets, or other jewelry do n...
belong with a Lumberjane uniform.

...CES

HOW TO WEAR THE UNIFORM

To look well in a uniform demans first of ...
uniform be kept in good condition—clean ...
pressed. See that the skirt is the right length for your own
height and build, that the belt is adjusted to your waist,
that your shoes and stockings are in keeping with the
uniform, that you watch your posture and carry yourself
with dignity and grace. If the beret is removed indoors,
be sure that your hair is neat and kept in place with an
insonspicuous clip or ribbon. When you wear a
Lumberjane uniform you are identified as a member of
this organization and you should be doubly careful to
conduct yourself in a way that will show everyone that
courtesy and thoughtfullness are part of being a
Lumberjane. People are likely to judge a whole nation by
the selfishness of a few individuals, to criticize a whole
family because of the misconduct of one member, and to
feel unkindly toward and organization because of the

The uniform...
helps to crea...
in a group. I...
active life th...
another bond...
future, and pre...
in order to be...
Lumberjane pro...
Penniquiqul Thi... ...re Lady
Types, but m... ...s will wish to have one. They
can either bu... ...uniform, or make it themselves from
materials available at the trading post.

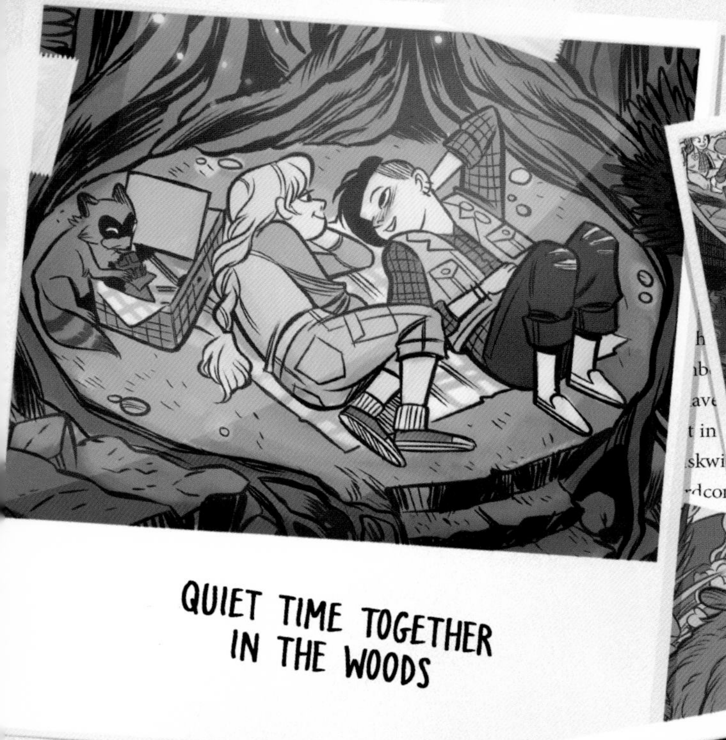

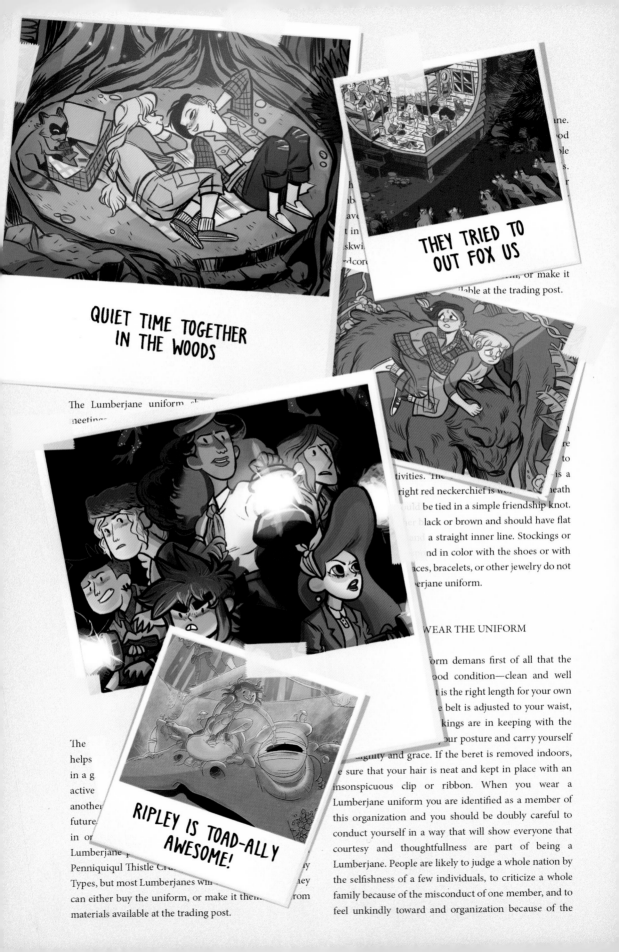

QUIET TIME TOGETHER IN THE WOODS

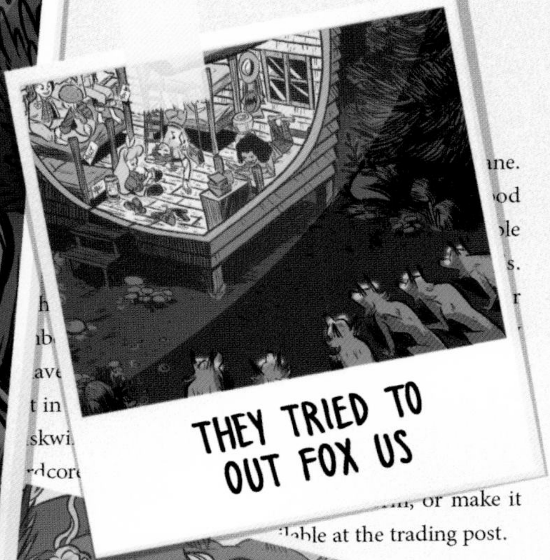

THEY TRIED TO OUT FOX US

...ne.
...od
...le
...s.
...r
...h
...nb
...ave
...t in
...skwi
...dcore
...m, or make it
...ilable at the trading post.

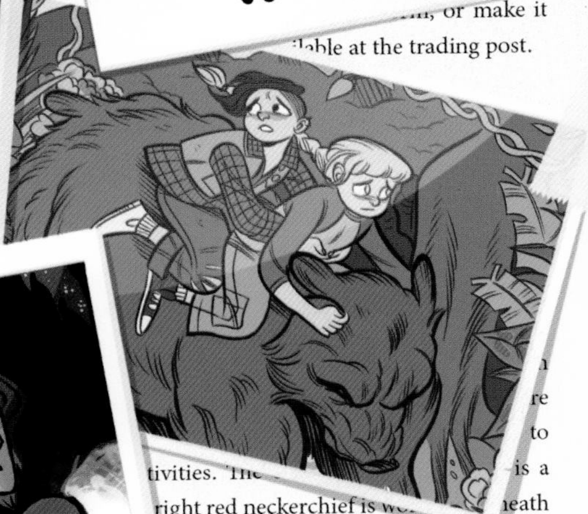

The Lumberjane uniform sh...
meeting...

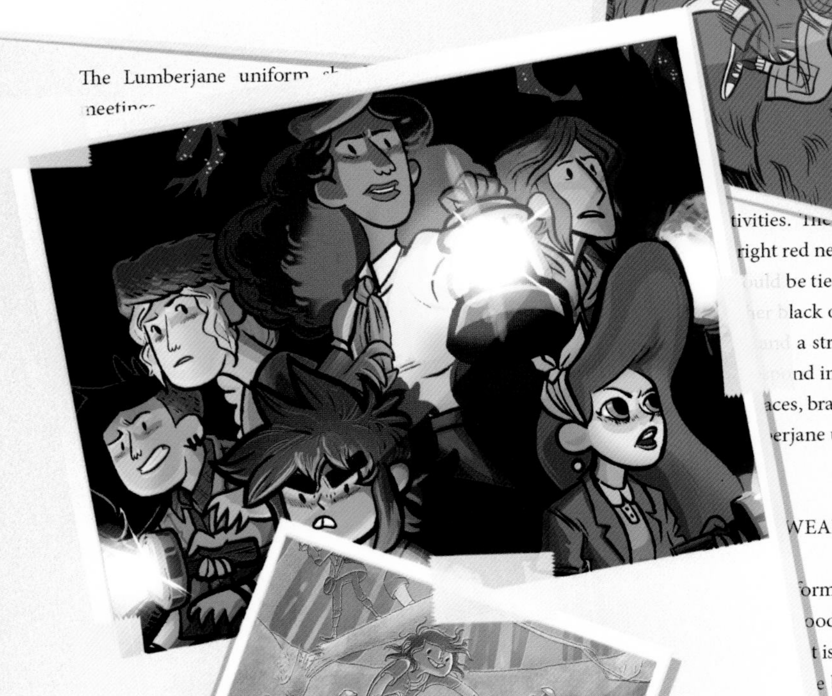

...n
...re
...to
...tivities. The ... is a
...right red neckerchief is wo... ...neath
...uld be tied in a simple friendship knot.
...her black or brown and should have flat
...and a straight inner line. Stockings or
...nd in color with the shoes or with
...aces, bracelets, or other jewelry do not
...berjane uniform.

...WEAR THE UNIFORM

...form demans first of all that the ...ood condition—clean and well ...t is the right length for your own ...e belt is adjusted to your waist, ...kings are in keeping with the ...our posture and carry yourself ...dignity and grace. If the beret is removed indoors, ...e sure that your hair is neat and kept in place with an insonspicuous clip or ribbon. When you wear a Lumberjane uniform you are identified as a member of this organization and you should be doubly careful to conduct yourself in a way that will show everyone that courtesy and thoughtfullness are part of being a Lumberjane. People are likely to judge a whole nation by the selfishness of a few individuals, to criticize a whole family because of the misconduct of one member, and to feel unkindly toward and organization because of the

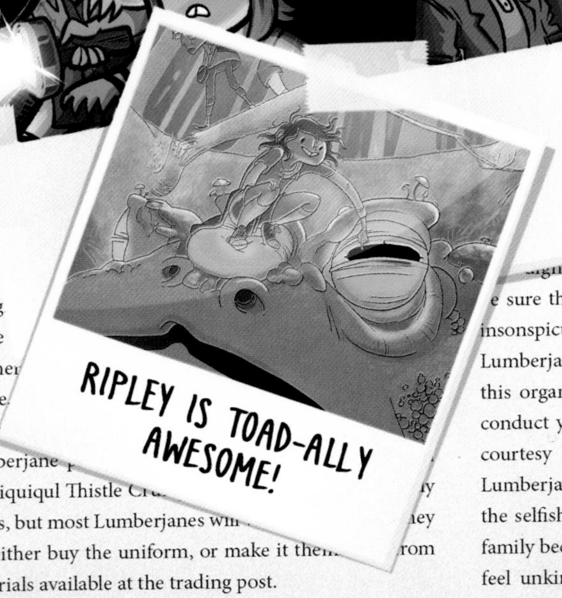

RIPLEY IS TOAD-ALLY AWESOME!

The ...
helps ...
in a g...
active ...
another...
future...
in or...
Lumberjane p...
Penniquiqul Thistle Cru... ...y
Types, but most Lumberjanes wil... ...hey
can either buy the uniform, or make it them... ...rom
materials available at the trading post.

SKETCHBOOK

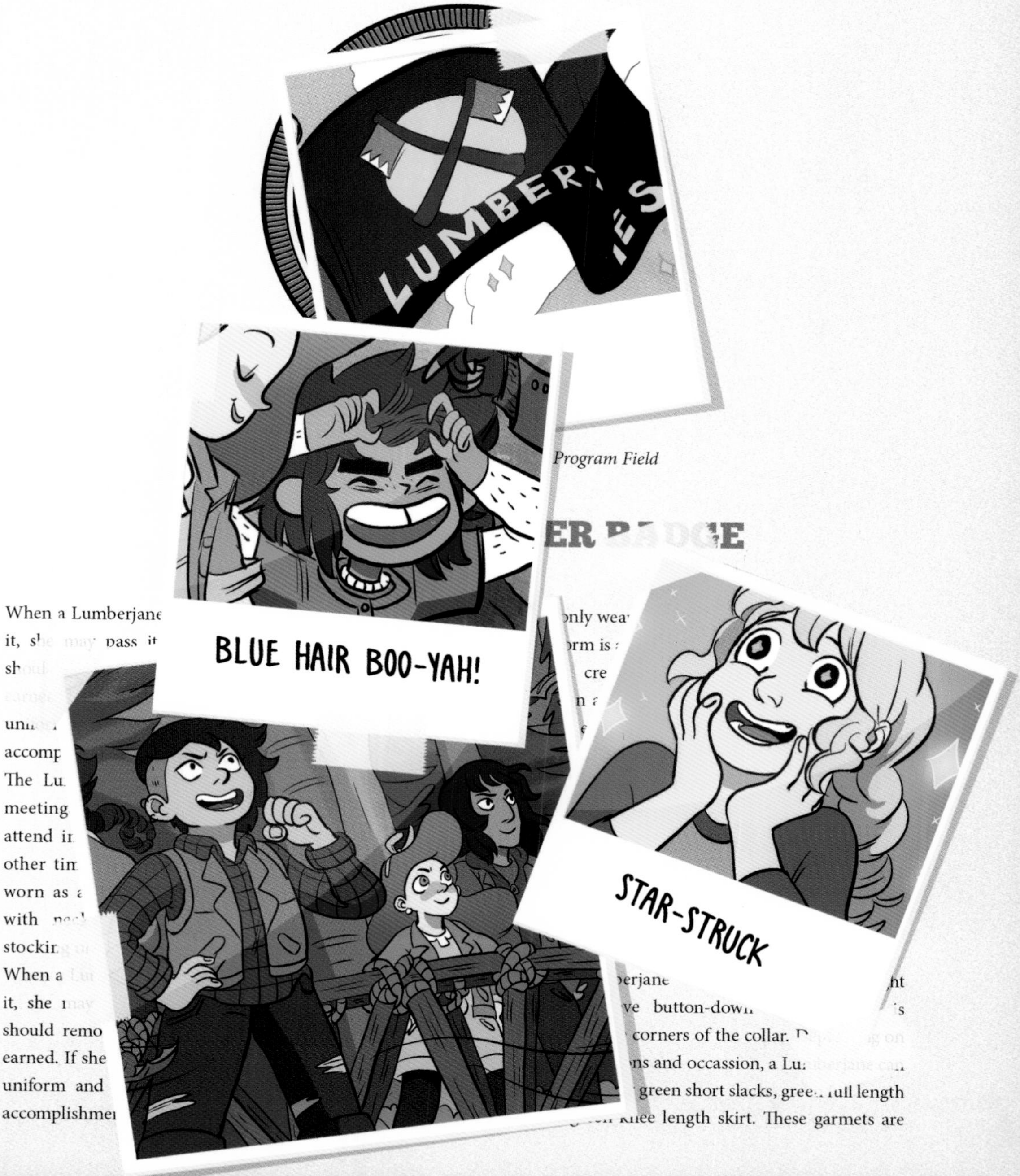
BLUE HAIR BOO-YAH!
STAR-STRUCK

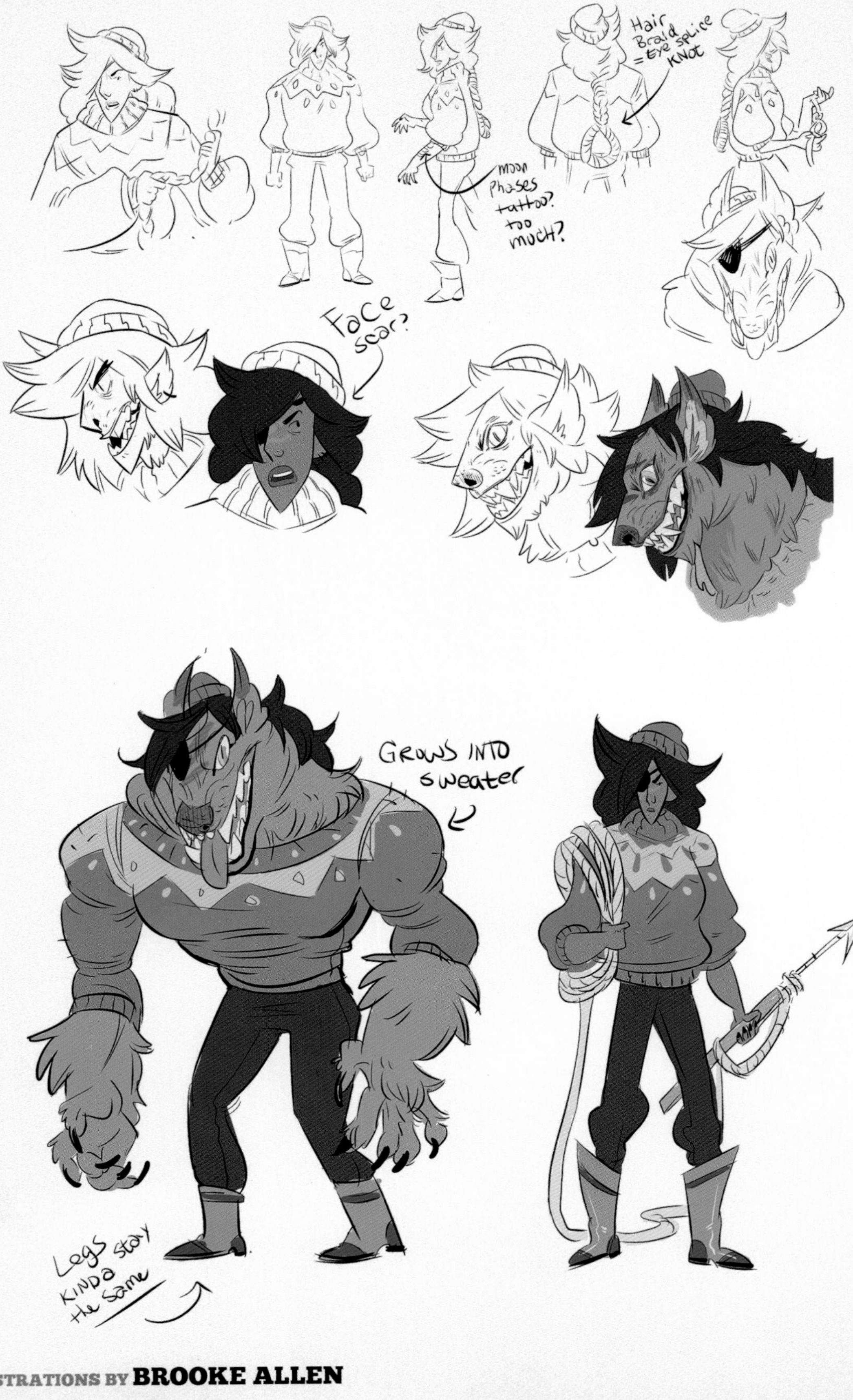

Hair Braid = Eye splice KNOT
moon phases tattoo? too much?
Face scar?
GROWS INTO sweater
Legs stay KINDA the same

ILLUSTRATIONS BY BROOKE ALLEN

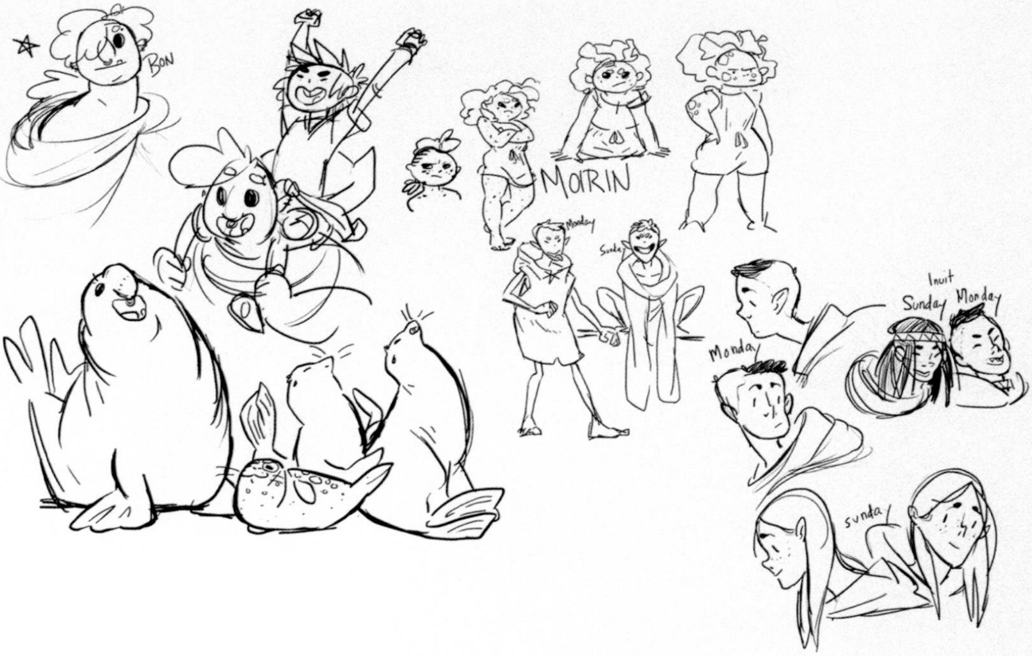
BON
MOIRIN
Inuit
Sunday
Monday
Monday
sunday

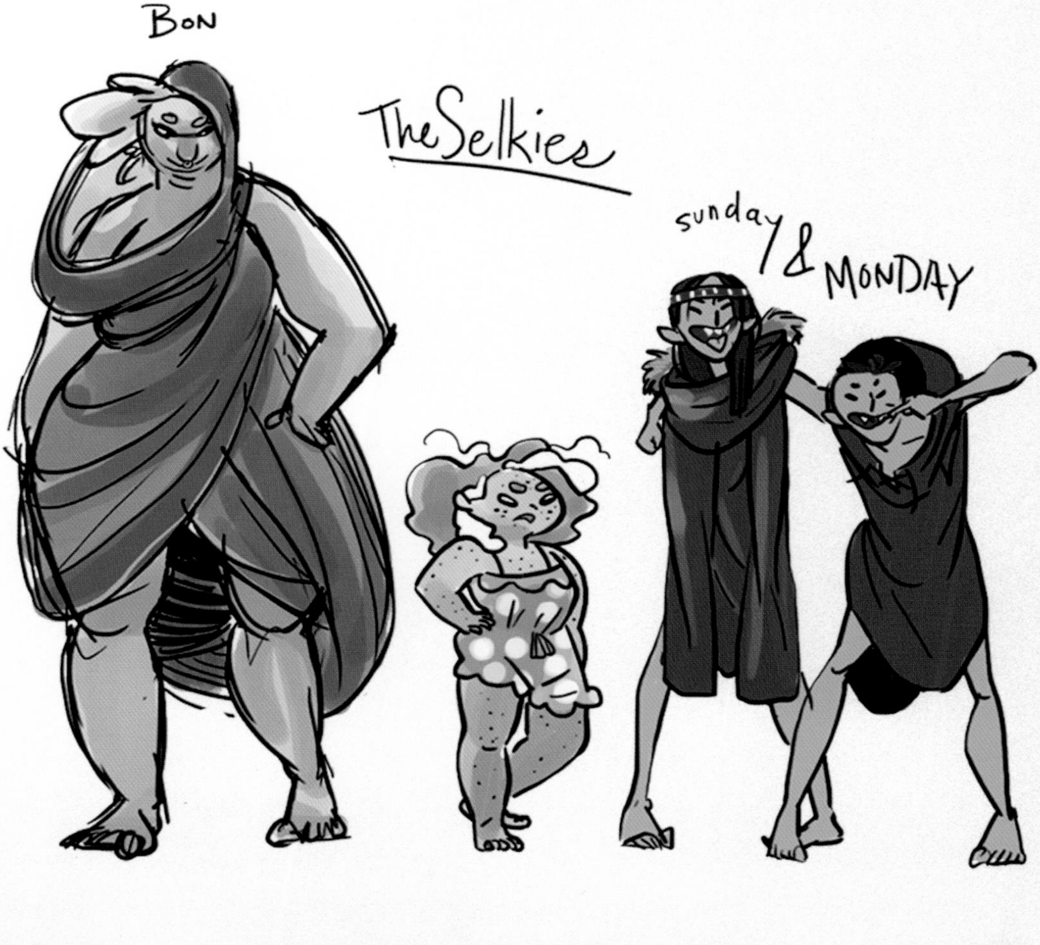
BON
The Selkies
sunday & MONDAY

ILLUSTRATIONS BY KAT LEYH

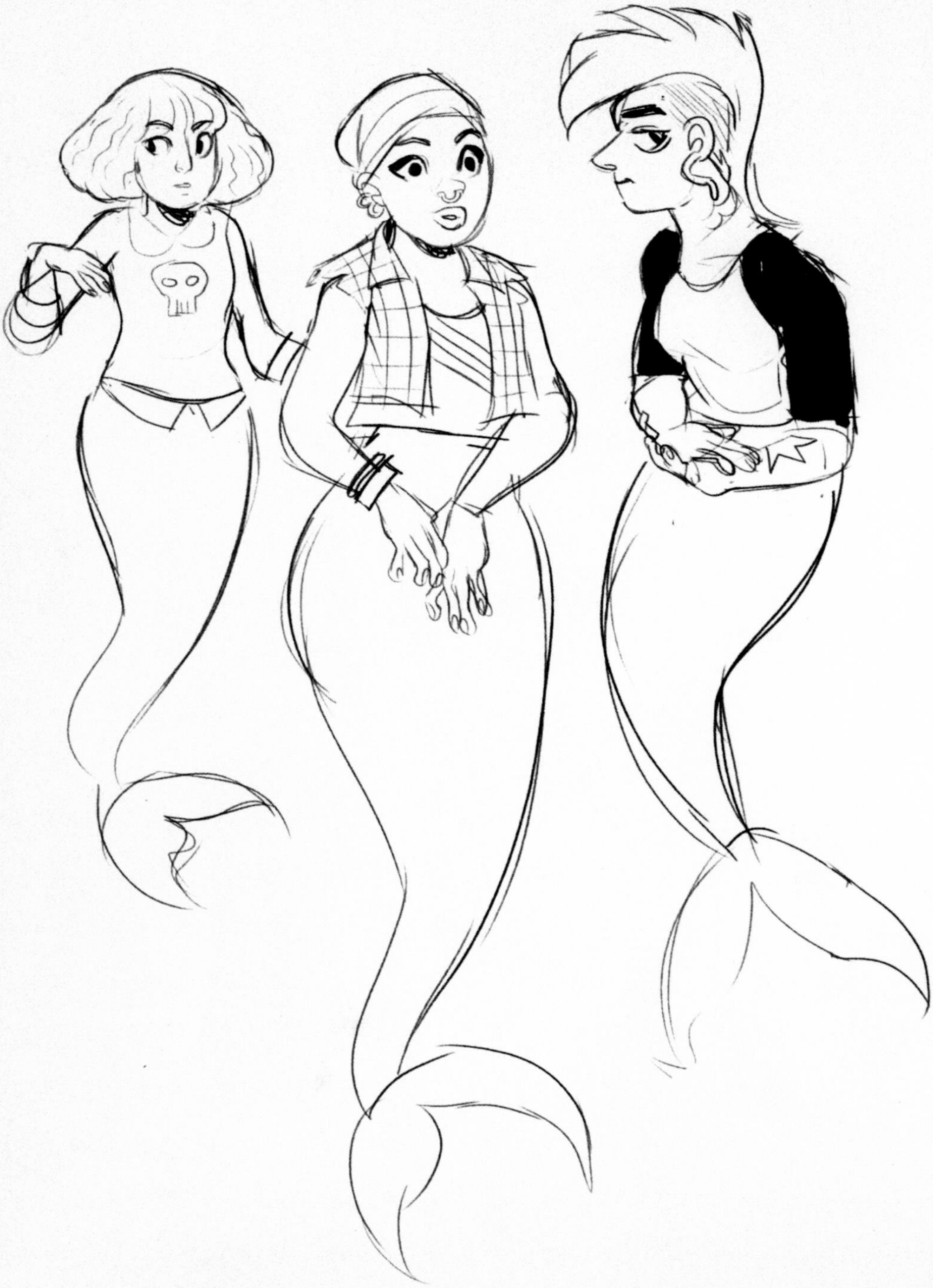

ILLUSTRATIONS BY **CAROLYN NOWAK**

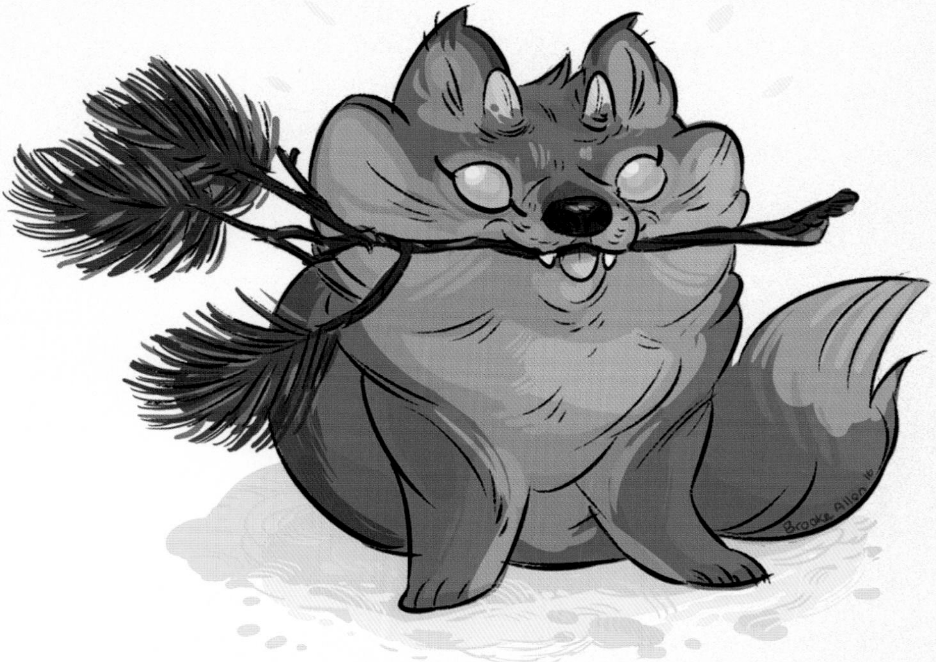
Brooke Allen

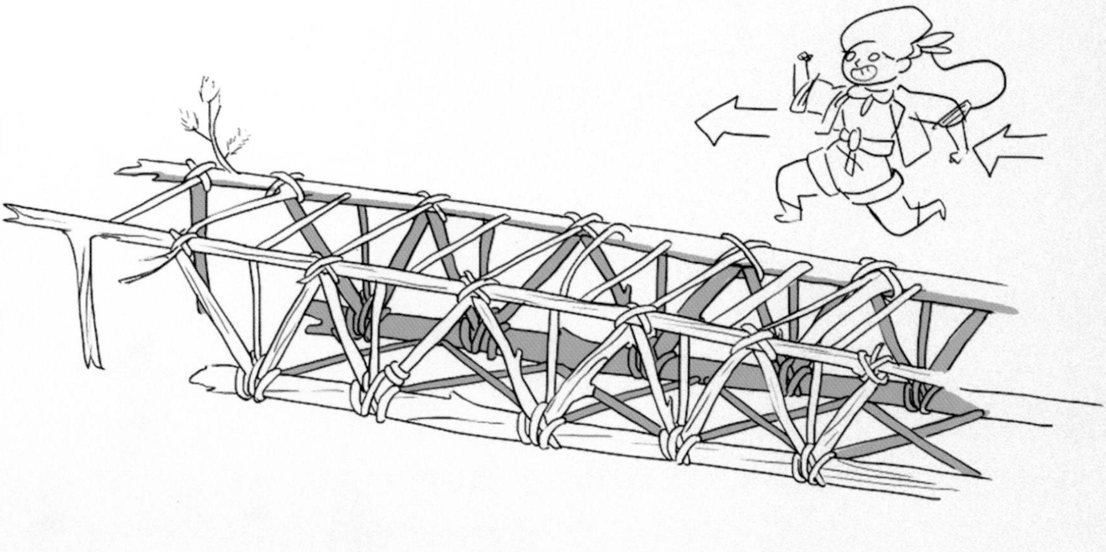

ILLUSTRATIONS BY BROOKE ALLEN & KAT LEYH

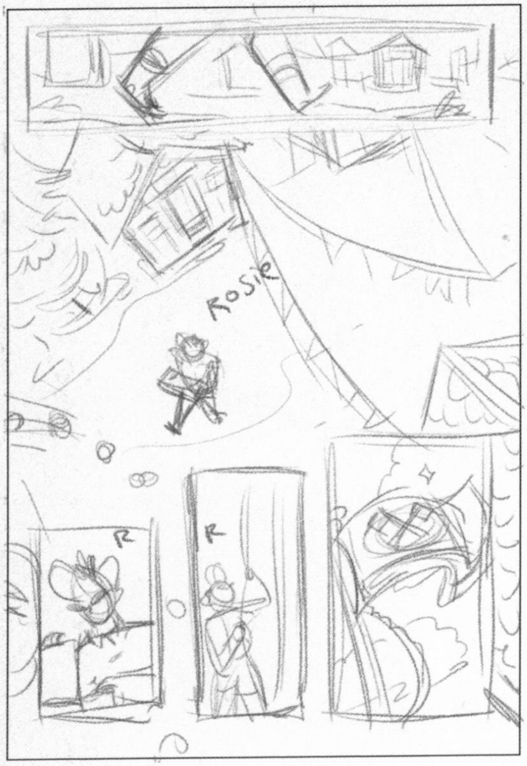
ROSIE
R
R

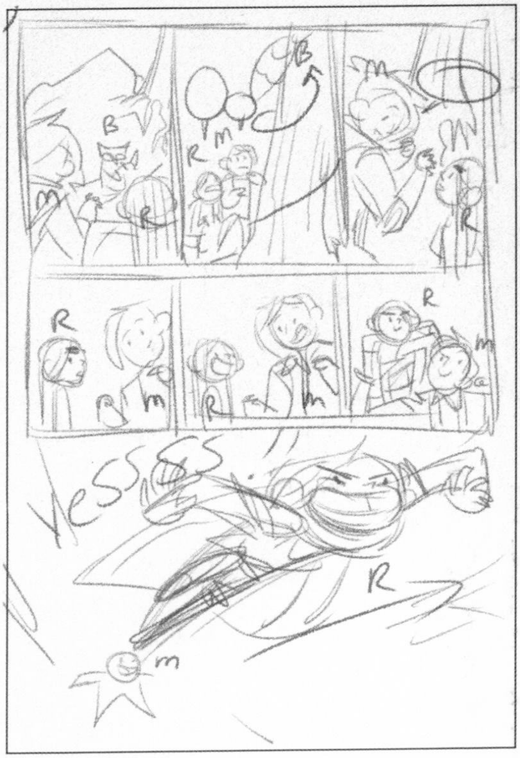
B
R
M
R
YESSSS
R
m

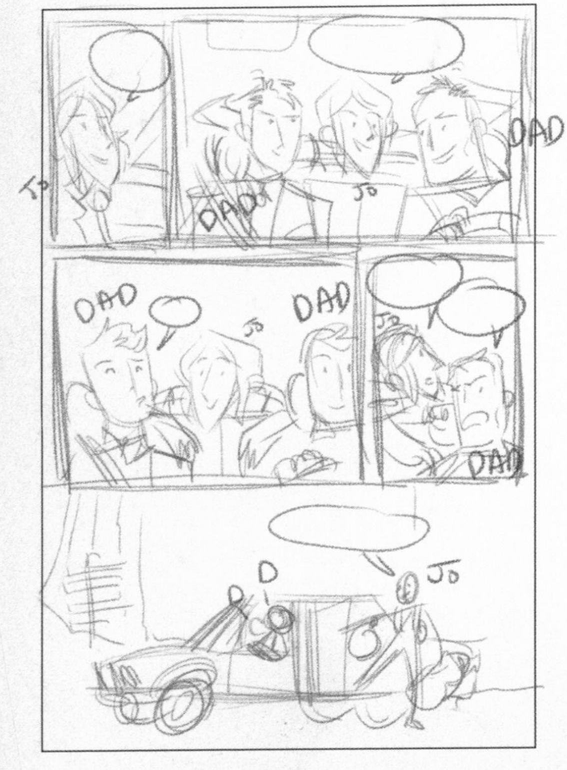
DAD
JO
DAD
JO
DAD
DAD
JO
DAD
D
JO

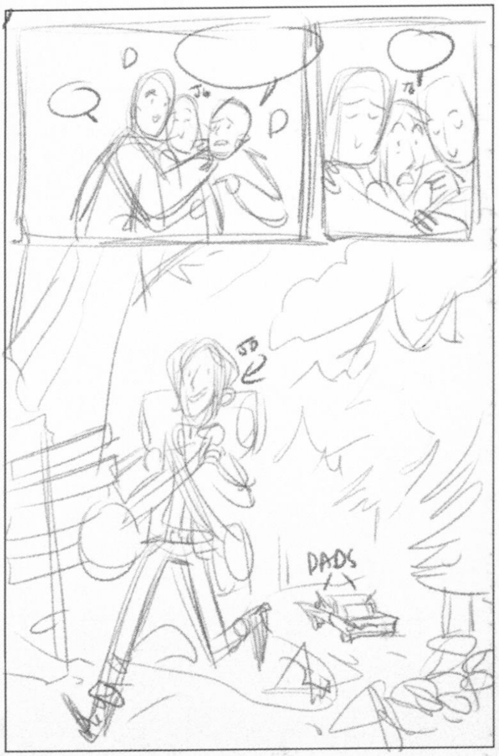
D
D
JO
DADS

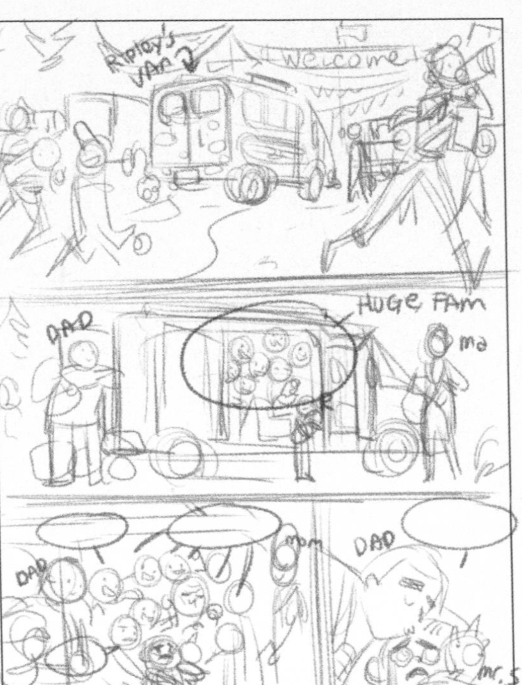
Ripley's VAN
Welcome
HUGE FAM
DAD
ma
R
DAD
mom
DAD
R
mr. S
R

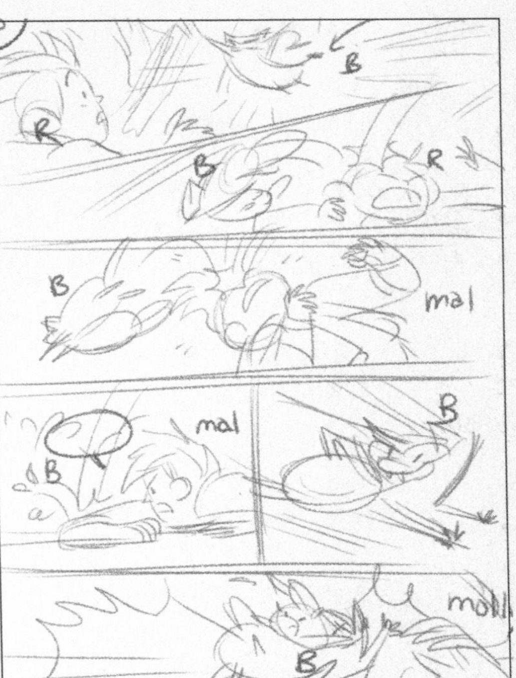
B
R
B
R
B
mal
mal
B
B
moll
B

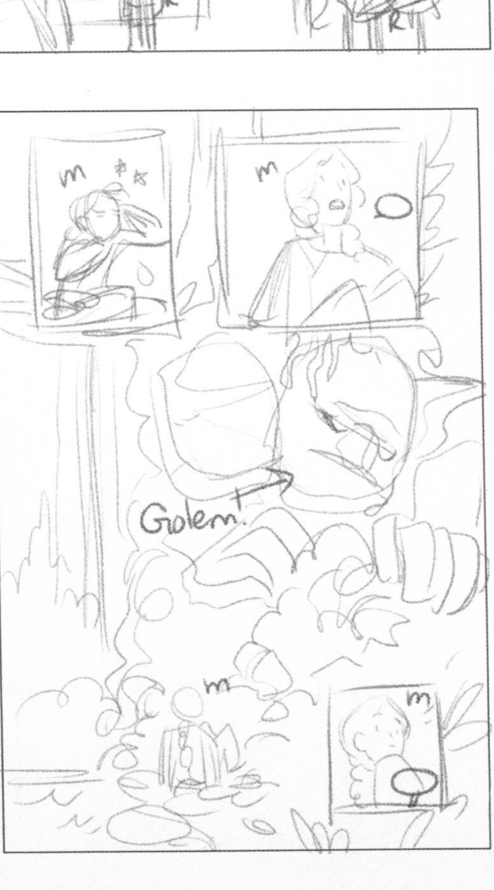
m
m
Golem
m
m

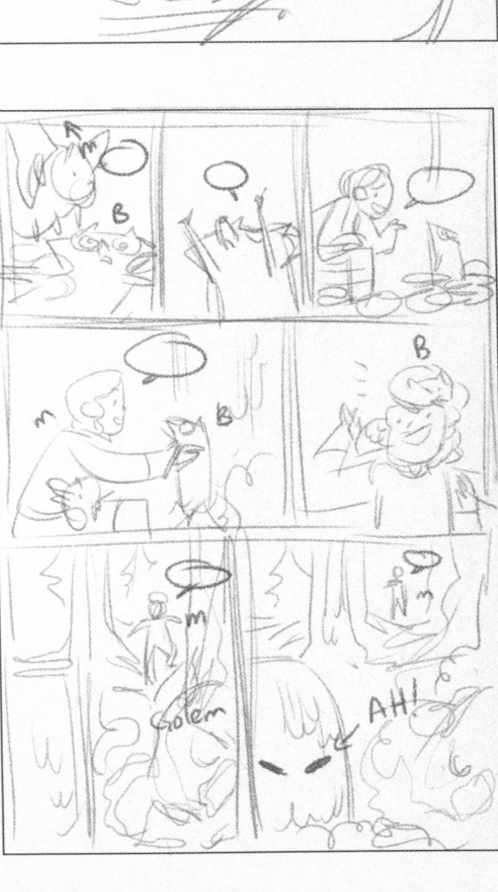
m
B
B
m
B
m
m
Golem
AH!

PENCILS BY BROOKE ALLEN

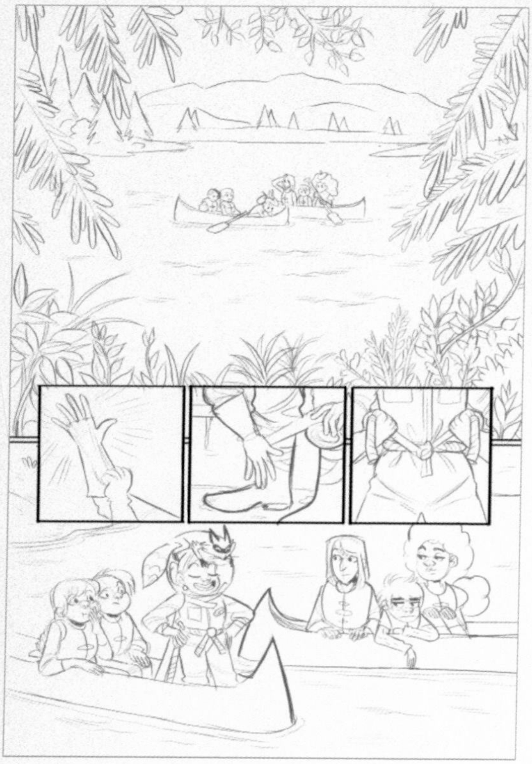

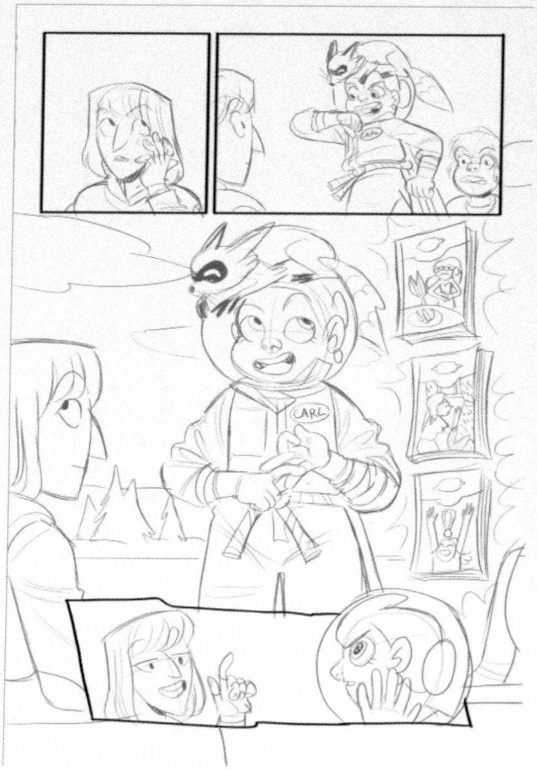
CARL

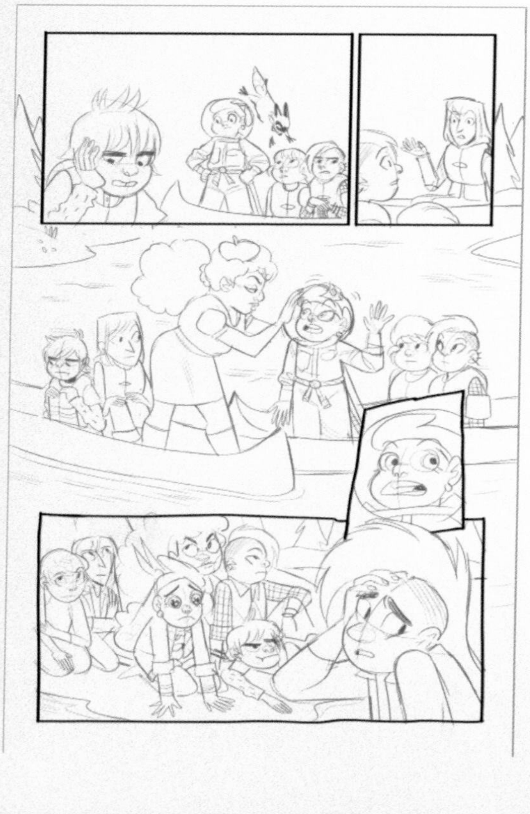

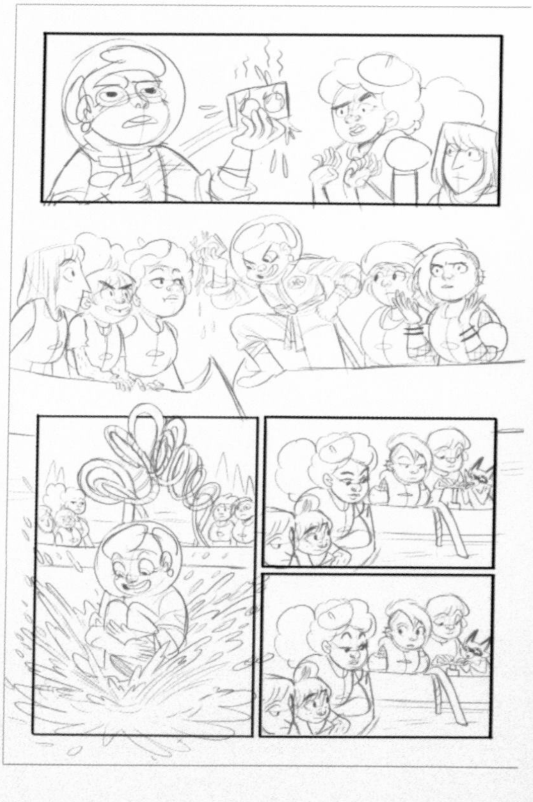

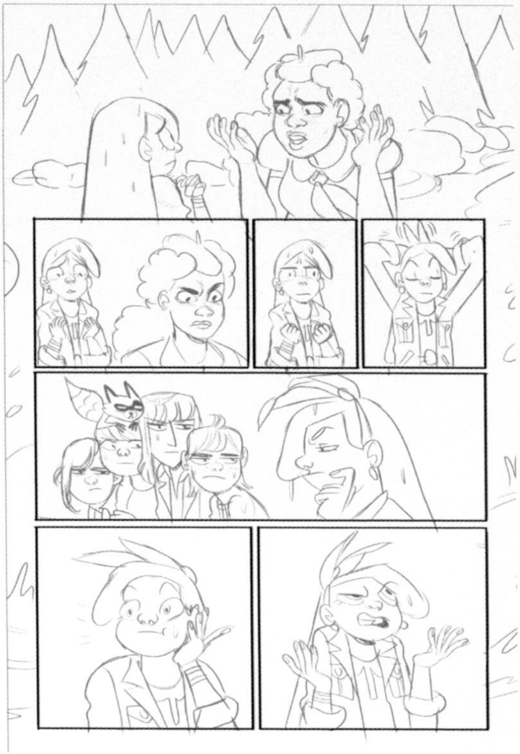

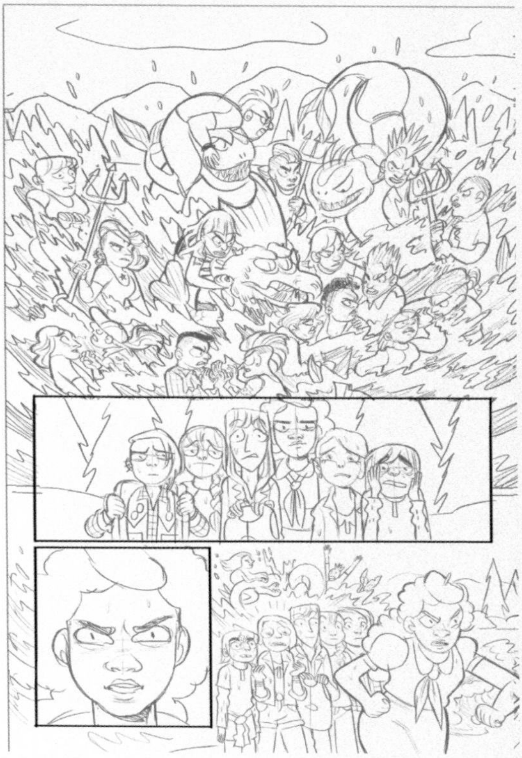

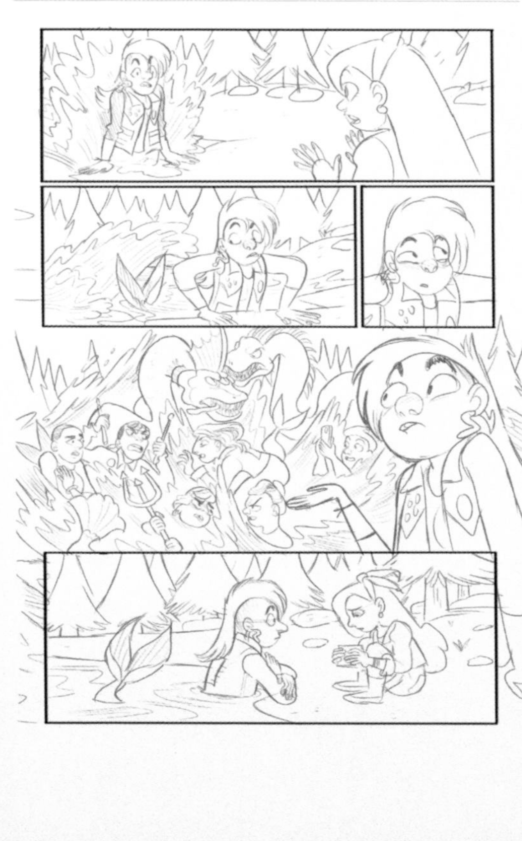

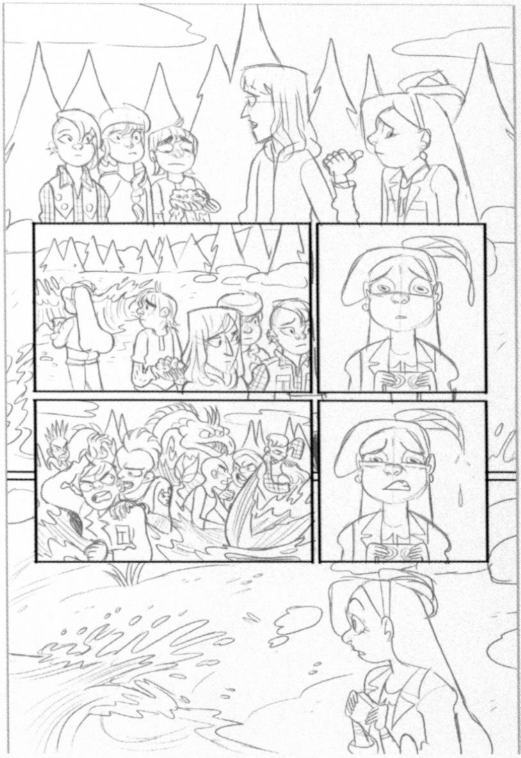

PENCILS BY **CAROLYN NOWAK**

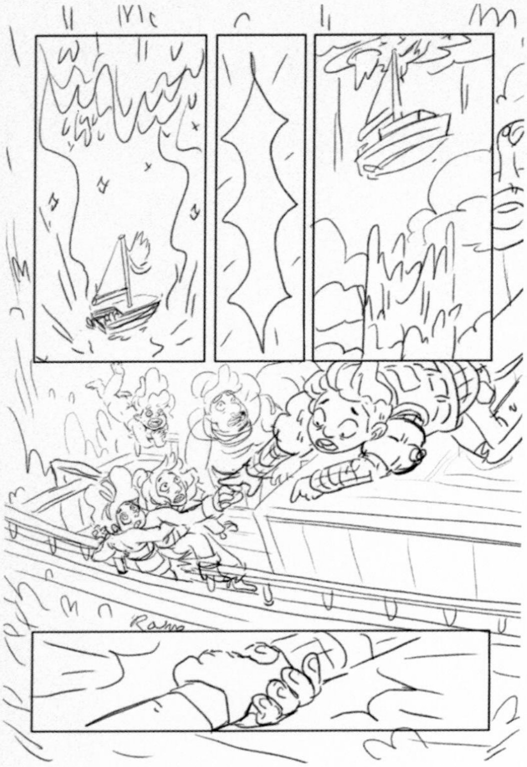

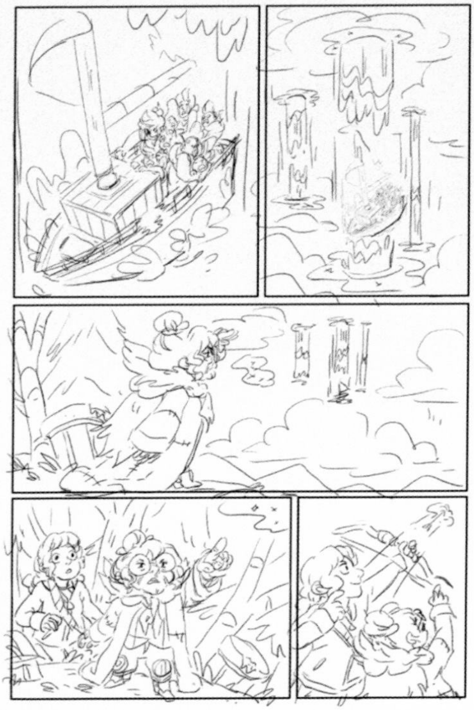

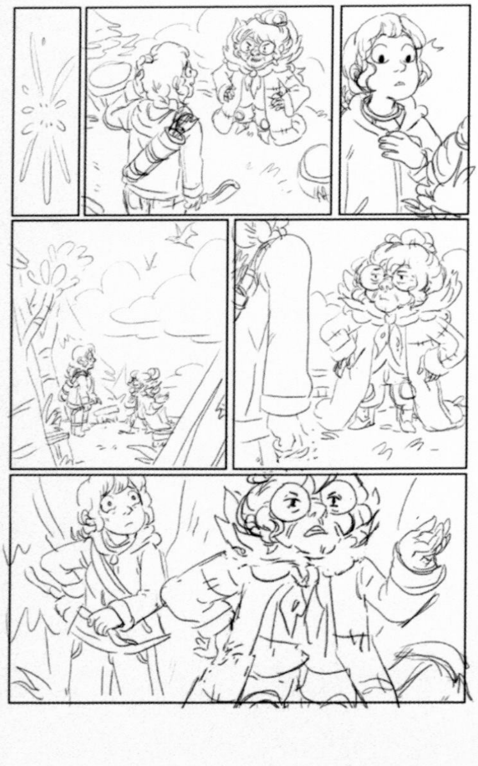

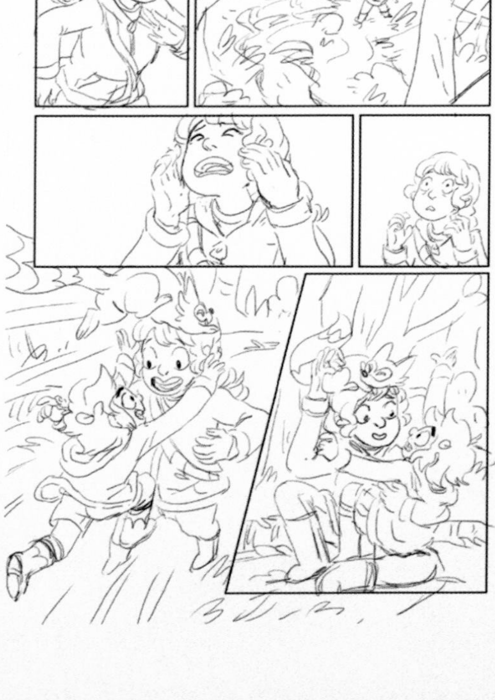

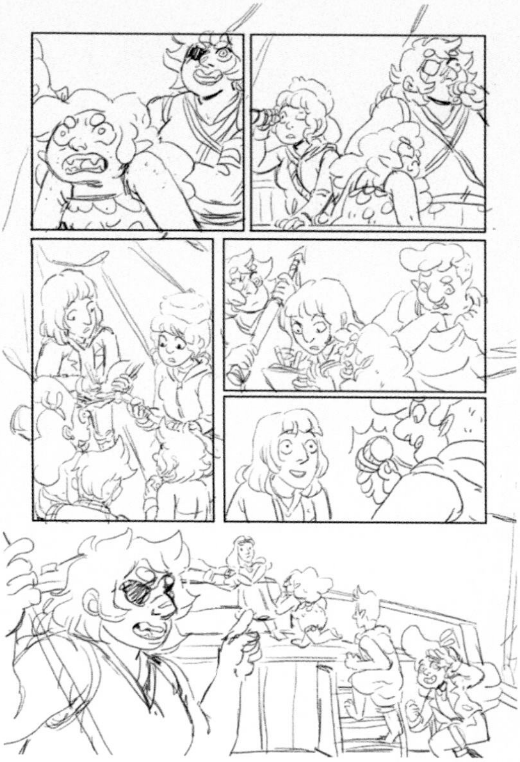

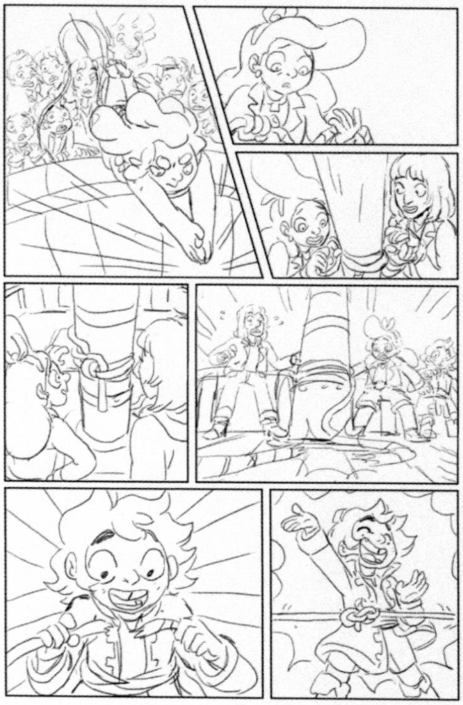

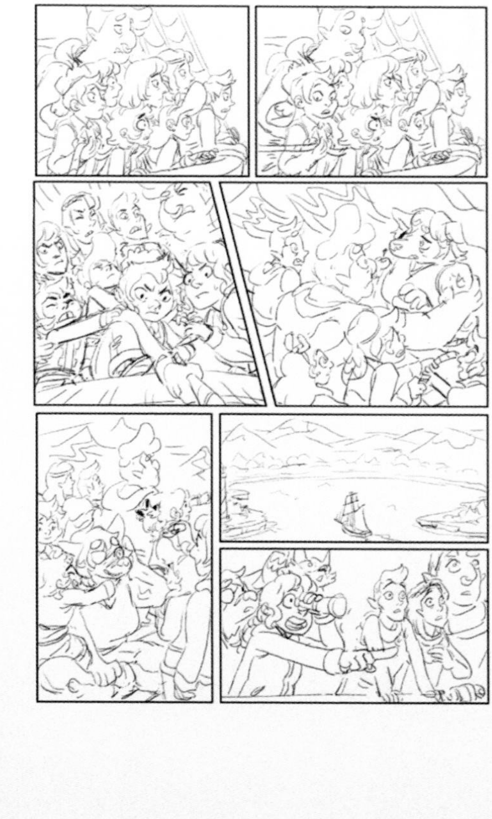

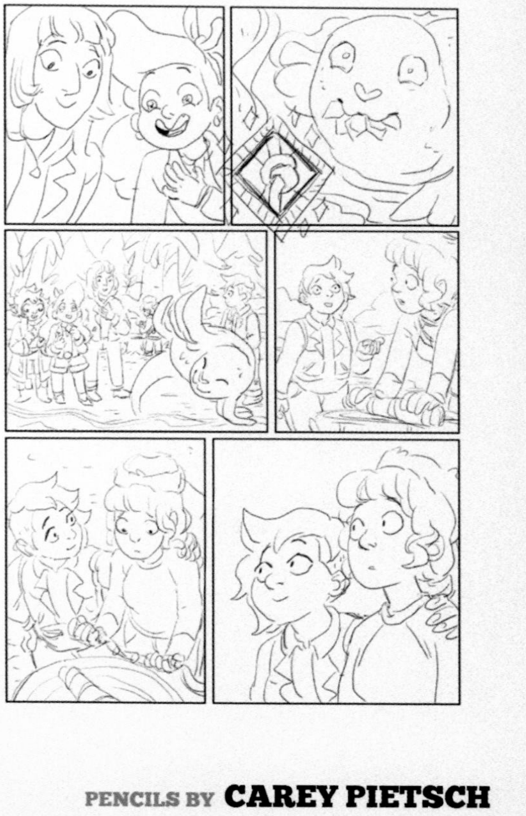

PENCILS BY CAREY PIETSCH

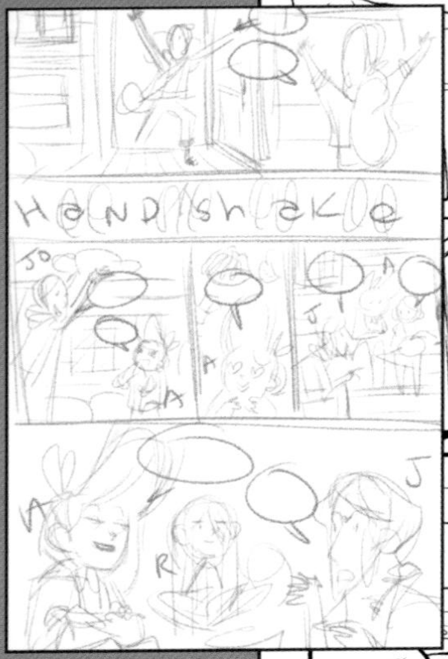

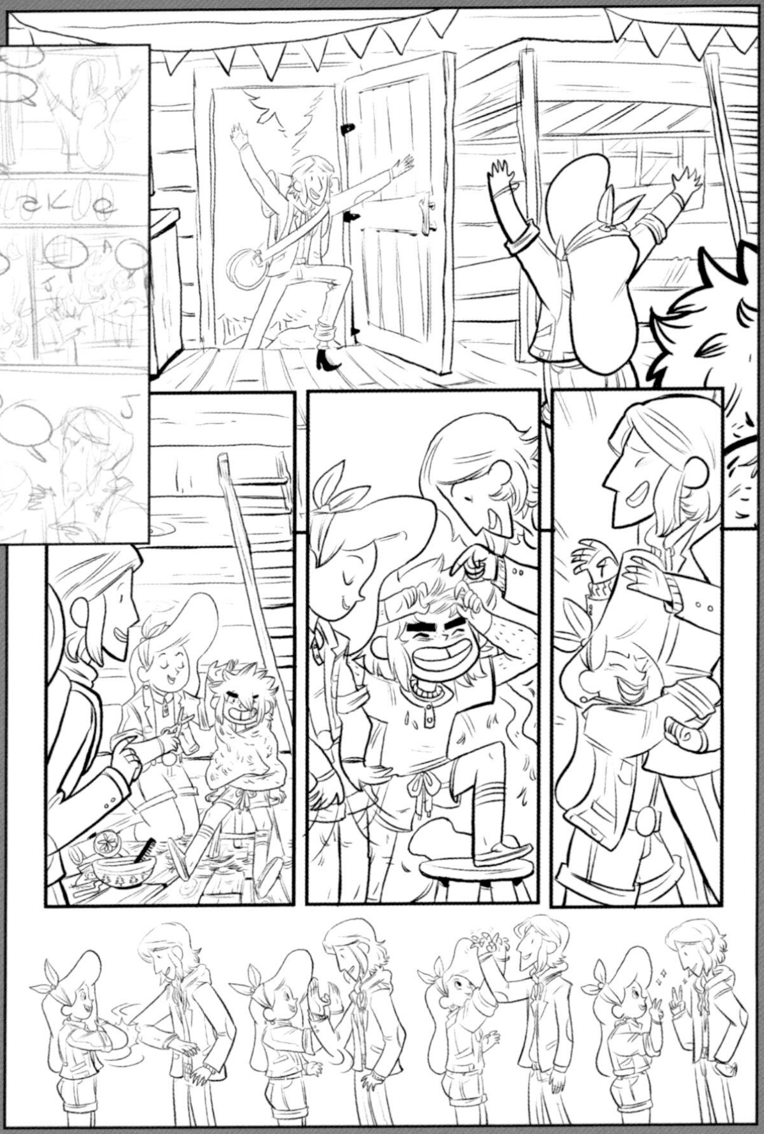

Issue Thirteen, Page Twelve

PANEL ONE: Back in the cabin. Jo is bursting in. April looks up, delighted, from where she is trimming Ripley's hair. Tufts of brown hair are scattered across the floor. Ripley's bangs have been dunked in blue dye and still look slightly wet.

JO: APRIL!

APRIL: JO!

PANEL TWO: Jo looks at Ripley, who is beaming - April proudly gestures to her work with a flourish.

JO: Whoa, what's going on over here?

APRIL: Me and Ripley are doing a MAKEOVER!

APRIL: THIS CAMP IS ALREADY THE BEST.

PANEL THREE: Ripley grabs her bangs and tugs on them in front of her face. April is

getting up, brushing stray hairs off her leggings.

      RIPLEY: LOOKIT MY BLUE HAIR.

      JO: Dude, you look TOTALLY hardcore.

PANEL FOUR: April grabs Jo around the middle and hoists her in a huge hug.

      APRIL: SECRET HANDSHAKE TIME!

      JO: AUGH!

PANEL FIVE: They do their secret handshake.

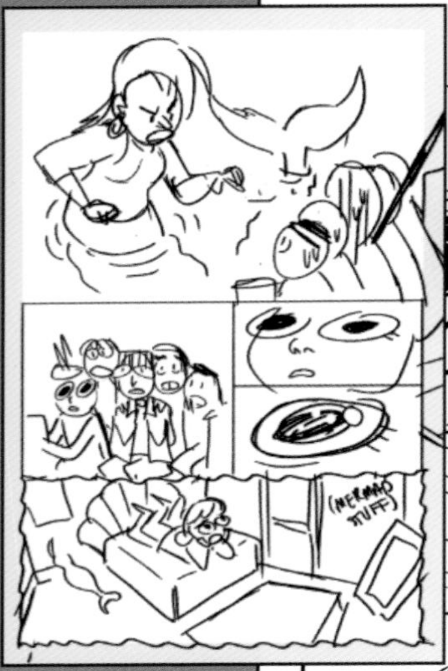

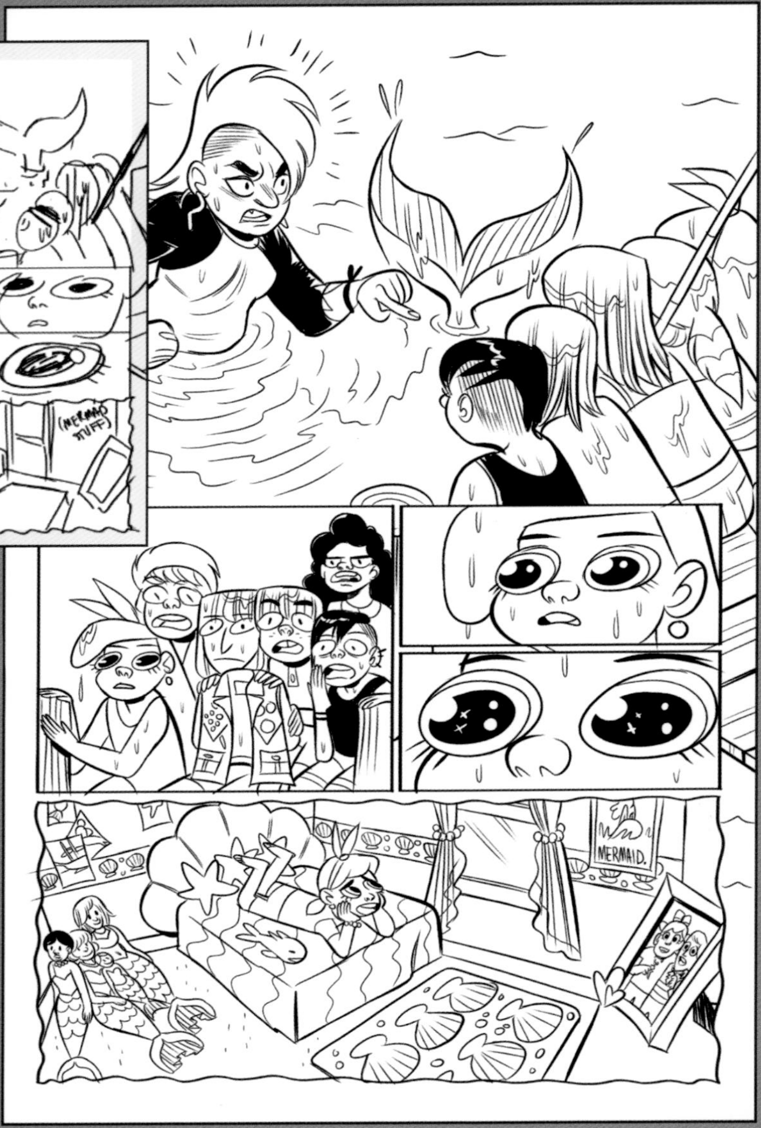
MERMAID.

Issue Eighteen, Page Seven

PANEL ONE: It's a mermaid! She's super punky, like a 90s lesbian of the old school. Tattooed, purple mohawk EVEN IN THE WATER. Fish-hook earrings, the works. Her tail is sticking out of the water, it is no mystery what she is.

HARLOW: Hey! What gives two-legs?! That's MINE!

PANEL TWO: Shot of the girls. They are all looking astonished. April looks EXTRA SHOCKED.

ALL BUT APRIL AND JEN: A MERMAID?!

JEN: NO. WAY. NOPE.

PANEL THREE: Close-up on April's face.

PANEL FOUR: Extreme close-up on April's eye.

PANEL FIVE: Gauzy memory panel! It's young April in her childhood room! She is surrounded

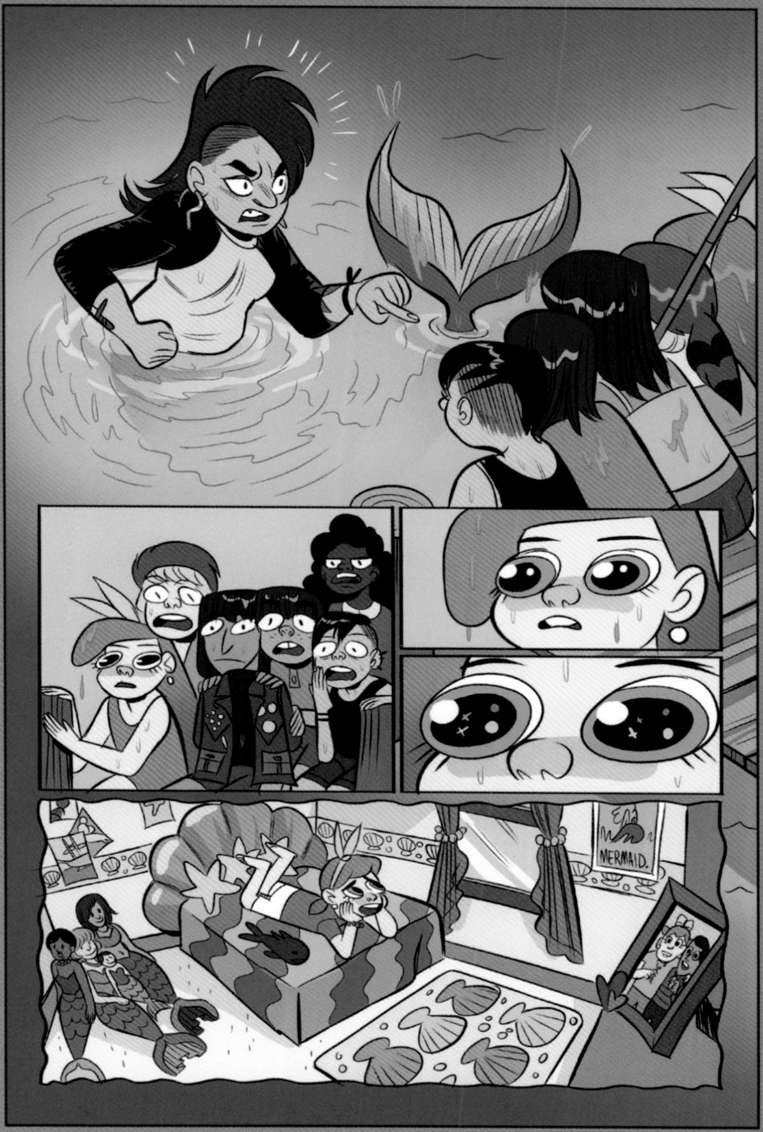
MERMAID.

by mermaid posters, dolls, stuffed animals, etc. Make sure there is a photo of her and pre-transition Jo somewhere. She is hugging a mermaid and sighing dreamily.

APRIL: I wish *I* could be a mermaid...

Issue Twenty, Page Five

PANEL ONE: It's Harlow! Aw yeah! She's looking very panicked!

    HARLOW: April! You're still here! I was on my way over--

PANEL TWO: Harlow is suddenly bashful.

    HARLOW: --to, er, y'know, check out the festival--

PANEL THREE: Harlow, even more embarrassed.

    HARLOW (small): --I mean, I didn't want to give Carter the satisfaction of not showing up--

    HARLOW (smaller): --and I did want to see Taylor play--

PANEL FOUR: Wide-shot of chaos. Harlow, recovering and gesturing at the chaos.

    HARLOW: Annnnnyway, what is...this all about?

PANEL FIVE:

APRIL: sigh…

APRIL(brackets small): I'm sorry, [special and amazing forever mermaid best friend] Harlow.

Issue Twenty-Three, Page Eight

PANEL ONE: Ripley POV through the spyglass. The color quality is a bit different. There is a huge bear outline/aura around the BW. Molly has an aura but it matches her outline.

> BEAR WOMAN: Eh, novelty wears off. But there's always something to do...
>
> RIPLEY: (off panel) Neat!

PANEL TWO: Ripley shifts the spyglass off to the side of Molly where she sees a huge moth settled under a leaf.

> BEAR WOMAN: (off panel) ...and it's always important.
>
> RIPLEY: GASP

PANEL THREE: Ripley moves the spyglass from her eye. She's looking at the moth with reverence, stars in her eyes.

> RIPLEY: Mothra.

PANEL FOUR: Molly is in the foreground speaking with BW, Ripley runs behind her, handing off the spyglass, but Molly is enthusiastically caught up in her conversation with BW. BW is cleaning her glasses.

    MOLLY: So you really are like a...guardian of the forest!!

    BEAR WOMAN: That's more or less the job title, sure.

PANEL FIVE: Same shot. Molly is enraptured by the conversation, BW is looking less frosty. Behind them the moth has taken off and Ripley is chasing after it.

    MOLLY: That is so cool!

PANEL SIX: The sun is beginning to come up. Ripley is in the foreground chasing the moth excitedly off frame, Bubbles with her. Behind her, Molly and BW are walking in the other direction, not looking back at her.

    BEAR WOMAN: The storm's moving east, let's keep going.

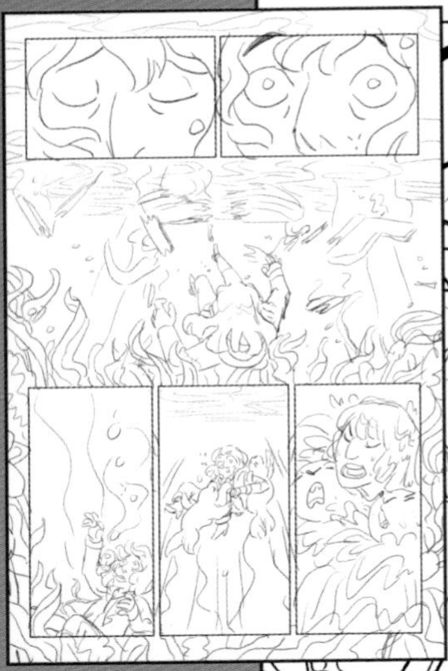

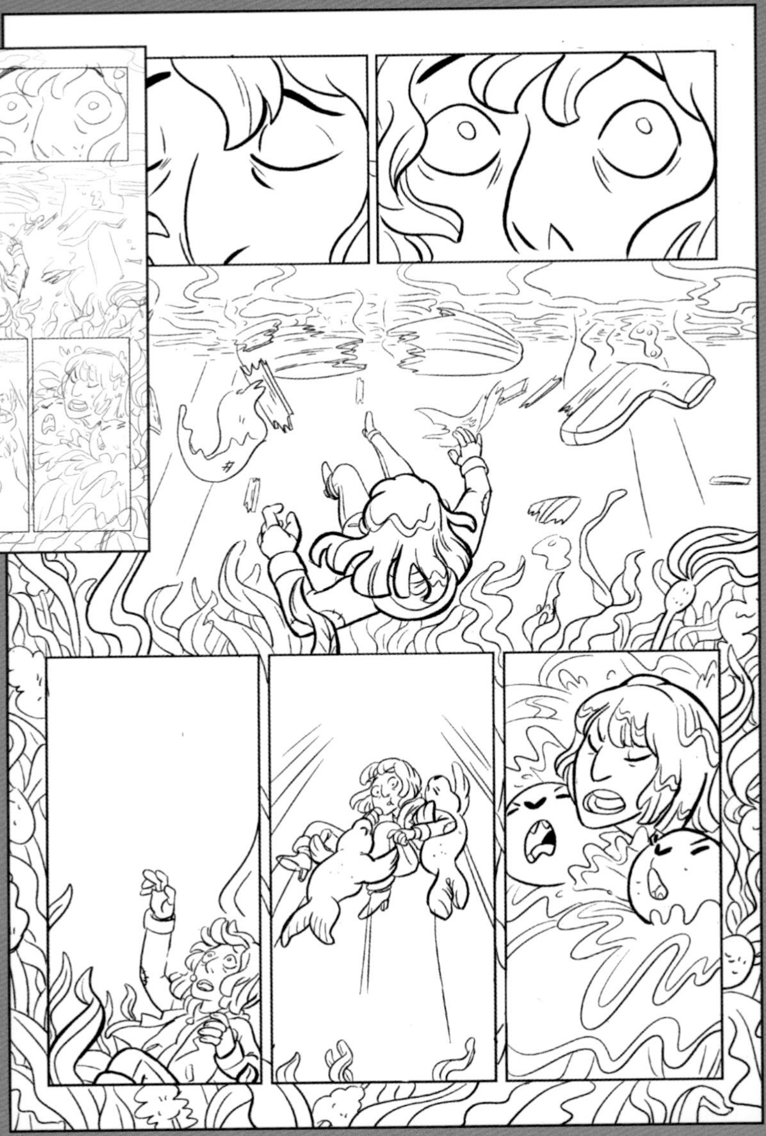

Issue Twenty-Four, Page One

PANEL ONE: Dark panel, CU of Jo's closed eyes.

PANEL TWO: Jo's eyes snap open. She's surprised by what she sees.

PANEL THREE: Big panel. Jo's small under the sea. Pieces of Karen's boat are floating around.

PANEL FOUR: Shot of Jo, near the bottom of the panel, sinking.

PANEL FIVE: She is suddenly swept up by Sunday and Monday as seals on either side of her.

PANEL SIX: Jo, Sunday, and Monday break the surface of the water. Jo is sputtering.

JO: KAF KAF

APRIL: (off panel) JO!!

LUMBERJANES FIELD MANUAL

ABOUT THE AUTHORS

SHANNON WATTERS

Shannon Watters is an editor lady by day and the co-creator of *Lumberjanes*...also by day. She helped guide KaBOOM!—BOOM! Studios' all-ages imprint—to commercial and critical success, and oversees BOOM! Box, an experimental imprint created "for the love of it." She has a great love for all things indie and comics, which is something she's been passionate about since growing up in the wilds of Arizona. When she's not working on comics she can be found watching classic films and enjoying the local cuisine.

ART BY BROOKE ALLEN

GRACE ELLIS

NOELLE STEVENSON

Grace Ellis is a writer most well-known for co-creating *Lumberjanes* and her work on the site *Autostraddle*. She is from Ohio and when she's not coming up with amazing mix-tapes, she's most likely enjoying camp stories, the zoo and The Great American Musical, of which she's sure to write a hit one someday.

Noelle Stevenson is the *New York Times* bestselling author of *Nimona*, has won two Eisner Awards for the series she co-created; *Lumberjanes*. She's been nominated for Harvey Awards, and was awarded the Slate Cartoonist Studio Prize for Best Web Comic in 2012 for *Nimona*. A graduate of the Maryland Institute College of Art, Noelle is a writer on Disney's *Wander Over Yonder*, she has written for Marvel and DC Comics. She lives in Los Angeles. In her spare time she can be found drawing superheroes and talking about bad TV. **www.gingerhaze.com**

ART BY **BROOKE ALLEN**

BROOKE ALLEN

KAT LEYH

Brooke Allen is a co-creator and the artist for *Lumberjanes* and when she is not drawing then she will most likely be found with a saw in her hand making something rad. Currently residing in the "for lovers" state of Virginia, she spends most of her time working on comics with her not-so-helpful assistant Linus...her dog.

Kat Leyh has been co-writer of *Lumberjanes* since issue 18 and cover artist since issue 24. Growing up in the woods, attending 4-H camp in the summers, and creating comics about supernatural queer characters have all led to her feeling right at home with the Lumberjanes! She's done various short comics for series like *Adventure Time* and *Bravest Warriors*, and her own series, *Supercakes*. When not making comics, she loves to cook, travel and explore!

ART BY **BROOKE ALLEN** AND **KAT LEYH**

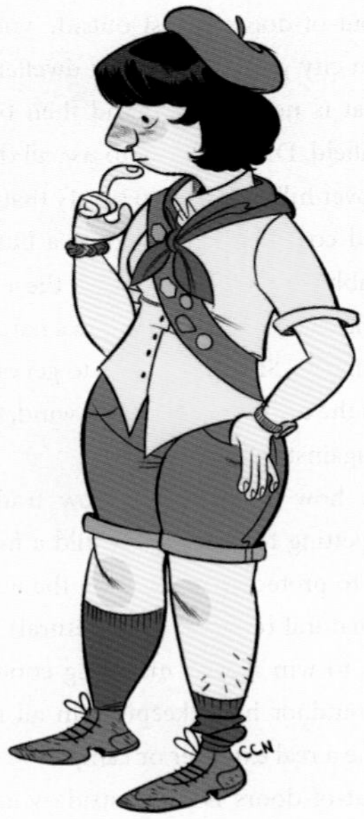
CCN

CAROLYN NOWAK

Carolyn Nowak is a cartoonist and illustrator who was born in Michigan and currently resides in the best state in the union (Michigan). Beyond *Lumberjanes* she's most proud of her own self-published comics. She thinks drawing is okay but if she could find someone to pay her to play DDR or watch and analyze T.V. all day she would quit with enthusiasm and never look back. Her only real goals are to live a long time, be happy and die in Michigan.

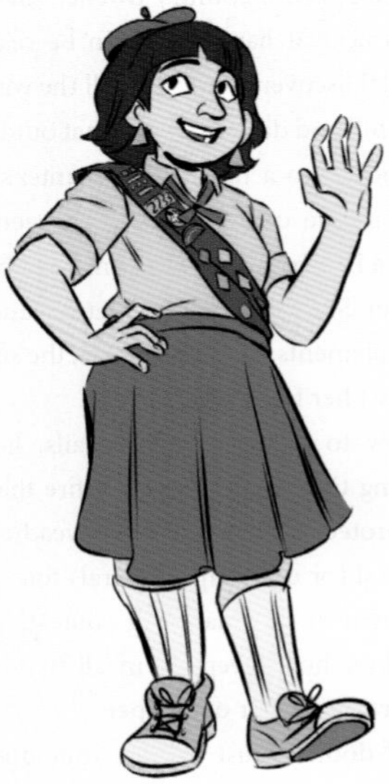

CAREY PIETSCH

Carey Pietsch is a Brooklyn-based cartoonist. She drew *Lumberjanes* #21-25, 29-32, the *Mages of Mystralia* webcomic, and is currently working on *The Adventure Zone: Here There Be Gerblins*. Carey also makes original comics about magic and empathy, plays too many tabletop games and listens to a lot of good podcasts about them. She's a for-real lifetime Girl Scout!

ART BY CAROLYN NOWAK AND CAREY PIETSCH

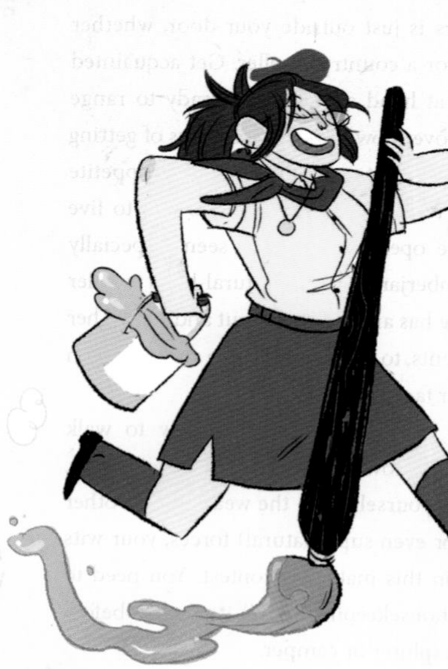

MAARTA LAIHO

Maarta Laiho is a freelance illustrator, who was somehow tricked into becoming a successful comics colorist. She is a graduate from the Savannah College of Art and Design with a BFA in Sequential Art. She, with her chinchilla sidekick, currently resides in the woods of midcoast Maine. In her spare time she draws her webcomic *Madwillow*, hoards houseplants, and complains about the snow.
www.PencilCat.net

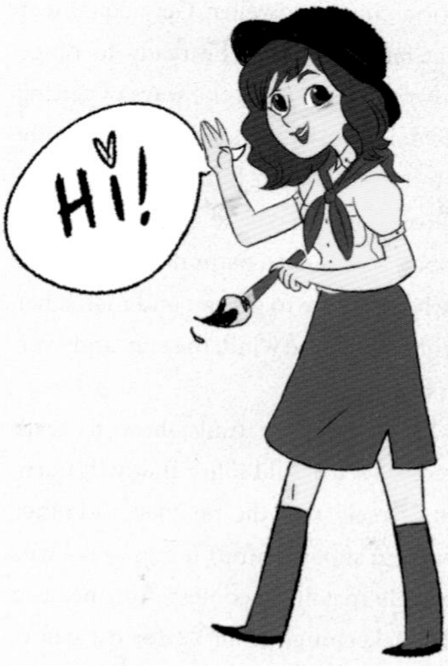
HI!

AUBREY AIESE

Aubrey Aiese is an illustrator and hand letterer from Brooklyn, New York currently living in Portland, Oregon. She loves eating ice cream, making comics, and playing with her super cute corgi pups, Ace and Penny. She's been nominated for a Harvey Award for her outstanding lettering on *Lumberjanes* and continues to find new ways to challenge herself in her field. She also puts an absurd amount of ketchup on her french fries.
www.lettersfromaubrey.com

ART BY BROOKE ALLEN

will co…

The …
It he… …E UNIFORM
appearan… …should be worn at camp
dress fo… …events when Lumberjanes
Further … …may also be worn at other
Lumber… …ons. It should be worn as a
to have … …the uniform dress with
part in … …rrect shoes, and stocking or
Thiskv… …out grows her uniform or
Hardo… …ng …ter Lumberjane.
have … …a she has
them … …her
…her

The …
yellow, short sle… …CES
emb…
the w…
choose…
slacks,…
made o…
out-of-do…
green bere…
the colla…
Shoes ma…
heels, roun… …ngs or
socks shoul… …th the shoes or wi…
the uniform. Ne… …es, bracelets, or other jewelry do
belong with a Lumberjane uniform.

HOW TO WEAR THE UNIFORM

To look well in a uniform demans first of…
uniform be kept in good condition—clean…
pressed. See that the skirt is the right length for your own
height and build, that the belt is adjusted to your waist,
that your shoes and stockings are in keeping with the
uniform, that you watch your posture and carry yourself
with dignity and grace. If the beret is removed indoors,
be sure that your hair is neat and kept in place with an
insconspicuous clip or ribbon. When you wear a
Lumberjane uniform you are identified as a member of
this organization and you should be doubly careful to
conduct yourself in a way that will show everyone that
courtesy and thoughtfullness are part of being a
Lumberjane. People are likely to judge a whole nation by
the selfishness of a few individuals, to criticize a whole
family because of the misconduct of one member, and to
feel unkindly toward and organization because of the

The unifor…
helps to cre…
in a group. …
active life th…
another bond…
future, and pr…
in order to b…
Lumberjane pr…
Penniquiqul Thi… …ore Lady
Types, but m… …es will wish to have one. They
can either bu… …ore…, or make it themselves from
materials available at the trading post.

LJ

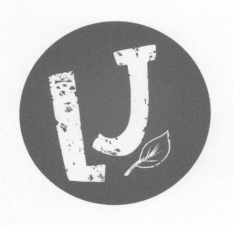